EVERYMAN'S LIBRARY
EDITED BY ERNEST RHYS

FICTION

RAVENSHOE BY
HENRY KINGSLEY

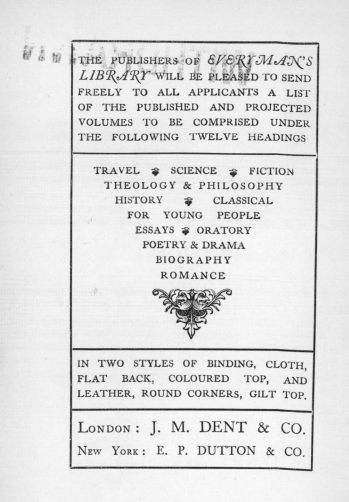

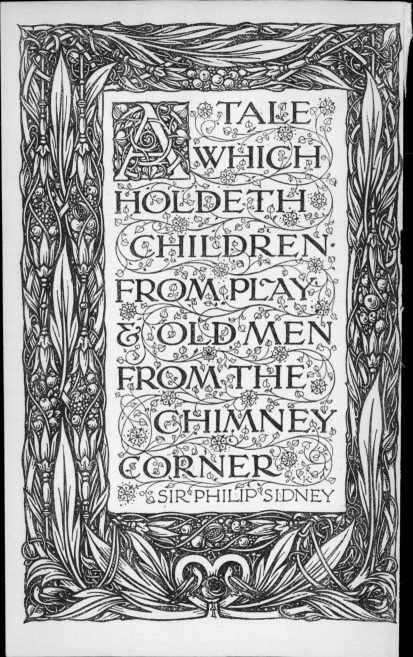

A TALE WHICH HOLDETH CHILDREN FROM PLAY & OLD MEN FROM THE CHIMNEY CORNER

SIR PHILIP SIDNEY

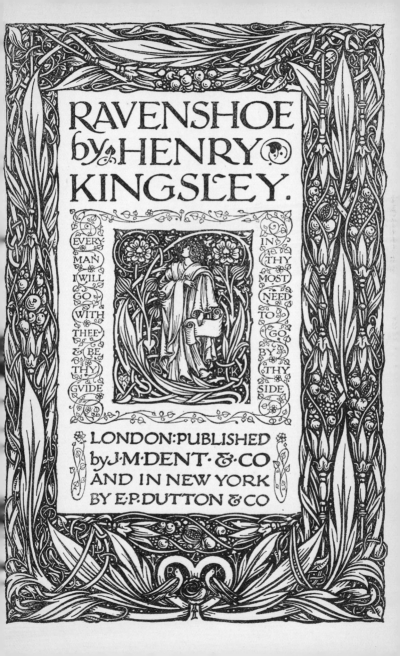

RAVENSHOE by HENRY KINGSLEY.

EVERY MAN I WILL GO WITH THEE & BE THY GVIDE

IN THY MOST NEED TO GO BY THY SIDE

LONDON: PUBLISHED by J·M·DENT·&·CO AND IN NEW YORK BY E·P·DUTTON & CO

First Edition, February 1906
Reprinted December 1906

RICHARD CLAY & SONS, LIMITED,
BREAD STREET HILL, E.C., AND
BUNGAY, SUFFOLK.

EDITOR'S NOTE

"Ravenshoe" was Henry Kingsley's second novel, and it appeared in 1862, when he was thirty-two years of age. It was one of his two favourites among his own works, and Charles Ravenshoe was one of his two favourite characters. Writing at the end of his novel "Stretton," he said : "The others come and go, and I love them well enough ; but the two who are with me always are the peaked-faced man Charles Ravenshoe and the lame French girl Mathilde." The last reference is to the later novel of "Mademoiselle Mathilde," a story of the French Revolution, which may also be added eventually to this series. One of the best tributes paid to Henry Kingsley's genius was that of "C. K. B.", who, writing to the *Academy* in 1901, said : "I first read 'Ravenshoe' at that period when absolute romance and absolute fact have to live together ; and very turbulent partners they make. The appeal of the book was instant and permanent. Even now after a dozen years I cannot read the story unmoved ; . . . each point holds me as of old, by sheer force of its human presentation, its resourceful dialogue, its unwearied vitality. In a word, the book is alive—the expression of a man who worked both with heart and head. He had something to say, and he said it." Henry Kingsley was Charles Kingsley's younger brother, and was born at Barnack, Northamptonshire, and his life was as stirring and adventurous, and in youth as restless, as his books would suggest. He left Oxford to go to the Australian gold-fields ; and returned five years later with small gold but rich experience. He wrote novels then—all too rapidly ; edited a paper at Edinburgh ; went out as war correspondent to the Franco-German War ; and died when

Editor's Note

he was only forty-six at Cuckfield, Sussex. The following is a List
of the published works of Henry Kingsley—

The Recollections of Geoffrey Hamlyn, 1859 ; Ravenshoe, 1862 ; Austin
Elliott, 1863 ; The Hillyars and the Burtons : a Story of Two Families,
1865 ; Leighton Court : a Country House Story, 1866 ; Silcote of Silcotes,
1867 ; Mademoiselle Mathilde, 1868 ; Biographical Introduction to the
"Globe" Edition of "Robinson Crusoe," 1868 ; Stretton, 1869 ; Tales
of Old Travels, re-narrated by H. K., 1869 ; Old Margaret, 1871 ; The
Lost Child, 1871 ; The Boy in Grey, 1871 ; Hetty, and other Stories,
1871 ; The Harveys, 1872 ; Hornby Mills, and other Stories, 1872 ;
Valentin : a French boy's story of Sedan, 1872 ; Reginald Hetherege,
1874 ; Number Seventeen, 1875 ; The Grange Garden : a Romance,
1876 ; Fireside Studies, 1876 ; The Mystery of the Island, 1877 ; Edition
of Novels, by C. K. Shorter, 1894, etc.

For eighteen months Kingsley was editor of the "Edinburgh Daily
Review," previous to going abroad as its correspondent during the Franco-
Prussian War.

RAVENSHOE

CHAPTER I

AN ACCOUNT OF THE FAMILY OF RAVENSHOE

I HAD intended to have gone into a family history of the
Ravenshoes, from the time of Canute to that of her present
Majesty, following it down through every change and revolution,
both secular and religious; which would have been deeply
interesting, but which would have taken more hard reading
than one cares to undertake for nothing. I had meant, I say,
to have been quite diffuse on the annals of one of our oldest
commoner families; but, on going into the subject, I found I
must either chronicle little affairs which ought to have been
forgotten long ago, or do my work in a very patchy and
inefficient way. When I say that the Ravenshoes have been
engaged in every plot, rebellion, and civil war, from about a
century or so before the Conquest to 1745, and that the history
of the house was marked by cruelty and rapacity in old times,
and in those more modern by political tergiversation of the
blackest dye, the reader will understand why I hesitate to say
too much in reference to a name which I especially honour.
In order, however, that I may give some idea of what the
hereditary character of the family is, I must just lead the reader's
eye lightly over some of the principal events of their history.

The great Irish families have, as is well known, a banshee,
or familiar spirit, who, previous to misfortune or death, flits
moaning round the ancestral castle. Now although the Ravenshoes, like all respectable houses, have an hereditary lawsuit;
a feud (with the Humbys of Hele); a ghost (which the present
Ravenshoe claims to have repeatedly seen in early youth); and
a buried treasure: yet I have never heard that they had a
banshee. Had such been the case, that unfortunate spirit

would have had no sinecure of it, but rather must have kept howling night and day for nine hundred years or so, in order to have got through her work at all. For the Ravenshoes were almost always in trouble, and yet had a facility of getting out again, which, to one not aware of the cause, was sufficiently inexplicable. Like the Stuarts, they had always taken the losing side, and yet, unlike the Stuarts, have always kept their heads on their shoulders, and their house over their heads. Lady Ascot says that, if Ambrose Ravenshoe had been attainted in 1745, he'd have been hung as sure as fate : there was evidence enough against him to hang a dozen men. I myself, too, have heard Squire Densil declare, with great pride, that the Ravenshoe of King John's time was the only Baron who did not sign Magna Charta; and if there were a Ravenshoe at Runnymede, I have not the slightest doubt that such was the case. Through the Rose wars, again, they were always on the wrong side, whichever that might have been, because your Ravenshoe, mind you, was not bound to either side in those times, but changed as he fancied fortune was going. As your Ravenshoe was the sort of man who generally joined a party just when their success was indubitable—that is to say, just when the reaction against them was about to set in—he generally found himself among the party which was going down hill, who despised him for not joining them before, and opposed to the rising party, who hated him because he had declared against them. Which little game is common enough in this present century among some men of the world, who seem, as a general rule, to make as little by it as ever did the Ravenshoes.

Well, whatever your trimmers make by their motion now-a-days, the Ravenshoes were not successful either at liberal conservatism, or conservative liberalism. At the end of the reign of Henry VII. they were as poor as Job, or poorer. But, before you have time to think of it, behold, in 1530, there comes you to court a Sir Alured Ravenshoe, who incontinently begins cutting in at the top of the tune, swaggering, swearing, dressing, fighting, dicing, and all that sort of thing, and, what is more, paying his way in a manner which suggests successful burglary as the only solution. Sir Alured, however, as I find, had done no worse than marry an old maid (Miss Hincksey, one of the Staffordshire Hinckseys) with a splendid fortune; which fortune set the family on its legs again for some generations. This Sir Alured seems to have been an audacious rogue. He made great interest with the king, who was so far pleased with his activity in athletic sports that he gave him a post in Ireland. There our Ravenshoe was so fascinated by the charming manners of the Earl of Kildare that he even accompanied that nobleman on a visit to Desmond ; and, after a twelvemonth's unauthorized residence in the interior of Ireland, on his return to England he was put into the Tower for six months to " consider himself."

This Alured seems to have been a deuce of a fellow, a very good type of the family. When British Harry had that difference we wot of with the Bishop of Rome, I find Alured to have been engaged in some five or six Romish plots, such as, had the king been in possession of facts, would have consigned him to a rather speedy execution. However, the king seems to have looked on this gentleman with a suspicious eye, and to have been pretty well aware what sort of man he was, for I find him writing to his wife, on the occasion of his going to Court— "The King's Grace looked but sourly upon me, and said it should go hard, but that the pitcher which went so oft to the well should be broke at last. Thereto I making answer, ' that that should depend on the pitcher, whether it were iron or clomb,' he turned on his heel, and presently departed from me."

He must have been possessed of his full share of family audacity to sharpen his wits on the terrible Harry, with such an unpardonable amount of treason hanging over him. I have dwelt thus long on him, as he seems to have possessed a fair share of the virtues and vices of his family—a family always generous and brave, yet always led astray by bad advisers. This Alured built Ravenshoe House, as it stands to this day, and in which much of the scene of this story is laid.

They seem to have got through the Gunpowder Plot pretty well, though I can show you the closet where one of the minor conspirators, one Watson, lay *perdu* for a week or so after that gallant attempt, more I suspect from the effect of a guilty conscience than any thing else, for I never heard of any distinct charge being brought against him. The Forty-five, however, did not pass quite so easily, and Ambrose Ravenshoe went as near to lose his head as any one of the family since the Conquest. When the news came from the north about the alarming advance of the Highlanders, it immediately struck Ambrose that this was the best opportunity for making a fool of himself that could possibly occur. He accordingly, without hesitation or consultation with any mortal soul, rang the bell for his butler, sent for his stud-groom, mounted every man about the place (twenty or so), armed them, grooms, gardeners,

and all, with crossbows and partisans from the armoury, and
rode into the cross, at Stonnington, on a market-day, and
boldly proclaimed the Pretender king.   It soon got about that
" the Squire " was making a fool of himself, and that there was
some fun going ; so he shortly found himself surrounded by
a large and somewhat dirty rabble, who, with cries of "Well
done, old rebel ! " and "Hurrah for the Pope ! " escorted him,
his terror-stricken butler, and his shame-stricken grooms, to the
Crown and Sceptre.   As good luck would have it, there happened to be in the town that day no less a person than Lord
Segur, the leading Roman Catholic nobleman of the county.
He, accompanied by several of the leading gentlemen of the
same persuasion, burst into the room where the squire sat,
overpowered him, and, putting him bound into a coach, carried
him off to Segur Castle, and locked him up.   It took all the
strength of the Popish party to save him from attainder.   The
Church rallied right bravely round the old house, which had
always assisted her with sword and purse, and never once had
wavered in its allegiance.   So, while nobler heads went down,
Ambrose Ravenshoe's remained on his shoulders.

Ambrose died in 1759.

John (Monseigneur) in 1771.

Howard in 1800.   He first took the Claycomb hounds.

Petre in 1820.   He married Alicia, only daughter of Charles,
third Earl of Ascot, and was succeeded by Densil, the first of
our dramatis personæ—the first of all this shadowy line that we
shall see in the flesh.   He was born in the year 1783, and
married, first in 1812, at his father's desire, a Miss Winkleigh,
of whom I know nothing ; and second, at his own desire, in
1823, Susan, fourth daughter of Lawrence Petersham, Esq., of
Fairford Grange, county Worcester, by whom he had issue—

Cuthbert, born 1826.

Charles, born 1831.

Densil was an only son.   His father, a handsome, careless,
good-humoured, but weak and superstitious man, was entirely
in the hands of the priests, who during his life were undisputed
masters of Ravenshoe.   Lady Alicia was, as I have said, a
daughter of Lord Ascot, a Staunton, as staunchly Protestant
a house as any in England.   She, however, managed to fall in
love with the handsome young Popish Squire, and to elope
with him, changing not only her name, but, to the dismay of
her family, her faith also, and becoming, pervert-like, more
actively bigoted than her easy-going husband.   She brought
little or no money into the family ; and, from her portrait,

appears to have been exceedingly pretty, and monstrously silly.

To this strong-minded couple was born, two years after their marriage, a son, who was called Densil.

This young gentleman seems to have got on much like other young gentlemen till the age of twenty-one, when it was determined by the higher powers in conclave assembled that he should go to London, and see the world ; and so, having been cautioned duly how to avoid the flesh and the devil, to see the world he went. In a short time intelligence came to the confessor of the family, and through him to the father and mother, that Densil was seeing the world with a vengeance ; that he was the constant companion of the Right Honourable Viscount Saltire, the great dandy of the Radical Atheist set, with whom no man might play picquet and live ; that he had been upset in a tilbury with Mademoiselle Vaurien of Drury-lane at Kensington turnpike ; that he had fought the French *émigré*, a Comte de Hautenbas, apropos of the Vaurien afore-mentioned—in short, that he was going on at a deuce of a rate : and so a hurried council was called to deliberate what was to be done.

" He will lose his immortal soul," said the priest.

" He will dissipate his property," said his mother.

" He will go to the devil," said his father.

So Father Clifford, good man, was despatched to London, with post horses, and ordered to bring back the lost sheep *vi et armis*. Accordingly, at ten o'clock one night, Densil's lad was astounded by having to admit Father Clifford, who demanded immediately to be led to his master.

Now this was awkward, for James well knew what was going on upstairs ; but he knew also what would happen, sooner or later, to a Ravenshoe servant who trifled with a priest, and so he led the way.

The lost sheep which the good father had come to find was not exactly sober this evening, and certainly not in a very good temper. He was playing *écarté* with a singularly handsome, though supercilious-looking man, dressed in the height of fashion, who, judging from the heap of gold beside him, had been winning heavily. The priest trembled and crossed himself—this man was the terrible, handsome, wicked, witty, Atheistical, radical Lord Saltire, whose tongue no woman could withstand, and whose pistol no man dared face ; who was currently believed to have sold himself to the deuce, or, indeed, as some said, to be the deuce himself.

A more cunning man than poor simple Father Clifford would have made some common-place remark and withdrawn, after a short greeting, taking warning by the impatient scowl that settled on Densil's handsome face. Not so he. To be defied by a boy whose law had been his word for ten years past never entered into his head, and he sternly advanced towards the pair.

Densil inquired if anything were the matter at home. And Lord Saltire, anticipating a scene, threw himself back in his chair, stretched out his elegant legs, and looked on with the air of a man who knows he is going to be amused, and composes himself thoroughly to appreciate the entertainment.

"Thus much, my son," said the priest; "your mother is wearing out the stones of the oratory with her knees, praying for her first-born, while he is wasting his substance, and perilling his soul, with debauched Atheistic companions, the enemies of God and man."

Lord Saltire smiled sweetly, bowed elegantly, and took snuff.

"Why do you intrude into my room, and insult my guest?" said Densil, casting an angry glance at the priest, who stood calmly like a black pillar, with his hands before him. "It is unendurable."

"*Quem Deus vult*," &c. Father Clifford had seen that scowl once or twice before, but he would not take warning. He said—

"I am ordered not to go westward without you. I command you to come."

"Command me! command a Ravenshoe!" said Densil furiously.

Father Clifford, by way of mending matters, now began to lose *his* temper.

"You would not be the first Ravenshoe who has been commanded by a priest; ay, and has had to obey too," said he.

"And you will not be the first jack-priest who has felt the weight of a Ravenshoe's wrath," replied Densil brutally.

Lord Saltire leant back, and said to the ambient air, "I'll back the priest, five twenties to one."

This was too much. Densil would have liked to quarrel with Saltire, but that was death—he was the deadest shot in Europe. He grew furious, and beyond all control. He told the priest to go (further than purgatory); grew blasphemous, emphatically renouncing the creed of his forefathers, and, in fact, all other creeds. The priest grew hot and furious too, retaliated in no measured terms, and finally left the room with his ears stopped, shaking the dust off his feet as he went. Then Lord Saltire drew up to the table again, laughing.

"Your estates are entailed, Ravenshoe, I suppose?" said he.

"No."

"Oh! It's your deal, my dear fellow."

Densil got an angry letter from his father in a few days, demanding full apologies and recantations, and an immediate return home. Densil had no apologies to make, and did not intend to return till the end of the season. His father wrote declining the honour of his further acquaintance, and sending him a draft for fifty pounds to pay outstanding bills, which he very well knew amounted to several thousands. In a short time the great Catholic tradesmen, with whom he had been dealing, began to press for money in a somewhat insolent way; and now Densil began to see that, by defying and insulting the faith and the party to which he belonged, he had merely cut himself off from rank, wealth, and position. He had defied the *partie prêtre*, and had yet to feel their power. In two months he was in the Fleet prison.

His servant (the title "tiger" came in long after this), a half groom, half valet, such as men kept in those days—a simple lad from Ravenshoe, James Horton by name—for the first time in his life disobeyed orders; for, on being told to return home by Densil, he firmly declined doing so, and carried his top boots and white neckcloth triumphantly into the Fleet, there pursuing his usual avocations with the utmost nonchalance.

"A very distinguished fellow that of yours, Curly" (they all had nicknames for one another in those days), said Lord Saltire. "If I were not Saltire, I think I would be Jim. To own the only clean face among six hundred fellow-creatures is a pre-eminence, a decided pre-eminence. I'll buy him of you."

For Lord Saltire came to see him, snuff-box and all. That morning Densil was sitting brooding in the dirty room with the barred windows, and thinking what a wild free wind would be sweeping across the Downs this fine November day, when the door was opened, and in walks me my lord, with a sweet smile on his face.

He was dressed in the extreme of fashion—a long-tailed blue coat with gold buttons, a frill to his shirt, a white cravat, a wonderful short waistcoat, loose short nankeen trousers, low shoes, no gaiters, and a low-crowned hat. I am pretty correct, for I have seen his picture, dated 1804. But you must please to remember that his lordship was in the very van of the fashion, and that probably such a dress was not universal for two or three years afterwards. I wonder if his well-known audacity would be sufficient to make him walk along one of the public thoroughfares in such a dress, to-morrow, for a heavy bet—I fancy not.

He smiled sardonically—"My dear fellow," he said, "when a man comes on a visit of condolence, I know it is the most wretched taste to say, 'I told you so;' but do me the justice to allow that I offered to back the priest five to one. I had been coming to you all the week, but Tuesday and Wednesday I was at Newmarket; Thursday I was shooting at your cousin Ascot's: yesterday I did not care about boring myself with you; so I have come to-day because I was at leisure and had nothing better to do."

Densil looked up savagely, thinking he had come to insult him: but the kindly compassionate look in the piercing grey eye belied the cynical curl of the mouth, and disarmed him. He leant his head upon the table and sobbed.

Lord Saltire laid his hand kindly on his shoulder, and said—

"You have been a fool, Ravenshoe; you have denied the faith of your forefathers. Pardieu, if I had such an article I would not have thrown it so lightly away."

"*You* talk like this? Who next? It was your conversation led me to it. Am I worse than you? What faith have you, in God's name?"

"The faith of a French Lycée, my friend; the only one I ever had. I have been sufficiently consistent to that, I think."

"Consistent indeed," groaned poor Densil.

"Now, look here," said Saltire; "I may have been to blame in this. But I give you my honour, I had no more idea that you would be obstinate enough to bring matters to this pass, than I had that you would burn down Ravenshoe House because I laughed at it for being old-fashioned. Go home, my poor little Catholic pipkin, and don't try to swim with iron pots like Wrekin and me. Make submission to that singularly *distingué*-looking old turkey-cock of a priest, kiss your mother, and get your usual autumn's hunting and shooting."

"Too late! too late, now!" sobbed Densil.

"Not at all, my dear fellow," said Saltire, taking a pinch of snuff; "the partridges will be a little wild, of course—that you must expect; but you ought to get some very pretty pheasant and cock-shooting. Come, say yes. Have your debts paid, and get out of this infernal hole. A week of this would tame the devil, I should think."

" If you think you could do anything for me, Saltire."

Lord Saltire immediately retired, and reappeared, leading in a lady by her hand. She raised the veil from her head, and he saw his mother. In a moment she was crying on his neck ; and, as he looked over her shoulder, he saw a blue coat passing out of the door, and that was the last of Lord Saltire for the present.

It was no part of the game of the priests to give Densil a cold welcome home. Twenty smiling faces were grouped in the porch to welcome him back ; and among them all none smiled more brightly than the old priest and his father. The dogs went wild with joy, and his favourite peregrine scolded on the falconer's wrist, and struggled with her jesses, shrilly reminding him of the merry old days by the dreary salt marsh, or the lonely lake.

The past was never once alluded to in any way by any one in the house. Old Squire Petre shook hands with faithful James, and gave him a watch, ordering him to ride a certain colt next day, and see how well forward he could get him. So next day they drew the home covers, and the fox, brave fellow, ran out to Parkside, making for the granite walls of Hessitor. And, when Densil felt his nostrils filled once more by the free rushing mountain air, he shouted aloud for joy, and James's voice alongside of him said—

" This is better than the Fleet, sir."

And so Densil played a single-wicket match with the Holy Church, and, like a great many other people, got bowled out in the first innings. He returned to his allegiance in the most exemplary manner, and settled down to the most humdrum of young country gentlemen. He did exactly what every one else about him did. He was not naturally a profligate or vicious man ; but there was a wild devil of animal passion in him, which had broken out in London, and which was now quieted by dread of consequences, but which he felt and knew was there, and might break out again. He was a changed man. There was a gulf between him and the life he had led before he went to London. He had tasted of liberty (or rather, not to profane that Divine word, of licentiousness), and yet not drunk long enough to make him weary of the draught. He had heard the dogmas he was brought up to believe infallible turned to unutterable ridicule by men like Saltire and Wrekin ; men who, as he had the wit to see, were a thousand times cleverer and better informed than Father Clifford or Father Dennis. In short, he had found out, as a great many others have, that Popery won't hold water, and so, as a *pis aller*, he adopted Saltire's creed—that religion was necessary for the government of States, that one religion was as good as another, and that, *cæteris paribus*, the best religion was the one which secured the professor £10,000 a year; and therefore Densil was a devout Catholic.

It was thought by the allied powers that he ought to marry. He had no objection, and so he married a young lady, a Miss Winkleigh—Catholic, of course—about whom I can get no information whatever. Lady Ascot says that she was a pale girl, with about as much air as a milkmaid; on which two facts I can build no theory as to her personal character. She died in 1816, childless; and in 1820 Densil lost both his father and mother, and found himself, at the age of thirty-seven, master of Ravenshoe and master of himself.

He felt the loss of the old folks most keenly, more keenly than that of his wife. He seemed without a stay or holdfast in the world, for he was a poorly-educated man, without resources; and so he went on moping and brooding until good old Father Clifford, who loved him dearly, got alarmed, and recommended travels. He recommended Rome, the cradle of the faith, and to Rome he went.

He stayed at Rome a year; at the end of which time he appeared suddenly at home with a beautiful young wife on his arm. As Father Clifford, trembling and astonished, advanced to lay his hand upon her head, she drew up, laughed, and said, "Spare yourself the trouble, my dear sir; I am a Protestant."

I have had to tell you all this, in order to show you how it came about that Densil, though a Papist, bethought of marrying a Protestant wife to keep up a balance of power in his house. For, if he had not married this lady, the hero of this book would never have been born; and this greater proposition contains the less, "that if he had never been born, his history would never have been written, and so this book would have had no existence."

CHAPTER II

SUPPLEMENTARY TO THE FOREGOING

THE second Mrs. Ravenshoe was the handsome dowerless daughter of a Worcester squire, of good standing, who, being blessed with an extravagant son, and six handsome daughters, had lived for several years abroad, finding society more accessible, and consequently, the matrimonial chances of the "Petersham girls" proportionately greater than in England. She was a handsome, proud woman, not particularly clever, or particularly agreeable, or particularly anything, except particularly self-possessed. She had been long enough looking after an establishment to know thoroughly the value of one, and had seen quite enough of good houses to know that a house without a mistress is no house at all. Accordingly, in a very few days the house felt her presence, submitted with the best grace to her not unkindly rule, and in a week they all felt as if she had been there for years.

Father Clifford, who longed only for peace, and was getting very old, got very fond of her, heretic as she was. She, too, liked the handsome, gentlemanly old man, and made herself agreeable to him, as a woman of the world knows so well how to do. Father Mackworth, on the other hand, his young coadjutor since Father Dennis's death, an importation of Lady Alicia's from Rome, very soon fell under her displeasure. The first Sunday after her arrival, she drove to church, and occupied the great old family pew, to the immense astonishment of the rustics, and, after afternoon service, caught up the old vicar in her imperious off-hand way, and will he nil he, carried him off to dinner—at which meal he was horrified to find himself sitting with two shaven priests, who talked Latin and crossed themselves. His embarrassment was greatly increased by the behaviour of Mrs. Ravenshoe, who admired his sermon, and spoke on doctrinal points with him as though there were not a priest within a mile. Father Mackworth was imprudent enough to begin talking at him, and at last said something unmistakably impertinent; upon which Mrs. Ravenshoe put her glass in her eye, and favoured him with such a glance of haughty astonishment as silenced him at once.

This was the beginning of hostilities between them, if one can give the name of hostilities to a series of infinitesimal annoyances on the one side, and to unmeasurable and barely concealed contempt on the other. Mackworth, on the one hand, knew that she understood and despised him, and he hated her. She, on the other hand, knew that he knew it, but thought him too much below her notice, save now and then that she might put down with a high hand any, even the most distant, approach to a tangible impertinence. But she was no match for him in the arts of petty, delicate, galling annoyances.

There he was her master; he had been brought up in a good
school for that, and had learnt his lesson kindly. He found
that she disliked his presence, and shrunk from his smooth,
lean face with unutterable dislike. From that moment he was
always in her way, overwhelming her with oily politeness,
rushing across the room to pick up anything she had dropped,
or to open the door, till it required the greatest restraint to
avoid breaking through all forms of politeness, and bidding
him begone. But why should we go on detailing trifles like
these, which in themselves are nothing, but accumulated, are
unbearable?

So it went on, till one morning, about two years after the
marriage, Mackworth appeared in Clifford's room, and, yawning,
threw himself into a chair.

"Benedicite," said Father Clifford, who never neglected
religious etiquette on any occasion.

Mackworth stretched out his legs and yawned, rather rudely,
and then relapsed into silence. Father Clifford went on reading.
At last Mackworth spoke.

"I'll tell you what, my good friend, I am getting sick of
this; I shall go back to Rome."

"To Rome?"

"Yes, back to Rome," repeated the other impertinently, for
he always treated the good old priest with contemptuous
insolence when they were alone. "What is the use of staying
here, fighting that woman? There is no more chance of
turning her than a rock, and there is going to be no family."

"You think so?" said Clifford.

"Good heavens, does it look like it? Two years, and not a
sign; besides, should I talk of going, if I thought so. *Then*
there would be a career worthy of me; then I should have a
chance of deserving well of the Church, by keeping a wavering
family in her bosom. And I could do it, too: every child
would be a fresh weapon in my hands against that woman.
Clifford, do you think that Ravenshoe is safe?"

He said this so abruptly that Clifford coloured and started.
Mackworth at the same time turned suddenly upon him, and
scrutinized his face keenly.

"Safe!" said the old man; "what makes you fear otherwise?"

"Nothing special," said Mackworth; "only I have never
been easy since you told me of that London escapade years
ago."

"He has been very devout ever since," said Clifford. "I
fear nothing."

"Humph! Well, I am glad to hear it," said Mackworth. "I shall go to Rome. I'd sooner be gossiping with Alphonse and Pierre in the cloisters than vegetating here. My talents are thrown away."

He departed down the winding steps of the priest's turret, which led to the flower garden. The day was fine, and a pleasant seat a short distance off invited him to sit. He could get a book he knew from the drawing-room, and sit there. So, with habitually noiseless tread, he passed along the dark corridor, and opened the drawing-room door.

Nobody was there. The book he wanted was in the little drawing-room beyond, separated from the room he was in by a partly-drawn curtain. The priest advanced silently over the deep piled curtain and looked in.

The summer sunlight, struggling through a waving bower of climbing plants and the small panes of a deeply mullioned window, fell upon two persons, at the sight of whom he paused, and, holding his breath, stood, like a black statue in the gloomy room, wrapped in astonishment.

He had never in his life heard these twain use any words beyond those of common courtesy towards one another; he had thought them the most indifferent, the coldest pair, he had even seen. But now! now, the haughty beauty was bending from her chair over her husband, who sat on a stool at her feet; her arm was round his neck, and her hand was in his; and, as he looked, she parted the clustering black curls from his forehead and kissed him.

He bent forward and listened more eagerly. He could hear the surf on the shore, the sea-birds on the cliffs, the nightingale in the wood; they fell upon his ear, but he could not distinguish them; he waited only for one of the two figures before him to speak.

At last Mrs. Ravenshoe broke silence, but in so low a voice that even he, whose attention was strained to the uttermost, could barely catch what she said.

"I yield, my love," she said; "I give you this one, but mind, the rest are mine. I have your solemn promise for that?"

"My solemn promise," said Densil, and kissed her again.

"My dear," she resumed, "I wish you could get rid of that priest, that Mackworth. He is irksome to me."

"He was recommended to my especial care by my mother," was Densil's reply. "If you could let him stay I should much rather."

"Oh, let him stay!" said she; "he is too contemptible for me to annoy myself about. But I distrust him, Densil. He has a lowering look sometimes."

"He is talented and agreeable," said Densil; "but I never liked him."

The listener turned to go, having heard enough, but was arrested by her continuing—

"By the bye, my love, do you know that that impudent girl Norah has been secretly married this three months?"

The priest listened more intently than ever.

"Who to?" asked Densil.

"To James, your keeper."

"I am glad of that. That lad James stuck to me in prison, Susan, when they all left me. She is a fine, faithful creature, too. Mind you give her a good scolding."

Mackworth had heard enough apparently, for he stole gently away through the gloomy room, and walked musingly upstairs to Father Clifford.

That excellent old man took up the conversation just where it had left off.

"And when," said he, "my brother, do you propose returning to Rome?"

"I shall not go to Rome at all," was the satisfactory reply, followed by a deep silence.

In a few months, much to Father Clifford's joy and surprise, Mrs. Ravenshoe bore a noble boy, which was named Cuthbert. Cuthbert was brought up in the Romish faith, and at five years old had just begun to learn his prayers of Father Clifford, when an event occurred equally unexpected by all parties. Mrs. Ravenshoe was again found to be in a condition to make an addition to her family.

CHAPTER III

IN WHICH OUR HERO'S TROUBLES BEGIN

IF you were a lazy yachtsman, sliding on a summer's day, before a gentle easterly breeze, over the long swell from the Atlantic, past the south-westerly shores of the Bristol Channel, you would find, after sailing all day beneath shoreless headlands of black slate, that the land suddenly fell away and sunk down, leaving, instead of beetling cliffs, a lovely amphitheatre of hanging wood and lawn, fronted by a beach of yellow sand—a pleasing contrast to the white surf and dark crag to which your eye had got accustomed.

This beautiful semicircular basin is about two miles in diameter, surrounded by hills on all sides, save that which is open to the sea. East and west the headlands stretch out a mile or more, forming a fine bay open to the north ; while behind, landward, the downs roll up above the woodlands, a bare expanse of grass and grey stone. Half way along the sandy beach, a trout stream comes foaming out of a dark wood, and finds its way across the shore in fifty sparkling channels ; and the eye, caught by the silver thread of water, is snatched away above and beyond it, along a wooded glen, the cradle of the stream, which pierces the country landward for a mile or two, till the misty vista is abruptly barred by a steep blue hill which crosses the valley at right angles. A pretty little village stands at the mouth of the stream, and straggles with charming irregularity along the shore for a considerable distance westward ; while behind, some little distance up the glen, a handsome church tower rises from among the trees. There are some fishing boats at anchor, there are some small boats on the beach, there is a coasting schooner beached and discharging coal, there are some fishermen lounging, there are some nets drying, there are some boys bathing, there are two grooms exercising four handsome horses ; but it is not upon horses, men, boats, ship, village, church, or stream, that you will find your eye resting, but upon a noble, turreted, deep-porched, grey stone mansion, that stands on the opposite side of the stream, about a hundred feet above the village.

On the east bank of the little river, just where it joins the sea, abrupt lawns of grass and fern, beautifully broken by groups of birch and oak, rise above the dark woodlands, at the culminating point of which, on a buttress which runs down from the higher hills behind, stands the house I speak of, the north front looking on the sea, and the west on the wooded glen before mentioned—the house on a ridge dividing the two. Immediately behind again the dark woodlands begin once more, and above them is the moor.

The house itself is of grey stone, built in the time of Henry VIII. The façade is exceedingly noble, though irregular ; the most striking feature in the north or sea front being a large dark porch, open on three sides, forming the basement of a high stone tower, which occupies the centre of the building. At the north-west corner (that towards the village) rises another tower of equal height; and behind, above the irregular groups of chimneys, the more modern cupola of the stables shows itself as the highest point of all, and gives, combined with the other towers, a charming air of irregularity to the whole. The windows are mostly long, low, and heavily mullioned, and the walls are battlemented.

On approaching the house, you find that it is built very much after the fashion of a college, with a quadrangle in the centre. Two sides of this, the north and west, are occupied by the house, the south by the stables, and the east by a long and somewhat handsome chapel, of greater antiquity than the rest of the house. The centre of this quad, in place of the trim grass-plat, is occupied by a tan lunging ring, in the middle of which stands a granite basin filled with crystal water from the hills. In front of the west wing, a terraced flower-garden goes step by step towards the stream, till the smooth-shaven lawns almost mingle with the wild ferny heather turf of the park, where the dappled deer browse, and the rabbit runs to and fro busily. On the north, towards the sea, there are no gardens; but a noble gravel terrace, divided from the park only by a deep rampart, runs along beneath the windows; and to the east the deer-park stretches away till lawn and glade are swallowed up in the encroaching woodland.

Such is Ravenshoe Hall at the present day, and such it was on the 10th of June, 1831 (I like to be particular), as regards the still life of the place; but, if one had then regarded the living inhabitants, one would have seen signs of an unusual agitation. Round the kitchen door stood a group of female servants talking eagerly together; and, at the other side of the court, some half-dozen grooms and helpers were evidently busy on the same theme, till the appearance of the stud-groom entering the yard suddenly dispersed them right and left; to do nothing with superabundant energy.

To them also entered a lean, quiet-looking man, aged at this time fifty-two. We have seen him before. He was our old friend Jim, who had attended Densil in the Fleet prison in old times. He had some time before this married a beautiful Irish Catholic waiting-maid of Lady Alicia's, by whom he had a daughter, now five years old, and a son aged one week. He walked across the yard to where the women were talking, and addressed them.

"How is my lady to-night?" said he.

"Holy Mother of God!" said a weeping Irish housemaid, "she's worse."

"How's the young master?"

"Hearty, a darling; crying his little eyes out, he is, a-bless him."

"He'll be bigger than Master Cuthbert, I'll warrant ye," said a portly cook.

"When was he born?" asked James.

"Nigh on two hours," said the other speaker.

At this conjuncture a groom came running through the passage, putting a note in his hat as he went; he came to the stud-groom, and said hurriedly, "A note for Dr. Marcy at Lanceston, sir. What horse am I to take?"

"Trumpeter. How is my lady?"

"Going, as far as I can gather, sir."

James waited until he heard him dash full speed out of the yard, and then till he saw him disappear like a speck along the mountain road far aloft; then he went into the house, and, getting as near to the sick room as he dared, waited quietly on the stairs.

It was a house of woe, indeed! Two hours before, one feeble, wailing little creature had taken up his burthen, and begun his weary pilgrimage across the unknown desolate land that lay between him and the grave—for a part of which you and I are to accompany him; while his mother even now was preparing for her rest, yet striving for the child's sake to lengthen the last few weary steps of her journey, that they two might walk, were it never so short a distance, together.

The room was very still. Faintly the pure scents and sounds stole into the chamber of death from the blessed summer air without: gently came the murmur of the surf upon the sands; fainter and still fainter came the breath of the dying mother. The baby lay beside her and her arm was round its body. The old vicar knelt by the bed, and Densil stood with folded arms and bowed head, watching the face which had grown so dear to him, till the light should die out from it for ever. Only those four in the chamber of death!

The sighing grew louder, and the eye grew once more animated. She reached out her hand, and, taking one of the vicar's laid it upon the baby's head. Then she looked at Densil, who was now leaning over her, and with a great effort spoke.

"Densil, dear, you will remember your promise?"

"I will swear it, my love."

A few more laboured sighs, and a greater effort : " Swear it to me, love."

He swore that he would respect the promise he had made, so help him God !

The eyes were fixed now, and all was still. Then there was a long sigh ; then there was a long silence ; then the vicar rose from his knees, and looked at Densil. There were but three in the chamber now.

*   *   *   *   *   *

Densil passed through the weeping women, and went straight to his own study. There he sat, tearless, musing much about her who was gone.

How he had grown to love that woman, he thought—her that he had married for her beauty and her pride, and had thought so cold and hard ! He remembered how the love of her had grown stronger, year by year, since their first child was born. How he had respected her for her firmness and consistency ; and how often, he thought, had he sheltered his weakness behind her strength ! His right hand was gone, and he was left alone to do battle by himself !

One thing was certain. Happen what would, his promise should be respected, and this last boy, just born, should be brought up a Protestant as his mother had wished. He knew the opposition he would have from Father Mackworth, and determined to brave it. And, as the name of that man came into his mind, some of his old fierce, savage nature broke out again, and he almost cursed him aloud.

" I hate that fellow ! I should like to defy him, and let him do his worst. I'd do it, now she's gone, if it wasn't for the boys. No, hang it, it wouldn't do. If I'd told him under seal of confession, instead of letting him grub it out, he couldn't have hung it over me like this. I wish he was——"

If Father Mackworth had had the slightest inkling of the state of mind of his worthy patron towards him, it was very certain that he would not have chosen that very moment to rap at the door. The most acute of us make a mistake some-times ; and he, haunted with vague suspicions since the con-versation he had overheard in the drawing-room before the birth of Cuthbert, grew impatient, and determined to solve his doubts at once, and, as we have seen, selected the singularly happy moment when poor passionate Densil was cursing him to his heart's content.

" Brother, I am come to comfort you," he said, opening the door before Densil had time, either to finish the sentence written above, or to say "Come in." "This is a heavy affliction, and the heavier because——"

"Go away," said Densil, pointing to the door.

"Nay, nay," said the priest, "hear me——"

"Go away," said Densil, in a louder tone. "Do you hear me? I want to be alone, and I mean to be. Go!"

How recklessly defiant weak men get when they are once fairly in a rage? Densil, who was in general civilly afraid of this man, would have defied fifty such as he now.

"There is one thing, Mr. Ravenshoe," said the priest, in a very different tone, "about which I feel it my duty to speak to you, in spite of the somewhat unreasonable form your grief has assumed. I wish to know what you mean to call your son."

"Why?"

"Because he is ailing, and I wish to baptize him."

"You will do nothing of the kind, sir," said Densil, as red as a turkey-cock. "He will be baptized in proper time in the parish church. He is to be brought up a Protestant."

The priest looked steadily at Densil, who, now brought fairly to bay, was bent on behaving like a valiant man, and said slowly—

"So my suspicions are confirmed, then, and you have determined to hand over your son to eternal perdition" (he didn't say perdition, he used a stronger word, which we will dispense with, if you have no objection).

"Perdition, sir!" bawled Densil; "how dare you talk of a son of mine in that free-and-easy sort of way? Why, what my family has done for the Church ought to keep a dozen generations of Ravenshoes from a possibility of perdition, sir. Don't tell me."

This new and astounding theory of justification by works, which poor Densil had broached in his wrath, was overheard by a round-faced, bright-eyed, curly-headed man about fifty, who entered the room suddenly, followed by James. For one instance you might have seen a smile of intense amusement pass over his merry face; but in an instant it was gone again, and he gravely addressed Densil.

"My dear Mr. Ravenshoe, I must use my authority as doctor, to request that your son's spiritual welfare should for the present yield to his temporal necessities. You must have a wet-nurse, my good sir."

Densil's brow had grown placid in a moment beneath the doctor's kindly glance. "God bless me," he said, "I never thought of it. Poor little lad! poor little lad!"

"I hope, sir," said James, "that you will let Norah have the young master. She has set her heart upon it."

"I have seen Mrs. Horton," said the doctor, "and I quite approve of the proposal. I think it, indeed, a most special providence that she should be able to undertake it. Had it been otherwise, we might have been undone."

"Let us go at once," said the impetuous Densil. "Where is the nurse? where is the boy?" And, so saying, he hurried out of the room, followed by the doctor and James.

Mackworth stood alone, looking out of the window, silent. He stood so long that one who watched him peered from his hiding-place more than once to see if he were gone. At length he raised his arm and struck his clenched hand against the rough granite window-sill so hard that he brought blood. Then he moodily left the room.

As soon as the room was quiet, a child about five years old crept stealthily from a dark corner where he had lain hidden, and with a look of mingled shyness and curiosity on his face, departed quietly by another door.

Meanwhile, Densil, James, and the doctor, accompanied by the nurse and baby, were holding their way across the court-yard towards a cottage which lay in the wood beyond the stables. James opened the door, and they passed into the inner room.

A beautiful woman was sitting propped up by pillows, nursing a week-old child. The sunlight, admitted by a half-open shutter, fell upon her, lighting up her delicate features, her pale pure complexion, and bringing a strange sheen on her long loose black hair. Her face was bent down, gazing on the child which lay on her breast; and at the entrance of the party she looked up, and displayed a large lustrous dark blue eye, which lighted up with infinite tenderness as Densil, taking the wailing boy from the nurse, placed it on her arm beside the other.

"Take care of that for me, Norah," said Densil. "It has no mother but you now."

"Acushla ma chree," she answered; "bless my little bird. Come to your nest, alanna, come to your pretty brother, my darlin'."

The child's wailing was stilled now, and the doctor remarked, and remembered long afterwards, that the little waxen fingers, clutching uneasily about, came in contact with the little hand of the other child, and paused there. At this moment, a beautiful little girl, about five years old, got on the bed, and nestled her peachy cheek against her mother's. As they went out, he turned and looked at the beautiful group once more, and then he followed Densil back to the house of mourning.

Reader, before we have done with those three innocent little faces, we shall see them distorted and changed by many passions, and shall meet them in many strange places. Come, take my hand, and we will follow them on to the end.

CHAPTER IV

FATHER MACKWORTH

I HAVE noticed that the sayings and doings of young gentlemen before they come to the age of, say seven or eight, are hardly interesting to any but their immediate relations and friends. I have my eye, at this moment, on a young gentleman of the mature age of two, the instances of whose sagacity and eloquence are of greater importance, and certainly more pleasant, to me, than the projects of Napoleon, or the orations of Bright. And yet I fear that even his most brilliant joke, if committed to paper, would fall dead upon the public ear; and so, for the present, I shall leave Charles Ravenshoe to the care of Norah, and pass on to some others who demand our attention more.

The first thing which John Mackworth remembered was his being left in the *loge* of a French school at Rouen by an English footman. Trying to push back his memory farther, he always failed to conjure up any previous recollection to that. He had certainly a very indistinct one of having been happier, and having lived quietly in pleasant country places with a kind woman who talked English; but his first decided impression always remained the same—that of being, at six years old, left friendless, alone, among twenty or thirty French boys older than himself.

His was a cruel fate. He would have been happier apprenticed to a collier. If the man who sent him there had wished to inflict the heaviest conceivable punishment on the poor, unconscious little innocent, he could have done no more than simply left him at that school. We shall see how he found out at last who his benefactor was.

English boys are sometimes brutal to one another (though

not so often as some wish to make out), and are always rough. Yet I must say, as far as my personal experience goes, the French boy is entirely master in the art of tormenting. He never strikes ; he does not know how to clench his fist. He is an arrant coward, according to an English schoolboy's definition of the word : but at pinching, pulling hair, ear pulling, and that class of annoyance, all the natural ingenuity of his nation comes out, and he is superb ; add to this a combined insolent studied sarcasm, and you have an idea of what a disagreeable French schoolboy can be.

To say that the boys at poor John Mackworth's school put all these methods of torture in force against him, and ten times more, is to give one but a faint idea of his sufferings. The English at that time were hated with a hatred which we in these sober times have but little idea of ; and, with the cannon of Trafalgar ringing as it were in their ears, these young French gentlemen seized on Mackworth as a lawful prize providentially delivered into their hands. We do not know what he may have been under happier auspices, or what he may be yet with a more favourable start in another life ; we have only to do with what he was. Six years of friendless persecution, of life ungraced and uncheered by domestic love, of such bitter misery as childhood alone is capable of feeling or enduring, transformed him from a child into a heartless, vindictive man.

And then, the French schoolmaster having roughly finished the piece of goods, it was sent to Rome to be polished and turned out ready for the market. Here I must leave him ; I don't know the process. I have seen the article when finished and am familiar with it. I know the trade mark on it as well as I know the Tower mark on my rifle. I may predicate of a glass that it is Bohemian ruby, and yet not know how they gave it the colour. I must leave descriptions of that system to Mr. Steinmetz, and men who have been behind the scenes.

The red-hot ultramontane thorough-going Catholicism of that pretty pervert, Lady Alicia, was but ill satisfied with the sensible, old English, cut-and-dried notions of the good Father Clifford. A comparison of notes with two or three other great ladies, brought about a consultation, and a letter to Rome, the result of which was that a young Englishman of presentable exterior, polite manners, talking English with a slight foreign accent, made his appearance at Ravenshoe, and was installed as her ladyship's confessor, about eighteen months before her death.

His talents were by no means ordinary. In very few days

he had gauged every intellect in the house, and found that he was by far the superior of all in wit and education ; and he determined that as long as he stayed in the house he would be master there.

Densil's jealous temper sadly interfered with this excellent resolution ; he was immensely angry and rebellious at the slightest apparent infringement of his prerogative, and after his parents' death treated Mackworth in such an exceedingly cavalier manner, that the latter feared he should have to move, till chance threw into his hand a whip wherewith he might drive Densil where he would. He discovered a scandalous liaison of poor Densil's, and in an indirect manner let him know that he knew all about it. This served to cement his influence until the appearance of Mrs. Ravenshoe the second, who, as we have seen, treated him with such ill-disguised contempt, that he was anything but comfortable, and was even meditating a retreat to Rome, when the conversation he overheard in the drawing-room made him pause, and the birth of the boy Cuthbert confirmed his resolution to stay.

For now, indeed, there was a prospect open to him. Here was this child delivered over to him like clay to a potter, that he might form it as he would. It should go hard but that the revenues and county influence of the Ravenshoes should tend to the glory of the Church as heretofore. Only one person was in his way, and that was Mrs. Ravenshoe ; after her death he was master of the situation with regard to the eldest of the boys. He had partly guessed, ever since he overheard the conversation of Densil and his wife, that some sort of bargain existed between them about the second child ; but he paid little heed to it. It was, therefore, with the bitterest anger that he saw his fears confirmed, and Densil angrily obstinate on the matter ; for supposing Cuthbert were to die, all his trouble and anxiety would avail nothing, and the old house and lands would fall to a Protestant heir, the first time in the history of the island. Father Clifford consoled him.

Meanwhile, his behaviour towards Densil was gradually and insensibly altered. He became the free and easy man of the world, the amusing companion, the wise counsellor. He saw that Densil was of a nature to lean on some one, and he was determined it should be on him ; so he made himself necessary. But he did more than this ; he determined he would be beloved as well as respected, and with a happy audacity he set to work to win that poor wild foolish heart to himself, using such arts of pleasing as must have been furnished by his own mother wit, and could never have been learned in a hundred years from a Jesuit college. The poor heart was not a hard one to win ; and, the day they buried poor Father Clifford in the mausoleum, it was with a mixture of pride at his own talents, and contemptuous pity for his dupe, that Mackworth listened to Densil as he told him that he was now his only friend, and besought him not to leave him—which thing Mackworth promised, with the deepest sincerity, he would not do.

CHAPTER V

RANFORD

Master Charles, blessed with a placid temper and a splendid appetite, throve amazingly. Before you knew where you were, he was in tops and bottoms ; before you had thoroughly realized that, he was learning his letters ; then there was hardly time to turn round, before he was a rosy-cheeked boy of ten.

From the very first gleam of reason, he had been put solely and entirely under the care of Mr. Snell, the old vicar, who had been with his mother when she died, and a Protestant nurse, Mrs. Varley. Faithfully had these two discharged their sacred trust ; and, if love can repay such services, right well were they repaid.

A pleasant task they had, though, for a more lovable little lad than Charles there never was. His little heart seemed to have an infinite capacity of affection for all who approached him. Everything animate came before him in the light of a friend, to whom he wished to make himself agreeable, from his old kind tutor and nurse down to his pony and terrier. Charles had not arrived at the time of life when it was possible for him to quarrel about women ; and so he actually had no enemies as yet, but was welcomed by pleasant and kind faces wherever he went. At one time he would be at his father's knee, while the good-natured Densil made him up some fishing tackle ; next you would find him in the kennel, with the whipper-in, feeding the hounds, half-smothered by their boisterous welcome ; then the stables would own him for a time, while the lads were cleaning up and feeding ; then came a sudden flitting to one of the keeper's lodges ; and anon he would be down on the sands wading with half a dozen fisher-boys as happy as himself—but welcomed and beloved everywhere.

Sunday was a right pleasant day for him. After seeing his father shave, and examining his gold-topped dressing-case from top to bottom—amusements which were not participated in by Cuthbert, who had grown too manly—he would haste through his breakfast, and with his clean clothes hurry down the village towards the vicarage, which stood across the stream near the church. Not to go in yet, you will observe, because the sermon, he well knew, was getting its finishing touches, and the vicar must not be disturbed. No, the old stone bridge would bring him up; and there he would stay looking at the brown crystal-clear water rushing and seething among the rocks, lying dark under the oak-roots, and flashing merrily over the weir, just above the bridge; till "flick!" a silver bar would shoot quivering into the air, and a salmon would light on the top of the fall, just where the water broke, and would struggle on into the still pool above, or be beaten back by the force, to resume his attempt when he had gained breath. The trout, too, under the bridge, bless the rogues, they knew it was Sunday well enough—how they would lie up there in the swiftest places, where glancing liquid glorified the poor pebbles below into living amber, and would hardly trouble themselves to snap at the great fat, silly stoneflies that came floating down. Oh! it was a terrible place for dawdling was that stone bridge on a summer sabbath morn.

But now would the country folks come trooping in from far and near, for Ravenshoe was the only church for miles, and however many of them there were, every one had a good West-country greeting for him. And, as the crowd increased near the church door, there was so much to say and hear, that I am afraid the prayers suffered a little sometimes.

The villagers were pleased enough to see the lad in the old carved horse-box (not to be irreverent) of a pew, beneath the screen in the chancel, with the light from the old rose window shining on his curly brown hair. The older ones would think of the haughty beautiful lady who sat there so few years ago, and oftentimes one of the more sagacious would shake his head and mutter to himself, "Ah! if *he* were heir."

Any boy who reads this story, and I hope many will read it, is hereby advertised that it is exceedingly wrong to be inattentive in church in sermon time. It is very naughty to look up through the windows at the white clouds flying across the blue

sky, and think how merrily the shadows are sweeping over the
upland lawn, where the pewits' nests are, and the blackcock is
crowing on the grey stones among the heather. No boy has
any right to notice another boy's absence, and spend sermon-
time in wondering whether he is catching crabs among the
green and crimson sea-weed on the rocks, or bathing in the still
pool under the cliff. A boy had better not go to church at all,
if he spends his time in thinking about the big trout that lies
up in one of the pools of the woodland stream, and whether
he will be able to catch a sight of him again by creeping gently
through the hazel and king fern. Birds' nests, too, even though
it be the ringousel's, who is to lay her last egg this blessed day,
and is marked for spoliation to-morrow, should be banished
from a boy's mind entirely during church time. Now, I am
sorry to say, that Charley was very much given to wander in
church, and, when asked about the sermon by the vicar next
day, would look rather foolish. Let us hope that he will be a
warning to all sinners in this respect.

Then, after church, there would be dinner, at his father's
lunch time, in the dark old hall, and there would be more to tell
his father and brother than could be conveniently got through at
that meal; then there was church again, and a long stroll in the
golden sunshine along the shore. Ah, happy summer sabbaths!

The only two people who were ever cold to Charley, were
his brother and Mackworth. Not that they were openly unkind, but there was between both of them and himself an
indefinable gulf, an entire want of sympathy, which grieved
him sometimes, though he was as yet too young to be much
troubled by it. He only exhausted all his little arts of pleasing
towards them to try and win them; he was indefatigable in
running messages for Cuthbert and the chaplain; and once,
when kind grandaunt Ascot (she was a Miss Headstall, daughter
of Sir Cingle Headstall, and married Lord George Ascot,
brother of Lady Alicia, Densil's mother) sent him a pineapple
in a box, he took it to the priest and would have had him take
it. Mackworth refused it, but looked on him not unkindly for
a few minutes, and then turned away with a sigh. Perhaps he
was trying to recall the time so long, long ago, when his own
face was as open and as innocent as that. God knows!
Charles cried a little, because the priest wouldn't take it, and,
having given his brother the best slice, ate the rest in the stable,
with the assistance of his foster brother, and two of the pad
grooms. Thereby proving himself to be a lad of low and
dissipated habits.

Cuthbert was at this time a somewhat good-looking young fellow of sixteen. Neither of the brothers was what would be called handsome, though, if Charley's face was the most pleasing, Cuthbert certainly had the most regular features. His forehead was lofty, although narrow, and flat at the sides; his cheek bones were high, and his nose was aquiline, not ill-formed, though prominent, starting rather suddenly out below his eyes; the lips were thin, the mouth small and firmly closed, and the chin short and prominent. The *tout ensemble* was hardly pleasing even at this youthful period; the face was too much formed and decided for so young a man.

Cuthbert was a reserved methodical lad, with whom no one could find fault, and yet whom few liked. He was studious and devout to an extent rare in one so young; and although a capital horseman, and a good shot, he but seldom indulged in those amusements, preferring rather a walk with the steward, and soon returning to the dark old library to his books and Father Mackworth. There they two would sit, like two owls, hour after hour, appearing only at meals, and talking French to one another, noticing Charley but little; who, however, was always full of news, and would tell it, too, in spite of the inattention of the strange couple. Densil began to respect and be slightly afraid of his eldest son, as his superior in learning and in natural abilities; but I think Charles had the biggest share in his heart.

Aunt Ascot had a year before sent to Cuthbert to pay her a visit at Ranford, her son's, Lord Ascot's place, where she lived with him, he being a widower, and kept house for him. Ranford, we all know, or ought to know, contains the largest private racing stud in England, and the Ascot family for many generations had given themselves up entirely to sporting—so much so, that their marriages with other houses have been to a certain extent influenced by it; and so poor Cuthbert, as we may suppose, was quite like a fish out of water. He detested and despised the men he met there, and they, on their parts, such of them as chose to notice him, thought him a surly young book-worm; and, as for his grandaunt, he hated the very sound of that excellent lady's voice. Her abruptness, her homœopathic medicines, her Protestantism (which she was always airing), and her stable-talk, nearly drove him mad; while she, on the other hand, thought him one of the most disagreeable boys she had ever met with in her life. So the visit was rather a failure than otherwise, and not very likely to be repeated. Nevertheless, her ladyship was very fond of young faces, and so in a twelvemonth, she wrote to Densil, as follows :—

"I am one mass of lumbago all round the small of my back, and I find nothing like opodeldoc after all. The pain is very severe, but I suppose you would comfort me, as a heretic, by saying it is nothing to what I shall endure in a few years' time. Bah! I have no patience with you Papists, packing better people than yourselves off somewhere in that free-and-easy way. By-the-bye, how is that father confessor of yours, Markworth, or some such name—mind me, Ravenshoe, that fellow is a rogue, and you being, like all Ravenshoes, a fool, there is a pair of you. Why, if one of Ascot's grooms was to smile as that man does, or to whine in his speech as that man does, when he is talking to a woman of rank, I'd have him discharged on the spot, without warning, for dishonesty.

"Don't put a penny on Ascot's horse at Chester; he will never stay over the Cup course. Curfew, in my opinion, looks by no means badly for the Derby; he is scratched for the Two Thousand—which was necessary, though I am sorry for it, &c., &c., &c.

"I wish you would send me your boy, will you? Not the eldest: the Protestant one. Perhaps he mayn't be such an insufferable coxcomb as his brother."

At which letter Densil shook his honest sides with uproarious laughter. "Cuthbert, my boy," he said, "you have won your dear aunt's heart entirely; though she, being determined to mortify the flesh with its affections, does not propose seeing you again, but asks for Charley. The candour of that dear old lady increases with her age. You seem to have been making your court, too, father; she speaks of your smile in the most unqualified terms."

"Her ladyship must do me the honour to quiz me," said Mackworth. "If it is possible to judge by her eye, she must like me about as well as a mad dog."

"For my part, father," said Cuthbert, curling up the corners of his thin lips sardonically, "I shall be highly content to leave my dear aunt in the peaceable enjoyment of her favourite society of grooms, horse-jockies, black-legs, dissenting ministers, and such-like. A month in that house, my dear Charley, will qualify you for a billiard-marker; and, after a course of six weeks, you will be fit to take the situation of croupier in a low hell on a race-course. How you will enjoy yourself, my dear !"

"Steady, Cuthbert, steady," said his father; "I can't allow you to talk like that about your cousin's house. It is a great house for field sports, but there is not a better conducted house in the kingdom."

Cuthbert lay over the sofa to fondle a cat, and then continued speaking very deliberately, in a slightly louder voice,

"I will allow my aunt to be the most polite, intellectual, delicate-minded old lady in creation, my dearest father, if you wish it; only, not having been born (I beg her pardon, dropped) in a racing stable, as she was herself, I can hardly appreciate her conversation always. As for my cousin, I consider him a splendid sample of an hereditary legislator. Charley, dear, you won't go to Church on Sunday afternoon at Ranford; you will go into the croft with your cousin Ascot to see the chickens fed. Ascot is very curious in his poultry, particularly on Sunday afternoon. Father, why does he cut all the cocks' tails square?"

"Pooh, pooh," said Densil, "what matter? many do it besides him. Don't you be squeamish, Cuthbert—though, mind you, I don't defend cock-fighting on Sunday."

Cuthbert laughed and departed, taking his cat with him.

Charles had a long coach journey of one day, and then an awful and wonderful journey on the Great Western Railway as far as Twyford—alighting at which place, he was accosted by a pleasant-looking, fresh-coloured boy, dressed in close-fitting cord trousers, a blue handkerchief, spotted with white, and a Scotch cap; who said—

"Oh! I'm your cousin Welter. I'm the same age as you, and I'm going to Eton next half. I've brought you over Tiger, because Punch is lame, and the station-master will look after your things; so we can come at once."

The boys were friends in two minutes; and going out, there was a groom holding two ponies—on the prettiest of which Charley soon found himself seated, and jogging on with his companion towards Henley. I like to see two honest lads, just introduced, opening their hearts to one another, and I know nothing more pleasant than to see how they rejoice as each similarity of taste comes out. By the time these two had got to Henley Bridge, Lord Welter had heard the name of every horse in the Ravenshoe stables, and Charley was rapidly getting learned in Lord Ascot's racing stud. The river at Henley distracted his attention for a time, as the biggest he had seen, and he asked his cousin, "Did he think the Mississippi was much bigger than that now?" and Lord Welter supposed, "Oh dear yes, a great deal bigger," he should say. Then there was more conversation about dogs and guns, and pleasant country

B

places to ride through ; then a canter over a lofty breezy down, and then the river again, far below, and at their feet the chimneys of Ranford.

The house was very full ; and, as the boys came up there was a crowd of phaetons, dog-carts, and saddle-horses, for the people were just arriving home for dinner after the afternoon drive, and, as they had all been to the same object of attraction that afternoon, they had all come in together and were loitering about talking, some not yet dismounted, and some on the steps. Welter was at home at once, and had a word with every one ; but Charles was left alone, sitting on his pony, feeling very shy ; till, at last, a great brown man with a great brown moustache, and a gruff voice, came up to him and lifted him off the horse, holding him out at arm's length for inspection.

" So you are Curly Ravenshoe's boy, eh ? " said he.

" Yes, sir."

" Ha ! " said the stranger, putting him down, and leading him towards the door ; " just tell your father you saw General Mainwaring, will you, and that he wanted to know how his old friend was."

Charles looked at the great brown hand which was in his own, and thought of the Afghan war, and of all the deeds of renown that that hand had done, and was raising his eyes to the general's face, when they were arrested half-way by another face, not the general's.

It was that of a handsome, grey-headed man, who might have been sixty, he was so well *conservé*, but who was actually far more. He wore his own white hair, which contrasted strongly with a pair of delicate thin black eyebrows. His complexion was florid, with scarcely a wrinkle, his features were fine and regular, and a pair of sparkling dark grey eyes gave a pleasant light to his face. His dress was wondrously neat, and Charles looking on him, guessed, with a boy's tact, that he was a man of mark.

" Whose son did you say he was, general ? " said the stranger.

" Curly's ! " said Mainwaring, stopping and smiling.

" No, really ! " said the other ; and then he looked fixedly at Charles, and began to laugh, and Charley, seeing nothing better to do, looked up at the grey eyes and laughed too, and this made the stranger worse ; and then, to crown the joke, the general began to laugh too, though none of them had said a syllable more than what I have written down ; and at last the ridiculous exhibition finished up by the old gentleman taking a great pinch of snuff from a gold box, and turning away.

Charles was much puzzled, and was still more so when, in an hour's time, having dressed himself, and being on his way downstairs to his aunt's room, who had just come in, he was stopped on the landing by this same old gentleman, beautifully dressed for dinner, who looked on him as before.

He didn't laugh this time, but he did worse. He utterly "dumbfounded" Charley, by asking abruptly—

"How's Jim?"

"He is very well, thank you, sir. His wife Norah nursed me when mamma died."

"Oh, indeed," said the other; "so he hasn't cut your father's throat yet, or anything of that sort?"

"Oh, dear, no," said Charles horrified; "bless you, what can make you think of such things? Why, he is the kindest man in the world."

"I don't know," said the old gentleman thoughtfully; "that excessively faithful kind of creature is very apt to do that sort of thing. I should discharge any servant of mine who exhibited the slightest symptoms of affection as a dangerous lunatic;" with which villainous sentiment he departed.

Charles thought what a strange old gentleman he was for a short time, and then slid down the banisters. They were better banisters than those at Ravenshoe, being not so steep, and longer; so he went up and slid down again;[1] after which he knocked at his aunt's door.

It was with a beating heart that he waited for an answer. Cuthbert had described Lady Ascot as such a horrid old ogress, that he was not without surprise when a cheery voice said, "Come in;" and entering a handsome room, he found himself in presence of a noble-looking old lady, with grey hair, who was knitting in an upright, old-fashioned chair.

"So you are Charles Ravenshoe, eh?" she began. "Why, my dear, you must be perished with cold and hunger. I should have come in before, but I didn't expect you so soon. Tea will be here directly. You ain't a beauty my dear, but I think I shall like you. There never was but one really handsome Ravenshoe, and that was poor Petre, your grandfather. Poor Alicia made a great fool of herself, but she was very happy with him. Welter, you naughty boy, be still."

The Right Honourable Viscount Welter wanted his tea, and was consequently troublesome and fractious. He had picked a quarrel with his grandmother's terrier, which he averred had

---

[1] The best banisters for sliding down are broad oak ones, with a rib in the middle. This new narrow sort, which is coming in, are wretched.

bitten him in the leg, and he was now heating the poker, in order, he informed the lady, to burn the place out, and prevent hydrophobia. Whether he would have done so or not, we shall never know now, for, tea coming in at that moment, he instantly sat down at table, and called to Charles to do likewise.

"Call Miss Adelaide, will you, Sims?" said Lady Ascot; and presently there came tripping into the room the loveliest little blonde fairy, about ten years old, that ever you saw. She fixed her large blue eyes on Charley, and then came up and gave him a kiss, which he, the rogue, returned with interest, and then, taking her seat at the table, she turned to Welter, and hoped he was going to be good.

Such, however, it soon appeared, was not his lordship's intention. He had a guest at table, and he was bound in honour to show off before him, besides having to attend to his ordinary duty of frightening his grandmother as nearly into fits as was safe. Accordingly, he began the repast by cramming buns into his mouth, using the handle of his knife as a rammer, until the salvation of his life appeared an impossibility, at which point he rose and left the room with a rapid, uneven step. On his reappearance he began drinking, but, having caught his grandmother's eye, over his teacup, he winked at her, and then held his breath till he was purple, and she began to ring her hands in despair. All this time he was stimulated by Charles's laughter and Adelaide's crying out, continually, "Oh, isn't he a naughty boy, Lady Ascot? oh, do tell him not to do it." But the crowning performance of this promising young gentleman—the feat which threw everything else into the shade, and which confirmed Charley in his admiration of his profound talents—was this. Just as a tall, grave, and handsome footman was pouring water into the teapot, and while her ladyship was inspecting the operation with all the interest of an old tea-maker, at that moment did Lord Welter contrive to inflict on the unfortunate man a pinch on the leg, of such a shrewdly agonizing nature as caused him to gnash his teeth in Lady Ascot's face, to cry aloud, "Oh, Lord!" to whirl the kettle within an inch of her venerable nose, and finally to gyrate across the room on one leg, and stand looking like the king of fools.

Lady Ascot, who had merely seen the effect, and not the cause, ordered him promptly to leave the room, whereupon Welter explained, and afterwards continued to Charles, with an off-hand candour quite his own, as if no such person as his grandmother was within a hundred miles—

"You know, Charley, I shouldn't dare to behave like this if my tutor was at home; she'd make nothing of telling him, now. She's in a terrible wax, but she'll be right by the time he comes back from his holidays; won't you, grandma?"

"You wicked boy," she replied. "I hope Hawtrey will cure you; Keate would have, I know."

The boys slid on the banisters; then they went to dessert. Then they went upstairs, and looked over Welter's cricket apparatus, fishing tackle, and so on; and then they went into the billiard-room, which was now lighted up and full of guests.

There were two tables in the room, at one of which a pool was getting up, while the other was empty. Welter was going to play pool, and Charles would have liked to do so too, being a very tolerable player; only he had promised his old tutor not to play for money till he was eighteen, and so he sat in the corner by the empty table, under the marking board, with one leg gathered under him, and instantly found himself thinking about the little girl he had seen upstairs.

Once or twice he was surprised to find himself thinking so much about her, but he found it a pleasant subject, too, for he had sat in his corner more than half-an-hour without changing it, when he became aware that two men were taking down cues from the rack, and were going to play at his table.

They were his two friends of the afternoon, General Mainwaring and the grey-headed man who laughed. When they saw him they seemed glad, and the old gentleman asked him why he wasn't playing.

"I mustn't play pool," he answered. "I should like to mark for you."

"Well said, my hero," said the general: "and so Jim's an honest man, is he?"

Charles saw that the old gentleman had told the general what had passed on the stairs, and wondered why he should take such an interest in him; but he soon fell to thinking about little Adelaide again, and marking mechanically, though correctly.

He was aroused by the general's voice. "Who did you mark that last miss to, my little man?" he said.

"To the old gentleman," said Charles, and then blushed at the consciousness of having said a rude thing.

"That is one for you, Methuselah," said the general.

"Never mind," said the old gentleman, "I have one great source of pride, which no one can rob me of, I am twelve years older than I look."

They went on playing. "By-the-by," said the general, "who is that exceedingly pretty child that the old lady has got with her?"

"A child she has adopted," said the old gentleman. "A grand-daughter of an old friend who died in poverty. She is a noble-hearted old soul, the jockey, with all her absurdities."

"Who was she?" said the general. ("That was rather a fluke, was it not?")

"She? Why, a daughter of old Cingle Headstall's, the mad old Cheshire baronet—you don't remember him, of course, but your father knew him. Drove his tandem round and round Berkeley Square for four hours on a foggy night, under the impression he was going home to Hounslow, and then fired at the watchman who tried to put him right, taking him for a highwayman. The son went to France, and was lost sight of in the revolution; so the girl came in for what money there was : not very much, I take it. This poor thing, who was pretty and clever enough, but without education, having been literally brought up in a stable, captivated the sagacious Ascot, and made him a capital wife."

"I suppose she'll portion this girl, then; you say she had money?"

"H'm," said the old gentleman, "there's a story about the aforesaid money, which is told in different ways, but which amounts to this, that the money is no more. Hallo, our marker is getting sleepy."

"Not at all, sir," said Charles. "If you will excuse me a moment, I will come back."

He ran across to Lord Welter, who was leaning on his cue. "Can you tell me," said he, "who is that old gentleman?"

"Which old gentleman?"

"That one, with the black eyebrows, playing with General Mainwaring. There, he is taking snuff."

"Oh, *him?*" said Welter; "that is Lord Saltire."

CHAPTER VI

THE WARREN HASTINGS

TIME, the inexorable, kept mowing away at poor Charles's flowers until the disagreeable old creature had cut them all

down but two or three, and mowed right into the morning
when it was necessary that he should go home; and then
Charles, looking forward through his tears, could see nothing
at first but the very commonest grass. For was he not going
to leave Adelaide, probably never to see her again? In short,
Charles was in love, and going to separate from the object of
his affections for the first time; at which I request you not to
laugh, but just reflect how old you were yourself when you first
fell in love.

The little flirt, she must have waited till she heard him
coming out of his room, and then have pretended to be coming
upstairs all in a hurry. He got a kiss or a dozen, though, and
a lock of hair, I believe; but he hadn't much time to think
about it, for Lord Ascot was calling out for him, and when he
got into the hall, there was all the household to see him off.
Everybody had a kind word for him; the old lady cried; Lord
Saltire and the general shook hands; Lord Welter said it was
a beastly sell; and Lord Ascot hummed and hawed, and told
him to tell his father he had been a good boy. They were all
sorry he was going, and he left as though he was leaving old
friends; but the carriage was there, and the rain was pouring
down; and, with one last look at the group of faces, he was in
the carriage and away.

It was a terrible day, though he did not notice it at first.
He was thinking how pleasant it was that the people were all
so kind to him, just as kind as they were at home. He thought
of Adelaide, and wondered whether she would ever think of
him. He was rather glad that Welter was a naughty boy (not
really naughty, you know), because she would be less likely to
like him. And then he thought how glad the people at home
would be to see him; and then he looked out of the window.
He had left Lord Ascot's carriage and got into the train some
time before this. Now he saw that the train was going very
slowly, and nothing was visible through the driving rain. Then
he tried to remember whether he had heard his father speak of
Lord Saltire, and what he had heard about him; and thinking
about this, the train stopped.—Swindon.

He got out to go to the refreshment room, and began
wondering what the noise was which prevented him from
hearing any one when they spoke, and why the people looked
scared, and talked in knots. Then he found that it was the
wind in the roof, and some one told him that a chimney had
been blown across the line, and they must wait till it was
removed.

All the day the brave engine fought westward against the wind, and two hours after time Charles found himself in the coach which would take him to Stonnington. The night crept on, and the coach crawled on its way through the terrible night, and Charles slept. In the cold pitiless morning, as they were going over a loftily exposed moor, the coach, though only going foot's pace, stood for a moment on two wheels, and then fell crashing over on to a heap of road-side stones, awaking Charles, who, being unhurt, lay still for a minute or so, with a faint impression of having been shaken in his sleep, and, after due reflection, made the brilliant discovery that the coach was upset.

He opened the door over his head and jumped out. For an instant he was blinded by the stinging rain, but turned his back to it; and then, for the first time, he became aware that this was the most terrible gale of wind he had ever seen in his lifetime.

He assisted the coachman and guard, and the solitary outside passenger, to lead the poor horses along the road. They fought on for about two hundred yards, and came to an alehouse, on the sight of which Charles knew that they were two stages short of where he thought they had been, for this was the Watershed Inn, and the rain from its roof ran partly into the Bristol Channel and partly into the British.

After an hour's rest here Charles was summoned to join the coach in the valley below, and they crawled on again. It was a weary day over some very bleak country. They saw in one place a cottage unroofed on a moor, and the terrified family crouched down beneath the tottering walls. In the valleys great trees were down across the road, which were cross-cut and moved by country men, who told of oaks of three hundred years fallen in the night, and of corn stacks hurried before the blast like the leaves of autumn. Still, as each obstacle was removed, there was the guard up blowing his horn cheerily, and Charles was inside with a jump, and on they went.

At last, at three o'clock, the coach drove under the gate of the "Chichester Arms," at Stonnington, and Charles, jumping out, was received by the establishment with the air of people who had done a clever thing, and were ready to take their meed of praise with humility. The handsome landlady took great credit to herself for Charles's arrival—so much so, that one would have thought she herself had, single-handed, dragged the coach from Exeter. "*She* had been sure all along that Mr. Charles would come." A speech which, with the cutting glance that accompanied it, goaded the landlord to retort in a voice wheezy with good living, and to remind her that she had said, not ten minutes before, that she was quite sure he wouldn't; whereupon the landlady loftily begged him not to expose himself before the servants. At which the landlord laughed, and choked himself; at which the landlady slapped him on the back, and laughed too; after which they went in.

His father, the landlord told him, had sent his pony over, as he was afraid of a carriage on the moor to-day, and that, if he felt at all afraid to come on, he was to sleep where he was. Charles looked at the comfortable parlour and hesitated; but, happening to close his eyes an instant, he saw as plain as possible the library at home, and the flickering fire-light falling on the crimson and oak furniture, and his father listening for him through the roaring wind; and so he hesitated no longer, but said he would push on, and that he would wish to see his servant while he took dinner.

The landlord eyed him admiringly with his head on one side, and proceeded to remark that corn was down another shilling; that Squire West had sold his chesnut mare for one hundred and twenty pounds; and that if he kept well under the walls going home he would be out of the wind; that his missis was took poorly in the night with spasms, and had been cured by two wine-glasses of peppermint; that a many chimney-pots was blown down, and that old Jim Baker had heard tell as a pig was blowed through a church window. After which he poked the fire and retired.

Charles was hard at his dinner when his man came in. It was the oldest of the pad grooms—a man with grizzled hair, looking like a white terrier; and he stood before him smoothing his face with his hand.

"Hallo, Michael," said Charley, "how came you to come?"

"Master wouldn't send no other, sir. It's an awful day down there; there's above a hundred trees down along the road."

"Shall we be able to get there?"

"As much as we shall, sir."

"Let us try. Terrible sea, I suppose?"

"Awful to look at, sir. Mr. Mackworth and Mr. Cuthbert are down to look at it."

"No craft ashore?"

"None as yet. None of our boats is out. Yesterday morning a Pill boat, 52, stood in to see where she was, and beat out again, but that was before it came on so bad."

So they started. They pushed rapidly out of the town, and up a narrow wooded valley which led to the moor which lay between them and Ravenshoe. For some time they were well enough sheltered, and made capital way, till the wood began to grow sparer, and the road to rise abruptly. Here the blast began to be more sensibly felt, and in a quarter of a mile they had to leap three uprooted trees; before them they heard a rushing noise like the sea. It was the wind upon the moor.

Creeping along under the high stone walls, and bending down, they pushed on still, until, coming to the open moor, and receiving for the first time the terrible tornado full in their faces, the horses reared up and refused to proceed; but, being got side by side and their heads being homeward, they managed to get on, though the rain upon their faces was agonising.

As they were proceeding thus, with Michael on the windward side, Charles looked up, and there was another horseman beside him. He knew him directly; it was Lloyd's agent.

"Anything wrong, Mr. Lewis? Any ship ashore?" he shouted.

"Not yet, sir," said the agent. "But there'll be many a good sailor gone to the bottom before to-morrow morning, I am thinking. This is the heaviest gale for forty years."

By degrees they descended to more sheltered valleys, and after a time found themselves in the court-yard of the hall. Charles was caught up by his father; Lloyd's agent was sent to the housekeeper's room; and very soon Charles had forgotten all about wind and weather, and was pouring into his father's ear all his impressions of Ranford.

"I am glad you liked it," said Densil, "and I'll be bound they liked you. You ought to have gone first. Cuthbert don't suit them."

"Oh, Cuthbert's too clever for them," said Charles; "they are not at all clever people, bless you!" And only just in time too, for Cuthbert walked into the room.

"Well, Charley," he said coolly, "so you're come back. Well, and what did you think of Welter, eh? I suppose he suited you?"

"I thought him very funny, Cuthbert," said Charles, timidly.

"I thought him an abominable young nuisance," said Cuthbert. "I hope he hasn't taught you any of his fool's tricks."

Charles wasn't to be put off like this; so he went and kissed his brother, and then came back to his father. There was a long dull evening, and when they went to complines, he went to bed. Up in his room he could hear that the wind was worse than ever, not rushing up in great gusts and sinking again, as in ordinary gales, but keeping up one continued unvarying scream against the house, which was terrible to hear.

He got frightened at being alone; afraid of finding some ghostly thing at his elbow, which had approached him unheard through the noise. He began, indeed, to meditate upon going downstairs, when Cuthbert, coming into the next room, reassured him, and he got into bed.

This wasn't much better, though, for there was a thing in a black hood came and stood at the head of his bed; and, though he could not see it, he could feel the wind of its heavy draperies as it moved. Moreover, a thing like a caterpillar, with a cat's head, about two feet long, came creep—creeping up the counterpane, which he valiantly smote, and found it to be his handkerchief—and still the unvarying roar went on till it was unendurable.

He got up and went to his brother's room, and was cheered to find a light burning; he came softly in and called "Cuthbert."

"Who is there?" asked he, with a sudden start.

"It's I," said Charles; "can you sleep?"

"Not I," saith Cuthbert, sitting up. "I can hear people talking in the wind. Come into bed; I'm so glad you're come."

Charles lay down by his brother, and they talked about ghosts for a long time. Once their father came in with a light from his bed-room next door, and sat on the bed talking, as if he, too, was glad of company, and after that they dozed off and slept.

It was in the grey light of morning that they awoke together and started up. The wind was as bad as ever, but the whole house was still, and they stared terrified at one another.

"What was it?" whispered Charles.

Cuthbert shook his head, and listened again. As he was opening his mouth to speak it came again, and they knew it was that which woke them. A sound like a single footstep on the floor above, light enough, but which shook the room. Cuthbert was out of bed in an instant, tearing on his clothes. Charles jumped out too, and asked him, "What is it?"

"A gun!"

Charles well knew what awful disaster was implied in those words. The wind was N.W., setting into the bay. The ship that fired that gun was doomed.

He heard his father leap out of bed, and ring furiously at his bell. Then doors began to open and shut, and voices and rapid footsteps were heard in the passage. In ten minutes the whole terrified household were running hither and thither, about they hardly knew what. The men were pale, and some of the women were beginning to whimper and wring their hands; when Densil, Lewis the agent, and Mackworth came rapidly down the staircase and passed out. Mackworth came back, and told the women to put on hot water and heat blankets. Then Cuthbert joined him, and they went together; and directly after Charles found himself between two men-servants, being dragged rapidly along towards the low headland which bounded the bay on the east.

When they came to the beach, they found the whole village pushing on in a long straggling line the same way as themselves. The men were walking singly, either running or going very fast ; and the women were in knots of twos and threes, straggling along and talking excitedly, with much gesticulation.

"There's some of the elect on board, I'll be bound," Charles heard one woman say, "as will be supping in glory this blessed night."

"Ay, ay," said an old woman. "I'd sooner be taken to rest sudden, like they're going to be, than drag on till all the faces you know are gone before."

"My boy," said another, "was lost in a typhoon in the China sea. Darn they lousy typhoons ! I wonder if he thought of his mother afore he went down."

Among such conversation as this, with the terrible, ceaseless thunder of the surf upon the left, Charles, clinging tight to his two guardians, made the best weather of it he could, until they found themselves on the short turf of the promontory, with their faces seaward, and the water right and left of them. The cape ran out about the third of a mile, rather low, and then abruptly ended in a cone of slate, beyond which, about two hundred yards at sea, was that terrible sunken rock, "The Wolf," on to which, as sure as death, the flowing tide carried every stick which was embayed. The tide was making ; a ship was known to be somewhere in the bay ; it was blowing a hurricane ; and what would you more ?

They hurried along as well as they could among the sharp slates which rose through the turf, until they came to where the people had halted. Charles saw his father, the agent, Mackworth, and Cuthbert together, under a rock ; the villagers were standing around, and the crowd was thickening every moment.

Every one had his hand over his eyes, and was peering due to windward, through the driving scud.

They had stopped at the foot of the cone, which was between them and the sea, and some more adventurous had climbed partly up it, if, perhaps, they might see further than their fellows ; but in vain : they all saw and heard the same—a blinding white cauldron of wind-driven spray below, and all around, filling every cranny—the howling storm.

A quarter of an hour since she fired last, and no signs of her yet. She must be carrying canvas and struggling for life, ignorant of the four-knot stream. Some one says she may have gone down—hush ! who spoke ?

Old Sam Evans had spoken. He had laid his hand on the squire's shoulder, and said, "There she is." And then arose a hubbub of talking from the men, and every one crowded on his neighbour and tried to get nearer. And the women moved hurriedly about, some moaning to themselves, and some saying, "Ah, poor dear !" "Ah, dear Lord ! there she is, sure enough."

She hove in sight so rapidly that, almost as soon as they could be sure of a dark object, they saw that it was a ship—a great ship about 900 tons ; that she was dismasted, and that her decks were crowded. They could see that she was unmanageable, turning her head hither and thither as the sea struck her, and that her people had seen the cliff at the same moment, for they were hurrying aft, and crowding on to the bulwarks.

Charles and his guardians crept up to his father's party. Densil was standing silent, looking on the lamentable sight ; and, as Charles looked at him, he saw a tear run down his cheek, and heard him say, "Poor fellows !" Cuthbert stood staring intently at the ship, with his lips slightly parted. Mackworth, like one who studies a picture, held his elbow in one hand, and kept the other over his mouth ; and the agent cried out, "A troop-ship, by gad. Dear ! dear !"

It is a sad sight to see a fine ship beyond control. It is like seeing one one loves gone mad. Sad under any circumstances ; how terrible it is when she is bearing on with her, in her mad Bacchante's dance a freight of living human creatures, to untimely destruction !

As each terrible feature and circumstance of the catastrophe became apparent to the lookers-on, the excitement became more intense. Forward and in the waist, there was a considerable body of seamen clustered about under the bulwarks— some half-stripped. In front of the cuddy door, between the poop and the mainmast, about forty soldiers were drawn up,

with whom were three officers, to be distinguished by their
blue coats and swords. On the quarter-deck were seven or
eight women, two apparently ladies, one of whom carried a
baby. A well-dressed man, evidently the captain, was with
them ; but the cynosure of all eyes was a tall man in white
trousers, at once and correctly judged to be the mate, who
carried in his arms a little girl.

The ship was going straight upon the rock, now only marked
as a whiter spot upon the whitened sea, and she was fearfully
near it, rolling and pitching, turning her head hither and
thither, fighting for her life. She had taken comparatively
little water on board as yet ; but now a great sea struck her
forward, and she swung with her bow towards the rock, from
which she was distant not a hundred yards. The end was
coming. Charles saw the mate slip off his coat and shirt, and
take the little girl again. He saw the lady with the baby rise
very quietly and look forward ; he saw the sailors climbing on
the bulwarks ; he saw the soldiers standing steady in two
scarlet lines across the deck ; he saw the officers wave their
hands to one another ; and then he hid his face in his hands,
and sobbed as if his heart would break.

They told him after how the end had come : she had lifted
up her bows defiantly, and brought them crashing down upon
the pitiless rock as though in despair. Then her stern had
swung round, and a merciful sea broke over her, and hid her
from their view, though above the storm they plainly heard her
brave old timbers crack ; then she floated off, with bulwarks
gone, sinking, and drifted out of sight round the headland, and,
though they raced across the headland, and waited a few
breathless minutes for her to float round into sight again, they
never saw her any more. The Warren Hastings had gone
down in fifteen fathom. And now there was a new passion
introduced into the tragedy to which it had hitherto been a
stranger—Hope. The wreck of part of the mainmast and half
the main topmast, which they had seen, before she struck,
lumbering the deck, had floated off, and there were three, four,
five men clinging to the futtock shrouds ; and then they saw
the mate with the child hoist himself on to the spar, and part
his dripping hair from his eyes.

The spar had floated into the bay, into which they were
looking, into much calmer water ; but, directly to leeward, the
swell was tearing at the black slate rocks, and in ten minutes it
would be on them. Every man saw the danger, and Densil,
running down to the water's edge, cried—

" Fifty pounds to any one who will take 'em a rope ! Fifty gold sovereigns down to-night ! Who's going ? "

Jim Matthews was going, and had been going before he heard of the fifty pounds—that was evident ; for he was stripped, and out on the rocks, with the rope round his waist. He stepped from the bank of slippery seaweed into the heaving water, and then his magnificent limbs were in full battle with the tide. A roar announced his success. As he was seen clambering on to the spar, a stouter rope was paid out ; and very soon it and its burden were high and dry upon the little half-moon of land which ended the bay.

Five sailors, the first mate, and a bright-eyed little girl, were their precious prize. The sailors lay about upon the sand, and the mate, untying the shawl that bound her to him, put the silent and frightened child into the hands of a woman that stood close by.

The poor little thing was trembling in every limb. " If you please," she said to the woman, " I should like to go to mamma. She is standing with baby on the quarter-deck. Mr. Archer, will you take me back to mamma, please ? She will be frightened if we stay away."

" Well, adeary me," said the honest woman, " she'll break my heart, a darling ; mamma's in heaven, my tender, and baby too."

" No, indeed," said the child, eagerly ; " she's on the quarter-deck. Mr. Archer, Mr. Archer ! "

The mate, a tall, brawny, whiskerless, hard-faced man, about six-and-twenty, who had been thrust into a pea-coat, now approached.

" Where's mamma, Mr. Archer ? " said the child.

" Where's mamma, my lady-bird ? Oh, dear ! oh, dear ! "

" And where's the ship, and Captain Dixon, and the soldiers ? "

" The ship, my pretty love," said the mate, putting his rough hand on the child's wet hair ; " why the good ship, Warren Hastings, Dixon master, is a-sunk beneath the briny waves, my darling ; and all on board of her, being good sailors and brave soldiers, is doubtless at this moment in glory."

The poor little thing set up a low wailing cry, which went to the hearts of all present ; then the women carried her away, and the mate, walking between Mackworth and Densil, headed the procession homeward to the hall.

" She was the Warren Hastings, of 900 tons," he said, " from Calcutta, with a detachment of the 120th on board. The old

story—dismasted, both anchors down, cables parted, and so
on. And now I expect you know as much as I do. This little
girl is daughter to Captain Corby, in command of the troops.
She was always a favourite of mine, and I determined to get
her through. How steady those sojers stood, by jingo, as
though they were on parade! Well, I always thought something was going to happen, for we had never a quarrel the
whole voyage, and that's curious with troops. Capital crew,
too. Ah, well, they are comfortable enough now, eh, sir?"

That night the mate arose from his bed like a giant refreshed with wine, and posted off to Bristol to "her owners,"
followed by a letter from Densil, and another from Lloyd's
agent of such a nature that he found himself in command of a
ship in less than a month. Periodically, unto this day, there
arrive at Ravenshoe, bows and arrows (supposed to be
poisoned), paddles, punkahs, rice-paper screens; a malignant
kind of pickle, which causeth the bowels of him that eateth of
it to burn; wicked-looking old gods of wood and stone; models
of Juggernaut's car; brown earthenware moonshees, translating
glazed porcelain bibles; and many other Indian curiosities, all
of which are imported and presented by the kind-hearted
Archer.

In a fortnight the sailors were gone, and, save a dozen or
so of new graves in the churchyard, nothing remained to tell of
the Warren Hastings but the little girl saved so miraculously—
little Mary Corby.

She had been handed over at once to the care of the kind-
hearted Norah, Charles's nurse, who instantaneously loved her
with all her great warm heart, and about three weeks after the
wreck gave Charles these particulars about her, when he went
to pay her a visit in the cottage behind the kennels.

After having hugged him violently, and kissed him till he
laughingly refused to let her do it again till she had told him
the news, she began—"The beauty-boy, he gets handsomer
every day" (this might be true, but there was great room for
improvement yet), "and comes and sees his old nurse, and who
loves him so well, alanna?· It's little I can tell ye about the
little girl, me darlin'. She's nine years old, and a heretic, like
yer own darlin' self, and who's to gainsay ye from it? She's
book-learned enough, and play she says she can, and I axed
her would she like to live in the great house, and she said no.
She liked me, and wanted to stay with me. She cries about
her mother, a dear, but not so much as she did, and she's now
inside and asleep. Come here, Avick."

She bent down her handsome face to Charles's ear and whispered, "If my boy was looking out for a little wee fairy wife, eh?"

Charles shook his hair, and laughed, and there and then told Norah all about Adelaide, which attachment Norah highly approved of, and remarked that he'd be old enough to be married before he knew where he was.

In spite of Densil's letters and inquiries, no friends came forward to claim little Mary. Uncle Corby, when in possession of facts, was far too much a man of business to do anything of the kind. In a very short time Densil gave up inquiring, and then he began dreading lest she should be taken from him, for he had got wonderfully fond of the quiet, pale, bright-eyed little creature. In three months she was considered as a permanent member of the household, and the night before Charles went to school he told her of his grand passion. His lordship considered this step showed deep knowledge of the world, as it would have the effect of crushing in the bud any rash hopes which Mary might have conceived; and, having made this provision for her peace of mind, he straightway departed to Shrewsbury school.

CHAPTER VII

IN WHICH CHARLES AND LORD WELTER DISTINGUISH THEMSELVES AT THE UNIVERSITY

It is a curious sensation, that of meeting, as a young man of two or three-and-twenty, a man one has last seen as a little lad of ten, or thereabouts. One is almost in a way disappointed. You may be asked out to dinner to meet a man called, say, Jones (or if you like the name better, Delamere D'Eresby), whom you believe to be your old friend Jones, and whom you have not seen for a month or so; and on getting to the house find it is not your Jones at all, but another Jones, whom you don't know. He may be cleverer, handsomer, more agreeable than your old friend—a man whom you are glad to know; and yet you are disappointed. You don't meet the man you expected, and you are rather disposed to be prejudiced against his representative.

So it is when you meet a friend in manhood whom you have not seen since you were at school. You have been picturing to yourself the sort of man your friend must have developed into, and you find him different from what you thought. So, instead of foregathering with an old friend, you discover that you have to make a new acquaintance.

You will now have to resume the acquaintance of Charles Ravenshoe at two and twenty. I hope you will not be much disappointed in him. He was a very nice boy, if you re-member, and you will see immediately that he has developed into a very nice young man indeed. It is possible that I may not be about to introduce him to you under the most favourable circumstances ; but he created those circumstances for himself, and must abide by them. As it is not my intention to follow him through any part of his University life, but only to resume his history when he quits it, so it becomes imperatively neces-sary for me to state, without any sort of disguise, the reason why he did leave it. And, as two or three other important characters in the story had something to do with it, I shall do so more at length than would at first seem necessary.

It was nine o'clock on the 6th of November. The sun, which had been doing duty for Her Majesty all night at Calcutta, Sydney, &c., had by this time reached Oxford, and was shining aslant into two pretty little Gothic windows in the inner, or library quadrangle of St. Paul's College, and illuminat-ing the features of a young man who was standing in the middle of the room and scratching his head.

He was a stout-built fellow, not particularly handsome, but with a very pleasing face. His hair was very dark brown, short and curling ; his forehead was broad and open, and below it were two uncommonly pleasant-looking dark grey eyes. His face was rather marked, his nose very slightly aquiline, and plenty of it, his mouth large and good-humoured, which, when opened to laugh, as it very frequently was, showed a splendid set of white teeth, which were well contrasted with a fine healthy brown and red complexion. Altogether a very pleasant young fellow to look on, and looking none the worse just now for an expression of droll perplexity, not unmixed with a certain amount of terror, which he had on his face.

It was Charles Ravenshoe.

He stood in his shirt and trousers only, in the midst of a scene of desolation so awful, that I who have had to describe some of the most terrible scenes and circumstances conceiv-able, pause, before attempting to give any idea of it in black and white. Every moveable article in the room—furniture, crockery, fender, fire-irons—lay in one vast heap of broken confusion in the corner of the room. Not a pane of glass remained in the windows; the bedroom door was broken down; and the door which opened into the corridor was minus the two upper panels. Well might Charles Ravenshoe stand there and scratch his head!

"By George," he said at last, soliloquising, "how deuced lucky it is that I never get drunk! If I had been screwed last night, those fellows would have burnt the college down. What a devil that Welter is when he gets drink into him; and Marlowe is not much better. The fellows were mad with fighting, too. I wish they hadn't come here and made hay afterwards. There'll be an awful row about this. It's all up, I am afraid. It's impossible to say, though."

At this moment a man appeared in the passage, and, looking in through the broken door, as if from a witness-box, announced, "The dean wishes to see you at once, sir." And exit.

Charles replied by using an expression then just coming into use among our youth, "All serene!" dressed himself by putting on a pilot coat, a pair of boots, and a cap and gown, and with a sigh descended into the quadrangle.

There were a good many men about, gathered in groups. The same subject was in everybody's mouth. There had been, the night before, without warning or apparent cause, the most frightful disturbance which, in the opinion of the porter, had graced the college for fifty years. It had begun suddenly, at half-past twelve, and had been continued till three. The dons had been afraid to come and interfere, the noise was so terrible. Five out-college men had knocked out at a quarter to three, refusing to give any name but the dean's. A rocket had been let up, and a five-barrel revolver had been let off, and—Charles Ravenshoe had been sent for.

A party of young gentlemen, who looked very seedy and guilty, stood in his way, and as he came up shook their heads sorrowfully; one, a tall one, with large whiskers, sat down in the gravel walk, and made as though he would have cast dust upon his head.

"This is a bad job, Charley," said one of them.

"Some heads must fall," said Charles; "I hope mine is not among the number. Rather a shame if it is, eh?"

The man with the big whiskers shook his head. "The state of your room," he said.

" Who has seen it ? " eagerly asked Charles.

" Sleeping innocent ! " replied the other, " the porter was up there by eight o'clock, and at half-past the dean himself was gazing on your unconscious face as you lay peacefully sleeping in the arms of desolation."

Charles whistled long and loud, and proceeded with a sinking heart towards the dean's rooms.

A tall pale man, with a hard marked countenance, was sitting at his breakfast, who, as soon as he saw his visitor, regarded him with the greatest interest, and buttered a piece of toast.

" *Well*, Mr. Ravenshoe," was his remark.

" I believe you sent for me, sir," said Charles, adding to himself, " Confound you, you cruel old brute, you are amusing yourself with my tortures."

" This is a pretty business," said the dean.

Charles would be glad to know to what he alluded.

" Well," said the dean, laughing, " I don't exactly know where to begin. However, I am not sure it much matters. You will be wanted in the common room at two. The proctor has sent for your character also. Altogether, I congratulate you. Your career at the University has been brilliant ; but, your orbit being highly elliptical, it is to be feared that you will remain but a short time above the horizon. Good morning."

Charles rejoined the eager knot of friends outside ; and, when he spoke the awful word, "common room," every countenance wore a look of dismay. Five more, it appeared, were sent for, and three were wanted by the proctor at eleven. It was a disastrous morning.

There was a large breakfast in the rooms of the man with the whiskers, to which all the unfortunates were of course going. One or two were in a state of badly-concealed terror, and fidgetted and were peevish, until they got slightly tipsy. Others laughed a good deal, rather nervously, and took the thing pluckily—the terror was there, but they fought against it ; but the behaviour of Charles extorted applause from everybody. He was as cool and as merry as if he was just going down for the long vacation ; he gave the most comical account of the whole proceedings last night from beginning to end, as he was well competent to do, being the only sober man who had witnessed them ; he ate heartily and laughed naturally, to the admiration of every one.

One of the poor fellows who had shown greatest signs of terror, and who was as near crying as he could possibly be without actually doing so, looked up and complimented him on his courage, with an oath.

"In me, my dear Dick," said Charles, good-naturedly, "you see the courage of despair. Had I half your chances I should be as bad as you. I know there are but a few more ceremonies to be gone through, and then——"

The other rose and left the room.

"Well," said he, as he went, with a choking voice, "I expect my old governor will cut his throat, or something; I'm fifteen hundred in debt." And so the door closed on the poor lad, and the party was silent.

There came in now a young man, to whom I wish especially to call your attention. He was an ordinary young man enough, in the morning livery of a groom. He was a moderately well-looking fellow, and there seems at first nothing in any way remarkable about him. But look at him again, and you are struck with a resemblance to some one you know, and yet at first you hardly know to whom. It is not decidedly, either, in any one feature, and you are puzzled for a time, till you come to the conclusion that every one else does. That man is a handsome likeness of Charles Ravenshoe.

This is Charles's foster-brother William, whom we saw on a former occasion taking refreshment with that young gentleman, and who had for some time been elevated to the rank of Mr. Charles's "lad." He had come for orders.

There were no orders but to exercise the horses, Charles believed; he would tell him in the afternoon if there were, he added sorrowfully.

"I saw Lord Welter coming away from the proctor's, sir," said William. "He told me to ask what train you were going down by. His lordship told me to say, sir, that Lord Welter of Christchurch would leave the University at twelve to-morrow, and would not come into residence again till next Michaelmas term."

"By Jove," said Charles, "he has got a dose! I didn't think they'd have given him a year. Well, here goes."

Charles went to the proctor's, but his troubles there were not so severe as he had expected. He had been seen fighting several times during the evening, but half the University had been doing the same. He had been sent home three times, and had reappeared; that was nothing so very bad. On his word of honour he had not tripped up the marshal; Brown himself thought he must have slipped on a piece of orange peel. Altogether it came to this; that Ravenshoe of Paul's had better be in by nine for the rest of term, and mind what he was about for the future.

But the common room at two was the thing by which poor Charles was to stand or fall. There were terrible odds against him—the master and six tutors. It was no use, he said, sniveling, or funking the thing; so he went into battle valiantly.

THE MASTER opened the ball, in a voice suggestive of mild remonstrance. In all his experience in college life, extending over a period of forty-five years, he had never even heard of proceedings so insubordinate, so unparalleled, so—so monstrous, as had taken place the night before, in a college only a twelvemonth ago considered to be the quietest in the University. A work of fiction of a low and vicious tendency, professing to describe scenes of headlong riot and debauchery at the sister University, called, he believed, "Peter Priggins," had been written, and was, he understood, greatly read by the youth of both seats of learning; but he was given to understand that the worst described in that book sank into nothing, actually dwindled into insignificance, before last night's proceedings. It appeared, he continued (referring to a paper through his gold eye-glasses), that at half-past twelve a band of intoxicated and frantic young men had rushed howling into the college, refusing to give their names to the porter (among whom was recognised Mr. Ravenshoe); that from that moment a scene of brutal riot had commenced in the usually peaceful quadrangle, and had continued till half-past three; loaded weapons had been resorted to, and fireworks had been exhibited; and, finally, that five members of another college had knocked out at half-past three, stating to the porter (without the slightest foundation) that they had been having tea with the dean. Now, you know, really and truly, it simply resolved itself into this. Were they going to keep St. Paul's College open, or were they not? If the institution which had flourished now for above five hundred years was to continue to receive undergraduates, the disturbers of last night must be sternly eliminated. In the last case of this kind, where a man was only convicted of—eh, Mr. Dean?—pump handle—thank you—was only convicted of playfully secreting the handle of the college pump, rustication had been inflicted. In this case the college would do its duty, however painful.

Charles was understood to say that he was quite sober, and had tried to keep the fellows out of mischief.

THE MASTER believed Mr. Ravenshoe would hardly deny having let off a rocket on the grass-plat.

Charles was ill-advised enough to say that he did it to keep the fellows quiet; but the excuse fell dead, and there was a slight pause. After which,

THE DEAN rose, with his hands in his pockets, and remarked that this sort of thing was all mighty fine, you know; but they weren't going to stand it, and the sooner this was understood the better. He, for one, as long as he remained dean of that college, was not going to have a parcel of drunken young idiots making a row under his windows at all hours in the morning. He should have come out himself last night, but that he was afraid, positively afraid, of personal violence; and the odds were too heavy against him. He, for one, did not want any more words about it. He allowed the fact of Mr. Ravenshoe being perfectly sober, though whether that could be pleaded in extenuation was very doubtful. (Did you speak, Mr. Bursar? No, I beg pardon, I thought you did.) He proposed that Mr. Ravenshoe should be rusticated for a year, and that the Dean of Christchurch should be informed that Lord Welter was one of the most active of the rioters. That promising young nobleman had done them the honour to create a disturbance in the college on a previous occasion, when he was, as last night, the guest of Mr. Ravenshoe.

Charles said that Lord Welter had been rusticated for a year.

THE DEAN was excessively glad to hear it, and hoped that he would stay at home and give his family the benefit of his high spirits. As there were five other gentlemen to come before them, he would suggest that they should come to a determination.

THE BURSAR thought that Mr. Ravenshoe's plea of sobriety should be taken in extenuation. Mr. Ravenshoe had never been previously accused of having resorted to stimulants. He thought it should be taken in extenuation.

THE DEAN was sorry to be of a diametrically opinion.

. No one else taking up the cudgels for poor Charles, the Master said he was afraid he must rusticate him.

Charles said he hoped they wouldn't.

THE DEAN gave a short laugh, and said that, if that was all he had to say, he might as well have held his tongue. And then the Master pronounced sentence of rustication for a year, and Charles, having bowed, withdrew.

CHAPTER VIII

JOHN MARSTON

CHARLES returned to his room a little easier in his mind than when he left it. There still remained one dreadful business to get over—the worst of all; that of letting his father know. Non-University men sneer at rustication; they can't see any particular punishment in having to absent yourself from your studies for a term or two. But do they think that the Dons don't know what they are about? Why, nine spirited young fellows out of ten would snap their fingers at rustication if it wasn't for the *home* business. It is breaking the matter to the father, his just anger, and his mother's still more bitter reproaches. It must all come out, the why and the wherefore, without concealment or palliation. The college write a letter to justify themselves, and then a mine of deceit is sprung under the parents' feet, and their eyes are opened to things they little dreamt of. This, it appears, is not the first offence. The college has been long-suffering, and has pardoned when it should have punished repeatedly. The lad who was thought to be doing so well has been leading a dissipated, riotous life, and deceiving them all. This is the bitterest blow they have ever had. How can they trust him again?—And so the wound takes long to heal and sometimes is never healed at all. That is the meaning of rustication.

A majority of young fellows at the University deceive their parents, especially if they come of serious houses. It is almost forced upon them sometimes, and in all cases the temptation is strong. It is very unwise to ask too many questions. Home questions are, in some cases, unpardonable. A son can't tell a father, as one man can tell another, to mind his own business. No. The father asks the question suddenly, and the son lies, perhaps for the first time in his life. If he told the truth, his father would knock him down.

Now Charles was a little better off than most young fellows in this respect. He knew his father would scold about the rustication, and still more at his being in debt. He wasn't much afraid of his father's anger. They two had always been too familiar to be much afraid of one another. He was much more afraid of the sarcasms of Mackworth, and he not a little dreaded his brother; but with regard to his father he felt but slight uneasiness.

He found his scout and his servant William trying to get the room into some order, but it was hopeless. William looked up with a blank face as he came in, and said—

"We can't do no good, sir; I'd better go for Herbert's man, I suppose?"

"You may go, William," said Charles, "to the stables, and prepare my horses for a journey. Ward, you may pack up my things, as I go down to-morrow. I am rusticated."

They both looked very blank, especially William, who, after a long pause, said—

"I was afraid of something happening yesterday after Hall, when I see my lord—— " here William paused abruptly, and, looking up, touched his head to some one who stood in the doorway.

It was a well-dressed, well-looking young man of about Charles's age, with a handsome, hairless florid face and short light hair. Handsome though his face was, it was hardly pleasing in consequence of a certain lowering of the eyebrows which he indulged in every moment—as often, indeed, as he looked at any one—and also of a slight cynical curl at the corners of the mouth. There was nothing else noticeable about Lord Welter except his appearance of great personal strength, for which he was somewhat famous.

"Hallo, Welter!" shouted Charles, "yesterday was an era in the annals of intoxication. Nobody ever was so drunk as you. I did all I could for you, more fool I, for things couldn't be worse than they are, and might be better. If I had gone to bed instead of looking after you, I shouldn't have been rusticated."

"I'm deuced sorry, Charley, I am 'pon my soul. It is all my confounded folly, and I shall write to your father and say so. You are coming home with me, of course?"

"By jove, I never thought of it. That wouldn't be a bad plan, eh? I might write from Ranford, you know. Yes, I think I'll say yes. William, you can take the horses over to-morrow. That is a splendid idea of yours. I was thinking of going to London."

"Hang London in the hunting season," said Lord Welter. "By George, how the governor will blow up. I wonder what my grandmother will say. Somebody has told her the world is coming to an end next year. I hope there'll be another Derby. She has cut homœopathy and taken to vegetable practice. She has deuced near slaughtered her maid with an overdose of Linum Catharticum, as she calls it. She goes digging about in waste places like a witch, with a big footman to carry the spade. She is a good old body, though ; hanged if she ain't."

" What does Adelaide think of the change in Lady Ascot's opinions, medical and religious ? "

" She don't care, bless you. She laughs about the world coming to an end, and as for the physic, she won't stand that. She has pretty much her own way with the old lady, I can tell you, and with every one else, as far as that goes. She is an imperious little body ; I'm afraid of her.—How do, Marston ? "

This was said to a small, neatly-dressed, quiet-looking man, with a shrewd, pleasant face, who appeared at this moment, looking very grave. He returned Welter's salutation, and that gentleman sauntered out of the room after having engaged Charles to dinner at the Cross at six. The new comer then sat down by Charles, and looked sorrowfully in his face.

" So it has come to this, my poor boy," said he, " and only two days after our good resolutions. Charley, do you know what Issachar was like ? "

" No."

" He was like a strong ass stooping between two burdens," replied the other, laughing. " I know somebody who is, oh, so very like him. I know a fellow who could do capitally in the schools and in the world, who is now always either lolling about reading novels, or else flying off in the opposite extreme, and running, or riding, or rowing like a madman. Those are his two burdens, and he is a dear old ass also, whom it is very hard to scold, even when one is furiously angry with him."

" It's all true, Marston ; it's all true as Gospel," said Charles.

" Look how well you did at Shrewsbury," continued Marston, " when you were forced to work. And now, you haven't opened a book for a year. Why don't you have some object in life, old fellow ? Try to be captain of the University Eight or the Eleven ; get a good degree ; anything. Think of last Easter vacation, Charley. Well, then, I won't——Be sure that pot-house work won't do. What earthly pleasure can there be in herding with men of that class, your inferiors in everything except strength ? and you can talk quite well enough for any society ? "

" It ain't my fault," broke in Charles piteously. " It's a good deal more the fault of the men I'm with. That Easter vacation business was planned by Welter. He wore a velveteen shooting-coat and knee-breeches, and called himself——"

"That will do, Charley; I don't want to hear any of that gentleman's performances. I entertain the strongest personal dislike for him. He leads you into all your mischief. You often quarrel; why don't you break with him?"

"I can't."

"Because he is a distant relation? Nonsense. Your brother never speaks to him."

"It isn't that."

"Do you owe him money?"

"No, it's the other way, by Jove! I can't break with that man. I can't lose the run of Ranford. I must go there. There's a girl there I care more about than all the world beside; if I don't see her I shall go mad."

Marston looked very thoughtful. "You never told me of this," he said; "and she has—she has refused you, I suppose?"

"Ay! how did you guess that?"

"By my mother wit. I didn't suppose that Charles Ravenshoe would have gone on as he has, under other circumstances."

"I fell in love with her," said Charley, rocking himself to and fro, "when she was a child. I have never had another love but her; and the last time I left Ranford I asked her—you know—and she laughed in my face, and said we were getting too old for that sort of nonsense. And, when I swore I was in earnest, she only laughed the more. And I'm a desperate beggar, by Jove, and I'll go and enlist, by Jove."

"What a brilliant idea!" said Marston. "Don't be a fool, Charley. Is this girl a great lady?"

"Great lady! Lord bless you, no; she's a dependant without a sixpence."

"Begin all over again with her. Let her alone a little, Perhaps you took too much for granted, and offended her. Very likely she has got tired of you. By your own confession, you have been making love to her for ten years; that must be a great bore for a girl, you know. I suppose you are thinking of going to Ranford now?"

"Yes, I am going for a time."

"The worst place you could go to; much better go home to your father. Yours is a quiet, staid, wholesome house; not such a bear-garden as the other place—but, let us change the subject. I am sent after you."

"By whom?"

"Musgrave. The University Eight is going down, and he

wants you to row four. The match with Cambridge is made up."

"Oh, hang it!" said poor Charles. "I can't show after this business. Get a waterman; do, Marston. They will know all about it by this time."

"Nay, I want you to come; do come, Charles. I want you to contrast these men with the fellows you were with last night, and to see what effect three such gentlemen and scholars as Dixon, Hunt, and Smith have in raising the tone of the men they are thrown among."

On the barge Charles met the others of the Eight—quiet, staid, gentlemanly men, every one of whom knew what had happened, and was more than usually polite in consequence. Musgrave, the captain, received him with manly courtesy. He was sorry to hear Ravenshoe was going down—had hoped to have had him in the Eight at Easter; however, it couldn't be helped; hoped to get him at Henley; and so on. The others were very courteous too, and Charles soon began to find that he himself was talking in a different tone of voice, and using different language from that which he would have been using in his cousin's rooms; and he confessed this to Marston that night.

Meanwhile the University Eight, with the little blue flag at her bows, went rushing down the river on her splendid course. Past heavy barges and fairy skiffs; past men in dingys, who ran high and dry on the bank to get out of the way; and groups of dandys, who ran with them for a time. And before any man was warm—Iffley. Then across the broad mill-pool and through the deep crooks, out into the broads, and past the withered beds of reeds which told of coming winter. Bridges, and a rushing lasher—Sandford. No rest here. Out of the dripping well-like lock. Get your oars out and away again, past the yellowing willows, past the long wild grey meadows, swept by the singing autumn wind. Through the swirling curves and eddies, onward under the westering sun towards the woods of Nunenham.

It was so late when they got back, that those few who had waited for them—those faithful few who would wait till midnight to see the Eight come in—could not see them, but heard afar off the measured throb and rush of eight oars as one, as they came with rapid stroke up the darkening reach. Charles and Marston walked home together.

"By George," said Charles, "I should like to do that and nothing else all my life. What a splendid stroke Musgrave gives you, so marked, and so long, and yet so lively. Oh, I should like to be forced to row every day like the watermen."

"In six or seven years you would probably row as well as a waterman. At least, I mean, as well as some of the second-rate ones. I have set my brains to learn steering, being a small weak man ; but I shall never steer as well as little Tims, who is ten years old. Don't mistake a means for an end——"

Charles wouldn't always stand his friend's good advice, and he thought he had had too much of it to-day. So he broke out into sudden and furious rebellion, much to Marston's amusement, who treasured up every word he said in his anger, and used them afterwards with fearful effect against him.

"I don't care for you," bawled Charles ; "you're a greater fool than I am, and be hanged to you. You're going to spend the best years of your life, and ruin your health, to get a first. A first ! A first ! Why that miserable little beast, Lock, got a first. A fellow who is, take him all in all, the most despicable little wretch I know ! If you are very diligent you may raise yourself to *his* level ! And when you have got your precious first, you will find yourself utterly unfit for any trade or profession whatever (except the Church, which you don't mean to enter). What do you know about modern languages or modern history ? If you go into the law, you have got to begin all over again. They won't take you in the army ; they are not such *muffs*. And this is what you get for your fifteen hundred pounds ! "

Charles paused, and Marston clapped his hands and said, "hear, *hear* ! " which made him more angry still.

"I shouldn't care if I *was* a waterman. I'm sick of all this pretension and humbug ; I'd sooner be anything than what I am, with my debts, and my rustication, and keeping up appearances. I wish I was a billiard marker ; I wish I was a jockey ; I wish I was Alick Reed's Novice ; I wish I was one of Barclay and Perkin's draymen. Hang it ! I wish I was a cabman ! Queen Elizabeth was a wise woman, and she was of my opinion."

"Did Queen Elizabeth wish she was a cabman ? " asked Marston gravely.

"No, she didn't," said Charles, very tartly. "She wished she was a milkmaid, and I think she was quite right. Now then."

"So you would like to be a milkmaid ? " said the inexorable Marston. "You had better try another Easter vacation with Welter. Mrs. Sherrat will get you a suit of cast-off clothes from some of the lads. Here's the 'Cross,' where you dine. Bye, bye ! "

John Marston knew, and knew well, nearly every one worth knowing in the University. He did not appear particularly rich; he was not handsome; he was not brilliant in conversation; he did not dress well, though he was always neat; he was not a cricketer, a rower, or a rider; he never spoke at the Union; he never gave large parties; no one knew anything about his family; he never betted; and yet he was in the best set in the University.

There was, of course, some reason for this; in fact, there were three good and sufficient reasons, although above I may seem to have exhausted the means of approach to good University society. First, He had been to Eton as a town boy, and had been popular there. Second, He had got one of the great open scholarships. And third, his behaviour had always been most correct and gentlemanly.

A year before this he had met Charles as a freshman in Lord Welter's rooms, and had conceived a great liking for him. Charles had just come up with a capital name from Shrewsbury, and Marston hoped that he would have done something; but no. Charles took up with riding, rowing, driving, &c. &c. not to mention the giving and receiving of parties, with all the zest of a young fellow with a noble constitution, enough money, agreeable manners, and the faculty of excelling to a certain extent in every sport he took in hand.

He very soon got to like and respect Marston. He used to allow him to blow him up, and give him good advice when he wouldn't take it from any one else. The night before he went down Marston came to his rooms, and tried to persuade him to go home, and not to "the training stables," as he irreverently called Ranford; but Charles had laughed and laughed, and joked, and given indirect answers, and Marston saw that he was determined, and discontinued pressing him.

CHAPTER IX

ADELAIDE

The next afternoon Lord Welter and Charles rode up to the door at Ranford. The servants looked surprised; they were not expected. His lordship was out shooting; her ladyship was in the poultry-yard; Mr. Pool was in the billiard-room with Lord Saltire.

"The deuce!" said Lord Welter; "that's lucky, I'll get him to break it to the governor."

The venerable nobleman was very much amused by the misfortunes of these ingenuous youths, and undertook the commission with great good nature. But, when he had heard the cause of the mishap, he altered his tone considerably, and took on himself to give the young men what was for him a severe lecture. He was sorry that this had come out of a drunken riot; he wished it . . . which, though bad enough, did not carry the disgrace with it that the other did. Let them take the advice of an old fellow who had lived in the world, ay, and moved with the world, for above eighty ye and take care not to be marked, even by their own set, drinking men. In his day, he allowed, drinking was entire *de rigueur;* and indeed nothing could be more proper and correct than the whole thing they had just described to him, if it had happened fifty years ago. But now a drunken row was an anachronism. Nobody drank now. He had made a point of watching the best young fellows, and none of them drank. He made a point of taking the time from the rising young fellows, as every one ought to, who wished to go with the world. In his day, for instance, it was the custom to talk with considerable freedom on sacred subjects, and he himself had been somewhat notorious for that sort of thing; but look at him now: he conformed with the times, and went to church. Every one went to church now. Let him call their attention to the fact that a great improvement had taken place in public morals of late years.

So the good-natured old heathen gave them what, I dare say, he thought was the best of advice. He is gone now to see what his system of morality was worth. I am very shy of judging him, or the men of his time. It gives me great pain to hear the men of the revolutionary era spoken of flippantly. The time was so exceptional. The men at that time were a race of giants. One wonders how the world got through that time at all. Six hundred millions of treasure spent by Britain alone! How many millions of lives lost none may guess. What wonder if there were hell-fire clubs and all kinds of monstrosities. Would any of the present generation have attended the fête of the goddess of reason, if they had lived at that time, I wonder? Of course they wouldn't.

Charles went alone to the poultry-yard; but no one was

there except the head keeper, who was administering medicine
to a cock, whose appearance was indictable—that is to say, if
the laws against cock-fighting were enforced. Lady Ascot had
gone in; so Charles went in too, and went upstairs to his
aunt's room.

One of the old lady's last fancies was sitting in the dark, or
in a gloom so profound as to approach to darkness. So
Charles, passing out of a light corridor, and shutting the door
behind him, found himself unable to see his hand before him.
Confident, however, of his knowledge of locality, he advanced
with such success that he immediately fell crashing headlong
over an ottoman; and in his descent, imagining that he was
falling into a pit or gulf of unknown depth, uttered a wild cry
of alarm. Whereupon the voice of Lady Ascot from close by
answered, "Come in," as if she thought she heard somebody
knock.

"Come up, would be more appropriate, aunt," said Charles.
"Why do you sit in the dark? I've killed myself, I believe."

"Is that you, Charles?" said she. "Why brings you over?
My dear, I am delighted. Open a bit of the window, Charles,
and let me see you."

Charles did as he was desired; and, as the strong light from
without fell upon him, the old lady gave a deep sigh.

"Ah, dear, so like poor dear Petre about the eyes. There
never was a handsome Ravenshoe since him, and there never
will be another. You were quite tolerable as a boy, my dear;
but you've got very coarse, very coarse and plain indeed.
Poor Petre!"

"You're more unlucky in the light than you were in the
darkness, Charles," said a brisk, clear, well-modulated voice
from behind the old lady. "Grandma seems in one of her
knock-me-down moods to-day. She had just told me that I
was an insignificant chit, when you made your graceful and
noiseless entrance, and saved me anything further."

If Adelaide had been looking at Charles when she spoke,
instead of at her work, she would have seen the start which he
gave when he heard her voice. As it was, she saw nothing
of it; and Charles, instantly recovering himself, said in the
most nonchalant voice possible:

"Hallo, are you here? How do you contrive to work in
the dark?"

"It is not dark to any one with eyes," was the curt reply.
"I can see to read."

Here Lady Ascot said that, if she had called Adelaide a

chit, it was because she had set up her opinion against that of such a man as Dr. Going; that Adelaide was a good and dutiful girl to her; that she was a very old woman, and perhaps shouldn't live to see the finish of next year; and that her opinion still was that Charles was very plain and coarse, and she was sorry she couldn't alter it.

Adelaide came rapidly up and kissed her, and then went and stood in the light beside Charles.

She had grown into a superb blonde beauty. From her rich brown crêpé hair to her exquisite little foot, she was a model of grace. The nose was delicately aquiline, and the mouth receded slightly, while the chin was as slightly prominent; the eyes were brilliant, and were concentrated on their object in a moment; and the eye-brows surmounted them in a delicately but distinctly marked curve. A beauty she was, such as one seldom sees; and Charles, looking on her, felt that he loved her more madly than ever, and that he would die sooner than let her know it.

"Well, Charles," she said, "you don't seem overjoyed to see me."

"A man can't look joyous with broken shins, my dear Adelaide. Aunt, I've got some bad news for you. I am in trouble."

"Oh, dear," said the old lady, "and what is the matter now? Something about a woman, I suppose. You Ravenshoes are always——"

"No, no, aunt. Nothing of the kind. Adelaide, don't go, pray; you will lose such a capital laugh. I've got rusticated, aunt."

"That is very comical, I dare say," said Adelaide, in a low voice; "but I don't see the joke."

"I thought you would have had a laugh at me, perhaps," said Charles; "it is rather a favourite amusement of yours."

"What, in the name of goodness, makes you so disagreeable and cross to-day, Charles? You were never so before, when anything happened. I am sure I am very sorry for your misfortune, though I really don't know its extent. Is it a very serious thing?"

"Serious, very. I don't much like going home. Welter is in the same scrape; who is to tell her?"

"This is the way," said Adelaide; "I'll show you how to manage her."

All this was carried on in a low tone, and very rapidly. The old lady had just begun in a loud, querulous, scolding voice to Charles, when Adelaide interrupted her with—

" I say, grandma, Welter is rusticated too."

Adelaide good-naturedly said this to lead the old lady's wrath from Charles, and throw it partly on to her grandson; but however good her intentions, the execution of them was unsuccessful. The old lady fell to scolding Charles; accusing him of being the cause of the whole mishap, of leading Welter into every mischief, and stating her opinion that he was an innocent and exemplary youth, with the fault only of being too easily led away. Charles escaped as soon as he could, and was followed by Adelaide.

" This is not true, is it ? " she said. " It is not your fault ? "

" My fault, partly, of course. But Welter would have been sent down before, if it hadn't been for me. He got me into a scrape this time. He mustn't go back there. You mustn't let him go back."

" I let him go back, forsooth ! What on earth can I have to do with his lordship's movements ? " she said, bitterly. " Do you know who you are talking to ?—a beggarly orphan."

" Hush ! don't talk like that, Adelaide. Your power in this house is very great. The power of the only sound head in the house. You could stop anything you like from happening."

They had come together at the conservatory door ; and she put her back against it, and held up her hand to bespeak his attention more particularly.

" I wish it was true, Charles ; but it isn't. No one has any power over Lord Ascot. Is Welter much in debt ? "

" I should say, a great deal," was Charles's reply. " I think I ought to tell you. You may help him to break it to them."

" Ay, he always comes to me for that sort of thing. Always did from a child. I'll tell you what, Charles, there's trouble coming or come on this house. Lord Ascot came home from Chester looking like death ; they say he lost fearfully both there and at Newmarket. He came home quite late, and went up to grandma ; and there was a dreadful scene. She hasn't been herself since. Another blow like it will kill her. I suspect my lord's bare existence depends on this colt winning the Derby. Come and see it gallop," she added, suddenly throwing her flashing eyes upon his, and speaking with an animation and rapidity very different from the cold stern voice in which she had been telling the family troubles. " Come, and let us have some oxygen. I have not spoken to a man for a month. I have been leading a life like a nun's ; no, worse than any nun's ; for I have been bothered and humiliated by—ah ! such wretched trivialities. Go and order horses. I will join you directly."

So she dashed away and left him, and he hurried to the yard. Scarcely were the horses ready when she was back again, with the same stern, cold expression on her face, now more marked, perhaps, from the effect of the masculine habit she wore. She was a consummate horsewoman, and rode the furious black Irish mare, which was brought out for her, with ease and self-possession, seeming to enjoy the rearing and plunging of the sour-tempered brute far more than Charles, her companion, did, who would rather have seen her on a quieter horse.

A sweeping gallop under the noble old trees, through a deep valley, and past a herd of deer, which scudded away through the thick-strewn leaves, brought them to the great stables, a large building at the edge of the park, close to the downs. Twenty or thirty long-legged, elegant, nonchalant-looking animals, covered to the tips of their ears with cloths, and ridden each by a queer-looking brown-faced lad, were in the act of returning from their afternoon exercise. These Adelaide's mare, " Molly Asthore," charged and dispersed like a flock of sheep ; and then, Adelaide pointing with her whip to the downs, hurried past the stables towards a group they saw a little distance off.

There were only four people—Lord Ascot, the stud-groom and two lads. Adelaide was correctly informed ; they we going to gallop the Voltigeur colt (since called Haphaza), and the cloths were now coming off him. Lord Ascot an the stud groom mounted their horses, and joined our pai who were riding slowly along the measured mile the way t horse was to come.

Lord Ascot looked very pale and worn ; he gave Charles a kindly greeting, and made a joke with Adelaide ; but his hands fidgeted with his reins, and he kept turning back towards the horse they had left, wondering impatiently what was keeping the boy. At last they saw the beautiful beast shake his head, give two or three playful plunges, and then come striding rapidly towards them, over the short, springy turf.

Then they turned, and rode full speed : soon they heard the mighty hollow-sounding hoofs behind, that came rapidly towards them, devouring space. Then the colt rushed by them in his pride, with his chin on his chest, hard held, and his hind feet coming forward under his girth every stride, and casting the turf behind him in showers. Then Adelaide's horse, after a few mad plunges, bolted, overtook the colt, and actually raced him for a few hundred yards ; then the colt was pulled up on a breezy hill, and they all stood a little together talking and congratulating one another on the beauty of the horse.

Charles and Adelaide rode away together over the downs, intending to make a little détour, and so lengthen their ride. They had had no chance of conversation since they parted at the conservatory door, and they took it up nearly where they had left it. Adelaide began, and, I may say, went on, too, as she had most of the talking.

" I should like to be a duchess ; then I should be mistress of the only thing I am afraid of."

" What is that ? "

" Poverty," said she ; "that is my only terror, and that is my inevitable fate."

" I should have thought, Adelaide, that you were too high-spirited to care for that, or anything."

" Ah, you don't know ; all my relations are poor. *I* know what it is ; *I* know what it would be for a beauty like me."

" You will never be poor or friendless while Lady Ascot lives."

" How long will that be ? My home now depends very much on that horse ; oh, if I were only a man, I should welcome poverty ; it would force me to action."

Charles blushed. Not many days before, Marston and he had had a battle royal, in which the former had said, that the only hope for Charles was that he should go two or three times without his dinner, and be made to earn it, and that as long as he had a " magma to bless himself with, he would always be a lazy, useless humbug ; and now here was a young lady uttering the same atrocious sentiments. He called attention to the prospect.

Three hundred feet below them, Father Thames was winding along under the down and yellow woodlands, past chalk quarry and grey farm-house, blood-red beneath the setting sun ; a soft, rich, autumnal haze was over everything ; the smoke from the distant village hung like a curtain of pearl across the valley ; and the long, straight, dark wood that crowned the high grey wold, was bathed in a dim purple mist, on its darkest side ; and to perfect the air of dreamy stillness, some distant bells sent their golden sound floating on the peaceful air. It was a quiet day in the old age of the year ; and its peace seemed to make itself felt on these two wild young birds ; for they were

theless, treating Adelaide almost with rudeness, and flinging about his words so carelessly, that sometimes she would look suddenly up indignant, and make some passionate reply, and sometimes she would rise and leave the room—for aught I know, in tears.

It was a sad house to stay in ; and his heart began to yearn for his western home in spite of Adelaide. After a short time came a long letter from his father, a scolding loving letter, in which Densil showed plainly that he was trying to be angry, and could not, for joy at having his son home with him—and concluded by saying that he should never allude to the circumstance again, and by praying him to come back at once from that wicked, cock-fighting, horse-racing Ranford. There was an inclosure for Lord Saltire, the reading of which caused his lordship to take a great deal of snuff, in which he begged him, for old friendship's sake, to send his boy home to him, as he had once sent him home to his father. And so Lord Saltire appeared in Charles's dressing-room before dinner one day, and, sitting down, said that he was come to take a great liberty, and, in fact, was rather presuming on his being an old man, but he hoped that his young friend would not take it amiss from a man old enough to be his grandfather, if he recommended him to leave that house, and go home to his father's. Ranford was a most desirable house in every way ; but, at the same time, it was what he believed the young men of the day called a fast house ; and he would not conceal from his young friend that his father had requested him to use his influence to make him return home ; and he did beg his old friend's son to believe that he was actuated by the best of motives.

"Dear Lord Saltire," said Charles, taking the old man's hand ; "I am going home to-morrow ; and you don't know how heartily I thank you for the interest you always take in me."

"I know nothing," said Lord Saltire, "more pleasing to a battered old fellow like myself than to contemplate the ingenuousness of youth, and you must allow me to say that your ingenuousness sits uncommonly well upon you—in fact, is very becoming. I conceived a considerable interest in you the first time I saw you, on that very account. I should like to have had a son like you, but it was not to be. I had a son, who was all that could be desired by the most fastidious person, brought up in a far better school than mine ; but he got shot in his first duel, at one-and-twenty. I remember to have been considerably annoyed at the time," continued the old gentleman, taking a pinch of snuff, and looking steadily at Charles without moving a muscle, "but I dare say it was all for the best ; he might have run in debt, or married a woman with red hair, or fifty things. Well, I wish you good day, and beg your forgiveness once more for the liberty I have taken."

Charles slipped away from the dinner table early that evening, and, while Lady Ascot was having her after-dinner nap, had a long conversation with Adelaide in the dark, which was very pleasant to one of the parties concerned, at any rate.

"Adelaide, I am going home to-morrow."

"Are you really ? Are you going so suddenly ? "

"I am, positively. I got a letter from home to-day. Are you very sorry or very glad ? "

"I am very sorry, Charles. You are the only friend I have in the world to whom I can speak as I like. Make me a promise."

"Well ? "

"This is the last night we shall be together. Promise that you won't be rude and sarcastic as you are sometimes—almost always, now, to poor me—but talk kindly, as we used to do."

"Very well," said Charles. "And you promise you won't be taking such a black view of the state of affairs as you do in general. Do you remember the conversation we had the day the colt was tried ? "

"I remember."

"Well, don't talk like that, you know."

"I won't promise that. The time will come very soon when we shall have no more pleasant talks together."

"When will that be ? "

"When I am gone out for a governess."

"What wages will you get ? You will not get so much as some girls, because you are so pretty and so wilful, and you will lead them such a deuce of a life."

"Charles, you said you wouldn't be rude."

"I choose to be rude. I have been drinking wine, and we are in the dark, and aunt is asleep and snoring, and I shall say just what I like."

"I'll wake her."

"I should like to see you. What shall we talk about ? What an old Roman Lord Saltire is. He talked about his son who was killed, to me to-day, just as I should talk about a pointer dog."

"Then he thought he had been showing some signs of weakness. He always speaks of his son like that when he thinks he has been betraying some feeling."

"I admire him for it," said Charles.—"So you are going to be a governess, eh?"

"I suppose so."

"Why don't you try being barmaid at a public-house? Welter would get you a place directly; he has great influence in the licensed victualling way. You might come to marry a commercial traveller, for anything you know."

"I would not have believed this," she said, in a fierce, low voice. "You have turned against me and insult me, because—— Unkind, unjust, ungentlemanlike."

He heard her passionately sobbing in the dark, and the next moment he had her in his arms, and was covering her face with kisses.

"Lie there, my love," he said; "that is your place. All the world can't harm or insult my Adelaide while she is there. Why did you fly from me and repulse me, my darling, when I told you I was your own true love?"

"Oh, let me go, Charles," she said, trying, ever so feebly, to repulse him. "Dear Charles, pray do; I am frightened."

"Not till you tell me you love me, false one."

"I love you more than all the world."

"Traitress! And why did you repulse me and laugh at me?"

"I did not think you were in earnest."

"Another kiss for that wicked, wicked falsehood. Do you know that this rustication business has all come from the despair consequent on your wicked behaviour the other day?"

"You said Welter caused it, Charles. But oh, please let me go."

"Will you go as a governess now?"

"I will do nothing but what you tell me."

"Then give me one, your own, own self, and I will let you go."

Have the reader's feelings of horror, indignation, astonishment, outraged modesty, or ridicule, given him time to remember that all this went on in the dark, within six feet of an unconscious old lady? Such, however, was the case. And scarcely had Adelaide determined that it was time to wake her, and barely had she bent over her for that purpose, when the door was thrown open, and—enter attendants with lights. Now, if the reader will reflect a moment, he will see what an awful escape they had; for the chances were about a thousand to one in favour of two things having happened : 1st, the groom of the chambers might have come into the room half a minute sooner ; and 2nd, they might have sat as they were half a minute longer ; in either of which cases, Charles would have been discovered with his arm around Adelaide's waist, and a fearful scandal would have been the consequence. And I mention this as a caution to young persons in general, and to remind them that, if they happen to be sitting hand in hand, it is no use to jump apart and look very red just as the door opens, because the incomer can see what they have been about as plain as if he had been there. On this occasion, also, Charles and Adelaide set down as usual to their own sagacity what was the result of pure accident.

Adelaide was very glad to get away after tea, for she felt rather guilty and confused. On Charles offering to go, however, Lady Ascot, who had been very silent and glum all tea-time, requested him to stay, as she had something serious to say to him. Which set that young gentleman speculating whether she could possibly have been awake before the advent of candles, and caused him to await her pleasure with no small amount of trepidation.

Her ladyship began, by remarking that digitalis was invaluable for palpitation, and that she had also found camomile, combined with gentle purgatives, efficient for the same thing, when suspected to proceed from the stomach. She opined that, if this weather continued, there would be heavy running for the Cambridgeshire, and Commissioner would probably stand as well as any horse. And then, having, like a pigeon, taken a few airy circles through stable-management, theology, and agriculture, she descended on her subject, and frightened Charles out of his five wits, by asking him if he didn't think Adelaide a very nice girl.

Charles decidedly thought she was a very nice girl ; but he rather hesitated, and said—" Yes, that she was charming."

" Now, tell me, my dear," said Lady Ascot, manœuvring a great old fan, " for young eyes are quicker than old ones. Did you ever remark anything between her and Welter ? "

Charles caught up one of his legs and exclaimed, " The devil ! "

" What a shocking expression, my dear ! Well, I agree with you. I fancy I have noticed that they have entertained a decided preference for one another. Of course, Welter will be throwing himself away, and all that sort of thing, but he is pretty sure to do that. I expect, every time he comes home, that he will bring a wife from behind the bar of a public-house. Now Adelaide——"

" Aunt! Lady Ascot! Surely you are under a mistake. I never saw anything between them."

" H'm."

" I assure you I never did. I never heard Welter speak of her in that sort of way, and I don't think she cares for him."

" What reason have you for thinking *that*? "

" Well—why, you know it's hard to say. The fact is, I have rather a partiality for Adelaide myself, and I have watched her in the presence of other men."

" Oho! Do you think she cares for you? Do you know she won't have a sixpence? "

" We shall have enough to last till next year, aunt; and then the world is to come to an end, you know, and we shan't want anything."

" Never you mind about the world, sir. Don't you be flippant and impertinent, sir. Don't evade my question, sir. Do **you** think Adelaide cares for you, sir? "

Charles looked steadily and defiantly at his aunt, and asked her whether she didn't think it was very difficult to find out what a girl's mind really was—whereby we may conclude that he was profiting by Lord Saltire's lesson on the command of feature.

" This is too bad, Charles," broke out Lady Ascot, " to put me off like this, after your infamous and audacious conduct of this evening—after kissing and hugging that girl under my very nose——"

" I thought it! " said Charles, with a shout of laughter. " I thought it, you were awake all the time! "

" I was not awake all the time, sir——"

" You were awake quite long enough, it appears, aunty. Now, what do you think of it? "

At first Lady Ascot would think nothing of it, but that the iniquity of Charles's conduct was only to be equalled by the baseness and ingratitude of Adelaide's; but by degrees she was brought to think that it was possible that some good might come of an engagement; and, at length, becoming garrulous on this point, it leaked out by degrees, that she had set her heart on it for years, that she had noticed for some time Charles's partiality for her with the greatest pleasure, and recently had feared that something had disturbed it. In short, that was her pet scheme, and that she had been coming to an explanation that very night, but had been anticipated.

CHAPTER XI

GIVES US AN INSIGHT INTO CHARLES'S DOMESTIC RELATIONS
AND SHOWS HOW THE GREAT CONSPIRATOR SOLILOQUISEI
TO THE GRAND CHANDELIER

IT may be readily conceived that a considerable amount of
familiarity existed between Charles and his servant and foster-
brother William. But, to the honour of both of them be it said,
there was more than this—a most sincere and hearty affection,
a feeling for one another which, we shall see, lasted through
everything. Till Charles went to Shrewsbury he had never
had another playfellow. He and William had been allowed to
paddle about on the sand, or ride together on the moor, as they
would, till a boy's friendship had arisen, sufficiently strong to
obliterate all considerations of rank between them. This had
grown with age, till William had become his confidential agent
at home during his absence, and Charles had come to depend
very much on his account of the state of things at head-quarters.
He had also another confidential agent, to whom we shall be
immediately introduced. She, however, was of another sex and
rank.

William's office was barely a pleasant one. His affection for
his master led him most faithfully to attend to his interests;
and, as a Catholic, he was often brought into collision with
Father Mackworth, who took a laudable interest in Charles's
affairs, and considered himself injured on two or three occasions
by the dogged refusal of William to communicate the substance
and result of a message forwarded through William, from
Shrewsbury, to Densil, which seemed to cause the old gentleman
some thought and anxiety. William's religious opinions, however, had got to be somewhat loose, and to sit somewhat easily
upon him, more particularly since his sojourn in Oxford. He
had not very long ago confided to Charles, in a private sitting,
that the conviction which was strong on his mind was that
Father Mackworth was not to be trusted, God forgive him for
saying so; and, on being pressed by Charles to state why, he
point-blank refused to give any reason whatever, but repeated
his opinion with redoubled emphasis. Charles had a great
confidence in William's shrewdness, and forebore to press him,

but saw that something had occurred which had impressed the above conviction on William's mind most strongly.

He had been sent from Oxford to see how the land lay at home, and had met Charles at the Rose and Crown at Stonnington, with saddle horses. No sooner were they clear of the town than William, without waiting for Charles's leave, put spurs to his horse and rode up alongside of him.

" What is your news, William ? "

" Nothing very great. Master looks bothered and worn."

" About this business of mine."

" The priest goes on talking about it, and plaguing him with it, when he wants to forget it."

" The deuce take him ! He talks about me a good deal."

" Yes ; he has begun about you again. Master wouldn't stand it the other day, and told him to hold his tongue, just like his own self. Tom heard him. They made it up afterwards, though."

" What did Cuthbert say ? "

" Master Cuthbert spoke up for you, and said he hoped there wasn't going to be a scene, and that you weren't coming to live in disgrace, for that would be punishing every one in the house for you."

" How's Mary ? "

" She's well. Master don't trust her out of his sight much. They will never set him against you while she is there. I wish you would marry her, Master Charles, if you can give up the other one."

Charles laughed, and told him he wasn't going to do anything of the sort. Then he asked, " Any visitors ? "

" Ay ; one Father Tiernay, a stranger."

" What sort of man ? "

" A real good one. I don't think our man likes him, though."

They had now come to the moor's edge, and were looking down on the amphitheatre which formed the domain of Ravenshoe. Far and wide the tranquil sea, vast, dim, and grey, flooded bay and headland, cave and islet. Beneath their feet slept the winter woodlands ; from whose brown bosom rose the old house, many-gabled, throwing aloft from its chimneys hospitable columns of smoke, which hung in the still autumn air, and made a hazy cloud on the hill-side. Everything was so quiet that they could hear the gentle whisper of the ground-swell, and the voices of the children at play upon the beach, and the dogs barking in the kennels.

" How calm and quiet the old home looks, William," said Charles ; " I like to get back here after Oxford."

" No wine parties here. No steeplechases. No bloomer balls," said William.

" No ! and no chapels and lectures, and being sent for by the Dean," said Charles.

" And none of they dratted bones, neither," said William, with emphasis.

" Ahem ! why no ! Suppose we ride on."

So they rode down the road through the woodland to the lodge, and so through the park—sloping steeply up on their left, with many a clump of oak and holly, and many a broad patch of crimson fern. The deer stood about in graceful groups, while the bucks belled and rattled noisily, making the thorn-thickets echo with the clatter of their horns. The rabbits scudded rapidly across the road, and the blackbird fled screaming from the mountain ash tree, now all afire with golden fruit. So they passed on until a sudden sweep brought them upon the terrace between the old grey house and the murmuring sea.

Charles jumped off and William led the horses round to the stable. A young lady in a straw hat and brown gloves, with a pair of scissors and a basket, standing half-way up the steps, came down to meet him, dropping the basket, and holding out the brown gloves before her. This young lady he took in his arms, and kissed ; and she, so far from resenting the liberty, after she was set on her feet again, held him by both hands, and put a sweet dark face towards his, as if she wouldn't care if he kissed her again. Which he immediately did.

It was not a very pretty face, but oh ! such a calm, quiet, pleasant one. There was scarcely a good feature in it, and yet the whole was so gentle and pleasing, and withal so shrewd and *espiègle*, that to look at it once was to think about it till you looked again ; and to look again was to look as often as you had a chance, and to like the face the more each time you looked. I said there was not a good feature in the face. Well, I misled you ; there was a pair of calm, honest, black eyes, a very good feature indeed, and which, once seen, you were not likely to forget. And also, when I tell you that this face and eyes belonged to the neatest, trimmest little figure imaginable, I hope I have done my work sufficiently well to make you envy that lucky rogue Charles, who, as we know, cares for no woman in the world but Adelaide, and who, between you and me, seems to be much too partial to this sort of thing.

" A thousand welcomes home, Charley," said the pleasant

little voice which belonged to this pleasant little personage.
"Oh! I am so glad you're come."

"You'll soon wish me away again. I'll plague you."

"I like to be plagued by you, Charley. How is Adelaide?"

"Adelaide is all that the fondest lover could desire" (for they
had no secrets, these two), "and either sent her love or meant
to do so."

"Charles, dearest," she said eagerly, "come and see him now!
come and see him with me!"

"Where is he?"

"In the shrubbery, with Flying Childers."

"Is he alone?"

"All alone, except the dog."

"Where are *they*?"

"They are gone out coursing. Come on; they will be back
in an hour, and the Rook never leaves him. Come, come."

It will be seen that these young folks had a tolerably good
understanding with one another, and could carry on a conversation about "third parties" without even mentioning their names.
We shall see how this came about presently; but, for the present,
let us follow these wicked conspirators, and see in what deep plot
they are engaged.

They passed rapidly along the terrace, and turned the corner
of the house to the left, where the west front overhung the river
glen, and the broad terraced garden went down step by step
towards the brawling stream. This they passed, and, opening an
iron gate, came suddenly into a gloomy maze of shrubbery that
stretched its long vistas up the valley.

Down one dark alley after another they hurried. The yellow
leaves rustled beneath their feet, and all nature was pervaded
with the smell of decay. It was hard to believe that these bare
damp woods were the same as those they had passed through
but four months ago, decked out with their summer bravery—an
orchestra to a myriad birds. Here and there a bright berry
shone out among the dull-coloured twigs, and a solitary robin
quavered his soft melancholy song alone. The flowers were
dead, the birds were flown or mute, and brave, green leaves
were stamped under foot; everywhere decay, decay.

In the dampest, darkest walk of them all, in a far-off path,
hedged with holly and yew, they found a bent and grey old man
walking with a toothless, grey, old hound for his silent companion. And, as Charles moved forward with rapid elastic
step, the old man looked up, and tottered to meet him, showing
as he did so, the face of Densil Ravenshoe.

"Now, the Virgin be praised," he said, "for putting it in your head to come so quick, my darling. Whenever you go away now, I am in terror lest I should die and never see you again. I might be struck with paralysis, and not know you, my boy. Don't go away from me again."

"I should like never to leave you any more, father dear. See how well you get on with my arm. Let us come out into the sun; why do you walk in this dismal wood?"

"Why?" said the old man, with sudden animation, his grey eye kindling as he stopped, "Why? I come here because I can catch sight of a woodcock, lad! I sprang one by that holly just before you came up. Flip flap, and away through the hollies like a ghost! Cuthbert and the priest are away coursing. Now you are come, surely I can get on the grey pony, and go up to see a hare killed. You will lead him for me, won't you? I don't like to trouble *them*."

"We can go to-morrow, dad, after lunch, you and I, and William. We'll have Leopard and Blue-ruin—by George, it will be like old times again."

"And we'll take our little quiet bird on *her* pony, won't we?" said Densil, turning to Mary. "She's such a good little bird, Charley. We sit and talk of you many an hour. Charley, can't you get me down on the shore, and let me sit there? I got Cuthbert to take me down once; but Father Mackworth came and talked about the Immaculate Conception through his nose all the time. I didn't want to hear him talk; I wanted to hear the surf on the shore. Good man! he thought he interested me, I dare say."

"I hope he is very kind to you, father?"

"Kind! I assure you, my dear boy, he is the kindest creature; he never lets me out of his sight; and so attentive!"

"He'll have to be a little less attentive in future, confound him!" muttered Charles. "There he is. Talk of the devil! Mary, my dear," he added aloud, "go and amuse the Rooks for a little, and let us have Cuthbert to ourselves."

The old man looked curious at the idea of Mary talking to the rooks; but his mind was drawn off by Charles having led him into a warm, southern corner, and set him down in the sun.

Mary did her errand well; for, in a few moments, Cuthbert advanced rapidly towards them. Coming up, he took Charles's hand, and shook it with a faint, kindly smile.

He had grown to be a tall and somewhat handsome young man—certainly handsomer than Charles. His face, even now he was warmed by exercise, was very pale, though the complexion was clear and healthy. His hair was slightly gone from his forehead, and he looked much older than he really was. The moment that the smile was gone his face resumed the expression of passionless calm that it had borne before ; and, sitting down by his brother, he asked him how he did.

"I am as well, Cuthbert," said Charles, "as youth, health, a conscience of brass, and a whole world full of friends can make me. *I'm* all right, bless you. But you look very peaking and pale. Do you take exercise enough?"

"I? Oh, dear, yes. But I am very glad to see you, Charles. Our father misses you. Don't you, father?"

"Very much, Cuthbert."

"Yes. I bore him. I do, indeed. I don't take interest in the things he does. I can't ; it's not my nature. You and he will be as happy as kings talking about salmon, and puppies, and colts."

"I know, Cuthbert ; I know. You never cared about those things as we do."

"No, never, brother ; and now less than ever. I hope you will stay with me—with us. You are my own brother. I will have you stay here," he continued in a slightly raised voice ; "and I desire that any opposition or impertinence you may meet with may be immediately reported to me."

"It will be immediately reported to those who use it, and in a way they won't like, Cuthbert. Don't you be afraid ; I shan't quarrel. Tell me something about yourself, old boy."

"I can tell you but little to interest you, Charles. You are of this world, and rejoice in being so. I, day by day, wean myself more and more from it, knowing its worthlessness. Leave me to my books and my religious exercises, and go on your way. The time will come when your pursuits and pleasures will turn to bitter dust in your mouth, as mine never can. When the world is like a howling wilderness to you, as it will be soon, then come to me and I will show you where to find happiness. At present you will not listen to me."

"Not I," said Charles. "Youth, health, talent, like yours— are these gifts to despise?"

"They are clogs to keep me from higher things. Study, meditation, life in the past with those good men who have walked the glorious road before us—in these consist happiness. Ambition! I have one earthly ambition—to purge myself from earthly affections, so that, when I hear the cloister-gate close behind me for ever, my heart may leap with joy, and I may feel that I am in the antechamber of heaven."

Charles was deeply affected, and bent down his head. " Youth, love, friends, joy in this beautiful world—all to be buried between four dull white walls, my brother ! "

" This beautiful earth, which is beautiful indeed—alas ! how I love it still ! shall become a burden to us in a few years. Love ! the greater the love, the greater the bitterness. Charles, remember *that*, one day, will you, when your heart is torn to shreds? I shall have ceased to love you then more than any other fellow-creature ; but remember my words. You are leading a life which can only end in misery, as even the teachers of the false and corrupt religion which you profess would tell you. If you were systematically to lead the life you do now, it were better almost that there were no future. You are not angry, Charles ? "

There was such a spice of truth in what Cuthbert said that it would have made nine men in ten angry. I am pleased to record of my favourite Charles that he was not ; he kept his head bent down, and groaned.

" Don't be hard on our boy, Cuthbert," said Densil ; " he is a good boy, though he is not like you. It has always been so in our family—one a devotee and the other a sportsman. Let us go in, boys ; it gets chill."

Charles rose up, and, throwing his arms round his brother's neck, boisterously gave him a kiss on the cheek ; then he began laughing and talking at the top of his voice, making the nooks and angles in the grey old façade echo with his jubilant voice.

Under the dark porch they found a group of three—Mackworth ; a jolly-looking, round-faced, Irish priest, by name Tiernay ; and Mary. Mackworth received Charles with a pleasant smile, and they joined in conversation together heartily. Few men could be more agreeable than Mackworth, and he chose to be agreeable now. Charles was insensibly carried away by the charm of his frank, hearty manner, and for a time forgot who was talking to him.

Mackworth and Charles were enemies. If we reflect a moment, we shall see that it could hardly be otherwise.

Charles's existence, holding, as he did, the obnoxious religion, was an offence to him. He had been prejudiced against him from the first : and, children not being very slow to find out who are well disposed towards them, or the contrary, Charles had early begun to regard the priest with distrust and dislike. So a distant, sarcastic line of treatment on the one hand and childish insolence and defiance on the other, had grown at last into something very like hatred on both sides. Every soul in the house adored Charles but the priest; and, on the other hand, the priest's authority and dignity were questioned by none but Charles. And, all these small matters being taken into consideration, it is not wonderful, I say, that Charles and the priest were not good friends even before anything had occurred to bring about any open rupture.

Charles and Mackworth seldom met of late years without a "sparring match." On this day, however—partly owing, perhaps, to the presence of a jolly good-humoured Irish priest —they got through dinner pretty well. Charles was as brave as a lion, and, though by far the priest's inferior in scientific "sparring," had a rough, strong, effective method of fighting, which was by no means to be despised. His great strength lay in his being always ready for battle. As he used to tell his crony William, he would as soon fight as not; and often, when rebuked by Cuthbert for what he called insolence to the priest, he would exclaim, "I don't care; what did he begin at me for? If he lets me alone, I'll let him alone." And, seeing that he had been at continual war with the reverend gentleman for sixteen years or more, I think it speaks highly for the courage of both parties that neither had hitherto yielded When Charles afterwards came to know what a terrible card the man had held in his hand, he was struck with amazement at his self-possession in not playing it, despite his interest.

Mackworth was hardly so civil after dinner as he was before; but Cuthbert was hoping that Charles and he would get on without a battle-royal, when a slight accident brought on a general engagement, and threw all his hopes to the ground. Densil and Mary had gone up to the drawing-room, and Charles, having taken as much wine as he cared for, rose from the table, and sauntered towards the door, when Cuthbert quite innocently asked him where he was going.

Charles said also in perfect good faith that he was going to smoke a cigar, and talk to William.

Cuthbert asked him, Would he get William or one of them to give the grey colt a warm mash with some nitre in it; and Charles said he'd see it done for him himself; when, without warning or apparent cause, Father Mackworth said to Father Tiernay,

"This William is one of the grooms. A renegade, I fancy! I believe the fellow is a Protestant at heart. He and Mr. Charles Ravenshoe are very intimate; they kept up a constant correspondence when apart, I assure you."

Charles faced round instantly, and confronted his enemy with a smile on his lips; but he said not a word, trying to force Mackworth to continue.

"Why don't you leave him alone?" said Cuthbert.

"My dear Cuthbert," said Charles, "pray don't humiliate me by interceding; I assure you I am greatly amused. You see he doesn't speak to me; he addressed himself to Mr. Tiernay."

"I wished," said Mackworth, "to call Father Tiernay's attention, as a stranger to this part of the world, to the fact of a young gentleman's corresponding with an illiterate groom in preference to any member of his family."

"The reason I do it," said Charles, speaking to Tiernay, but steadily watching Mackworth to see if any of his shafts hit, "is to gain information. I like to know what goes on in my absence. Cuthbert here is buried in his books, and does not know everything."

No signs of flinching there. Mackworth sat with a scornful smile on his pale face, without moving a muscle.

"He likes to get information," said Mackworth, "about his village amours, I suppose. But, dear me, he can't know anything that the whole parish don't know. I could have told him that that poor deluded fool of an underkeeper was going to marry Mary Lee, after all that had happened. He will be dowering a wife for his precious favourite some day."

"My precious favourite, Father Tiernay," said Charles, still closely watching Mackworth, "is my foster-brother. He used to be a great favourite with our reverend friend; his pretty sister Ellen is so still, I believe."

This was as random an arrow as ever was shot, and yet it went home to the feather. Charles saw Mackworth give a start and bite his lip, and knew that he had smote him deep; he burst out laughing.

"With regard to the rest, Father Tiernay, any man who says that there was anything wrong between me and Mary Lee tells, saving your presence, a lie. It's infernally hard if a man mayn't play at love-making with the whole village for a confidant, and the whole matter a merry joke, but one must be accused of all sorts of villainy. Isn't ours a pleasant household, Mr. Tiernay?"

Father Tiernay shook his honest sides with a wondering laugh, and said, "Faix it is. But I hope ye'll allow me to put matters right betune you two. Father Mackworth begun on the young man; he was going out to his dudeen as peaceful as an honest young gentleman should. And some of the best quality are accustomed to converse their grooms in the evening over their cigar. I myself can instance Lord Mountdown, whose hospitality I have partook frequent. And I'm hardly aware of any act of parliament, brother, whereby a young man shouldn't kiss a pretty girl in the way of fun, as I've done myself, sure. Whist now, both on ye! I'll come with ye, ye heretic, and smoke a cigar meself."

"I call you to witness that he insulted me," said Mackworth, turning round from the window.

"I wish you would let him alone, Father," said Cuthbert, peevishly; "we were getting on very happily till you began. Do go, Charles, and smoke your cigar with Father Tiernay."

"I am waiting to see if he wants any more," said Charles, with a laugh. "Come on, Father Tiernay, and I'll show you the miscreant, and his pretty sister, too, if you like."

"I wish he hadn't come home," said Cuthbert, as soon as he and Mackworth were alone together. "Why do you and he fight like cat and dog? You make me perfectly miserable. I know he is going to the devil, in a worldly point of view, and that his portion will be hell necessarily as a heretic; but I don't see why you should worry him to death, and make the house miserable to him."

"It is for his good."

"Nonsense," rejoined Cuthbert. "You make him hate you; and I don't think you ought to treat a son of this house in the way you treat him. You are under obligations to this house. Yes, you are. I won't be contradicted now. I will have my say when I am in this temper, and you know it. The devil is not dead yet by a long way, you see. Why do you rouse him?"

"Go on, go on."

"Yes, I will go on. I'm in my own house, I believe. But the eleven thousand virgins, more or less, of the holy St. Ursula, virgin and martyr, that brother of mine is a brave fellow. Why, he cares as much for you as for a little dog barking at him. And you're a noble enemy for any man. You'd better let him alone, I think; you won't get much out of him. Adieu."

"What queer wild blood there is in these Ravenshoes," said Mackworth to himself, when he was alone. "A younger hand than myself would have been surprised at Cuthbert's kicking after so much schooling. Not I. I shall never quite tame him, though he is broken in enough for all practical purposes.

He will be on his knees to-morrow for this. I like to make him kick; I shall do it sometimes for amusement; he is so much easier managed after one of these tantrums. By Jove! I love the man better every day; he is one after my own heart. As for Charles, I hate him, and yet I like him after a sort. I like to break a pointless lance with that boy, and let him fancy he is my equal. It amuses me.

"I almost fancy that I could have fallen in love with that girl Ellen. I was uncommon near it. I must be very careful. What a wild hawk she is! What a magnificent move that was of hers, risking a prosecution for felony on one single throw, and winning. How could she have guessed that there was anything there? She couldn't have guessed it. It was an effort of genius. It was a splendid move.

"How nearly that pigheaded fool of a young nobleman has gone to upset my calculations! His namesake the chessplayer could not have done more mischief by his talents than his friend had by stupidity. I wish Lord Ascot could get ruined as quickly as possible, and then my friend would be safe out of the way. But he won't."

CHAPTER XII

CONTAINING A SONG BY CHARLES RAVENSHOE, AND ALSO FATHER TIERNAY'S OPINION ABOUT THE FAMILY

CHARLES and the good-natured Father Tiernay wandered out across the old court-yard, towards the stables—a pile of buildings in the same style as the house, which lay back towards the hill. The moon was full, although obscured by clouds, and the whole court-yard was bathed in a soft yellow light. They both paused for a moment to look at the fine old building, standing silent for a time; and then Charles startled the contemplative priest by breaking into a harsh scornful laugh, as unlike his own cheery Ha! Ha! as it was possible to be.

"What are you disturbing a gentleman's meditations in that way for?" said the Father. "Is them your Oxford manners? Give me ye'r cigar-case, ye haythen, if ye can't appreciate the beauties of nature and art combined—laughing like that at the cradle of your ancestors, too."

Charles gave him the cigar-case, and rolled out in a rich bass voice—

> "The old falcon's nest
>   Was built up on the crest
> Of the cliff that hangs over the sea ;
>   And the jackdaws and crows,
>   As every one knows,
> Were confounded respectful to he, to he—e—e."

"Howld yer impudence, ye young heretic doggrel-writer ; can't I see what ye are driving at ? "

> "But the falcon grew old,
>   And the nest it grew cold,
> And the carrion birds they grew bolder ;
>   So the jackdaws and crows,
>   Underneath his own nose,
> Gave both the young falcons cold shoulder."

"Bedad," said the good-natured Irishman, "some one got hot shoulder to-day. Aren't ye ashamed of yourself, singing such ribaldry, and all the servants hearing ye ? "

"Capital song, Father ; only one verse more."

> "The elder was quelled,
>   But the younger rebelled ;
> So he spread his white wings and fled over the sea.
>   Said the jackdaws and crows,
>   'He'll be hanged I suppose,
> But what in the deuce does that matter to we ? ' "

There was something in the wild, bitter tone in which he sang the last verse that made Father Tiernay smoke his cigar in silence as they sauntered across the yard, till Charles began again.

"Not a word of applause for my poor impromptu song? Hang it, I'd have applauded anything you sang."

"Don't be so reckless and bitter, Mr. Ravenshoe," said Tiernay, laying his hand on his shoulder. " I can feel for you, though there is so little in common between us. You might lead a happy, peaceful life if you were to come over to us ; which you will do, if I know anything of my trade, in the same day that the sun turns pea-green. *Allons*, as we used to say over the water ; let us continue our travels."

"Reckless ! I am not reckless. The jolly old world is very wide, and I am young and strong. There will be a wrench when the tooth comes out; but it will soon be over, and the toothache will be cured."

Tiernay remained silent a moment, and then in an absent manner sang this line, in a sweet low voice—

"For the girl of my heart that I'll never see more."

"She must cast in her lot with me," said Charles. "Ay, and she will do it, too. She will follow me to the world's end, sir. Are you a judge of horses? What a question to ask of an Irishman! Here are the stables."

The lads were bedding down, and all the great building was alive with the clattering of busy feet and the neighing of horses. The great Ravenshoe Stud was being tucked up for the night; and over that two thousand pounds' worth of horse-flesh at least six thousand pounds' worth of fuss was being made, under the superintendence of the stud groom, Mr. Dickson.

The physical appearance of Mr. Dickson was as though you had taken an aged Newmarket jockey and put a barrel of oysters, barrel and all, inside his waistcoat. His face was thin; his thighs were hollow; calves to his legs he had none. He was all stomach. Many years had elapsed since he had been brought to the verge of dissolution by severe training; and since then all that he had eaten, or drunk, or done, had flown to his stomach, producing a tympanitic action in that organ, astounding to behold. In speech he was, towards his superiors, courteous and polite; towards his equals, dictatorial; towards his subordinates, abusive, not to say blasphemous. To this gentleman Charles addressed himself, inquiring if he had seen William: and he, with a lofty, though courteous, sense of injury, inquired in a loud tone of voice, of the stable-men generally, if any one had seen Mr. Charles's pad-groom.

In a dead silence which ensued, one of the lads was ill-advised enough to say that he didn't exactly know where he was; which caused Mr. Dickson to remark that, if that was all he had to say, he had better go on with his work, and not make a fool of himself—which the man did, growling out something about always putting his foot in it.

"Your groom comes and goes pretty much as he likes, sir," said Mr. Dickson. "I don't consider him as under my orders. Had he been so, I should have felt it my duty to make complaint on more than one occasion; he is a little too much of a gentleman for *my* stable, sir."

"Of course, my good Dickson," interrupted Charles, "the

fact of his being my favourite makes you madly jealous of him ;
that is not the question now.   If you don't know where he is,
be so good as to hold your tongue."

Charles was only now and then insolent and abrupt with servants, and they liked him the better for it.   It was one of
Cuthbert's rules to be coldly, evenly polite, and, as he thought,
considerate to the whole household ; and yet they did not like
him half so well as Charles, who would sometimes, when anything went wrong, " kick up," what an intelligent young Irish
footman used to call " the divvle's own shindy."   Cuthbert,
they knew, had no sympathy for them, but treated them, as he
treated himself, as mere machines; while Charles had that
infinite capacity of good-will which none are more quick to
recognise than servants and labouring people.   And on this
occasion, though Mr. Dickson might have sworn a little more
than usual after Charles's departure, yet his feeling, on the
whole, was that he was sorry for having vexed the young gentleman by sneering at his favourite.

But Charles, having rescued the enraptured Father Tiernay
from the stable, and having listened somewhat inattentively to a
long description of the Curragh of Kildare, led the worthy priest
round the back of the stables, up a short path through the wood,
and knocked at the door of a long, low keeper's lodge, which
stood within a stone's throw of the other buildings, in an open,
grassy glade, through which flowed a musical, slender stream of
water.   In one instant, night was hideous with rattling chains
and barking dogs, who made as though they would tear the
intruders to pieces ; all except one foolish pointer pup, who was
loose, and who, instead of doing his duty by barking, came
feebly up, and cast himself on his back at their feet, as though
they were the car of Juggernaut, and he was a candidate for
paradise.   Finding that he was not destroyed, he made a
humiliating feint of being glad to see them, and nearly over-
threw the priest by getting between his legs.   But Charles, finding that his second summons was unanswered, lifted the latch,
and went into the house.

The room they entered was dark, or nearly so, and at the
first moment appeared empty : but, at the second glance, they
made out that a figure was kneeling before the dying embers of
the fire, and trying to kindle a match by blowing on the coals.

" Hullo ! " said Charles.

" William, my boy," said a voice which made the priest start,
" Where have you been, lad ? "

At the same moment a match was lit, and then a candle ; as

the light blazed up, it fell on the features of a grey headed old man, who was peering through the darkness at them, and the priest cried, "Good God! Mr. Ravenshoe!"

The likeness for one moment was very extraordinary; but, as the eye grew accustomed to the light, one saw that the face was the face of a taller man than Densil, and one, too, who wore the dress of a gamekeeper. Charles laughed at the priest, and said—

"You were struck, as many have been, by the likeness. He has been so long with my father that he has the very trick of his voice, and the look of the eye. Where have you been to-night, James?" he added affectionately. "Why do you go out so late alone? If any of those mining rascals were to be round poaching, you might be killed."

"I can take care of myself yet, Master Charles," said the old man, laughing; and, to do him justice, he certainly looked as if he could.

"Where is Nora?"

"Gone down to young James Holby's wife; she is lying-in."

"Pretty early, too. Where's Ellen?"

"Gone up to the house."

"See, Father, I shall be disappointed in showing you the belle of Ravenshoe; and now you will go back to Ireland, fancying you can compete with us."

Father Tiernay was beginning a story about five Miss Moriartys, who were supposed to rival in charms and accomplishments, any five young ladies in the world, when his eye was attracted by a stuffed hare in a glass case, of unusual size and very dark colour.

"That, sir," said James, the keeper, in a bland, polite, explanatory tone of voice, coming and leaning over him, "is old Mrs. Jewel, that lived in the last cottage on the right hand side, under the cliff. I always thought that it had been Mrs. Simpson, but it was not. I shot this hare on the Monday, not three hundred yards from Mrs. Jewel's house; and on the Wednesday the neighbours noticed the shutters hadn't been down for two days, and broke the door open; and there she was, sure enough, dead in her bed. I had shot her as she was coming home from some of her devilries. A quiet old soul she was, though. No, I never thought it had been she."

It would be totally impossible to describe the changes through which the broad, sunny face of Father Tiernay went, during the above astounding narration; horror, astonishment, inquiry, and humour were so strangely blended. He looked into the face of the old gamekeeper, and met the expression of a man who had mentioned an interesting fact, and had contributed to the scientific experience of the listener. He looked at Charles, and met no expression whatever; but the latter said—

"Our witches in these parts, Father, take the form of some inferior animal when attending their Sabbath or general meetings, which I believe are presided over by an undoubted gentleman, who is not generally named in polite society. In this case, the old woman was caught sneaking home under the form of a hare, and promptly rolled over by James; and here she is."

Father Tiernay said, "Oh, indeed!" but looked as if he thought the more.

"And there's another of them out now, sir," said the keeper; "and, Master Charles dear, if you're going to take the grey hounds out to-morrow, do have a turn at that big black hare under Birch Tor——"

"A black hare!" said Father Tiernay, aghast.

"Nearly coal-black, your reverence," said James. "She's a witch, your reverence, and who she is the blessed saints only know. I have seen her three or four times. If the master was on terms with Squire Humby to Hele, we might have the harriers over and run her down. But that can't be, in course. If you take Blue-ruin and Lightning out to-morrow, Master Charles, and turn her out of the brambles under the rocks, and leave the Master and Miss Mary against the corner of the stone wall to turn her down the gully, you must have her."

The look of astonishment had gradually faded from Father Tiernay's face. It is said that one of the great elements of power in the Roman Catholic priesthood, is that they can lend themselves to any little bit of—well, of mild deception—which happens to be going. Father Tiernay was up to the situation. He looked from the keeper to Charles with a bland and stolid expression of face, and said—

"If she is a witch, mark my words, the dogs will never touch her. The way would be to bite up a crooked sixpence and fire at her with that. I shall be there to see the sport. I never hunted a witch yet."

"Has your reverence ever seen a white polecat?" said the keeper.

"No, never," said the priest; "I have heard of them though. My friend, Mr. Moriarty, of Castledown (not Mountdown Castle, ye understand; that is the sate of my Lord Mountdown, whose blessed mother was a Moriarty, the heavens be her bed), claimed to have seen one; but, bedad, no one else ever saw it, and he said it turned brown again as the season came round. May the—may the saints have my sowl if I believe a word of it."

"*I* have one, your reverence; and it is a rarity, I allow. Stoats turn white often in hard winters, but polecats rarely. If your reverence and your honour will excuse me a moment, I will fetch it. It was shot by my Lord Welter when he was staying here last winter. A fine shot is my lord, your reverence, for so young a man."

He left the room, and the priest and Charles were left alone together.

"Does he believe all this rubbish about witches?" said Father Tiernay.

"As firmly as you do the liquefaction of the blood of——"

"There, there; we don't want all that. Do you believe in it?"

"Of course I don't," said Charles; "but why should I tell him so?"

"Why do you lend yourself to such humbug?"

"Why do you?"

"Begorra. I don't know. I am always lending I lent a low-browed, hang-jawed spalpeen of a Belgian priest two pound the other day, an sorra a halfpenny of it will me mother's son ever see again. Hark!"

There were voices approaching the lodge—the voices of two uneducated persons quarrelling; one that of a man, the other of a woman. They both made so much out in a moment. Charles recognised the voices, and would have distracted the priest's attention, and given those without warning that there were strangers within; but in his anxiety to catch what was said, he was not ready enough, and they both heard this.

The man's voice said fiercely, "You did."

The woman's voice said after a wild sob, "I did not."

"You did. I saw you. You are a liar as well as——"

"I swear I didn't; Strike me dead, Bill, if there's been anything wrong."

"No. If I thought there had, I'd cut his throat first and yours after."

"If it had been *him*, Bill, you wouldn't have used me like this."

"Never you mind that."

"You want to drive me mad. You do. You hate me. Master Charles hates me. Oh, I wish I was mad."

"I'd sooner see you chained by the waist in the straw than see what I saw to-night." Then followed an oath.

The door was rudely opened, and there entered first of all our old friend, Charles's groom, William, who seemed beside himself with passion, and after him a figure which struck the good Irishman dumb with amazement and admiration—a girl as beautiful as the summer morning, with her bright brown hair tangled over her forehead, and an expression of wild terror and wrath on her face, such as one may conceive the old sculptor wished to express, when he tried, and failed, to carve the face of the Gorgon.

She glared on them both in her magnificent beauty only one moment. Yet that look, as of a lost soul of another world, mad, hopeless, defiant, has never passed from the memory of either of them.

She was gone in an instant into an inner room, and William was standing looking savagely at the priest. In another moment his eyes had wandered to Charles, and then his face grew smooth and quiet, and he said—

"We've been quarrelling, sir ; don't you and this good gentle man say anything about it. Master Charles, dear, she drives me mad sometimes. Things are not going right with her."

Charles and the priest walked thoughtfully home together.

"Allow me to say, Ravenshoe," said the priest, "that as an Irishman, I consider myself a judge of remarkable establishments. I must say honestly that I have seldom or never met with a great house with so many queer elements about it as yours. You are all remarkable people. And, on my honour, I think that our friend Mackworth is the most remarkable man of the lot."

CHAPTER XIII

THE BLACK HARE

IT was a glorious breezy November morning ; the sturdy oaks alone held on to the last brown remnants of their summer finery ; all the rest of the trees in the vast sheets of wood which clothed the lower parts of the downs overhanging Ravenshoe had changed the bright colours of autumn for the duller, but not less beautiful, browns and purples of winter. Below, in the park, the deer were feeding among the yellow fern brakes, and

the rabbits were basking and hopping in the narrow patches of
slanting sun-light, which streamed through the leafless trees.
Aloft, on the hill, the valiant blackcock led out his wives and
family from the wortle-grown rocks, to flaunt his plumage in the
warmest corner beneath the Tor.

And the Tors, too, how they hung aloft above the brown
heather, which was relieved here and there by patches of dead
brown, king-fern ; hung aloft like brilliant, clearly-defined
crystals, with such mighty breadths of light and shadow as Sir
Charles Barry never could accomplish, though he had West-
minster Abbey to look at every day.

Up past a narrow sheep-path, where the short grass faded on
the one side into feathery broom, and on the other into brown
heather and grey stone, under the shadow of the Tor which lay
nearest to Ravenshoe, and overhung those dark woods in which
we saw Densil just now walking with his old hound ; there was
grouped, on the morning after the day of Charles's arrival, a
happy party, every one of whom is already known to the reader.
Of which circumstance I, the writer, am most especially glad.
For I am already as tired of introducing new people to you as
my lord chamberlain must be of presenting strangers to Her
Majesty at a levée.

Densil first, on a grey cob, looking very old and feeble, straining his eyes up the glen whither Charles, and James, the old
keeper, had gone with the greyhounds. At his rein stood
William, whom we knew at Oxford. Beside the old man sat
Mary on her pony, looking so radiant and happy, that, even if
there had been no glorious autumn sun overhead, one glance
at her face would have made the dullest landscape in Lancashire
look bright. Last, not least, the good Father Tiernay, who sat
on his horse, hatless, radiant, scratching his tonsure.

" And so you're determined to back the blue dog, Miss
Mary," said he.

" I have already betted a pair of gloves with Charles, Mr.
Tiernay," said Mary, "and I will be rash enough to do
so with you. Ruin is the quickest striker we have ever
bred."

" I know it ; they all say so," said the priest ; " but come, I
must have a bet on the course. I will back Lightning."

" Lightning is the quicker dog," said Densil ; " but Ruin !
you will see him lie behind the other dog all the run, and strike
the hare at last. Father Mackworth, a good judge of a dog,
always backs him against the kennel."

" Where is Father Mackworth ? "

" I don't know," said Densil. " I am surprised he is not with us ; he is very fond of coursing."

" His reverence, sir," said William, " started up the moor about an hour ago. I saw him going."

" Where was he going to ? "

" I can't say, sir. He took just over past the rocks on the opposite side of the bottom from Mr. Charles."

" I wonder," said Father Tiernay, " whether James will find his friend, the witch, this morning."

" Ah," said Densil, "he was telling me about that. I am sure I hope not."

Father Tiernay was going to laugh, but didn't.

" Do you believe in witches, then, Mr. Ravenshoe ? "

" Why, no," said Densil, stroking his chin thoughtfully, " I suppose not. It don't seem to me now, as an old man, a more absurd belief than this new electro-biology and table-turning. Charles tells me that they use magic crystals at Oxford, and even claim to have raised the devil himself at Merton ; which, at this time of day, seems rather like reverting to first principles. But I am not sure I believe in any of it. I only know that, if any poor old woman has sold herself to Satan, and taken it into her head to transform herself into a black hare, my greyhounds won't light upon her. She must have made such a deuced hard bargain that I shouldn't like to cheat her out of any of the small space left her between this and, and—thingamy."

William, as a privileged servant, took the liberty of remarking that old Mrs. Jewel didn't seem to have been anything like a match for Satan in the way of a bargain, for she had had hard times of it seven years before she died. From which—

Father Tiernay deduced the moral lesson, that that sort of thing didn't pay ; and—

Mary said she didn't believe a word of such rubbish, for old Mrs. Jewel was as nice an old body as ever was seen, and had worked hard for her living, until her strength failed, and her son went down in one of the herring-boats.

Densil said that his little bird was too positive. There was the Witch of Endor, for instance—

Father Tiernay, who had been straining his eyes and attention at the movements of Charles and the greyhounds, and had only caught the last word, said with remarkable emphasis and distinctness—

> " A broomstick of the Witch of Endor,
>   Well shod wi' brass,"

and then looked at Densil as though he had helped him out of a difficulty, and wanted to be thanked. Densil continued without noticing him—

"There was the Witch of Endor. And 'thou shalt not suffer a witch to live.' If there weren't such things as witches, you know, St. Paul wouldn't have said that."

"I don't think it was St. Paul, papa, was it?" said Mary.

"It was one of them, my love; and, for that matter I consider St. Peter quite as good as St. Paul, if not better. St. Peter was always in trouble, I know; but he was the only one who struck a blow for the good cause, all honour to him. Let me see, he married St. Veronica, didn't he?"

"Marry St. Veronica, virgin and martyr?" said the priest, aghast. "My good sir, you are really talking at random."

"Ah, well, I may be wrong; she was virgin, but she was no martyr."

"St. Veronica," said Father Tiernay dogmatically and somewhat sulkily, "was martyred under Tiberius; no less than that."

"I bet you what you like of it," cried Densil, "she died——"

But what was Densil's opinion about the last days of St. Veronica will for ever remain a mystery; for at this moment there came a "See, HO!" from Charles; in the next a noble hare had burst from a tangled mass of brambles at his feet; in another the two dogs were on her haunches, and Charles, carrying two little flags furled in his hand, had dashed at the rough rocks on the bottom of the valley, had brought his horse on his nose, recovered him, and was half way up the hill after the flying greyhounds.

It was but a short course. Puss raced for some broken ground under the hill, opposite to where our party stood. She was too close pressed, and doubled back for the open, but, meeting James, turned as a last desperate chance back to her first point. Too late; the dogs were upon her. There was a short scuffle, and then Charles, rising in his saddle, unfurled his blue flag, and waved it.

"Hurrah!" cried Mary, clapping her hands, "two pairs of gloves this morning: where will he try now, I wonder? Here comes James; let us ask him."

James approached them with the dead hare, and Densil asked where he was going to try. He said, just where they were.

Densil asked, had he seen Father Mackworth? and he was in the act of saying that he was gone over the down, when a shout from Charles, and a still louder one from James, made them all start. A large *black hare* had burst from the thorns at Charles's feet, and was bowling down the glen straight towards them, with the dogs close behind her.

"The witch," shouted James, "the witch! we shall know who she is now."

It seemed very likely indeed. Densil broke away from William, and, spurring his pony down the sheep path at the risk of his neck, made for the entrance of the wood. The hare, one of such dark colour that she looked almost black, scudded along in a parallel direction, and dashed into the grass ride just in front of Densil; they saw her flying down it, just under the dogs' noses, and then they saw her dash into a cross ride, one of the dogs making a strike at her as she did so; then hare and greyhounds disappeared round the corner.

"She's dead, sir, confound her; we shall have her now, the witch!"

They all came round the corner pell-mell. Here stood the dogs, panting and looking foolishly about them, while in front of them, a few yards distant, stood Father Mackworth, looking disturbed and flushed, as though he had been running.

Old James stared aghast; William gave a long whistle; Mary, for a moment, was actually terrified. Densil looked puzzled, Charles amused; while Father Tiernay made the forest ring with peal after peal of uproarious laughter.

"I am afraid I have spoilt sport, Mr. Ravenshoe," said Mackworth, coming forward; "the hare ran almost against my legs, and doubled into the copse, puzzling the dogs. They seemed almost inclined to revenge themselves on me for a moment."

"Ha, ha!" cried the jolly priest, not noticing, as Charles did, how confused the priest was. "So we've caught you sneaking home from your appointment with your dear friend."

"What do you mean, sir, by appointment? You are over-stepping the bounds of decorum, sir. Mr. Ravenshoe, I beg you to forgive me for inadvertently spoiling your sport."

"Not at all, my dear Father," said Densil, thinking it best, from the scared look of old James, to enter into no further explanations; "we have killed one hare, and now I think it is time to come home to lunch."

"Don't eat it all before I come; I must run up to the Tor; I have dropped my whip there," said Charles. "James, ride my horse home; you look tired. I shall be there on foot in half the time."

He had cast the reins to James, and was gone, and they all turned homewards together.

Charles, fleet of foot, was up on the Tor in a few minutes, and had picked up his missing property; then he sat him down on a stone, thinking.

"There is something confoundedly wrong somewhere, and I should like to find out what it is. What had that Jack priest been up to, that made him look so queer? And also, what was the matter between Ellen and William last night? Whom has she been going on with? I will go down. I wish I could find some trace of him. One thing I know, and one thing only, that he hates me worse than poison; and that his is not likely to be a passive hatred."

The wood into which Charles descended was of very large extent, and composed of the densest copse, intersected by long straight grass rides. The day had turned dark and chilly; and a low moaning wind began to sweep through the bare boughs, rendering still more dismal the prospect of the long-drawn vistas of damp grass and rotting leaves.

He passed musing on from one ride to another, and in one of them came in sight of a low, white building, partly ruinous, which had been built in the deepest recesses of the wood for a summer-house. Years ago Cuthbert and Charles used to come and play there on happy summer holidays—play at being Robinson Crusoe and what not; but there had been a fight with the poachers there, and one of their young men had been kicked in the head by one of the gang, and rendered idiotic; and Charles had seen the blood on the grass next morning; and so they voted it a dismal place, and never went near it again. Since then it had been taken possession of by the pheasants to dust themselves in. Altogether it was a solitary, ghostly sort of place; and, therefore, Charles was considerably startled, on looking in at the low door, to see a female figure, sitting unmoveable in the darkest corner.

It was not a ghost, for it spoke. It said, "Are you come back to upbraid me again? I know my power, and you shall never have it." And Charles said, "Ellen!"

She looked up, and began to cry. At first a low, moaning cry, and afterwards a wild passionate burst of grief.

He drew her towards him, and tried to quiet her, but she drew away. "Not to-day," she cried, "not to-day."

"What is the matter, pretty one? What is the matter, sister?" said Charles.

"Call me sister again," she said, looking up. "I like that name. Kiss me, and call me sister, just for once."

"Sister dear," said Charles kindly, kissing her on the forehead, "what is the matter?"

"I have had a disagreement with Father Mackworth, and he has called me names. He found me here walking with Master Cuthbert."

"With Cuthbert?"

"Ay, why not? I might walk with you or him any time, and no harm. I must go."

Before Charles had time to say one word of kindness, or consolation, or wonder, she had drawn him towards her, given him a kiss, and was gone down the ride towards the house. He saw her dress flutter round the last corner, and she disappeared.

CHAPTER XIV

LORD SALTIRE'S VISIT, AND SOME OF HIS OPINIONS

THERE followed on the events above narrated two or three quiet months—a time well remembered by Charles as one of the quietest and most peaceful in his life, in all the times which followed. Every fine day there was a ramble with his father through the kennels and stables, and down through the wood, or over the farm. Charles, who at Oxford thought no day complete, after riding with the drag, or Drakes, or rowing to Sandford; without banquier, vingt-et-un, or loo, till three o'clock in the morning, now found, greatly to his astonishment, that he got more pleasure by leaning over a gate with his father, and looking at fat beasts and pigs, chewing a straw the while. A noisy wine-party, where he met the same men he had met the night before, who sang the same songs, and told the same silly stories, was well enough; but he began to find that supper in the oak dining-room, sitting between Mary and his father, and talking of the merest trifles, was a great deal pleasanter. Another noticeable fact was that Father Mackworth's sarcasms were turned off with a good-natured laugh, and that battle was on all occasions refused to the worthy priest. In short, Charles, away from company and dissipation, was himself. The good, worthy fellow, whom I learnt to like years ago. The man whose history I am proud to write.

Lord Saltire had arrived meanwhile; he had written to Densil, to say that he was horribly bored; that he wished, as an ethical study, to settle, once for all, the amount of boredom a man could stand without dying under it; that, having looked carefully about him, to select a spot and a society where that object could be obtained, he had selected Ravenshoe, as being the most eligible; that he should wish his room to have a south aspect; and that his man would arrive with his things three days after date. To this Densil had written an appropriate reply, begging his kind old friend to come and make his house his home; and Lord Saltire had arrived one evening, when every one was out of the way but Mary, who received him in the hall.

She was in some little trepidation. She had read and heard enough of "the wild prince and Poyns," and of Lord Saltire's powers of sarcasm, to be thoroughly frightened at her awful position. She had pictured to herself a terrible old man, with overhanging eyebrows, and cruel gleaming eyes beneath them. Therefore she was astonished to see a gentleman, old it is true, but upright as a young oak, of such remarkable personal beauty, and such a pleasant expression of countenance, as she had never seen before.

She was astonished, I said; but, mind you, Mary was too much of a lady to show too much of it. She sailed towards him through the gloom of the old hall with a frank smile, and just that amount of admiration which paid Lord Saltire the truest compliment he had had for many a day.

"Mr. Ravenshoe will be sorry to have missed receiving you, my lord," she said.

"If Mr. Ravenshoe is sorry," he said, "I certainly am not. Mr. Ravenshoe has done me the honour to show me the most beautiful thing in his house first. I rather think that is a pretty compliment, Miss Corby, unless I am getting out of practice."

"That is a very pretty compliment, indeed," she answered, laughing. "I most heartily thank you for it. I know nothing in life so pleasant as being flattered. May I introduce Father Mackworth?"

Lord Saltire would be delighted. Father Mackworth came forward, and Mary saw them look at one another. She saw at a glance that either they had met before, or there was some secret which both of them knew. She never forgot Mackworth's defiant look, or Lord Saltire's calm considerate glance, which said as plain as words, "This fellow knows it."

This fellow knew it—had known it for years. The footman who had left Mackworth at the lodge of the French Lycée, the nameless domestic, who formed the last link with his former life—this man had worn Lord Saltire's livery, and he remembered it.

"I see," said Lord Saltire, "that Miss Corby is prepared for walking. I guess that she is going to meet Mr. Ravenshoe, and, if my surmise is correct, I beg to be allowed to accompany her."

"You are wonderfully correct, my lord. Cuthbert and Charles are shooting pheasants in the wood, and Mr. Ravenshoe is with them on his pony. If you will walk with me, we shall meet them."

So the grand old eagle and the pretty sweet-voiced robin passed out on to the terrace, and stood looking together, under the dull December sky, at the whispering surges. Right and left the misty headlands seemed to float on the quiet grey sea, which broke in sighs at their feet, as the long majestic groundswell rolled in from the ocean; and these two stood there for a minute or more without speaking.

"The new school of men," said Lord Saltire at last, looking out to sea, "have perhaps done wisely in thinking more of scenery and the mere externals of nature than we did. We lived the life of clubs and crowds, and we are going to our places one after another. There are but few left now. These Stephensons and Paxtons are fine men enough. *They* are fighting inert matter, but *we* fought the armies of the Philistine. We had no time for botany and that sort of thing; which was unfortunate. You young folks shouldn't laugh at us though."

"I laugh at you!" she said suddenly and rapidly; "laugh at the giants who warred with the gods. My lord, the men of our time have not shown themselves equal to their fathers."

Lord Saltire laughed.

"No, not yet," she continued; "when the time comes they will. The time has not come yet."

"Not yet," Miss Corby. "It will come—mind the words of a very old man; an old fellow who has seen a confounded deal of the world."

"Are we to have any more wars, Lord Saltire?"

"Wars such as we never dreamt of, young lady."

"Is all this new inauguration of peace to go for nothing?"

"Only as the inauguration of a new series of wars, more terrible than those which have gone before."

"France and England combined can give the law to Europe."

Lord Saltire turned upon her and laughed. "And so you actually believe that France and England can really combine for anything more important than a raid against Russia. Not that they will ever fight Russia, you know. There will be no fight. If they threaten loud enough, Russia will yield. Nicholas knows his weakness, and will give way. If he is fool enough to fight the Western powers, it will end in another *duel à l'outrance* between France and England. They will never work together for long. If they do, Europe is enslaved, and England lost."

"But why, Lord Saltire?"

"Well, well; I think so. Allow me to say that I was not prepared to find a deep-thinking, though misguided politician in such an innocent-looking young lady. God defend the dear old land, for every fresh acre I see of it confirms my belief that it is the first country in the world."

They were crossing the old terraced garden towards the wood, where they heard the guns going rapidly, and both were silent for a minute or so. The leafless wood was before them, and the village at their feet. The church spire rose aloft among the trees. Some fisherman patriarch had gone to his well-earned rest that day, and the bell was tolling for him. Mary looked at the quiet village, at the calm winter sea, and then up at the calm stern face of the man who walked beside her, and said—

"Tell me one thing, Lord Saltire; you have travelled in many countries. Is there any land, east or west, that can give us what this dear old England does—settled order, in which each man knows his place and his duties? It is so easy to be good in England."

"Well, no. It is the first country in the world. A few bad harvests would make a hell of it, though. Has Ravenshoe got many pheasants down here?"

And, so talking, this strange pair wandered on towards the wood, side by side.

Charles was not without news in his retirement, for a few friends kept him pretty well *au fait* with what was going on in the world. First, there was news from Oxford; one sort of which was communicated by Charles Marston, and another sort by one Marker of Brazenose, otherwise known as

"Bodger," though, why, I know not, nor ever could get any one to tell me. He was purveyor of fashionable intelligence, while Charles Marston dealt more in example and advice. About this time the latter wrote as follows:—

"How goes Issachar? Is the ass stronger or weaker than formerly? Has my dearly-beloved ass profited, or otherwise, by his stay at Ranford? How is the other ass, my Lord Welter? He is undoubtedly a fool, but I think an honest one, so long as you keep temptation out of his way. He is shamefully in debt; but I suppose, if their horse wins the Derby, he will pay; otherwise I would sooner be my lord than his tradesman. How goes the 'grand passion'—has Chloe relented? She is a great fool if she does. Why, if she refuses you, she may marry Lord Welter, and he may settle his debts on her. A word in your ear. I have an invitation to Ranford. I must go, I suppose. The dear old woman, whose absurdities your honour is pleased to laugh at, has been always kind to me and mine; and I shall go. I shall pay my just tribute of flattery to the noble honest old soul, who is struggling to save a falling house. Don't you laugh at Lady Ascot, you impudent young rascal. I have no doubt that she offers some prominent points for the exercise of your excellency's wit, but she is unmeasurably superior to you, you young scapegrace.

"Bless your dear old face; how I long to see it again! I am coming to see it. I shall come to you at the beginning of the Christmas vacation. I shall come to you a beaten man, Charley. I shall only get a second. Never mind; I would sooner come to you and yours and hide my shame, than to any one else.

"Charles, old friend, if I get a third, I shall break my heart. Don't show this letter to any one. I have lost the trick of Greek prose. Oh, old Charley! believe this, that the day once lost can never, never come back any more! They preach a future hell; but what hell could be worse than the eternal contemplation of opportunities thrown away—of turning-points in the affairs of a man's life, when, instead of rising, he has fallen —not by a bold stroke like Satan, but by laziness and neglect."

Charles was very sorry, very grieved and vexed, to find his shrewd old friend brought to this pass by over-reading, and over-anxiety about a subject, which, to a non-university man, does not seem of such vital importance. He carried the letter to his father, in spite of the prohibition contained in it, and he found his father alone with the good, honest Father Tiernay;

to whom, not thinking that thereby he was serving his friend ill, he read it aloud.

"Charley dear," said his father, half rising from his chair, "he must come to us my boy ; he must come here to us, and stay with us till he forgets his disappointment. He is a noble lad. He has been a good friend to my boy ; and, by George, the house is his own."

"I don't think, dad," said Charles, looking from Densil to Father Tiernay, "that he is at all justified in the dark view he is taking of matters. The clever fellows used to say that he was safe of his first. You know he is going in for mathematics as well."

"He is a good young man, any way," said Father Tiernay ; "his sentiments do honour to him ; and none the worst of them is his admiration for my heretic young friend here, which does him most honour of all. Mr. Ravenshoe, I'll take three to one against his double first ; pity he ain't a Catholic. What the divvle do ye Prothestants mean by absorbing (to use no worse language) the rints and revenues left by Catholic testators for the good of the hooly Church, for the edication of heretics ? Tell me that, now."

"The other letter from Oxford was of a very different tenor. Mr. Marker, of Brazenose, began by remarking that—

"He didn't know what was come over the place ; it was getting confoundedly slow, somehow. They had had another Bloomer ball at Abingdon, but the thing was a dead failure, sir. Jemmy Dane, of University, had driven two of them home in a cart, by way of Nunenham. He had passed the Pro's at Magdalen turnpike, and they never thought of stopping him, by George. Their weak intellects were not capable of conceiving such glorious audacity. Both the Proctors were down at Coldharbour turnpike, stopping every man who came from Abingdon way. Toreker, of Exeter, was coming home on George Simmond's Darius, and, seeing the Proctors in the light of the turnpike gate, had put his horse at a fence (Charles would remember it, a stubbed hedge and a ditch), and got over the back water by the White House, and so home by the Castle. Above forty men had been rusticated over this business, and some good fellows too." (Here followed a list of names, which I could produce, if necessary ; but seeing that some names on the list are now rising at the bar or in the Church, think it better not.) "Pembroke had won the fours, very much in consequence of Exeter having gone round the flag, and, on being made to row again, of fouling them in the gut. The water was out heavily, and had spoilt the boating. The Christ Church grind had been slow, but the best that year. L——n was going down, and they said was going to take the Pychley. C——n was pretty safe of his first—so reading men said. Martin of Trinity had got his testamur, at which event astonishment, not unmixed with awe, had fallen on the University generally. That he himself was in for his *vivâ voce* two days after date, and he wished himself out of the hands of his enemies."

There was a postscript, which interested Charles as much as all the rest of the letter put together. It ran thus :—

" By the bye, Welter has muckered ; you know that by this time. But, worse than that, they say that Charles Marston's classical first is fishy. The old cock has over-worked himself, they say."

Lord Saltire never went to bed without having Charles up into his dressing-room for a chat. " Not having," as his lordship most truly said, " any wig to take off, or any false teeth to come out, I cannot see why I should deny myself the pleasure of my young friend's company at night. Every evening, young gentleman, we are one day older and one day wiser. I myself have got so confoundedly wise with my many years, that I have nothing left to learn. But it amuses me to hear your exceedingly *naïve* remarks on things in general, and it also flatters and soothes me to contrast my own consummate wisdom with your folly. Therefore I will trouble you to come up to my dressing-room every night, and give me your crude reflections on the events of the day."

So Charles came up one night, with Mr. Marker's letter, which he read to Lord Saltire, while his valet was brushing his hair ; and then Charles, by way of an easily answered question, asked Lord Saltire, What did he think of his friend's chances ?

" I must really remark," said Lord Saltire, " even if I use unparliamentary language, which I should be very sorry to do, that that is one of the silliest questions I ever had put to me. When I held certain seals, I used to have some very foolish questions put to me (which, by the way, I never answered), but I don't know that I ever had such a foolish question put to me as that. Why, how on earth can I have any idea of what your friend's chances are ? Do be reasonable."

" Dear Lord Saltire, don't be angry with me. Tell me, as far as your experience can, how far a man who knows his work, by George, as well as a man can know it, is likely to fail through nervousness. You have seen the same thing in Parliament.

You know how much mischief nervousness may do.   Now, do give me your opinion."

"Well, you are putting your question in a slightly more reasonable form; but it is a very silly one yet.   I have seen a long sort of man, with black hair, and a hook nose, like long Montague, for instance, who has been devilishly nervous till he got on his legs, and has then astonished every one, and no one more than myself, not so much by his power of declamation as by the extraordinary logical tenacity with which he clung to his subject.   Yes, I don't know but what I have heard more telling and logical speeches from unprepared men than I ever have from one of the law lords.   But I am a bad man to ask.   I never was in the lower house.   About your friend's chance; —well, I would not give two-pence for it; in after life he may succeed.   But, from what you have told me, I should prepare myself for a disappointment."

Very shortly after this, good Lord Saltire had to retire for a time into the upper chamber; he had a severe attack of gout.

There had been no more quarrelling between Father Mackworth and Charles; peace was proclaimed,—an armed truce; and Charles was watching, watching in silence.   Never since he met her in the wood had he had an opportunity of speaking to Ellen.   She always avoided him.   William, being asked confidentially by Charles what he thought was the matter, said that Ellen had been "carrin on" with some one, and he had been blowing her up; which was all the explanation he offered.   In the meantime, Charles lived under the comforting assurance that there was mischief brewing, and that Mackworth was at the bottom of it.

CHAPTER XV·

CHARLES'S "LIDDELL AND SCOTT"

A GROWING anxiety began to take possession of Charles shortly before Christmas, arising from the state of his father's health.   Densil was failing.   His memory was getting defective, and his sense dulled.   His eye always was searching for Charles, and he was uneasy at his absence.   So it was with a vague sense of impending misfortune that he got a letter from the dean of his college, summoning him back after the Christmas vacation.

Mr. Dean said, "That Mr. Ravenshoe's case had been re-considered, and that, at the warm, and, he thought, misguided, intercession of the Bursar, a determination had been come to, to allow Mr. Ravenshoe to come into residence again for the Lent term. He trusted that this would be a warning, and that, while there was time, he would arrest himself in that miserable career of vice and folly which could only have one termination —utter ruin in this world and in the next."

A college "Don," by long practice, acquires a power of hurting a young man's feelings, utterly beyond competition, save by a police magistrate. Charles winced under this letter; but the same day Mary, coming singing downstairs as was her wont, was alarmed by the descent of a large opaque body of considerable weight down the well of the staircase, which lodged in the wood basket at the bottom, and which, on examination, she found to be a Liddell and Scott's Lexicon. At which she rejoiced; for she concluded that Charles had taken to reading again, though why he should begin by throwing his books down stairs she could not well understand, until he joined her and explained that he had been dusting it on the landing, and that it had slipped out of his hand.

"What a crack it came down," added he; "I wish Father Mackworth's head had been underneath it."

"I have no doubt of it, young gentleman," said the priest quietly from behind; and there he was with his hand on the library door, and in he went and shut it behind him.

Mary and Charles were both awfully disconcerted. Mary felt horribly guilty; in fact, if the priest had remained quiet one moment more, he would undoubtedly have heard one or two candid and far from complimentary remarks about himself from that young lady, which would have made his ears tingle.

"Confound him," said Charles; "how he glides about! He learned that trick, and a few others, at that precious Jesuit College of his. They teach them that sort of thing as the old Jews teach the young pickpockets. The old father inquisitor puts the door ajar with a bell against it, and they all have to come in one after another. The one who rings it gets dropped on to like blazes."

Mary was going to ask what exact amount of personal suffering being dropped on to like blazes involved; but Charles stopped her and took her hand.

"Mary dear," he said, "do you ever think of the future?"

"Night and day, Charles—night and day."

"If he dies, Mary? When he dies?"

"Night and day, brother," she answered, taking one of his great brown hands between her two white little palms. "I dream in my sleep of the new regime which is to come, and I see only trouble, and again trouble."

"And then?"

"There is a God in heaven, Charles."

"Ay, but Mary, what will you do?"

"I?" and she laughed the merriest little laugh ever you heard. "Little me? Why go for a governess, to be sure. Charles, they shall love me so that this life shall be a paradise. I will go into a family where there are two beautiful girls; and, when I am old and withered, there shall be two nurseries in which I shall be often welcome, where the children shall come babbling to my knee, the darlings, and they shall tell me how they love me, almost as well as their mother. There is my future. Would you change it?"

Charles was leaning against the oak banister; and, when he saw her there before him, when he saw that valiant, true-hearted face, in the light which streamed from the old window above, he was rebuked, and bent down his head on the rail. The Dean's letter of that morning had done something; but the sight of that brave little woman, so fearless with all the world before her, did more. She weak, friendless, moneyless, and so courageous! He with the strong arm, so cowardly! It taught him a lesson indeed, a lesson he never forgot. But oh! for that terrible word—too late!

Ah! too late! What word is so terrible as that? You will see what I mean soon. That is the cry which one writer puts in the mouths of the lost spirits in hell. God's mercy is infinite, and it is yet a question whether it were better for Charles to have fallen into the grove of ordinary life, or to have gone through those humiliating scenes through which we must follow him.

"Charley dear," said Mary, laying her hand on his shoulder, "it is not about myself I am thinking; it is about you. What are you going to do when he is gone? are you going into the Church?"

"Oh, no!" said Charles, "I couldn't bear the idea of that."

"Then, why are you at Oxford?"

"To get an education, I suppose."

"But what use will a university education be to you, Charles! Have you no plans?"

"I give you my word, my dear Mary, that I am as much in the dark about the future as a five days-old puppy."

"Has he made any provision for you?"

"Oh, yes! I am to have six thousand."

"Do you know that the estate is involved, Charles?"

"No."

"I believe it is. There has been a great deal of state kept up here, and I believe it is the case."

"Cuthbert would soon bring that round."

"I tremble to think of the future, Charles. Are your debts at Oxford heavy?"

"Pretty well. Five hundred would clear me."

"Don't get any more in debt, that's a dear."

"No, Mary dear, I won't. I don't care for the future. I shall have £180 a year. That will be enough for William and me. Then I shall go to the bar, and make a deuce of a lot of money, and marry Adelaide. Then you will come to live with us, and we shall have such jolly times of it.—Take that, you villain!"

This last elegant apostrophe was addressed to William (who at that moment had come in by the side door), and was accompanied by the dexterous delivery of the Liddell and Scott, in the manner of a cricket ball. Our friend William stood to catch it in a style worthy of Box, with his knees a yard apart, and one palm over the other; but as luck would have it, he missed it, and it alighted full on the shins of Father Mackworth, who had selected that time for coming out of the library; and so it lay sillily open at λαμ, γεμ, at his feet.

Mackworth really thought that it was intentional, and was furious. He went back into the library; and Charles, seeing what must come, followed him, while Mary fled upstairs. There was no one in the room but Cuthbert and Father Tiernay.

"I will be protected from insult in this house," began Mackworth; "twice to-day I have been insulted by Mr. Charles Ravenshoe, and I demand protection."

"What have you been doing, Charley?" said Cuthbert. "I thought you two had given up quarrelling. You will wear my life out. Sometimes, what with one thing and another, I wish I were dead. Oh! if the great problem were solved! Surely my brother may avoid brawling with a priest, a man sacred by his office, though of another faith. Surely my brother has taste enough to see the propriety of that."

"Your brother has no taste or sense, sir," said Father Mackworth. "He has no decency. He has no gentlemanly feeling. Within ten minutes he has dropped a book downstairs, and lamented, to my face, that it hadn't fallen on my head; and just now he has thrown the same book at me, and hit me with it."

"I thank God, Charles," said poor weary Cuthbert, "that our father is spared this. It would kill him. Brother, brother, why do you vex me like this? I have always stood on your side, Charley. Don't let me be killed with these ceaseless brawls."

"They will soon cease, sir," said Father Mackworth; "I leave this house to-morrow."

"Cuthbert, hear me now. I never intended to insult him."

"Why did you throw your book at him, Charley? It is not decorous. You must know when you wound him you wound me. And I have fought such battles for you, Charley."

"Cuthbert! brother! do hear me. And let him hear me. And let Father Tiernay hear me. Cuthbert, you know I love you. Father Tiernay you are a good and honest man; hear what I have to say. You Mackworth, you are a scoundrel. You are a double-dyed villain. What were you doing with that girl in the wood, the day you hunted the black hare a month ago? Cuthbert, tell me, like an honest gentleman, did you ever walk in the wood with Ellen?"

"I?" said Cuthbert, scared; "I never walked with Ellen there. I have walked with Mary there, brother. Why should I not?"

"There, look at the lie that this man has put into her mouth. She told me that he had found you and her walking together there."

"I am not answerable for any young woman's lies," said Father Mackworth. "I decline to continue this discussion. It is humiliating. As for you, you poor little moth," he said, turning to Charles, "when the time comes, I will crush you with my thumb against the wall. My liking for your father prevents my doing my duty as yet. In that I err. Wait."

Charles had been in a passion before this; but, seeing danger, and real danger, abroad, he got cool, and said—

"Wait."

And they both waited, and we shall see who waited the longest.

"I have done it now, Mary dear," said Charles, returning upstairs with the unlucky lexicon. "It is all over now."

"Has there been a scene?"

"A terrible scene. I swore at him, and called him a villain."

"Why did you do that, Charles? Why are you so violent? You are not yourself, Charles, when you give way to your temper like that."

"Well, I'll tell you, my robin. He is a villain."

"I don't think so, Charles. I believe he is a high-minded man."

"I know he is not, birdie. At least, I believe he is not."

"I believe him to be so, Charles."

"I know him to be otherwise; at least, I think so."

"Are you doing him justice, Charley dear? Are you sure you are doing him justice?"

"I think so."

"Why?"

"I cannot tell you, Mary. When the end of all things comes, and you and I are thrown abroad like two corks on the great sea, you will know. But I cannot tell you."

"I believe, dear, that you are so honest that you would not do injustice even to him. But, oh! be sure that you are right. Hush! Change the subject. What were you going to read when that unlucky book fell downstairs?"

"Demosthenes."

"Let me come in and sit with you, Charley dear, and look out the words; you don't know how clever I am. Is it the 'De Coronâ'?"

Charley took her hand and kissed it; and so they two poor fools went on with their Demosthenes.

CHAPTER XVI

MARSTON'S ARRIVAL

THE night after the terrible lexicon quarrel, which, you will observe, arose entirely from Charles's good resolution to set to work reading—whereby we should take warning not to be too sanguine of good resolutions, taken late, bringing forth good fruit—the very evening, I say, after this fracas, Charles, his father, and Mary, were sitting in the library together. Of course Densil had heard nothing of the disturbance, and was, good old gentleman, as happy as you please; all his elements of pleasure

were there. Father Mackworth was absent. Father Tiernay
was throwing his whole hearty soul into a splendid copy of
Bewick's Birds, date 1799. Cuthbert was before the upper
fireplace, beyond the pillar, poring over goodness only knows
what monkish lore; while close to him was bird Mary sewing,
and Charles reading aloud a book, very often quoted in every-
day life unconsciously.

Charles read how Mr. Quilp begged Mr. Brass would take
particular care of himself, or he would never forgive him; how
there was a dog in the lane who had killed a boy on Tuesday,
and bitten a man on Friday; how the dog lived on the right
hand side, but generally lurked on the left, ready for a spring;
and they were laughing over Mr. Brass's horror, when there
came a noise of wheels on the gravel.

"That is Marston, father, for a thousand pounds," said
Charles.

He hurried into the hall, as the men were undoing the door;
Mary, dropping her work, went after him; and Densil taking
his stick, came too. Cuthbert looked up from the further end
of the room, and then bent his head over his book again.
Father Tiernay looked up, inquisitive and interested, but sat
still. They who followed into the hall saw this.

Charles stood in front of the hall door, and out of the winter's
darkness came a man, with whom, as Mary once playfully said,
she had fallen in love at once. It was Marston.

Charles went up to him quickly with both hands out, and
said—

"We are so glad."

"It is very kind of you. God bless you; how did you
know it?"

"We know nothing, my dear Marston, except that you are
welcome. Now put me out of my pain."

"Why, well," said the other, "I don't know how it has
happened: but I have got my double first."

Charles gave a wild cheer, and the others were all on him
directly—Densil, Tiernay, Cuthbert, and all. Never was such
a welcome; not one of them, save Charles, had ever seen him
before, yet they welcomed him as an old friend.

"You have not been to Ranford then?" said Charles.

"Why, no. I did not feel inclined for it after so much
work. I must take it on my way back."

Lord Saltire's gout was better to-night, and he was down
stairs. He proceeded to remark that, having been in ——;
well, he wouldn't shock Miss Corby by saying where—for a day

or so, he had suddenly, through no merit of his own, got promoted back into purgatory. That, having fought against the blue devils, and come down stairs, for the sole purpose of making himself disagreeable, he had been rewarded, for that display of personal energy and self-sacrifice, by most unexpectedly meeting a son of his old friend, Jackdaw Marston. He begged to welcome his old friend's son, and to say that, by Jove, he was proud of him. His young friend's father had not been a brilliant scholar, as his young friend was ; but had been one of the first whist-players in England. His young friend had turned his attention to scholastic honours, in preference to whist, which might or might not be a mistake : though he believed he was committing no breach of trust in saying that the position had been thrust on his young friend from pecuniary motives. Property had an infernal trick of deteriorating. His own property had not happened to deteriorate (none knew why, for he had given it every chance) ; but the property of his young friend's father having deteriorated in a confounded rapid sort of way, he must say that it was exceedingly creditable in his young friend to have made such a decided step towards bringing matters right again as he had.

"My father's son, my Lord, thanks you for your kind remembrance of his father. I have always desired to see and meet my father's old friends, of whom you, Mr. Ravenshoe, were among the kindest. We have given up the greater vices lately, my Lord, but we do our best among the smaller ones."

There was a quiet supper, at which Lord Saltire consented to stay, provided no one used the expression "cheese"; in which case he said he should have to retire. There wasn't cheese on the table, but there was more than cheese ; there was scolloped cockles, and Lord Saltire ate some. He said at the time that they would have the same effect on him as swallowing the fireshovel. But, to relieve your mind at once, I may tell you that they didn't do him any harm at all, and he was as well as ever next morning.

Father Tiernay said grace ; and, when the meal was half over, in came Father Mackworth. Densil said, "Father Mackworth, Mr. Marston ;" and Marston said, after a moment's glance at him, "How do you do, sir?"

Possibly a more courteous form of speaking to a new acquaintance might have been used. But Marston had his opinions about Father Mackworth, and had no objection that the holy father should know them.

"We got, Mary," said Cuthbert suddenly, "more cocks than

pheasants to-day. Charles killed five couple, and I four. I was very vexed at being beaten by Charles, because I am so much the better shot."

Charles looked up and met his eyes—a look he never forgot. Accompanying the apparent petulance of the remark was a look of love and pity and sorrow. It pleased him, above everything, during the events which were to come, to recall that look, and say, "Well, he liked me once."

That evening Charles and Marston retired to Charles's study (a deal of study had been carried on there, you may depend), and had a long talk over future prospects. Charles began by telling him all about Madam Adelaide, and Marston said, "Oh, indeed! what are you going to do, Charley, boy, to keep her? She comes out of an extravagant house, you know."

"I must get called to the bar."

"Hard work for nothing, for many years, you know."

"I know. But I won't go into the Church; and what else is there?"

"Nothing I know of, except billiard marking and steeple-chase riding."

"Then, you approve of it?"

"I do most heartily. The work will be good for you. You have worked before, and can do it again. Remember how well you got on at Shrewsbury."

Then Charles told him about the relations between him-self and Father Mackworth, and what had happened that day.

"You and he have had disgraceful scenes like this before, haven't you?"

"Yes, but never so bad as this."

"He is a very passionate man, isn't he? You took utterly wrong grounds for what you did to-day. Don't you see that you have no earthly grounds for what you said, except your own suspicions? The girl's own account of the matter seems natural enough. That she was walking with your most saint-like brother, and the priest found them, and sent them to the right-about with fleas in their ears."

"I believe that man to be a great villain," said Charles.

"So may I," said the other, "but I shan't tell him so till I can prove it. As for that quarrel between William and his sister the night you came home, that proves nothing, except that she has been going too far with some one. But who? What have you been doing that empowers him to say that he will crush you like a moth?"

"Oh, bravado, I take it! You should have seen how mad he looked when he said it."

"I am glad I did not. Let us talk no more about him. Is that sweet little bird Mary Corby?"

"You know it is."

"Well, so I do know, but I wanted an excuse for saying the name over again. Charles, you are a fool."

"That is such a very novel discovery of yours," said Charles, laughing. "What have I been a-doing on now?"

"Why didn't you fall in love with Mary Corby instead of Madam Adelaide?"

"I am sure I don't know. Why, I never thought of such a thing as that."

"Then you ought to have done so. Now go to bed."

CHAPTER XVII

IN WHICH THERE IS ANOTHER SHIPWRECK

TIME jogged on very pleasantly to the party assembled at Ravenshoe that Christmas. There were woodcocks and pheasants in the woods; there were hares, snipes and rabbits on the moor. In the sea there were fish; and many a long excursion they had in the herring-boats—sometimes standing boldly out to sea towards the distant blue island in the main, sometimes crawling lazily along under the lofty shoreless cliffs which towered above their heads from 200 to 1,100 feet high.

It was three days before Christmas-day, and they were returning from fishing along the coast, and were about ten miles or so from home. I say returning, though in fact there was not a breath of wind, and the boat was drifting idly along on the tide. Two handsome simple-looking young men were lolling by the useless tiller; an old man, hale and strong as a lion, with a courteous highbred look about him, was splicing a rope; and a tall, pale, black-haired man was looking steadily seaward, with his hands in his pockets, while Charles and Marston were standing in the bows smoking.

"What a curious dreamy, dosy, delicious kind of winter you have down here," said Marston.

"I am very fond of it," said Charles; it keeps you in

continual hope for the spring that is coming. In the middle of frost and snow and ice one is apt to lose one's faith in waving boughs and shady pools."

" I have had such a quiet time with you down here, Charley. I am so pleased with the way in which you are going on. You are quite an altered man. I think we shall both look back to the last few quiet weeks as a happy time."

Here the tall dark man, who was looking out to sea, suddenly said—

"Rain and hail, snow and tempest, stormy wind fulfilling His word."

"Ay, ay," said the old man; "going to blow to-night I expect."

" We shall go home pretty fast, may be."

"Not us, Master Charles, dear," said the tall man. "We are going to have it from south and by west, and so through west round to north. Before which time there'll be souls in glory, praise be to God."

The old man took off his hat reverently.

"There won't be amuch surf on when we beaches she," said one of the young men. "It won't get up afore the wind be full round west for an hour."

"You're a spaking like a printed buke, Jan," said the old man.

"I'm a thinking differently, Master Evans," said the dark man. "It will chop round very sudden, and be west before we know where we are. I speak with humility to a man who has seen the Lord's wonders in the deep so many years longer nor me. But I think, under God, I am right."

"You must in general be right. They as converses with the Lord night and day, day and night, like as you do, knows likely more of his works nor we, as ain't your gifts."

"The Lord has vouchsafed me nothing in the way of a vision, about this afternoon, Master Evans."

"Didn't 'ee dream never at all last night?" said one of the young men: "Think 'ee now."

"Nought to bear on wind or weather, Jan. I judges from the glass. It's a dropping fast."

Jan would have had more faith in one of Matthew's dreams, and didn't seem to think much of the barometer. Meanwhile Marston had whispered Charles—

"Who is Matthews? What sect is he?"

"Oh, he's a Brianite."

"What is that?"

" A sort of Ranter, I believe."

Marston looked up, and saw the two great black eyes under the lofty forehead fixed full upon him. With the instinct of a gentleman, he said at once—

" I was asking Mr. Charles what sect you were of; that was all. He tells me you are a Brianite, and I had never heard of that sect before. I hope you will let me talk to you about your matters of belief some day."

Matthews took off his hat, and said—That with the Lord's will he would speak to his honour. " Will your honour bear with a poor fisherman, ignorant of the world's learning, but who has had matters revealed to him by the Lord in dreams and visions of the night? Peter was only a fisherman, your honour, and, oh, if we could only hear him speak now !"

He paused, and looked again to seaward. Charles had gone again into the bow, and Marston was standing among the men right aft. Suddenly Matthews turned again upon him and said—

" In the beaching of this here boat to-night, your honour, there may be danger. In such case my place will be alongside of him," pointing to Charles. " There'd be a many kind hearts aching, if aught happened to him. You stick close to these young men. They'll see after you, sir."

" You keep close alongside of we, sir. You hold on of we, sir. We'll see you all right, sir," said the two young men.

" But, my dear good souls, I am as good a swimmer as any in England, and as active as a cat. Pray, don't mind me."

" You keep hold of we and run, sir," said one of the young men, " that's all you're a'got to do, sir."

" I shall most certainly run," said Marston, laughing, " but I decline drowning any one but myself——"

Charles said at this moment, " Do come here and look at this."

It was worth looking at, indeed. They were about a mile from shore, floating about anyhow on an oily smooth sea; for the tide had changed, and they were making no headway. Before them one of the noblest headlands on the coast, an abrupt cone of slate, nigh a thousand feet high, covered almost entirely with grass, sloped suddenly into the water; and in advance of it, but slightly on one side, a rugged mound of black rock, nearly six hundred feet, stood out into the sea, and contrasted its horrid jagged lines with the smooth green of the peak behind. Round its base, dividing it from the glossy sea, ran a delicate line of silver—the surf caused by the groundswell; and in front the whole promontory was dimly mirrored in the quietly heaving ocean.

"What a noble headland," said Marston; "is that grass on the further peak too steep to walk upon?"

"There's some one a'walking on it now," said old Evans. "There's a woman a'walking on it."

None could see it but he, except Matthews, who said he couldn't tell if it was a sheep or no.

Charles got out his glass, and the old man was right. A woman was walking rapidly along the peak, about the third of the way down.

"What a curious place for a woman to be in!" he remarked. "It is almost terrible to look at."

"I never saw any one there before, save the shepherd," said the old man.

"It's a sheep-path," said one of the young ones. "I have been along there myself. It is the short way round to Coombe."

Charles would have thought more of the solitary female figure on that awful precipice, but that their attention was diverted by something else. From the south-westward black flaws of wind began to creep towards them, alternated with long irregular bands of oily calm. Soon the calm bands disappeared, and the wind reached them. Then they had steerage, and in a very short time were roaring out to sea close hauled, with a brisk and ever increasing breeze.

They saw that they would have to fetch a very long leg, and make a great offing, in order to reach Ravenshoe at all. The wind was freshening every moment, changing to the west, and the sea was getting up. It took them three hours to open Ravenshoe Bay; and, being about five miles from the shore, they could see that already there was an ugly side-surf sweeping in, and that the people were busy on the beach hauling up their boats out of harm's way.

"How beautifully these craft sail," said Marston, as they were all hanging on by her weather gunwale, and the green sea was rushing past to leeward, almost under their feet, in sheets of angry foam.

"It is amazing what speed is got out of them on a wind," said Charles, "but they are dangerous craft."

"Why so?"

"These lug-sails are so awkward in tacking, you will see."

They ran considerably past Ravenshoe and about six miles to sea, when the word was given to go about. In an instant the half deck was lumbered with the heavy red sails; and, after five minutes of unutterable confusion, she got about. Marston was expecting her to broach to every moment during this long five minutes, but fortune favoured them. They went freer on this tack, for the wind was now north of west, and the brave little craft went nearly before it at her finest pace. The men kept on her as much sail as she could stand, but that was very little; fast as they went, the great seas went faster, as though determined to be at the dreadful rendezvous before the boat. Still the waves rose higher and the wind howled louder. They were nearing the shore rapidly.

Now they began to see, through the mist, the people gathered on the shore, densest at one point, but with a few restless stragglers right and left of that point, who kept coming and going. The spot was where they expected to come ashore. They were apparently the last boat out, and all the village was watching them with the deepest anxiety.

They began to hear a sound other than the howling of the wind in the rigging, and the rush of waters around them—a continuous thunder, growing louder each moment as the boat swept onward. The thunder of the surf upon the sand. And, looking forward, they could see just the top of it as it leapt madly up.

It was a nervous moment. They stood ready in their shirts and trousers, for a rush, should it be necessary. And the old man was at the helm. They saw the seas begin to curl. Then they were in the middle of them. Then the water left them on the sand, and three brave fellows from the shore dashed to hook on the tackles; but they were too late. Back with a roar like a hungry lion came the sea; the poor boat broached to, and took the whole force of the deluge on her broadside. In a moment more, blinded and stunned, they were all in the water, trying to stand against the backward rush which took them near midthigh. Old Master Evans was nearest to Marston; he was tottering to fall when Marston got hold of him, and saved him. The two young men got hold of both of them. Then three men from the shore dashed in and got hold of Charles; and then, as the water went down and they dared move their feet, they all ran for their lives. Marston and his party got on to dry land on their feet, but Charles and his assistants were tumbled over and over, and washed up ignominiously covered with sand. Charles, however, soon recovered himself, and, looking round to thank those who had done him this service, found that one of them was William, who, when the gale had come on, had, with that blind indifference to the stud-groom's personal feelings which we have seen him exhibit before, left his work, and dressed in a Jersey and blue trousers, and come down to lend a hand. He had come in time to help his foster-brother out of the surf.

"I am so very thankful to you," said Charles to the two others. "I will never forget you. I should have been drowned but for you. William, when I am in trouble I am sure to find you at my elbow."

"You won't find me far off, Master Charles," said William. They didn't say any more to one another those two. There was no need.

The tall man, Matthews had been cast up with a broken head, and, on the whole, seemed rather disappointed at not finding himself in paradise. He had stumbled in leaping out of the boat, and hurt his foot, and had had a hard time of it, poor fellow.

As Charles and William stood watching the poor boat breaking up, and the men venturing their lives to get the nets out of her, a hand was laid on Charles's shoulder, and, turning round, he faced Cuthbert.

"Oh, Charles, Charles, I thought I had lost you. Come home and let us dry you, and take care of you. William, you have risked your life for one who is very dear to us. God reward you for it! Brother, you are shivering with cold, and you have nothing but your trousers and Jersey on, and your head and feet are bare, and your poor hair is wet and full of sand; let me carry you up, Charles, the stones will cut your feet. Let me carry you, Charles. I used to do it when you were little."

There was water in Charles's eyes (the salt water out of his hair, you understand), as he answered—

"I think I can walk, Cuthbert; my feet are as hard as iron."

"No, but I must carry you," said Cuthbert. "Get up, brother."

Charles prepared to comply, and Cuthbert suddenly pulled off his shoes and stockings, and made ready.

"Oh, Cuthbert, don't do that," said Charles, "you break my heart."

"Do let me, dear Charles. I seldom ask you a favour. If I didn't know that it wasn't acceptable to God, do you think I would do it?"

Charles hesitated one moment; but he caught William's eye, and William's eye and William's face said so plainly, "do it," that Charles hesitated no longer, but got on his brother's back. Cuthbert ordered William, who was barefoot, to put on his discarded shoes and stockings, which William did; and then Cuthbert went toiling up the stony path towards the hall, with his brother on his back—glorying in his penance.

Is this ridiculous? I cannot say I can see it in this light. I may laugh to scorn the religion that teaches men that, by artificially producing misery and nervous terror, and in that state flying to religion as a comfort and refuge, we may in any way glorify God, or benefit ourselves. I can laugh, I say, at a form of religion like this; but I cannot laugh at the men who believe in it, and act up to it. No. I may smoke my pipe, and say that the fool Cuthbert Ravenshoe took off his shoes, and gave them to the groom, and carried a twelve-stone brother for a quarter of a mile barefoot, and what a fool he must be, and so forth. But the sneer is a failure, and the laugh dies away; and I say, "Well, Cuthbert, if you are a fool, you are a consistent and manly one at all events."

Let us leave these three toiling up the steep rocky path, and take a glance elsewhere. When the gale had come on, little Mary had left Densil, and, putting on her bonnet, gone down to the beach. She had asked the elder fishermen whether there would be any danger in beaching the boat, and they had said in chorus, "Oh, bless her sweet ladyship's heart, no. The young men would have the tackles on her and have her up, oh, ever so quick;" and so she had been reassured, and walked up and down. But, as the wind came stronger and stronger, and she had seen the last boat taken in half full of water—and as the women kept walking up and down uneasily, with their hands under their aprons—and as she saw many an old eagle eye, shaded by a horny hand, gazing anxiously seawards at the two brown sails plunging about in the offing—she had lost heart again, and had sat her down on a windlass apart, with a pale face, and a sick heart.

A tall gaunt brown woman came up to her and said—

"My lady mustn't fret. My lady would never do for a fisherman's wife. Why, my dear tender flesh, there's a hundred strong arms on the beach now, as would fetch a Ravenshoe out of anywhere a'most. 'Tis a cross surf, Miss Mary; but, Lord love ye, they'll have the tackles on her afore she's in it. Don't ye fret dear, don't ye fret."

But she had sat apart and fretted nevertheless; and, when she saw the brown bows rushing madly through the yellow surf, she had shut her eyes and prayed, and had opened them to see the boat on her beam ends, and a dozen struggling figures in the pitiless water.

Then she had stood up and wrung her hands.

They were safe. She heard that, and she buried her face in her hands, and murmured a prayer of thanksgiving.

Some one stood beside her. It was Marston, bareheaded and barefooted.

"Oh, thank God," she said.

"We have given you a sad fright."

"I have been terribly frightened. But you must not stand dripping there. Please, come up, and let me attend you"

So she got him a pair of shoes, and they went up together. The penance procession had passed on before; and a curious circumstance is this, that, although on ordinary occasions Marston was as lively a talker as need be, on this occasion he was an uncommonly stupid one, as he never said one word all the way up to the hall, and then separated from her with a formal little salutation.

CHAPTER XVIII

MARSTON'S DISAPPOINTMENT

MARY did not wonder at Marston's silence. She imagined that perhaps he had been sobered by being cast on the shore so unceremoniously, and thought but little more of it. Then she dressed for dinner, and went and stood in one of the deep windows of the hall, looking out.

The great fire which leapt and blazed in the hall chimney was fast superseding the waning daylight outside. It was very pleasant to look at the fire, and the firelight on wall and ceiling, on antler and armour, and then to get behind the curtain and look out into the howling winter's evening, over the darkening raging sea, and the tossing trees, and think how all the boats were safe in, and the men sitting round the pleasant fires with their wives and children, and that the dogs were warm in the kennels, and the horses in the stable; and to pity the poor birds, and hope they had good warm nooks and corners to get to; and then to think of the ships coming up the channel, and hope they might keep a good offing.

This brought her to thinking, for the first time, of her own little self—how, so many years ago, she had been cast up like a little piece of sea-weed out of that awful ocean. She thought of the *Warren Hastings*, and how she and Charles, on summer-days, went out gathering shells on the rocks, used to look over to where the ship lay beneath the sea, and wonder whereabout it was. Then she had a kindly smile on her face as she thought of Mr. Archer, the brave and good (now I am happy to say Captain Archer), and looked over the hall to a hideous and diabolical graven image, which he had sent the year before, among some very valuable presents, and had begged her to be particularly careful of, as he had risked his life in getting it; and which she and Charles had triumphantly placed in the hall, and maintained there, too, in spite of the sarcasms of Father Mackworth, and the pious horror of the servants and villagers. And so she went on thinking—thinking of her dead parents, of the silence maintained by her relations, of old Densil's protection, and then of the future. That protection must cease soon, and then—

A governess! There were many stories about governesses not being well treated. Perhaps it was their own fault, or they were exceptional cases. She would like the nursery best, and to keep away from the drawing-room altogether. "Yes," she said, "I will *make* them love me; I will be so gentle, patient, and obliging. I am not afraid of the children—I know I can win *them*—or of my mistress much; I believe I can win *her*. I am most afraid of the superior servants; but, surely, kindness and submission will win them in time.

"My sheet-anchor is old Lady Ascot. She got very fond of me during that six months I staid with her; and she is very kind. Surely she will get me a place where I shall be well treated! and, if not, why then—I shall only be in the position of thousands of other girls. I must fight through it. There is another life after this.

"It will be terribly hard parting from all the old friends though! After that, I think I shall have no heart left to suffer with. Yes; I suppose the last details of the break-up will be harder to bear than anything which will follow. That will tear one's heart terribly. That over, I suppose my salary will keep me in drawing materials, and give me the power, at every moment of leisure, of taking myself into fairyland.

"I suppose actual destitution is impossible. I should think so. Yes, yes; Lady Ascot would take care of that. If that were to come though? They say a girl can always make fourpence a day by her needle. How I would fight, and strive, and toil! And then how sweet death would be!"

She paused, and looked out on the darkened ocean. "And yet," she thought again, "I would follow—follow him to the world's end—

> "'Across the hills, and far away,
>   Beyond their utmost purple rim;
> Beyond the night, across the day,
>   The happy princess followed him.'"

A door opened into the hall, and a man's step was on the stone floor; she raised the curtain to see who it was. It was Marston; and he came straight towards her, and stood beside her, looking out over the wild stormy landscape.

"Miss Corby," he said, "I was coming to try and find you."

"You are very lucky in your search," she said, smiling on him. "I was alone here with the storm; and, if I had not raised the curtain, you would never have seen me. How it blows! I am glad you are not out in this. This is one of your lucky days."

"I should be glad to think so. Will you listen to me for a few minutes, while I tell you something?"

"Surely," she said. "Who is there that I would sooner listen to?"

"I fear I shall tire your patience now, though. I am a comparatively poor man."

"And what of that, my dear Mr. Marston? You are rich in honour, in future prospects. You have a noble future before you."

"Will you share it, Mary?"

"Oh! what do you mean?"

"Will you be my wife? I love you beyond all the riches and honours of the world—I love you as you will never be loved again. It is due to you and to myself to say that, although I call myself poor, I have enough to keep you like a lady, and all my future prospects beside. Don't give me a hasty answer, but tell me is it possible you can become my wife?"

"Oh, I am so sorry for this!" said poor Mary. "I never dreamt of this. Oh no! it is utterly and entirely impossible, Mr. Marston—utterly and hopelessly impossible! You must forgive me, if you can; but you must never, never think about me more."

"Is there no hope?" said Marston.

"No hope, no hope!" said Mary. "Please never think

about me any more, till you have forgiven me ; and then, with
your children on your knee, think of me as a friend who loves
you dearly."

"I shall think of you till I die. I was afraid of this : it is
just as I thought."

"What did you think ? "

"Nothing—nothing ! Will you let me kiss your hand ? "

"Surely ; and God bless you ! "

"Are we to say good-bye for ever, then ? " said poor Marston.

"I hope not. I should be sorry to think that," said poor
Mary, crying. "But you must never speak to me like this
again, dear Mr. Marston. God bless you, once more ! "

Charles was dressing while this scene was going on, and was
thinking, while brushing his hair, what there was for dinner,
and whether there would be a turbot or not, and whether the
cook would send in the breast of the venison. The doe,
Charles sagely reflected, had been killed five days before, and
the weather had been warm : surely That Woman would let
them have the breast. He was a fool not to have told her of
it in the morning before he went out; but she was such an
obstinate old catamaran that she very likely wouldn't have done
it. "There was no greater mistake," this young Heliogabalus
proceeded to remark, "than hanging your breasts too long.
Now, your haunch, on the other hand——" but we cannot
follow him into such a vast and important field of speculation.
"There will be a couple of cocks, though—pretty high, near
about the mark——"

The door opened, and in walked Father Mackworth.

"Hallo, Father ! " said Charles. "How are you ? Did you
hear of our spill to-day? We were deuced near done for, I
assure you."

"Charles," said the priest, "your nature is frank and noble.
I was in terror to-day lest you should go to your account bearing
me malice."

"A Ravenshoe never bears malice, Father," said Charles.

"A Ravenshoe never does, I am aware," said Father Mackworth, with such a dead equality of emphasis, that Charles
could not have sworn that he laid any on the word "Ravenshoe."

"But I have got an apology to make to you, Father," said
Charles : "I have to apologize to you for losing my temper
with you the other day, and breaking out into I can't say what
tirade of unjust anger. I pray you to forgive me. We don't
love one another, you know. How can we ? But I behaved

like a blackguard, as I always do when I am in a passion. Will you forgive me?"

"I had forgotten the circumstance." ("Good heaven!" said Charles to himself, "can't this man help lying?") "But if I have anything to forgive, I freely do so. I have come to ask for a peace. As long as your father lives, let there be outward peace between us, if no more."

"I swear there shall," said Charles. "I like you to-night, sir, better than ever I did before, for the kindness and consideration you show to my father. When he is gone there will be peace between us, for I shall leave this house, and trouble you no more."

"I suppose you will," said Father Mackworth, with the same deadness of emphasis remarked before. And so he departed.

"That is a manly young fellow, and a gentleman," thought Father Mackworth. "Obstinate and headstrong, without much brains; but with more brains than the other, and more education. The other will be very troublesome and headstrong; but I suppose I shall be able to manage him."

What person do you think Father Mackworth meant by the "other"? He didn't mean Cuthbert.

At dinner Densil was garrulous, and eager to hear of their shipwreck. He had made a great rally the last fortnight, and was his old self again. Lord Saltire, whose gout had fled before careful living and moderate exercise, informed them, after the soup, that he intended to leave them after four days' time, as he had business in another part of the country. They were rather surprised at his abrupt departure, and he said that he was very sorry to leave such pleasant society, in which he had been happier than he had been for many years.

"There is a pleasant, innocent, domestic sort of atmosphere which radiates from you, my old friend," he said, "such as I seldom or never get away from you or Mainwaring, grim warrior though he be (you remember him at Ranford, Charles?). But the law of the Medes and Persians is not amenable to change, and I go on Thursday."

The post arrived during dinner, and there was a letter for Charles. It was from Ranford. "Welter comes on Thursday, father—the very day Lord Saltire goes. How annoying!"

"I must try to bear up under the affliction!" said that nobleman, taking snuff, and speaking very drily.

"Where is he to go, I wonder?" mused Mary, aloud. "He must go into the west wing, for he always smokes in his bedroom."

Charles expected that Cuthbert would have had a sneer at Welter, whom he cordially disliked; but Cuthbert had given up sneering lately. "Not much more reading for you, Charles!" he said.

"I am afraid not," said Charles. "I almost wish he wasn't coming; we were very happy before."

Charles was surprised to see Marston so silent at dinner. He feared he might have offended him, but couldn't tell how. Then he wondered to see Mary so silent, too, for she generally chirruped away like a lark; but he didn't refer the two similar phenomena to a common cause, and so he arrived at no conclusion.

When Lord Saltire went to bed that night, he dismissed Charles from attendance, and took Marston's arm; and, when they were alone together, he thus began—

"Does your shrewdness connect my abrupt departure with the arrival of Lord Welter?"

"I was inclined to, my lord; but I do not see how you were to have known it."

"I heard yesterday from Lady Ascot."

"I am sorry he is coming," said Marston.

"So am I. I can't stay in the house with him. The contrast of his loud coarse voice and stable slang to the sort of quiet conversation we have had lately would be intolerable; besides, he is an atrocious young ruffian, and will ruin our boy if he can."

"Charles won't let him now, Lord Saltire."

"Charles is young and foolish. I am glad, however, that Welter does not go back to Oxford with him. But there will be Welter's set in their glory, I suppose, unless some of them have got hung. I would sooner see him at home. He is naturally quiet and domestic. I suppose he was in a sad set up there."

"He was in a very good set, and a very bad one. He was a favourite everywhere."

"He had made some acquaintances he ought to be proud of, at least," said Lord Saltire, in a way which made honest Marston blush. "I wish he wasn't going to Ranford."

"Report says," said Marston, "that affairs are getting somewhat shaky there: Welter's tradesmen can't get any money."

Lord Saltire shook his head significantly, and then said, "Now I want to speak to you about yourself. Did not you have a disappointment to-day?"

"Yes, my lord."

"Ha!"

They both sat silent for a moment.

"How did you guess that, Lord Saltire?"

"I saw what was going on; and, by your manner and hers to-day, I guessed something had taken place. Is there no hope for you?"

"None."

"I feared not; but what right had I to tell you so?"

"Perhaps, my lord, I should not have believed you if you had," said Marston smiling.

"What man would have? You are not angry?"

"How could I be? The world is out of joint, that is all."

"You are a true gentleman. I swear to you," said the old man, eagerly, "that there is no one in fault. She has given her honest little heart away—and what wonder!—but, believe me, that you are behaving as a man should behave, in not resenting it. If you were a heathen and a Frenchman (synonymous terms, my dear boy), you might find it your duty to cut somebody's throat; but, being a Christian and a gentleman, you will remain a true friend to somebody who loves you dearly, and is worth loving in return. This sort of thing cuts a man up confoundedly. It happened to me once; but, believe me, you will get over it."

"I mean to do so. How kind and generous you are to me? How shall I ever repay you?"

"By kindness to those I love," said the old man. "I take this opportunity of telling you that your fortunes are my particular care. I cannot get you the wife you love, but I am rich and powerful, and can do much. Not another word. Go to bed, sir—to bed."

Marston, sitting on his bedside that night, said aloud to himself, "And so that is that dicing old *roué*, Saltire, is it? Well, well; it is a funny world. What a noble fellow he would have been if he had had a better chance. Nay, what a noble fellow he is. I am ten years older since this morning" (he wasn't, but he thought it). And so he said his prayers like an honest man, and prayed for the kind old heathen who had such a warm heart; and then, being nowise ashamed to do so, he prayed that he might sleep well; and for a time he forgot all about his disappointment, and slept like a child.

Lord Saltire's valet was a staid and sober-minded gentleman of sixty-four. Generally, when he was putting his lordship to bed, he used to give him the news of the day; but to-night

Lord Saltire said, "Never mind the news, Simpson, if you please; I am thinking of something." My lord used to wear a sort of muffler, like a footless stocking, to keep his old knees warm in bed. He remained silent till he got one on, and then, without taking the other from the expectant Simpson, he addressed the fire-irons aloud—

"This is a pretty clumsy contrivance to call a world!" he said, with profound scorn. "Look here (to the poker), here's as fine a lad as ever you saw, goes and falls in love with a charming girl, who cares no more for him than the deuce. He proposes to her, and is refused. Why? because she has given her heart away to another fine young fellow, who don't care twopence for her, and has given *his* heart away to the most ambitious young Jezebel in the three kingdoms, who I don't believe cares so very much for him! I am utterly disgusted with the whole system of mundane affairs! Simpson, give me that muffler, if you please; and pray don't wake me before nine. I must try to sleep off the recollection of some of this folly."

CHAPTER XIX

ELLEN'S FLIGHT

AFTER all the fatigues and adventures of the day before, Charles slept well—long pleasant dreams of roaming in sunny places on summer days fell to his happy lot—and so he was not pleased when he found himself shaken by the shoulder.

It was William come to wake him. Charles was at once alarmed to see him there, and started up, saying—

"Is anything the matter, Will? Is my father ill?"

"The master's well, I trust, Master Charles. I want to tell you something that I want others to find out for themselves."

"What is it?" said Charles, seriously alarmed, for he had had his suspicions lately, though he had dreaded to give them a name.

"Ellen is gone!"

"My dear lad," said Charles, hurriedly, "what makes you think so. Since when have you missed her?"

"Since yesterday afternoon."

"Have you been in her room?"

E

"Yes. She has not been to bed, and the window is open just as it was yesterday morning at bed-making time."

"Hush—wait! There may be time yet. Go down and saddle two horses at once. I will tell you what I know as we ride, but there is not time now. Tell me only one thing: Is there any one she would be likely to go to at Coombe?"

"No one that I know off."

William departed to get the horses. Charles had suddenly thought of the solitary female figure he had seen passing along the dizzy sheep-path the day before, and he determined to follow that till he lost sight of it.

"For the poor dear girl's sake—for the honour of this old house—I wonder who is at the bottom of all this? I must tell Marston," he said, when he was out on the landing. "George, tell them to get me some coffee instantly. I am going out hunting."

Marston thought as Charles did. The right thing to do would be to follow her, see that she wanted for nothing, and leave her brother with her for a time. "He won't quarrel with her now, you'll see. He is a good fellow, mind you, Charles, though he did lose his temper with her that night."

So they rode forth side by side into the wild winter's morning. The rain had ceased for a time, but the low dark clouds were hurrying swiftly before the blast, and eddying among the loftier tors and summits. The wind was behind them, and their way was east, across the lofty downs.

"William," said Charles, at last, "who is at the bottom of this?"

"I don't know, Master Charles. If I did there would be mischief, unless it was one of two."

"Ay, Will, but it ain't. You don't think it is Cuthbert?"

"No, no! He, forsooth! Father Mackworth knows, I believe, more than we do."

"You do not suspect him?"

"Certainly not. I did, but I don't now. I suspect he knows, as I said, more than we do. He has been speaking harshly to her about it."

They had arrived at the hill round which Charles suspected he had seen her pass the day before. It was impossible to pass round the promontory on horseback in the best of weathers; now doubly so. They would have to pass inland of it. They both pulled up their horses and looked. The steep slope of turf, the top of which, close overhead, was hid by flying mists, trended suddenly downwards, and disappeared. Eight hundred feet below was the raging sea.

As they stood there, the same thought came across both of them. It was a dreadful place. They neither spoke at all, but spurred on faster, till the little grey village of Coombe, down at their feet, sheltered from the storm by the lofty hills around, opened to their view; and they pushed on down the steep rocky path.

No. No one had seen her yesterday at such a time. The streets would have been full of the miners coming from work; or, if she had come earlier, there would have been plenty of people to see her. It was a small place, and no stranger, they said, could ever pass through it unnoticed.

And, though they scoured the country far and wide, and though for months after the fishermen fished among the quiet bays beneath the cliffs in fear, lest they should find there something which should be carried in silent awe up the village, and laid quietly in the old churchyard, beneath the elm; yet Ellen was gone—gone from their ken like a summer cloud. They thought it a pious fraud to tell Densil that she was gone —with some excuse, I forget what, but which satisfied him. In a conclave held over the matter, Cuthbert seemed only surprised and shocked, but evidently knew nothing of the matter. Father Mackworth said that he expected something of the kind for some little time, and William held his peace. The gossips in the village laid their heads together, and shook them. There was but one opinion there.

> Never again shall she put garland on;
> Instead of it she'll wear sad cypress now,
> And bitter elder broken from the bough.

Nora—poor old Nora—took to her bed. Father Mackworth was with her continually, but she sank and sank. Father Mackworth was called away across the moors, one afternoon, to an outlying Catholic tenant's family; and, during his absence, William was sent to Charles to pray him to come, in God's name, to his mother. Charles ran across at once, but Nora was speechless. She had something to say to Charles, but the great Sower, which shall sow us all in the ground, and tread us down, had his hand heavy on her, and she could not speak. In the morning, when the gale had broken, and the white seabirds were soaring and skimming between the blue sky and the noble green rolling sea, and the ships were running up channel, and the fishing-boats were putting out gaily from the pier, and all nature was brilliant and beautiful, old Nora lay dead, and her secret with her.

"Master Charles," said William, as they stood on the shore together, "she knew something, and Ellen knows it too, I very much suspect. The time will come, Master Charles, when we shall have to hunt her through the world, and get the secret from her."

"William, I would go many weary journeys to bring poor Ellen back into the ways of peace. The fact of her being your sister would be enough to make me do that."

CHAPTER XX

RANFORD AGAIN

CHARLES, though no genius, had a certain amount of common sense, and, indeed, more of that commodity than most people gave him credit for. Therefore he did not pursue the subject with William. Firstly, because he did not think he could get any more out of him (for William had a certain amount of sturdy obstinacy in his composition); and secondly, because he knew William was, in the main, a sensible fellow, and loved the ground he stood on. Charles would never believe that William would serve him falsely; and he was right.

He told Marston of the curious words which William had used, and Marston had said—

"I don't understand it. The devil is abroad. Are you coming into any money at your father's death?"

"I am to have £180 a year."

"I wouldn't give £50 a year for your chance of it. What is this property worth?"

"£9,000 a year. The governor has lived very extravagantly. The stable establishment is fit for a duke now; and, then, look at the servants."

"He is not living up to ten thousand a year now, I should say."

"No; but it is only the other day he gave up the hounds. They cost him two thousand a year; and, while he had them, the house was carried on very extravagantly. The governor has a wonderful talent for muddling away money; and, what is more, I believe he was bit with the railways. You know, I believe, the estate is involved."

"Bathershin. But still, Cuthbert won't marry, and his life is a bad one, and you are a heretic, my poor little innocent."

"And then?"

"Heaven only knows what then. I am sure I don't. At what time does the worthy and intellectual Welter arrive?"

"He will be here about six."

"Two hours' more rational existence for one, then. After that a smell as of ten thousand stables and fifty stale copies of *Bell's Life* in one's nose, till his lordship takes his departure. I don't like your cousin, Charles."

"What an astounding piece of news! He says you are a conceited prig, and give yourself airs."

"He never said a wiser or truer thing in his life. I am exactly that; and he is a fifth-class steeplechase rider, with a title."

"How you and he will fight!"

"So I expect. That is, if he has the courage for battle, which I rather doubt. He is terribly afraid of me."

"I think you are hard on poor Welter," said Charles; "I do, indeed. He is a generous, good-hearted fellow."

"Oh! we are all generous, good-hearted fellows," said Marston, "as long as we have plenty of money and good digestions. You are right, though, Charley. He is what you say, as far as I know; but the reason I hate him is this:—You are the dearest friend I have, and I am jealous of him. He is in eternal antagonism to me. I am always trying to lead you right, and he is equally diligent in leading you into wrong."

"Well, he sha'n't lead me into any more, I promise you now. Do be civil to him."

"Of course I will, you gaby. Did you think I was going to show fight in your house?"

When Marston came down to dinner there was Lord Welter, sitting beside old Densil, and kindly amusing him with all sorts of gossip—stable and other.

"How do, Marston?" said he, rising and coming forward.

"How d'ye do, Lord Welter?" said Marston.

"I am very glad to meet you here," said Lord Welter, with a good-humoured smile, "although I am ashamed to look you in the face. Marston, my dear Mr. Ravenshoe, is Charles's good genius, and I am his evil one; I am always getting

Charles into mischief, and he is always trying to keep him out of it. Hitherto, however, I have been completely successful, and he has made a dead failure."

Old Densil laughed. "You are doing yourself injustice, Welter," he said. "Is he not doing himself an injustice, Mr. Marston?"

"Not in the least, sir," said Marston. And the two young men shook hands more cordially than they had ever done before.

That evening Welter fulfilled Mary's prophecy, that he would smoke in his bed-room, and not only smoked there himself, but induced Charles to come and do so also. Marston was not in the humour for the style of conversation he knew he should have there, and so he retired to bed, and left the other two to themselves.

"Well, Charles," said Welter. "Oh, by the bye, I have got a letter for you from that mysterious madcap, Adelaide. She couldn't send it by post; that would not have been mysterious and underhand enough for her. Catch hold."

Charles caught hold, and read his letter. Welter watched him curiously from under the heavy eyebrows, and, when he had finished, said—

"Come, put that away, and talk. That sort of thing is pretty much the same in all cases, I take it. As far as my own experience goes, it is always the same. Scold and whine and whimper; whimper, whine, and scold. How's that old keeper of yours?"

"He has lost his wife."

"Poor fellow! I remember his wife—a handsome Irish woman."

"My nurse?"

"Ay, ay. And the pretty girl Ellen; how is she?"

"Poor Ellen! She has run away, Welter; gone on the bad, I fear."

Lord Welter sat in just the same position, gazing on the fire. He then said, in a very deliberate voice—

"The deuce she is. I am sorry to hear that. I was in hopes of renewing our acquaintance."

The days flew by, and, as you know, there came no news from Ellen. The household had been much saddened by her disappearance, and by Nora's death, though not one of the number ever guessed what had passed between Mary and Marston. They were not a very cheerful household; scarce one of them but had some secret trouble. Father Tiernay came back after a week or so; and, if good-natured kindly chatter could have cheered them at all, he would have done it. But there was a settled gloom on the party, which nothing could overcome. Even Lord Welter, boisterous as his spirits usually were, seemed often anxious and distraught; and, as for poor Cuthbert, he would, at any time within the knowledge of man, have acted as a "damper" on the liveliest party. His affection for Charles seemed, for some reason, to increase day by day, but it was sometimes very hard to keep the peace between Welter and him. If there was one man beyond another that Cuthbert hated, it was Lord Welter; and sometimes, after dinner, such a scene as this would take place.

You will, perhaps, have remarked that I have never yet represented Cuthbert as speaking to Mary. The real fact is, that he never did speak to her, or to any woman, anything beyond the merest commonplaces—a circumstance which made Charles very much doubt the truth of Ellen's statement that the priest had caught them talking together in the wood. However, Cuthbert was, in his way, fond enough of the bonny little soul (I swear I am in love with her myself, over head and ears); and so, one day, when she came crying in, and told him—as being the first person she met—that her little bantam-cock had been killed by the dorking, Cuthbert comforted her, bottled up his wrath, till his father had gone into the drawing-room with her after dinner, and the others were sitting at their wine. Then he said, suddenly—

"Welter, did you have any cock-fighting to-day?"

"Oh, yes, by the bye, a splendid turn-up. There was a noble little bantam in an inclosed yard challenging a great dorking, and they both seemed so very anxious for sport that I thought it would be a pity to baulk them; so I just let the bantam out. I give you my word it is my belief that the bantam would have been the best man, but that he was too old. His attack was splendid; but he met the fate of the brave."

"You should not have done that, Welter," said Charles; "that was Mary's favourite bantam."

"I don't allow any cock-fighting at Ravenshoe, Welter," said Cuthbert.

"You don't allow it!" said Lord Welter, scornfully.

"No, by heaven!" said Cuthbert, "I don't allow it."

"Don't you!" said Welter; "you are not master here, nor ever will be. No Ravenshoe was ever master of his own house yet."

"I am absolute master here," said Cuthbert, with a rising colour. "There is no appeal against me here."

"Only to the priest," said Welter. (I must do him justice to say that neither Mackworth nor Tiernay was in the room, or he would not have said it.)

"You are insolent, Welter, and brutal. It is your nature to be so," said Cuthbert, fiercely.

Marston, who had been watching Welter all this time, saw a flash come from his eyes, and, for one moment a terrible savage setting of the teeth. "Ha, ha! my friend," thought he, "I thought that stupid face was capable of some such expression as that. I am obliged to you, my friend, for giving me one little glimpse of the devil inside."

"By gad, Cuthbert," said Lord Welter, "if you hadn't been at your own table, you shouldn't have said that, cousin or no cousin, twice."

"Stop, now," said Charles, "don't turn the place into a bear-pit. Cuthbert, do be moderate. Welter, you shouldn't have set the cocks fighting. Now, don't begin quarrelling again, you two, for heaven's sake!"

And so the peace was made: but Charles was very glad when the time came for the party to break up; and he went away to Ranford with Welter, preparatory to his going back to Oxford.

His father was quite his old self again, and seemed to have rallied amazingly; so Charles left him without much anxiety; and there were reasons we know of why his heart should bound when he heard the word Ranford mentioned, and why the raging speed of the Great Western Railway express seemed all too slow for him. Lord Ascot's horses were fast, the mail-phaeton was a good one, and Lord Welter's worst enemies could not accuse him of driving slow; yet the way from Didcot to Ranford seemed so interminably long that he said :—

"By Jove, I wish we had come by a slower train, and gone on to Twyford!"

"Why so?"

"I don't know. I think it is pleasanter driving through Wargrave and Henley."

Lord Welter laughed, and Charles wondered why. There were no visitors at Ranford; and, when they arrived, Welter of course, adjourned to the stables, while Charles ran upstairs and knocked at Lady Ascot's door.

He was bidden to come in by the old lady's voice. Her

black and tan terrier, who was now so old that his teeth and
voice were alike gone, rose from the hearth, and went through
the motion and outward semblance of barking furiously at
Charles, though without producing any audible sound. Lady
Ascot rose up and welcomed him kindly.

" I am so glad to see your honest face, my dear boy. I have
been sitting here all alone so long. Ascot is very kind, and
comes and sits with me, and I give him some advice about his
horses, which he never takes. But I am very lonely."

" But where is Adelaide, aunt dear ? "

" She's gone."

" Gone ! My dear aunt, where to ? "

" Gone to stay ten days with Lady Hainault."

Here was a blow.

" I know you are very disappointed, my poor boy, and I
told Welter so expressly to tell you in my last letter. He is so
shockingly careless and forgetful ! "

" So Welter knew of it," said Charles to himself. " And
that is what made him laugh at my hurry. It is very ungentle-
manly behaviour."

But Charles's anger was like a summer cloud. " I think,
aunt," he said, " that Welter was having a joke with me ; that
was all. When will she be back ? "

" The end of next week."

" And I shall be gone to Oxford. I shall ride over to
Casterton and see her."

" You knew Hainault at Shrewsbury ? Yes. Well, you
had better do so, child. Yes, certainly."

" What made her go, aunt, I wonder ? "

" Lady Hainault was ill, and would have her, and I was
forced to let her go."

Oh, Lady Ascot, Lady Ascot, you wicked old fibster !
Didn't you hesitate, stammer, and blush, when you said that ?
I am very much afraid you didn't. Hadn't you had, three
days before, a furious *fracas* with Adelaide about something,
and hadn't it ended by her declaring that she would claim the
protection of Lady Hainault ? Hadn't she ordered out the
pony-carriage and driven off with a solitary bandbox and what
I choose to call a crinoline-chest ? And hadn't you and Lady
Hainault had a brilliant passage of arms over her ladyship's
receiving and abetting the recalcitrant Adelaide ?

Lady Ascot was perfectly certain of one thing—that Charles
would never hear about this from Adelaide ; and so she lied
boldly and with confidence. Otherwise, she must have made

a dead failure, for few people had practised that great and difficult art so little as her ladyship.

That there had been a furious quarrel between Lady Ascot and Adelaide about this time, I well know from the best authority. It had taken place just as I have described it above. I do not know for certain the cause of it, but can guess; and, as I am honestly going to tell you all I know, you will be able to make as good a guess as I hereafter.

Lady Ascot said furthermore, that she was very uneasy in her mind about Ascot's colt, which she felt certain would not stay over the Derby course. The horse was not so well ribbed up as he should be, and had hardly quarter enough to suit her. Talking of that, her lumbago had set in worse than ever since the frost had come on, and her doctor had had the impudence to tell her that her liver was deranged, whereas, she knew it proceeded from cold in the small of her back. Talking of the frost, she was told that there had been a very good sheet of ice on the carp-pond, where Charles might have skated, though she did hope he would never go on the ice till it was quite safe—as, if he were to get drowned, it would only add to her vexation, and surely she had had enough of that, with that audacious chit of a girl, Adelaide, who was enough to turn one's hair grey; though for that matter it had been grey for many years, as all the world might see.

"Has Adelaide been vexing you, aunt dear?" interrupted Charles.

"No, my dear boy, no," replied the old woman. "She is a little tiresome sometimes, but I dare say it is more my fault than hers."

"You will not be angry with her, aunt dear? You will be long-suffering with her, for my sake?"

"Dear Charles," said the good old woman weeping, "I will forgive her till seventy times seven. Sometimes, dear, she is high-spirited, and tries my temper. And I am very old, dear, and very cross and cruel to her. It is all my fault, Charles, all my fault."

Afterwards, when Charles knew the truth, he used to bless the memory of this good old woman, recalling this conversation, and knowing on which side the fault lay. At this time, blindly in love as he was with Adelaide, he had sense enough left to do justice.

"Aunt, dear," he said, "you are old, but you are neither cross nor cruel. You are the kindest and most generous of women. You are the only mother I ever had, aunt. I dare say Adelaide is tiresome sometimes; bear with her for my sake. Tell me some more about the horses. God help us, they are an important subject enough in this house now!"

Lady Ascot said, having dried her eyes and kissed Charles, that she had seen this a very long time: that she had warned Ascot solemnly, as it was a mother's duty to do, to be careful of Ramoneur blood, and that Ascot would never listen to her ; that no horse of that breed had ever been a staying horse ; that she believed, if the truth could be got at, that the Pope of Rome had been, indirectly, perhaps, but certainly, the inventor of produce stakes, which had done more to ruin the breed of horses, and consequently the country, than fifty reform bills. Then her ladyship wished to know if Charles had read Lord Mount E——'s book on the battle of Armageddon, and, on receiving a negative answer, gave a slight abstract of that most prophetical production, till the gong sounded, and Charles went up to dress for dinner.

CHAPTER XXI

CLOTHO, LACHESIS, AND ATROPOS

THE road from Ranford to Casterton, which is the name of Lord Hainault's place, runs through about three miles of the most beautiful scenery. Although it may barely come up to Cookham or Cliefden, yet it surpasses the piece from Wargrave to Henley, and beats Pangbourne hollow. Leaving Ranford Park, the road passes through the pretty village of Ranford. And in the street of Ranford, which is a regular street, the principal inn is the White Hart, kept by Mrs. Foley.

Here, in summer, all through the long glorious days, which seem so hard to believe in in winter time, come anglers, and live. Here they order their meals at impossible hours, and drive the landlady mad by not coming home to them. Here, too, they plan mad expeditions with the fishermen, who are now in all their glory, wearing bright-patterned shirts, scornful of half-crowns, and in a general state of obfuscation, in consequence of being plied with strange liquors by their patrons, out of flasks, when they are out fishing. Here, too, come artists, with beards as long as your arm, and pass the day under white umbrellas, in pleasant places by the waterside, painting.

The dark old porch of the inn stands out in the street, but the back of the house goes down to the river. At this porch there is generally a group of idlers, or an old man sunning himself, or a man on horseback, drinking. On this present occasion there were all three of these things, and also Lord Ascot's head keeper, with a brace of setters.

As Charles rode very slowly towards the group, the keeper and the groom on horseback left off talking. Charles fancied they had been talking about him, and I, who know every thing, also know that they had. When Charles was nearly opposite to him, the keeper came forward and said—

"I should like to show you the first trout of the season, sir. Jim, show Mr. Ravenshoe that trout."

A beautiful ten-pounder was immediately laid on the stones.

"He would have looked handsomer in another month, Jackson," said Charles.

"Perhaps he would, sir. My lady generally likes to get one as soon as she can."

At this stage the groom, who had been standing apart, came up, and touching his hat, put into Charles's hand a note.

It was in Adelaide's handwriting. The groom knew it, the keeper knew it, they all knew it, and Charles knew they knew it; but what cared he—all the world might know it. But they knew and had been talking of something else before he came up, which Charles did not know. If anything is going wrong, all the country side know it before the person principally concerned. And all the countryside knew that there had been a great and scandalous quarrel between Adelaide and Lady Ascot—all, except Charles.

He put the note in his pocket without opening it; he gave the groom half-a-crown; he bade good-bye to the keeper; he touched his hat to the loiterers; and then he rode on his way towards Casterton, down the village street. He passed the church among the leafless walnut-trees, beneath the towering elms, now noisy with building rooks; and then, in the broad road under the lofty chalk downs, with the elms on his left, and glimpses of the flashing river between their stems, there he pulled up his horse and read his love letter.

"DEAR CHARLES,—" Ain't you very cross at my having been away when you came? I don't believe you are, for you are never cross. I couldn't help it, Charles, dear. Aunt wanted me to go.

" Aunt is very cross and tiresome. She don't like me as well as she used. You mustn't believe all she says, you know. It ain't one word of it true. It is only her fancy.

" Do come over and see me. Lord Hainault ") this, I must tell you, reader, is the son, not the husband, of Lady Ascot's most cherished old enemy) " is going to be married, and there will be a great wedding. She is that long Burton girl, whom you may remember. I have always had a great dislike for her ; but she has asked me to be bridesmaid, and of course one can't refuse. Lady Emily Montfort is ' with me,' as the lawyers say, and of course she will have her mother's pearls in her ugly red hair."—

Charles couldn't agree as to Lady Emily's hair being red. He had thought it the most beautiful hair he had ever seen in his life.—

" *Pour moi*, I shall wear a camelia, if the gardener will give me one. How I wish I had jewels to beat hers ! She can't wear the Cleveland diamonds as a bridesmaid ; that is a comfort. Come over and see me. I am in agony about what aunt may have said to you.

" ADELAIDE."

The reader may see more in this letter than Charles did. The reader may see a certain amount of selfishness and vanity in it : Charles did not. He took up his reins and rode on ; and, as he rode, said, " By Jove, Cuthbert shall lend me the emeralds ! "

He hardly liked asking for them ; but he could not bear the idea of Lady Emily shining superior to Adelaide in consequence of her pearls. Had he been a wise man (which I suppose you have, by this time, found out that he is decidedly not. Allow me to recommend this last sentence in a grammatical point of view), he would have seen that, with two such glorious creatures as Adelaide and Lady Emily, no one would have seen whether they were clothed in purple and fine linen, or in sackcloth and ashes. But Charles was a fool. He was in love, and he was riding out to see his love.

The Scotchman tells us about Spey leaping out a glorious giant from among the everlasting hills ; the Irishman tells you of Shannon rambling on past castle and mountain, gathering new beauty as he goes ; the Canadian tells you of the great river which streams over the cliff between Erie and Ontario; and the Australian tells you of Snowy pouring eternally from his great curtain of dolomite, seen forty miles away by the lonely traveller on the dull grey plains; but the Englishman tells you of the Thames, whose valley is the cradle of Freedom, and the possessors of which are the arbiters of the world.

And along the Thames valley rode Charles. At first the road ran along beneath some pleasant sunny heights; but, as it gradually rose, the ground grew more abrupt, and, on the right, a considerable down, with patches of gorse and juniper, hung over the road; while, on the left, the broad valley stretched away to where a distant cloud of grey smoke showed where lay the good old town of Casterton. Now the road entered a dark beech wood beneath lofty banks, where the squirrels, merry fellows, ran across the road and rattled up the trees, and the air was faint with the scent of last year's leaves. Then came a break in the wood to the right, and a vista up a long-drawn valley, which ended in a chalk cliff. Then a break in the wood to the left, and a glance at the flat meadows, the gleaming river, and the dim grey distance. Then the wood again denser and darker than ever. Then a sound, at first faint and indistinct, but growing gradually upon the ear, until it could be plainly heard above the horse's footfall. Then suddenly the end of the wood and broad open sunlight. Below, the weirs of Casterton, spouting by a hundred channels, through the bucks and under the mills. Hard by, Casterton town, lying, a tumbled mass of red brick and grey flint, beneath a faint soft haze of smoke, against the vast roll in the land called Marldown. On the right, Casterton Park, a great wooded promontory, so steep that one can barely walk along it, clothed with beech and oak from base to summit, save in one place, where a bold lawn of short grass, five hundred feet high, stoops suddenly down towards the meadows, fringed at the edges with broom and fern, and topped with three tall pines—the landmark for ten miles along the river.

A lodge, the white gate of which is swung open by a pretty maiden; a dark oak wood again, with a long vista, ended by the noble precipitous hill on which the house stands; a more open park, with groups of deer lying about and feeding; another dark wood, the road now rising rapidly; rabbits, and a pot-valiant cock-pheasant standing in the middle of the way, and "currucking," under the impression that Charles is in possession of all his domestic arrangements, and has come to disturb them; then the smooth gravel road, getting steeper and steeper; then the summit; one glimpse of a glorious panorama; then the front door and footmen.

Charles sent his card in, and would be glad to know if Lady Hainault could see him. While he waited for an answer, his horse rubbed its nose against its knee and yawned, while the footmen on the steps looked at the rooks. They knew all about it too. (The footmen, I mean, not the rooks); though I wouldn't swear against a rook's knowing anything, mind you.

Lady Hainault would see Mr. Ravenshoe—which was lucky, because, if she wouldn't have done so, Charles would have been obliged to ask for Adelaide. So Charles's horse was led to the stable, and Charles was led by the butler through the hall, and shown into a cool and empty library, to purge himself of earthly passions, before he was admitted to The Presence.

Charles sat himself down in the easiest chair he could find, and got hold of " Ruskin's Modern Painters." That is a very nice book : it is printed on thick paper, with large print; the reading is very good, full of the most beautiful sentiments ever you heard ; and there are also capital plates in it. Charles looked through the pictures : he didn't look at the letter-press, I know—for, if he had, he would have been so deeply enchained with it that he wouldn't have done what he did— get up, and look out of the window. The window looked into the flower-garden. There he saw a young Scotch gardener, looking after his rose-trees. His child, a toddling bit of a thing, four years old (it must have been his first, for he was a very young man), was holding the slips of matting for him; and glancing up between whiles at the great façade of the house, as though wondering what great people were inside, and whether they were looking at him. This was a pretty sight to a good whole-hearted fellow like Charles ; but he got tired of looking at that even, after a time ; for he was anxious and not well at ease. And so, after his watch had told him that he had waited half an hour, he rang the bell.

The butler came almost directly.

" Did you tell Lady Hainault that I was here? " said Charles.

" My lady was told, sir."

" Tell her again, will you ? " said Charles, and yawned.

Charles had time for another look at Ruskin, and another

look at the gardener and his boy, before the butler came back and said, " My lady is disengaged, sir."

Charles was dying to see Adelaide, and was getting very impatient ; but he was, as you have seen, a very contented sort of fellow : and, as he had fully made up his mind not to leave the house without a good half-hour with her, he could afford to wait. He crossed the hall behind the butler, and then went up the great staircase, and through the picture-gallery. Here he was struck by seeing the original of one of the prints he had seen downstairs, in the book, hanging on the wall among others. He stopped the butler and asked, " What picture is that ? "

" That, sir," said the butler, hesitatingly, " that, sir—that is the great Turner, sir. Yes, sir," he repeated, after a glance at a Francia on the one side and a Rembrandt on the other, " yes, sir, that *is* the great Turner, sir."

Charles was shown into a boudoir on the south side of the house, where sat Lady Hainault, an old and not singularly agreeable looking woman, who was doing crochet-work, and her companion, a strong-minded and vixenish-looking old maid, who was also doing crochet-work. They looked so very like two of the Fates, weaving woe, that Charles looked round for the third sister, and found her not.

" How d'ye do, Mr. Ravenshoe ? " said Lady Hainault. " I hope you haven't been kept waiting ? "

" Not at all," said Charles ; and if that was not a deliberate lie, I want to know what is.

If there was any one person in the world for whom Charles bore a cherished feeling of dislike, it was this virtuous old lady. Charles loved Lady Ascot dearly, and Lady Hainault was her bitterest enemy. That would have been enough ; but she had a horrid trick of sharpening her wit upon young men, and saying things to them in public which gave them a justifiable desire to knock her down and jump on her, as the Irish reapers do to their wives ; and she had exercised this talent on Charles once at Ranford, and he hated her as much as he could hate any one, and that was not much. Lord Saltire used to say that he must give her the credit of being the most infernally disagreeable woman in Europe. Charles thought, by the twitching of her long fingers over her work, that she was going to be disagreeable now, and he was prepared. But, to Charles's great astonishment, the old lady was singularly gracious.

" And how," she said, " is dear Lady Ascot ? I have been

coming, and coming, for a long time, but I have never gone so far this winter."

"Lucky for aunt!" thought Charles. Then there was a pause, and a very awkward one.

Charles said, very quietly, "Lady Hainault, may I see Miss Summers?"

"Surely! I wonder where she is. Miss Hicks, ring the bell."

Charles stepped forward and rang, and Miss Hicks, as Clotho, who had half-risen, sat down again, and wove her web grimly.

Atropos appeared after an interval, looking as beautiful as the dawn. So Charles was looking too intently at her to notice the quick eager glances that the old women threw at her as she came into the room. His heart leapt up as he went forward to meet her ; and he took her hand and pressed it, and would have done so if all the furies in Pandemonium were there to prevent him.

It did not please her ladyship to see this ; and so Charles did it once more, and then they sat down together in a window.

"And how am I looking?" said Adelaide, gazing at him full in the face. "Not a single pretty compliment for me after so long? I require compliments; I am used to them. Lady Hainault paid me some this morning."

Lady Hainault, as Lachesis, laughed and wove. Charles thought, " I suppose she and Adelaide have been having a shindy. She and aunt fall out sometimes."

Adelaide and Charles had a good deal of quiet conversation in the window ; but what two lovers could talk with Clotho and Lachesis looking on, weaving? I, of course, know perfectly well what they talked of, but it is hardly worth setting down here. I find that lovers' conversations are not always interesting to the general public. After a decent time, Charles rose to go, and Adelaide went out by a side door.

Charles made his adieux to Clotho and Lachesis, and departed at the other end of the room. The door had barely closed on him, when Lady Hainault, eagerly thrusting her face towards Miss Hicks, hissed out—

" Did I give her time enough? Were her eyes red? Does he suspect anything?"

" You gave her time enough, I should say," said Miss Hicks, deliberately. "I didn't see that her eyes were red. But he must certainly suspect that you and she are not on the best of terms, from what she said."

" Do you think he knows that Hainault is at home ? Did he ask for Hainault ? "

" I don't know," said Miss Hicks.

" She shall not stop in the house. She shall go back to Lady Ascot. I won't have her in the house," said the old lady, furiously.

" Why did you have her here, Lady Hainault ? "

" You know perfectly well, Hicks. You know I only had her to spite old Ascot. But she shall stay here no longer."

" She must stay for the wedding now," said Miss Hicks.

" I suppose she must," said Lady Hainault ; " but, after that, she shall pack. If the Burton people only knew what was going on, the match would be broken off."

" I don't believe anything is going on," said Miss Hicks, " at least, not on his side. You are putting yourself in a passion for nothing, and you will be ill after it."

" I am not putting myself in a passion, and I won't be ill, Hicks ! And you are impudent to me, as you always are. I tell you that she must be got rid of, and she must marry that young booby, or we are all undone. I say that Hainault is smitten with her."

" I say he is not, Lady Hainault. I say that what there is is all on her side."

" She shall go back to Ranford after the wedding. I was a fool to have such a beautiful vixen in the house at all."

We shall not see much more of Lady Hainault. Her son is about to marry the beautiful Miss Burton, and make her Lady Hainault. We shall see something of her by and bye.

The wedding came off the next week. A few days previously, Charles rode over to Casterton and saw Adelaide. He had with him a note and jewel-case. The note was from Cuthbert, in which he spoke of her as his future sister, and begged her to accept the loan of " these few poor jewels." She was graciously pleased to do so ; and Charles took his leave very soon, for the house was turned out of the windows, and the next day but one " the long Burton girl " became Lady Hainault, and Lady Ascot's friend became Dowager. Lady Emily did not wear pearls at the wedding. She wore her own splendid golden hair, which hung round her lovely face like a glory. None who saw the two could say which was the most beautiful of these two celebrated blondes — Adelaide, the imperial, or Lady Emily, the gentle and the winning.

But, when Lady Ascot heard that Adelaide had appeared at the wedding with the emeralds, she was furious. "She has gone," said that deeply injured lady—"she, a penniless girl, has actually gone, and, without my consent or knowledge, borrowed the Ravenshoe emeralds, and flaunted in them at a wedding. That girl would dance over my grave, Brooks."

"Miss Adelaide," said Brooks, "must have looked very well in them, my lady!" for Brooks was good-natured, and wished to turn away her ladyship's wrath.

Lady Ascot turned upon her and withered her. She only said, "Emeralds upon pink! Heugh!" But Brooks was withered, nevertheless.

I cannot give you any idea as to how Lady Ascot said "Heugh!" as I have written it above. We don't know how the Greeks pronounced the amazing interjections in the Greek plays. We can only write them down.

"Perhaps the jewels were not remarked, my lady," said the maid, making a second and worse shot.

"Not remarked, you foolish woman!" said the angry old lady. "Not remark a thousand pounds' worth of emeralds upon a girl who is very well known to be a pensioner of mine. And I daren't speak to her or we shall have a scene with Charles. I am glad of one thing, though; it shows that Charles is thoroughly in earnest. Now let me get to bed, that's a good soul; and don't be angry with me if I am short-tempered, for heaven knows I have enough to try me! Send one of the footmen across to the stable to know if Mahratta has had her nitre. Say that I insist on a categorical answer. Has Lord Ascot come home?"

"Yes, my lady."

"He might have come and given me some news about the horse. But there, poor boy, I can forgive him."

CHAPTER XXII

THE LAST GLIMPSE OF OXFORD

OXFORD. The front of Magdalen Hall, about which said the least the soonest mended. On the left, further on, All Souls, which seems to have been built by the same happy hand which built the new courts of St. John's, Cambridge (for they are about equally bad). On the right, the Clarendon and the Schools, blocking out the western sky. Still more to the right, a bit of Exeter, and all Brazenose. In front, the Radcliff, the third dome in England, and, beyond, the straight façade of St. Mary's, gathering its lines upward ever, till tired of window and buttress, of crocket, finial, gargoyle, and all the rest of it, it leaps up aloft in one glorious crystal, and carries up one's heart with it into the heaven above.

Charles Ravenshoe and Marston. They stood side by side on the pavement, and their eyes roamed together over the noble mass of architecture, passing from the straight lines and abrupt corner of the Radcliff, on to the steeple of St. Mary's. They stood silent for a moment, and then Marston said—

"Serve him right."

"Why?" said Charles.

"Because he had no business to be driving tandem at all. He can't afford it. And besides, if he could, why should he defy the authorities by driving tandem? Nobody would drive tandem if it wasn't forbidden."

"Well, he is sent down, and therefore your virtue may spare him."

"Sent down!" said Marston, testily, "he never ought to have come up. He was only sent here to be pitchforked through the Schools, and get a family living."

"Well, well," said Charles; "I was very fond of him."

"Pish!" said Marston. Whereat Charles laughed uproariously, and stood in the gutter. His mirth was stopped by his being attacked by a toothless black-and-tan terrier, who was so old that he could only bark in a whisper, but whose privilege it was to follow about one of the first divinity scholars of the day, round the sunniest spots in the town. The dog having been appeased, Charles and Marston stood aside, and got a kindly smile from the good old man, in recognition of their having touched their caps to him.

"Charley," said Marston, "I am so glad to hear of your going on so well. Mind you, if you had stuck to your work sooner, you would have had more than a second in Moderations. You must, and you shall, get a first, you know. I will have it."

"Never, my boy, never," said Charles; "I haven't read for it."

"Nonsense. You are a great fool; but you may get your first."

Thereupon Charles laughed again, louder than before, and wanted to know what his friend had been eating to upset his liver. To which Marston answered "Bosh!" and then they went down Oriel Lane, "And so by Merton," as the fox-hunters say, to Christ Church Meadow.

"I am glad you are in the University eight," said Marston; "it will do you a vast deal of good. You used to over-value that sort of thing, but I don't think that you do so now. You can't row or ride yourself into a place in the world, but that is no reason why you should not row or ride. I wish I was heavy enough to row. Who steers to-day?"

"The great Panjandrum."

"I don't like the great Panjandrum. I think him slangy. And I don't pardon slang in any one beyond a very young bachelor."

"I am very fond of him," said Charles, "and you are bilious, and out of humour with every one in heaven and earth, except apparently me. But, seriously speaking, old man, I think you have had something to vex you, since you came up yesterday. I haven't seen you since you were at Ravenshoe, and you are deucedly altered, do you know?"

"I am sure you are wrong, Charles. I have had nothing— Well, I never lie. I have been disappointed in something, but I have fought against it so, that I am sure you must be wrong. I cannot be altered."

"Tell me what has gone wrong, Marston. Is it in money matters? If it is, I know I can help you there."

"Money. Oh! dear no," said Marston. "Charley, you are a good fellow. You are the best fellow I ever met, do you know? But I can't tell you what is the matter now."

"Have I been doing anything?" said Charles, eagerly.

"You have been doing a great deal to make me like and respect you, Charles; but nothing to make me unhappy. Now answer me some questions, and let us change the subject. How is your father?"

"Dear old dad is very well. I got a letter from him to-day."

"And how is your brother?"

"Well in health, but weak in mind, I fear. I am very much afraid that I shall be heir to Ravenshoe."

"Why? Is he going mad?"

"Not a bit of it, poor lad. He is going into a religious house, I am afraid. At least he mentioned that sort of thing the last time he wrote to me, as if he were trying to bring me face to face with the idea; and be sure my dearly beloved Father Mackworth will never let the idea rest."

"Poor fellow! And how is Adelaide the beautiful?"

"*She's* all right," said Charles. "She and aunt are the best friends in the world."

"They always were, weren't they?"

"Why, you see," said Charles, "sometimes aunt was cross, and Adelaide is very high-spirited, you know, exceedingly high-spirited."

"Indeed?"

"Oh, yes, very, very much so; she didn't take much nonsense from Lady Hainault, I can tell you."

"Well," said Marston, "to continue my catechizing, how is William?"

"He is very well. Is there no one else you were going to ask after?"

"Oh, yes. Miss Corby?"

"She is pretty well, I believe, in health, but she does not seem quite so happy as she was," said Charles, looking at Marston, suddenly.

He might as well have looked at the Taylor building, if he expected any change to take place in Marston's face. He regarded him with a stony stare, and said—

"Indeed. I am sorry to hear that."

"Marston," said Charles, "I once thought that there was something between you and her."

"That is a remarkable instance of what silly notions get into vacant minds," said Marston steadily. Whereat Charles laughed again.

At this point, being opposite the University barge, Charles was hailed by a West-countryman of Exeter, whom we shall call Lee, who never met with Charles without having a turn at talking Devonshire with him. He now began at the top of his voice, to the great astonishment of the surrounding dandies.

"Where be gwine? Charles Ravenshoe, where be gwine?"

"We'm gwine for a ride on the watter, Jan Lee."

"Be gwine in the 'Varsity eight, Charles Ravenshoe?"

"Iss, sure."

"How do 'e feel? Don't 'e feel afeard?"

"Ma dear soul, I've got such a wambling in my innards, and——"

"We are waiting for you, Ravenshoe," said the captain; and, a few minutes after, the University eight rushed forth on her glorious career, clearing her way through the crowd of boats, and their admiring rowers towards Iffley.

And Marston sat on the top of the University barge, and watched her sweeping on towards the distance, and then he said to himself—

"Ah! there goes the man I like best in the world, who don't care for the woman I love best in the world, who is in love with the man before mentioned, who is in love with a woman who don't care a hang for him. There is a certain left-handedness in human affairs."

CHAPTER XXIII[1]

THE LAST GLIMPSE OF THE OLD WORLD

PUTNEY BRIDGE at half-an-hour before high tide; thirteen or fourteen steamers; five or six thousand boats, and fifteen or twenty thousand spectators. This is the morning of the great University race, about which every member of the two great Universities, and a very large section of the general public, have been fidgeting and talking for a month or so.

The bridge is black, the lawns are black, every balcony and window in the town is black; the steamers are black with a swarming, eager multitude, come to see the picked youths of the upper class try their strength against one another. There are two friends of ours nearly concerned in the great event of the day. Charles is rowing three in the Oxford boat, and Marston is steering. This is a memorable day for both of them, and more especially for poor Charles.

Now the crowd surges to and fro, and there is a cheer. The men are getting into their boats. The police-boats are busy clearing the course. Now there is a cheer of admiration, Cambridge dashes out, swings round, and takes her place at the bridge.

Another shout. Oxford sweeps majestically out and takes

[1] The short description of the University boat-race which begins this chapter was written two years ago, from the author's recollection of the race of 1852. It would do for a description of this year's race, quite as well as of any other year, substituting "Cambridge" for "Oxford," according to the year.

her place by Cambridge. Away go the police-galleys, away go all the London club-boats, at ten miles an hour down the course. Now the course is clear, and there is almost a silence.

Then a wild hubbub; and people begin to squeeze and crush against one another. The boats are off; the fight has begun; then the thirteen steamers come roaring on after them, and their wake is alive once more with boats.

Everywhere a roar and a rushing to and fro. Frantic crowds upon the towing-path, mad crowds on the steamers, which make them sway and rock fearfully. Ahead Hammersmith Bridge, hanging like a black bar, covered with people as with a swarm of bees. As an eye-piece to the picture, two solitary flying boats, and the flashing oars, working with the rapidity and regularity of a steam-engine.

"Who's in front?" is asked by a thousand mouths; but who can tell? We shall see soon. Hammersmith Bridge is stretching across the water not a hundred yards in front of the boats. For one half-second a light shadow crosses the Oxford boat, and then it is out into the sunlight beyond. In another second the same shadow crosses the Cambridge boat. Oxford is ahead.

The men with light-blue neckties say that, "By George, Oxford can't keep that terrible quick stroke going much longer"; and the men with dark-blue ties say, "Can't she, by Jove!" Well, we shall know all about it soon, for here is Barnes Bridge. Again the shadow goes over the Oxford boat, and then one, two, three, four seconds before the Cambridge men pass beneath it. Oxford is winning! There is a shout from the people at Barnes, though the πολλοί don't know why. Cambridge has made a furious rush, and nearly drawn up to Oxford; but it is useless. Oxford leaves rowing, and Cambridge rows ten strokes before they are level. Oxford has won!

Five minutes after, Charles was on the wharf in front of the Ship Inn, at Mortlake, as happy as a king. He had got separated from his friends in the crowd, and the people round him were cheering him, and passing flattering remarks on his personal appearance, which caused Charles to laugh, and blush, and bow, as he tried to push through his good-natured persecutors, when he suddenly, in the midst of a burst of laughter caused by a remark made by a drunken bargeman, felt somebody clasp his arm, and, turning round, saw William.

He felt such a shock that he was giddy and faint. "Will," he said, "what is the matter?"

"Come here, and I'll tell you."

He forced his way to a quieter place, and then turned round to his companion—"Make it short, Will; that's a dear fellow, I can stand the worst."

"Master was took very bad two days ago, Master Charles; and Master Cuthbert sent me off for you at once. He told me directly I got to Paddington to ask for a telegraph-message, so that you might hear the last accounts; and here it is.

He put what we now call a "telegram" into Charles's hand, and the burden of it was mourning and woe. Densil Ravenshoe was sinking fast, and all that steam and horse-flesh could do would be needed, if Charles would see him alive.

"Will, go and find Mr. Marston for me, and I will wait here for you. How are we to get back to Putney?"

"I have got a cab waiting."

William dashed into the inn, and Charles waited. He turned and looked at the river.

There it was winding away past villa and park, bearing a thousand boats upon its bosom. He looked once again upon the crowded steamers and the busy multitude, and even in his grief felt a rush of honest pride as he thought that he was one of the heroes of the day. And then he turned, for William was beside him again. Marston was not to be found.

"I should like to have seen him again," he said; "but we must fly, Will, we must fly!"

Had he known under what circumstances he was next to see a great concourse of people, and under what circumstances he was next to meet Marston, who knows but that in his ignorance and shortsightedness he would have chosen to die where he stood in such a moment of triumph and honour?

In the hurry of departure he had no time to ask questions. Only when he found himself in the express train, having chosen to go second-class with his servant, and not be alone, did he find time to ask how it had come about.

There was but little to be told. Densil had been seized after breakfast, and at first so slightly that they were not much alarmed. He had been put to bed, and the symptoms had grown worse. Then William had been despatched for Charles, leaving Cuthbert, Mary, and Father Mackworth at his bedside. All had been done that could be done. He seemed to be in no pain, and quite contented. That was all. The telegraph told the rest. Cuthbert had promised to send horses to Crediton, and a relay forty miles nearer home.

The terrible excitement of the day, and the fact that he had eaten nothing since breakfast, made Charles less able to bear up against the news than he would otherwise have been. Strange thoughts and fears began to shape themselves in his head, and to find voices in the monotonous jolting of the carriage.

Not so much the fear of his father's death. That he did not fear, because he knew it would come ; and, as to that, the bitterness of death was past, bitter, deeply bitter, as it was ; but a terror lest his father should die without speaking to him —that he should never see those dear lips wreathe into a smile for him any more.

Yesterday he had been thinking of this very journey—of how, if they won the race, he would fly down on the wings of the wind to tell them, and how the old man would brighten up with joy at the news. Yesterday he was a strong, brave man ; and now what deadly terror was this at his heart ?

" William, what frightens me like this ? "

" The news I brought you, and the excitement of the race. And you have been training hard for a long time, and that don't mend a man's nerves ; and you are hungry."

" Not I."

" What a noble race it was ! I saw you above a mile off. I could tell the shape of you that distance, and see how you was pulling your oar through. I knew that my boy was going to be in the winning boat, Lord bless you ! before the race was rowed. And when I saw Mr. C—— come in with that tearing, licking quick stroke of his, I sung out for old Oxford, and pretty nearly forgot the photograph for a bit."

" Photograph, Will ? what photograph ? "

" Telegraph, I mean. It's all the same."

Charles couldn't talk, though he tried. He felt an anxiety he had never felt before. It was so ill-defined that he could not trace it to its source. He had a right to feel grief, and deep anxiety to see his father alive ; but this was sheer terror, and at what ?

At Swindon, William got out and returned laden with this and with that, and forced Charles to eat and drink. He had not tasted wine for a long time, so he had to be careful with it ; but it seemed to do him no good. But, at last, tired nature did something for him, and he fell asleep.

When he awoke it was night, and at first he did not remember where he was. But rapidly his grief came upon him ; and up, as it were out of a dark gulf, came the other nameless terror and took possession of his heart.

There was a change at Exeter; then at Crediton they met with their first relay of horses, and, at ten o'clock at night, after a hasty supper, started on their midnight ride. The terror was gone the moment Charles was on horseback.

The road was muddy and dark, often with steep banks on each side; but a delicious April moon was overhead, and they got on bravely. At Bow there was a glimpse of Dartmoor towering black, and a fresh puff of westerly wind, laden with scents of spring. At Hatherleigh, there were fresh horses, and one of the Ravenshoe grooms waiting for them. The man had heard nothing since yesterday, so at one o'clock they started on again. After this, there were none but cross-country roads, and dangerous steep lanes; so they got on slowly. Then came the morning with voice of ten thousand birds, and all the rich perfume of awaking nature. And then came the woods of home, and they stood on the terrace, between the old house and the sea.

The white surf was playing and leaping around the quiet headlands; the sea-birds were floating merrily in the sunshine; the April clouds were racing their purple shadows across the jubilant blue sea; but the old house stood blank and dull. Every window was closed and not a sound was heard.

For Charles had come too late. Densil Ravenshoe was dead.

CHAPTER XXIV

THE FIRST GLIMPSE OF THE NEW WORLD

In the long dark old room with the mullioned windows looking out on the ocean, in the room that had been Charles's bedroom, study, and playroom, since he was a boy, there sat Charles Ravenshoe, musing, stricken down with grief, and forlorn.

There were the fishing-rods and the guns, there were the books and the homely pictures in which his soul had delighted. There was "The Sanctuary and the Challenge" and Bob Coombes in his outrigger. All were there. But Charles Ravenshoe was not there. There was another man in his place, bearing his likeness, who sat and brooded with his head on his hands.

Where was the soul which was gone? Was he an infant in a new cycle of existence? or was he still connected with the scenes and people he had known and loved so long? Was he present? Could he tell at last the deep love that one poor foolish heart had borne for him? Could he know now the deep, deep grief that tore that poor silly heart, because its owner had not been by to see the last faint smile of intelligence flutter over features that he was to see no more?

"Father! Father! Where are you? Don't leave me all alone, father." No answer! only the ceaseless beating of the surf upon the shore.

He opened the window, and looked out. The terrace the woods, the village, and beyond, the great unmeasurable ocean! What beyond that?

What was this death, which suddenly made that which we loved so well, so worthless? Could they none of them tell us? One there was who triumphed over death and the grave, and was caught up in His earthly body. Who is this Death that he should triumph over us? Alas, poor Charles! There are evils worse than death. There are times when death seems to a man like going to bed. Wait!

There was a picture of Mary's, of which he bethought himself. One we all know. Of a soul being carried away by angels to heaven. They call it St. Catherine, though it had nothing particular to do with St. Catherine, that I know of; and he thought he would go see it. But, as he turned, there stood Mary herself before him.

He held out his hands towards her, and she came and sat beside him, and put her arm round his neck. He kissed her! Why not? They were as brother and sister.

He asked her why she had come.

"I knew you wanted me," she said.

Then she, still with her arm round his neck, talked to him about what had just happened. "He asked for you soon after he was taken on the first day, and told Father Mackworth to send off for you. Cuthbert had sent two hours before, and he said he was glad, and hoped that Oxford would win the race——"

"Charles," said Mary again, "do you know that old James has had a fit, and is not expected to live?"

"No."

"Yes, as soon as he heard of our dear one's death he was taken. It has killed him."

"Poor old James!"

They sat there some time, hand in hand, in sorrowful communion, and then Charles said suddenly—

"The future, Mary! The future, my love?"

"We discussed that before, Charles dear. There is only one line of life open to me."

"Ah!"

"I shall write to Lady Ascot to-morrow. I heard from Adelaide the other day, and she tells me that young Lady Hainault is going to take charge of poor Lord Charles's children in a short time; and she will want a nursery governess; and I will go."

"I would sooner you were there than here, Mary. I am very glad of this. She is a very good woman. I will go and see you there very often."

"Are you going back to Oxford, Charles?"

"I think not."

"Do you owe much money there?"

"Very little now. He paid it almost all for me."

"What shall you do?"

"I have not the remotest idea. I cannot possibly conceive. I must consult Marston."

There passed a weary week—a week of long brooding days and sleepless nights, while outside the darkened house the bright spring sun flooded all earth with light and life, and the full spring wind sang pleasantly through the musical woods, and swept away inland over heather and crag.

Strange sounds began to reach Charles in his solitary chamber; sounds which at first made him fancy he was dreaming, they were so mysterious and inexplicable. The first day they assumed the forms of solitary notes of music, some almost harsh, and some exquisitely soft and melodious. As the day went on they began to arrange themselves into chords, and sound slightly louder, though still a long way off. At last, near midnight, they seemed to take form, and flow off into a wild, mournful piece of music, the like of which Charles had never heard before; and then all was still.

Charles went to bed, believing either that the sounds were supernatural or that they arose from noises in his head. He came to the latter conclusion, and thought sleep would put an end to them; but, next morning, when he had half opened the shutters, and let in the blessed sunlight, there came the sound again—a wild, rich, triumphant melody, played by some hand, whether earthly or unearthly, that knew its work well.

"What is that, William?"

" Music."

" Where does it come from ? "

" Out of the air. The pixies make such music at times.
Maybe it's the saints in glory with their golden harps,
welcoming Master and Father."

" Father ! "

" He died this morning at daybreak ; not long after his old
master, eh ? He was very faithful to him. He was in prison
with him once, I've heard tell. I'll be as faithful to you,
Charles, when the time comes."

And another day wore on in the darkened house, and still
the angelic music rose and fell at intervals, and moved the
hearts of those that heard it strangely.

"Surely," said Charles to himself, " that music must sound
louder in one place than another." And then he felt himself
smiling at the idea that he half believed it to be supernatural.

He rose and passed on through corridor and gallery, still
listening as he went. The music had ceased, and all was
still.

He went on through parts of the house he had not been in
since a boy. This part of the house was very much deserted ;
some of the rooms he looked into were occupied as inferior
servants' bedrooms ; some were empty, and all were dark.
Here was where he, Cuthbert, and William would play hide-
and-seek on wet days ; and well he remembered each nook and
lair. A window was open in one empty room, and it looked
into the court-yard. They were carrying things into the chapel,
and he walked that way.

In the dark entrance to the dim chapel a black figure stood
aside to let him pass ; he bowed, and did so, but was barely in
the building when a voice he knew said, " It is Charles," and
the next moment he was clasped by both hands, and the kind
face of Father Tiernay was beaming before him.

" I am so glad to see you, Father Tiernay. It is so kind of
you to come."

"You look pale and worn," said the good man ; "you have
been fretting. I won't have that, now that I am come. I will
have you out in the air and sunshine, my boy, along the
shore——"

The music again ! Not faint and distant as heretofore, but
close overhead, crashing out into a mighty jubilate, which
broke itself against rafter and window in a thousand sweet
echoes. Then, as the noble echoes began to sink, there arose
a soft flute-like note which grew more intense until the air was

filled with passionate sound; and it trilled and ran, and paused, and ran on, and died you knew not where.

"I can't stand much of that, Father Tiernay," said Charles. "They have been mending the organ, I see. That accounts for the music I have heard. I suppose there will be music at the funeral, then."

"My brother Murtagh," said Father Tiernay, "came over yesterday morning from Lord Segur's. He is organist there, and he mended it. Bedad, he is a sweet musician. Hear what Sir Henry Bishop says of him."

There came towards them, from the organ-loft, a young man, wearing a long black coat and black bands with white edges, and having of his own one of the sweetest, kindliest faces eye ever rested on. Father Tiernay looked on him with pride and affection, and said—

"Murty, my dear brother, this is Mr. Charles Ravenshoe, me very good friend, I hope you'll become acquaintances, for the reason that two good fellows should know one another."

"I am almost afraid," said the young man, with a frank smile, "that Charles Ravenshoe has already a prejudice against me for the disagreeable sounds I was making all day yesterday in bringing the old organ into work again."

"Nay, I was only wondering where such noble bursts of melody came from," said Charles. "If you had made all the evil noises in Pandemonium, they would have been forgiven for that last piece of music. Do you know that I had no idea the old organ could be played on. Years ago, when we were boys, Cuthbert and I tried to play on it; I blew for him, and he sounded two or three notes, but it frightened us, and we ran away, and never went near it again."

"It is a beautiful old instrument," said young Tiernay; "will you stand just here, and listen to it?"

Charles stood in one of the windows, and Father Tiernay beside him. He leant his head on his arm, and looked forth eastward and northward, over the rolling woods, the cliffs, and the bright blue sea.

The music began with a movement soft, low, melodious, beyond expression, and yet strong, firm, and regular as of a thousand armed men marching to victory. It grew into volume and power till it was irresistible, yet still harmonious and perfect. Charles understood it. It was the life of a just man growing towards perfection and honour.

It wavered and fluttered, and threw itself into sparkling sprays and eddies. It leapt and laughed with joy unutterable, yet still through all the solemn measure went on. Love had come to gladden the perfect life, and had adorned without disturbing it.

Then began discords and wild sweeping storms of sound, harsh always, but never unmelodious: fainter and fainter grew the melody, till it was almost lost. Misfortunes had come upon the just man, and he was bending under them.

No. More majestic, more grand, more solemn than ever the melody re-asserted itself: and again, as though purified by a furnace, marched solemnly on with a clearness and sweetness greater than at first. The just man had emerged from his sea of troubles ennobled. Charles felt a hand on his shoulder. He thought it had been Father Tiernay. Father Tiernay was gone. It was Cuthbert.

"Cuthbert! I am so glad you have come to see me. I was not surprised because you would not see me before. You didn't think I was offended, brother, did you? I know you. I know you!

Charles smoothed his hair and smiled pleasantly upon him. Cuthbert stood quite still and said nothing.

"Cuthbert," said Charles, "you are in pain. In bodily pain, I mean."

"I am. I spent last night on these stones praying, and the cold has got into my very bones."

"You pray for the dead, I know," said Charles. "But why destroy the health God has given you because a good man has gone to sleep?"

"I was not praying for him as much as for you."

"God knows I want it, dear Cuthbert. But can you benefit me by killing yourself?"

"Who knows? I may **try**. How long is it since we were boys together, Charles?"

"How long? Let me see. Why, it is nineteen years at least since I can first remember you."

"I have been sarcastic and distant with you sometimes, Charles, but I have never been unkind."

"Cuthbert! I never had an unkind word or action from you. Why do you say this?"

"Because——Charles, do you remember the night the *Warren Hastings* came ashore?"

"Ay," said Charles, wonderingly.

"In future, when you call me to mind, will you try to think of me as I was then, not as I have been lately. We slept together, you remember, through the storm, and he sat on the bed. God has tried me very hard. Let us hope that heaven will be worth the winning. After this you will see me no more in private. Good-bye!"

Charles thought he knew what he meant, and had expected it. He would not let him go for a time.

CHAPTER XXV

FATHER MACKWORTH BRINGS LORD SALTIRE TO BAY, AND WHAT CAME OF IT

OLD James was to be buried side by side with his old master in the vault under the altar. The funeral was to be on the grandest scale, and all the Catholic gentry of the neighbourhood, and most of the Protestant, were coming. Father Mackworth, it may be conceived, was very busy, and seldom alone. All day he and the two Tiernays were arranging and ordering. When thoroughly tired out, late at night, he would retire to his room and take a frugal supper (Mackworth was no glutton) and sit before the fire musing.

One night, towards the middle of the week, he was sitting thus before the fire when the door opened, and some one came in ; thinking it was the servant, he did not look round ; but, when the supposed servant came up to the fire-place and stood still, he cast his eyes suddenly up, and they fell upon the cadaverous face of Cuthbert.

He looked deadly pale and wan as he stood with his face turned to the flickering fire, and Mackworth felt deep pity for him. He held an open letter towards Mackworth, and said—

" This is from Lord Saltire. He proposes to come here the night before the funeral and go away in Lord Segur's carriage with him after it is over. Will you kindly see after his rooms, and so on ? Here is the letter."

" I will," said Mackworth. " My dear boy, you look deadly ill."

" I wish I were dead."

" So do all who hope for heaven," said Mackworth.

" Who would not look worn and ill with such a scene hanging over their heads ? "

" Go away and avoid it."

F

"Not I. A Ravenshoe is not a coward. Besides, I want to see him again. How cruel you have been! Why did you let him gain my heart? I have little enough to love."

There was a long pause—so long that a bright-eyed little mouse ran out from the wainscot and watched. Both their eyes were bent on the fire, and Father Mackworth listened with painful intentness for what was to come.

"He shall speak first," he thought. "How I wonder——"

At last Cuthbert spoke slowly, without raising his eyes.

"Will nothing induce you to forego your purpose?"

"How can I forego it, Cuthbert, with common honesty? I have foregone it long enough."

"Listen now," said Cuthbert, unheedingly: "I have been reckoning up what I can afford, and I find that I can give you five thousand pounds down for that paper, and five thousand more in bills of six, eight, and twelve months. Will that content you?"

Father Mackworth would have given a finger to have answered promptly "No," but he could not. The offer was so astounding, so unexpected, that he hesitated long enough to make Cuthbert look round, and say—

"Ten thousand pounds is a large sum of money, Father."

It was, indeed; and Lord Saltire coming next week! Let us do the man justice; he acted with a certain amount of honour. When you have read this book to the end you will see that ten thousand pounds was only part of what was offered to him. He gave up it all because he would not lower himself in the eyes of Cuthbert, who had believed in him so long.

"I paused," said he, "from astonishment, that a gentleman could have insulted me by such a proposition."

"Your pause," said Cuthbert, "arose from hesitation, not from astonishment. I saw your eyes blaze when I made you the offer. Think of ten thousand pounds. You might appear in the world as an English Roman Catholic of fortune. Good heavens! with your talent you might aspire to the cardinal's chair!"

"No, no, no!" said Mackworth fiercely. "I did hesitate, and I have lied to you; but I hesitate no longer. I won't have the subject mentioned to me again, sir. What sort of a gentleman are you to come to men's rooms in the dead of the night, with your father lying dead in the house, and tempt men to felony? I will not."

"God knows," said Cuthbert, as he passed out, "whether I have lost heaven in trying to save him."

Mackworth heard the door close behind him, and then looked eagerly towards it. He heard Cuthbert's footsteps die along the corridor, and then, rising up, he opened it and looked out. The corridor was empty. He walked hurriedly back to the fireplace.

"Shall I call him back?" he said. "It is not too late. Ten thousand pounds! A greater stake than I played for; and now, when it is at my feet, I am throwing it away. And for what? For honour, after I have acted the——" (he could not say the word). "After I have gone so far. I must be a gentleman. A common rogue would have jumped at the offer. By heaven! there are some things better than money. If I were to take his offer he would know me for a rogue. And I love the lad. No, no! let the fool go to his prayers. I will keep the respect of one man at least.

"What a curious jumble and puzzle it all is, to be sure. Am I any worse than my neighbours? I have made a desperate attempt at power, for a name, and an ambition; and then, because the ball comes suddenly at my feet, from a quarter I did not expect, I dare not strike it because I fear the contempt of one single pair of eyes from which I have been used to receive nothing but love and reverence.

"Yet, he cannot trust me, as I thought he did, or he would not have made the offer to me. And then he made it in such a confident way that he must have thought I was going to accept it. That is strange. He has never rebelled lately. Am I throwing away substance for shadow? I have been bound to the Church body and soul from my boyhood, and I must go on. I have refused a cardinal's chair this night. But who will ever know it?

"I must go about with my Lord Saltire. I could go at him with more confidence if I had ten thousand pounds in the bank though, in case of failure. I am less afraid of that terrible old heretic than I am of those great eyes of Cuthbert's turned on me in scorn. I have lived so long among gentlemen that I believe myself to be one. He knows, and he shall tell.

"And, if all fails, I have served the Church, and the Church shall serve me. What fools the best of us are! Why did I ever allow that straightforward idiot Tiernay into the house? He hates me, I know. I rather like the fool. He will take the younger one's part on Monday; but I don't think my gentleman will dare to say too much."

After this soliloquy, the key to which will appear very shortly, Father Mackworth took off his clothes and got into bed.

The day before the funeral, Cuthbert sent a message to Charles, to beg that he would be kind enough to receive Lord Saltire; and, as the old man was expected at a certain hour, Charles, about ten minutes before the time, went down to the bottom of the hall steps on to the terrace, to be ready for him when he came.

Oh the glorious wild freshness of the sea and sky after the darkened house! The two old capes right and left; the mile-long stretch of sand between them; and the short crisp waves rolling in before the westerly wind of spring! Life and useful action in the rolling water; budding promise in the darkening woods; young love in every bird's note!

William stood beside him before he had observed him. Charles turned to him, and took his arm in his.

"Look at this," he said.

"I am looking at it."

"Does it make you glad and wild?" said Charles. "Does it make the last week in the dark house look like twenty years? Are the two good souls which are gone looking at it now, and rejoicing that earth should still have some pleasure left for us?"

"I hope not," said William, turning to Charles.

"And why?" said Charles, and wondering rather what William would say.

"I wouldn't," said William, "have neither of their hearts broke with seeing what is to come."

"Their hearts broke!" said Charles, turning full round on his foster-brother. "Let them see how we behave under it, William. That will never break their hearts, my boy."

"Charles," said William, earnestly, "do you know what is coming?"

"No; nor care."

"It is something terrible for you, I fear," said William.

"Have you any idea what it is?" said Charles.

"Not the least. But look here. Last night, near twelve, I went down to the chapel, thinking to say an ave before the coffin, and there lay Master Cuthbert on the stones. So I kept quiet and said my prayer. And of a sudden he burst out and said, 'I have risked my soul and my fortune to save him; Lord, remember it!'"

"Did he say that, William?"

"The very words."

"Then he could not have been speaking of me," said Charles. "It is possible that by some means I may not come into the property I have been led to expect; but that could not have referred to me. Suppose I was to leave the house, penniless, to-morrow morning, William, should I go alone? I am very strong and very patient, and soon learn anything. Cuthbert would take care of me. Would you come with me, or let me go alone?"

"You know. Why should I answer?"

"We might go to Canada and settle. And then Adelaide would come over when the house was ready; and you would marry the girl of your choice; and our boys would grow up to be such friends as you and I are. And then my boy should marry your girl, and——"

Poor dreaming Charles, all unprepared for what was to come!

A carriage drove on to the terrace at this moment, with Lord Saltire's solemn servant on the box.

Charles and William assisted Lord Saltire to alight. His lordship said that he was getting devilish stiff and old, and had been confoundedly cut up by his old friend's death, and had felt bound to come down to show his respect to the memory of one of the best and honestest men it had ever been his lot to meet in a tolerably large experience. And then, standing on the steps, went on—

"It is very pleasant to me to be greeted by a face I like as yours, Charles. I was gratified at seeing your name in the *Times* as being one of the winners of the great boat-race the other day. My man pointed it out to me. That sort of thing is very honourable to a young fellow, if it does not lead to a neglect of other duties, in which case it becomes very mischievous: in yours it has not. That young man is, I believe, your foster-brother. Will he be good enough to go and find Miss Corby, and tell her that Lord Saltire wants her to come and walk with him on the terrace? Give me your shoulder." William ran right willingly on his errand.

"Your position here, Charles," continued Lord Saltire, "will be a difficult one."

"It will, indeed, my lord."

"I intend you to spend most of your time with me in future. I want some one to take care of me. In return for boring you all day, I shall get you the run of all the best houses, and make a man of you. Hush! not a word now! Here comes our Robin Redbreast. I am glad I have tempted her out into the air and the sunshine. How peaked you look, my dear! How are you?"

Poor Mary looked pale and wan, indeed, but brightened up

at the sight of her old friend. They three walked and talked in the fresh spring morning an hour or more.

That afternoon came a servant to Lord Saltire with a note from Father Mackworth, requesting the honour of ten minutes' conversation with Lord Saltire in private.

"I suppose I must see the fellow," said the old man to himself.

"My compliments to Mr. Mackworth, and I am alone in the library. The fool," continued he, when the man had left the room, "why doesn't he let well alone ? I hate the fellow. I believe he is as treacherous as his mother. If he broaches the subject, he shall have the whole truth."

Meanwhile, Father Mackworth was advancing towards him through the dark corridors, and walking slower, and yet more slow, as he neared the room where sat the grim old man. He knew that there would be a fencing match ; and of all the men in broad England he feared his lordship most. His determination held, however ; though, up to the very last, he had almost determined to speak only about comparatively indifferent subjects, and not about that nearest to his heart.

"How do you do, my good sir ?" said Lord Saltire, as he came in ; "I have to condole with you on the loss of our dear old friend. We shall neither of us have a better one, sir."

Mackworth uttered some common-places ; to which Lord Saltire bowed, without speaking, and then sat with his elbows on the arms of his chair, making a triangle of his two forefingers and thumbs, staring at Father Mackworth.

"I am going, Lord Saltire, to trouble you with some of my early reminiscences as a boy."

Lord Saltire bowed, and settled himself easily in his chair, as one does who expects a good story. Mackworth went on—

"One of my earliest recollections, my lord, is of being at a French lycée."

"The fault of those establishments," said Lord Saltire, pensively, "is the great range of subjects which are superficially taught. I ask pardon for interrupting you. Do you take snuff ? "

Mackworth declined, with great politeness, and continued—

"I was taken to that school by a footman in livery."

"Upon my honour, then, I owe you an apology. I thought, of course, that the butler had gone with you. But, in a large house, one never really knows what one's people are about."

Father Mackworth did not exactly like this. It was perfectly evident to him, not only that Lord Saltire knew all about his birth and parentage, but also was willing to tell.

"Lord Saltire," he said, "I have never had a parent's care, or any name but one I believe to be fictitious. You can give me a name—give me, perhaps, a parent—possibly a brother. Will you do this for me?"

"I can do neither the one thing nor the other, my good sir. I entreat you, for your own sake, to inquire no further."

There was a troubled expression in the old man's face as he answered. Mackworth thought he was gaining his point, and pressed on.

"Lord Saltire, as you are a gentleman, tell me who my parents were;" and, as he said this, he rose up and stood before him, folding his arms.

"Confound the impudent, theatrical jackanapes!" thought Lord Saltire. "His mother all over. I will gratify your curiosity, sir," he said aloud, angrily. "You are the illegitimate son of a French ballet-dancer."

"But who was my father, my lord? Answer me that, on your honour."

"Who was your father? *Pardieu*, that is more than I can tell. If any one ever knew it must have been your mother. You are assuming a tone with me, sir, which I don't intend to put up with. I wished to spare you a certain amount of humiliation. I shall not trouble myself to do so now, for many reasons. Now listen to me, sir—to the man who saved you from the kennel, sir—and drop that theatrical attitude. Your mother was my brother's mistress, and a clever woman in her way; and meeting her here and there, in the green-room and where not, and going sometimes to her house with my brother, I had a sort of acquaintance with her, and liked her as one likes a clever brilliant woman of that sort. My brother died. Some time after your mother fell into poverty and disgrace under circumstances into which I should advise you not to inquire, and on her death-bed recommended you to my care as an old acquaintance, praying that you might be brought up in her own religion. The request was, under the circumstances, almost impudent; but remembering that I had once liked the woman, and calling to mind the relation she had held to poor dear John, I complied, and did for you what I have done. You were a little over a twelvemonth old at the time of your mother's death, and my brother had been dead nearly or quite five years. Your mother had changed her protector thrice during that time. Now, sir!"

Mackworth stood before Lord Saltire all this time as firm as a rock. He had seen from the old man's eye that every word was terribly true, but he had never flinched—never a nerve in his face had quivered; but he had grown deadly pale. When Lord Saltire had finished he tried to speak, but found his mouth as dry as dust. He smiled, and, with a bow, reaching past Lord Saltire, took up a glass of lemonade which stood at his elbow and drank it. Then he spoke clearly and well.

"You see how you have upset me, my lord. In seeking this interview, I had some hopes of having forced a confession from your lordship of my relationship with you, and thereby serving my personal ambition. I have failed. It now remains to me to thank you heartily and frankly for the benefits I have received from you, and to beg you to forgive my indiscretion."

"You are a brave man, sir," said Lord Saltire. "I don't think you are an honest one. But I can respect manliness."

"You have a great affection for Charles Ravenshoe, my lord?"

"Yes," said Lord Saltire; "I love Charles Ravenshoe more than any other human being."

"Perhaps the time may come, my lord, when he will need all your love and protection."

"Highly possible. I am in possession of the tenor of his father's will; and those who try to set that will aside, unless they have a very strong case, had better consider that Charles is backed up by an amount of ready money sufficient to ruin the Ravenshoe estate in law."

"No attempt of the kind will be made, my lord. But I very much doubt whether your lordship will continue your protection to that young man. I wish you good afternoon."

"That fellow," said Lord Saltire, "has got a card to play which I don't know of. What matter? I can adopt Charles, and he may defy them. I wish I could give him my title; but that will be extinct. I am glad little Mary is going to Lady Hainault. It will be the best place for her till she marries. I wish that fool of a boy had fallen in love with her. But he wouldn't."

Mackworth hurried away to his room; and, as he went, he said, "I have been a fool. A fool. I should have taken Cuthbert's offer. None but a fool would have done otherwise. A cardinal's chair thrown to the dogs!"

"I could not do it this morning; but I can do it now. The son of a figurante, and without a father! Perhaps he will offer it again."

" If he does not, there is one thing certain. That young ruffian Charles is ruined. Ah, ah! my Lord Saltire, I have you there! I should like to see that old man's face when I play my last card. It will be a finer sight than Charles's. You'll make him your heir, will you, my lord? Will you make him your groom?"

He went to his desk, took out an envelope, and looked at it. He looked at it long, and then put it back. "It will never do to tempt him with it. If he were to refuse his offer of this morning, I should be ruined. Much better to wait and play out the ace boldly. I can keep my hold over *him :* and William is mine, body and soul, if he dies."

With which reflections the good Father dressed for dinner.

CHAPTER XXVI

THE GRAND CRASH

THE funeral was over. Charles had waited with poor weeping Mary to see the coffin carried away under the dark grim archway of the vault, and had tried to comfort her who would not be comforted. And, when the last wild wail of the organ had died away, and all the dark figures but they two had withdrawn from the chapel, there stood those two poor orphans alone together.

It was all over, and they began for the first time to realise it; they began to feel what they lost. King Densil was dead and King Cuthbert reigned. When a prime minister dies the world is shaken; when a county member dies the county is agitated, and the opposition electors, till lately insignificant, rise suddenly into importance, and the possible new members are suddenly great men. So, when a mere country gentleman dies, the head of a great family dies, relations are changed entirely between some score or two of persons. The dog of to-day is not the dog of yesterday. Servants are agitated, and remember themselves of old impertinences, and tremble. Farmers wonder what the new Squire's first move will be. Perhaps, even the old hound wonders whether he is to keep his old place by the fire or no, and younger brothers bite their nails, and wonder too, about many things.

Charles wondered profoundly in his own room that afternoon, whither he had retired after having dismissed Mary at her door with a kiss. In spite of his grief he wondered what was coming, and tried to persuade himself that he didn't care. From this state of mind he was aroused by William, who told him that Lord Segur was going and Lord Saltire with him, and that the latter wanted to speak to him.

Lord Saltire had his foot on the step of the carriage. "Charles, my dear boy," he said, "the moment things are settled, come to me at Segur Castle. Lord Segur wants you to come and stay there while I am there."

Lord Segur, from the carriage, hoped Charles would come and see them at once.

"And mind, you know," said Lord Saltire, "that you don't do anything without consulting me. Let the little bird pack off to Lady Ascot's and help to blow up the grooms. Don't let her stay moping here. Now, good-bye, my dear boy. I shall see you in a day or so."

And so the old man was gone. And, as Charles watched the carriage, he saw the sleek grey head thrust from the window, and the great white hand waved to him. He never forgot that glimpse of the grey head and white hand, and he never will.

A servant came up to him, and asked him, Would he see Mr. Ravenshoe in the library? Charles answered Yes, but was in no hurry to go. So he stood a little longer on the terrace, watching the bright sea, and the gulls, and the distant island. Then he turned into the darkened house again, and walked slowly towards the library door.

Some one else stood in the passage—it was William, with his hand on the handle of the door.

"I waited for you, Master Charles," he said; "they have sent for me too. Now you will hear something to your advantage."

"I care not," said Charles, and they went in.

Once, in lands far away, there was a sailor lad, a good-humoured, good-looking, thoughtless fellow, who lived alongside of me, and with whom I was always joking. We had a great liking for one another. I left him at the shaft's mouth at two o'clock one summer's day, roaring with laughter at a story I had told him; and at half-past five I was helping to wind up the shattered corpse, which when alive had borne his name. A flake of gravel had come down from the roof of the drive and killed him, and his laughing and story-telling were over for ever. How terrible these true stories are! Why do I tell this one? Because, whenever I think of this poor lad's death, I find myself not thinking of the ghastly thing that came swinging up out of the darkness into the summer air, but of the poor fellow as he was the morning before. I try to think how he looked, as leaning against the windlass with the forest behind and the mountains beyond, and if, in word or look, he gave any sign of his coming fate before he went gaily down into his tomb.

So it was with Charles Ravenshoe. He remembers part of the scene that followed perfectly well; but he tries more than all to recall how Cuthbert looked, and how Mackworth looked before the terrible words were spoken. After it was all over he remembers, he tells me, every trifling incident well. But his memory is a little gone about the first few minutes which elapsed after he and William came into the room. He says that Cuthbert was sitting at the table very pale, with his hands clasped on the table before him, looking steadily at him without expression on his face; and that Mackworth leant against the chimney-piece, and looked keenly and curiously at him.

Charles went up silently and kissed his brother on the forehead. Cuthbert neither moved nor spoke. Charles greeted Mackworth civilly, and then leant against the chimney-piece by the side of him and said what a glorious day it was. William stood at a little distance, looking uneasily from one to another.

Cuthbert broke silence. "I sent for you," he said.

"I am glad to come to you, Cuthbert, though I think you sent for me on business, which I am not very well up to to-day."

"On business," said Cuthbert: "business which must be gone through with to-day, though I expect it will kill me."

Charles, by some instinct (who knows what? it was nothing reasonable, he says) moved rapidly towards William, and laid his hand on his shoulder. I take it, that it arose from that curious gregarious feeling that men have in times of terror. He could not have done better than to move towards his truest friend, whatever it was.

"I should like to prepare you for what is to come," continued Cuthbert, speaking calmly, with the most curious distinctness; "but that would be useless. The blow would be equally severe whether you expect it or not. You two who stand there were nursed at the same breast. That groom, on whose shoulder you have your hand now, is my real brother.

You are no relation to me ; you are the son of the faithful old servant whom we buried to-day with my father."

Charles said, Ho ! like a great sigh. William put his arm round him, and, raising his finger, and looking into his face with his calm, honest eyes, said with a smile—

"This was it then. We know it all now."

Charles burst out into a wild laugh, and said, "Father Mackworth's ace of trumps ! He has inherited a talent for melodrama from his blessed mother. Stop. I beg your pardon, sir, for saying that; I said it in a hurry. It was blackguardly. Let's have the proofs of this, and all that sort of thing, and witnesses too, if you please. Father Mackworth, there have been such things as prosecutions for conspiracy. I have Lord Saltire and Lord Ascot at my back. You have made a desperate cast, sir. My astonishment is that you have allowed your hatred for me to outrun your discretion so far. This matter will cost some money before it is settled."

Father Mackworth smiled, and Charles passed him, and rang the bell. Then he went back to William and took his arm.

"Fetch the Fathers Tiernay here immediately," said Charles to the servant who answered the bell.

In a few minutes the worthy priests were in the room. The group was not altered. Father Mackworth still leant against the mantel-piece, Charles and William stood together, and Cuthbert sat pale and calm with his hands clasped together.

Father Tiernay looked at the disturbed group and became uneasy. "Would it not be better to defer the settlement of any family disagreements to another day ? On such a solemn occasion——"

"The ice is broken, Father Tiernay," said Charles. "Cuthbert, tell him what you have told me."

Cuthbert, clasping his hands together, did so, in a low, quiet voice.

"There," said Charles, turning to Father Tiernay, "what do you think of that ? "

"I am so astounded and shocked, that I don't know what to say," said Father Tiernay ; "your mind must be abused, my dear sir. The likeness between yourself and Mr. Charles is so great that I cannot believe it. Mackworth, what have you to say to this ? "

"Look at William, who is standing beside Charles," said the priest quietly, "and tell me which of those two is most like Cuthbert."

"Charles and William are very much alike, certainly," said Tiernay; "but——"

"Do you remember James Horton, Tiernay?" said Mackworth.

"Surely."

"Did you ever notice the likeness between him and Densil Ravenshoe?"

"I have noticed it, certainly; especially one night. One night I went to his cottage last autumn. Yes—well?"

"James Horton was Densil Ravenshoe's half-brother. He was the illegitimate son of Petre."

"Good God!"

"And the man whom you call Charles Ravenshoe, whom I call Charles Horton, is his son."

Charles was looking eagerly from one to the other, bewildered.

"Ask him, Father Tiernay," he said, "what proofs he has. Perhaps he will tell us."

"You hear what Mr. Charles says, Mackworth. I address you because you have spoken last. You must surely have strong proofs for such an astounding statement."

"I have his mother's handwriting," said Father Mackworth.

"My mother's, sir," said Charles, flushing up, and advancing a pace towards him.

"You forget who your mother was," said Mackworth. "Your mother was Norah, James Horton's wife. She confessed to me the wicked fraud she practised, and has committed that confession to paper. I hold it. You have not a point of ground to stand on. Fifty Lord Saltires could not help you one jot. You must submit. You have been living in luxury and receiving an expensive education when you should have been cleaning out the stable. So far from being overwhelmed at this, you should consider how terribly the balance is against you."

He spoke with such awful convincing calmness that Charles's heart died away within him. He knew the man.

"Cuthbert," he said, "you are a gentleman. Is this true?"

"God knows how terribly true it is," said Cuthbert quietly. Then there was a silence, broken by Charles in a strange thick voice, the like of which none there had heard before.

"I want to sit down somewhere. I want some drink. Will, my own boy, take this d——d thing from round my neck? I can't see; where is there a chair? Oh, God!"

He fell heavily against William, looking deadly white, without sense or power. And Cuthbert looked up at the priest, and said, in a low voice—

"You have killed him."

Little by little he came round again, and rose on his feet, looking round him as a buck or stag looks when run to soil, and is watching to see which dog will come, with a piteous wild look, despairing and yet defiant. There was a dead silence.

"Are we to be allowed to see this paper?" said Charles at length.

Father Mackworth immediately handed it to him, and he read it. It was completely conclusive. He saw that there was not a loophole to creep out of. The two Tiernays read it, and shook their heads. William read it and turned pale. And then they all stood staring blankly at one another.

"You see, sir," said Father Mackworth, "that there are two courses open to you. Either on the one hand, to acquiesce in the truth of this paper; or, on the other, to accuse me in a court of justice of conspiracy and fraud. If you were to be successful in the latter course, I should be transported out of your way, and the matter would end so. But any practical man would tell you, and you would see in your calmer moments, that no lawyer would undertake your case. What say you, Father Tiernay?"

"I cannot see what case he has, poor dear," said Father Tiernay. "Mackworth," he added suddenly.

Father Mackworth met his eye with a steady stare, and Tiernay saw there was no hope of explanation there.

"On the other hand," continued Father Mackworth, "if this new state of things is quietly submitted to (as it must be ultimately, whether quietly or otherwise you yourself will decide), I am authorized to say that the very handsomest provision will be made for you, and that, to all intents and purposes, your prospects in the world will not suffer in the least degree. I am right in saying so, I believe, Mr. Ravenshoe?"

"You are perfectly right, sir," said Cuthbert in a quiet, passionless voice. "My intention is to make a provision of three hundred a year for this gentleman, whom, till the last few days, I believed to be my brother. Less than twenty-four hours ago, Charles, I offered Father Mackworth ten thousand pounds for this paper, with a view to destroy it. I would, for your sake, Charles, have committed an act of villainy which would have entailed a life's remorse, and have robbed William, my own brother, of his succession. You see what a poor weak rogue I am, and what a criminal I might become with a little

temptation. Father Mackworth did his duty, and refused me.
I tell you this to show you that he is, at all events, sincere
enough in his conviction of the truth of this."

"You acted like yourself, Cuthbert. Like one who would
risk body and soul for one you loved."

He paused ; but they waited for him to speak again. And
very calmly, in a very low voice, he continued—

"It is time that this scene should end. No one's interest
will be served by continuing it. I want to say a very few
words, and I want them to be considered as the words, as it
were, of a dying man ; for no one here present will see me
again till the day when I come back to claim a right to the
name I have been bearing so long—and that day will be
never."

Another pause. He moistened his lips, which were dry and
cracked, and then went on—

"Here is the paper, Father Mackworth ; and may the Lord
of Heaven be judge between us if that paper be not true !"

Father Mackworth took it, and looking him steadily in the
face, repeated his words, and Charles's heart sank lower yet as
he watched him, and felt that hope was dead.

"May the Lord of Heaven be judge between us two,
Charles, if that paper be not true ! Amen."

"I utterly refuse," Charles continued, "the assistance which
Mr. Ravenshoe has so nobly offered. I go forth alone into the
world to make my own way, or to be forgotten. Cuthbert and
William, you will be sorry for a time, but not for long. You
will think of me sometimes of dark winter nights, when the wind
blows, won't you ? I shall never write to you, and shall never
return here any more. Worse things than this have happened
to men, and they have not died."

All this was said with perfect self-possession, and without
a failure in the voice. It was magnificent despair. Father
Tiernay, looking at William's face, saw there a sort of sarcastic
smile, which puzzled him amazingly.

"I had better," said Charles, "make my will. I should like
William to ride my horse Monté. He has thrown a curb, sir,
as you know," he said, turning to William ; "but he will serve
you well, and I know you will be gentle with him."

William gave a short, dry laugh.

"I should have liked to take my terrier away with me, but I
think I had better not. I want to have nothing with me to
remind me of this place. My greyhound and the pointers I
know you will take care of. It would please me to think that

William had moved into my room, and had taken possession of all my guns, and fishing-rods, and so on. There is a double-barrelled gun left at Venables', in St. Aldate's, at Oxford, for repairs. It ought to be fetched away.

"Now, sir," he said, turning to Cuthbert, "I should like to say a few words about money matters. I owe about £150 at Oxford. It was a great deal more at one time, but I have been more careful lately. I have the bills upstairs. If that could be paid——"

"To the utmost farthing, my dear Charles," said Cuthbert; "but——"

"Hush!" said Charles, "I have five-and-twenty pounds by me. May I keep that?"

"I will write you a cheque for five hundred. I shall move your resolution, Charles," said Cuthbert.

"Never, so help me God!" said Charles; "it only remains to say good-bye. I leave this room without a hard thought towards any one in it. I am at peace with all the world. Father Mackworth, I beg your forgiveness. I have been often rude and brutal to you. I suppose that you always meant kindly to me. Good-bye."

He shook hands with Mackworth, then with the Tiernays; then he offered his hand to William, who took it smiling; and, lastly, he went up to Cuthbert, and kissed him on the cheek, and then walked out of the door into the hall.

William, as he was going, turned as though to speak to Cuthbert, but Cuthbert had risen, and he paused a moment.

Cuthbert had risen, and stood looking wildly about him; then he said, "Oh, my God, he is gone!" And then he broke through them, and ran out into the hall, crying, "Charles, Charles, come back! Only one more word, Charles." And then they saw Charles pause, and Cuthbert kneel down before him, calling him his own dear brother, and saying he would die for him. And then Father Tiernay hastily shut the library door, and left those two wild hearts out in the old hall together alone.

Father Tiernay came back to William, and took both his hands. "What are you going to do?" he said.

"I am going to follow him wherever he goes," said William. "I am never going to leave him again. If he goes to the world's end, I will be with him."

"Brave fellow!" said Tiernay. "If he goes from here, and is lost sight of, we may never see him again. If you go with him, you may change his resolution."

" That I shall never do," said William; "I know him too well. But I'll save him from what I am frightened to think of. I will go to him now. I shall see you again directly; but I must go to him."

He passed out into the hall. Cuthbert was standing alone, and Charles was gone.

CHAPTER XXVII

THE COUP DE GRACE

In the long watches of the winter night, when one has awoke from some evil dream, and lies sleepless and terrified with the solemn pall of darkness around one—on one of those deadly, still dark nights, when the window only shows a murky patch of positive gloom in contrast of the nothingness of the walls, when the howling of a tempest round chimney and roof would be welcomed as a boisterous companion—in such still dead times only, one realizes that some day we shall lie in that bed and not think at all : that the time will come soon when we must die.

Our preachers remind us of this often enough, but we cannot realize it in a pew in broad daylight. You must wake in the middle of the night to do that, and face the thought like a man, that it will come, and come to ninety-nine in a hundred of us, not in a maddening clatter of musketry as the day is won ; or in carrying a line to a stranded ship, or in such like glorious times, when the soul is in mastery over the body ; but in bed, by slow degrees. It is in darkness and silence only that we realize this ; and then let us hope that we humbly remember that death has been conquered for us, and that in spite of our unworthiness we may defy him. And after that sometimes will come the thought, "Are there no evils worse even than death?"

I have made these few remarks (I have made very few in this story, for I want to suggest thought, not to supply it ready-made) because Charles Ravenshoe has said to me in his wild way, that he did not fear death, for he had died once already.

I did not say anything, but waited for him to go on.

"For what," he continued, "do you make out death even at the worst? A terror, then a pang, more or less severe; then a total severance of all ties on earth, an entire and permanent loss of everything one has loved. After that, remorse and useless regret, and the horirble torture of missed opportunities without number thrust continually before one. The monotonous song of the fiends, 'Too late! too late!' I have suffered all these things! I have known what very few men have known, and lived—despair; but perhaps the most terrible agony for a time was the feeling of *loss of identity*—that I was not myself; that my whole existence from babyhood had been a lie. This at times, at times only, mind you, washed away from me the only spar to which I could cling—the feeling that I was a gentleman. When the deluge came, that was the only creed I had, and I was left alone, as it were, on the midnight ocean, out of sight of land, swimming with failing strength."

I have made Charles speak for himself. In this I know that I am right. Now we must go on with him through the gathering darkness without flinching; in terror, perhaps, but not in despair as yet.

It never for one moment entered into his head to doubt the truth of what Father Mackworth had set up. If he had had doubts even to the last, he had none after Mackworth had looked him compassionately in the face, and said, "God judge between us if this paper be not true!" Though he distrusted Mackworth, he felt that no man, be he never so profound an actor, could have looked so and spoken so if he were not telling what he believed to be the truth. And that he and Norah were mistaken he justly felt to be an impossibility. No. He was the child of Petre Ravenshoe's bastard son by an Irish peasant girl. He who but half an hour before had been heir to the proud old name, to the noble old house, the pride of the west country, to hundreds of acres of rolling woodland, to mile beyond mile of sweeping moorland, to twenty thriving farms, deep in happy valleys, or perched high up on the side of lofty downs, was now just this—a peasant, an impostor.

The tenantry, the fishermen, the servants, they would come to know all this. Had he died (ah! how much better than this), they would have mourned for him, but what would they say or think now? That he, the patron, the intercessor, the condescending young prince, should be the child of a waiting woman and a gamekeeper. Ah! mother, mother, God forgive you!

Adelaide; what would she think of this? He determined that he must go and see her, and tell her the whole miserable story. She was ambitious, but she loved him. Oh yes, she loved him. She could wait. There were lands beyond the sea, where a man could win a fortune in a few years, perhaps in one. There were Canada, and Australia, and India, where a man needed nothing but energy. He never would take one farthing from the Ravenshoes, save the twenty-five pounds he had. That was a determination nothing could alter. But why need he? There was gold to be won, and forest to be cleared, in happier lands.

Alas, poor Charles! He has never yet set foot out of England, and perhaps never will. He never thought seriously about it but this once. He never had it put before him strongly by any one. Men only emigrate from idleness, restlessness, or necessity; with the two first of these he was not troubled, and the last had not come yet. It would, perhaps, have been better for him to have gone to the backwoods or the diggings; but, as he says, the reason why he didn't was that he didn't. But at this sad crisis of his life it gave him comfort for a little to think about; only for a little, then thought and terror came sweeping back again.

Lord Saltire? He would be told of this by others. It would be Charles's duty not to see Lord Saltire again. With his present position in society, as a servant's son, there was nothing to prevent his asking Lord Saltire to provide for him, except—what was it? Pride? Well, hardly pride. He was humble enough, God knows; but he felt as if he had gained his goodwill, as it were, by false pretences, and that duty would forbid his presuming on that goodwill any longer. And would Lord Saltire be the same to a lady's-maid's son, as he would to the heir-presumptive of Ravenshoe? No; there must be no humiliation before those stern grey eyes. Now he began to see that he loved the owner of those eyes more deeply than he had thought; and there was a gleam of pleasure in thinking that, when Lord Saltire heard of his fighting bravely unassisted with the world, he would say, "That lad was a brave fellow; a gentleman after all."

Marston? Would this terrible business, which was so new and terrible as to be as yet only half appreciated—would it make any difference to him? Perhaps it might. But, whether or no, he would humble himself there, and take from him just reproaches for idleness and missed opportunities, however bitter they might be.

And Mary? Poor little Mary! Ah! she would be safe with that good Lady Hainault. That was all. Ah, Charles!

what pale little sprite was that outside your door now, listening, dry-eyed, terrified, till you should move? Who saw you come up with your hands clutched in your hair, like a madman, an hour ago, and heard you throw yourself upon the floor, and has waited patiently ever since to see if she could comfort you, were it never so little? Ah, Charles! Foolish fellow!

Thinking, thinking—now with anger, now with tears, and now with terror—till his head was hot and his hands dry, his thoughts began to run into one channel. He saw that action was necessary, and he came to a great and noble resolution, worthy of himself. All the world was on one side, and he alone on the other. He would meet the world humbly and bravely, and conquer it. He would begin at the beginning, and find his own value in the world, and then, if he found himself worthy, would claim once more the love and respect of those who had been his friends hitherto.

How he would begin he knew not, nor cared, but it must be from the beginning. And, when he had come to this resolution, he rose up and faced the light of day once more.

There was a still figure sitting in his chair, watching him. It was William.

"William! How long have you been here?"

"Nigh on an hour. I came in just after you, and you have been lying on the hearth-rug ever since, moaning."

"An hour? Is it only an hour?"

"A short hour."

"It seemed like a year. Why, it is not dark yet. The sun still shines, does it?"

He went to the window and looked out. "Spring," he said, "early spring. Fifty more of them between me and rest most likely. Do I look older, William?"

"You look pale and wild, but not older. I am amazed and stunned. I want you to look like yourself and help me, Charles. We must get away together out of this house."

"You must stay here, William; you are heir to the name and the house. You must stay here and learn your duty; I must go forth and dree my weary weird alone."

"You must go forth, I know; but I must go with you."

"William, that is impossible."

"To the world's end, Charles; I swear it by the holy Mother of God."

"Hush! You don't know what you are saying. Think of your duties."

"I know my duty. My duty is with you."

"William, look at the matter in another point of view. Will Cuthbert let you come with me?"

"I don't care. I am coming."

William was sitting where he had been in Charles's chair, and Charles was standing beside him. If William had been looking at Charles, he would have seen a troubled, thoughtful expression on his face for one moment, followed by a sudden look of determination. He laid his hand on William's shoulder, and said—

"We must talk this over again. I *must* go to Ranford and see Adelaide at once, before this news gets there from other mouths. Will you meet me at the old hotel in Convent Garden four days from this time?"

"Why there?" said William. "Why not at Henley?"

"Why not at London, rather?" replied Charles. "I must go to London. I mean to go to London. I don't want to delay about Ranford. No; say London."

William looked in his face for a moment, and then said—

"I'd rather travel with you. You can leave me at Wargrave, which is only just over the water from Ranford, or at Didcot, while you go on to Ranford. You must let me do that, Charles."

"We will do that, William, if you like."

"Yes, yes!" said William. "It must be so. Now you must come downstairs."

"Why?"

"To eat. Dinner is ready. I am going to tea in the servants' hall."

"Will Mary be at dinner, William?"

"Of course she will."

"Will you let me go for the last time? I should like to see the dear little face again. Only this once."

"Charles! Don't talk like that. All that this house contains is yours, and will be as long as Cuthbert and I are here. Of course you must go. This must not get out for a long while yet—we must keep up appearances."

So Charles went down into the drawing-room. It was nearly dark; and at first he thought there was no one there, but, as he advanced towards the fireplace, he made out a tall, dark figure, and saw that it was Mackworth.

"I am come, sir," he said, "to dinner in the old room for the last time for ever."

"God forbid!" said Mackworth. "Sir, you have behaved like a brave man to-day, and I earnestly hope that, as long as

I stay in this house, you will be its honoured guest. It would be simply nonsensical to make any excuses to you for the part I have taken. Even if you had not systematically opposed your interest to mine in this house, I had no other course open. You must see that."

"I believe I owe you my thanks for your forbearance so long," said Charles; "though that was for the sake of my father more than myself. Will you tell me, sir, now we are alone, how long have you known this?"

"Nearly eighteen months," said Father Mackworth promptly.

Mackworth was not an ill-natured man when he was not opposed, and, being a brave man himself, could well appreciate bravery in others. He had knowledge enough of men to know that the revelation of to-day had been as bitter a blow to a passionate, sensitive man like Charles, as he could well endure and live. And he knew that Charles distrusted him, and that all out-of-the-way expressions of condolence would be thrown away; and so, departing from his usual rule of conduct, he spoke for once in a way naturally and sincerely, and said: "I am very, very sorry. I would have done much to avoid this."

Then Mary came in and the Tiernays. Cuthbert did not come down. There was a long, dull dinner, at which Charles forced himself to eat, having a resolution before him. Mary sat scared at the head of the table, and scarcely spoke a word, and, when she rose to go into the drawing-room again, Charles followed her.

She saw that he was coming, and waited for him in the hall. When he shut the dining-room door after him she ran back, and putting her two hands on his shoulders, said—

"Charles! Charles! what is the matter?"

"Nothing, dear; only I have lost my fortune; I am penniless."

"Is it all gone, Charles?"

"All. You will hear how, soon. I just come out to wish my bird good-bye. I am going to London to-morrow."

"Can't you come and talk to me, Charles, a little?"

"No! not to-night. Not to-night."

"You will come to see me at Lady Hainault's in town, Charles?"

"Yes, my love; yes."

"Won't you tell me any more, Charles?"

"No more, my robin. It is good-bye. You will hear all about it soon enough."

"Good-bye."

A kiss, and he was gone up the old staircase towards his own room. When he gained the first landing he turned and looked at her once more, standing alone in the centre of the old hall in the light of a solitary lamp. A lonely, beautiful little figure, with her arms drooping at her sides, and the quiet, dark eyes turned towards him, so lovingly ! And there, in his ruin and desolation, he began to see, for the first time, what others, keener-eyed, had seen long ago. Something that might have been, but could not be now ! And so, saying, " I must not see her again," he went up to his own room, and shut the door on his misery.

Once again he was seen that night. William invaded the stillroom, and got some coffee, which he carried up to him. He found him packing his portmanteau, and he asked William to see to this and to that for him, if he should sleep too long. William made him sit down and take coffee and smoke a cigar, and sat on the footstool at his feet, before the fire, complaining of cold. They sat an hour or two, smoking, talking of old times, of horses and dogs, and birds and trout, as lads do, till Charles said he would go to bed, and William left him.

He had hardly got to the end of the passage, when Charles called him back, and he came.

" I want to look at you again," said Charles ; and he put his two hands on William's shoulders, and looked at him again. Then he said, " Good night," and went in.

William went slowly away, and, passing to a lower storey, came to the door of a room immediately over the main entrance, above the hall. This room was in the turret above the porch. It was Cuthbert's room.

He knocked softly, and there was no answer ; again, and louder. A voice cried querulously, " Come in," and he opened the door.

Cuthbert was sitting before the fire with a lamp beside him and a book on his knee. He looked up and saw a groom before him, and said, angrily—

" I can give no orders to-night. I will not be disturbed to-night."

" It is me, sir," said William.

Cuthbert rose at once. " Come here, brother," he said, "and let me look at you. They told me just now that you were with our brother Charles."

" I stayed with him till he went to bed, and then I came to you."

" How is he ? "

" Very quiet—too quiet."

" Is he going away ? "

" He is going in the morning."

" You must go with him, William," said Cuthbert eagerly.

" I came to tell you that I must go with him, and to ask you for some money."

" God bless you. Don't leave him. Write to me every day. Watch and see what he is inclined to settle to, and then let me know. You must get some education too. You will get it with him as well as anywhere. He must be our first care."

William said yes. He must be their first care. He had suffered a terrible wrong.

" We must get to be as brothers to one another, William," said Cuthbert. " That will come in time. We have one great object in common—Charles ; and that will bring us together. The time was, when I was a fool, that I thought of being a saint, without human affections. I am wiser now. People near death see many things which are hidden in health and youth."

" Near death, Cuthbert ! " said William, calling him so for the first time. " I shall live, please God, to take your children on my knee."

" It is right that you should know, brother, that in a few short years you will be master of Ravenshoe. My heart is gone. I have had an attack to-night."

" But people who are ill don't always die," said William. " Holy Virgin ! you must not go and leave me all abroad in the world like a lost sheep."

" I like to hear you speak like that, William. Two days ago, I was moving heaven and earth to rob you of your just inheritance."

" I like you the better for that. Never think of that again. Does Mackworth know of your illness ? "

" He knows everything."

" If Charles had been a Catholic, would he have concealed this ? "

" No ; I think not. I offered him ten thousand pounds to hush it up."

" I wish he had taken it. I don't want to be a great man. I should have been far happier as it was. I was half a gentleman, and had everything I wanted. Shall you oppose my marrying when Charles is settled ? "

" You must marry, brother. I can never marry, and would

not if I could. You must marry, certainly. The estate is a little involved; but we can soon bring it right. Till you marry, you must be contented with four hundred a year."

William laughed. "I will be content and obedient enough, I warrant you. But, when I speak of marrying, I mean marrying my present sweetheart."

Cuthbert looked up suddenly. "I did not think of that. Who is she?"

"Master Evans's daughter, Jane."

"A fisherman's daughter," said Cuthbert. "William, the mistress of Ravenshoe ought to be a lady."

"The master of Ravenshoe ought to be a gentleman," was William's reply. "And, after your death (which I don't believe in, mind you), he won't be. The master of Ravenshoe then will be only a groom; and what sort of a fine lady would he buy with his money, think you? A woman who would despise him and be ashamed of him. No, by St. George and the dragon, I will marry my old sweetheart or be single!"

"Perhaps you are right, William," said Cuthbert; "and, if you are not, I am not one who has a right to speak about it. Let us in future be honest and straightforward, and have no more miserable *esclandres*, in God's name. What sort of a girl is she?"

"She is handsome enough for a duchess, and she is very quiet and shy."

"All the better. I shall offer not the slightest opposition. She had better know what is in store for her."

"She shall; and the blessings of all the holy saints be on you! I must go now. I must be up at dawn."

"Don't go yet, William. Think of the long night that is before me. Sit with me, and let me get used to your voice. Tell me about the horses, or anything—only don't leave me alone yet."

William sat down with him. They sat long and late. When at last William rose to go, Cuthbert said,—

"You will make a good landlord, William. You have been always a patient, faithful servant, and you will make a good master. Our people will get to love you better than ever they would have loved me. Cling to the old faith. It has served us well so many hundred years. It seems as if God willed that Ravenshoe should not pass from the hands of the faithful. And now, one thing more; I must see Charles before he goes. When you go to wake him in the morning, call me, and I will go with you. Good night!"

In the morning they went up together to wake him. His window was open, and the fresh spring air was blowing in. His books, his clothes, his guns and rods, were piled about in their usual confusion. His dog was lying on the hearthrug, and stretched himself as he came to greet them. The dog had a glove at his feet, and they wondered at it. The curtains of his bed were drawn close. Cuthbert went softly to them and drew them aside. He was not there. The bed was smooth.

"Gone! gone!" cried Cuthbert. "I half feared it. Fly, William, for God's sake, to Lord Ascot's, to Ranford; catch him there, and never leave him again. Come, and get some money, and begone. You may be in time. If we should lose him after all—after all."

William needed no second bidding. In an hour he was at Stonnington. Mr. Charles Ravenshoe had arrived there at daybreak, and had gone on in the coach which started at eight. William posted to Exeter, and at eleven o'clock in the evening saw Lady Ascot at Ranford. Charles Ravenshoe had been there that afternoon, but was gone. And then Lady Ascot, weeping wildly, told him such news as made him break from the room with an oath, and dash through the scared servants in the hall and out into the darkness, to try to overtake the carriage he had discharged, and reach London.

The morning before, Adelaide had eloped with Lord Welter.

CHAPTER XXVIII

FLIGHT

WHEN William left Charles in his room at Ravenshoe, the latter sat down in his chair and began thinking.

The smart of the blow, which had fallen so heavily at first, had become less painful. He knew by intuition that it would be worse on the morrow, and on many morrows; but at present it was alleviated. He began to dread sleeping, for fear of the waking.

He dreaded the night and dreams; and, more than all, the morrow and the departure. He felt that he ought to see Cuthbert again, and he dreaded that. He dreaded the servants seeing him go. He had a horror of parting from all he had known so long, formally. It was natural. It would be so much pain to all concerned; were it not better avoided? He thought of all these things, and tried to persuade himself that these were the reasons which made him do what he had as good as determined to do an hour or two before, what he had in his mind when he called William back in the corridor—to go away alone, and hide and mope like a wounded stag for a little time.

It was his instinct to do so. Perhaps it would have been the best thing for him. At all events, he determined on it, and packed up a portmanteau and carpet-bag, and then sat down again, waiting.

"Yes," he said to himself, "it will be better to do this. I must get away from William, poor lad. He must not follow my fortunes, for many reasons."

His dog had been watching him, looking, with his bright loving eyes, first at him and then at his baggage, wondering what journey they were going on now. When Charles had done packing, and had sat down again in his chair, before the fire, the dog leapt up in his lap unbidden, and laid his head upon his breast.

"Grip, Grip!" said Charles, "I am going away to leave you for ever, Grip. Dogs don't live so long as men, my boy; you will be quietly under the turf and at rest when I shall have forty long years more to go through with."

The dog wagged his tail and pawed his waistcoat. He wanted some biscuit. Charles got him some, and then went on talking.

"I am going to London, old dog. I am going to see what the world is like. I shan't come back before you are dead, Grip, I expect. I have got to win money and a name for the sake of one who is worth winning it for. Very likely I shall go abroad, to the land where the stuff comes from they make sovereigns of, and try my luck at getting some of the yellow rubbish. And she will wait in the old house at Ranford."

He paused here. The thought came upon him. "Would it not be more honourable to absolve Adelaide from her engagement? Was he acting generously in demanding of her to waste the best part of her life in waiting till a ruined man had won fortune and means?"

The answer came, "She loves me. If I can wait, why not she?"

"I have wronged her by such a thought, Grip. Haven't I, my boy?"—And so on. I needn't continue telling you the

nonsense Charles talked to his dog. Men will talk nonsense
to their dogs and friends when they are in love ; and such nonsense is but poor reading at any time. To us who know what
had happened, and how worthless and false Adelaide was, it
would be merely painful and humiliating to hear any more of
it. I only gave you so much to show you how completely
Charles was in the dark, poor fool, with regard to Adelaide's
character, and to render less surprising the folly of his behaviour
after he heard the news at Ranford.

Charles judged every one by his own standard. She had
told him that she loved him ; and perhaps she did, for a time.
He believed her. As for vanity, selfishness, fickleness, calculation, coming in and conquering love, he knew it was impossible
in his own case, and so he conceived it impossible in hers. I
think I have been very careful to impress on you that Charles
was not wise. At all events, if I have softened matters so far
hitherto as to leave you in doubt, his actions, which we shall
have to chronicle immediately, will leave not the slightest doubt
of it. I love the man. I love his very faults in a way. He is a
reality to me, though I may not have the art to make him so to
you. His mad, impulsive way of forming a resolution, and
his honourable obstinacy in sticking to that resolution afterwards, even to the death, are very great faults ; but they are,
more or less, the faults of men who have made a very great
figure in the world, or I have read history wrong. Men with
Charles Ravenshoe's character, and power of patience and application superadded, turn our very brilliant characters for the
most part. Charles had not been drilled into habits of application early enough. Densil's unthinking indulgence had done
him much harm, and he was just the sort of boy to be spoilt at
school—a favourite among the masters and the boys ; always
just up to his work and no more. It is possible that Eton in
one way, or Rugby in another, might have done for him what
Shrewsbury certainly did not. At Eton, thrown at once into a
great, free republic, he might have been forced to fight his way up
to his proper place, which, I believe, would not have been a low
one. At Rugby he would have had his place to win all the same ;
but to help him he would have had all the traditionary school
policy which a great man has left behind him as an immortal
legacy. It was not to be. He was sent to a good and manly
school enough, but one where there was for him too little of
competition. Shrewsbury is, in most respects, the third of the
old schools in England ; but it was, unluckily, not the school
for him. He was too great a man there.

At Oxford, too, he hardly had a fair chance. Lord Welter was there before him, and had got just such a set about him as one would expect from that young gentleman's character and bringing up. These men were Charles's first and only acquaintances at the University. What chance was there among them for correcting and disciplining himself? None. The wonder was, that he came out from among them without being greatly deteriorated. The only friend Charles ever had who could guide him on the way to being a man was John Marston. But John Marston, to say the truth, was sometimes too hard and didactic, and very often roused Charles's obstinacy through want of tact. Marston loved Charles, and thought him better than the ninety and nine who need no repentance ; but it did not fall to Marston's lot to make a man of Charles. Some one took that in hand who never fails.

This is the place for my poor apology for Charles's folly. If I had inserted it before, you would not have attended to it, or would have forgotten it. If I have done my work right, it is merely a statement of the very conclusion you must have come to. In the humiliating scenes which are to follow, I only beg you to remember that Charles Horton was Charles Ravenshoe once ; and that, while he was a gentleman, the people loved him well.

Once, about twelve o'clock, he left his room, and passed through the house to see if all was quiet. He heard the grooms and footmen talking in the servants' hall. He stole back again to his room, and sat before the fire.

In half-an-hour he rose again, and put his portmanteau and carpet-bag outside his room door. Then he took his hat and rose to go.

One more look round the old room! The last for ever! The present overmastered the past, and he looked round almost without recognition. I doubt whether at great crises men have much time for recollecting old associations. I looked once into a room, which had been my home ever since I was six years old, for five-and-twenty years, knowing I should never see it again. But it was to see that I had left nothing behind me. The coach was at the door, and they were calling for me. Now I could draw you a correct map of all the blotches and cracks in the ceiling, as I used to see them when I lay in bed of a morning. But then, I only shut the door and ran down the passage, without even saying " good-bye, old bedroom." Charles Ravenshoe looked round the room thoughtlessly, and then blew out the candle, went out, and shut the door.

The dog whined and scratched to come after him; so he went back again. The old room bathed in a flood of moonlight, and, seen through the open window, the busy chafing sea, calling to him to hasten.

He took a glove from the table, and, laying it on the hearthrug, told the dog to mind it. The dog looked wistfully at him and lay down. The next moment he was outside the door again.

Through long moonlit corridors, down the moonlit hall, through dark passages, which led among the sleeping household, to the door in the priest's tower. The household slept, old men and young men, maids and matrons, quietly, and dreamt of this and of that. And he, who was yesterday nigh master of all, passed out from among them, and stood alone in the world, outside the dark old house, which he had called his home.

Then he felt the deed was done. Was it only the night-wind from the north that laid such a chill hand on his heart? Busy waves upon the shore talking eternally,—" We have come in from the Atlantic, bearing messages; we have come over foundered ships and the bones of drowned sailors, and we tell our messages and die upon the shore."

Shadows that came sweeping from the sea, over lawn and flower-bed, and wrapped the old mansion like a pall for one moment, and then left it shining again in the moonlight, clear, pitiless. Within, warm rooms, warm beds, and the bated breath of sleepers, lying secure in the lap of wealth and order. Without, hard, cold stone. The great world around awaiting to devour one more atom. The bright unsympathizing stars, and the sea, babbling of the men it had rolled over, whose names should never be known.

Now the park, with herds of ghostly startled deer, and the sweet scent of growing fern; and then the rush of the brook, the bridge, and the vista of woodland above; and then the sleeping village.

CHAPTER XXIX

CHARLES'S RETREAT UPON LONDON

PASSING out of the park, Charles set down his burden at the door of a small farm-house at the further end of the village, and knocked. For some time he stood waiting for an answer, and heard no sound save the cows and horses moving about in the warm straw-yard. The beasts were in their home. No terrible new morrow for them. He was without in the street; his home irrevocable miles behind him ; still not a thought of flinching or turning back. He knocked again.

The door was unbarred. An old man looked out, and recognised him with wild astonishment.

"Mr. Charles! Good lord a-mercy! My dear tender heart, what be doing out at this time a-night? With his port-mantle, too, and his carpet bag! Come in, my dear soul, come in. An' so pale and wild! Why, you'm overlooked, Master Charles."

"No, Master Lee, I ain't overlooked. At least not that I know of——"

The old man shook his head, and reserved his opinion.

"—— But I want your gig to go to Stonnington."

"To-night?"

"Ay, to-night. The coach goes at eight in the morning; I want to be there before that."

"Why do'ee start so soon? They'll be all abed in the *Chichester Arms.*"

"I know. I shall get into the stable. I don't know where I shall get. I must go. There is trouble at the Hall."

"Ay! ay! I thought as much, and you'm going away into the world?"

"Yes."

The old man said "Ay! ay!" again, and turned to go up-stairs. Then he held his candle over his head, and looked at Charles; and then went upstairs muttering to himself.

Presently was aroused from sleep a young Devonshire giant, half Hercules, half Antinous, who lumbered down the stairs and into the room, and made his obeisance to Charles with an air of wonder in his great sleepy black eyes, and departed to get the gig.

Of course his first point was Ranford. He got there in the afternoon. He had in his mind at this time, he thinks (for he does not remember it all very distinctly), the idea of going to Australia. He had an idea, too, of being eminently practical and business-like; and so he did a thing which may appear to be trifling, but which was important—one cannot say how much so. He asked for Lord Ascot instead of Lady Ascot.

Lord Ascot was in the library. Charles was shown in to him. He was sitting before the fire, reading a novel. He looked very worn and anxious, and jumped up nervously when Charles was announced. He dropped his book on the floor, and came forward to him, holding out his right hand.

"Charles," he said, "you will forgive me any participation in this. I swear to you——"

Charles thought that by some means the news of what had happened at Ravenshoe had come before him, and that Lord Ascot knew all about Father Mackworth's discovery. Lord Ascot was thinking about Adelaide's flight; so they were at cross purposes.

"Dear Lord Ascot," said Charles, "how could I think of blaming you, my kind old friend?"

"It is devilish gentlemanly of you to speak so, Charles," said Lord Ascot. "I am worn to death about that horse, Haphazard, and other things; and this has finished me. I have been reading a novel to distract my mind. I must win the Derby, you know; by Gad, I must."

"Whom have you got, Lord Ascot?"

"Wells."

"You couldn't do better, I suppose?"

"I suppose not. You don't know—I'd rather not talk any more about it, Charles."

"Lord Ascot, this is, as you may well guess, the last time I shall ever see you. I want you to do me a favour."

"I will do it, my dear Charles, with the greatest pleasure. Any reparation——"

"Hush, my lord! I only want a certificate. Will you read this which I have written in pencil, and, if you conscientiously can, copy in your own hand, and sign it. Also, if I send to you a reference, will you confirm it?"

Lord Ascot read what Charles had written, and said—

"Yes, certainly. You are going to change your name then?"

"I must bear that name now; I am going abroad."

Lord Ascot wrote—

"The undermentioned Charles Horton I have known ever since he was a boy. His character is beyond praise in every way. He is a singularly bold and dexterous rider, and is thoroughly up to the management of horses.

"Ascot."

"You have improved upon my text, Lord Ascot," said Charles. "It is like your kindheartedness. The mouse may offer to help the lion, my lord; and, although the lion may know how little likely it is that he should require help, yet he may take it as a sign of goodwill on the part of the poor mouse. Now, good-bye, my lord; I must see Lady Ascot, and then be off."

Lord Ascot wished him kindly good-bye, and took up his novel again. Charles went alone up to Lady Ascot's room.

He knocked at the door, and received no answer; so he went in. Lady Ascot was there, although she had not answered him. She was sitting upright by the fire, staring at the door, with her hands folded on her lap. A fine brave-looking old lady at all times, but just now, Charles thought, with that sweet look of pity showing itself principally about the corners of the gentle old mouth, more noble-looking than ever!

"May I come in, Lady Ascot?" said Charles.

"My dearest own boy! You must come in and sit down. You must be very quiet over it. Try not to make a scene, my dear. I am not strong enough. It has shaken me so terribly. I heard you had come, and were with Ascot. And I have been trembling in every limb. Not from terror so much of you in your anger, as because my conscience is not clear. I may have hidden things from you, Charles, which you ought to have known." And Lady Ascot began crying silently.

Charles felt the blood going from his cheeks to his heart. His interview with Lord Ascot had made him suspect something further was wrong than what he knew of, and his suspicions were getting stronger every moment. He sat down quite quietly, looking at Lady Ascot, and spoke not one word. Lady Ascot, wiping her eyes, went on; and Charles's heart began to beat with a dull heavy pulsation, like the feet of those who carry a coffin.

"I ought to have told you what was going on between them before she went to old Lady Hainault. I ought to have told you of what went on before Lord Hainault was married. I can never forgive myself, Charles. You may upbraid me, and I will sit here and make not one excuse. But I must say that I never for one moment thought that she was anything more than light-headed. I,—oh, Lord! I never dreamt it would have come to this."

"Are you speaking of Adelaide, Lady Ascot?" said Charles.

"Of course I am," she said, almost peevishly. "If I had ever——"

"Lady Ascot," said Charles quietly, "you are evidently speaking of something of which I have not heard. What has Adelaide done?"

The old lady clasped her hands above her head. "Oh, weary, weary day! And I thought that he had heard it all, and that the blow was broken. The cowards! they have left it to a poor old woman to tell him at last."

"Dear Lady Ascot, you evidently have not heard of what a terrible fate has befallen me. I am a ruined man, and I am very patient. I had one hope left in the world, and I fear that you are going to cut it away from me. I am very quiet, and will make no scene; only tell me what has happened."

"Adelaide!—be proud, Charles, be angry, furious—you Ravenshoes can!—be a man, but don't look like that. Adelaide, dead to honour and good fame, has gone off with Welter!"

Charles walked towards the door.

"That is enough. Please let me go. I can't stand any more at present. You have been very kind to me and to her, and I thank you and bless you for it. The son of a bastard blesses you for it. Let me go—let me go!"

Lady Ascot had stepped actively to the door, and had laid one hand on the door and one on his breast. "You shall not go," she said, "till you have told me what you mean!"

"How? I cannot stand any more at present."

"What do you mean by being the son of a bastard?"

"I am the son of James, Mr. Ravenshoe's keeper. He was the illegitimate son of Mr. Petre Ravenshoe."

"Who told you this?" said Lady Ascot.

"Cuthbert."

"How did he know it?"

Charles told her all.

"So the priest has found that out, eh?" said Lady Ascot. "It seems true"; and, as she said so, she moved back from the door. "Go to your old bedroom, Charles. It will always be ready for you while this house is a house. And come down to me presently. Where is Lord Saltire?"

"At Lord Segur's."

Charles went out of the room, and out of the house, and was seen no more. Lady Ascot sat down by the fire again.

"The one blow has softened the other," she said. "I will never keep another secret after this. It was for Alicia's sake and for Petre's that I did it, and now see what has become of it. I shall send for Lord Saltire. The boy must have his rights, and shall, too."

So the brave old woman sat down and wrote to Lord Saltire. We shall see what she wrote to him in the proper place. Not now. She sat calmly and methodically writing, with her kind old face wreathing into a smile as she went on. And Charles, the madman, left the house, and posted off to London, only intent on seeking to lose himself among the sordid crowd, so that no man he had ever called a friend should set eyes on him again.

CHAPTER XXX

MR. SLOANE

CHARLES RAVENSHOE had committed suicide—committed suicide as deliberately as any maddened wretch had done that day in all the wide miserable world. He knew it very well, and was determined to go on with it. He had not hung himself, or drowned himself, but he had committed deliberate suicide, and he knew—knew well—that his obstinacy would carry him through to the end.

What is suicide nine cases out of ten? Any one can tell you. It is the act of a mad, proud coward, who flies, by his own deed, not from humiliation or disgrace, but, as he fancies, from feeling the consequences of them—who flies to unknown, doubtful evils, sooner than bear positive, present, undoubted ones. All this had Charles done, buoying him up with this excuse and that excuse, and fancying that he was behaving, the cur, like Bayard, or Lieutenant Willoughby—a greater than Bayard—all the time.

The above is Charles's idea of the matter himself, put in the third person for form's sake. I don't agree with all he says about himself. I don't deny that he did a very foolish thing, but I incline to believe that there was something noble and self-reliant in his doing it. Think a moment. He had only two courses open to him—the one (I put it coarsely) to eat humble pie, to go back to Cuthbert and Mackworth and accept their offers; the other to do as he had done—to go alone into the world, and stand by himself. He did the latter, as we shall see. He could not face Ravenshoe, or any connected with it, again. It had been proved that he was an unwilling impostor, of base, low blood, and his sister—ah! one more pang, poor heart!—his sister Ellen, what was she?

Little doubt—little doubt! Better for both of them if they had never been born! He was going to London, and, perhaps, might meet her there! All the vice and misery of the country got thrown into that cesspool. When anything had got too foul for the pure country air, men said, Away with it; throw it into the great dunghill, and let it rot there. Was he not going there himself? It was fit she should be there before him! They would meet for certain!

How would they meet? Would she be in silks and satins, or in rags? flaunting in her carriage, or shivering in an archway? What matter? Was not shame the heritage of the "lower orders"? The pleasures of the rich must be ministered to by the "lower orders," or what was the use of money or rank? He was one of the lower orders now. He must learn his lesson; learn to cringe and whine like the rest of them. It would be hard, but it must be learnt. The dogs rose against it some-times, but it never paid.

The devil was pretty busy with poor Charles in his despair, you see. This was all he had left after three and twenty years of careless idleness and luxury. His creed had been, "I am a Ravenshoe," and lo! one morning, he was a Ravenshoe no longer. A poor crow, that had been fancying himself an eagle. A crow! "By heavens," he thought, "he was not even that." A nonentity, turned into the world to find his own value! What were honour, honesty, virtue to him? Why, nothing—words! He must truckle and pander for his living. Why not go back and truckle to Father Mackworth? There was time yet.

No!

Why not? Was it pride only? We have no right to say what it was. If it was only pride, it was better than nothing. Better to have that straw only to cling to, than to be all alone in the great sea with nothing. We have seen that he has done nothing good, with circumstances all in his favour; let us see if he can in any way hold his own, with circumstances all against him.

"America?" he thought once. "They are all gentlemen there. If I could only find her, and tear her jewels off, we would go there together. But she must be found—she must be found. I will never leave England till she goes with me. We shall be brought together. We shall see one another. I love her as I never loved her before. What a sweet, gentle little love she was! My darling! And, when I have kissed her, I never dreamed she was my sister. My pretty love!

Ellen, Ellen, I am coming to you. Where are you, my love?"

He was alone, in a railway carriage, leaning out to catch the fresh wind, as he said this. He said it once again, this time aloud. "Where are you, my sister?"

Where was she? Could he have only seen! *We* may be allowed to see, though *he* could not. Come forward into the great Babylon with me, while he is speeding on towards it; we will rejoin him in an instant.

In a small luxuriously furnished hall, there stands a beautiful woman, dressed modestly in the garb of a servant. She is standing with her arms folded, and a cold, stern, curious look on her face. She is looking towards the hall-door, which is held open by a footman. She is waiting for some one who is coming in; and two travellers enter, a man and a woman. She goes up to the woman, and says quietly, "I bid you welcome, madam." Who are these people? Is that waiting-woman Ellen? and these travellers, are they Lord Welter and Adelaide? Let us get back to poor Charles; better be with him than here!

We must follow him closely. We must see why, in his despair, he took the extraordinary resolution that he did. Not that I shall take any particular pains to follow the exact process of his mind in arriving at his determination. If the story has hitherto been told well, it will appear nothing extraordinary, and, if otherwise, an intelligent reader would very soon detect any attempt at bolstering up ill-told facts by elaborate, soul-analyzing theories.

He could have wished the train would have run on for ever; but he was aroused by the lights growing thicker and more brilliant, and he felt that they were nearing London, and that the time for action was come.

The great plunge was taken, and he was alone in the cold street—alone, save for the man who carried his baggage. He stood for a moment or so, confused with the rush of carriages of all sorts which were taking the people from the train, till he was aroused by the man asking him where he was to go to.

Charles said, without thinking, "The Warwick Hotel," and thither they went. For a moment he regretted that he had said so, but the next moment he said aloud, "Let us eat and drink, for to-morrow we die!"

The man turned round and begged his pardon. Charles did not answer him; and the man went on, wondering what sort of a young gentleman he had got hold of.

The good landlord was glad to see him. Would he have

dinner?—a bit of fish and a lamb chop, for instance? Then it suddenly struck Charles that he was hungry—ravenous. He laughed aloud at the idea; and the landlord laughed too, and rubbed his hands. Should it be whiting or smelts now? he asked.

"Anything," said Charles, "so long as you feed me quick. And give me wine, will you, of some sort; I want to drink. Give me sherry, will you? And I say, let me taste some now, and then I can see if I like it. I am very particular about my wine, you must know."

In a few minutes a waiter brought in a glass of wine, and waited to know how Charles liked it. He told the man he could go, and he would tell him at dinner-time. When the man was gone, he looked at the wine with a smile. Then he took it up, and poured it into the coal-scuttle.

"Not yet," he said, "not yet! I'll try something else before I try to drink my troubles away." And then he plunged into the *Times*.

He had no sooner convinced himself that Lord Aberdeen was tampering with the honour of the country by not declaring war, than he found himself profoundly considering what had caused that great statesman to elope with Adelaide, and whether, in case of a Russian war, Lady Ascot would possibly convict Father Mackworth of having caused it. Then Lady Ascot came into the room with a large bottle of medicine and a Testament, announcing that she was going to attend a sick gun-boat. And then, just as he began to see that he was getting sleepy, to sleep he went, fast as a top.

Half-an-hour's sleep restored him, and dinner made things look different. "After all," he said, as he sipped his wine, "here is only the world on the one side and I on the other. I am utterly reckless, and can sink no further. I will get all the pleasure out of life that I can, honestly; for I am an honest man still, and mean to be. I love you, Madame Adelaide, and you have used me worse than a hound, and made me desperate. If he marries you, I will come forward some day and disgrace you. If you had only waited till you knew everything, I could have forgiven you. I'll get a place as a footman, and talk about you in the servants' hall. All London shall know you were engaged to me."

"Poor dear, pretty Adelaide: as if I would ever hurt a hair of your head, my sweet love! Silly——"

The landlord came in. There was most excellent company in the smoking-room. Would he condescend to join them?

Company and tobacco ! Charles would certainly join them ; so he had his wine carried in.

There was a fat gentleman, with a snub nose, who was a Conservative. There was a tall gentleman, with a long nose, who was Liberal. There was a short gentleman, with no particular kind of nose, who was Radical. There was a handsome gentleman, with big whiskers, who was commercial ; and there was a gentleman with bandy legs, who was horsy.

I strongly object to using a slang adjective, if any other can be got to supply its place ; but by doing so sometimes one avoids a periphrasis, and does not spoil one's period. Thus, I know of no predicate for a gentleman with a particular sort of hair, complexion, dress, whiskers, and legs, except the one I have used above, and so it must stand.

As Providence would have it, Charles sat down between the landlord and the horsy man, away from the others. He smoked his cigar, and listened to the conversation.

The Conservative gentleman coalesced with the Liberal gentleman on the subject of Lord Aberdeen's having sold the country to the Russians ; the Radical gentleman also came over to them on that subject ; and for a time the Opposition seemed to hold an overwhelming majority, and to be merely allowing Aberdeen's Government to hold place longer, that they might commit themselves deeper. In fact, things seemed to be going all one way, as is often the case in coalition ministries just before a grand crash, when the Radical gentleman caused a violent split in the cabinet, by saying that the whole complication had been brought about by the machinations of the aristocracy—which assertion caused the Conservative gentleman to retort in unmeasured language ; and then the Liberal gentleman, trying to trim, found himself distrusted and despised by both parties. Charles listened to them, amused for the time to hear them quoting, quite unconsciously, whole sentences out of their respective leading papers, and then was distracted by the horsy man saying to him—

"Darn politics ! What horse will win the Derby, sir ?"

"Haphazard," said Charles, promptly. This, please to remember, was Lord Ascot's horse, which we have seen before.

The landlord immediately drew closer up.

The horsy man looked at Charles, and said, " H'm ; and what has made my lord scratch him for the Two Thousand, sir ?"

And so on. We have something to do with Haphazard's

winning the Derby, as we shall see ; and we have still more to do with the result of Charles's conversation with the "horsy man." But we have certainly nothing to do with a wordy discussion about the various horses which stood well for the great race (wicked, lovely darlings, how many souls of heroes have they sent to Hades !), and so we will spare the reader. The conclusion of their conversation was the only important part of it.

Charles said to the horsy man on the stairs, "Now you know everything. I am penniless, friendless, and nameless. Can you put me in the way of earning my living honestly ? "

And he said, "I can, and I will. This gentleman is a fast man, but he is rich. You'll have your own way. Maybe, you'll see some queer things, but what odds ? "

"None to me," said Charles ; "I can always leave him."

"And go back to your friends, like a wise young gentleman, eh ? " said the other, kindly.

"I am not a gentleman," said Charles. "I told you so, before. I am a gamekeeper's son ; I swear to you I am. I have been petted and pampered till I look like one, but I am not."

"You are a deuced good imitation," said the other. "Good night ; come to me at nine, mind."

At this time, Lady Ascot had despatched her letter to Lord Saltire, and had asked for Charles. The groom of the chambers said that Mr. Ravenshoe had left the house immediately after his interview with her ladyship, three hours before.

She started up—"Gone !—Whither ? "

"To Twyford, my lady."

"Send after him, you idiot ! Send the grooms after him on all my lord's horses. Send a lad on Haphazard, and let him race the train to London. Send the police ! He has stolen my purse, with ten thousand gold guineas in it !—I swear he has. Have him bound hand and foot, and bring him back, on your life. If you stay there, I will kill you ! "

The violent old animal nature, dammed up so long by creeds and formulas, had broken out at last. The decorous Lady Ascot was transformed in one instant into a terrible, grey-headed, magnificent old Alecto, hurling her awful words abroad in a sharp, snarling voice, that made the hair of him that heard it to creep upon his head. The man fled, and shut Lady Ascot in alone.

She walked across the room, and beat her withered old hands

against the wall. "Oh, miserable, wicked old woman!" she cried aloud. "How surely have your sins found you out! After concealing a crime for so many years, to find the judgment fall on such an innocent and beloved head! Alicia, Alicia, I did this for your sake. Charles, Charles, come back to the old woman before she dies, and tell her you forgive her."

CHAPTER XXXI

LIEUTENANT HORNBY

CHARLES had always been passionately fond of horses and of riding. He was a consummate horseman, and was so perfectly accomplished in everything relating to horses, that I really believe that in time he might actually have risen to the dizzy height of being stud-groom to a great gentleman or nobleman. He had been brought up in a great horse-riding house, and had actually gained so much experience, and had so much to say on matters of this kind, that once, at Oxford, a promising young nobleman cast, so to speak, an adverse opinion of Charles into George Simmonds' own face. Mr. Simmonds looked round on the offender mildly and compassionately, and said, "If any undergraduate *could* know, my lord, that undergraduate's name would be Ravenshoe of Paul's. But he is young, my lord. And, in consequence, ignorant." His lordship didn't say anything after that.

I have kept this fact in the background rather, hitherto, because it has not been of any very great consequence. It becomes of some consequence now, for the first time. I enlarged a little upon Charles being a rowing man, because rowing and training had, for good or for evil, a certain effect on his character. (Whether for good or for evil, you must determine for yourselves.) And I now mention the fact of his being a consummate horseman, because a considerable part of the incidents which follow arise from the fact.

Don't think for one moment that you are going to be bored by stable talk. You will have simply none of it. It only amounts to this—that Charles, being fond of horses, took up with a certain line of life, and in that line of life met with certain adventures which have made his history worth relating.

When he met the "horsy" man next morning, he was not dressed like a gentleman. In his store he had some old clothes, which he used to wear at Ravenshoe, in the merry old days when he would be up with daylight to exercise the horses on the moor—cord trousers, and so on, which, being now old and worn, made him look uncommonly like a groom out of place. And what contributed to the delusion was, that for the first time in his life he wore no shirt collar, but allowed his blue-spotted neck-cloth to border on his honest red face, without one single quarter of an inch of linen. And, if it ever pleases your lordship's noble excellence to look like a blackguard for any reason, allow me to recommend you to wear a dark neck-tie and no collar. Your success will be beyond your utmost hopes.

Charles met his new friend in the bar, and touched his hat to him. His friend laughed, and said, that would do, but asked how long he thought he could keep that sort of thing going. Charles said, as long as was necessary; and they went out together.

They walked as far as a street leading out of one of the largest and best squares (I mean B—lg—e Sq—e, but I don't like to write it at full length), and stopped at the door of a handsome shop. Charles knew enough of London to surmise that the first floor was let to a man of some wealth; and he was right.

The door was opened, and his friend was shown up stairs, while he was told to wait in the hall. Now Charles began to perceive, with considerable amusement, that he was acting a part—that he was playing, so to speak, at being something other than what he really was, and that he was perhaps over-doing it. In this house, which yesterday he would have entered as an equal, he was now playing at being a servant. It was immensely amusing. He wiped his shoes very clean, and sat down on a bench in the hall, with his hat between his knees, as he had seen grooms do. It is no use wondering; one never finds out anything by that. But I do wonder, nevertheless, whether Charles, had he only known in what relation the master of that house stood to himself, would or would not have set the house on fire or cut its owner's throat. When he did find out, he did neither the one thing nor the other; but he had been a good deal tamed by that time.

Presently a servant came down, and, eyeing Charles curiously as a prospective fellow-servant, told him civilly to walk up stairs. He went up. The room was one of a hand-

some suite, and overlooked the street. Charles saw at a
glance that it was the room of a great dandy. A dandy, if
not of the first water, most assuredly high up in the second.
Two things only jarred on his eye in his hurried glance round
the room. There was too much bric-a-brac, and too many
flowers. "I wonder if he is a gentleman," thought Charles.
His friend of the night before was standing in a respectful
attitude, leaning on the back of a chair, and Charles looked
round for the master of the house, eagerly. He had to cast
his eyes downward to see him, for he was lying back on an
easy chair, half hidden by the breakfast-table.

There he was—Charles's master : the man who was going to
buy him. Charles cast one intensely eager glance at him, and
was satisfied. " He will do at a pinch," said he to himself.

There were a great many handsome and splendid things in
that room, but the owner of them was by far the handsomest
and most splendid thing there.

He was a young man, with very pale and delicate features,
and a singularly amiable cast of face, who wore a moustache,
with the long whiskers which were just then coming into
fashion ; and he was dressed in a splendid uniform of blue,
gold, and scarlet, for he had been on duty that morning, and
had just come in. His sabre was cast upon the floor before
him, and his shako was on the table. As Charles looked at
him, he passed his hand over his hair. There was one ring
on it, but *such* a ring ! "That's a high-bred hand enough,"
said Charles to himself. "And he hasn't got too much
jewellery on him. I wonder who the deuce he is ? "

"This is the young man, sir," said Charles's new friend.

Lieutenant Hornby was looking at Charles, and after a
pause, said—

"I take him on your recommendation, Sloane. I have
no doubt he will do. He seems a good fellow. You are a
good fellow, ain't you ? " he continued, addressing Charles
personally, with that happy graceful insolence which is the
peculiar property of prosperous and entirely amiable young
men, and which charms one in spite of oneself.

Charles replied, " I am quarrelsome sometimes among my
equals, but I am always good-tempered among horses."

"That will do very well. You may punch the other two
lads' heads as much as you like. They don't mind me ;
perhaps they may you. You will be over them. You will
have the management of everything. You will have unlimited
opportunities of robbing and plundering me, with an entire

absence of all chance of detection. But you won't do it. It isn't your line, I saw at once. Let me look at your hand."

Charles gave him the great ribbed paw which served him in that capacity. And Hornby said—

"Ha! Gentleman's hand. No business of mine. Don't wear that ring, will you? A groom mustn't wear such rings as that. Any character?"

Charles showed him the letter Lord Ascot had written.

"Lord Ascot, eh? I know Lord Welter, slightly."

"The deuce you do!" thought Charles.

"Were you in Lord Ascot's stables?"

"No, sir. I am the son of Squire Ravenshoe's gamekeeper. The Ravenshoes and my Lord Ascot's family are connected by marriage. Ravenshoe is in the west country, sir. Lord Ascot knows me by repute, sir, and has a good opinion of me."

"It is perfectly satisfactory. Sloane, will you put him in the way of his duties? Make the other lads understand that he is master, will you? You may go."

CHAPTER XXXII

SOME OF THE HUMOURS OF A LONDON MEWS

So pursuing the course of our story, we have brought ourselves to the present extraordinary position. That Charles Ravenshoe, of Ravenshoe, in the county Devonshire, Esquire, and some time of St. Paul's College, Oxford, has hired himself out as groom to Lieutenant Hornby, of the 140th Hussars, and that also the above-named Charles Ravenshoe was not, and never had been, Charles Ravenshoe at all, but somebody else all the time, to wit, Charles Horton, a gamekeeper's son, if indeed he was even this, having been christened under a false name.

The situation is so extraordinary and so sad, that having taken the tragical view of it in the previous chapter, we must of necessity begin to look on the brighter side of it now. And this is the better art, because it is exactly what Charles began to do himself. One blow succeeded the other so rapidly, the utter bouleversement of all that he cared about in the world. Father, friends, position, mistress, all lost in one day, had brought on a kind of light-hearted desperation, which had the effect of making him seek company, and talk boisterously and loud all day. It was not unnatural in so young and vigorous a man. But if he woke in the night, there was the cold claw grasping his heart. Well, I said we would have none of this at present, and we won't.

Patient old earth, intent only on doing her duty in her set courses, and unmindful of the mites which had been set to make love or war on her bosom, and the least of whom was worth her whole well-organized mass, had rolled on, and on, until by bringing that portion of her which contains the island of Britain, gradually in greater proximity to the sun, she had produced that state of things on that particular part of her which is known among mortals as spring. Now, I am very anxious to please all parties. Some people like a little circumlocution, and for them the above paragraph was written; others do not, and for them, I state that it was the latter end of May, and beg them not to read the above flight of fancy, but to consider it as never having been written.

It was spring. On the sea-coast, the watchers at the lighthouses and the preventive stations began to walk about in their shirt-sleeves, and trim up their patches of spray-beaten garden, hedged with tree-mallow and tamarisk, and to thank God that the long howling winter nights were past for a time. The fishermen shouted merrily one to another as they put off from the shore, no longer dreading a twelve hours' purgatory of sleet and freezing mist and snow; saying to one another how green the land looked, and how pleasant mackerel time was after all. Their wives, light-hearted at the thought that the wild winter was past, and that they were not widows, brought their work out to the doors, and gossiped pleasantly in the sun, while some of the bolder boys began to paddle about in the surf, and try to believe that the Gulf Stream had come in, and that it was summer again, and not only spring.

In inland country places the barley was all in and springing, the meadows were all bush-harrowed, rolled, and laid up for hay; nay, in early places, brimful of grass, spangled with purple orchises, and in moist rich places golden with marsh marigold, over which the south-west wind passed pleasantly, bringing a sweet perfume of growing vegetation, which gave those who smelt it a tendency to lean against gates, and stiles, and such places, and think what a delicious season it was, and wish it were to last for ever. The young men began to slip away from work somewhat early of an evening, not (as now) to the parade ground, or the butts, but to take their turn at the wicket on the green, where Sir John (our young landlord) was to be found in a scarlet flannel shirt, bowling away like a catapult, at all comers, till the second bell began to ring, and he had to dash off and dress. Now lovers walking by moonlight in deep banked lanes began to notice how dark and broad the shadows grew, and to wait at the lane's end by the river, to listen to the nightingale, with his breast against the thorn, ranging on from height to height of melodious passion, petulant at his want of art, till he broke into one wild jubilant burst, and ceased, leaving night silent, save for the whispering of new-born insects, and the creeping sound of reviving vegetation.

Spring. The great renewal of the lease. The time when nature-worshippers made good resolutions, to be very often broken before the leaves fall. The time the country becomes once more habitable and agreeable. Does it make any difference in the hundred miles of brick and mortar called London, save, in so far as it makes every reasonable Christian pack up his portmanteau and fly to the green fields, and lovers' lanes before-mentioned (though it takes two people for the latter sort of business)? Why, yes; it makes a difference to London certainly, by bringing somewhere about 10,000 people, who have got sick of shooting and hunting through the winter months, swarming into the west end of it, and making it what is called full.

I don't know that they are wrong after all, for London is a mighty pleasant place in the season (we don't call it spring on the paving-stones). At this time the windows of the great houses in the squares begin to be brilliant with flowers; and, under the awnings of the balconies, one sees women moving about in the shadow. Now, all through the short night, one hears the ceaseless low rolling thunder of beautiful carriages, and in the daytime also the noise ceases not. All through the west end of the town there is a smell of flowers, of fresh-watered roads, and Macassar oil; while at Covent Garden, the scent of the peaches and pine-apples begins to prevail over that of rotten cabbage-stalks. The fiddlers are all fiddling away at concert pitch for their lives, the actors are all acting their very hardest, and the men who look after the horses, have never a minute to call their own, day or night.

It is neither to dukes nor duchesses, to actors nor fiddlers, that we must turn our attention just now, but to a man who was sitting in a wheelbarrow, watching a tame jackdaw.

The place was a London mews, behind one of the great squares—the time was afternoon. The weather was warm and sunny. All the proprietors of the horses were out riding or driving, and so the stables were empty and the mews were quiet.

This was about a week after Charles's degradation, almost the first hour he had to himself in the daytime, and so he sat pondering on his unhappy lot.

Lord Ballyroundtower's coachman's wife was hanging out the clothes. She was an Irishwoman off the estate (his lordship's Irish residences, I see on referring to the peerage, are, "The Grove," Blarney, and "Swatewathers," near Avoca). When I say that she was hanging out the clothes, I am hardly correct, for she was only fixing the lines up to do so, and being of short stature, and having to reach was naturally showing her heels, and the jackdaw perceiving this, began to hop stealthily across the yard. Charles saw what was coming and became deeply interested. He would not have spoken for his life. The jackdaw sidled up to her, and began digging into her tendon Achilles with his hard bill with a force and rapidity which showed that he was fully aware of the fact, that the amusement, like most pleasant things, could not last long, and must therefore be made the most of. Some women would have screamed and faced round at the first assault. Not so our Irish friend. She endured the anguish until she had succeeded in fastening the clothes-line round the post, and then she turned round on the jackdaw, who had fluttered away to a safe distance, and denounced him.

"Bad cess to ye, ye impident divvle, sure its Sathan's own sister's son ye are, ye dirty prothestant, pecking at the hales of an honest woman, daughter of my lord's own man, Corny O'Brine, as was a dale bether nor them as sits on whale-barrows and sets ye on too't—" (this was levelled at Charles, so he politely took off his cap, and bowed).

"Though, God forgive me, there's some sitting on whale-barrows as should be sitting in drawing-rooms, may be (here the jackdaw raised one foot, and said 'Jark'). Get out ye baste; don't ye hear me blessed lady's own bird swearing at ye, like a gentleman's bird as he is. A pretty dear."

This was strictly true. Lord Ballyroundtower's brother, the Honourable Frederick Mulligan, was a lieutenant in the navy. A short time before this, being on the Australian station, and wishing to make his sister-in-law a handsome present, he had commissioned a Sydney Jew bird-dealer to get him a sulphur-

crested cockatoo, price no object, but the best talker in the
colony. The Jew faithfully performed his behest; he got
him the best talking cockatoo in the colony, and the Hon.
Fred, brought it home in triumph to his sister-in-law's drawing
room in Belgrave Square.

The bird was a beautiful talker. There was no doubt about
that. It had such an amazingly distinct enunciation. But
then the bird was not always discreet. Nay, to go further,
the bird never *was* discreet. He had been educated by a
convict bullock-driver, and finished off by the sailors on board
H.M.S. *Actæon;* and really you know, sometimes he did say
things he ought not to have said. It was all very well
pretending that you couldn't hear him, but it rendered conversation
impossible. You were always in agony at what was to
come next. One afternoon, a great many people were there,
calling. Old Lady Hainault was there. The bird was worse
than ever. Every body tried to avoid a silence, but it came,
inexorably. That awful old woman, Lady Hainault, broke it
by saying that she thought Fred Mulligan must have been
giving the bird private lessons himself. After that you know
it wouldn't do. Fred might be angry, but the bird must go to
the mews.

So there the bird was, swearing dreadfully at the jackdaw.
At last her ladyship's pug-dog who was staying with the
coachman for medical treatment, got excited, bundled out of
the house, and attacked the jackdaw. The jackdaw formed
square to resist cavalry, and sent the dog howling into the
house again quicker than he came out. After which the bird
barked and came and sat on the dunghill by Charles.

The mews itself, as I said, was very quiet, with a smell
of stable, subdued by a fresh scent of sprinkled water; but at
the upper end it joined a street leading from Belgrave Square
towards the Park, which was by no means quiet, and which
smelt of geraniums and heliotropes. Carriage after carriage
went blazing past the end of the mews, along the street, like
figures across the disk of a magic lanthorn. Some had scarlet
breeches, and some blue; and there were pink bonnets, and
yellow bonnets, and Magenta bonnets; and Charles sat on the
wheelbarrow by the dunghill, and looked at it all, perfectly
contented.

A stray dog lounged in out of the street. It was a cur dog
—that any one might see. It was a dog which had bit its
rope and run away, for the rope was round its neck now; and
it was a thirsty dog, for it went up to the pump and licked the

stones. Charles went and pumped for it, and it drank. Then, evidently considering that Charles, by his act of good nature, had acquired authority over its person, and having tried to do without a master already, and having found it wouldn't do, it sat down beside Charles and declined to proceed any further.

There was a public-house at the corner of the mews, where it joined the street; and on the other side of the street you could see one house, No. 16. The footman of No. 16 was in the area, looking through the railings. A thirsty man came to the public-house on horseback, and drank a pot of beer at a draught, turning the pot upside down. It was too much for the footman, who disappeared.

Next came a butcher with a tray of meat, who turned into the area of No. 16, and left the gate open. After him came a blind man, led by a dog. The dog, instead of going straight on, turned down the area steps after the butcher. The blind man thought he was going round the corner. Charles saw what would happen; but, before he had time to cry out, the blind man had plunged headlong down the area steps and disappeared, while from the bottom, as from the pit, arose the curses of the butcher.

Charles and others assisted the blind man up, gave him some beer, and sent him on his way. Charles watched him. After he had gone a little way, he began striking spitefully at where he thought his dog was, with his stick. The dog was evidently used to this amusement, and dexterously avoided the blows. Finding vertical blows of no avail, the blind man tried horizontal ones, and caught an old gentleman across the shins, making him drop his umbrella and catch up his leg. The blind man promptly asked an alms from him, and, not getting one, turned the corner; and Charles saw him no more.

The hot street and, beyond, the square, the dusty lilacs and laburnums, and the crimson hawthorns. What a day for a bathe! outside the gentle surf, with the sunny headlands right and left, and the moor sleeping quietly in the afternoon sunlight, and Lundy, like a faint blue cloud on the Atlantic horizon, and the old house—— He was away at Ravenshoe on a May afternoon.

They say poets are never sane; but are they ever mad? Never. Even old Cowper saved himself from actual madness by using his imagination. Charles was no poet; but he was a good day-dreamer, and so now, instead of maddening himself in his squalid brick prison, he was away in the old bay, bathing and fishing, and wandering up the old stream, breast high among king-fern under the shadowy oaks.

Bricks and mortar, carriages and footmen, wheelbarrows and dunghills, all came back in one moment, and settled on his outward senses with a jar. For there was a rattle of horse's feet on the stones, and the clank of a sabre, and Lieutenant Hornby, of the 140th Hussars (Prince Arthur's Own), came branking into the yard, with two hundred pounds' worth of trappings on him, looking out for his servant. He was certainly a splendid fellow, and Charles looked at him with a certain kind of pride, as on something that he had a share in.

"Come round to the front door, Horton, and take my horse up to the barracks" (the Queen had been to the station that morning, and his guard was over).

Charles walked beside him round into Grosvenor Place. He could not avoid stealing a glance up at the magnificent apparition beside him ; and, as he did so, he met a pair of kind grey eyes looking down on him.

"You mustn't sit and mope there, Horton," said the lieutenant ; "it never does to mope. I know it is infernally hard to help it, and of course you can't associate with servants, and that sort of thing, at first ; but you will get used to it. If you think I don't know you are a gentleman, you are mistaken. I don't know who you are, and shall not try to find out. I'll lend you books or anything of that sort ; but you mustn't brood over it. I can't stand seeing my fellows wretched, more especially a fellow like you."

If it had been to save his life, Charles couldn't say a word. He looked up at the lieutenant and nodded his head. The lieutenant understood him well enough, and said to himself—

"Poor fellow ! "

So there arose between these two a feeling which lightened Charles's servitude, and which before the end came, had grown into a liking. Charles's vengeance was not for Hornby, for the injury did not come from him. His vengeance was reserved for another, and we shall see how he took it.

CHAPTER XXXIII

A GLIMPSE OF SOME OLD FRIENDS

HITHERTO I have been able to follow Charles right on without leaving him for one instant : now, however, that he is reduced to sitting on a wheelbarrow in a stable-yard, we must see a little less of him. He is, of course, our principal object; but he has removed himself from the immediate sphere of all our other acquaintances, and so we must look up some of them, and see how far they, though absent, are acting on his destiny —nay, we must look up every one of them sooner or later, for there is not one who is not in some way concerned in his adventures past and future.

By reason of her age, her sex, and her rank, my Lady Ascot claims our attention first. We left the dear old woman in a terrible taking, on finding that Charles had suddenly left the house and disappeared. Her wrath gave way to tears, and her tears to memory. Bitterly she blamed herself now for what seemed, years ago, such a harmless deceit. It was not too late. Charles might be found; would come back, surely—would come back to his poor old aunt ! He would never—hush ! it won't do to think of that !

Lady Ascot thought of a brilliant plan, and put it into immediate execution. She communicated with Mr. Scotland Yard, the eminent ex-detective officer, forwarding a close description of Charles, and a request that he might be found, alive or dead, immediately. Her efforts were crowned with immediate and unlooked-for success. In a week's time the detective had discovered, not one Charles Ravenshoe, but three, from which her ladyship might take her choice. But the worst of it was that neither of the three was Charles Ravenshoe. There was a remarkable point of similarity between Charles and them, certainly ; and that point was, that they were all three young gentlemen under a cloud, and had all three dark hair and prominent features. Here the similarity ended.

The first of the cases placed so promptly before her ladyship by Inspector Yard presented some startling features of similarity with that of Charles. The young gentleman was from the West of England, had been at College somewhere, had been extravagant ("God bless him, poor dear! when lived a Ravenshoe that wasn't?" thought Lady Ascot), had been crossed in love, the inspector believed (Lady Ascot thought she had got her fish), and was now in the Coldbath Fields Prison, doing two years' hard labour for swindling, of which two months were yet to run. The Inspector would let her ladyship know the day of his release.

This could not be Charles: and the next young gentleman offered to her notice was a worse shot than the other. He also was dark-haired; but here at once all resemblance ceased. This one had started in life with an ensigncy in the line. He had embezzled the mess funds, had been to California, had enlisted, deserted, and sold his kit, been a billiard-marker, had come into some property, had spent it, had enlisted again, had been imprisoned for a year and discharged—here Lady Ascot would read no more, but laid down the letter, saying, "Pish!"

But the inspector's cup was not yet full. The unhappy man was acting from uncertain information, he says. He affirmed, throughout all the long and acrimonious discussion which followed, that his only instructions were to find a young gentleman with dark hair and a hook nose. If this be the case, he may possibly be excused for catching a curly-headed little Jew of sixteen, who was drinking himself to death in a public-house off Regent Street, and producing him as Charles Ravenshoe. His name was Cohen, and he had stolen some money from his father and gone to the races. This was so utterly the wrong article, that Lady Ascot wrote a violent letter to the ex-inspector, of such an extreme character, that he replied by informing her ladyship that he had sent her letter to his lawyer. A very pretty quarrel followed, which I have not time to describe.

No tidings of Charles! He had hidden himself too effectually. So the old woman wept and watched—watched for her darling who came not, and for the ruin that she saw settling down upon her house like a dark cloud, that grew evermore darker.

And little Mary had packed up her boxes and passed out of the old house, with the hard, bitter world before her. Father Mackworth had met her in the hall, and had shaken hands with her in silence. He loved her, in his way, so much, that he cared not to say anything. Cuthbert was outside, waiting to hand her to her carriage. When she was seated he said, "I shall write to you, Mary, for I can't say all I would." And then he opened the door and kissed her affectionately; then the carriage went on, and before it entered the wood, she had a glimpse of the grey old house, and Cuthbert on the steps before the porch, bareheaded, waving his hand ; then it was among the trees, and she had seen the last of him for ever ; then she buried her face in her hands, and knew, for the first time, perhaps, how well she had loved him.

She was going, as we know, to be nursery-governess to the orphan children of Lord Hainault's brother. She went straight to London to assume her charge. It was very late when she got to Paddington. One of Lord Hainault's carriages was waiting for her, and she was whirled through "the season" to Grosvenor Square. Then she had to walk alone into the great lighted hall, with the servants standing right and left, and looking at nothing, as well-bred servants are bound to do. She wished for a moment that the poor little governess had been allowed to come in a cab.

The groom of the chambers informed her that her ladyship had gone out, and would not be home till late ; that his lordship was dressing ; and that dinner was ready in Miss Corby's room whenever she pleased.

So she went up. She did not eat much dinner ; the steward's-room boy in attendance had his foolish heart moved to pity by seeing how poor an appetite she had, when he thought what *he* could have done in that line too.

Presently she asked the lad where was the nursery. The second door to the right. When all was quiet, she opened her door, and thought she would go and see the children asleep. At that moment the nursery-door opened, and a tall, handsome, quiet-looking man came out. It was Lord Hainault ; she had seen him before.

"I like this," said she, as she drew back. "It was kind of him to go and see his brother's children before he went out ; " and so she went into the nursery.

An old nurse was sitting by the fire sewing. The two elder children were asleep ; but the youngest, an audacious young sinner of three, had refused to do anything of the kind until the cat came to bed with him. The nursery cat being at that time out a-walking on the leads, the nursemaid had been dispatched to borrow one from the kitchen. At this state of affairs Mary entered. The nurse rose and curtsied, and the rebel clambered on her knee, and took her into his confidence. He told her that that day, while walking in the square, he had seen a chimney-sweep ; that he had called to Gus and Flora to come and look ; that Gus had been in time and seen him go round the corner, but that Flora had come too late, and cried, and so Gus had lent her his hoop, and she had left off, &c., &c. After a time he requested to be allowed to say his prayers to her: to which the nurse objected, on the theological ground that he had said them twice already that evening, which was once more than was usually allowed. Soon after this the little head lay heavy on Mary's arm, and the little hand loosed its hold on hers, and the child was asleep.

She left the nursery with a lightened heart; but, nevertheless, she cried herself to sleep. "I wonder, shall I like Lady Hainault; Charles used to. But she is very proud, I believe. I cannot remember much of her.—How those carriages growl and roll, almost like the sea at dear old Ravenshoe." Then, after a time, she slept.

There was a light in her eyes, not of dawn, which woke her. A tall, handsome woman, in silk and jewels, came and knelt beside her and kissed her; and said that, now her old home was broken up, she must make one there, and be a sister to her, and many other kind words of the same sort. It was Lady Hainault (the long Burton girl, as Madam Adelaide called her) come home from her last party; and in such kind keeping I think we may leave little Mary for the present.

CHAPTER XXXIV

IN WHICH FRESH MISCHIEF IS BREWED

CHARLES's duties were light enough; he often wished they had been heavier. There were such long idle periods left for thinking and brooding. He rather wondered at first why he was not more employed. He never was in attendance on the lieutenant, save in the daytime. One of the young men under him drove the brougham, and was out all night and in bed all day; and the other was a mere stable-lad from the country. Charles's duty consisted almost entirely in dressing himself about two o'clock, and loitering about town after his master; and, after he had been at this work about a fortnight, it seemed to him as if he had been at it a year or more.

Charles soon found out all he cared to know about the lieutenant. He was the only son and heir of an eminent solicitor, lately deceased, who had put him into the splendid regiment to which he belonged, in order to get him into good society. The young fellow had done well enough in that way. He was amazingly rich, amazingly handsome, and passionately fond of his profession, at which he really worked hard ; but he was terribly fast. Charles soon found that out; and the first object which he placed before himself, when he began to awaken from the first dead torpor which came on him after his fall ; was to gain influence with him and save him from ruin.

"He is burning the candle at both ends," said Charles. "He is too good to go to the deuce. In time, if I am careful, he may listen to me."

And, indeed, it seemed probable. From the very first, Hornby had treated Charles with great respect and consideration. Hornby knew he was a gentleman. One morning, before Charles had been many days with him, the brougham had not come into the mews till seven o'clock ; and Charles, going to his lodgings at eight, had found him in uniform, bolting a cup of coffee before going on duty. There was a great pile of money, sovereigns and notes, on the dressing-table, and he caught Charles looking at it.

Hornby laughed. "What are you looking at with that solemn face of yours?" said he.

"Nothing, sir," said Charles.

"You are looking at that money," said Hornby ; "and you are thinking it would be as well if I didn't stay out all night playing—eh?"

"I might have thought so, sir," said Charles. "I did think so."

"Quite right, too. Some day I will leave off, perhaps."

And then he rattled out of the room, and Charles watched him riding down the street, all blue, and scarlet, and gold, a brave figure, with the world at his feet.

"There is time yet," said Charles.

The first time Charles made his appearance in livery in the street he felt horribly guilty. He was in continual terror lest he should meet some one he knew ; but, after a time, when he found that day after day he could walk about and see never a familiar face, he grew bolder. He wished sometimes he could see some one he knew from a distance, so as not to be recognised—it was so terribly lonely.

Day after day he saw the crowds pass him in the street, and recognised no one. In old times, when he used to come to London on a raid from Oxford, he fancied he used to recognise an acquaintance at every step; but now, day after day went on, and he saw no one he knew. The world had become to him like a long uneasy dream of strange faces.

After a very few days of his new life, there began to grow on him a desire to hear of those he had left so abruptly; a desire which was at first mere curiosity, but which soon developed into a yearning regret. At first, after a week or so, he began idly wondering where they all were, and what they thought of his disappearance; and at this time, perhaps, he may have felt a little conceited in thinking how he occupied their thoughts, and of what importance he had made himself by his sudden disappearance. But his curiosity and vanity soon wore away, and were succeeded by a deep gnawing desire to hear something of them all—to catch hold of some little thread, however thin, which should connect him with his past life, and with those he had loved so well. He would have died in his obstinacy sooner than move one inch towards his object: but every day, as he rode about the town, dressed in the livery of servitude, which he tried to think was his heritage, and yet of which he was ashamed, he stared hither and thither at the passing faces, trying to find one, were it only that of the meanest servant, which should connect him with the past.

At last, and before long, he saw some one.

One afternoon he was under orders to attend his master on horseback, as usual. After lunch, Hornby came out, beautifully dressed, handsome and happy, and rode up Grosvenor Place into the park. At the entrance to Rotten Row he joined an old gentleman and his two daughters, and they rode together, chatting pleasantly. Charles rode behind with the other groom, who talked to him about the coming Derby, and would have betted against Haphazard at the current odds. They rode up and down the Row twice, and then Hornby, calling Charles, gave him his horse and walked about by the Serpentine, talking to every one, and getting a kindly welcome from great and small; for the son of a great attorney, with wealth, manners, and person, may get into very good society, if he is worth it; or, quite possibly, if he isn't.

Then Hornby and Charles left the Park, and, coming down Grosvenor Place, passed into Pall Mall. Here Hornby went into a club, and left Charles waiting in the street with his horse half an hour or more.

Then he mounted again, and rode up St. James's Street into Piccadilly. He turned to the left; and, at the bottom of the hill, not far from Halfmoon Street, he went into a private house, and, giving Charles his reins, told him to wait for him; and so Charles waited there, in the afternoon sun, watching what went by.

It was a sleepy afternoon, and the horses stood quiet, and Charles was a contented fellow, and he rather liked dozing there and watching the world go by. There is plenty to see in Piccadilly on an afternoon in the season, even for a passer-by; but, sitting on a quiet horse, with nothing to do or think about, one can see it all better. And Charles had some humour in him, and so he was amused at what he saw, and would have sat there an hour or more without impatience.

Opposite to him was a great bonnet-shop, and in front of it was an orange-woman. A grand carriage dashed up to the bonnet-shop, so that he had to move his horses, and the orange-woman had to get out of the way. Two young ladies got out of the carriage, went in, and (as he believes) bought bonnets, leaving a third, and older one, sitting in a back seat, who nursed a pug dog, with a blue riband. Neither the coachman nor footman belonging to the carriage seemed to mind this lady. The footman thought he would like some oranges; so he went to the orange-woman. The orange-woman was Irish, for her speech betrayed her, and the footman was from the county Clare; so those two instantly began comparing notes about those delectable regions, to such purpose, that the two ladies, having, let us hope, suited themselves in the bonnet way, had to open their own carriage-door and get in, before the footman was recalled to a sense of his duties—after which he shut the door and they drove away.

Then there came by a blind man. It was not the same blind man that Charles saw fall down the area, because that blind man's dog was a brown one, with a curly tail, and this one's dog was black with no tail at all. Moreover, the present dog carried a basket, which the other one did not. Otherwise they were so much alike (all blind men are), that Charles might have mistaken one for the other. This blind man met with no such serious accident as the other, either. Only, turning into the public-house at the corner, opposite Mr. Hope's, the dog lagged behind, and, the swing-doors closing between him and his master, Charles saw him pulled through by his chain, and nearly throttled.

Next there came by Lord Palmerston, with his umbrella on his shoulder, walking airily arm-in-arm with Lord John Russell. They were talking together; and, as they passed, Charles heard Lord Palmerston say that it was much warmer on this side of

the street than on the other. With which proposition Lord John
Russell appeared to agree ; and so they passed on westward.

After this there came by three prize fighters, arm-in-arm ;
each of them had a white hat and a cigar ; two had white bull-
dogs, and one a black and tan terrier. They made a left wheel,
and looked at Charles and his horses, and then they made a
right wheel and looked into the bonnet-shop ; after which they
went into the public-house into which the blind man had gone
before ; and, from the noise which immediately arose from inside,
Charles came to the conclusion, that the two white bull-dogs
and the black and tan terrier had set upon the blind man's dog,
and touzled him.

After the prize-fighters came Mr. Gladstone, walking very
fast. A large Newfoundland dog with a walking-stick in
his mouth, blundered up against him, and nearly threw him
down. Before he got under way again, the Irish orange-woman
bore down on him, and faced him with three oranges in each
hand, offering them for sale. Did she know, with the sagacity
of her nation, that he was then on his way to the house, to
make a Great Statement, and that he would want oranges ? I
cannot say. He probably got his oranges at Bellamy's, for he
bought none of her. After him came a quantity of indifferent
people ; and then Charles's heart beat high—for here was
some one coming whom he knew with a vengeance.

Lord Welter, walking calmly down the street, with his big
chest thrown out, and his broad, stupid face in moody repose.
He was thinking. He came so close to Charles that, stepping
aside to avoid a passer-by, he whitened the shoulder of his
coat against the pipe-clay on Charles's knee ; then he stood
stock still within six inches of him, but looking the other way
towards the houses.

He pulled off one of his gloves and bit his nails. Though
his back was towards Charles, still Charles knew well what
expression was on his face as he did that. The old cruel
lowering of the eyebrows, and pinching in of the lips was there,
he knew. The same expression as that which Marston
remarked the time he quarrelled with Cuthbert once at
Ravenshoe—mischief !

He went into the house where Charles's master, Hornby,
was ; and Charles sat and wondered.

Presently there came out on to the balcony above, six or seven
well-dressed young men, who lounged with their elbows on the
red cushions which were fixed to the railing, and talked, looking
at the people in the street.

Lord Welter and Lieutenant Hornby were together at the end. There was no scowl on Welter's face now ; he was making himself agreeable. Charles watched him and Hornby ; the conversation between them got eager, and they seemed to make an appointment. After that they parted, and Hornby came downstairs and got on his horse.

They rode very slowly home. Hornby bowed right and left to the people he knew, but seemed absent. When Charles took his horse at the door, he said suddenly to Charles—

"I have been talking to a man who knows something of you, I believe—Lord Welter."

"Did you mention me to him, sir ? "

"No ; I didn't think of it."

"You would do me a great kindness if you would not do so, sir."

"Why," said Hornby, looking suddenly up.

"I am sorry I cannot enter into particulars, sir ; but, if I thought he would know where I was, I should at once quit your service and try to lose myself once more."

"Lose yourself ? "

"Yes, sir."

"H'm ! " said Hornby thoughtfully. "Well, I know there is something about you which I don't understand. I ain't sure it is any business of mine though. I will say nothing. You are not a man to chatter about anything you see. Mind you don't. You see how I trust you." And so he went in, and Charles went round to the stable.

"Is the brougham going out to-night ? " he asked of his fellow-servant.

"Ordered at ten," said the man. "Night-work again, I expect. I wanted to get out too. Consume the darned card-playing. Was you going anywhere to-night ? "

"Nowhere," said Charles.

"It's a beautiful evening," said the man. "If you should by chance saunter up towards Grosvenor Square, and could leave a note for me, I should thank you very much ; upon my soul I should."

I don't think Charles ever hesitated at doing a good-natured action in his life. A request to him was like a command. It came as natural to him now to take a dirty, scrawled love-letter from a groom to a scullery-maid as in old times it did to lend a man fifty pounds. He said at once he would go with great pleasure.

The man (a surly fellow enough at ordinary times) thanked him heartily ; and, when Charles had got the letter, he sauntered away in that direction slowly, thinking of many things.

"By Jove!" he said to himself, "my scheme of hiding does not seem to be very successful. Little more than a fortnight gone, and I am thrown against Welter. What a strange thing!"

It was still early in the afternoon—seven o'clock, or there-abouts—and he was opposite Tattersall's. A mail phaeton, with a pair of splendid horses, attracted his attention and diverted his thoughts. He turned down. Two eminent men on the turf walked passed him up the nearly empty yard, and he heard one say to the other—

"Ascot will run to win; that I know. He *must*. If Haphazard can stay, he is safe."

To which the other said, "Pish!" and they passed on.

"There they are again," said Charles, as he turned back. "The very birds of the air are talking about them. It gets interesting, though—if anything could ever be interesting again."

St. George's Hospital. At the door was a gaudily dressed, handsome young woman, who was asking the porter could she see some one inside. No. The visiting hours were over. She stood for a few minutes on the steps, impatiently biting her nails, and then fluttered down the street.

What made him think of his sister Ellen? She must be found. That was the only object in the world, so to speak. There was nothing to be done, only to wait and watch.

"I shall find her some day, in God's good time."

The world had just found out that it was hungry, and was beginning to tear about in wheeled vehicles to its neighbours' houses to dinner. As the carriages passed Charles, he could catch glimpses of handsome girls, all a mass of white muslin, swan's-down fans, and fal-lals, going to begin their night's work; of stiff dandies, in white ties, yawning already; of old ladies in jewels, and old gentlemen buttoned up across the chest, going, as one might say, to see fair play among the young people. And then our philosophical Charles pleased himself by picturing how, in two months more, the old gentlemen would be among their turnips, the old ladies among their flowers and their poor folks, the dandies creeping, creeping, weary hours through the heather, till the last maddening moment when the big stag was full in view, sixty yards off; and (prettiest thought of all), how the girls, with their thick shoes on, would be gossiping with old Goody Blake and Harry Gill, or romping with the village school-children on the lawn. Right, old Charles, with all but the dandies! For now the apotheosis of dandies was approaching. The time was coming when so many of them should disappear into that black thunder-cloud to the south, and be seen no more in park or club, in heather or stubble.

But, in that same year, the London season went on much as usual; only folks talked of war, and the French were more popular than they are now. And through the din and hubbub poor Charles passed on like a lost sheep, and left his fellow-servant's note at an area in Grosvenor Square.

"And which," said he to the man who took it, with promises of instant delivery, "is my Lord Hainault's house, now, for instance?"

Lord Hainault's house was the other side of the square; number something. Charles thanked the man, and went across. When he had made it out he leant back against the railings of the square, and watched it.

The carriage was at the door. The coachman, seeing a handsomely-dressed groom leaning against the rails, called to him to come over and alter some strap or another. Charles ran over and helped him. Charles supposed her ladyship was going out to dinner. Yes, her ladyship was now coming out. And, almost before Charles had time to move out of the way, out she came, with her head in the air, more beautiful than ever, and drove away.

He went back to his post from mere idleness. He wondered whether Mary had come there yet or not. He had half a mind to inquire, but was afraid of being seen. He still leant against the railings of the gate, as I said, in mere idleness, when he heard the sound of children's voices in the square behind.

"That woman," said a child's voice, "was a gipsy-woman. I looked through the rails, and I said, 'Hallo, ma'am, what are you doing there?' And she asked me for a penny. And I said I couldn't give her anything, for I had given three half-pence to the Punch and Judy, and I shouldn't have any more money till next Saturday. Which was quite true, Flora, as you know."

"But, Gus," said another child's voice, "if she had been a gipsy-woman she would have tried to steal you, and make you beg in the streets; or else she would have told your fortune in coffee-grounds. I don't think she was a real gipsy."

"I should like to have my fortune told in the coffee-grounds," said Gus; "but, if she had tried to steal me, I should have kicked her in the stomach. There is a groom outside there ; let us ask him. Grooms go to the races, and see heaps of gipsies ! I say, sir."

Charles turned. A child's voice was always music to him. He had such a look on his face as he turned to them, that the children had his confidence in an instant. The gipsy question was laid before him instantly, by both Gus and Flora, with immense volubility, and he was just going to give an oracular opinion through the railings, when a voice—a low, gentle voice, which made him start—came from close by.

"Gus and Flora, my dears, the dew is falling. Let us go in."

"There is Miss Corby," said Gus. "Let us run to her."

They raced to Mary. Soon after the three came to the gate, laughing, and passed close to him. The children were clinging to her skirt and talking merrily. They formed a pretty little group as they went across the street, and Mary's merry little laugh comforted him. "She is happy there," he said ; " best as it is ! "

Once, when halfway across the street, she turned and looked towards him, before he had time to turn away. He saw that she did not dream of his being there, and went on. And so Charles sauntered home through the pleasant summer evening, saying to himself, " I think she is happy; I am glad she laughed."

" Three meetings in one day ! I shall be found out, if I don't mind. I must be very careful."

CHAPTER XXXV

IN WHICH AN ENTIRELY NEW, AND, AS WILL BE SEEN HERE-AFTER, A MOST IMPORTANT CHARACTER IS INTRODUCED

THE servants, I mean the stable-servants, who lived in the mews where Charles did, had a club ; and, a night or two after he had seen Mary in the square, he was elected a member of it. The duke's coachman, a wiry, grey, stern-looking, elderly man, waited upon him and informed him of the fact. He said that such a course was very unusual—in fact, without precedent. Men, he said, were seldom elected to the club until they were known to have been in good service for some years ; but he (coachman) had the ear of the club pretty much, and had brought him in triumphant. He added that he could see through a brick wall as well as most men, and that, when he see a *gentleman* dressed in a livery, moping and brooding about the mews, he had said to himself that he wanted a little company, such as it was, to cheer him up, and so he had requested the club, &c.; and the club had done as he told them.

"Now this is confoundedly kind of you," said Charles; "but I am not a gentleman; I am a gamekeeper's son."

"I suppose you can read Greek, now, can't you?" said the coachman.

Charles was obliged to confess he could.

"Of course," said the coachman; "all gamekeepers' sons is forced to learn Greek, in order as they may slang the poachers in an unknown tongue. Fiddle-dedee! I know all about it; leastwise, guess. Come along with me; why, I've got sons as old as you. Come along."

"Are they in service?" said Charles, by way of something to say.

"Two of 'em are, but one's in the army."

"Indeed!" said Charles, with more interest.

"Ay; he is in your governor's regiment."

"Does he like it?" said Charles. "I should like to know him."

"Like it?—don't he?" said the coachman. "See what society he gets into. I suppose there ain't no gentlemen's sons troopers in that regiment, eh? Oh dear no. Don't for a moment suppose it, young man. Not at all."

Charles was very much interested by this news. He made up his mind there and then that he would enlist immediately. But he didn't; he only thought about it.

Charles found that the club was composed of about a dozen coachmen and superior pad-grooms. They were very civil to him, and to one another. There was nothing to laugh at. There was nothing that could be tortured into ridicule. They talked about their horses and their business quite naturally. There was an air of kindly fellowship, and a desire for mutual assistance among them, which, at times, Charles had not noticed at the university. One man sang a song, and sang it very prettily, too, about stag-hunting. He had got so far as—

> As every breath with sobs he drew,
> The labouring buck strained full in view,

when the door opened, and an oldish groom came in.

The song was not much attended to now. When the singer had finished, the others applauded him, but impatiently ; and then there was a general exclamation of " Well ? "

" I've just come down from the corner. There has been a regular run against Haphazard, and no one knows why. Something wrong with the horse, I suppose, because there's been no run on any other in particular, only against him."

" Was Lord Ascot there ? " said some one.

" Ah, that he was. Wouldn't bet, though, even at the long odds. Said he'd got every sixpence he was worth on the horse, and would stand where he was ; and that's true, they say. And master says, likewise, that Lord Welter would have taken 'em, but that his father stopped him."

" That looks queerish," said some one else.

" Ay, and wasn't there a jolly row, too ? "

" Who with ? " asked several.

" Lord Welter and Lord Hainault. It happened outside, close to me. Lord Hainault was walking across the yard, and Lord Welter came up to him and said, ' How d'ye do, Hainault ? ' and Lord Hainault turned round and said, quite quiet, ' Welter, you are a scoundrel ! ' And Lord Welter said, ' Hainault, you are out of your senses ; ' but he turned pale, too, and he looked—Lord ! I shouldn't like to have been before him—and Lord Hainault says, ' You know what I mean ; ' and Lord Welter says, ' No, I don't ; but, by Gad, you shall tell me ' ; and then the other says, as steady as a rock, ' I'll tell you. You are a man that one daren't leave a woman alone with. Where's that Casterton girl ? Where's Adelaide Summers ? Neither a friend's house, nor your own father's house, is any protection for a woman against you.' ' Gad,' says Lord Welter, ' you were pretty sweet on the last-named yourself, once on a time.' "

" Well ! " said some one, " and what did Lord Hainault say ? "

" He said, ' You are a liar and a scoundrel, Welter.' And then Lord Welter came at him ; but Lord Ascot came between them, shaking like anything, and says he, ' Hainault, go away, for God's sake ; you don't know what you are saying.—Welter, be silent.' But they made no more of he than——" (here our friend was at a loss for a simile).

" But how did it end ? " asked Charles.

" Well," said the speaker, " General Mainwaring came up, and laid his hand on Lord Welter's shoulder, and took him off pretty quiet. And that's all I know about it."

It was clearly all.   Charles rose to go, and walked by himself from street to street, thinking.

Suppose he *was* to be thrown against Lord Welter, how should he act? what should he say? Truly it was a puzzling question. The anomaly of his position was never put before him more strikingly than now. What could he say? what could he do?

After the first shock, the thought of Adelaide's unfaithfulness was not so terrible as on the first day or two; many little unamiable traits of character, vanity, selfishness, and so on, unnoticed before, began to come forth in somewhat startling relief. Anger, indignation, and love, all three jumbled up together, each one by turns in the ascendant, were the frames of mind in which Charles found himself when he began thinking about her. One moment he was saying to himself, "How beautiful she was!" and the next, "She was as treacherous as a tiger; she never could have cared for me." But, when he came to think of Welter, his anger overmastered everything, and he would clench his teeth as he walked along, and for a few moments feel the blood rushing to his head and singing in his ears. Let us hope that Lord Welter will not come across him while he is in that mood, or there will be mischief.

But his anger was soon over. He had just had one of these fits of anger as he walked along; and he was, like a good fellow, trying to conquer it by thinking of Lord Welter as he was as a boy, and before he was a villain, when he came before St. Peter's Church, in Eaton Square, and stopped to look at some fine horses which were coming out of Salter's.

At the east end of St. Peter's Church there is a piece of bare white wall in a corner, and in front of the wall was a little shoeblack.

He was not one of the regular brigade, with a red shirt, but an "Arab" of the first water. He might have been seven or eight years old, but was small. His whole dress consisted of two garments; a ragged shirt with no buttons, and half of one sleeve gone, and a ragged pair of trousers, which, small as he was, were too small for him, and barely reached below his knees. His feet and head were bare; and under a wild, tangled shock of hair looked a pretty, dirty, roguish face, with a pair of grey, twinkling eyes, which was amazingly comical. Charles stopped, watching him, and, as he did so, felt what we have most of us felt, I dare say—that, at certain times of vexation and anger, the company and conversation of children is the best thing for us.

H

The little man was playing at fives against the bare wall, with such tremendous energy, that he did not notice that Charles had stopped, and was looking at him. Every nerve in his wiry lean little body was braced up to the game; his heart and soul were as deeply enlisted in it, as though he were captain of the eleven, or stroke of the eight.

He had no ball to play with, but he played with a brass button. The button flew hither and thither, being so irregular in shape, and the boy dashed after it like lightning. At last, after he had kept up five-and-twenty or so, the button flew over his head, and lighted at Charles's feet.

As the boy turned to get it, his eyes met Charles's, and he stopped, parting the long hair from his forehead, and gazing on him till the beautiful little face, beautiful through dirt and ignorance and neglect, lit up with a smile, as Charles looked at him, with the kind, honest old expression. And so began their acquaintance, almost comically at first.

Charles don't care to talk much about that boy now. If he ever does, it is to recall his comical, humorous sayings and doings in the first part of their strange friendship. He never speaks of the end, even to me.

The boy stood smiling at him, as I said, holding his long hair out of his eyes; and Charles looked on him and laughed, and forgot all about Welter and the rest of them at once.

"I want my boots cleaned," he said.

The boy said, "I can't clean they dratted top-boots. I cleaned a groom's boots a Toosday, and he punched my block because I blacked the tops. Where did that button go?"

And Charles said, "You can clean the lower part of my boots, and do no harm. Your button is here against the lamp-post."

The boy picked it up, and got his apparatus ready. But, before he began, he looked up in Charles's face, as if he was going to speak; then he began vigorously, but in half a minute looked up again, and stopped.

Charles saw that the boy liked him, and wanted to talk to him; so he began, severely—

"How came you to be playing fives with a brass button, eh?"

The boy struck work at once, and answered, "I ain't got no ball."

"If you begin knocking stamped pieces of metal about in the street," continued Charles, "you will come to chuck-farthing; and from chuck-farthing to the gallows is a very short step indeed, I can assure you."

The boy did not seem to know whether Charles was joking or not. He cast a quick glance up at his face; but, seeing no sign of a smile there, he spat on one of his brushes and said,—

"Not if you don't cheat, it ain't."

Charles suffered the penalty, which usually follows on talking nonsense, of finding himself in a dilemma. So he said imperiously,—

"I shall buy you a ball to-morrow; I am not going to have you knocking buttons about against people's walls in broad daylight, like that."

It was the first time that the boy had ever heard nonsense talked in his life. It was a new sensation. He gave a sharp look up into Charles's face again, and then went on with his work.

"Where do you live, my little mannikin?" said Charles directly, in that quiet pleasant voice I know so well.

The boy did not look up this time. It was not very often, possibly, that he got spoken to so kindly by his patrons; he worked away, and answered that he lived in Marquis Court, in Southwark.

"Why do you come so far then?" asked Charles.

The boy told him why he plodded so wearily, day after day, over here in the West-end. It was for family reasons, into which I must not go too closely. Somebody, it appeared, still came home, now and then, just once in a way, to see her mother, and to visit the den where she was bred; and there was still left one who would wait for her, week after week—still one pair of childish feet, bare and dirty, that would patter back beside her—still one childish voice that would prattle with her on her way to her hideous home, and call her sister.

"Have you any brothers?"

Five altogether. Jim was gone for a sojer, it appeared, and Nipper was sent over the water. Harry was on the cross—

"On the cross?" said Charles.

"Ah!" the boy said, "he goes out cly-faking, and such. He's a prig, and a smart one, too. He's fly, is Harry."

"But what is cly-faking?" said Charles.

"Why a-prigging of wipes, and sneeze-boxes, and ridicules, and such."

Charles was not so ignorant of slang as not to understand what his little friend meant now. He said—

"But *you* are not a thief, are you?"

The boy looked up at him frankly and honestly, and said—

"Lord bless you, no! I shouldn't make no hand of that, I ain't brave enough for that!"

He gave the boy twopence, and gave orders that one penny was to be spent in a ball. And then he sauntered listlessly away—every day more listless, and not three weeks gone yet.

His mind returned to this child very often. He found himself thinking more about the little rogue than he could explain. The strange babble of the child, prattling so innocently, and, as he thought, so prettily, about vice, and crime, and misery ; about one brother transported, one a thief —and you see he could love his sister even to the very end of it all. Strange babble indeed from a child's lips.

He thought of it again and again, and then, dressing himself plainly, he went up to Grosvenor Square, where Mary would be walking with Lord Charles Herries's children. He wanted to hear *them* talk.

He was right in his calculations; the children were there. All three of them this time ; and Mary was there too. They were close to the rails, and he leant his back on them, and heard every word.

"Miss Corby," said Gus, "if Lady Ascot is such a good woman, she will go to heaven when she dies ? "

"Yes, indeed, my dear," said Mary.

"And when grandma dies, will she go to heaven, too ? " said the artful Gus, knowing as well as possible that old Lady Hainault and Lady Ascot were deadly enemies.

"I hope so, my dear," said Mary.

"But does Lady Ascot hope so ? Do you think grandma would be happy if——"

It became high time to stop Master Gus, who was getting on too fast. Mary having bowled him out, Miss Flora had an innings.

"When I grow up," said Flora, "I shall wear knee-breeches and top-boots, and a white bull-dog, and a long clay pipe, and I shall drive into Henley on a market-day and put up at the Catherine Wheel."

Mary had breath enough left to ask why.

"Because Farmer Thompson at Casterton dresses like that, and he is such a dear old darling. He gives us straw-berries and cream ; and in his garden are gooseberries and peacocks ; and the peacocks' wives don't spread out their tails like their husbands do,—the foolish things. Now, when I am married——"

Gus was rude enough to interrupt her here. He remarked—

"When Archy goes to heaven, he'll want the cat to come to

bed with him ; and, if he can't get her, there will be a pretty noise."

"My dears," said Mary, "you must not talk any more nonsense ; I can't permit it."

"But, my dear Miss Corby," said Flora, "we haven't been talking nonsense, have we ? I told you the truth about Farmer Thompson."

"I know what she means," said Gus ; "we have been saying what came into our heads, and it vexes her. It is all nonsense, you know, about your wearing breeches and spreading out your tail like a peacock ; we mustn't vex her."

Flora didn't answer Gus, but answered Mary by climbing on to her knee and kissing her. "Tell us a story, dear," said Gus.

"What shall I tell ?" said Mary.

"Tell us about Ravenshoe," said Flora ; "tell us about the fishermen, and the priest that walked about like a ghost in the dark passages ; and about Cuthbert Ravenshoe, who was always saying his prayers ; and about the other one who won the boat race."

"Which one ?" said silly Mary.

"Why, the other ; the one you like best. What was his name ?"

"Charles !"

How quietly and softly she said it ! The word left her lips like a deep sigh. One who heard it was a gentleman still. He had heard enough, perhaps too much, and walked away towards the stable and the public-house, leaving her in the gathering gloom of the summer's evening under the red haw-thorns, and laburnums, among the children. And, as he walked away, he thought of the night he left Ravenshoe, when the little figure was standing in the hall all alone. "She might have loved me and I her," he said, "if the world were not out of joint ; God grant it may not be so !" And, although he said, "God grant that she may not," he really wished it had been so ; and from this very time Mary began to take Adelaide's place in his heart.

Not that he was capable of falling in love with any woman at this time. He says he was crazy, and I believe him to a certain extent. It was a remarkably lucky thing for him that he had so diligently neglected his education. If he had not, and had found himself in his present position, with three or four times more of intellectual cravings to be satisfied, he would have gone mad, or taken to drinking. I, who write, have seen the thing happen.

But, before the crash came, I have seen Charles patiently spending the morning cutting gun-wads from an old hat, in preference to going to his books. It was this interest in trifles which saved him just now. He could think at times, and had had education enough to think logically; but his brain was not so active but that he could cut gun-wads for an hour or so; though his friend William could cut one-third more gun-wads out of an old hat than he.

He was thinking now, in his way, about these children—about Gus and Flora on the one hand, and the little shoeblack on the other. Both so innocent and pretty, and yet so different. He had taken himself from the one world and thrown himself into the other. There were two worlds and two standards—gentlemen and non-gentlemen. The "lower orders" did not seem to be so particular about the character of their immediate relations as the upper. That was well, for he belonged to the former now, and had a sister. If one of Lord Charles Herries's children had gone wrong, Gus and Flora would never have talked of him or her to a stranger. He must learn the secret of this armour which made the poor so invulnerable. He must go and talk to the little shoeblack.

He thought that was the reason why he went to look after the little rogue next day; but that was not the real reason. The reason was, that he had found a friend in a lower grade than himself, who would admire him and look up to him. The first friend of that sort he had made since his fall. What that friend accidentally saved him from, we shall see.

CHAPTER XXXVI

THE DERBY

HORNBY was lying on his back on the sofa in the window, and looking out. He had sent for Charles, and Charles was standing beside him; but he had not noticed him yet. In a minute Charles said, "You sent for me, sir."

Hornby turned sharply round. "By Jove, yes!" he said, looking straight at him; "Lord Welter is married."

Charles did not move a muscle, and Hornby looked disappointed. Charles only said—

"May I ask who she is, sir?"

"She is a Miss Summers. Do you know anything of her?"

Charles knew Miss Summers quite well by sight—had attended her while riding, in fact. A statement which, though strictly true, misled Hornby more than fifty lies.

"Handsome?"

"Remarkably so. Probably the handsomest (he was going to say 'girl,' but said 'lady,') I ever saw in my life."

"H'm!" and he sat silent a moment, and gave Charles time to think. "I am glad he has married her, and before to-morrow, too."

"Well," said Hornby again, "we shall go down in the drag to-morrow. Ferrers will drive, he says. I suppose he had better; he drives better than I. Make the other two lads come in livery, but come in black trousers yourself. Wear your red waistcoat; you can button your coat over it, if it is necessary."

"Shall I wear my cockade, sir?"

"Yes; that won't matter. Can you fight?"

Charles said to himself, "I suppose we shall be in Queer-street to-morrow, then"; but he rather liked the idea. "I used to like it," said he aloud. "I don't think I care about it now. Last year, at Oxford, I and three other University men, three Pauls and a Brazenose, had a noble stramash on Folly-bridge. That is the last fighting I have seen."

"What College were you at?" said Hornby, looking out of the window; "Brazenose?"

"Paul's," said Charles without thinking.

"Then you are the man Welter was telling me about—Charles Ravenshoe."

Charles saw it was no good to fence, and said "Yes."

"By Jove!" said Hornby, "yours is a sad story. You must have ridden out with Lady Welter more than once, I take it."

"Are you going to say anything to Lord Welter, sir?"

"Not I. I like you too well to lose you. You will stick by me, won't you?"

"I will," said Charles, "to the death. But oh, Hornby, for my sake mind those d——d bones!"

"I will. But don't be an ass: I don't play half as much as you think."

"You are playing with Welter now, sir; are you not?"

"You are a pretty dutiful sort of a groom, I don't think," said Hornby, looking round and laughing good-naturedly. "What the dickens do you mean by cross-questioning me like that? Yes, I am. There—and for a noble purpose too."

Charles said no more, but was well pleased enough. If Hornby had only given him a little more of his confidence!

"I suppose," said Hornby, "if Haphazard don't win to-morrow, Lord Ascot will be a beggar."

"They say," said Charles, "that he has backed his own horse through thick and thin, sir. It is inconceivable folly; but things could not be worse at Ranford, and he stands to win some sum on the horse, as they say, which would put everything right; and the horse is favourite."

"Favourites never win," said Hornby; "and I don't think that Lord Ascot has so much on him as they say."

So, the next day they went to the Derby. Sir Robert Ferrers, of the Guards drove (this is Inkerman Bob, and he has got a patent cork leg now, and a Victoria Cross, and goes a-shooting on a grey cob); and there was Red Maclean, on furlough from India; and there was Lord Swansea, youngest of existing Guardsmen, who blew a horn, and didn't blow it at all well; and there were two of Lieutenant Hornby's brother-officers, besides the Lieutenant: and behind, with Hornby's two grooms and our own Charles, dressed in sober black, was little Dick Ferrers, of the Home Office, who carried a peashooter, and pea-shot the noses of the leading horses of a dragful of Plungers, which followed them—which thing, had he been in the army, he wouldn't have dared to do. And the Plungers swore, and the dust flew, and the wind blew, and Sir Robert drove, and Charles laughed, and Lord Swansea gave them a little music, and away they went to the Derby.

When they came on the course, Charles and his fellow-servants had enough to do to get the horses out and see after them. After nearly an hour's absence he got back to the drag, and began to look about him.

The Plungers had drawn up behind them, and were lolling about. Before them was a family party—a fine elderly gentleman, a noble elderly lady, and two uncommonly pretty girls, and they were enjoying themselves. They were too well bred to make a noise; but there was a subdued babbling sound of laughter in that carriage, which was better music than that of a little impish German who, catching Charles's eye, played the accordion and waltzed before him, as did Salome before Herod, but with a different effect.

The carriage beyond that was a very handsome one, and in it sat a lady most beautifully dressed, alone. By the step of the carriage were a crowd of men—Hornby, Hornby's brother-officers, Sir Robert Ferrers, and even little Dick Ferrers.

Nay, there was a Plunger there; and they were all talking and laughing at the top of their voices.

Charles, goose as he was, used to be very fond of Dickens's novels. He used to say that almost everywhere in those novels you came across a sketch, may be unconnected with the story, as bold and true and beautiful as those chalk sketches of Raphael in the Taylor—scratches which, when once seen, you could never forget any more. And, as he looked at that lady in the carriage, he was reminded of one of Dickens's masterpieces in that way, out of the "Old Curiosity Shop"—of a lady sitting in a carriage all alone at the races, who bought Nell's poor flowers, and bade her go home and stay there, for God's sake.

Her back was towards him, of course; yet he guessed she was beautiful. "She is a fast woman, God help her!" said he; and he determined to go and look at her.

He sauntered past the carriage, and turned to look at her. It was Adelaide.

As faultlessly beautiful as ever, but ah—how changed! The winning petulance, so charming in other days, was gone from that face for ever. Hard, stern, proud, defiant, she sat there upright, alone. Fallen from the society of all women of her own rank, she knew—who better?—that not one of these men chattering around her would have borne to see her in the company of his sister, viscountess though she were, countess and mother of earls as she would be. They laughed, and lounged, and joked before her; and she tolerated them, and cast her gibes hither and thither among them, bitterly and contemptuously. It was her first appearance in the world. She had been married three days. Not a woman would speak to her: Lord Welter had coarsely told her so that morning; and bitterness and hatred were in her heart. It was for this she had bartered honour and good fame. She had got her title, flung to her as a bone to a dog by Welter; but her social power, for which she had sold herself, was lower, far lower, than when she was poor Adelaide Summers.

It is right that it should be so, as a rule; in her case it was doubly right.

Charles knew all this well enough. And at the first glance at her face he knew that "the iron had entered into her soul" (I know no better expression), and he was revenged. He had ceased to love her, but revenge is sweet—to some.

Not to him. When he looked at her, he would have given

his life that she might smile again, though she was no more to him what she had been. He turned, for fear of being seen, saying to himself—

"Poor girl! Poor dear Adelaide! She must lie on the bed she has made. God help her!"

Haphazard was the first favourite—*facile princeps*. He was at two and a half to one. Bill Sykes, at three and a half, was a very dangerous horse. Then came Carnarvon, Lablache, Lickpitcher, Ivanhoe, Ben Caunt, Bath-bun, Hamlet, Allfours, and Colonel Sibthorp. The last of these was at twenty to one. Ben Caunt was to make the running for Haphazard, so they said; and Colonel Sibthorp for Bill Sykes.

So he heard the men talking round Lady Welter's carriage. Hornby's voice was as loud as any one's, and a pleasant voice it was; but they none of them talked very low. Charles could hear every word.

"I am afraid Lady Welter will never forgive me," said Hornby, "but I have bet against the favourite."

"I beg your pardon," said Adelaide.

"I have bet against your horse, Lady Welter."

"My horse?" said Adelaide, coolly and scornfully. "My horses are all post-horses, hired for the day to bring me here. I hope none of them are engaged in the races, as I shall have to go home with a pair only, and then I shall be disgraced for ever."

"I mean Haphazard."

"Oh, that horse?" said Adelaide; "that is Lord Ascot's horse, not mine. I hope you may win. You ought to win something, oughtn't you? Welter has won a great deal from you, I believe."

The facts were the other way. But Hornby said no more to her. She was glad of this, though she liked him well enough, for she hoped that she had offended him by her insolent manner. But they were at cross-purposes.

Presently Lord Welter came swinging in among them; he looked terribly savage and wild, and Charles thought he had been drinking. Knowing what he was in this mood, and knowing also the mood Adelaide was in, he dreaded some scene. "But they cannot quarrel so soon," he thought.

"How d'ye do?" said Lord Welter to the knot of men round his wife's carriage. "Lady Welter, have your people got any champagne, or anything of that sort?"

"I suppose so; you had better ask them."

She had not forgotten what he had said to her that morning

so brutally. She saw he was madly angry, and would have liked to make him commit himself before these men. She had fawned, and wheedled, and flattered for a month ; but now she was Lady Welter, and he should feel it.

Lord Welter looked still more savage but said nothing. A man brought him some wine ; and, as he gave it to him, Adelaide said, as quietly as though she were telling him that there was some dust on his coat,—

"You had better not take too much of it : you seem to have had enough already. Sir Robert Ferrers here is very taciturn in his cups, I am told ; but you make such a terrible to-do when you are drunk."

They should feel her tongue, these fellows ! They might come and dangle about her carriage-door, and joke to one another, and look on her beauty as if she were a doll; but they should feel her tongue ; Charles's heart sank within him as he heard her. Only a month gone, and she desperate.

But of all the mischievous things done on that race-course that day—and they were many—the most mischievous and uncalled-for was Adelaide's attack upon Sir Robert Ferrers, who, though very young, was as sober, clever, and discreet a young man as any in the Guards, or in England. But Adelaide had heard a story about him ; to wit, that, going to dinner at Greenwich with a number of friends, and having taken two glasses or so of wine at his dinner, he got it into his head that he was getting tipsy ; and refused to speak another word all the evening for fear of committing himself.

The other men laughed at Ferrers. And Lord Welter chose to laugh too ; he was determined that his wife should not make a fool of him. But now every one began to draw off and take their places for the race. Little Dick Ferrers, whose whole life was one long effort of good nature, stayed by Lady Welter, though horribly afraid of her, because he did not like to see her left alone. Charles forced himself into a front position against the rails, with his friend Mr. Sloane, and held on thereby, intensely interested. He was passionately fond of horse-racing ; and he forgot everything, even his poor, kind old friend Lord Ascot, in scrutinising every horse as it came by from the Warren, and guessing which was to win.

Haphazard was the horse, there could be no doubt. A cheer ran all along the line, as he came walking majestically down, as though he knew he was the hero of the day. Bill Sykes and Carnarvon were as good as good could be ; but Haphazard was better. Charles remembered Lady Ascot's tearful warning about his not being able to stay; but he laughed it to scorn. The horse had furnished so since then! Here he came, flying past them like a whirlwind, shaking the earth, and making men's ears tingle with the glorious music of his feet on the turf. Haphazard, ridden by Wells, must win! Hurrah for Wells!

As the horse came slowly past again, he looked up to see the calm stern face; but it was not there. There were Lord Ascot's colours, dark blue and white sash; but where was Wells? The jockey was a smooth-faced young man, with very white teeth, who kept grinning and touching his cap at every other word Lord Ascot said to him. Charles hurriedly borrowed Sloane's card, and read,—

"Lord Ascot's Haphazard——J. Brooks."

Who, in the name of confusion, was J. Brooks? All of a sudden he remembered. It was one of Lord Ascot's own lads. It was the very lad that rode Haphazard on the day that Adelaide and he rode out to the Downs, at Ranford, to see the horse gallop. Lord Ascot must be mad.

"But Wells was to have ridden Haphazard, Mr. Sloane," said Charles.

"He wouldn't," said Sloane, and laughed sardonically. But there was no time for Charles to ask why he laughed, for the horses were off.

Those who saw the race were rather surprised that Ben Caunt had not showed more to the front at first to force the running; but there was not much time to think of such things. As they came round the corner, Haphazard, who was lying sixth, walked through his horses and laid himself alongside of Bill Sykes. A hundred yards from the post, Bill Sykes made a push, and drew a neck a-head; in a second or so more Haphazard had passed him, winning the Derby by a clear length; and poor Lord Ascot fell headlong down in a fit, like a dead man.

Little Dicky Ferrers in the excitement of the race, had climbed into the rumble of Adelaide's carriage, peashooter and all; and, having cheered rather noisily as the favourite came in winner, he was beginning to wonder whether he hadn't made a fool of himself, and what Lady Welter would say when she found where he had got to, when Lord Welter broke through the crowd, and came up to his wife, looking like death.

"Get home, Adelaide! You see what has happened, and know what to do. Lady Welter, if I get hold of that boy, Brooks, to-night, in a safe place, I'll murder him, by—— !"

" I believe you will, Welter. Keep away from him, unless you are a madman. If you anger the boy it will all come out. Where is Lord Ascot ? "

" Dead, they say, or dying. He is in a fit."

" I ought to go to him, Welter, in common decency."

" Go home I tell you. Get the things you know of packed and taken to one of the hotels at London Bridge. Any name will do. Be at home to-night, dressed, in a state of jubilation ; and keep a couple of hundred pounds in the house. Here, you fellows ! her ladyship's horses—look sharp ! "

Poor little Dicky Ferrers had heard more than he intended, but Lord Welter, in his madness, had not noticed him. He didn't use his peashooter going home, and spoke very little. There was a party of all of them in Hornby's rooms that night, and Dicky was so dull at first, that his brother made some excuse to get him by himself, and say a few eager, affectionate words to him.

" Dick, my child, you have lost some money. How much ? You shall have it to-morrow."

" Not a halfpenny, Bob ; but I was with Lady Welter just after the race, and I heard more than I ought to have heard."

" You couldn't help it, I hope ? "

" I ought to have helped it ; but it was so sudden, I couldn't help it. And now I can't ease my mind by telling anybody."

" I suppose it was some rascality of Welter's," said Sir Robert, laughing. " It don't much matter ; only don't tell any one, you know." And then they went in again, and Dicky never told any one till soon every one knew.

For it came out soon that Lord Ascot had been madly betting, by commission, against his own horse, and that forty years' rents of his estates wouldn't set my lord on his legs again. With his usual irresolution, he had changed his policy—partly owing, I fear, to our dear old friend Lady Ascot's perpetual croaking about " Ramoneur blood," and its staying qualities. So, after betting such a sum on his own horse as gave the betting world confidence, and excusing himself by pleading his well-known poverty from going further, he had hedged, by commission ; and, could his horse have lost, he would have won enough to have set matters right at Ranford. He dared not ask a great jockey to ride for him under such circumstances, and so he puffed one of his own lads to the world, and broke with Wells. The lad had sold him like a sheep. Meanwhile, thinking himself a man of honour, poor fool ! he had raised every farthing possible on his estate to meet his engagements

on the turf in case of failure—in case of his horse winning by
some mischance, if such a thing could be. And so it came
about that the men of the turf were all honourably paid, and
he and his tradesmen were ruined. The estates were entailed ;
but for thirty years Ranford must be in the hands of strangers.
Lord Welter, too, had raised money, and lost fearfully by the
same speculation.

There are some men who are always in the right place when
they are wanted—always ready to do good and kind actions—
and who are generally found " to the fore " in times of trouble.
Such a man was General Mainwaring. When Lord Ascot fell
down in a fit, he was beside him, and, having seen him doing
well, and having heard from him, as he recovered, the fearful
extent of the disaster, he had posted across country to Ranford
and told Lady Ascot.

She took it very quietly.

"Win or lose," she said, "it is all one to this unhappy house.
Tell them to get out my horses, dear general, and let me go to
my poor darling Ascot. You have heard nothing of Charles
Ravenshoe, general ? "

"Nothing, my dear lady."

Charles had brushed his sleeve in the crowd that day, and
had longed to take the dear old brown hand in his again, but
dare not ! Poor Charles ! If he had only done so !

So the general and Lady Ascot went off together, and nursed
Lord Ascot ; and Adelaide, pale as death, but beautiful as ever,
was driven home through the dust and turmoil, clenching her
hands impatiently together at every stoppage on the road.

CHAPTER XXXVII

LORD WELTER'S MÉNAGE

THERE was a time, a time we have seen, when Lord Welter
was a merry, humorous, thoughtless boy. A boy, one would
have said, with as little real mischief in him as might be. He
might have made a decent member of society, who knows ?
But to do him justice, he had had everything against him from
his earliest childhood. He had never known what a mother
was, or a sister. His earliest companions were grooms and
gamekeepers ; and his religious instruction was got mostly from

his grandmother, whose old-fashioned Sunday-morning lectures and collect learnings, so rigidly pursued that he dreaded Sunday of all days in the week, were succeeded by cock-fighting in the Croft with his father in the afternoon, and lounging away the evening among the stable-boys. As Lord Saltire once said, in the former part of this story, " Ranford was what the young men of the day called an uncommon fast house."

Fast enough, in truth. "All downhill and no drag on." Welter soon defied his grandmother. For his father he cared nothing. Lord Ascot was so foolishly fond of the boy that he never contradicted him in anything, and used even to laugh when he was impudent to his grandmother, whom, to do Lord Ascot justice, he respected more than any living woman. Tutors were tried, of whom Welter, by a happy combination of obstinacy and recklessness, managed to vanquish three, in as many months. It was hopeless. Lord Ascot would not hear of his going to school. He was his only boy, his darling. He could not part with him ; and, when Lady Ascot pressed the matter, he grew obstinate, as he could at times, and said he would not. The boy would do well enough ; he had been just like him at his age, and look at him now !

Lord Ascot was mistaken. He had not been quite like Lord Welter at his age. He had been a very quiet sort of boy indeed. Lord Ascot was a great stickler for blood in horses, and understood such things. I wonder he could not have seen the difference between the sweet, loving face of his mother, capable of violent, furious passion though it was, and that of his coarse, stupid, handsome, gipsy-looking wife, and judged accordingly. He had engrafted a new strain of blood on the old Staunton stock, and was to reap the consequences.

What was to become of Lord Welter was a great problem, still unsolved ; when, one night, shortly before Charles paid his first visit to Ranford, vice Cuthbert, disapproved of, Lord Ascot came up, as his custom was, into his mother's dressing-room, to have half-an-hour's chat with her before she went to bed.

"I wonder, mother dear," he said, "whether I ought to ask old Saltire again, or not ? He wouldn't come last time, you know. If I thought he wouldn't come, I'd ask him."

"You must ask him," said Lady Ascot, brushing her grey hair, "and he will come."

"*Very* well," said Lord Ascot. "It's a bore ; but you must have some one to flirt with, I suppose."

Lady Ascot laughed. In fact, she had written before, and told him that he *must* come, for she wanted him ; and come he did.

"Now, Maria," said Lord Saltire, on the first night, as soon as he and Lady Ascot were seated together on a quiet sofa, "what is it? Why have you brought me down to meet this mob of jockeys and gamekeepers? A fortnight here, and not a soul to speak to but Mainwaring and yourself. After I was here last time, dear old Lady Hainault croaked out in a large crowd that some one smelt of the stable."

"Dear old soul," said Lady Ascot. "What a charming, delicate wit she has. You will have to come here again, though. Every year, mind."

"Kismet," said Lord Saltire. "But what is the matter?"

"What do you think of Ascot's boy?"

"Oh, Lord!" said Lord Saltire. "So I have been brought all this way to be consulted about a schoolboy. Well, I think he looks an atrocious young cub, as like his dear mamma as he can be. I always used to expect that she would call me a pretty gentleman, and want to tell my fortune."

Lady Ascot smiled: *she* knew her man. She knew he would have died for her and hers.

"He is getting very troublesome," said Lady Ascot. "What would you reco——"

"Send him to Eton," said Lord Saltire.

"But he is very high-spirited, James, and——"

"*Send him to Eton.* Do you hear, Maria?"

"But Ascot won't let him go," said Lady Ascot.

"Oh, he won't, won't he?" said Lord Saltire. "Now, let us hear no more of the cub, but have our picquet in peace."

The next morning Lord Saltire had an interview with Lord Ascot, and two hours afterwards it was known that Lord Welter was to go to Eton at once.

And so, when Lord Welter met Charles at Twyford, he told him of it.

At Eton, he had rapidly found other boys brought up with the same tastes as himself, and with these he consorted. A rapid interchange of experiences went on among these young gentlemen; which ended in Lord Welter, at all events, being irreclaimably vicious.

Lord Welter had fallen in love with Charles, as boys do, and their friendship had lasted on, waning as it went, till they permanently met again at Oxford. There, though their intimacy was as close as ever, the old love died out, for a time, amidst riot and debauchery. Charles had some sort of creed about women; Lord Welter had none. Charles drew a line at a certain point, low down it might be, which he never passed; Welter set no bounds anywhere. What Lord Hainault said of him at Tattersall's was true. One day, when they had been arguing on this point rather sharply, Charles said—

"If you mean what you say, you are not fit to come into a gentleman's house. But you don't mean it, old cock; so don't be an ass."

He did mean it, and Charles was right. Alas! that ever he should have come to Ravenshoe!

Lord Welter had lived so long in the house with Adelaide that he never thought of making love to her. They used to quarrel, like Benedict and Beatrice. What happened was her fault. She was worthless. Worthless. Let us have done with it. I can expand over Lord Saltire and Lady Ascot, and such good people, but I cannot over her, more than is necessary.

Two things Lord Welter was very fond of—brawling and dicing. He was an arrant bully; very strong, and perfect in the use of his fists, and of such courage and tenacity that, having once begun a brawl, no one had ever made him leave it, save as an unqualified victor. This was getting well known now. Since he had left Oxford and had been living in London, he had been engaged in two or three personal encounters in the terribly fast society to which he had betaken himself, and men were getting afraid of him. Another thing was, that, drink as he would, he never played the worse for it. He was a lucky player. Sometimes, after winning money of a man, he would ask him home to have his revenge. That man generally went again and again to Lord Welter's house, in St. John's Wood, and did not find himself any the richer. It was the most beautiful little gambling den in London, and it was presided over by one of the most beautiful, witty, fascinating women ever seen. A woman with whom all the men fell in love; so staid, so respectable, and charmingly behaved. Lord Welter always used to call her Lady Welter; so they all called her Lady Welter too, and treated her as though she were.

But this Lady Welter was soon to be dethroned to make room for Adelaide. A day or two before they went off together, this poor woman got a note from Welter to tell her to prepare for a new mistress. It was no blow to her. He had prepared her for it for some time. There might have been tears, wild tears, in private; but what cared he for the

tears of such an one? When Lord Welter and Adelaide
came home, and Adelaide came with him into the hall, she
advanced towards her, dressed as a waiting-woman, and said
quietly—

"You are welcome home, madam."

It was Ellen, and Lord Welter was the delinquent, as you
have guessed already. When she fled from Ravenshoe, she
was flying from the anger of her supposed brother William;
for he thought he knew all about it; and, when Charles and
Marston saw her passing round the cliff, she was making her
weary way on foot towards Exeter to join him in London.
After she was missed, William had written to Lord Welter,
earnestly begging him to tell him if he had heard of her. And
Welter had written back to him that he knew nothing, on his
honour. Alas for Welter's honour, and William's folly in
believing him!

Poor Ellen! Lord Welter had thought that she would have
left the house, and had good reason for thinking so. But,
when he got home, there she was, all her finery cast away,
dressed plainly and quietly. And there she stayed, waiting on
Adelaide, demure and quiet as a waiting-woman should be.
Adelaide had never been to Ravenshoe, and did not know
her. Lord Welter had calculated on her going; but she
stayed on. Why?

You must bear with me, indeed you must, at such times as
these. I touch as lightly as I can; but I have undertaken to
tell a story, and I must tell it. These things are going on
about us, and we try to ignore them, till they are thrust
rudely upon us, as they are twenty times a year. No English
story about young men could be complete without bringing in
subjects which some may think best left alone. Let us
comfort ourselves with one great, undeniable fact,—the immense
improvement in morals which has taken place in the last ten
years. The very outcry which is now raised against such
relations shows plainly one thing at least—that undeniable
facts are being winked at no longer, and that some reform is
coming. Every younger son who can command £200 a year
ought to be allowed to marry in his own rank in life, whatever
that may be. They will be uncomfortable, and have to save
and push; and a very good thing for them. They won't lose
caste. There are some things worse than mere discomfort.
Let us look at bare facts, which no one dare deny. There is
in the great world, and the upper middle-class world too, a
crowd of cadets; younger sons, clerks, officers in the army,

and so on; non-marrying men, as the slang goes, who are
asked out to dine and dance with girls who are their equals
in rank, and who have every opportunity of falling in love
with them. And yet if one of this numerous crowd were to
dare to fall in love with, and to propose to, one of these girls,
he would be denied the house. It is the fathers and mothers
who are to blame, to a great extent, for the very connexions
they denounce so loudly. But yet the very outcry they are
raising against these connexions is a hopeful sign.

Lieutenant Hornby, walking up and down the earth to see
what mischief he could get into, had done a smart stroke of
business in that way, by making the acquaintance of Lord
Welter at a gambling-house. Hornby was a very good fellow.
He had two great pleasures in life. One, I am happy to say,
was soldiering, at which he worked like a horse, and the other,
I am very sorry to say, was gambling, at which he worked a
great deal harder than he should. He was a marked man
among professional players. Every one knew how awfully
rich he was, and every one in succession had a "shy" at him.
He was not at all particular. He would accept a battle with
any one. Gaming men did all sorts of dirty things to get
introduced to him, and play with him. The greater number
of them had their wicked will; but the worst of it was that he
always won. Sometimes, at a game of chance, he might lose
enough to encourage his enemies to go on; but at games of
skill no one could touch him. His billiard playing was simply
masterly. And Dick Ferrers will tell you, that he and Hornby,
being once, I am very sorry to say, together at G—n—ch
F—r, were accosted in the park by a skittle-sharper, and that
Hornby (who would, like Faust, have played chess with Old
Gooseberry) allowed himself to be taken into a skittle-ground,
from which he came out in half-an-hour victorious over the
skittle-sharper, beating him easily.

In the heyday of his fame, Lord Welter was told of him,
and saying, "Give me the daggers," got introduced to him.
They had a tournament at *écarté*, or billiards, or something
or another of that sort, it don't matter; and Lord Welter
asked him up to St. John's Wood, where he saw Ellen.

He lost that night liberally, as he could afford to; and, with
very little persuasion, was induced to come there the next.
He lost liberally again. He had fallen in love with Ellen.

Lord Welter saw it, and made use of it as a bait to draw on
Hornby to play. Ellen's presence was, of course, a great
attraction to him, and he came and played; but unluckily for

Lord Welter, after a few nights his luck changed, or he took more care, and he began to win again; so much so that, about the time when Adelaide came home, my Lord Welter had had nearly enough of Lieutenant Hornby, and was in hopes that he should have got rid of Ellen and him together; for his lordship was no fool about some things, and saw plainly this— that Hornby was passionately fond of Ellen, and, moreover, that poor Ellen had fallen deeply in love with Hornby.

So, when he came home, he was surprised and angry to find her there. She would not go. She would stay and wait on Adelaide. She had been asked to go; but had refused sharply the man she loved. Poor girl, she had her reasons; and we shall see what they were. Now you know what I meant when I wondered whether or no Charles would have burnt Hornby's house down if he had known all. But you will be rather inclined to forgive Hornby presently, as Charles did when he came to know everything.

But the consequence of Ellen's staying on as a servant to Adelaide brought this with it, that Hornby determined that he would have the *entrée* of the house at St. John's Wood, at any price. Lord Welter guessed this, and guessed that Hornby would be inclined to lose a little money in order to gain it. When he brushed Charles's knee in Piccadilly he was deliberating whether or no he should ask him back there again. As he stood unconsciously almost touching Charles, he came to the determination that he would try what bargain he could make with the honour of Charles's sister, whom he had so shamefully injured already. And Charles saw them make the appointment together in the balcony. How little he guessed for what!

Lord Hainault was right. Welter was a scoundrel. But Hornby was not, as we shall see.

Hornby loved play for play's sake. And, extravagant dandy though he was, the attorney blood of his father came out sometimes so strong in him that, although he would have paid any price to be near, and speak to Ellen, yet he could not help winning, to Lord Welter's great disgust, and his own great amusement. Their game, I believe, was generally *picquet* or *écarté*, and at both these he was Lord Welter's master. What with his luck and his superior play, it was very hard to lose decently sometimes; and sometimes, as I said, he would cast his plans to the winds, and win terribly. But he always repented when he saw Lord Welter get savage, and lost dutifully, though at times he could barely keep his countenance. Nevertheless the balance he allowed to Lord Welter made a very important item in that gentleman's somewhat precarious income.

But, in spite of all his sacrifices, he but rarely got even a glimpse of Ellen. And, to complicate matters, Adelaide, who sat by and watched the play, and saw Hornby purposely losing at times, got it into her silly head that he was in love with her. She liked the man; who did not? But she had honour enough left to be rude to him. Hornby saw all this, and was amused. I often think that it must have been a fine spectacle, to see the honourable man playing with the scoundrel, and give him just as much line as he chose. And when I call Hornby an honourable man, I mean what I say, as you will see.

This was the state of things when the Derby crash came. At half-past five on that day, the Viscountess Welter dashed up to her elegant residence in St. John's Wood, in a splendid barouche, drawn by four horses, and when "her people" came and opened the door and let down the steps, lazily descended, and, followed by her footman bearing her fal-lals, lounged up the steps as if life were really too ennuyant to be borne any longer. Three hours afterwards, a fierce eager woman, plainly dressed, with a dark veil, was taking apartments in the Bridge Hotel, London Bridge, for Mr. and Mrs. Staunton, who were going abroad in a few days; and was overseeing, with her confidential servant, a staid man in black, the safe stowage of numerous hasped oak boxes, the most remarkable thing about which was their great weight. The lady was Lady Welter, and the man was Lord Welter's confidential scoundrel. The landlord thought they had robbed Hunt and Roskell's, and were off with the plunder, till he overheard the man say, "I think that is all, my lady;" after which he was quite satisfied. The fact was that all the Ascot race plate, gold salvers and épergnes, silver cups rough with designs of the chase, and possibly also some of the Ascot family jewels, were so disgusted with the state of things in England, that they were thinking of going for a little trip on the Continent. What should a dutiful wife do but see to their safe stowage? If any enterprising burglar had taken it into his head to "crack" that particular "crib" known as the Bridge Hotel, and got clear off with the "swag," he might have retired on the hard-earned fruits of a well-spent life into happier lands—might have been "run" for M.L.C., or possibly for Congress in a year or two. Who can tell?

And, also, if Lord Welter's confidential scoundrel had taken it into his head to waylay and rob his lordship's noble consort on her way home—which he was quite capable of doing—and if he also had got clear off, he would have found himself a better man by seven hundred and ninety-four pounds, three half-crowns, and a three-penny piece; that is, if he had done it before her ladyship had paid the cabman. But both the burglar and the valet missed the tide, and the latter regrets it to this day.

At eleven o'clock that night, Lady Welter was lolling leisurely on her drawing-room sofa, quite bored to death. When Lord Welter and Hornby, and Sir Robert Ferrers and some Dragoons came in, she was yawning, as if life was really too much of a plague to be endured. Would she play loo? Oh, yes; anything after such a wretched, lonely evening. That was the game where you had three cards, wasn't it, and you needn't go on unless you liked. Would Welter or some one lend her some money. She had got a three-penny piece and a shilling somewhere or another, but that would not be enough, she supposed. Where was Sir Robert's little brother? Gone to bed? How tiresome; she had fallen in love with him, and had set her heart on seeing him to-night. And so on.

Lord Welter gave her a key, and told her there was some money in his dressing-case. As she left the room, Hornby, who was watching them, saw a quick look of intelligence pass between them, and laughed in his sleeve.

I have been given to understand that guinea unlimited loo is a charming pursuit, soothing to the feelings, and highly improving to the moral tone. I speak from hearsay, as circumstances over which I have no control have prevented my ever trying it. But this I know—that, if Lord Welter's valet had robbed his master and mistress, when they went to bed that night, instead of netting seven hundred and ninety-four, seven, nine, he would have netted eleven hundred and forty-six, eight, six; leaving out the three-penny piece. But he didn't do it; and Lord and Lady Welter slept that sleep which is the peculiar reward of a quiet conscience undisturbed.

But, next morning, when Charles waited on Hornby, in his dressing-room, the latter said—

"I shall want you to-night, lad. I thought I might have last night; but, seeing the other fellows went, I left you at home. Be ready at half-past six. I lost a hundred and twenty pounds last night. I don't mean to afford it any longer. I shall stop it."

"Where are we to go to, sir?"

"To St. John's Wood. We shall be up late. Leave the servants' hall, and come up and lie in the hall, as if you were asleep. Don't let yourself be seen. No one will notice you."

Charles little thought where he was going.

CHAPTER XXXVIII

THE HOUSE FULL OF GHOSTS

CHARLES had really no idea where he was going. Although he knew that Hornby had been playing with Lord Welter, yet he thought, from what Hornby had said, that he would not bring him into collision with him ; and indeed he did not— only taking Charles with him as a reserve in case of accidents, for he thoroughly distrusted his lordship.

At half-past six in the evening Hornby rode slowly away, followed by Charles. He had told Charles that he should dine in St. John's Wood at seven, and should ride there, and Charles was to wait with the horses. But it was nearly seven, and yet Hornby loitered, and seemed undetermined. It was a wild, gusty evening, threatening rain. There were very few people abroad, and those who were rode or walked rapidly. And yet Hornby dawdled irresolutely, as though his determination were hardly strong enough yet.

At first he rode quite away from his destination, but by degrees his horse's head got changed into the right direction ; then he made another detour, but a shorter one; at last he put spurs to his horse, and rode resolutely up the short carriage-drive before the door, and, giving the reins to Charles, walked firmly in.

Charles put up the horses and went into the servants' hall, or the room which answered that end in the rather small house of Lord Welter. No one was there. All the servants were busy with the dinner, and Charles was left unnoticed.

By and by a page, noticing a strange servant in passing the door, brought him some beer, and a volume of the Newgate Calendar. This young gentleman called his attention to the print of a lady cutting up the body of her husband with a chopper, assisted by a young Jew, who was depicted "walking off with a leg," like one of the Fans (the use of which seems to be, to cool the warm imagination of other travellers into proper limits), while the woman was preparing for another effort. After having recommended Charles to read the letterpress thereof, as he would find it tolerably spicy, he departed, and left him alone.

The dinner was got over in time; and after a time there was silence in the house—a silence so great that Charles rose and left the room. He soon found his way to another ; but all was dark and silent, though it was not more than half-past nine.

He stood in the dark passage, wondering where to go, and determined to turn back to the room from which he had come. There was a light there, at all events.

There was a light, and the Newgate Calendar. The wild wind, that had eddied and whirled the dust at the street corners, and swept across the park all day, had gone down, and the rain had come on. He could hear it drip, drip, outside ; it was very melancholy. Confound the Newgate Calendar.

He was in a very queer house, he knew. What did Hornby mean by asking him the night before whether or no he could fight, and whether he would stick to him ? Drip, drip ; otherwise a dead silence. Charles's heart began to beat a little faster.

Where were all the servants ? He had heard plenty of them half an hour ago. He had heard a French cook swearing at English kitchen-girls, and had heard plenty of other voices ; and now—the silence of the grave. Or of Christie and Manson's on Saturday evening ; or of the Southern Indian Ocean in a calm at midnight ; or of anything else you like ; similes are cheap.

He remembered now that Hornby had said, " Come and lie in the hall as if asleep ; no one will notice you." He determined to do so. But where was it ? His candle was flickering in its socket, and, as he tried to move it, it went out.

He could scarcely keep from muttering an oath, but he did. His situation was very uncomfortable. He did not know in what house he was—only that he was in a quarter of the town in which there were not a few uncommonly queer houses. He determined to grope his way to the light.

He felt his way out of the room and along a passage. The darkness was intense, and the silence perfect. Suddenly a dull red light gleamed in his eyes, and made him start. It was the light of the kitchen fire. A cricket would have been company, but there was none.

He continued to advance cautiously. Soon a ghostly square of very dim grey light on his left showed him where was a long narrow window. It was barred with iron bars. He was just thinking of this, and how very queer it was, when he uttered a loud oath, and came crashing down. He had fallen upstairs.

He had made noise enough to waken the seven sleepers; but those gentlemen did not seem to be in the neighbourhood, or, at all events, if awakened gave no sign of it. Dead silence. He sat on the bottom stair and rubbed his shins, and in spite of a strong suspicion that he had got into a scrape, laughed to himself at the absurdity of his position.

"Would it be worth while, I wonder," he said to himself, "to go back to the kitchen and get the poker? I'd better not, I suppose. It would be so deuced awkward to be caught in the dark with a poker in your hand. Being on the premises for the purpose of committing a felony—that is what they would say; and then they would be sure to say that you were the companion of thieves, and had been convicted before. No. Under this staircase, in the nature of things, is the housemaid's cupboard. What should I find there as a weapon of defence? A dust-pan. A great deal might be done with a dust-pan, mind you, at close quarters. How would it do to arrange all her paraphernalia on the stairs, and cry fire, so that mine enemies, rushing forth, might stumble and fall, and be taken unawares? But that would be acting on the offensive, and I have no safe grounds for pitching into anyone yet."

Though Charles tried to comfort himself by talking nonsense, he was very uncomfortable. Staying where he was, was intolerable; and he hardly dared to ascend into the upper regions unbidden. Besides, he had fully persuaded himself that a disturbance was imminent, and though a brave man, did not like to precipitate it. He had mistaken the character of the house he was in. At last, taking heart, he turned and felt his way upstairs. He came before a door through the keyhole of which the light streamed strongly; he was deliberating whether to open it or not, when a shadow crossed it, though he heard no noise, but a minute after the distant sound of a closing door. He could stand it no longer. He opened the door, and advanced into a blaze of light.

He entered a beautiful flagged hall, frescoed and gilded.

There were vases of flowers round the walls, and strips of
Indian matting on the pavement. It was lit by a single
chandelier, which was reflected in four great pier-glasses
reaching to the ground, in which Charles's top-boots and brown
face were re-duplicated most startlingly. The *tout ensemble*
was very beautiful; but what struck Charles was the bad taste of
having an entrance-hall decorated like a drawing-room. "That
is just the sort of thing they do in these places," he thought.

There were only two hats on the entrance table; one of
which he was rejoiced to recognise as that of his most respected
master. "May the deuce take his silly noddle for bringing me
to such a place!" thought Charles.

This was evidently the front hall spoken of by Hornby;
and he remembered his advice to pretend to go to sleep.
So he lay down on three hall-chairs, and put his hat over
his eyes.

Hall-chairs are hard; and, although Charles had just been
laughing at the proprietor of the house for being so lavish in
his decorations, he now wished that he had carried out his
system a little farther, and had cushions to his chairs. But
no; the chairs were *de rigueur*, with crests on the back of them.
Charles did not notice whose.

If a man pretends to go to sleep, and, like the Marchioness
with her orange-peel and water, "makes believe very much,"
he may sometimes succeed in going to sleep in good earnest.
Charles imitated the thing so well, that in five minutes he was
as fast off as a top.

Till a night or two before this, Charles had never dreamt of
Ravenshoe since he had left it. When the first sharp sting of
his trouble was in his soul, his mind had refused to go back
farther than to the events of a day or so before. He had
dreamt long silly dreams of his master, or his fellow-servants,
or his horses, but always, all through the night, with a dread
on him of waking in the dark. But, as his mind began to
settle and his pain got dulled, he began to dream about
Ravenshoe, and Oxford, and Shrewsbury again; and he no
longer dreaded the waking as he did, for the reality of his life
was no longer hideous to him. With the fatal "plasticity" of
his nature, he had lowered himself, body and soul, to the level
of it.

But to-night, as he slept on these chairs, he dreamt of
Ravenshoe, and of Cuthbert, and of Ellen. And he woke,
and she was standing within ten feet of him, under the
chandelier.

He was awake in an instant, but he lay as still as a mouse, staring at her. She had not noticed him, but was standing in profound thought. Found, and so soon! His sister! How lovely she was, standing, dressed in light pearl grey, like some beautiful ghost, with her speaking eyes fixed on nothing. She moved now, but so lightly that her footfall was barely heard upon the matting. Then she turned and noticed him. She did not seemed surprised at seeing a groom stretched out asleep on the chairs—she was used to that sort of thing, probably—but she turned away, gliding through a door at the further end of the hall, and was gone.

Charles's heart was leaping and beating madly, but he heard another door open, and lay still.

Adelaide came out of a door opposite to the one into which Ellen had passed. Charles was not surprised. He was beyond surprise. But, when he saw her and Ellen in the same house, in one instant, with the quickness of lightning, he understood it all. It was Welter had tempted Ellen from Ravenshoe. Fool! fool! he might have prevented it once if he had only guessed.

If he had any doubt as to where he was now, it was soon dispelled. Lord Welter came rapidly out of the door after Adelaide, and called her in a whisper, " Adelaide."

"Well," she said, turning round sharply.

"Come back, do you hear?" said Lord Welter. "Where the deuce are you going?"

"To my own room."

"Come back, I tell you," said Lord Welter, savagely, in a low voice. "You are going to spoil everything with your confounded airs."

"I shall not come back. I am not going to act as a decoy-duck to that man, or any other man. Let me go, Welter."

Lord Welter was very near having to let her go with a vengeance. Charles was ready for a spring, but watched, and waited his time. Lord Welter had only caught her firmly by the wrist to detain her. He was not hurting her.

"Look you here, my Lady Welter," he said, slowly and distinctly. "Listen to what I've got to say, and don't try the shadow of a tantrum with me, for I won't have it for one moment. I don't mind your chaff and nonsense in public; it blinds people, it is racy and attracts people; but in private I am master, do you hear? Master. You know you are afraid of me, and have good cause to be, by Jove! You are shaking now. Go back to that room."

"I won't, I won't, I won't. Not without you, Welter. How can you use me so cruelly, Welter? Oh, Welter, how can you be such a villain?"

"You conceited fool," said Lord Welter, contemptuously. "Do you think he wants to make love to you?"

"You know he does, Welter; you know it," said Adelaide passionately.

Lord Welter laughed good-naturedly. (He could be good-natured.) He drew her towards him and kissed her. "My poor little girl," he said, "if I thought that, I would break his neck. But it is utterly wide of the truth. Look here, Adelaide; you are as safe from insult as my wife, as you were at Ranford. What you are not safe from is my own temper. Let us be friends in private and not squabble so much, eh? You are a good shrewd, clever wife to me. Do keep your tongue quiet. Come in and mark what follows."

They had not noticed Charles, though he had been so sure that they would, that he had got his face down on the chair, covered with his arms, feigning sleep. When they went into the room again, Charles caught hold of a coat which was on the back of a chair, and, curling himself up, put it over him. He would listen, listen, listen for every word. He had a right to listen now.

In a minute a bell rang twice. Almost at the same moment some one came out of the door through which Lord Welter had passed, and stood silent. In about two minutes another door opened, and some one else came into the hall.

A woman's voice—Ellen's—said, "Oh, are you come again?"

A man's voice—Lieutenant Hornby's—said in answer, "You see I am. I got Lady Welter to ring her bell twice for you, and then to stay in that room, so that I might have an interview with you."

"I am obliged to her ladyship. She must have been surprised that I was the object of attraction. She fancied herself so."

"She was surprised. And she was more so when I told her what my real object was."

"Indeed," said Ellen bitterly. "But her ladyship's surprise does not appear to have prevented her from assisting you."

"On the contrary," said Hornby, "she wished me God speed—her own words."

"Sir, you are a gentleman. Don't disgrace yourself and me—if I can be disgraced—by quoting that woman's blasphemy before me. Sir, you have had your answer. I shall go."

"Ellen, you must stay. I have got this interview with you to-night, to ask you to be my wife. I love you as I believe woman was never loved before, and I ask you to be my wife."

"You madman! You madman!"

"I am no madman. I was a madman when I spoke to you before; I pray your forgiveness for that. You must forget that. I say that I love you as a woman was never loved before. Shall I say something more, Ellen?"

"Say on."

"You love me."

"I love you as man was never loved before; and I swear to you that I hope I may lie stiff and cold in my unhonoured coffin, before I'll ruin the man I love by tying him to such a wretch as myself."

"Ellen, Ellen, don't say that. Don't take such vows, which you will not dare to break afterwards. Think, you may regain all that you have lost, and marry a man who loves you—ah, so dearly!—and whom you love too."

"Ay; there's the rub. If I did not love you, I would marry you to-morrow. Regain all I have lost, say you? Bring my mother to life again, for instance, or walk among other women again as an honest one? You talk nonsense, Mr. Hornby— nonsense. I am going."

"Ellen! Ellen! Why do you stay in this house? Think once again."

"I shall never leave thinking; but my determination is the same. I tell you, as a desperate woman like me dare tell you, that I love you far too well to ruin your prospects, and I love my own soul too well ever to make another false step. I stayed in this house because I loved to see you now and then, and hear your voice; but now I shall leave it."

"See me once more, Ellen—only once more!"

"I will see you once more. I will tear my heart once more, if you wish it. You have deserved all I can do for you, God knows. Come here the day after to-morrow; but come without hope, mind. A woman who has been through what I have can trust herself. Do you know that I am a Catholic?"

"No."

"I am. Would you turn Catholic if I were to marry you?" God forgive poor Hornby! He said, "Yes." What will not men say at such times?

"Did I not say you were a madman? Do you think I would ruin you in the next world, as well as in this? Go away, sir;

and, when your children are round you, humbly bless God's mercy for saving you, body and soul, this night."

"I shall see you again?"

"Come here the day after to-morrow; but come without hope."

She passed through the door, and left him standing alone. Charles rose from his lair, and coming up to him, laid his hand on his shoulder.

"You have heard all this," said poor Hornby.

"Every word," said Charles. "I had a right to listen, you know. She is my sister."

"Your sister?"

Then Charles told him all. Hornby had heard enough from Lord Welter to understand it.

"Your sister! Can you help me, Horton? Surely she will hear reason from you. Will you persuade her to listen to me?"

"No," said Charles. "She was right. You are mad. I will not help you do an act which you would bitterly repent all your life. You must forget her. She and I are disgraced, and must get away somewhere, and hide our shame together."

What Hornby would have answered, no man can tell; for at this moment Adelaide came out of the room, and passed quickly across the hall, saying good night to him as she passed. She did not recognise Charles, or seem surprised at seeing Hornby talking to his groom. Nobody who had lived in Lord Welter's house a day or two was surprised at anything.

But Charles, speaking to Hornby more as if he were master than servant, said, "Wait here;" and, stepping quickly from him, went into the room where Lord Welter sat alone, and shut the door. Hornby heard it locked behind him, and waited in the hall, listening intensely for what was to follow.

"There'll be a row directly," said Hornby to himself; "and that chivalrous fool, Charles, has locked himself in. I wish Welter did not send all his servants out of the house at night. There'll be murder done here some day."

He listened and heard voices, low as yet—so low that he could hear the dripping of the rain outside. Drip—drip! The suspense was intolerable. When would they be at one another's throats?

CHAPTER XXXIX

CHARLES'S EXPLANATION WITH LORD WELTER

THERE is a particular kind of Ghost or Devil, which is represented by an isosceles triangle (more or less correctly drawn) for the body; straight lines turned up at the ends for legs; straight lines divided into five at the ends for arms; a round O, with arbitrary dots for the features, for a head; with a hat, an umbrella, and a pipe. Drawn like this, it is a sufficiently terrible object. But if you take an ace of clubs, make the club represent the head, add horns, and fill in the body and limbs as above, in deep black, with the feather end of the pen, it becomes simply appalling, and will strike terror into the stoutest heart.

Is this the place, say you, for talking such nonsense as this? if you must give us balderdash of this sort, could not you do so in a chapter with a less terrible heading than this one has? And I answer, Why not let me tell my story my own way? Something depends even on this nonsense of making devils out of the ace of clubs.

It was rather a favourite amusement of Charles's and Lord Welter's, in old times at Ranford. They used, on rainy afternoons, to collect all the old aces of clubs (and there were always plenty of them to be had in that house, God help it), and make devils out of them, each one worse than the first. And now, when Charles had locked the door, and advanced softly up to Welter, he saw, over his shoulder, that he had got an ace of clubs, and the pen and ink, and was making a devil.

It was a trifling circumstance enough, perhaps; but there was enough of old times in it to alter the tone in which Charles said, "Welter," as he laid his hand on his shoulder.

Lord Welter was a bully; but he was as brave as a lion, with nerves of steel. He neither left off his drawing, nor looked up; he only said—"Charley, boy, come and sit down till I have finished this fellow. Get an ace of clubs and try your own hand. I am out of practice."

Perhaps even Lord Welter might have started when he heard Charles's voice, and felt his hand on his shoulder; but he had had one instant—only one instant—of preparation. When he heard the key turn in the door, he had looked in a pier-glass opposite to him, and seen who and what was coming, and then gone on with his employment. Even allowing for this moment's preparation, we must give him credit for the nerve of one man in ten thousand; for the apparition of Charles Ravenshoe was as unlooked for as that of any one of Charles Ravenshoe's remote ancestors.

You see, I call him Charles Ravenshoe still. It is a trick. You must excuse it.

Charles did not sit down and draw devils; he said, in a quiet, mournful tone,

"Welter, Welter, why have you been such a villain?"

Lord Welter found that a difficult question to answer. He let it alone, and said nothing.

"I say nothing about Adelaide. You did not use me well there; for, when you persuaded her to go off with you, you had not heard of my ruin."

"On my soul, Charles, there was not much persuasion wanted there."

"Very likely. I do not want to speak about that, but about Ellen, my sister. Was anything ever done more shamefully than that?"

Charles expected some furious outbreak when he said that. None came. What was good in Lord Welter came to the surface, when he saw his old friend and playmate there before him, sunk so far below him in all that this world considers worth having, but rising so far above him in his fearless honour and manliness. He was humbled, sorry, and ashamed. Bitter as Charles's words were, he felt they were true, and had manhood enough left not to resent them. To the sensation of fear, as I have said before, Lord Welter was a total stranger, or he might have been nervous at being locked up in a room alone, with a desperate man, physically his equal, whom he had so shamefully wronged. He rose and leant against the chimney-piece, looking at Charles.

"I did not know she was your sister, Charles. You must do me that justice."

"Of course you did not. If——"

"I know what you are going to say—that I should not have dared. On my soul, Charles, I don't know; I believe I dare do anything. But I tell you one thing—of all the men who walk this earth, you are the last I would willingly wrong. When I went off with Adelaide, I knew she did not care six-pence for you. I knew she would have made you wretched. I knew better than you, because I never was in love with her, and you were, what a heartless, ambitious jade it was! She sold herself to me for the title I gave her, as she had tried to sell herself to that solemn prig, Hainault, before. And I bought her, because a handsome, witty, clever wife is a valuable chattel to a man like me, who has to live by his wits."

"Ellen was as handsome and as clever as she. Why did not you marry her?" said Charles bitterly.

"If you will have the real truth, Ellen would have been Lady Welter now, but——"

Lord Welter hesitated. He was a great rascal, and he had a brazen front, but he found a difficulty in going on. It must be, I should fancy, very hard work to tell all the little ins and outs of a piece of villany one has been engaged in, and to tell, as Lord Welter did on this occasion, the exact truth.

"I am waiting," said Charles, "to hear you tell me why she was not made Lady Welter."

"What, you will have it then? Well, she was too scrupulous. She was too honourable a woman for this line of business. She wouldn't play, or learn to play—d—n it, sir, you have got the whole truth now, if that will content you."

"I believe what you say, my lord. Do you know that Lieutenant Hornby made her an offer of marriage to-night."

"I supposed he would," said Lord Welter.

"And that she has refused him?"

"I guessed that she would. She is your own sister. Shall you try to persuade her?"

"I would see her in her coffin first."

"So I suppose."

"She must come away from here, Lord Welter. I must keep her and do what I can for her. We must pull through it together somehow."

"She had better go from here. She is too good for this hole. I must make provision for her to live with you."

"Not one halfpenny, my lord. She has lived too long in dependence and disgrace already. We will pull through together alone."

Lord Welter said nothing, but he determined that Charles should not have his way in this respect.

Charles continued, "When I came into this room to-night I came to quarrel with you. You have not allowed me to do so, and I thank you for it." Here he paused, and then went on in a lower voice, "I think you are sorry, Welter; are you not? I am sure you are sorry. I am sure you wouldn't have done it if you had foreseen the consequences, eh?"

Lord Welter's coarse under-lip shook for half a second, and his big chest heaved once; but he said nothing.

"Only think another time; that is all. Now do me a favour; make me a promise."

"I have made it."

"Don't tell any human soul you have seen me. If you do, you will only entail a new disguise and a new hiding on me. You have promised."

"On my honour."

"If you keep your promise, I can stay where I am. How is —Lady Ascot?"

"Well. Nursing my father."

"Is he ill?"

"Had a fit the day before yesterday. I heard this morning from them. He is much better, and will get over it."

"Have you heard anything from Ravenshoe?"

"Not a word. Lord Saltire and General Mainwaring are both with my father, in London. Grandma won't see either me or Adelaide. Do you know she has been moving heaven and earth to find you?"

"Good soul! I won't be found, though. Now, good-night!"

And he went. If any one had told him three months before that he would have been locked in the same room with a man who had done him such irreparable injury, and have left it at the end of half an hour with a quiet "good-night," he would most likely have beaten that man there and then. But he was getting tamed very fast. Ay, he was already getting more than tamed; he was in a fair way to get broken-hearted.

"I will not see her to-night, sir," he said to Hornby, whom he found with his head resting on the table; "I will come to-morrow and prepare her for leaving this house. You are to see her the day after to-morrow; but without hope, remember."

He roused a groom from above the stable to help him to saddle the horses. "Will it soon be morning?" he asked.

"Morning," said the lad; "it's not twelve o'clock yet. It's a dark night, mate, and no moon. But the nights are short now. The dawn will be on us before we have time to turn in our beds."

He rode slowly home after Hornby. "The night is dark, but the dawn will be upon us before we can turn in our beds!" Only the idle words of a sleepy groom, yet they echoed in his ears all the way home. The night is dark indeed; but it will be darker yet before the dawn, Charles Ravenshoe.

CHAPTER XL

A DINNER PARTY AMONG SOME OLD FRIENDS

LADY HAINAULT (*née* Burton, not the Dowager) had asked some one to dinner, and the question had been whom to ask to meet him. Mary had been called into consultation, as she generally was on most occasions, and she and Lady Hainault had made up a list together. Every one had accepted, and was coming; and here were Mary and Lady Hainault, dressed for dinner, alone in the drawing-room with the children.

"We could not have done better for him, Mary, I think. You must go in to dinner with him."

"Is Mary going to stop down to dinner?" said the youngest boy; "what a shame! I shan't say my prayers to-night if she don't come up."

The straightforward Gus let his brother know what would be the consequences of such neglect hereafter, in a plain-spoken way peculiarly his own.

"Gus! Gus! don't say such things," said Lady Hainault.

"The hymn-book says so, aunt," said Gus, triumphantly; and he quoted a charming little verse of Dr. Watts, beginning, "There is a dreadful Hell."

Lady Hainault might have been puzzled what to say, and Mary would not have helped her, for they had had an argument about that same hymn-book (Mary contending that one or two of the hymns were as well left alone at first), when Flora struck in and saved her aunt, by remarking—

"I shall save up my money and buy some jewels for Mary like aunt's, so that when she stays down to dinner some of the men may fall in love with her, and marry her."

"Pooh! you silly goose," said Gus, "those jewels cost sixty million thousand pounds a-piece. I don't want her to be married till I grow up, and then I shall marry her myself. Till then, I shall buy her a yellow wig, like grandma Hainault's, and then nobody will want to marry her."

"Be quiet, Gus," said Lady Hainault.

It was one thing to say "Be quiet, Gus," and it was another thing to make him hold his tongue. But, to do Gus justice, he was a good fellow, and never acted "*enfant terrible*" but to the most select and private audience. Now he had begun: "I wish some one would marry grandma," when the door was thrown open, the first guest was announced, and Gus was dumb.

"General Mainwaring." The general sat down between Lady Hainault and Mary, and, while talking to them, reached out his broad brown hand and lifted the youngest boy on his knee, who played with his ribands, and cried out that he would have the orange and blue one, if he pleased; while Gus and Flora came and stood at his knee.

He talked to them both sadly in a low voice about the ruin which had come on Lord Ascot. There was worse than mere ruin, he feared. He feared there was disgrace. He had been with him that morning. He was a wreck. One side of his face was sadly pulled down, and he stammered in his speech. He would get over it. He was only three-and-forty. But he would not show again in society, he feared. Here was somebody else; they would change the subject.

Lord Saltire. They were so glad to see him. Every one's face had a kind smile on it as the old man came and sat down among them. His own smile was not the least pleasant of the lot, I warrant you.

"So you are talking about poor Ascot, eh?" he said. "I don't know whether you were or not; but, if you were, let us talk about something else. You see, my dear Miss Corby, that my prophecy to you on the terrace at Ravenshoe is falsified. I said they would not fight, and lo! they are as good as at it."

They talked about the coming war, and Lord Hainault came in and joined them. Soon after, another guest was announced.

Lady Ascot. She was dressed in dark grey silk, with her white hair simply parted under a plain lace cap. She looked so calm, so brave, so kind, so beautiful, as she came with firm strong step in at the door, that they one and all rose and came towards her. She had always been loved by them all; how much more deeply was she loved now, when her bitter troubles had made her doubly sacred!

Lord Saltire gave her his arm, and she came and sat down among them with her hands calmly folded before her.

"I was determined to come and see you to-night, my dear," she said. "I should break down if I couldn't see some that I loved. And to-night, in particular" (she looked earnestly at Lord Saltire). "Is he come yet?"

"Not yet, dear grandma," said Mary.

"No one is coming besides, I suppose?" asked Lady Ascot.

"No one; we are waiting for him."

The door was opened once more, and they all looked

curiously round. This time the servant announced, perhaps in a somewhat louder tone than usual, as if he were aware that they were more interested—

" Mr. Ravenshoe."

A well-dressed, gentlemanly-looking man came into the room, bearing such a wonderful likeness to Charles Ravenshoe, that Lady Hainault and General Mainwaring, the only two who had never seen him before, started, and thought they saw Charles himself. It was not Charles, though; it was our old friend, William, whilom pad-groom to Charles Ravenshoe, Esquire, now himself William Ravenshoe, Esquire, of Ravenshoe.

He was the guest of the evening. He would be heir to Ravenshoe himself some day; for they had made up their minds that Cuthbert would never marry. Ravenshoe, as Cuthbert was managing it now, would be worth ten or twelve thousand a year, and, if these new tin lodes came to anything, perhaps twenty. He had been a stable-helper, said old Lady Hainault—the companion of the drunken riots of his foster-brother impostor, and that quiet gentlemanly creature Welter. If he entered the house, she left it. To which young Lady Hainault had replied that some one must ask him to dinner in common decency, if it was only for the sake of that dear Charles, who had been loved by every one who knew him. That she intended to ask him to dinner, and that, if her dear mother-in-law objected to meet him, why the remedy lay with herself. Somebody must introduce him to some sort of society; and Lord Hainault and herself had made up their minds to do it, so that further argument on the subject would be wasted breath. To which the Dowager replied that she really wished, after all, that Hainault had married that pretty chit of a thing, Adelaide Summers, as he was thinking of doing; as she, the Dowager, could not have been treated with greater insolence even by her, bold as she was. With which Parthian piece of spite she had departed to Casterton with Miss Hicks, and had so goaded and snapped at that unfortunate reduced gentle-woman by the way, that at last Hicks, as her wont was, had turned upon her and given her as good as she brought. If the Dowager could have heard Lady Hainault telling her lord the whole business that night, and joking with him about his alleged *penchant* for Adelaide and heard the jolly laugh that those two good souls had about it, her ladyship would have been more spiteful still.

But, nevertheless, Lady Hainault was very nervous about William. When Mary was consulted, she promptly went bail

for his good behaviour, and pled his case so warmly that the
tears stood in her eyes.   Her old friend William !   What
innocent plots she and he had hatched together against the
priest in the old times.   What a bond there was between them
in their mutual love for him who was lost to them.

But Lady Hainault would be on the safe side ; and so only
the party named above were asked.   All old friends of the
family.

Before dinner was announced they were all at their ease
about him.   He was shy certainly, but not awkward.   He
evidently knew that he was asked there on trial, and he
accepted his position.   But he was so handsome (handsomer
than poor Charles), he was so gentle and modest, and—
perhaps, too, not least—had such a well modulated voice, that,
before the evening was over he had won every one in the
room.   If he knew anything of a subject he helped the conversation quietly, as well as he could ; if he had to confess
ignorance (which was seldom, for he was among well-bred
people) he did so frankly, but unobtrusively.   He was a great
success.

One thing puzzled him, and pleased him.   He knew that
he was a person of importance, and that he was the guest of
the evening.   But he soon found that there was another cause
for his being interesting to them all, more powerful than his
curious position, or his prospective wealth ; and that was his
connexion with Charles Ravenshoe, now Horton.   *He* was the
hero of the evening.   Half William's light was borrowed from
him.   He quickly became aware of it, and it made him
happy.

How strange it is that some men have the power of winning
such love from all they meet.   I knew one, gone from us now
by a glorious death, who had that faculty.   Only a few knew
his great worth and goodness ; and yet, as his biographer most
truly says, those who once saw his face never forgot it.
Charles Ravenshoe had that faculty also, though, alas, his
value, both in worth and utility, was far inferior to that of the
man to whom I have alluded above.[1]   But he had the same
infinite kindness towards everything created ; which is part of
the secret.

The first hint that William had, as to how deeply important
a person Charles was among the present company, was given
him at dinner.   Various subjects had been talked of indiffer-

[1] I mean C. M.

ently, and William had listened, till Lord Hainault said to William,

"What a strange price people are giving for cobs! I saw one sold to day at Tattersall's for ninety guineas."

William answered, "Good cobs are very hard to get, Lord Hainault. I could get you ten good horses over fifteen, for one good cob."

Lord Saltire said, "My cob is the best I ever had; and a sweet-tempered creature. Our dear boy broke it for me at Ravenshoe."

"Dear Charles," said Lady Ascot. "What a splendid rider he was! Dear boy! He got Ascot to write him a certificate about that sort of thing before he went away. Ah, dear!"

"I never thought," said Lord Saltire, quietly, "that I ever should have cared half as much for anybody as I do for that lad. Do you remember, Mainwaring," he continued, speaking still lower, while they all sat hushed, "the first night I ever saw him, when he marked for you and me at billiards, at Ranford? I don't know why, but I loved the boy from the first moment I saw him. Both there and ever afterwards, he reminded me so strongly of Barkham. He had just the same gentle, winning way with him that Barkham had. Barkham was a little taller, though, I fancy," he went on, looking straight at Lady Ascot, and taking snuff. "Don't you think so, Maria?"

No one spoke for a moment.

Lord Barkham had been Lord Saltire's only son. He had been killed in a duel at nineteen, as I have mentioned before. Lord Saltire very rarely spoke of him, and, when he did, generally in a cynical manner. But General Mainwaring and Lady Ascot knew that the memory of that poor boy was as fresh in the true old heart after forty years, as it was on the morning when he came out from his dressing-room, and met them carrying his corpse upstairs.

"He was a good fellow," said Lord Hainault, alluding to Charles. "He was a very good fellow."

"This great disappointment which I have had about him," said Lord Saltire, in his own dry tone, "is a just judgment on me for doing a good-natured and virtuous action many years ago. When his poor father Densil was in prison, I went to see him, and reconciled him with his family. Poor Densil was so grateful for this act of folly on my part, that I grew personally attached to him; and hence all this misery. Disinterested actions are great mistakes, Maria, depend upon it."

When the ladies were gone upstairs, William found Lord
Saltire beside him. He talked to him a little time, and then
finished by saying—

"You are modest and gentlemanly, and the love you bear
for your foster-brother is very pleasing to me indeed. I am
going to put it to the test. You must come and see me to-
morrow morning. I have a great deal to say to you."

"About him, my lord? Have you heard of him?"

"Not a word. I fear he has gone to America or Australia.
He told Lord Ascot he should do so."

"I'll hunt him to the world's end, my lord," said true
William. "And Cuthbert shall pray for me the while. I fear
you are right. But we shall find him soon."

When they went up into the drawing-room, Mary was sitting
on a sofa by herself. She looked up to William, and he went
and sat down by her. They were quite away from the rest,
together.

"Dear William," said Mary, looking frankly at him, and
laying her hand on his.

"I am so glad," said William, "to see your sweet face again.
I was down at Ravenshoe last week. How they love you
there! An idea prevails among old and young that dear
Cuthbert is to die, and that I am to marry you, and that we
are to rule Ravenshoe triumphantly. It was useless to represent to them that Cuthbert would not die, and that you and I
most certainly never would marry one another. My dearest
Jane Evans was treated as a thing of nought. You were
elected mistress of Ravenshoe unanimously."

"How is Jane?"

"Pining, poor dear, at her school. She don't like it."

"I should think not," said Mary. "Give my dear love to
her. She will make you a good wife. How is Cuthbert?"

"Very well in health. No more signs of his heart
complaint, which never existed. But he is peaking at getting
no tidings from Charles. Ah, how he loved him! May I call
you 'Mary'?"

"You must not dare to call me anything else. No tidings
of him yet?"

"None. I feel sure he is gone to America. We will get
him back, Mary. Never fear."

They talked till she was cheerful, and at last she said—

"William, you were always so well-mannered; but how—
how—have you got to be so gentlemanly in so short a time?"

"By playing at it," said William, laughing. "The stud-groom at Ravenshoe used always to say I was too much of a gentleman for him. In twenty years' time I shall pass muster in a crowd. Good-night."

And Charles was playing at being something other than a gentleman all the time. We shall see who did best in the end.

CHAPTER XLI

CHARLES'S SECOND EXPEDITION TO ST. JOHN'S WOOD

What a happy place a man's bed is—probably the best place in which he ever finds himself. Very few people will like to deny that, I think ; that is to say, as a general rule. After a long day's shooting in cold weather, for instance ; or half a night on deck among the ice, when the fog has lifted, and the ghastly cold walls are safe in sight ; or after a fifty mile ride in the bush, under a pouring rain ; or after a pleasant ball, when you have to pull down the blind, that the impudent sun may not roast you awake in two hours ; for in all these cases, and a hundred more, bed is very pleasant ; but you know as well as I do, that there are times when you would sooner be on a frozen deck, or in the wildest bush in the worst weather, or waltzing in the hall of Eblis with Vathek's mama, or almost in your very grave, than in bed, and awake.

Oh, the weary watches ! when the soul, which in sleep would leave the tortured body to rest and ramble off in dreams, holds on by a mere thread, yet a thread strong enough to keep every nerve in tense agony. When one's waking dreams of the past are as vivid as those of sleep, and there is always present, through all, the dreadful lurking thought that one is awake, and that it is all real. When, looking back, every kindly impulsive action, every heartily spoken word, makes you fancy that you have only earned contempt where you merit kindness. When the past looks like a hell of missed opportunities, and the future like another black hopeless hell of uncertainty and imminent misfortune of all kinds ! Oh, weary watches. Let us be at such times on the bleakest hill-side, in the coldest night that ever blew, rather than in the warmest bed that money will buy.

When you are going to have a night of this kind, you seldom

know it beforehand, for certain. Sometimes, if you have had much experience in the sort of thing—if you have lost money, or gone in debt, or if your sweetheart has cut you very often— you may at least guess, before you get your boots off, that you are going to have a night of it ; in which case, read yourself to sleep *in bed*. Never mind burning the house down (that would be rather desirable as a distraction from thought); but don't read till you are sleepy with your clothes on, and then undress, because, if you do, you will find, by the time you have undressed yourself, that you are terribly wide awake, and, when the candle is blown out, you will be all ready for a regular Walpurgis night.

Charles, poor lad, had not as yet had much experience of Walpurgis nights. Before his catastrophe he had never had one. He had been used to tumble tired into his bed, and sleep a heavy dreamless sleep till an hour before waking. Then, indeed, he might begin to dream of his horses, and his dogs, and so on, and then gradually wake into a state more sweet than the sweetest dream—that state in which sense is awake to all outward objects, but in which the soul is taking its few last airy flutters round its home, before coming to rest for the day. But, even since then, he had not had experience enough to make him dread the night. The night he came home from St. John's Wood, he thought he would go to bed and sleep it off. Poor fellow !

A fellow-servant slept in the same room with him—the younger and better-tempered of the two (though Charles had no complaint against either of them). The lad was asleep ; and, before Charles put out the light, he looked at him. His cheek was laid on his arm, and he seemed so calm and happy that Charles knew that he was not there, but far away. He was right. As he looked, the lad smiled, and babbled of something in his dream. Strange ! the soul had still sufficient connexion with the body to make it smile.

"I wonder if Miss Martineau or Mr. Atkinson ever watched the face of one who slept and dreamt," said Charles, rambling on as soon as he had got into bed. "Pish ! why that fellow's body is the mere tool of his soul. His soul is out a-walking, and his body is only a log. Hey, that won't do ; that's as bad as Miss Martineau. I should have said that his body is only a fine piece of clockwork. But clockwork don't smile of itself. My dear Madam, and Mr. Atkinson, I am going to leave my body behind, and be off at Ravenshoe in five minutes. That is to say, I am going to sleep."

He was, was he? Why no, not just at present. If he had meant to do so, he had, perhaps, better not have bothered himself about "Letters on the laws of man's nature"; for, when he had done his profound cogitations about them, as above, he thought he had got a——well, say a pulex, in his bed. There was no more a pulex than there was a scorpion; but he had an exciting chase after an imaginary one, like our old friend Mr. Sponge after an imaginary fox at Laverick Wells. After this, he had an irritation where he couldn't reach, that is to say, in the middle of his back: then he had the same complaint where he could reach, and used a certain remedy (which is a pretty way of saying that he scratched himself); then he had the cramp in his right leg; then he had the cramp in his left leg; then he grew hot all over, and threw the clothes off; then he grew cold all over, and pulled them on again; then he had the cramp in his left leg again; then he had another flea hunt, cramp, irritation in back, heat, cold, and so on, all over; and then, after half an hour, finding himself in a state of feverish despondency, he fell into a cheerful train of thought, and was quite inclined to look at his already pleasant prospects from a hopeful point of view.

Poor dear fellow! You may say that it is heartless to make fun of him just now, when everything is going so terribly wrong. But really my story is so very sad, that we must try to make a little feeble fun where we can, or it would be unreadable.

He tried to face the future, manfully. But lo, there was no future to face—it was all such a dead, hopeless blank. Ellen must come away from that house, and he must support her; but how? It would be dishonourable for him to come upon the Ravenshoes for a farthing; and it would be dishonourable for her to marry that foolish Hornby. And these two courses, being dishonourable, were impossible. And there he was brought up short.

But would either course be dishonourable? Yes, yes, was the answer each weary time he put the question to himself; and there the matter ended. Was there one soul in the wide world he could consult? Not one. All alone in the weary world, he and she. Not one friend for either of them. They had made their beds, and must lie on them. When would the end of it all come? What would the end be?

There was a noise in the street. A noise of a woman scolding, whose voice got louder and louder, till it rose into a scream. A noise of a man cursing and abusing her; then a louder scream, and a sound of blows. One, two, then a heavy fall, and silence. A drunken, homeless couple had fallen out in the street, and the man had knocked the woman down. That was all. It was very common. Probably the woman was not much hurt. That sort of woman got used to it. The police would come and take them to the station. There they were. The man and woman were being taken off by two constables, scolding and swearing. Well, well !

Was it to come to that ? There were bridges in London, and under them runs the river. Charles had come over one once, after midnight. He wished he had never seen the cursed place. He remembered a fluttering figure which had come and begged a halfpenny of him to pay the toll, and get home. He had given her money, and then, by a sudden impulse, followed her till she was safe off the bridge. Ugly thoughts, Charles ! ugly thoughts ! Will the dawn never come ? Why, the night is not half over yet.

God in His mercy sets a limit to human misery in many ways. I do not believe that the condemned man, waiting through the weary night for the gallows, thinks all night through of his fate. We read generally in those accounts of the terrible last night (which are so rightly published in the newspapers— they are the most terrifying part of the punishment), that they conversed cheerfully, or slept, or did something, showing that they half forgot for a time what was coming. And so, before the little window grew to a lighter grey, poor Charles had found some relief from his misery. He was between sleep and waking, and he had fulfilled his challenge to Miss Martineau, though later than he intended. He had gone to Ravenshoe.

There it was, all before him. The dawn behind the eastern headland had flooded the amphitheatre of hills, till the crags behind the house had turned from grey to gold, and the vane upon the priest's tower shone like a star. The sea had changed from black to purple, and the fishing boats were stealing lazily homewards, over the rolling gentle groundswell. The surf was whispering to the sand of their coming. As window after window blazed out before the sun, and as woodland and hill-side, stream and park, village and lonely farm in the distant valley, waked before the coming day, Charles watched, in his mind's eye, the dark old porch, till there came out a figure in black, and stood solitary in the terrace gazing seawards. And as he said, "Cuthbert," he fell into a dreamless, happy sleep.

He determined that he would not go to see Ellen till the

afternoon. Hornby was on duty in the morning, and never saw Charles all day; he avoided him as though on purpose. Charles, on his part, did not want to meet him till he had made some definite arrangement, and so was glad of it. But, towards two o'clock, it came across his mind that he would saunter round to St. Peter's Church, and see the comical little imp of a boy who was generally to be found there, and beguile a quarter of an hour by listening to his prattle.

He had given up reading. He had hardly opened a book since his misfortune. This may seem an odd thing to have to record about a gentleman, and to a certain extent a scholar; but so it was. He wanted to lower himself, and he was beginning to succeed. There was an essential honesty in him, which made him hate to appear what he was not; and this feeling, carried to an absurd extent, prevented his taking refuge in the most obvious remedy for all troubles except hunger : books. He did not know, as I do, that determined reading : reading of anything, even the advertisements in a newspaper ; will stop all cravings except those of the stomach, and will even soften them ; but he guessed it, nevertheless. "Why should I read it?" said he. "I must learn to do as the rest of them." And so he did as the rest of them, and "rather loafed away his time than otherwise."

And he was more inclined to "loaf" than usual this day, because he very much dreaded what was to come. And so he dawdled round to St. Peter's Church, and came upon his young friend, playing at fives with the ball he had given him, as energetically as he had before played with the brass button. Shoeblacks are compelled to a great deal of unavoidable "loafing"; but certainly this one loafed rather energetically, for he was hot and frantic in his play.

He was very glad to see Charles. He parted his matted hair from his face, and looked at him admiringly with a pleasant smile ; then he suddenly said—

"You was drunk last night, won't you?"

Charles said, No—that he never got drunk.

"Won't you really, though?" said the boy; "you look as tho' you had a been. You looks wild about the eyes"; and then he hazarded another theory to account for Charles's appearance, which Charles also negatived emphatically.

"I gave a halfpenny for this one," said the boy, showing him the ball, "and I spent the other halfpenny." Here he paused, expecting a rebuke, apparently; but Charles nodded kindly at him, and he was encouraged to go on, and to communicate a

piece of intelligence with the air of one who assumes that his
hearer is *au fait* with all the movements of the great world, and
will be interested.

"Old Biddy Flanigan's dead."

"No! is she?" said Charles, who, of course, had not the
wildest idea who she was, but guessed her to be an aged, and
—probably a dissipated Irishwoman.

"Ah! I believe you," said the boy. "And they was a-waking
on her last night, down in our court (he said "dăŏne in ăŏur
cawt"). They waked me sharp enough; but, as for she!
she's fast."

"What did she die of?" asked Charles.

"Well, she died mostly along of Mr. Malone's bumble foot,
I fancy. Him and old Biddy was both drunk a-fighting on the
stairs, and she was a step below he; and he being drunk, and
bumble-footed too, lost his balance, and down they come
together, and the back of her head come against the door-
scraper, and there she was. Wake she!" he added with scorn,
"not if all the Irish and Rooshans in France was to put stones
in their stockings, and howl a week on end, they wouldn't wake
her."

"Did they put stones in their stockings?" asked Charles,
thinking that it was some papist form of penance.

"Miss Ophelia Flanigan, she put half a brick in her
stocking end, so she did, and come at Mr. Malone for to break
his head with it, and there were a hole in the stocking, and the
brick flew out, and hit old Denny Moriarty in the jaw, and
broke it. And he worn't a doing nothink, he worn't; but was
sitting in a corner decent and quiet, blind drunk, a singing to
his self; and they took he to Guy's orspital. And the pleece
come in, and got gallus well kicked about the head, and then
they took they to Guy's orspital; and then Miss Flanigan fell
out of winder into the airy, and then they took she to Guy's
orspital; and there they is, the whole bilin of 'em in bed
together, with their heads broke, a-eating of jelly and a-drinking
of sherry wind; and then in comes a mob from Rosemary-
lane, and then they all begins to get a bit noisy and want to
fight, and so I hooked it."

"Then there are a good many Irish in your court?" said
Charles.

"Irish! ah! I believe you. They're all Irish there except
we and Billy Jones's lot. The Emperor of Rooshar is a nigger;
but his lot is mostly Irish, but another bilin of Irish from Mr.
Malone's lot. And one on 'em plays the bagpipes, with a

bellus, against the water-butt of a Sunday evening, when they're off the lay. And Mr. Malone's lot heaves crockery and broken vegetables at him out of winder, by reason of their being costermongers, and having such things handy; so there's mostly a shine of a Sunday evening."

"But who are Mr. Malone, and Billy Jones, and the Emperor of Russia?"

"They keeps lodging houses," said the boy. "Miss Ophelia Flanigan is married on Mr. Malone, but she keeps her own name, because her family's a better one nor his'n, and she's ashamed of him. They gets on very well when they're sober, but since they've been a making money they mostly gets drunk in bed of a morning, so they ain't so happy together as they was."

"Does she often attack him with a brick in the foot of a stocking?" asked Charles.

"No," said the boy, "she said her papa had taught her that little game. She used to fist hold of the poker, but he got up to that, and spouted it. So now they pokes the fire with a mopstick, which ain't so handy to hit with, and softer."

Charles walked away northward, and thought what a charming sort of person Miss Ophelia Flanigan must be, and how he would rather like to know her for curiosity's sake. The picture he drew of her in his mind was not exactly like the original, as we shall see.

It was very pleasant summer weather—weather in which an idle man would be inclined to dawdle, under any circumstances; and Charles was the more inclined to dawdle, because he very much disliked the errand on which he went. He could loiter at street corners now with the best of them, and talk to any one who happened to be loitering there too. He was getting on.

So he loitered at street corners, and talked. And he found out something to-day for the first time. He had been so absorbed in his own troubles that all rumours had been to him like the buzzing of bees; but to-day he began to appreciate that this rumour of war was no longer a mere rumour, but likely to grow into an awful reality.

If he were only free, he said to himself. If he could only provide for poor Ellen. "Gad, if they could get up a regiment of fellows in the same state of mind as I am!"

He went into a public-house, and drank a glass of ale. They were talking of it there. "Sir Charles Napier is to have the fleet," said one man, "and if he don't bring Cronstadt about their ears in two hours, I am a Dutchman. As for Odessa——"

A man in seedy black, who (let us hope) had seen better days, suggested Sebastopol.

The first man had not heard of Sebastopol. It could not be a place of much importance, or he must have heard of it. Talk to him about Petersburg and Moscow, and he would listen to you.

This sort of talk, heard everywhere on his slow walk, excited Charles ; and, thinking over it, he came to the door of Lord Welter's house, and rang.

The door was barely opened, when he saw Lord Welter himself in the hall, who called to him by his Christian name, and bade him come in. Charles followed Lord Welter into a room, and, when the latter turned round, Charles saw that he was disturbed and anxious.

"Charles," he said, " Ellen is gone ! "

Charles said " Where ? " for he hardly understood him.

"Where? God knows ! She must have left the house soon after you saw her last night. She left this note for me. Take it and read it. You see I am free from blame in this matter."

Charles took it and read it.

" My Lord,

" I should have consented to accept the shelter of your roof for a longer period, were it not that, by doing so, I should be continually tempted to the commission of a dishonourable action—an action which would bring speedy punishment on myself, by ruining too surely the man whom, of all others in the world, I love and respect.

" Lieutenant Hornby has proposed marriage to me. Your lordship's fine sense of honour will show you at once how impossible it is for me to consent to ruin his prospects by a union with such a one as myself. Distrusting my own resolution, I have fled, and henceforth I am dead to him and to you.

" Ah ! Welter, Welter ! you yourself might have been loved as he is, once ; but that time is gone by for ever. I should have made you a better wife than Adelaide. I might have loved you myself once, but I fell more through anger and vanity than through love.

" My brother, he whom we call Charles Ravenshoe, is in this weary world somewhere. I have an idea that you will meet him. You used to love one another. Don't let him quarrel with you for such a worthless straw as I am. Tell him I always loved him as a brother. It is better that we should not meet yet. Tell him that he must make his own place in the world before we meet, and then I have something to say to him.

" Mary, the Mother of God, and the blessed saints before the throne, bless you and him, here and hereafter."

Charles had nothing to say to Lord Welter, not one word. He saw that the letter was genuine. He understood that Welter had had no time to tell her of his coming, and that she was gone; neither Welter nor he knew where, or were likely to know; that was all. He only bid him good-bye, and walked home again.

When you know the whole story, you will think that Charles's run of ill luck at this time is almost incredible; but I shall call you to witness that it is not so. This was the first stroke of real ill luck that he had had. All his other misfortunes came from his mad determination of alienating himself from all his friends. If he had even left Lord Welter free to have mentioned that he had been seen, all might have gone well, but he made him promise secrecy; and now, after having, so to speak, made ill luck for himself, and lamented over it, here was a real stroke of it with a vengeance, and he did not know it. He was not anxious about Ellen's future; he felt sure at once that she was going into some Roman Catholic refuge, where she would be quiet and happy. In fact, with a new fancy he had in his head, he was almost content to have missed her. And Ellen, meanwhile, never dreamt either of his position or state of mind, or she would have searched him out at the end of the world. She thought he was just as he always had been, or, perhaps, turning his attention to some useful career, with Cuthbert's assistance; and she thought she would wait, and wait she did; and they went apart, not to meet till the valley of the shadow of death had been passed, and life was not so well worth having as it had been.

But as for our old friend, Father Mackworth. As I said once before, " It's no use wondering, but I do wonder," whether Father Mackworth, had he known how near Ellen and Charles had been to meeting the night before, would not have whistled "Lillibulero," as Uncle Toby did in times of dismay; that is, if he had known the tune.

CHAPTER XLII

RAVENSHOE HALL, DURING ALL THIS

THE villagers at Ravenshoe, who loved Charles, were very much puzzled and put out by his sudden disappearance. Although they had little or no idea of the real cause of his absence, yet it was understood to be a truth, not to be gainsayed, that it was permanent. And as it was a heavily-felt misfortune to them, and as they really had no idea why he was gone, or where he was gone to, it became necessary that they should comfort themselves by a formula. At which time Master Lee, up to Slarrow, erected the theory, that Master Charles was gone to the Indies—which was found to be a doctrine so comfortable to the souls of those that adopted it, as being hazy and vague, and as leaving his return an open question, that it was unanimously adopted; and those who ventured to doubt it, were treated as heretics and heathens.

It was an additional puzzle to them to find that William had turned out to be a gentleman, and a Ravenshoe; a fact which could not, of course, be concealed from them, though the other facts of the case were carefully hushed up—not a very difficult matter in a simple feudal village, like Ravenshoe. But, when William appeared, after a short absence, he suffered greatly in popularity, from the belief that he had allowed Charles to go to the Indies by himself. Old Master James Lee, of Tor Head, old Master James Lee, of Withycombe Barton, and old Master James Lee, up to Slarrow, the three great quidnuncs of the village, were sunning themselves one day under the wall which divides part of the village from the shore, when by there came, talking earnestly together, William, and John Marston.

The three old men raised their hats, courteously. They were in no distinguishable relation to one another, but, from similarity of name and age, always hunted in a leash. (Sporting men will notice a confusion here about the word "leash," but let it pass.) When no one was by, I have heard them fall out and squabble together about dates, or such like; but, when others were present, they would, so to speak, trump one another's tricks to any amount. And if, on these occasions, any one of the three took up an untenable position, the other two would lie him out of it like Jesuits, and only fall foul of him when they were alone together—which, to say the least of it, was neighbourly and decent.

"God save you, gentlemen," said old Master Lee up to Slarrow, who was allowed to commit himself by the other two, who were waiting to be "down on him" in private. "Any news from the Indies lately?"

William and Marston stopped, and William said—

"No, Master Lee, we have not heard from Captain Archer for seven months, or more."

"I ask your pardon," said Lee up to Slarrow; "I worn't a speaking of he. I was speaking of our own darling boy, Master Charles. When be he a-coming back to see we?"

"When, indeed!" said William. "I wish I knew, Master Lee."

"They Indies," said the old man, "is well enough; but what's he there no more than any other gentleman? Why don't he come home to his own. Who's a-keeping on him away?"

William and John Marston walked on without answering. And then the two other Master Lees fell on to Master Lee up to Slarrow, and verbally ill treated him—partly because he had got no information out of William, and partly because, having both sat quiet and given him plenty of rope, he had not hanged himself. Master Lee up to Slarrow had evil times of it that blessed spring afternoon, and ended by "dratting" both his companions, for a couple of old fools. After which they adjourned to the public-house and hard cider, sent them to drink for their sins.

"They'll never make a scholar of me, Marston," said William; "I will go on at it for a year, but no more. I shall away soon to hunt up Charles. Is there any police in America?"

Marston answered absently, Yes; he believed so; but was evidently thinking of something else.

They had gone sauntering out for a walk together. Marston had come down from Oxford the day before (after an examination for an Exeter fellowship, I believe) for change of air; and he thought he would like to walk with William up to the top of the lofty promontory, which bounded Ravenshoe-bay on the west, and catch the pleasant summer breeze coming in from the Atlantic.

On the loftiest point of all, with the whispering blue sea on three sides of them, four hundred feet below, there they sat down on the short sheep-eaten turf, and looked westward.

Cape after cape stretched away under the afternoon sun, till the last seemed only a dark cloud floating on the sea. Beyond that cape there was nothing but water for three thousand weary miles. The scene was beautiful enough, but very melancholy; a long coastline, trending away into dim distance, on a quiet sunny afternoon, is very melancholy. Indeed, far more melancholy than the same place in a howling gale: when the nearest promontory only, is dimly visible, a black wall, echoing the thunder of bursting waves, and when sea, air, and sky, like the three furies, are rushing on with mad, destructive unanimity.

They lay, these two, on the short turf, looking westward; and, after a time, John Marston broke silence. He spoke very low and quietly, and without looking at William.

"I have something very heavy on my mind, William. I am not a fool, with a morbid conscience, but I have been very wrong. I have done what I never can undo. I loved that fellow, William!"

William said "Ay."

"I know what you would say. You would say, that every one who ever knew Charles loved him; and you are right. He was so utterly unselfish, so entirely given up to trying to win others, that every one loved him, and could not help it. The cleverest man in England, with all his cleverness, could not gain so many friends as Charles."

William seemed to think this such a self-evident proposition, that he did not think it worth while to say anything.

"And Charles was not clever. And what makes me mad with myself is this. I had influence over him, and I abused it. I was not gentle enough with him. I used to make fun of him, and be flippant, and priggish, and dictatorial, with him. God help me! And now he has taken some desperate step, and, in fear of my ridicule, has not told me of it. I felt sure he would come to me, but I have lost hope now. May God forgive me—God forgive me!"

In a few moments William said, "If you pause to think, Marston, you will see how unjust you are to yourself. He could not be afraid of me, and yet he has never come near me."

"Of course not," said Marston. "You seem hardly to know him so well as I. He fears that you would make him take money, and that he would be a burthen on you. I never expected that he would come back to you. He knows that you would never leave him. He knows, as well as you know yourself, that you would sacrifice all your time and your opportunities of education to him. And, by being dependent on you, he would be dependent on Father Mackworth—the only man in the world he dislikes and distrusts."

William uttered a form of speech concerning the good father, which is considered by foreigners to be merely a harmless national *façon de parler*—sometimes, perhaps, intensive, when the participle is used, but in general no more than expletive. In this case, the speaker was, I fear, in earnest, and meant what he said most heartily.

Marston never swore, but he certainly did not correct William for swearing, in this case, as he should have done. There was a silence for a time. After a little, William laid his hand on Marston's shoulder, and said—

"He never had a truer friend than you. Don't you blame yourself."

"I do ; and shall until I find him."

"Marston," said William, "what *has* he done with himself ? Where the deuce is he gone ?"

"Lord Saltire and I were over the same problem for two hours the other night, and we could make nothing of it, but that he was gone to America or Australia. He hardly took money enough with him to keep him till now. I can make nothing of it. Do *you* think he would be likely to seek out Welter ?"

"If he were going to do so, he would have done so by now, and we must have heard of it. No," said William.

"He was capable of doing very odd things," said Marston. "Do you remember that Easter vacation, when he and Lord Welter and Mowbray went away together ?"

"Remember !" said William. "Why, I was with them ; and glorious fun it was. Rather fast fun though—too fast by half. We went up and lived on the Severn and Avon Canal, among the bargemen, dressing accordingly. Charles had nothing to do with that folly, beyond joining in it, and spending the day in laughing. That was Lord Welter's doing. The bargees nicknamed Lord Welter 'the sweep,' and said he was a good fellow, but a terrible blackguard. And so he was—for that time, at all events."

Marston laughed, and, after a time, said, "Did he ever seem to care about soldiering ? Do you think he was likely to enlist ?"

"It is possible," said William ; "it is quite possible. Yes, he has often talked to me about soldiering. I mind—I remember, I should say—that he once was hot about going into the army, but he gave it up because it would have taken him away from Mr. Ravenshoe too much."

They turned and walked homewards, without speaking a word all the way. On the bridge they paused and leant upon the coping, looking into the stream. All of a sudden William laid his hand on Marston's arm, and, looking in his face, said—

"Every day we lose, I feel he is getting farther from us. I don't know what may happen. I shall go and seek him. I will get educated at my leisure. Only think of what may be happening now! I was a fool to have given it up so soon, and to have tried waiting till he came to us. He will never come. I must go and fetch him. Here is Cuthbert, too, good fellow, fretting himself to death about it. Let us go and talk to him."

And John Marston said, "Right, true heart; let us go."

Of all their acquaintances there was only one who could have given them any information—Lord Welter; and he, of all others, was the very last they dreamt of going to. You begin to see, I dare say, that, when Charles is found, my story will nearly be at an end. But my story is not near finished yet, I assure you.

Standing where they were on the bridge, they could look along the village street. It was as neat a street as one ever sees in a fishing village; that is to say, rather an untidy one, for, of all human employments, fishing involves more lumber and mess than any other. Everything past use was "hit," as they say in Berkshire, out into the street; and of the inorganic part of this refuse, that is to say, tiles, bricks, potsherds, and so on, the children built themselves shops and bazaars, and sold one another the organic orts, that is to say, cabbage-stalks, fish-bones, and orange-peel, which were paid for in mussel-shells. And, as Marston and William looked along this street, as one may say, at high market time, they saw Cuthbert come, slowly riding along among the children, and the dogs, and the pigs, and the herring-bones, and brickbats.

He was riding a noble horse, and was dressed with his usual faultless neatness and good taste, as clean as a new pin from top to toe. As he came along, picking his way gently among the children, the fishermen and their wives came out right and left from their doors, and greeted him kindly. In olden times they would not have done this, but it had got about that he was pining for the loss of his brother, and their hearts had warmed to him. It did not take much to make their hearts warm to a Ravenshoe; though they were sturdy, independent rogues enough at times. I am a very great admirer of the old feudal feeling, when it is not abused by either party. In parts of

Australia, where it, or something near akin to it, is very strong indeed, I have seen it act on high and low most beneficially; giving to the one side a sense of responsibility, and to the other a feeling of trust and reliance. "Here's 'Captain Dash,' or 'Colonel Blank,' or 'Mr. So-and-so,' and he won't see me wronged, I know. I have served him and his father for forty years, and he's a *gentleman*, and so were his father before him." That is a sort of thing you will hear often enough in Australia. And even on the diggings, with all the leaven of Americanism and European Radicalism one finds there, it is much easier for a warden to get on with the diggers if he comes of a known colonial family, than if he is an unknown man. The old colonial diggers, the people of the greatest real weight, talk of them, and the others listen and mark. All people, prate as they may, like a guarantee for respectability. In the colonies, such a guarantee is given by a man's being tolerably well off, and "come of decent people." In England, it is given, in cases, by a man and a man's forefathers having been good landlords and honest men. Such a guarantee is given by such people as the Ravenshoes, but that is not the whole secret of *their* influence. That comes more from association—a feeling strong enough, as one sees, to make educated and clever men use their talents and eloquence towards keeping a school in a crowded, unhealthy neighbourhood, instead of moving it into the country; merely because, as far as one can gather from their speeches, they were educated at it themselves, twenty years ago. Hereby visiting the sins of the fathers on the children, with a vengeance!

"Somewhat too much of this." It would be stretching a point to say that Cuthbert was a handsome man, though he was very near being so, indeed. He was tall, but not too slender, for he had developed in chest somewhat since we first knew him. His face was rather pale, but his complexion perfectly clear; save that he had a black mark round his eyes. His features were decidedly marked, but not so strongly as Charles's; and there was an air of stately repose about him, showing itself in his way of carrying his head perfectly upright, and the firm, but not harsh, settling of his mouth, with the lower lip slightly pouting, which was very attractive. He was a consummate horseman, too, and, as I said, perfectly dressed; and, as he came towards them, looking apparently at nothing, both William and Marston thought they had never seen a finer specimen of a gentleman.

He had strangely altered in two months. As great a change

had come over him as comes over a rustic when the drill-sergeant gets him and makes a soldier of him. There is the same body, the same features, the same hair and eyes. Bill Jones is Bill Jones, if you are to believe his mother. But Bill Jones the soldier is not Bill Jones the ploughboy. He is quite a different person. So, since the night when Charles departed, Cuthbert had not been the Cuthbert of former times. He was no longer wayward and irritable; he was as silent as ever, but he had grown so staid, so studiously courteous to every one, so exceedingly humble-minded and patient with every one, that all save one or two wondered at the change in him.

He had been passionately fond of Charles, though he had seldom shown it, and was terribly cut up at his loss. He had greatly humiliated himself to himself by what was certainly his felonious offer to Father Mackworth; and he had found the estate somewhat involved, and had determined to set to work and bring it to rights. These three causes had made Cuthbert Ravenshoe a humbler and better man than he had ever been before.

"William," he said, smiling kindly on him, "I have been seeing after your estate for you. It does me good to have some one to work for. You will die a rich man."

William said nothing. One of Cuthbert's fixed notions was, that he would die young and childless. He claimed to have a heart-complaint, though it really appeared without any foundation. It was a fancy which William had combated at first, but now acquiesced in, because he found it useless to do otherwise.

He dismounted and walked with him. "Cuthbert," said William, "we have been thinking about Charles."

"I am always thinking about him," said Cuthbert; "is there no way of finding him?"

"I am going. I want you to give me some money and let me go."

"You had better go at once, William. You had better try if the police can help you. We are pretty sure that he has gone to America, unless he has enlisted. In either case it is very possible we may find him. Aunt Ascot would have succeeded if she had not lost her temper. Don't you think I am right, my dear Marston?"

"I do, indeed, Ravenshoe," said Marston. "Don't you think now, Mr. Mackworth, that, if a real push is made, and with judgment, we may find Charles again?"

They had reached the terrace, and Father Mackworth was

standing in front of the porch. He said he believed it was perfectly possible. "Nay," he said, "possible! I am as sure of seeing Charles Horton back here again, as I am that I shall eat my dinner to-day."

"And I," said Cuthbert, "am equally sure that we shall see poor Ellen back some day. Poor girl! she shall have a warm welcome."

Father Mackworth said he hoped it might be so. And the lie did not choke him.

"We are going to send William away again to look after him, father," said Cuthbert.

"He had much better stay at home and mind his education," said Mackworth.

William had his back towards them, and was looking out to sea, whistling. When the priest spoke he turned round sharply, and said—

"Hey? What's that?"

The priest repeated it.

"I suppose," said William, "that that is more my business than yours, is it not? I don't intend to go to school again, certainly not to you."

Cuthbert looked from one to the other of them and said nothing. A few days before this William and the priest had fallen out; and Mackworth, appealing, had been told with the greatest kindness and politeness by Cuthbert that he could not interfere. That William was heir to Ravenshoe, and that he really had no power over him whatever. Mackworth had said nothing then, but now he had followed Cuthbert into the library, and, when they were alone, said—

"Cuthbert, I did not expect this from you. You have let him insult me twice, and have not corrected him."

Cuthbert put his back against the door and said—

"Now you don't leave this room till you apologize for these wicked words. My dear old fellow, what a goose you are! Have not you and he always squabbled? Do fight it out with him, and don't try and force me to take a side. I ain't going to do it, you know, and so I tell you plainly. Give it to him. Who can do it so well as you? Remember what an altered position he is in. How can you expect me to take your part against him?"

Father Mackworth cleared his brow, and said, laughing, "You are right, Cuthbert. I'll go about with the rogue. He is inclined to kick over the traces, but I'll whip him in a little. I have had the whip hand of every Ravenshoe I have had to deal with yet, yourself included, and it's hard if I am to be beat by this new whipper-snapper."

Cuthbert said affectionately to him, "I think you love me, Mackworth. Don't quarrel with him more than you can help. I know you love me." And so Cuthbert went to seek John Marston.

Love him! Ay, that he did. John Mackworth could be cruel, hard, false, vindictive. He could cheat, and he could lie, if need were. He was heartless and ambitious. But he loved Cuthbert. It was a love which had taken a long time growing, but there it was, and he was half ashamed of it. Even to himself he would try to make out that it was mere selfishness and ambition—that he was gentle with Cuthbert, because he must keep his place at Ravenshoe. Even now he would try to persuade himself that such was the case—perhaps the more strongly, because he began to see now that there was a soft spot in his heart, and that Cuthbert was master of it. Since the night when Cuthbert had offered him ten thousand pounds, and he had refused it, Cuthbert had never been the same to him. And Mackworth, expecting to find his influence increased, found to his astonishment that from that moment it was *gone*. Cuthbert's intensely sensitive and proud nature revolted from the domination of a man before whom he had so lowered himself; and firmly, though humbly now, for he was altered by seeing how nearly he had been a villain, he let him see that he would walk in future in his own strength. Father Mackworth saw soon that Ravenshoe was a comfortable home for him, but that his power was gone. Unless!

And yet he knew he could exercise a power little dreamt of. It is in the power, possibly, of a condemned man to burn the prison down, and possibly his interest; but he has compunctions. Mackworth tried to persuade himself that the reason he did not use his power was that it would not be advisable. He was a cipher in the house, and knew by instinct that he would never be more. But in reality, I believe, he let his power sleep for Cuthbert's sake.

"Who could have thought," he said, "that the very thing which clinched my power, as I thought, should have destroyed it? Are not those people fools, who lay down rules for human action? Why, no. They are possibly right five times out of ten. But as for the other five! Bah!"

"No, I won't allow that. It was my own fault. I should have known his character better. But there, I could not have helped it, for he did it himself. I was passive."

And Cuthbert followed Marston into the hall and said, "You are not going away because William goes, Marston?"

"Do you want me?" said Marston.

"Yes," said Cuthbert. "You must stay with me. My time is short, and I must know as much of this world as I may. I have much to do; you must help me. I will be like a little child in your hands. I will die in the old faith; but I will learn something knew."

And so Marston stayed with him, and they two grew fast friends. Cuthbert had nothing to learn in this management of his estate; there he was Marston's master; but all that a shrewd young man of the world could teach a bookworm, so much Cuthbert got from Marston.

Marston one day met the village doctor, the very man whom we saw at the beginning of the book, putting out William (whom we then supposed to be Charles) to nurse. Marston asked him, "Was there any reality in this heart-complaint of Cuthbert's?"

"Not the very faintest shadow of a reality," said the doctor. "It is the most tiresome whimsy I ever knew. He has persuaded himself of it, though. He used to be very hypochondriac. He is as likely to live till eighty as you are."

CHAPTER XLIII

THE MEETING

THERE was ruin in the Ascot family, we know. And Lord Ascot, crippled with paralysis at six-and-forty, was lying in South Audley Street, nursed by Lady Ascot. The boxes, which we saw packed ready for their foreign tour at the London Bridge Hotel, were still there—not gone abroad yet, for the simple reason that Herodias had won the Oaks, and that Lord Welter had won, some said seven, others said seventy thousand pounds. (He had really won nine.) So the boxes might stay where they were a few days, and he might pursue his usual avocations in peace, all his debts of honour being satisfied.

He had barely saved himself from being posted. Fortunately for him, he had, on the Derby, betted chiefly with a few friends, one of whom was Hornby; and they waited and said nothing till after the Oaks, when they were paid, and Welter could hold up his head again. He was indebted to the generosity of Hornby and Sir Charles Ferrers for his honour—the very men whom he would have swindled. But he laughed and ate his dinner, and said they were good fellows, and thought no more of it.

The bailiffs were at Ranford. The servants were gone, and the horses were advertised at Tattersall's already. It was reported in the county that an aged Jew, being in possession, and prowling about the premises, had come into the poultry-yard, and had surreptitiously slain, cooked, and essayed to eat, the famous cock "Sampson," the champion bird of England, since his match with "Young Countryman." On being informed by the old keeper that my lord had refused sixty guineas for him a few weeks before, he had (so said the county) fled out of the house, tearing his hair, and knocked old Lady Hainault, who had also come prowling over in her pony-carriage, down the steps, flat on her back. Miss Hicks, who was behind with her shawls, had picked her up, they said, and "caught it."

If Adelaide was beautiful everywhere, surely she was more beautiful on horseback than anywhere else, and no one knew it better than herself. She was one of the few who appeared in the park in a low-crowned hat—a "wide-awake." They are not *de rigueur* even yet, I believe; but Adelaide was never very particular so long as she could look well. She had found out how splendid her perfect mask looked under the careless, irregular curves of such a head-dress, and how bright her banded hair shone in contrast with a black ostrich feather which drooped on her shoulder. And so she had taken to wear one since she had been Lady Welter, and had appeared in the park in it twice.

Lord Welter bethought himself once in these times—that is, just after the Oaks—that he would like to take his handsome wife out and show her in the park. His Hornby speculation had turned out ill; in fact, Hornby had altogether made rather a handsome sum out of him, and he must look for some one else. The some one else, a young Austrian, Pscechenyi by name, a young fellow of wealth, had received his advances somewhat coldly, and it became necessary to hang out Adelaide as a lure.

Lord Welter was aware that, if he had asked Adelaide to come and ride with him, on the ground of giving her an afternoon's amusement, and tried to persuade her to it by fair-spoken common-places, she would probably not have come ; and so he did nothing of the kind. He and his wife thoroughly understood one another. There was perfect confidence between them in everything. Towards one another they were perfectly sincere ; and this very sincerity begot a feeling of trust between them, which ultimately ripened into something better. They began life together without any professions of affection ; but out of use, and a similarity of character, there grew a liking in the end. She knew everything about Lord Welter, save one thing, which she was to know immediately, and which was of no importance ; and she was always ready to help him, provided, as she told him, " he didn't humbug," which his lordship, as we know, was not inclined to do, without her caution.

Lord Welter went into her dressing-room in the morning, and said—

" Here's a note from Pscechenyi. He won't come to-night."

" Indeed ! " said Adelaide, brushing her hair. " I did not give him credit for so much sense. Really, you know, he can't be such a fool as he looks."

" We must have him," said Lord Welter.

" Of course we must," said Adelaide " I really cannot allow such a fat goose to run about with a knife and fork in him any longer. Heigh ho ! Let's see. He affects Lady Brittlejug, don't he ? I am going to her party to-night, and I'll capture him for you, and bring him home to you from under her very nose. Now do try and make a better hand of him than you did of Hornby, or we shall all be in the workhouse together."

" I'll do my best," said Lord Welter, laughing. " But look here. I don't think you'll catch him so, you know. She looks as well as you by candlelight ; but she can't ride a hang. Come out in the park this afternoon. He will be there."

" Very well," said Adelaide ; " I suppose you know best. I shall be glad of a ride. Half-past two, then."

So, at the time appointed these two innocent lambkins rode forth to take the air. Lord Welter, big, burly, red-faced, good-humoured, perfectly dressed, and sitting on his horse as few others could sit, the model of a frank English nobleman. Adelaide, beautiful and fragile beyond description, perfect in dress and carriage, riding trustingly and lovingly in the shadow of her lord, the happy, timid bride all over. They had no groom. What should a poor simple couple like them want with a groom ? It was a beautiful sight, and many turned to look at them.

But Lord Saltire, who was looking out of the drawing-room

window of Lord Ascot's house in South Audley Street, as they passed, turned to Marston, and said very emphatically—

" Now, I do really wonder what infernal mischief those two are after. There is an air of pastoral simplicity about their whole get-up, which forebodes some very great—very great "—here he paused, took snuff, and looked Marston straight in the face—" obliquity of moral purpose."

Meanwhile, the unconscious innocents sauntered on into the park, under the Marble Arch, and down towards Rotten-row. When they got into the Row they had a canter. There was Pscechenyi riding with Hornby and Miss Buckjumper, but they gave them the " go by," and went softly on towards Kensington Gate. " Who is the woman in the hat and feathers ? " said everybody who didn't know. " Lady Welter," said everybody who did ; and, whatever else they said of her, they all agreed that she was wonderfully beautiful, and rode divinely. When they came slowly back, they found Hornby and the Austrian were standing against the rail talking to some ladies. They drew close up, and entered into conversation ; and Adelaide found herself beside Miss Buckjumper, now Lady Handlycross.

Adelaide was somewhat pleased to find herself at the side of this famous horsewoman and beauty. She was so sure that comparisons would be favourable to herself. And they were. If ever an exquisitely formed nose was, so to speak, put out of joint, that nose was in the middle of Miss Buckjumper's face that day. Nevertheless, she did not show anything. She had rather a respect for Adelaide, as being a successful woman. Was not she herself cantering for a coronet ? There was very soon a group round them, and Lord Welter's hoarse jolly laugh was heard continually. People, who were walking in the park to see the great people, paused outside the circle to look at her, and repassed again. Mr. Pelagius J. Bottom, of New York, whose father emigrated to Athens, and made a great fortune at the weaving business in the time of King Theseus, got on a bench, and looked at her through a double-barrelled opera-glass. There never was such a success. The Austrian thought no more of Hornby's cautions, thought no more of Miss Buckjumper or Lady Brittlejug. He was desperately in love, and was dying for some excuse to withdraw his refusal of this morning. Pelagius Jas. Bottom would have come, and mortgaged the paternal weaving business at the dice, but unfortunately his letters of introduction, being all addressed to respectable people, did not include one to Lord and Lady Welter. All the young fellows would have come and played all night, till church-time next morning, for her sake. As Lord Welter candidly told her that night, she was the best investment he had ever made.

They did not want all the young fellows though. Too many cooks spoil the broth. They only wanted the young Austrian, and so Lord Welter said, after a time, " I was in hopes of seeing you at my house to-night." That was quite enough. Fifty Hornbys would not have stopped him now.

Still they stood there talking. Adelaide was almost happy. Which of these staid women had such power as she? There was a look of pride and admiration even on Lord Welter's stupid face. Yes, it was a great success. Suddenly all people began to look one way and come towards the rails, and a buzz arose, " The Queen—the Queen ! "

Adelaide turned just as the outriders were opposite to her. She saw the dark claret-coloured carriage, fifty yards off, and she knew that Lady Emily Montford, who had been her sister-bridesmaid at Lady Hainault's wedding, was in waiting that day. Hornby declares the whole thing was done on purpose. Let us be more charitable, and suppose that her horse was startled at the scarlet coats of the outriders ; however it was, the brute took fright, stood on its hind legs, and bolted straight towards the royal carriage. She reigned it up within ten feet of the carriage step, plunging furiously. Raising her whip hand to push her hat more firmly on, she knocked it off, and sat there bareheaded, with one loop of her hair fallen down, a sight which no man who saw it ever forgot. She saw a look of amazed admiration in the Queen's face. She saw Lady Emily's look of gentle pity. She saw Her Majesty lean forward, and ask who it was. She saw her name pass Lady Emily's lips, and then she saw the Queen turn with a frown, and look steadily the other way.

Wrath and rage were in her heart, and showed themselves one instant in her face. A groom had run out and picked up her hat. She bent down to take it from him, and saw that it was Charles Ravenshoe.

Her face grew soft again directly. Poor thing ! she must have had a kind heart after all, crusted over as it was with vanity, pride, and selfishness. Now, in her anger and shame, she could have cried to see her old love so degraded. There was no time for crying, or for saying more than a few sharp words, for they were coming towards her.

" What nonsense is this, Charles ? " she said. " What is this masquerade ? Are you come to double my shame ? Go home

and take that dress off and burn it. Is your pride dead, that
you disgrace yourself like this in public? If you are desperate,
as you seem, why are you not at the war? They want desperate
men there. Oh! if I was a man!"

They parted then! no one but Lord Welter and Hornby
knew who Charles was. The former saw that Adelaide had
recognised him, and, as they rode simply home together, said—

"I knew poor Charles was a groom. He saw his sister the
other night at our house. I didn't tell you; I hardly know
why. I really believe, do you know, that the truth of the
matter is, Adelaide, that I did not want to vex you. Now!"

He looked at her as if he thought she would disbelieve him,
but she said—

"Nay, I do believe you, Welter. You are not an ill-natured
man, but you are selfish and unprincipled. So am I, perhaps
to a greater extent than you. At what time is that fool of a
German coming?"

"At half-past eleven."

"I must go to that woman Brittlejug's party. I must show
there, to keep friends with her. She has such a terrible
tongue; I will be back by twelve or so."

"I wish you could stay at home."

"I really dare not, my dear Welter. I must go. I will be
back in good time."

"Of course you will please yourself about it," said Lord
Welter, a thought sulkily. And, when he was by himself, he
said—

"She is going to see Charles Ravenshoe. Well, perhaps she
ought. She treated him d——d bad! And so did I."

CHAPTER XLIV

ANOTHER MEETING

LORD ASCOT had been moved into South Audley Street, his
town house, and Lady Ascot was there nursing him. General
Mainwaring was off for Varna. But Lord Saltire had been a
constant visitor, bringing with him very often Marston, who
was, you will remember, an old friend of Lady Ascot.

It was not at all an unpleasant house to be in. Lord Ascot
was crippled—he had been seized with paralysis at Epsom; and

he was ruined. But every one knew the worst, and felt relieved by thinking that things could get no worse than worst, and so must get better.

In fact, every one admitted to the family party about that time remembered it as a very happy and quiet time indeed. Lord Ascot was their first object, of course ; and a more gentle and biddable invalid than the poor fellow made can hardly be conceived. He was passionately fond of reading novels (a most reprehensible practice), and so was easily amused. Lord Saltire and he would play picquet ; and every evening there would be three hours of whist, until the doctor looked in the last thing, and Lord Ascot was helped to bed.

Marston was always set to play with Lord Ascot, because Lord Saltire and Lady Ascot would not play against one another. Lord Saltire was, of course, one of the best players in Europe ; and I believe that Lady Ascot was not the worst by any means. I can see the party now. I can see Lady Ascot laying down a card, and looking at the same time at her partner, to call his attention to her lead. And I can see Lord Saltire take out his snuff-box thereat, as if he were puzzled, but not alarmed. William would come sometimes and sit quietly behind Marston, or Lord Saltire, watching the game. In short, they were a very quiet pleasant party indeed.

One night—it was the very night in which Adelaide had lost her hat in the Park—there was no whist. Marston had gone down to Oxford suddenly, and William came in to tell them so. Lady Ascot was rather glad, she said, for she had a friend coming to tea, who did not play whist ; so Lord Saltire and Lord Ascot sat down to picquet, and William talked to his aunt.

"Who is your friend, Maria ? " asked Lord Saltire.

" A Mr. Bidder, a minister. He has written a book on the Revelations, which you really ought to read, James ; it would suit you."

They both laughed.

"About the seven seals, hey ? " said Lord Saltire ; " ' *septem phocæ*,' as I remember Machynleth translated it at Eton once. We called him ' Vitulina ' ever after. The name stuck to him through life with some of us. A capital name for him, too ! His fussy blundering in this war-business is just like his old headlong way of looking out words in his dictionary. He is an ass, Maria ; and I will bet fifty pounds that your friend, the minister, is another."

" How can you know ? at all events the man he brings with him is none."

"Another minister?"

"Yes, a Moravian missionary from Australia."

"Then certainly another ass, or he would have gone as missionary to a less abominably detestable hole. They were all burnt into the sea there the other day. Immediately after which the river rose seventy feet, and drowned the rest of them."

Soon after were announced Mr. Bidder and Mr. Smith. Mr. Bidder was an entirely unremarkable man; but Mr. Smith was one of the most remarkable men I have ever seen, or rather heard—for externally there was nothing remarkable about him, except a fine forehead, and a large expressive grey eye, which, when he spoke to you, seemed to come back from a long distance, and fix itself upon yours. In manners he was perfect. He was rather taciturn, though always delighted to communicate information about his travels, in a perfectly natural way. If one man wanted information on botany, or what not, he was there to give it. If another wanted to hear about missionary work, he was ready for him. He never spoke or acted untruthfully for one instant. He never acted the free and easy man of the world as some religious gentlemen of all sects feel it necessary to do sometimes, imitating the real thing as well as Paul Bedford would imitate Fanny Ellsler. What made him remarkable was his terrible earnestness, and the feeling you had that his curious language was natural, and meant something; something very important indeed.

He has something to do with the story. The straws in the gutter have to do with the history of a man like Charles, a man who leaves all things to chance. And this man Smith is very worthy of notice, and so I have said thus much about him, and am going to say more.

Mr. Bidder was very strong on the Russian war, which he illustrated by the Revelations. He was a good fellow, and well-bred enough to see that his friend Smith was an object of greater interest to Lady Ascot than himself; so he "retired into" a book of prints, and left the field clear.

Mr. Smith sat by Lady Ascot, and William drew close up. Lady Ascot began by a common place, of course.

"You have suffered great hardships among those savages, Mr. Smith, have you not?"

"Hardships! Oh, dear no, my dear lady. Our station was one of the pleasantest places in the whole earth, I believe; and we had a peaceful time. When the old man is strong in me I wish I was back there."

" You did not make much progress with them, I believe ? "

" None whatever. We found out after a year or two that it was hopeless to make them understand the existence of a God ; and after that we stayed on to see if we could bring them to some knowledge of agriculture, and save them from their inevitable extermination as the New Zealanders have been saved."

" And to no purpose ? "

" None. For instance, we taught them to plant our potatoes for us. They did it beautifully, but in the night they dug them up and ate them. And in due season we waited that our potatoes should grow, and they grew not. Then they came to Brother Hillyar, my coadjutor, an old man, now ruling ten cities for his master, and promised for rewards of flour to tell him why the potatoes did not grow. And he, loving them, gave them what they desired. And they told him that they dug them up while we slept. And for two days I went about my business, laughing in secret places, for which he tried to rebuke me, but could not, laughing himself. The Lord kept him waiting long, for he was seventy-four ; but, doubtless, his reward is the greater."

William said, " You brought home a collection of zoological specimens, I think. They are in the Museum."

"Yes. But what I could not bring over were my live pets. I and my wife had a menagerie of our own—a great number of beasts——"

Mr. Bidder, looking up from his book, catching the last sentence only, said the number of the beast was 666 ; and then turning round, held himself ready to strike into the conversation, thinking that the time was come when he should hide his light no longer.

" The natives are very low savages, are they not, Mr. Smith ? " said William. " I have heard that they cannot count above ten."

" Not so far as that," said Mr. Smith. " The tribe we were most among used to express all large unknown quantities by ' eighty-four ' ; [1] it was as x and y to them. That seems curious at first, does it not ? "

William said it did seem curious, their choosing that particular number. But Mr. Bidder, dying to mount his hobby-horse, and not caring how, said it was not at all curious. If you

[1] A fact with regard to one tribe, to the author's frequent confusion. Any number above two, whether of horses, cattle, or sheep, was always represented as being eighty-four. Invariably, too, with an adjective introduced after the word "four," which we don't use in a drawing-room.

multiplied the twelve tribes of Israel into the seven cities of refuge, there you were at once.

Mr. Smith said he thought he had made a little mistake. The number, he fancied, was ninety-four.

Lord Saltire, from the card-table, said that that made the matter clearer than before. For if you placed the Ten Commandments to the previous result you arrived at ninety-four, which was the number wanted. And his lordship, who had lost, and was consequently possibly cross, added that, if you divided the whole by the five foolish virgins, and pitched Tobit's dog, neck and heels, into the result, you would find yourself much about where you started.

Mr. Bidder, who, as I said, was a good fellow, laughed, and Mr. Smith resumed the conversation once more ; Lord Saltire seemed interested in what he said, and did not interfere with him.

"You buried poor Mrs. Smith out there," said Lady Ascot. "I remember her well. She was very beautiful as a girl."

"Very beautiful," said the missionary. "Yes; she never lost her beauty, do you know. That climate is very deadly to those who go there with the seeds of consumption in them. She had done a hard day's work before she went to sleep, though she was young. Don't you think so, Lady Ascot?"

"A hard day's work ; a good day's work, indeed. Who knows better than I?" said Lady Ascot. "What an awakening it must be from such a sleep as hers!"

"Beyond the power of human tongue to tell," said the missionary, looking dreamily as at something far away. "Show me the poet that can describe in his finest language the joy of one's soul when one wakes on a summer's morning. Who, then, can conceive or tell the unutterable happiness of the purified soul, waking face to face with the King of Glory?"

Lord Saltire looked at him curiously, and said to himself, "This fellow is in earnest. I have seen this sort of thing before. But seldom! Yes, but seldom!"

"I should not have alluded to my wife's death," continued the missionary, in a low voice, "but that her ladyship introduced the subject. And no one has a better right to hear of her than her kind old friend. She fell asleep on the Sabbath evening after prayers. We moved her bed into the verandah, Lady Ascot, that she might see the sunlight fade out on the tops of the highest trees—a sight she always loved. And from the verandah we could see through the tree stems Mount Joorma, laid out in endless folds of woodland, all purple and gold. And I thought she was looking at the mountain, but she was looking far beyond that, for she said, ' I shall have to wait thirty years for you, James, but I shall be very happy and very busy. The time will go quick enough for me, but it will be a slow, weary time for you, my darling. Go home from here, my love, into the great towns, and see what is to be done there.' And so she went to sleep.

"I rebelled for three days. I went away into the bush, with Satan at my elbow all the time, through dry places, through the forest, down by lonely creeksides, up among bald volcanic downs, where there are slopes of slippery turf, leading down to treacherous precipices of slag ; and then through the quartz ranges, and the reedy swamps, where the black swans float, and the spur-winged plover hovers and cackles ; all about I went among the beasts and the birds. But on the third day the Lord wearied of me, and took me back, and I lay on His bosom again like a child. He will always take you home, my lord, if you come. After three days, after thrice twenty years, my lord. Time is nothing to Him."

Lord Saltire was looking on him with kindly admiration.

"There is something in it, my lord. Depend upon it that it is not all a dream. Would not you give all your amazing wealth, all your honours, everything, to change places with me ? "

"I certainly would," said Lord Saltire. " I have always been of opinion that there was something in it. I remember," he continued, turning to William, "expressing the same opinion to your father in the Fleet Prison once, when he had quarrelled with the priests for expressing some opinions which he had got from me. But you must take up with that sort of thing very early in life if you mean it to have any reality at all. I am too old now ! " [1]

Lord Saltire said this in a different tone from his usual one. In a tone that we have never heard him use before. There was something about the man Smith which, in spite of his quaint language, softened every one who heard him speak. Lady Ascot says it was the grace of God. I entirely agree with her ladyship.

"I came home," concluded the missionary, "to try some

---

[1] Once for all, let me call every honest reader to witness, that, unless I speak in the first person, I am not bound to the opinions of any one of the characters in this book. I have merely made people speak, I think, as they would have spoken. Even in a story, consisting so entirely of incident as this, I feel it necessary to say so much, for no kind of unfairness is so common as that of identifying the opinions of a story-teller with those of his *dramatis personæ*.

city work. My wife's nephew, John Marston, whom I expected to see here to-night, is going to assist me in this work. There seems plenty to do. We are at work in Southwark at present."

Possibly it was well that the company, more particularly Lady Ascot, were in a softened and forgiving mood. For, before any one had resumed the conversation, Lord Ascot's valet stood in the door, and, looking at Lady Ascot with a face which said as plain as words, "It is a terrible business, my lady, but I am innocent," announced—

"Lady Welter."

Lord Saltire put his snuff-box into his right-hand trousers' pocket, and his pocket handkerchief into his left, and kept his hands there, leaning back in his chair, with his legs stretched out, and a smile of infinite wicked amusement on his face. Lord Ascot and William stared like a couple of gabies. Lady Ascot had no time to make the slightest change, either in feature or position, before Adelaide, dressed for the evening in a cloud of white and pink, with her bare arms loaded with bracelets, a swansdown fan hanging from her left wrist, sailed swiftly into the room, with outstretched hands, bore down on Lady Ascot, and began kissing her, as though the old lady were fruit of some sort, and she were a dove pecking at it.

"Dearest grandma!"—peck. "So glad to see you!"—peck. "Couldn't help calling in on you as I went to Lady Brittlejug's—and how well you are looking!"—peck, peck. "I can spare ten minutes—do tell me all the news, since I saw you. My dear Lord Ascot, I was so sorry to hear of your illness, but you look better than I expected. And how do *you* do, my dear Lord Saltire?"

Lord Saltire was pretty well, and was delighted to see Lady Welter apparently in the enjoyment of such health and spirits, and so on, aloud. But, secretly, Lord Saltire was wondering what on earth could have brought her here. Perhaps she only wanted to take Lady Ascot by surprise and force her into a recognition of her as Lady Welter. No. My lord saw there was something more than that. She was restless and absent with Lady Ascot. Her eye kept wandering in the middle of all her rattling talk ; but, wherever it wandered, it always came back to William, of whom she had hitherto taken no notice whatever.

"She has come after him. For what?" thought my lord. "I wonder if the jade knows anything of Charles."

Lady Ascot had steeled herself against this meeting. She

had determined, firstly, that no mortal power should ever induce her to set eyes on Adelaide again ; and, secondly, that she, Lady Ascot, would give her, Adelaide, a piece of her mind, which she should never forget to her dying day. The first of these rather contradictory determinations had been disposed of by Adelaide's audacity ; and as for the second ; why, the piece of Lady Ascot's mind which was to be given to Adelaide was, somehow, not ready ; but, instead of it, only silent tears, and withered, trembling fingers, which wandered lovingly over the beautiful young hand, and made the gaudy bracelets on the wrist click one against the other.

" What could I say, Brooks ? what could I do ? " said Lady Ascot to her maid that night, " when I saw her own self come back, with her own old way ? I love the girl more than ever, Brooks, I believe. She beat me. She took me by surprise. I could not resist her. If she had proposed to put me in a wheelbarrow, and wheel me into the middle of that disgrace- ful, that detestable woman Brittlejug's drawing-room, there and then, I should have let her do it, I believe. I might have begged for time to put on my bonnet ; but I should have gone."

She sat there ten minutes or more, talking. Then she said that it was time to go, but that she should come and see Lady Ascot on the morrow. Then she turned to William, to whom she had not been introduced, and asked, would he see her to her carriage ? Lord Saltire was next the bell, and, looking her steadily in the face, raised his hand slowly to pull it. Adelaide begged him eagerly not to trouble himself ; he, with a smile, promptly dropped his hand, and out she sailed on William's arm, Lord Saltire holding the door open, and shutting it after her, with somewhat singular rapidity.

" I hope none of those fools of servants will come blundering upstairs before she has said her say," he remarked aloud. " Give us some of your South African experiences, Mr. Smith. Did you ever see a woman beautiful enough to go clip a lion's claws single-handed, eh ? "

William, convoying Adelaide downstairs, had got no farther than the first step, when he felt her hand drawn from his arm ; he had got one foot on the step below, when he turned to see the cause of this. Adelaide was standing on the step above him, with her glorious face bent sternly, almost fiercely, down on his, and the hand from which the fan hung pointed towards him. It was as beautiful a sight as he had ever seen, and he calmly wondered what it meant. The perfect mouth was curved in scorn, and from it came sharp ringing words, decisive, hard, clear, like the sound of a hammer on an anvil.

"Are you a party to this shameful business, sir? you, who have taken his name, and his place, and his prospects in society. You, who professed, as I hear, to love him like another life, dearer than your own. You, who lay on the same breast with him— tell me, in God's name, that you are sinning in ignorance."

William, as I have remarked before, had a certain amount of shrewdness. He determined to let her go on. He only said, "You are speaking of Charles Ravenshoe."

"Ay," she said sharply; "of Charles Ravenshoe, sir—ex-stable-boy. I came here to-night to beard them all; to ask them did they know, and did they dare to suffer it. If they had not given me an answer, I would have said such things to them as would have made them stop their ears. Lord Saltire has a biting tongue, has he? Let him hear what mine is. But when I saw you among them, I determined to save a scene and speak to you alone. Shameful——"

William looked quietly at her. "Will your ladyship remark that I, that all of us, have been moving heaven and earth to find Charles Ravenshoe, and that we have been utterly unable to find him? If you have any information about him, would it not be as well to consider that the desperation caused by your treatment of him was the principal cause of his extraordinary resolution of hiding himself? And, instead of scolding me and others, who are doing all we can, to give us all the information in your power?"

"Well, well," she said, "perhaps you are right. Consider me rebuked, will you have the goodness? I saw Charles Ravenshoe to-day."

"To-day!"

"Ay, and talked to him."

"How did he look? was he pale? was he thin? Did he seem to want money? Did he ask after me? Did he send any message? Can you take me to where he is? Did he seem much broken down? Does he know we have been seeking him? Lady Welter, for God's sake, do something to repair the wrong you did him, and take me to where he is."

"I don't know where he is, I tell you. I saw him for just one moment. He picked up my hat in the Park. He was dressed like a groom. He came from I know not where, like a ghost from the grave. He did not speak to me. He gave me my hat, and was gone. I do not know whose groom he is, but I think Welter knows. He will tell me to-night. I dared not ask him to-day, lest he should think I was going to see him. When I tell him where I have been, and describe what has passed here, he will tell me. Come to me to-morrow morning, and he shall tell you ; that will be better. You have sense enough to see why."

"I see."

"Another thing. He has seen his sister Ellen. And yet another thing. When I ran away with Lord Welter, I had no idea of what had happened to him—of this miserable *esclandre*. But you must have known that before, if you were inclined to do me justice. Come to-morrow morning. I must go now."

And so she went to her carriage by herself after all. And William stood still on the stairs, triumphant. Charles was as good as found.

The two clergymen passed him on their way downstairs, and bade him good-night. Then he returned to the drawing-room and said—

"My lord, Lady Welter has seen Charles to-day, and spoken to him. With God's help, I will have him here with us to-morrow night."

It was half-past eleven. What Charles, in his headlong folly and stupidity, had contrived to do before this time, must be told in another chapter—no, I have not patience to wait. My patience is exhausted. One act of folly following another so fast would exhaust the patience of Job. If one did not love him so well, one would not be so angry with him. I will tell it here and have done with it. When he had left Adelaide, he had gone home with Hornby. He had taken the horses to the stable ; he had written a note to Hornby. Then he had packed up a bundle of clothes, and walked quietly off.

Round by St. Peter's Church—he had no particular reason for going there, except, perhaps, that his poor foolish heart yearned that evening to see some one who cared for him, though it were only a shoeblack. There was still one pair of eyes which would throw a light for one instant into the thick darkness which was gathering fast around him.

His little friend was there. Charles and he talked for a while, and at last he said—

"You will not see me again. I am going to the war. I am going to Windsor to enlist in the Hussars to-night."

"They will kill you," said the boy.

"Most likely," said Charles. "So we must say good-bye. Mind, now, you go to the school at night, and say that prayer

I gave you on the paper. We must say good-bye. We had better be quick about it."

The boy looked at him steadily. Then he began to draw his breath in long sighs—longer, longer yet, till his chest seemed bursting. Then out it all came in a furious hurricane of tears, and he leant his head against the wall, and beat the bricks with his clenched hand.

"And I am never to see you no more! no more! no more!"

"No more," said Charles. But he thought he might soften the poor boy's grief; and he did think, too, at the moment, that he would go and see the house where his kind old aunt lived before he went away for ever; so he said—

"I shall be in South Audley Street, 167, to-morrow at noon. Now, you must not cry, my dear. You must say good-bye."

And so he left him, thinking to see him no more. Once more, Charles, only once more, and then God help you!

He went off that night to Windsor, and enlisted in the 140th Hussars.

CHAPTER XLV

HALF A MILLION

AND so you see here we are all at sixes and sevens once more. Apparently as near the end of the story as when I wrote the adventures of Alured Ravenshoe at the Court of Henry the Eighth in the very first chapter. If Charles had had a little of that worthy's impudence, instead of being the shy, sensitive fellow he was, why, the story would have been over long ago. In point of fact, I don't know that it would ever have been written at all. So it is best as it is for all parties.

Although Charles had enlisted in Hornby's own regiment, he had craftily calculated that there was not the slightest chance of Hornby's finding it out for some time. Hornby's troop was at the Regent's Park. The head-quarters were at Windsor, and the only officer likely to recognise him was Hornby's captain. And so he went to work at his new duties with an easy mind, rather amused than otherwise, and wondering where and when it would all end.

From sheer unadulterated ignorance, I cannot follow him

during the first week or so of his career. I have a suspicion, almost amounting to a certainty, that, if I could, I should not. I do not believe that the readers of Ravenshoe would care to hear about sword-exercise, riding-school, stableguard, and so on. I can, however, tell you thus much, that Charles learnt his duties in a wonderfully short space of time, and was a great favourite with high and low.

When William went to see Adelaide by appointment the morning after his interview with her, he had an interview with Lord Welter, who told him, in answer to his inquiries, that Charles was groom to Lieutenant Hornby.

"I promised that I would say nothing about it," he continued, "but I think I ought; and Lady Welter has been persuading me to do so, if any inquiries were made, only this morning. I am deuced glad, Ravenshoe, that none of you have forgotten him. It would be a great shame if you had. He is a good fellow, and has been infernally used by some of us—by me, for instance."

William, in his gladness, said, "Never mind, my lord; let bygones be bygones. We shall all be to one another as we were before, please God. I have found Charles, at all events; so there is no gap in the old circle, except my father's. I had a message for Lady Welter."

"She is not down; she is really not well this morning, or she could have seen you."

"It is only this. Lady Ascot begs that she will come over to lunch. My aunt wished she would have stopped longer last night."

"Your aunt?"

"My aunt, Lady Ascot."

"Ah! I beg pardon; I am not quite used to the new state of affairs. Was Lady Welter with Lady Ascot last night?"

William was obliged to say yes, but felt as if he had committed an indiscretion by having said anything about it.

"The deuce she was!" said Lord Welter. "I thought she was somewhere else. Tell my father that I will come and see him to-day, if he don't think it would be too much for him."

"Ah, Lord Welter! you would have come before, if you had known——"

"I know, I know. You must know that I had my reasons for not coming. Well, I hope that you and I will be better acquainted in our new positions; we were intimate enough in our old."

When William was gone, Lord Welter went up to his wife's dressing-room and said—

"Lady Welter, you are a jewel. If you go on like this, you will be recognised, and we shall die at Ranford—you and I— a rich and respectable couple. If 'ifs and ands were pots and pans,' Lady Welter, we should do surprisingly well. If, for instance, Lord Saltire could be got to like me something better than a mad dog, he would leave my father the whole of his landed estate, and cut Charles Horton, whilom Ravenshoe, off with the comparatively insignificant sum of eighty thousand pounds, the amount of his funded property. Eh! Lady Welter?"

Adelaide actually bounded from her chair.

"Are you drunk, Welter?" she said.

"Seeing that it is but the third hour of the day, I am not, Lady Welter. Neither am I a fool. Lord Saltire would clear my father now, if he did not know that it would be more for my benefit than his. I believe he would sooner leave his money to a hospital than see me get one farthing of it."

"Welter," said Adelaide eagerly, "if Charles gets hold of Lord Saltire again, he will have the whole; the old man adores him. I know it; I see it all now; why did I never think of it before. He thinks he is like Lord Barkham, his son. There is time yet. If that man, William Ravenshoe, comes this morning, you must know nothing of Charles. Mind that. Nothing. They must not meet. He may forget him. Mind, Welter, no answer!"

She was walking up and down the room rapidly now, and Lord Welter was looking at her with a satirical smile on his face.

"Lady Welter," he said, "the man, William Ravenshoe has been here and got his answer. By this time, Charles is receiving his lordship's blessing."

"Fool!" was all that Adelaide could say.

"Well, hardly that," said Lord Welter. "At least, *you* should hardly call me so. I understood the position of affairs long before you. I was a reckless young cub not to have paid Lord Saltire more court in old times; but I never knew the state of our affairs till very shortly before the crash came, or I might have done so. In the present case, I have not been such a fool. Charles is restored to Lord Saltire through my instrumentality. A very good basis of operations, Lady Welter."

"At the risk of about half a million of money," remarked Adelaide.

"There was no risk in the other course, certainly," said Lord Welter, "for we should never have seen a farthing of it. And besides, Lady Welter——"

"Well!"

"I have your attention. Good. It may seem strange to you, who care about no one in heaven or earth, but I love this fellow, this Charles Horton. I always did. He is worth all the men I ever met put together. I am glad to have been able to give him a lift this morning. Even if I had not been helping myself, I should have done it all the same. That is comical, is it not? For Lord Saltire's landed property I shall fight. The campaign begins at lunch to-day, Lady Welter; so, if you will be so good as to put on your full war-paint and feathers, we will dig up the tomahawk, and be off on the war-trail in your ladyship's brougham. Good-bye for the present."

Adelaide was beaten. She was getting afraid of her husband; afraid of his strong masculine cunning, of his reckless courage, and of the strange apparition of a great brutal *heart* at the bottom of it all. What were all her fine-spun female cobwebs worth against such a huge, blundering, thieving hornet as he?

CHAPTER XLVI

TO LUNCH WITH LORD ASCOT

THAT same day, Lord Saltire and Lady Ascot were sitting in the drawing-room window, in South Audley Street, alone. He had come in, as his custom was, about eleven, and found her reading her great old Bible; he had taken up the paper and read away for a time, saying that he would not interrupt her; she, too, had seemed glad to avoid a *tête-à-tête* conversation, and had continued; but, after a few minutes, he had dropped the paper, and cried—

"The deuce!"

"My dear James," said she, "what is the matter?"

"Matter! why, we have lost a war-steamer, almost without a shot fired. The Russians have got the *Tiger*, crew and all. It is unbearable, Maria; if they are going to blunder like this at the beginning, where will it end?"

Lord Saltire was disgusted with the war from the very

beginning, in consequence of the French alliance, and so the present accident was as fuel for his wrath. Lady Ascot, as loyal a soul as lived, was possibly rather glad that something had taken up Lord Saltire's attention just then, for she was rather afraid of him this morning. She knew his great dislike for Lord Welter, and expected to be scolded for her weakness with regard to Adelaide the night before. Moreover, she had the guilty consciousness that she had asked Adelaide to come to lunch that morning, of which he did not yet know. So she was rather glad to have a subject to talk of, not personal.

"And when did it happen, my dear James?" she asked.

"On the twelfth of last month, Lady Ascot. Come and sit here in the window, and give an account of yourself, will you have the goodness?"

Now that she saw it must come, she was as cool and as careless as need be. He could not be hard on her. Charles was to come home to them that day. She drew her chair up, and laid her withered old hand on his, and the two grey heads were bent together. Grey heads but green hearts.

"Look at old Daventry," said Lord Saltire, "on the other side of the way. Don't you see him, Maria, listening to that organ? He is two years older than I am. He looks younger."

"I don't know that he does. He ought to look older. She led him a terrible life. Have you been to see him lately?"

"What business is that of yours? So you are going to take Welter's wife back into your good graces, eh, my lady?"

"Yes, James."

"'Yes, James!' I have no patience with you. You are weaker than water. Well, well, we must forgive her, I suppose. She has behaved generous enough about Charles, has she not? I rather admire her scolding poor William Ravenshoe. I must renew our acquaintance."

"She is coming to lunch to-day."

"I thought you looked guilty. Is Welter coming?"

Lady Ascot made no reply. Neither at that moment would Lord Saltire have heard her if she had. He was totally absorbed in the proceedings of his old friend Lord Daventry, before mentioned. That venerable dandy had listened to the organ until the man had played all his tunes twice through, when he had given him half a crown, and the man had departed. Immediately afterwards, a Punch and Judy had come, which Punch and Judy was evidently an acquaintance of his; for, on descrying him, it had hurried on with its attendant crowd, and breathlessly pitched itself in front of him, let down its green curtains, and plunged at once *in medias'res.* The back of the show was towards Lord Saltire; but, just as he saw Punch look round the corner, to see which way the Devil was gone, he saw two pickpockets advance on Lord Daventry from different quarters, with fell intentions. They met at his tail-coat pocket, quarrelled, and fought. A policeman bore down on them; Lord Daventry was still unconscious, staring his eyes out of his head. The affair was becoming exciting, when Lord Saltire felt a warm tear drop on his hand.

"James," said Lady Ascot, "don't be hard on Welter. I love Welter. There is good in him; there is, indeed. I know how shamefully he has behaved; but don't be hard on him, James."

"My dearest Maria," said Lord Saltire, "I would not give you one moment's uneasiness for the world. I do not like Welter. I dislike him. But I will treat him for your sake and Ascot's as though I loved him—there. Now about Charles. He will be with us to-day, thank God. What the deuce are we to do?"

"I cannot conceive," said Lady Ascot; "it is such a terrible puzzle. One does not like to move, and yet it seems such a sin to stand still."

"No answer to your advertisement, of course?" said Lord Saltire.

"None whatever. It seems strange, too, with such a reward as we have offered; but it was worded so cautiously, you see."

Lord Saltire laughed. "Cautiously, indeed. No one could possibly guess what it was about. It was a miracle of obscurity; but it won't do to go any farther yet." After a pause, he said —"You are perfectly certain of your facts, Maria, for the fiftieth time?"

"Perfectly certain. I committed a great crime, James. I did it for Alicia's sake. Think what my bringing up had been, how young I was, and forgive me if you can; excuse me if you cannot."

"Nonsense about a great crime, Maria. It was a great mistake, certainly. If you had only had the courage to have asked Petre one simple question! Alicia never guessed the fact, of course?"

"Never."

"Do you think, Maria, that by any wild possibility James or Norah knew?"

"How could they possibly? What a foolish question."

"I don't know. These Roman Catholics do strange things," said Lord Saltire, staring out of the window at the crowd.

"If she knew, why did she change the child?"

"Eh?" said Lord Saltire, turning round.

"You have not been attending," said Lady Ascot.

"No, I have not," said Lord Saltire; "I was looking at Daventry."

"Do you still," said Lord Saltire, "since all our researches and failures, stick to the belief that the place was in Hampshire?"

"I do, indeed, and in the north of Hampshire too."

"I wonder," said Lord Saltire, turning round suddenly, "whether Mackworth knows?"

"Of course he does," said Lady Ascot quietly.

"Hum," said Lord Saltire, "I had a hold over that man once; but I threw it away as being worthless. I wish I had made a bargain for my information. But what nonsense; how can he know?"

"Know?" said Lady Ascot, scornfully; "what is there a confessor don't know? Don't tell me that all Mackworth's power came from finding out poor Densil's *faux pas*. The man had a sense of power other than that."

"Then he never used it," said Lord Saltire. "Densil, dear soul, never knew."

"I said a *sense* of power," said Lady Ascot, "which gave him his consummate impudence. Densil never dreamt of it."

At this point the policeman had succeeded in capturing the two pickpockets, and was charging them before Lord Daventry. Lord Daventry audibly offered them ten shillings a-piece to say nothing about it; at which the crowd cheered.

"Would it be any use to offer money to the priest—say ten thousand pounds or so?" said Lord Saltire. "You are a religious woman, Maria, and as such are a better judge of a priest's conscience than I. What do you think?"

"I don't know," said Lady Ascot. "I don't know but what the man is high-minded, in his heathenish way. You know Cuthbert's story of his having refused ten thousand pounds to hush up the matter about Charles. His information would be a blow to the Popish Church in the West. He would lose position by accepting your offer. I don't know what his position may be worth. You can try him, if all else fails; not otherwise, I should say. We must have a closer search."

"When you come to think, Maria, he can't know. If Densil did not know, how could he?"

"Old Clifford might have known, and told him."

" If we are successful, and if Adelaide has no children—two improbable things," said Lord Saltire, "why then——"

" Why then——" said Lady Ascot. " But at the worst you are going to make Charles a rich man. Shall you tell William?"

" Not yet. Cuthbert should never be told, I say; but that is Charles's business. I have prepared William."

" Cuthbert will not live," said Lady Ascot.

"Not a chance of it, I believe. Marston says his heart-complaint does not exist, but I think differently."

At this moment, Lord Daventry's offer of money having been refused, the whole crowd moved off in procession towards the police-station. First came three little girls with big bonnets and babies, who, trying to do two things at once—to wit, head the procession by superior speed, and at the same time look round at Lord Daventry and the pickpockets—succeeded in neither, but only brought the three babies' heads in violent collision every other step. Next came Lord Daventry, resigned. Next the policeman, with a pickpocket in each hand, who were giving explanations. Next the boys; after them the Punch and Judy, which had unfortunately seen the attempt made, and must to the station as a witness, to the detriment of business. Bringing up the rear were the British public, who played practical jokes with one another. The dogs kept a parallel course in the gutter, and barked In turning the first corner, the procession was cut into, and for a time thrown into confusion, by a light-hearted costermonger, who, returning from a successful market with an empty barrow, drove it in among them with considerable velocity. After which they disappeared like the baseless fabric of a dream, only to be heard of again in the police reports.

"Lord and Lady Welter."

Lord Saltire had seen them drive up to the door; so he was quite prepared. He had been laughing intensely, but quite silently, at poor Lord Daventry's adventures, and so, when he turned round, he had a smile on his face. Adelaide had done kissing Lady Ascot, and was still holding both her hands with a look of intense mournful affection. Lord Saltire was so much amused by Adelaide's acting, and her simplicity in performing before himself, that, when he advanced to Lord Welter, he was perfectly radiant.

" Well, my dear scapegrace, and how do *you* do?" he said, giving his hand to Lord Welter; "a more ill-mannered fellow I never saw in my life. To go away and hide yourself with that lovely young wife of yours, and leave all us oldsters to bore one another to death. What the deuce do you mean by it? Eh, sir?"

Lord Welter did not reply in the same strain. He said—

"It is very kind of you to receive me like this. I did not expect it. Allow me to tell you, that I think your manner towards me would not be quite so cordial if you knew everything; there is a great deal that you don't know, and which I don't mean to tell you."

It is sometimes quite impossible, even for a writer of fiction, a man with *carte blanche* in the way of invention, to give the cause for a man's action. I have thought and thought, and I cannot for the life of me tell you why Lord Welter answered Lord Saltire like that, whether it was from deep cunning or merely from recklessness. If it was cunning, it was cunning of a high order. It was genius. The mixture of respect and kindness towards the person, and of carelessness about his favour was—well—very creditable. Lord Saltire did not think he was acting, and his opinion is of some value, I believe. But then, we must remember that he was prepared to think the best of Lord Welter that day, and must make allowances. I am not prepared with an opinion; let every man form his own. I only know that Lord Saltire tapped his teeth with his snuff-box and remained silent. Lord Welter, whether consciously or no, was nearer the half of a million of money than he had ever been before.

But Adelaide's finer sense was offended at her husband's method of proceeding. For one instant, when she heard him say what he did, she could have killed him. "Reckless, brutal, selfish," she said fiercely to herself, "throwing a duke's fortune to the winds by sheer obstinacy." (At this time she had picked up Lady Ascot's spectacles, and was playfully placing them on her venerable nose.) "I wish I had never seen him. He is maddening. If he only had some brains, where might not we be?" But the conversation of that morning came to her mind with a jar, and the suspicion with it, that he had more brains of a sort than she; that, though they were on a par in morality, there was a strength about him, against which her finesse was worthless. She knew she could never deceive Lord Saltire, and there was Lord Saltire tapping him on the knee with his snuff-box, and talking earnestly and confidentially to him. She was beginning to respect her husband. *He* dared face that terrible old man with his hundreds of thousands; *she* trembled in his presence.

Let us leave her, fooling our dear old friend to the top of her bent, and hear what the men were saying.

"I know you have been, as they say now, 'very fast,'" said Lord Saltire, drawing nearer to him. "I don't want to ask any questions which don't concern me. You have sense enough to know that it is worth your while to stand well with me. Will you answer me a few questions which do concern me?"

"I can make no promises, Lord Saltire. Let me hear what they are, will you?"

"Why," said Lord Saltire, "about Charles Ravenshoe."

"About Charles!" said Lord Welter, looking up at Lord Saltire. "Oh, yes; any number. I have nothing to conceal there. Of course you will know everything. I had sooner you knew it from me than another."

"I don't mean about Adelaide; let that go by. Perhaps I am glad that that is as it is. But have you known where Charles was lately? Your wife told William to come to her this morning; that is why I ask."

"I have known a very short time. When William Ravenshoe came this morning, I gave him every information. Charles will be with you to-day."

"I am satisfied."

"I don't care to justify myself, but if it had not been for me you would never have seen him. And more. I am not the first man, Lord Saltire, who has done what I have done."

"No, of course not," said Lord Saltire. "I can't fling the first stone at you; God forgive me."

"But you must see, Lord Saltire, that I could not have guessed that Ellen was his sister."

"Hey?" said Lord Saltire. "Say that again."

"I say that, when I took Ellen Horton away from Ravenshoe, I did not know that she was Charles's sister."

Lord Saltire fell back in his chair, and said—

"Good God!"

"It is very terrible, looked at one way, Lord Saltire. If you come to look at it another, it amounts to this, that she was only, as far as I knew, a gamekeeper's daughter. Do you remember what you said to Charles and me, when we were rusticated?"

"Yes. I said that one vice was considered more venial than another vice now-a-days; and I say so still. I had sooner that you had died of delirium tremens in a ditch than done this."

"So had not I, Lord Saltire. When I became involved with Adelaide, I thought Ellen was provided for; I, even then, had not heard this *esclandre* about Charles. She refused a splendid offer of marriage before she left me."

"We thought she was dead. Where is she gone?"

"I have no idea. She refused everything. She stayed on as Adelaide's maid, and left us suddenly. We have lost all trace of her."

"What a miserable, dreadful business!" said Lord Saltire.

"Very so," said Lord Welter. "Hadn't we better change the subject, my lord?" he added dryly. "I am not at all sure that I shall submit to much more cross-questioning. You must not push me too far, or I shall get savage."

"I won't," said Lord Saltire. "But, Welter, for God's sake, answer me two more questions. Not offensive ones, on my honour."

"Fifty, if you will; only consider my rascally temper."

"Yes, yes! When Ellen was with you, did she ever hint that she was in possession of any information about the Ravenshoes?"

"Yes; or rather, when she went, she left a letter, and in it she said that she had something to tell Charles."

"Good, good!" said Lord Saltire. "She may know. We must find her. Now, Charles is coming here to-day; had you better meet him, Welter?"

"We have met before. All that is past is forgiven between us."

"Met!" said Lord Saltire eagerly. "And what did he say to you? Was there a scene, Welter?"

Lord Welter paused before he answered, and Lord Saltire, the wise, looked out of the window. Once Lord Welter seemed going to speak, but there was a catch in his breath. The second attempt was more fortunate. He said, in a low voice—

"Why, I'll tell you, my lord. Charles Ravenshoe is broken-hearted."

"Lord and Lady Hainault."

And Miss Corby, and Gus, and Flora, and Archy, the footman might have added, but was probably afraid of spoiling his period.

It was rather awkward. They were totally unexpected, and Lord Hainault and Lord Welter had not met since Lord Hainault had denounced Lord Welter at Tattersall's. It was so terribly awkward that Lord Saltire recovered his spirits, and

looked at the two young men with a smile. The young men
disappointed him, however, for Lord Hainault said, " How
d'ye do, Welter?" and Lord Welter said, " How do, Hainault?" and the matter was settled, at all events for the
present.

When all salutations had been exchanged among the ladies,
and Archy had hoisted himself up into Mary's lap, and Lady
Hainault had imperially settled herself in a chair, with Flora
at her knee, exactly opposite Adelaide, there was a silence for
a moment, during which it became apparent that Gus had a
question to ask of Lady Ascot. Mary trembled, but the others
were not quite sorry to have the silence broken. Gus, having
obtained leave of the house, wished to know, whether or not
Satan, should he repent of his sins, would have a chance of
regaining his former position?

" That silly Scotch nursemaid has been reading Burns's
poems to him, I suppose," said Lady Hainault; "unless
Mary herself has been doing so. Mary prefers anything to
Watts's hymns, Lady Ascot."

" You must not believe one word Lady Hainault says, Lady
Ascot," said Mary. " She has been shamefully worsted in an
argument, and she is resorting to all sorts of unfair means to
turn the scales. I never read a word of Burns's poems in my
life."

" You will be pleased not to believe a single word Miss
Corby says, Lady Ascot," said Lady Hainault. " She has
convicted herself. She sings, ' The banks and braes of bonny
Doon '—very badly, I will allow, but still she sings it."

There was a laugh at this. Anything was better than the
silence which had gone before. It became evident that Lady
Hainault would not speak to Adelaide. It was very uncomfortable. Dear Mary would have got up another friendly passage
of arms with Lady Hainault, but she was too nervous. She
would have even drawn out Gus, but she saw that Gus, dear
fellow, was not in a humour to be trusted that morning. He
evidently was aware that the dogs of war were loose, and was
champing the bit like a war-horse. Lady Ascot was as nervous
as Mary, dying to say something, but unable. Lady Hainault
was calmly inexorable, Adelaide sublimely indifferent. If you
will also consider that Lady Ascot was awaiting news of Charles
—nay, possibly Charles himself—and that, in asking Adelaide
to lunch, she had overlooked the probability that William
would bring him back with him—that Lord Welter had come
without invitation, and that the Hainaults were totally unex-

pected—you will think that the dear old lady was in about as uncomfortable a position as she could be, and that any event, even the house catching fire, must change matters for the better.

Not at all. They say that, when things come to the worst, they must mend. That is undeniable. But when are they at the worst? Who can tell that? Lady Ascot thought they were at the worst now, and was taking comfort. And then the footman threw open the door, and announced—

" Lady Hainault and Miss Hicks."

At this point Lady Ascot lost her temper, and exclaimed aloud, "This is too much!" They thought old Lady Hainault did not hear her; but she did, and so did Hicks. They heard it fast enough, and remembered it too.

In great social catastrophes, minor differences are forgotten. In the Indian mutiny people spoke to one another, and made friends, who were at bitterest variance before. There are crises so terrible that people of all creeds and shades of political opinion must combine against a common enemy. This was one. When this dreadful old woman made her totally unexpected entrance, and when Lady Ascot showed herself so entirely without discretion as to exclaim aloud in the way she did, young Lady Hainault and Adelaide were so horrified, so suddenly quickened to a sense of impending danger, that they began talking loudly and somewhat affectionately to one another. And young Lady Hainault, whose self-possession was scattered to the four winds by this last misfortune, began asking Adelaide all about Lady Brittlejug's drum, in full hearing of her mamma-in-law, who treasured up every word she said. And, just as she became conscious of saying wildly that she was so sorry she could not have been there—as if Lady Brittlejug would ever have had the impudence to ask her—she saw Lord Saltire, across the room, looking quietly at her, with the expression on his face of one of the idols at Abou Simbel.

Turn Lady Ascot once fairly to bay, you would (if you can forgive slang) get very little change out of her. She came of valiant blood. No Headstall was ever yet known to refuse his fence. Even her poor brother, showing as he did traces of worn-out blood (the men always go a generation or two before the women), had been a desperate rider, offered to kick Fouquier Tinville at his trial, and had kept Simon waiting on the guillotine while he pared his nails. Her ladyship rose and accepted battle ; she advanced towards old Lady Hainault, and, leaning on her crutched stick, began—

"And how do you do, my dear Lady Hainault?"

She thought Lady Hainault would say something very disagreeable, as she usually did. She looked at her, and was surprised to see how altered she was. There was something about her looks that Lady Ascot did not like.

"My dear Lady Ascot," said old Lady Hainault, "I thank you. I am a very old woman. I never forget my friends, I assure you. Hicks, is Lord Hainault here?—I am very blind, you will be glad to hear, Lady Ascot. Hicks, I want Lord Hainault, instantly. Fetch him to me, you stupid woman. Hainault! Hainault!"

Our Lady Hainault rose suddenly, and put her arm round her waist. "Mamma," she said, "what do you want!"

"I want Hainault, you foolish girl. Is that him? Hainault, I have made the will, my dear boy. The rogue came to me, and I told him that the will was made, and that Britten and Sloane had witnessed it. Did I do right or not, eh? Ha! ha! I followed you here to tell you. Don't let that woman Ascot insult me, Hainault. She has committed a felony, that woman. I'll have her prosecuted. And all to get that chit Alicia married to that pale-faced papist, Petre Ravenshoe. She thinks I didn't know it, does she? I knew she knew it well enough, and I knew it too, and I have committed a felony too, in holding my tongue, and we'll both go to Bridewell, and——"

Lord Saltire here came up, and quietly offered her his arm. She took it and departed, muttering to herself.

I must mention here, that the circumstance mentioned by old Lady Hainault, of having made a will, had nothing to do with the story. A will had existed to the detriment of Lady Hainault and Miss Hicks, and she had most honourably made another in their favour.

Lady Ascot would have given worlds to unsay many things she had heretofore said to her. It was evident that poor old Lady Hainault's mind was failing. Lady Ascot would have prayed her forgiveness on her knees, but it was too late. Lady Hainault never appeared in public again. She died a short time after this, and, as I have mentioned before, left poor Miss Hicks a rich woman. Very few people knew how much good there was in the poor old soul. Let the Casterton tenantry testify.

On this occasion her appearance had, as we have seen, the effect of reconciling Lady Hainault and Adelaide. A very few minutes after her departure William entered the room, followed by Hornby, whom none of them had ever seen before.

They saw from William's face that something fresh was the matter. He introduced Hornby, who seemed concerned, and then gave an open note to Lord Saltire. He read it over, and then said—

"This unhappy boy has disappeared again. Apparently his interview with you determined him, my dear Lady Welter. Can you give us any clue? This is his letter"—

"DEAR LIEUTENANT,—I must say good-bye even to you, my last friend. I was recognised in your service to-day by Lady Welter, and it will not do for me to stay in it any longer. It was a piece of madness ever taking to such a line of life."

[Here there were three lines carefully erased. Lord Saltire mentioned it, and Hornby quietly said, "I erased those lines previous to showing the letter to any one; they referred to exceedingly private matters." Lord Saltire bowed and continued,]

"A hundred thanks for your kindness; you have been to me more like a brother than a master. We shall meet again, when you little expect it. Pray don't assist in any search after me; it will be quite useless.

"CHARLES HORTON."

Adelaide came forward as pale as death. "I believe I am the cause of this. I did not dream it would have made him alter his resolution so suddenly. When I saw him yesterday he was in a groom's livery. I told him he was disgracing himself, and told him, if he was desperate, to go to the war."

They looked at one another in silence.

"Then," Lady Ascot said, "he has enlisted, I suppose. I wonder what regiment?—could it be in yours, Mr. Hornby?"

"The very last in which he would, I should say," said Hornby, "if he wants to conceal himself. He must know that I should find him at once."

So Lady Ascot was greatly pooh-poohed by the other wise-acres, she being right all the time.

"I think," said Lord Saltire to Lady Ascot, "that perhaps we had better take Mr. Hornby into our confidence." She agreed, and after the Hainaults and Welters were gone, Hornby remained behind with them, and heard things which rather surprised him.

"Inquiries at the depôts of various regiments would be as good a plan as any. Meanwhile, I will give any assistance in my power. Pray, would it not be a good plan to advertise for him and state all the circumstances of the case?"

"Why, no," said Lord Saltire, "we do not wish to make known all the circumstances yet. Other interests have to be consulted, and our information is not yet complete. Complete! we have nothing to go on but mere surmise."

"You will think me inquisitive," said Hornby. "But you little know what a right (I had almost said) I have to ask these questions. Does the present Mr. Ravenshoe know of all this?"

"Not one word."

And so Hornby departed with William, and said nothing at all about Ellen. As they left the door a little shoe-black looked inquisitively at them, and seemed as though he would speak. They did not notice the child. He could have told them what they wanted to know, but how were they to guess that?

Impossible. Actually, according to the sagacious Welter, half a million pounds, and other things, going a-begging, and a dirty little shoe-black the only human being who knew where the heir was! A pig is an obstinate animal, likewise a sheep; but what pig or sheep was ever so provoking in its obstinacy as Charles in his good-natured, well-meaning, blundering stupidity? In a very short time you will read an advertisement put into the *Times* by Lady Ascot's solicitor, which will show the reason for some of the great anxiety which she and others felt to have him on the spot. At first Lady Ascot and Lord Saltire lamented his absence, from the hearty goodwill they bore him; but, as time wore on, they began to get deeply solicitous for his return for other reasons. Lady Ascot's hands were tied. She was in a quandary, and, when the intelligence came of his having enlisted, and there seemed nearly a certainty of his being shipped off to foreign parts, and killed before she could get at him, she was in a still greater quandary. Suppose, before being killed, he was to marry some one? "Good Heavens, my dear James, was ever an unfortunate wretch punished so before for keeping a secret?"

"I should say not, Maria," said Lord Saltire, coolly. "I declare I love the lad the better the more trouble he gives one. There never was such a dear obstinate dog. Welter has been making his court, and has made it well—with an air of ruffian-like simplicity, which was charming, because novel. I, even I, can hardly tell whether it was real or not. He has ten times the brains of his shallow-pated little wife, whose manœuvres, my dear Maria, I should have thought even you, not ordinarily a sagacious person, might have seen through."

"I believe the girl loves me; and don't be rude, James."

"I believe she don't care twopence for you; and I shall be as rude as I please, Maria."

Poor Lord Ascot had a laugh at this little battle between his mother and her old friend. So Lord Saltire turned to him and said—

"At half-past one to-morrow morning, you will be awakened by three ruffians in crape masks, with pistols, who will take you out of bed with horrid threats, and walk you upstairs and down in your shirt, until you have placed all your money and valuables into their hands. They will effect an entrance by removing a pane of glass, and introducing a small boy, disguised as a shoe-black, who will give them admittance."

"Good Gad?" said Lord Ascot, "what are you talking about?"

"Don't you see that shoe-black over the way?" said Lord Saltire. "He has been watching the house for two hours; the burglars are going to put him in at the back-kitchen window. There comes Daventry back from the police-station. I bet you a sovereign he has his boots cleaned."

Poor Lord Ascot jumped at the bet like an old war-horse. "I'd have given you three to one if you had waited."

Lord Daventry had indeed reappeared on the scene; his sole attendant was one of the little girls with a big bonnet and a baby, before mentioned, who had evidently followed him to the police-station, watched him in, and then accompanied him home—staring at him as at a man of dark experiences, a man not to be lost sight of on any account, lest some new and exciting thing should befall him meanwhile. This young lady, having absented herself some two hours on this errand, and having thereby deprived the baby of its natural nourishment, was now suddenly encountered by an angry mother, and, knowing what she had to expect, was forced to "dodge" her infuriated parent round and round Lord Daventry, in a way which made that venerable nobleman giddy, and caused him to stop, shut his eyes, and feebly offer them money not to do it any more. Ultimately the young lady was caught and cuffed, the baby was refreshed, and his lordship free.

Lord Saltire won his pound, to his great delight. Such an event as a shoe-black in South Audley Street was not to be passed by. Lord Daventry entered into conversation with our little friend, asked him if he went to school? if he could say the Lord's Prayer? how much he made in the day? whether his parents were alive? and ultimately had his boots cleaned, and gave the boy half-a-crown. After which he disappeared

from the scene, and, like many of our large staff of super-
numeraries, from this history for evermore—he has served his
turn with us.   Let us dismiss the kind-hearted old dandy, with
our best wishes.

Lord Saltire saw him give the boy the half-crown.   He saw
the boy pocket it as though it were a halfpenny ; and afterwards
continue to watch the house, as before.   He was more sure
than ever that the boy meant no good.   If he had known that
he was waiting for one chance of seeing Charles again, perhaps
he would have given him half-a-crown himself.   What a
difference one word from that boy would have made in our
story !

When they came back from dinner, there was the boy still
lying on the pavement, leaning against his box.   The little girl
who had had her ears boxed came and talked to him for a
time, and went on.   After a time she came back with a
quartern loaf in her hand, the crumbs of which she picked as
she went along, after the manner of children sent on an errand
to the baker's.   When she had gone by, he rose and leant
against the railings, as though lingering, loth to go.

Once more, later, Lord Saltire looked out, and the boy was
still there.   "I wonder what the poor little rogue wants?"
said Lord Saltire ; "I have half a mind to go and ask him."
But he did not.   It was not to be, my lord.   You might have
been with Charles the next morning at Windsor.   You might
have been in time if you had ; you will have a different sort of
meeting with him than that, if you meet him at all.   Beyond
the grave, my lord, that meeting must be.   Possibly a happier
one, who knows ? who dare say ?

The summer night closed in, but the boy lingered yet, to see,
if perchance he might, the only friend he ever had ; to hear, if
he might, the only voice which had ever spoken gently and
kindly to him of higher things : the only voice which had told
him that strange, wild tale, scarce believed as yet, of a glorious
immortality.

The streets began to get empty.   The people passed him—

> " Ones and twos,
> And groups ; the latest said the nights grew chill,
> And hastened ; but he loitered ; whilst the dews
> Fell fast, he loitered still."

CHAPTER XLVII

LADY HAINAULT'S BLOTTING-BOOK

IN the natural course of events I ought now to follow Charles in his military career, step by step. But the fact is that I know no more about the details of horse-soldiering than a marine, and, therefore, I cannot. It is within the bounds of possibility that the reader may congratulate himself on my ignorance, and it may also be possible that he has good reasons for so doing.

Within a fortnight after Hornby's introduction to Lord Saltire and Lady Ascot, he was off with the headquarters of his regiment to Varna. The depôt was at Windsor, and there, unknown to Hornby, was Charles drilling and drilling. Two more troops were to follow the head-quarters in a short time, and so well had Charles stuck to his duty that he was considered fit to take his place in one of them. Before his moustaches were properly grown, he found himself a soldier in good earnest.

In all his troubles this was the happiest time he had, for he had got rid of the feeling that he was a disgraced man. If he must wear a livery, he would wear the Queen's ; there was no disgrace in that. He was a soldier, and he would be a hero. Sometimes, perhaps, he thought for a moment that he, with his two thousand pounds' worth of education, might have been better employed than in littering a horse and swash-bucklering about among the Windsor taverns ; but he did not think long about it. If there were any disgrace in the matter, there was a time coming soon, by all accounts, when the disgrace would be wiped out in fire and blood. On Sunday, when he saw the Eton lads streaming up to the terrace, the old Shrewsbury days, and the past generally, used to come back to him rather unpleasantly ; but the bugle put it all out of his head again in a moment. Were there not the three most famous armies in the world gathering, gathering, for a feast of ravens ? Was not the world looking on in silence and awe, to see England, France and Russia locked in a death-grip ? Was not he to make one at the merry meeting ? Who could think at such a time as this ?

The time was getting short now. In five days they were to

start for Southampton, to follow the headquarters to Constantinople, to Varna, and so into the dark thunder-cloud beyond. He felt as certain that he would never come back again, as that the sun would rise on the morrow.

He made the last energetic effort that he made at all. It was like the last struggle of a drowning man. He says that the way it happened was this. And I believe him, for it was one of his own mad impulses, and, like all his other impulses, it came too late. They came branking into some pot-house, half-a-dozen of them, and talked aloud about this and that, and one young lad among them said, that "he would give a thousand pounds, if he had it, to see his sister before he went away, for fear she should think that he had gone off without thinking of her."

Charles left them and walked up the street. As he walked his purpose grew. He went straight to the quarters of a certain cornet, son to the major of the regiment, and asked to speak to him.

The cornet, a quiet, smooth-faced boy, listened patiently to what he had to say, but shook his head and told him he feared it was impossible. But, he said, after a pause, he would help him all he could. The next morning he took him to the major while he was alone at breakfast, and Charles laid his case before him so well that the kind old man gave him leave to go to London at four o'clock, and come back by the last train that same evening.

The Duchess of Cheshire's ball was the last and greatest which was given that season. It was, they say, in some sort like the Duchess of Richmond's ball before Waterloo. The story I have heard is that Lord George Barty persuaded his mother to give it, because he was sure that it would be the last ball he should ever dance at. At all events it was given, and he was right; for he sailed in the same ship with Charles four days after, and was killed at Balaclava. However, we have nothing to do with that. All we have to do with is the fact that it was a very great ball indeed, and that Lady Hainault was going to it.

Some traditions and customs grow by degrees into laws, ay, and into laws less frequently broken than those made and provided by Parliament. Allow people to walk across the corner of one of your fields for twenty years, and there is a right of way, and they may walk across that field till the crack of doom. Allow a man to build a hut on your property and live in it for twenty years, and you can't get rid of him. He gains a right there. (I never was annoyed in either of these ways myself, for reasons which I decline to mention; but it is the law, I believe.) There is no law to make the young men fire off guns at one's gate on the 5th of November, but they never miss doing it. (I found some of the men using their rifles for this purpose last year, and had to fulminate about it.) To follow out the argument, there was no rule in Lord Hainault's house that the children should always come in and see their aunt dress for a ball. But they always did; and Lady Hainault herself, though she could be perfectly determined, never dared to question their right.

They behaved very well. Flora brought in a broken picture-broom, which, stuck into an old straw hat of Archy's, served her for feathers. She also made unto herself a newspaper fan. Gus had an old twelfth-cake ornament on his breast for a star and a tape round his neck for a garter. In this guise they represented the Duke and Duchess of Cheshire, and received their company in a corner, as good as gold. As for Archy, he nursed his cat, sucked his thumb, and looked at his aunt.

Mary was "by way of" helping Lady Hainault's maid, but she was very clumsy about it, and her hands shook a good deal. Lady Hainault, at last looking up, saw that she was deadly pale and crying. So, instead of taking any notice, she dismissed the children as soon as she could, as a first step towards being left alone with Mary.

Gus and Flora, finding that they must go, changed the game, and made believe that they were at court, and that their aunt was the Queen. So they dexterously backed to the door and bowed themselves out. Archy was lord chamberlain, or gold stick, or what not, and had to follow them in the same way. He was less successful, for he had to walk backwards, sucking his thumb and nursing his cat upside down (she was a patient cat, and was as much accustomed to be nursed that way as any other). He got on very well till he came to the door, when he fell on the back of his head, crushing his cat and biting his thumb to the bone. Gus and Flora picked him up, saying that lord chamberlains never cried when they fell on the backs of their heads. But Archy, poor dear, was obliged to cry a little, the more so as the dear cat had bolted upstairs, with her tail as big as a fox's, and Archy was afraid she was angry with him, which seemed quite possible. So Mary had to go out and take him to the nursery. He would stop his crying, he said, if she would tell him the story of Ivedy Avedy. So she told it him quite to the end, where the baffled old sorcerer, Gongolo, gets into the plate-warmer with his three-farthings and the brass soup-ladle, shuts the door after him, and disappears for ever. After which she went down to Lady Hainault's room again.

Lady Hainault was alone now. She was sitting before her dressing-table with her hands folded, apparently looking at herself in the glass. She took no notice of what she had seen; though now they were alone together, she determined that Mary should tell her what was the matter—for, in truth, she was very anxious to know. She never looked at Mary when she came in; she only said—

"Mary, my love, how do I look?"

"I never saw you look so beautiful before," said Mary.

"I am glad of that. Hainault is so ridiculously proud of me, that I really delight in looking my best. Now, Mary, let me have the necklace; that is all, I believe, unless you would like me to put on a little rouge."

Mary tried to laugh, but could not. Her hands were shaking so that the jewels were clicking together as she held them. Lady Hainault saw that she must help her to speak, but she had no occasion; the necklace helped her.

It was a very singular necklace, a Hainault heirloom, which Lady Hainault always wore on grand occasions to please her husband. There was no other necklace like it anywhere, though some folks who did not own it said it was old-fashioned, and should be reset. It was a collar of nine points, the ends of brilliants, running upwards as the points broadened into larger rose diamonds. The eye, catching the end of the points, was dazzled with yellow light, which faded into red as the rays of the larger roses overpowered the brilliants; and at the upper rim the soft crimson haze of light melted, overpowered, into nine blazing great rubies. It seemed, however, a shame to hide such a beautiful neck by such a glorious bauble.

Mary was trying to clasp it on, but her fingers failed, and down went the jewels clashing on the floor. The next moment she was down too, on her knees, clutching Lady Hainault's hand and saying, or trying to say, in spite of a passionate burst of sobbing, "Lady Hainault, let me see him; let me see him, or I shall die."

Lady Hainault turned suddenly upon her, and laid her disengaged hand upon her hair. "My little darling," she said, "my pretty little bird."

"You must let me see him. You could not be so cruel. I

always loved him, not like a sister, oh! not like a sister, woe to me. As you love Lord Hainault; I know it now."

"My poor little Mary. I always thought something of this kind."

"He is coming to-night. He sails to-morrow or next day, and I shall never see him again."

"Sails! where for?"

"I don't know; he does not say. But you must let me see him. He don't dream I care for him, Lady Hainault. But I must see him, or I shall die."

"You shall see him; but who is it? Any one I know?"

"Who is it? Who could it be but Charles Ravenshoe?"

"Good God! Coming here to-night! Mary, ring the bell for Alwright. Send round to South Audley Street for Lord Saltire, or William Ravenshoe, or some of them. They are dying to catch him. There is something more in their eagerness than you or I know of. Send at once. Mary, or we shall be too late. When does he come? Get up, my dear. My poor little Mary. I am so sorry. Is he coming here? And how soon will he come, dear? Do be calm. Think what we may do for him. He should be here now. Stay, I will write a note—just one line. Where is my blotting-book? Alwright, get my blotting-book. And stay; say that, if any one calls for Miss Corby, he is to be shown into the drawing-room at once. Let us go there, Mary."

Alwright had meanwhile, not having heard the last sentence, departed to the drawing-room, and possessed herself of Lady Hainault's portfolio, meaning to carry it up to the dressing-room; then she had remembered the message about any one calling being shown up to the drawing-room, and had gandered down to the hall to give it to the porter; after which she gandered upstairs to the dressing-room again, thinking that Lady Hainault was there, and missing both her and Mary from having gone downstairs. So while she and Mary were looking for the blotting-book impatiently in the drawing-room, the door was opened, and the servant announced, "A gentleman to see Miss Corby."

He had discreetly said a gentleman, for he did not like to say an Hussar. Mary turned round and saw a man all scarlet and gold before her, and was frightened and did not know him. But when he said "Mary," in the old, old voice, there came such a rush of bygone times, bygone words, scenes, sounds meetings and partings, sorrows and joys, into her wild, warm little heart, that, with a low, loving, tender cry, she ran to him and hid her face on his bosom.[1]

And Lady Hainault swept out of the room after that unlucky blotting-book. And I intend to go after her, out of mere politeness, to help her to find it. I will not submit to be lectured for making an aposiopesis. If any think they could do this business better than I, let them communicate with the publishers, and finish the story for themselves. I decline to go into that drawing-room at present. I shall wander upstairs into my lady's chamber, after that goosey-gander Alwright, and see what she has done with the blotting-book.

Lady Hainault found the idiot of a woman in her dressing-room, looking at herself in the glass, with the blotting-book under her arm. The maid looked as foolish as people generally do who are caught looking at themselves in the glass. (How disconcerting it is to be found standing on a chair before the chimney-glass, just to have a look at your entire figure before going to a party![2]) But Lady Hainault said nothing to her; but, taking the book from under her arm, she sat down and fiercely scrawled off a note to Lord Saltire, to be opened by any of them, to say that Charles Ravenshoe was then in her house, and to come in God's name.

"I have caged their bird for them," she said out loud when she had just finished and was folding up the letter; "they will owe me a good turn for this."

The maid, who had no notion anything was the matter, had been surreptitiously looking in the glass again, and wondering whether her nose was really so very red after all. When Lady Hainault spoke thus aloud to herself, she gave a guilty start, and said, "Immediately, my lady," which, you will perceive, was not exactly appropriate to the occasion.

"Don't be a goose, my good old Alwright, and don't tread on my necklace, Alwright; it is close at your feet."

So it was. Lying where Mary had dropped it. Alwright thought she must have knocked it off the dressing-table; but, when Lady Hainault told her that Miss Corby had dropped it there, Alwright began to wonder why her ladyship had not thought it worth while to pick it up again.

---

[1] As a matter of curiosity, I tried to write this paragraph from the word "Mary" to the word "bosom," without using a single word derived from the Latin. After having taken all possible pains to do so, I found there were eight out of forty-eight. I think it is hardly possible to reduce the proportion lower, and I think it is undesirable to reduce it so low.

[2] Which is a crib from Sir E. B. L. B. L.

L

"Put it on while I seal this letter, will you? I cannot trust you, Alwright; I must go myself." She went out of the room and quickly downstairs to the hall. All this had taken but a few minutes; she had hurried as much as was possible, but the time seems longer to us, because, following my usual plan of playing the fool on important occasions, I have been telling you about the lady's-maid's nose. She went down quickly to the hall, and sent off one of the men to South Audley Street with her note, giving him orders to run all the way, and personally to see Lady Ascot, or some one else of those named. After this she came upstairs again.

When she came to the drawing-room door, Charles was standing at it. "Lady Hainault," he said, "would you come here, please? Poor Mary has fainted."

"Poor thing," said Lady Hainault. "I will come to her. One word, Mr. Ravenshoe. Oh, do think one instant of this fatal, miserable resolution of yours. Think how fond we have all been of you. Think of the love that your cousin and Lady Ascot bear for you, and communicate with them. At all events stay ten minutes more, and see one of them. I must go to poor Mary."

"Dear Lady Hainault, you will not change my resolution to stand alone. There is a source of disgrace you probably know nothing of. Besides, nothing short of an Order in Council could stop me now. We sail for the East in twenty-four hours."

They had just time for this, very hurriedly spoken, for poor little Mary had done what she never had done before in her life, fainted away. Lady Hainault and Charles went into the drawing-room.

Just before this, Alwright, coming downstairs, had seen her most sacred mistress standing at the drawing-room door, talking familiarly and earnestly to a common soldier. Her ladyship had taken his hand in hers, and was laying her other hand upon his breast. Alwright sat down on the stairs.

She was a poor feeble thing, and it was too much for her. She was Casterton-bred, and had a feeling for the honour of the family. Her first impulse was to run to Lord Hainault's dressing-room door and lock him in. Her next was to rock herself to and fro and moan. She followed the latter of these two impulses. Meanwhile, Lady Hainault had succeeded in bringing poor Mary to herself. Charles had seen her bending over the poor little lifeless body, and blessed her. Presently Lady Hainault said, "She is better now, Mr. Ravenshoe; will you come and speak to her?" There was no answer. Lady Hainault thought Charles was in the little drawing-room, and had not heard her. She went there. It was dimly lighted, but she saw in a moment that it was empty. She grew frightened, and hurriedly went out on to the stairs. There was no one there. She hurried down and was met by the weeping Alwright.

"He is safe out of the house, my lady," said that brilliant genius. "I saw him come out of the drawing-room, and I ran down and sent the hall porter on a message, and let him out myself. Oh, my lady! my lady!"

Lady Hainault was a perfect-tempered woman, but she could not stand this. "Alwright," she said, "you are a perfect, hopeless, imbecile idiot. Go and tell his lordship to come to me instantly. Instantly! do you hear? I wouldn't," she continued to herself when Alwright was gone, "face Lord Saltire alone after this for a thousand pounds."

What was the result of Charles's interview with Mary? Simply this. The poor little thing had innocently shown him, in a way he could not mistake, that she loved him with all her heart and soul. And when he left that room, he had sworn an oath to himself that he would use all his ingenuity to prevent her ever setting eyes on him again. "I am low and degraded enough now," he said to himself; "but if I gave that poor innocent child the opportunity of nourishing her love for me, I should be too low to live."

He did not contemplate the possibility, you see, of raising himself to her level. No. He was too much broken down for that. Hope was dead with him. He had always been a man of less than average strength of will; and two or three disasters—terrible disasters they were, remember—had made him such as we see him, a helpless, drifting log upon the sea of chance. What Lord Welter had said was terribly true, "Charles Ravenshoe is broken-hearted." But to the very last he was a just, honourable, true, kind-hearted man. A man in ten thousand. Call him fool, if you will. I cannot gainsay you there. But when you have said that, you have finished.

Did he love Mary? Yes, from this time forward, he loved her as she loved him; and, the darker the night grew, that star burned steadily and more steadily yet. Never brighter, perhaps, than when it gleamed on the turbid waters, which whelm the bodies of those to whose eyesight all stars have set for ever.

CHAPTER XLVIII

IN WHICH CUTHBERT BEGINS TO SEE THINGS IN A NEW LIGHT

THE stream at Ravenshoe was as low as they had ever seen it, said the keeper's boys who were allowed to take artists and strangers up to see the waterfall in the wood. The artists said that it was more beautiful than ever ; for now, instead of roaring headlong over the rocks in one great sheet beneath the quivering oak leaves, it streamed and spouted over and among the black slabs of slate in a million interlacing jets. Yes, the artists were quite satisfied with the state of things ; but the few happy souls who had dared to ask Cuthbert for a day or so of salmon-fishing were not so well satisfied by any means. While the artists were saying that this sort of thing, you know, was the sort of thing to show one how true it was that beauty, life and art, were terms co-ordinate, synonymous, inseparable—that these made up the sum of existence—that the end of existence was love, and what was love but the worship of the beautiful (or something of this sort, for your artist is but a mortal man, like the rest of us, and is apt, if you give him plenty of tobacco on a hot day, to get uncommon hazy in his talk)—while, I say, the artists were working away like mad, and uttering the most beautiful sentiments in the world, the anglers were, as old Master Lee, up to Slarrow, would have said, " dratting " the scenery, the water, the weather, the beer and existence generally, because it wouldn't rain. If it had rained, you see, the artists would have left talking about the beautiful, and begun " dratting " in turn, leaving the anglers to talk about the beautiful as best they might. Which fact gives rise to moral reflections of the profoundest sort. But every one, except the discontented anglers, would have said that it was heavenly summer weather. The hay was all got in without one drop of rain on it. And now, as one glorious, cloudless day succeeded another, all the land seemed silently swelling with the wealth of the harvest. Fed by gentle dews at night, warmed by the genial sun by day, the corn began to turn from grey to gold, and the distant valleys which spread away inland, folded in the mighty grey arms of the moor, shone out gallantly with acre beyond acre of yellow wheat and barley. A still, happy time.

And the sea! Who shall tell the beauty of the restless
Atlantic in such weather? For nearly three weeks there was
a gentle wind, now here, now there, which just curled the
water, and made a purple shadow for such light clouds as crept
across the blue sky above. Night and morning the fishing-
boats crept out and in. Never was such a fishing season.
The mouth of the stream was crowded with salmon, waiting
to get up the first fresh. You might see them as you sailed
across the shallow sand-bank, the Delta of the stream, which
had never risen above the water for forty years, yet which now,
so still had been the bay for three weeks, was within a foot of
the surface at low tide.

A quiet, happy time. The three old Master Lees lay all day
on the sand, where the fishing-boats were drawn up, and had
their meals brought to them by young male relatives, who
immediately pulled off every rag of clothes they had, and
went into the water for an hour or two. The minding of these
'ere clothes, and the looking out to sea, was quite enough
employment for these three old cronies. They never fell out
once for three weeks. They used to talk about the war, or the
cholera, which was said to be here, or there, or coming, or
gone. But they cared little about that. Ravenshoe was not
a cholera place. It had never come there before, and they
did not think that it was coming now. They were quite right;
it never came. Cuthbert used his influence, and got the folks
to move some cabbage stalks, and rotten fish, just to make sure,
as he said. They would have done more for him than that just
now; so it was soon accomplished. The juvenile population,
which is the pretty way of saying the children, might have
offered considerable opposition to certain articles of merchandise
being removed without due leave obtained and given; but,
when it was done, they were all in the water as naked as they
were born. When it was over they had good sense enough to
see that it could not be helped. These sweeping measures of
reform, however, are apt to bear hard on particular cases. For
instance, young James Lee, great-grandson of Master James
Lee, up to Slarrow, lost six dozen (some say nine, but that I
don't believe) of oyster shells, which he was storing up for a
grotto. Cuthbert very properly refunded the price of them,
which amounted to two-pence.

"Nonsense, again," you say. Why, no! What I have
written above is not nonsense. The whims and oddities of
a village; which one has seen with one's own eyes, and heard
with one's own ears, are not nonsense. I knew, when I began,

what I had to say in this chapter, and I have just followed on a train of images. And the more readily, because I know that what I have to say in this chapter must be said without effort to be said well.

If I thought I was writing for a reader who was going to criticise closely my way of telling my story, I tell you the honest truth, I should tell my story very poorly indeed. Of course I must submit to the same criticism as my betters. But there are times when I feel that I must have my reader go hand in hand with me. To do so, he must follow the same train of ideas as I do. At such times I write as naturally as I can. I see that greater men than I have done the same. I see that Captain Marryat, for instance, at a particular part of his noblest novel, "The King's Own," has put in a chapter about his grandmother and the spring tides, which, for perfect English and rough humour, it is hard to match anywhere.

I have not dared to pláy the fool, as he has, for two reasons. The first, that I could not play it so well, and the second, that I have no frightful tragedy to put before you, to counterbalance it, as he had. Well, it is time that this rambling came to an end. I hope that I have not rambled too far, and bored you. That would be very unfortunate just now.

Ravenshoe Bay again, then—in the pleasant summer drought I have been speaking of before. Father Mackworth and the two Tiernays were lying on the sand, looking to the sea. Cuthbert had gone off to send away some boys who were bathing too near the mouth of the stream and hunting his precious salmon. The younger Tiernay had recently taken to collect "common objects of the shore"—a pleasant, healthy mania which prevailed about that time. He had been dabbling among the rocks at the western end of the bay, and had just joined his brother and Father Mackworth with a tin-box full of all sorts of creatures, and he turned them out on the sand and called their attention to them.

"A very good morning's work, my brother," he said. "These anemones are all good and rare ones."

"Bedad," said the jolly priest, "they'd need be of some value, for they ain't pretty to look at; what's this cockle now wid the long red spike coming out of him?"

"Cardium tuberculatum."

"See here, Mackworth," said Tiernay, rolling over toward him on the sand with the shell in his hand. "Here's the rid-nosed oysther of Carlingford. Ye remember the legend about it, surely?"

"I don't, indeed," said Mackworth, angrily, pretty sure that Father Tiernay was going to talk nonsense, but not exactly knowing how to stop him.

"Not know the legend!" said Father Tiernay. "Why, when St. Bridget was hurrying across the sand, to attend St. Patrick in his last illness, poor dear, this divvle of a oysther was sunning himself on the shore, and, as she went by, he winked at her holiness with the wicked eye of 'um, and he says, says he, 'Nate ankles enough, anyhow,' he says. 'Ye're drunk ye spalpeen,' says St. Bridget, 'to talk like that to an honest gentlewoman.' 'Sorra a bit of me,' says the oysther. 'Ye're always drunk,' says St. Bridget. 'Drunk yourself,' says the oysther; 'I'm fastin' from licker since the tide went down.' 'What makes your nose so red, ye scoundrel?' says St. Bridget. 'No ridder nor your own,' says the oysther, getting angry. For the Saint was stricken in years, and red-nosed by rayson of being out in all weathers, seeing to this and to that. 'Yer nose is red through drink,' says she, 'and yer nose shall stay as rid as mine is now, till the day of judgment.' And that's the legend about St. Bridget and the Carlingford oysther, and ye ought to be ashamed that ye never heard it before."

"I wish, sir," said Mackworth, "that you could possibly stop yourself from talking this preposterous, indecent nonsense. Surely the first and noblest of Irish saints may claim exemption from your clumsy wit."

"Begorra, I'm catching it, Mr. Ravenshoe," said Tiernay.

"What for?" said Cuthbert, who had just come up.

"Why, for telling a legend. Sure, I made it up on the spot. But it is none the worse for that; d'ye think so now?"

"Not much the better, I should think," said Cuthbert, laughing.

"Allow me to say," said Mackworth, "that I never heard such shameless, blasphemous nonsense in my life."

The younger Tiernay was frightened, and began gathering up his shells and weeds. His handsome weak face was turned towards the great, strong, coarse face of his brother with a look of terror, and his fingers trembled as he put the sea-spoils into his box. Cuthbert, watching them both, guessed that sometimes Father Tiernay could show a violent, head-long temper, and that his brother had seen an outbreak of this kind and trembled for one now. It was only a guess, probably a good one; but there were no signs of such an outbreak now. Father Tiernay only lay back on the sand and laughed, without a cloud on his face.

"Bedad," he said, "I've been lying on the sand, and the sun has got into my stomach and made me talk nonsense. When I was a gossoon, I used to sleep with the pig; and it was a poor, feeble-minded pig, as never got fat on petaty skins. If folly's catchin', I must have caught it from that pig. Did ye ever hear the legend of St. Laurence O'Toole's wooden-legged sow, Mackworth?"

It was evident, after this, that the more Mackworth fulminated against good Father Tiernay's unutterable nonsense, the more he would talk; so he rose and moved sulkily away. Cuthbert asked him, laughing, what the story was.

"Faix," said Tiernay, "I ain't sure, principally because I haven't had time to invent it; but we've got rid of Mackworth, and can now discourse reasonable."

Cuthbert sent a boy up to the hall for some towels, and then lay down on the sand beside Tiernay. He was very fond of that man in spite of his reckless Irish habit of talking nonsense. He was not alone there. I think that every one who knew Tiernay liked him.

They lay on the sand together, those three; and when Father Mackworth's anger had evaporated he came back and lay beside them. Tiernay put his hand out to him, and Mackworth shook it, and they were reconciled. I believe Mackworth esteemed Tiernay, though they were so utterly unlike in character and feeling. I know that Tiernay had a certain admiration for Mackworth.

"Do you think now," said Tiernay, "that you Englishmen enjoy such a scene and such a time as this as much as we Irishmen do? I cannot tell. You talk better about it. You have a dozen poets to our one. Our best poet, I take it, is Tommy Moore. You class him as third-rate; but I doubt, mind you, whether you feel nature as acutely as we do."

"I think we do," said Cuthbert eagerly. "I cannot think that you can feel the beauty of the scene we are looking at more deeply than I do. You feel nature as in 'Silent O'Moyle;' we feel it as in Keats' 'St. Agnes' Eve!'"

He was sitting up on the sand, with his elbows on his knees and his face buried in his hands. None of them spoke for a time; and he, looking seaward, said, idly, in a low voice—

"'St. Agnes' Eve. Ah! bitter chill it was.
The owl, for all his feathers, was a-cold;
The hare limped, trembling, through the frozen grass;
And drowsy was the flock in woolly fold.'"

What was the poor lad thinking of? God knows. There

are times when one can't follow the train of a man's thoughts
—only treasure up their spoken words as priceless relics.

His beautiful face was turned towards the dying sun, and in
that face there was a look of such kindly, quiet peace that they
who watched it were silent, and waited to hear what he would
say.

The western headland was black before the afternoon sun,
and, far to sea, Lundy lay asleep in a golden haze.   All before
them the summer sea heaved between the capes and along the
sand, and broke in short crisp surf at their feet, gently moving
the seaweed, the sand, and the shells.

" ' St. Agnes' Eve,' " he said again.   " Ah, yes ! that is one of
the poems written by Protestants which help to make men
Catholics.   Nine-tenths of their highest religious imagery is
taken from Catholicism.   The English poets have nothing to
supply the place of it.   Milton felt it, and wrote about it ; yes,
after ranging through all heathendom for images, he comes
home to us at last—

> ' Let my due feet never fail
> To walk the studious cloisters pale,
> And love the high embowed roof,
> With antique pillars massy proof,
> And storied windows, richly dight,
> Casting a dim religious light.'

" Yes ; he could feel for that cloister life.   The highest form
of human happiness ! We have the poets with us, at all events.
Why, what is the most perfect bijou of a poem in the English
language ?   Tennyson's ' St. Agnes.'   He had to come to us."

The poor fellow looked across the sea, which was breaking
in crisp ripples at his feet among the seaweed, the sand and
the shells ; and as they listened they heard him say, almost
passionately—

> ' Break up the heavens, oh, Lord ! and far
> Through all yon starlight keen
> Draw me, thy bride, a glittering star
> In raiment white and clean.'

" They have taken our churches from us, and driven us into
Birmingham-built chapels.   They sneer at us, but they forget
that we built their arches and stained their glass for them.   Art
has revenged herself on them for their sacrilege by quitting
earth in disgust.   They have robbed us of our churches and
our revenues, and turned us out on the world.   Ay, but we are
revenged.   They don't know the use of them now they have
got them ; and the only men who could teach them, the

L 2

Tractarians, are abused and persecuted by them for their superior knowledge."

So he rambled on, looking seaward ; at his feet the surf playing with the sand, the seaweed, and the shells.

He made a very long pause, and then, when they thought that he was thinking of something quite different, he suddenly said—

" I don't believe it matters whether a man is buried in the chancel, or out of it. But they are mad to discourage such a feeling as that, and not make use of it. Am I the worse man because I fancy that, when I lay there so quiet, I shall hear above my head the footfalls of those who go to kneel around the altar ? What is it one of them says—

> ' Or where the kneeling hamlet drains
> The chalice of the grapes of God.' "

He very seldom spoke so much as this. They were surprised to hear him ramble on so ; but it was an afternoon in which it was natural to sit upon the shore and talk, saying straight on just what came uppermost—a quiet, pleasant afternoon ; an afternoon to lie upon the sand and conjure up old memories.

"I have been rambling, hav'n't I ?" he said presently. "Have I been talking aloud, or only thinking ? "

" You have been talking," said Tiernay, wondering at such a question.

"Have I ? I thought I had been only thinking. I will go and bathe, I think, and clear my head from dreams. I must have been quoting poetry, then ? " he added, smiling.

" Ay, and quoting it well too," said Tiernay.

A young fisherman was waiting with a boat, and the lad had come with his towels. He stepped lazily across the sand to the boat and they shoved off.

Besides the murmur of the surf upon the sand, playing with the shells and seaweed ; besides the shouting of the bathing boys ; besides the voices of the home-returning fishermen, carried sharp and distinct along the water ; besides the gentle chafing of the stream among the pebbles, was there no other sound upon the beach that afternoon ? Yes, a sound different to all these. A loud-sounding alarm drum, beating more rapidly and furiously each moment, but only heard by one man, and not heeded by him.

The tide drawing eastward, and a gentle wind following it, hardly enough to fill the sails of the lazy fishing-boats and keep them to their course. Here and there among the leeward part of the fleet, you might hear the sound of an oar working in the rowlocks, sleepily coming over the sea and mingling harmoniously with the rest.

The young man with Cuthbert rowed out a little distance, and then they saw Cuthbert standing in the prow undressing himself. The fishing-boats near him luffed and hurriedly put out oars, to keep away. The Squire was going to bathe, and no Ravenshoe man was ill-mannered enough to come near.

Those on the shore saw him standing stripped for one moment—a tall majestic figure. Then they saw him plunge into the water and begin swimming.

And then ;—it is an easy task to tell it. They saw his head go under water, and though they started on their feet and waited till seconds grew to minutes and hope was dead, it never rose again. Without one cry, without one struggle, without even one last farewell wave of the hand, as the familiar old landscape faded on his eyes for ever, poor Cuthbert went down ; to be seen no more till the sea gave up its dead. The poor wild, passionate heart had fluttered itself to rest for ever.

The surf still gently playing with the sand, the sea changing from purple to grey, and from grey to black, under the fading twilight. The tide sweeping westward the tall black headland, towards the slender-curved thread of the new moon, which grew more brilliant as the sun dipped to his rest in the red Atlantic.

Groups of fishermen and sea boys and servants, that followed the ebbing tide as it went westward, peering into the crisping surf to see something they knew was there. One group that paused among the tumbled boulders on the edge of the retreating surges, under the dark promontory, and bent over something which lay at their feet.

The naked corpse of a young man, calm and beautiful in death, lying quiet and still between two rocks, softly pillowed on a bed of green and purple seaweed. And a priest that stood upon the shore, and cried wildly to the four winds of heaven. "Oh, my God, I loved him ! My God ! my God ! I loved him ! "

CHAPTER XLIX

THE SECOND COLUMN OF "THE TIMES" OF THIS DATE, WITH OTHER MATTERS

" TOMATO.   Slam the door ! "

" EDWARD.   Come at once ; poor Maria is in sad distress. Toodlekins stole ! ! ! ! "

" J. B. can return to his deeply afflicted family if he likes, or remain away if he likes.   The A F, one and all, will view either course with supreme indifference.   Should he choose the former alternative, he is requested to be as quick as possible.   If the latter, to send the key of the cellaret."

" LOST.   A little black-and-tan lady's lap dog. Its real name is Pussy, but it will answer to the name of Toodlekins best. If any gentleman living near Kensal Green, or Kentish town, should happen, perfectly accidentally of course, to have it in his possession, and would be so good as to bring it to 997, Sloane Street, I would give him a sovereign and welcome, and not a single question asked, upon my honour."

IT becomes evident to me that the dog Toodlekins, mentioned in the second advertisement, is the same dog alluded to in the fourth ; unless you resort to the theory that two dogs were stolen on the same day, and that both were called Toodlekins. And you are hardly prepared to do that, I fancy. Consequently, you arrive at this, that the "Maria" of the second advertisement is the "little black-and-tan lady" of the fourth.   And that, in 1854, she lived at 997, Sloane Street. Who was she? Had she made a fortune by exhibiting herself in a caravan like Mrs. Gamp's spotted negress, and taken a house in Sloane Street, for herself, Toodlekins, and the person who advertised for Edward to come and comfort her? Again, who was Edward? Was he her brother? Was he something nearer and dearer? Was he enamoured of her person or her property? I fear the latter. Who could truly love a little black-and-tan lady?

Again.   The wording of her advertisement gives rise to this train of thought. Two persons must always be concerned in stealing a dog—the person who steals the dog, and the person who has the dog stolen ; because, if the dog did not belong to any one, it is evident that no one could steal it.   To put it more scientifically, there must be an active and a passive agent.   Now, I'll bet a dirty old dishcloth against the *New York Herald*, which is pretty even betting, that our little black and tan friend, Maria, had been passive agent in a dog-stealing case more than once before this, or why does she mention these two localities? But we must get on to the other advertisements.

"LOST. A large white bull-dog, very red about the eyes; desperately savage. Answers to the name of 'Billy.' The advertiser begs that any person finding him will be very careful not to irritate him. The best way of securing him is to make him pin another dog, and then tie his four legs together and muzzle him. Any one bringing him to the Coach and Horses, St. Martin's Lane, will be rewarded."

He seems to have been found the same day, and by some one who was a bit of a wag; for the very next advertisement runs thus:

"FOUND. A large white bull-dog, very red about the eyes; desperately savage. The owner can have him at once, by applying to Queen's Mews, Belgrave Street, and paying the price of the advertisement and the cost of a new pad-groom, aged 18, as the dog has bitten one so severely about the knee that it is necessary to sell him at once to drive a cab."

"LOST. Somewhere between Mile-end Road and Putney Bridge, an old leathern purse, containing a counterfeit sixpence, a lock of hair in a paper, and a twenty-pound note. Any one bringing the note to 267, Tylney Street, Mayfair, may keep the purse and the rest of its contents for their trouble."

This was a very shabby advertisement. The next, though coming from an attorney's office, is much more munificent. It quite makes one's mouth water, and envy the lucky fellow who would answer it.

"ONE HUNDRED GUINEAS REWARD. Register wanted. To parish clerks. Any person who can discover the register of marriage between Petre Ravenshoe, Esq., of Ravenshoe, in the county of Devon, and Maria Dawson, which is supposed to have been solemnised in or about the year 1778, will receive the above reward, on communicating with Messrs. Compton and Brogden, Solicitors, 2004, Lincoln's Inn Fields."

Tomato slammed the door as he was told. Edward dashed up to 997, Sloane Street, in a hansom cab, just as the little black and tan lady paid one sovereign to a gentleman in a velveteen shooting-coat, from Kentish Town, and hugged Toodlekins to her bosom. J. B. came home to his afflicted family with the key of the cellaret. The white bull-dog was restored to the prizefighter, and the groom-lad received shin-plaster and was sent home tipsy. Nay, even an honest man, finding that the note was stopped, took it to Tylney Street, and got half-a-crown. But no one ever answered the advertisement of Lord Saltire's solicitor about the marriage register. The long summer dragged on. The square grew dry and dusty;

business grew slack, and the clerks grew idle ; but no one came. As they sat there drinking ginger-beer, and looking out at the parched lilacs and laburnums, talking about the theatres, and the war, and the cholera, it grew to be a joke with them. When any shabby man in black was seen coming across the square, they would say to one another, "Here comes the man to answer Lord Saltire's advertisement." Many men in black, shabby and smart, came across the square and into the office ; but none had a word to say about the marriage of Petre Ravenshoe with Maria Dawson, which took place in the year 1778.

Once, during that long, sad summer, the little shoeblack thought he would saunter up to the house in South Audley Street, before which he had waited so long one night to meet Charles, who had never come. Not perhaps with any hope. Only that he would like to see the place which his friend had appointed. He might come back there some day ; who could tell ?

Almost every house in South Audley Street had the shutters closed. When he came opposite Lord Ascot's house, he saw the shutters were closed there too. But more ; at the second story there was a great painted board hung edgeways, all scarlet and gold. There was some writing on it too, on a scroll. He could spell a little, now, thanks to the ragged-school, and he spelt out "Christus Salvator meus." What could that mean ? he wondered.

There was an old woman in the area, holding two of the rails in her hands, and resting her chin on the kerbstone, looking along the hot, desolate street. Our friend went over and spoke to her.

" I say, missus," he said, " what's that thing up there ? "

" That's the scutching, my man," said she.

" The scutchings ! "

" Ah ! My Lord's dead. Died last Friday week, and they've took him down to the country house to bury him."

" My Lord ? " said the boy. " Was he the one as used to wear top-boots, and went for a soger ? "

The old woman had never seen my lord wear top-boots. Had hearn tell, though, as his father used to, and drive a coach and four in 'em. None of 'em hadn't gone for sogers, neither.

" But what's the scutching for ? " asked the boy.

They put it up for a year, like for a monument, she said. She couldn't say what the writing on it meant. It was my lord's motter, that was all she knowd. And, being a tender-hearted old woman, and not having the fear of thieves before her eyes, she had taken him down into the kitchen and fed him. When he returned to the upper regions, he was "collared" by a policeman, on a charge of "area sneaking," but, after explanations, was let go, to paddle home, barefooted, to the cholera-stricken court where he lived, little dreaming, poor lad, what an important part he was accidentally to play in this history hereafter.

They laid poor Lord Ascot to sleep in the chancel at Ranford, and Lady Ascot stood over the grave like a grey, old, storm-beaten tower. "It is strange, James," she said to Lord Saltire that day, "you and I being left like this, with the young ones going down around us like grass. Surely our summons must come soon, James. It's weary, weary waiting."

CHAPTER L

SHREDS AND PATCHES

LORD WELTER was now Lord Ascot. I was thinking at one time that I would continue to call him by his old title, as being the one most familiar to you. But, on second thoughts, I prefer to call him by his real name, as I see plainly that to follow the other course would produce still worse confusion. I only ask that you will bear his change of title in mind. The new Lady Ascot I shall continue to call Adelaide, choosing rather to incur the charge of undue familiarity with people so far above me in social position, than to be answerable for the inevitable confusion which would be caused by my speaking, so often as I shall have to speak, of two Ladies Ascot, with such a vast difference between them of age and character.

Colonel Whisker, a tenant of Lord Ascot's, had kindly placed his house at the disposal of his Lordship for his father's funeral. Never was there a more opportune act of civility, for Ranford was dismantled : and the doors of Casterton were as firmly closed to Adelaide as the gates of the great mosque at Ispahan to a Christian.

Two or three days after Lord Ascot's death, it was arranged that he should be buried at Ranford. That night the new

Lord Ascot came to his wife's dressing-room, as usual, to plot and conspire.

"Ascot," said she, "they are all asked to Casterton for the funeral. Do you think she will ask me?"

"Oh dear, no," said Lord Ascot.

"Why not?" said Adelaide. "She ought to. She is civil enough to me."

"I tell you I know she won't. He and I were speaking about it to-day."

He was looking over her shoulder into the glass, and saw her bite her lip.

"Ah," said she. "And what did he say?"

"Oh, he came up in his infernal, cold, insolent way, and said that he should be delighted to see me at Casterton during the funeral, but Lady Hainault feared that she could hardly find rooms for Lady Ascot and her maid."

"Did you knock him down? Did you kick him? Did you take him by the throat and knock his hateful head against the wall?" said Adelaide, as quietly as if she was saying "How d'ye do?"

"No, my dear, I didn't," said Lord Ascot. "Partly, you see, because I did not know how Lord Saltire would take it. And remember, Adelaide, I always told you that it would take years, years before people of that sort would receive you."

"What did you say to him?"

"Well, as much as you could expect me to say. I sneered as insolently, but much more coarsely than he could possibly sneer; and I said that I declined staying at any house where my wife was not received. And so we bowed and parted."

Adelaide turned round and said, "That was kind and manly of you, Welter. I thank you for that, Welter."

And so they went down to Colonel Whisker's cottage, for the funeral. The colonel probably knew quite how the land lay, for he was a man of the world, and so he had done a very good-natured action just at the right time. She and Lord Ascot lived for a fortnight there, in the most charming style; and Adelaide used to make him laugh, by describing what it was possible the other party were doing up at the solemn old Casterton. She used to put her nose in the air and imitate young Lady Hainault to perfection. At another time she would imitate old Lady Hainault and her disagreeable sayings equally well. She was very amusing that fortnight, though never affectionate. She knew that was useless; but she tried to keep Lord Ascot in good humour with her. She had a reason. She wanted to get his ear. She wanted him to confide entirely to her the exact state of affairs between Lord Saltire and himself. Here was Lord Ascot dead, Charles Ravenshoe probably at Alyden in the middle of the cholera, and Lord Saltire's vast fortune, so to speak, going a-begging. If he were to be clumsy now—now that the link formed by his father, Lord Ascot, between him and Lord Saltire was taken away—they were ruined indeed. And he was so terribly outspoken!

And so she strained her wits, till her face grew sharp and thin, to keep him in good humour. She had a hard task at times; for there was something lying up in the deserted house at Ranford which made Lord Ascot gloomy and savage now and then, when he thought of it. I believe that the man, coarse and brutal as he was, loved his father, in his own way, very deeply.

A night or so after the funeral, there was a dressing-room conference between the two; and, as the conversation which ensued was very important, I must transcribe it carefully.

When he came up to her, she was sitting with her hands folded on her lap, looking so perfectly beautiful that Lord Ascot, astonished and anxious as he was at that moment, remarked it, and felt pleased at, and proud of, her beauty. A greater fool than she might probably have met him with a look of love. She did not. She only raised her great eyes to his, with a look of intelligent curiosity.

He drew a chair up close to her, and said—

"I am going to make your hair stand bolt up on end, Adelaide, in spite of your bandoline."

"I don't think so," said she; but she looked startled, nevertheless.

"I am. What do you think of this?"

"This? I think that is the *Times* newspaper. Is there anything in it?"

"Read," said he, and pointed to the list of deaths. She read.

"Drowned, while bathing in Ravenshoe Bay, Cuthbert Ravenshoe, Esq., of Ravenshoe Hall. In the faith that his forefathers bled and died for.—R.I.P."

"Poor fellow!" she said, quietly. "So *he's* gone, and brother William, the groom, reigns in his stead. That is a piece of nonsense of the priest's, about their dying for the faith. I never heard that any of them did that. Also, isn't there something wrong about the grammar?"

"I can't say," said Lord Ascot. "I was at Eton, and hadn't the advantage that you had of learning English grammar. Did you ever play the game of trying to read the *Times* right across, from one column to another, and see what funny nonsense it makes?"

"No. I should think it was good fun."

"Do it now."

She did. Exactly opposite the announcement of Cuthbert's death, was the advertisement we have seen before—Lord Saltire's advertisement for the missing register.

She was attentive and eager enough now. After a time, she said, "Oho!"

Lord Ascot said, "Hey! what do you think of that, Lady Ascot?"

"I am all abroad."

"I'll see if I can fetch you home again. Petre Ravenshoe, in 1778, married a milkmaid. She remembered the duties of her position so far as to conveniently die before any of the family knew what a fool he had made of himself; but so far forgot them as to give birth to a boy, who lived to be one of the best shots, and one of the jolliest old cocks I ever saw— Old James, the Ravenshoe keeper. Now my dearly beloved grandmother Ascot is, at this present speaking, no less than eighty-six years old, and so, at the time of the occurrence, was a remarkably shrewd girl of ten. It appears that Petre Ravenshoe, sneaking away here and there with his pretty Protestant wife, out of the way of the priests, and finding life unendurable, not having had a single chance to confess his sins for two long years, came to the good-natured Sir Cingle Headstall, grandmamma's papa, and opened his griefs, trying to persuade him to break the matter to that fox-hunting old Turk of a father of his, Howard. Sir Cingle was too cowardly to face the old man for a time ; and, before the pair of them could summon courage to speak, the poor young thing died at Manger Hall, where they had been staying with the Head-stalls some months. This solved the difficulty, and nothing was said about the matter. Petre went home. They had heard reports about his living with a woman and having had a baby born. They asked very few questions about the child or his mother, and of course it was all forgotten conveniently, long before his marriage with my grandaunt, Lady Alicia Staunton, came on the tapis, which took place in 1782, when grandma was fourteen years of age. Now grandma had, as a girl of ten, heard this marriage of Petre Ravenshoe with Maria

Dawson discussed in her presence, from every point of view, by her father and Petre. Night and morning, at bed-time, at meal-times, sober, and very frequently drunk. She had heard every possible particular. When she heard of his second marriage (my mouth is as dry as dust with this talking; ring the bell, and send your maid down for some claret and water) —when she heard of his second marriage, she never dreamt of saying anything, of course—a chit of fourteen with a great liability to having her ears boxed. So she held her tongue. When afterwards my grandfather made love to her, she held it the tighter, for my grandaunt's sake, of whom she was fond. Petre, after a time, had the boy James home to Ravenshoe, and kept him about his own person. He made him his gamekeeper, treated him with marked favour and so on; but the whole thing was a sort of misprision of felony, and poor silly old grandma was a party to it."

"You are telling this very well, Ascot," said Adelaide. "I will, as a reward, go so far out of my usual habits as to mix you some claret and water. I am not going to be tender, you know; but I'll do so much. Now that's a dear, good fellow; go on."

"Now comes something unimportant, but inexplicable. Old Lady Hainault knew it, and held *her* tongue. How or why is a mystery we cannot fathom, and don't want to. Grandma says that she would have married Petre herself, and that her hatred for grandma came from the belief that grandma could have stopped the marriage with my grandaunt by speaking. After it was over she thinks that Lady Hainault had sufficient love left for Petre to hold her tongue. But this is nothing to the purpose. This James, the real heir of Ravenshoe, married an English girl, a daughter of a steward on one of our Irish estates, who had been born in Ireland, and was called Nora. She was, you see, Irish enough at heart; for she committed the bull of changing her own child, poor dear Charles, the real heir, for his youngest half-brother, William, by way of bettering his position, and then confessed the whole matter to the priest. Now this new discovery would blow the honest priest's boat out of the water; but:—"

"Yes!"

"Why, grandma can't, for the life of her, remember where they were married. She is certain that it was in the north of Hampshire, she says. Why or wherefore, she can't say. She says they resided the necessary time, and were married by license. She says she is sure of it, because she heard him,

more than once, say to her father that he had been so careful
of poor Maria's honour, that he sent her from Ravenshoe to
the house of the clergyman who married them, who was a
friend of his ; farther than this she knows nothing."

" Hence the advertisement, then. But why was it not
inserted before ? "

" Why, it appears that, when the whole *esclandre* took place,
and when you, my Lady Ascot, jilted the poor fellow for a man
who is not worth his little finger, she communicated with Lord
Saltire at once, and the result was that she began advertising
in so mysterious a manner that the advertisement was wholly
unintelligible. It appears that she and Lord Saltire agreed not
to disturb Cuthbert till they were perfectly sure of everything.
But, now he is dead, Lord Saltire has insisted on instantly
advertising in a sensible way. So you see his advertisement
appears actually in the same paper which contains Cuthbert's
death, the news of which William got the night before last by
telegraph."

" William, eh ? How does he like the cup being dashed
from his lips like this ? "

Lord Ascot laughed. " That ex-groom is a born fool, Lady
Ascot. He loves his foster-brother better than nine thousand
a year, Lady Ascot. He is going to start to Varna, and hunt
him through the army and bring him back."

" It is incredible," said Adelaide.

" I don't know. I might have been such a fool myself once,
who knows ? "

" Who knows indeed," thought Adelaide, " who knows
now ? " " So," she said aloud, " Charles is heir of Ravenshoe
after all."

" Yes. You were foolish to jilt him."

" I was. Is Alyden healthy ? "

" You know it is not. Our fellows are dying like dogs."

" Do you know what regiment he is in ? "

" They think, from Lady Hainault's and Mary Corby's
description, that it is the 140th."

" Why did not William start on this expedition before ? "

" I don't know. A new impulse. They have written to all
sorts of commanding officers, but he won't turn up till he
chooses, if I know him right."

" If William brings him back."

" Why, then he'll come into nine, or more probably twelve,
thousand a year. For those tin lodes have turned up
trumps."

"And the whole of Lord Saltire's property?"

"I suppose so."

"And we remain beggars."

"I suppose so," said Lord Ascot. "It is time to go to bed, Lady Ascot."

This is exactly the proper place to give the results of William's expedition to Varna. He arrived there just after the army had gone forward. Some men were left behind invalided, among whom were two or three of the 140th. One of these William selected as being a likely man from whom to make inquiries.

He was a young man, and, likely enough, a kind-hearted one; but when he found himself inquired of by a handsome, well-dressed young gentleman, obviously in search of a missing relative, a lying spirit entered into him, and he lied horribly. It appeared that he had been the intimate and cherished comrade of Charles Horton (of whom he had never heard in his life). That they had ridden together, drunk together, and slept side by side. That he had nursed him through the cholera, and then (seeing no other way out of the maze of falsehood in which he had entangled himself), that he assisted to bury him with his own hands. Lastly, lying on through mere recklessness, into desperation, and so into a kind of sublimity, he led William out of the town, and pointed out to him Charles's untimely grave. When he saw William pick some dry grass from the grave, when he saw him down on his knees, with his cheek on the earth, then he was sorry for what he had done. And, when he was alone, and saw William's shadow pass across the blazing white wall, for one instant, before he went under the dark gateway of the town, then the chinking gold pieces fell from his hand on the burning sandy ground, and he felt that he would have given them and ten times more, to have spoken the truth.

So Charles was dead and buried was he? Not quite yet, if you please. Who is this riding, one of a gallant train, along the shores of the bay of Eupatoria towards some dim blue mountains? Who is this that keeps looking each minute to the right, at the noble fleet which is keeping pace with the great scarlet and blue rainbow which men call the allied armies? At the great cloud of smoke floating angrily seaward, and the calm waters of the bay beaten into madness by three hundred throbbing propellers?

CHAPTER LI

IN WHICH CHARLES COMES TO LIFE AGAIN

HA! This was a life again. Better this than dawdling about at the heels of a dandy, or sitting on a wheelbarrow in a mews! There is a scent here sweeter than that of the dung-hill, or the dandy's essences—what is it? The smell of tar, and bilge water, and red herrings. There is a fresh whiff of air up this narrow street, which moves your hair, and makes your pulse quicken. It is the free wind of the sea. At the end of the street are ships, from which comes the clinking of cranes; pleasanter music sometimes than the song of nightingales.

Down the narrow street towards the wharf come the hussars. Charles is among them. On the wharf, in the confusion, foremost, as far as he dare, to assist. He was known as the best horseman in the troop, and, as such, was put into dangerous places. He had attracted great attention among the officers by his fearlessness and dexterity. The captain had openly praised him; and, when the last horse had been slung in, and the last cheer given, and the great ship was away down the river, on her message of wrath, and woe, and glory, Charles was looking back at Southampton spires, a new man with a new career before him.

The few months of degradation, of brooding misery, of listlessness and helplessness he had gone through, made this short episode in his life appear the most happy and most beautiful of all. The merest clod of a recruit in the regiment felt in some way ennobled and exalted: but as for Charles with his intensely sensitive, and romantic nature, he was quite, as the French say, *tête montée*. The lowest menial drudgery was exalted and glorified. Groom his horse and help clean the deck? Why not? That horse must carry him in the day of the merry meeting of heroes. Hard living, hard work, bad weather, disease, death: what were they, with his youth, health, strength, and nerve? Not to be thought of save with a smile. Yes! this expedition of his to the Crimea was the noblest, and possibly the happiest in his life. To use a borrowed simile, it was like the mournful, beautiful autumn sunset, before the dark night closes in. He felt like a boy at midsummer, exploring some wood, or distant valley, watched from a distance long and at last attained ; or as one feels when a stranger in a new land, one first rides forth alone into the forest on some distant expedition, and sees the new world, dreamt of and longed for all one's life, realized in all its beauty and wonder at last ; and expanding leaf by leaf before one. In a romantic state of mind. I can express it no better.

And really it is no wonder that a man, not sea-sick, should have been in a state of wonder, eager curiosity, kindliness, and, above all, high excitement—which four states of mind, I take it, make up together the state of mind called romantic, quixotic, or chivalrous ; which is a very pleasant state of mind indeed. For curiosity, there was enough to make the dullest man curious. Where were they going ? Where would the blow be struck ? Where would the dogs of war first fix their teeth ? Would it be a campaign in the field, or a siege, or what ? For kindliness : were not his comrades a good set of brave, free-hearted lads, and was not he the favourite among them ? As for wonder and excitement, there was plenty of that, and it promised to last. Why, the ship herself was a wonder. The biggest in the world, carrying 500 men and horses ; and every man in the ship knew, before she had been five hours at sea, that that quiet-looking commander of hers was going to race her out under steam the whole way. Who could tire of wondering at the glimpse one got down the iron-railed well into the machinery, at the busy cranks and leaping pistons, or, when tired of that, at the strange dim vista of swinging horses between decks ? Wonder and excitement enough here to keep twenty Don Quixotes going ! Her very name, too, was romantic—HIMALAYA.

A north-east wind and a mountain of rustling white canvas over-head. Blue water that seethed and creamed and roared past to leeward. A calm, and the Lizard to the north, a dim grey cape. A south-west wind, and above a mighty cobweb of sail-less rigging. Top-gallant masts sent down and yards close hauled. Still, through it all, the busy clack and rattle of the untiring engine.

A dim wild sunset, and scudding prophet clouds that hurried from the west across the crimson zenith, like witches towards a sabbath. A wind that rose and grew as the sun went down, and hummed loud in the rigging as the bows of the ship dipped into the trough of the waves, and failed almost into silence as she raised them. A night of storm and terror : in the morning, the tumbling broken seas of Biscay. A few fruit brigs scudding wildly here and there ; and a cape on a new land. A high round down, showing a gleam of green among the flying mists.

Sail set again before a northerly wind, and the ship rolling before it like a jolly drunkard. Then a dim cloud of smoke before them. Then the great steamer *Bussorah*, thundering forward against the wind, tearing furiously at the leaping seas with her iron teeth. A hurried glimpse of fluttering signals, and bare wet empty decks; and, before you had time to say what a noble ship she was, and what good weather she was making of it, only a cloud of smoke miles astern.

Now a dark line, too faint for landsmen's eyes, far ahead, which changed into a loom of land, which changed into a cloud, which changed into a dim peak towering above the sea mists, which changed into a tall crag, with a town, and endless tiers of white fortifications—Gibraltar.

Then a strong west wind for three days, carrying the ship flying before it with all plain sail set. And each day, at noon, a great excitement on the quarter-deck, among the officers. On the third day much cheering and laughter, and shaking of hands with the commander. Charles, catching an opportunity, took leave to ask his little friend the cornet, what it meant. The Himalaya had run a thousand miles in sixty-three hours.[1]

And now at sunrise an island is in sight, flat, bald, blazing yellow in the morning sun, with a solitary, flat-topped mass of buildings just in the centre, which the sailors say is Civita Vecchia; and, as they sweep round the southern point of it, a smooth bay opens, and there is a flat-roofed town rising in tiers from the green water—above heavier fortifications than those of Gibraltar, Charles thinks, but wrongly. Right and left, two great forts, St. Elmo and St. Angelo, say the sailors; and that flight of stone steps, winding up into the town, is the Nix Mangare stairs. A flood of historical recollections comes over Charles, and he recognises the place as one long known and very dear to him. On those very stairs, Mr. Midshipman Easy stood, and resolved that he would take a boat and sail to Gozo. What followed on his resolution is a matter of history. Other events have taken place at Malta, about which Charles was as well informed as the majority, but Charles did not think of them; not even of St. Paul and the viper, or the old windy dispute, in Greek Testament lecture, at Oxford, between

---

[1] The most famous voyage of the *Himalaya*, from Cork to Varna in twelve days, with the Fifth Dragoon Guards, took place in June. The voyage here described is, as will be perceived, a subsequent one, but equally successful, apparently.

this Melita and the other one off the coast of Illyricum. He thought of Midshipman Easy, and felt as if he had seen the place before.

I suppose that, if I knew my business properly, I should at this point represent Charles as falling down the companion-ladder and spraining his ancle, or as having over-eaten himself, or something of that sort, and so pass over the rest of the voyage by saying that he was confined to his bunk, and saw no more of it. But I am going to do nothing of the sort, for two reasons. In the first place, because he did not do anything of the kind ; and in the next, because he saw somebody at Constantinople, of whom I am sure you will be glad to hear again.

Charles had seen Tenedos golden in the east, and Lemnos purple in the west, as the sun went down ; then, after having steamed at half-speed through the Dardanelles, was looking the next evening at Constantinople, and at the sun going down behind the minarets, and at all that sort of thing, which is no doubt very beautiful, but of which one seems to have heard once or twice before. The ship was lying at anchor, with fires banked, and it was understood that they were waiting for a Queen's messenger.

They could see their own boat, which they had sent to wait for him at Scraglio Point. One of the sailors had lent Charles a telescope—a regular old brute of a telescope, with a crack across the object-glass. Charles was looking at the boat with it, and suddenly said, "There he is."

He saw a small grey-headed man, with moustaches, come quickly down and get into the boat, followed by some Turks with his luggage. This was Colonel Oldhoss, the Queen's messenger ; but there was another man with him, whom Charles recognised at once. He handed the telescope to the man next him, and walked up and down the deck rapidly.

"I *should* like to speak to him," he thought, "if it were only one word. Dear old fellow. But then he will betray me, and they will begin persecuting me at home, dear souls. I suppose I had better not. No. If I am wounded and dying I will send for him. I will not speak to him now."

The Queen's messenger and his companion came on board, and the ship got under way and steamed through the Bosphorus out into the wild, seething waves of the " Fena Kara degniz," and Charles turned in without having come near either of them. But in the chill morning, when the ship's head was north-west, and the dawn was flushing up on the distant

Thracian sierra, Charles was on deck, and, while pausing for an instant in his duties to look westward, and try to remember what country and what mountains lay to the north-west of Constantinople, a voice behind him said, quietly, "Go, find me Captain Croker, my man." He turned, and was face to face with General Mainwaring.

It was only for an instant, but their eyes met; the general started, but he did not recognise him. Charles's moustache had altered him so much that it was no great wonder. He was afraid that the general would seek him out again, but he did not. These were busy times. They were at Varna that night.

Men were looking sourly at one another. The French expedition had just come in from Kustendji in a lamentable state, and the army was rotting in its inactivity. You know all about that as well as I can tell you; what is of more importance to us is, that Lieutenant Hornby had been down with typhus, and was recovering very slowly, so that Charles's chances of meeting him were very small.

What am I to do with this three weeks or more at Varna to which I have reduced Charles, you, and myself? Say as little about it as need be, I should say. Charles and his company were, of course, moved up at once to the cavalry camp at Devna, eighteen miles off, among the pleasant hills and woodlands. Once, his little friend, the young cornet, who had taken a fancy for him, made him come out shooting with him to carry his bag. And they scrambled and clambered, and they tore themselves with thorns, and they fell down steep places, and utterly forgot their social positions towards one another. And they tried to carry home every object that was new to them, including a live turtle and a basaltic column. And they saw a green lizard, who arched his tail and galloped away like a racehorse, and a grey lizard, who let down a bag under his chin and barked at them like a dog. And the cornet shot a quail, and a hare, and a long-tailed francolin, like a pheasant, and a wood-pigeon. And, lastly, they found out that, if you turned over the stones, there were scorpions under them, who tucked their claws under their armpits, as a man folds his arms, and sparred at them with their tails, drawing their sting in and out, as an experienced boxer moves his left hand when waiting for an attack. Altogether, they had a glorious day in a new country, and did not remember in what relation they were to one another till they topped the hill above Devna by moonlight, and saw the two long lakes, stretching towards the sea, broken here and there into silver ripples by the oars of the commissariat boats. A happy innocent school-boy day—the sort of day which never comes if we prepare for it and anticipate it, but which comes without warning, and is never forgotten.

Another day the cornet had business in Varna, and he managed that Charles should come with him as orderly ; and with him, as another orderly, went the young lad who spoke about his sister in the pot-house at Windsor ; for this lad was another favourite of the cornet's, being a quiet gentlemanly lad, in fact, a favourite with everybody. A very handsome lad, too. And the three went branking bravely down the hill-side, through the woodlands, over the streaming plain, into the white dirty town. And the cornet must stay and dine with the mess of the 42nd, and so Charles and the other lad might go where they would. And they went and bathed, and then, when they had dressed, they stood together under the burning white wall, looking over the wicked Black Sea, smoking. And Charles told his comrade about Ravenshoe, about the deer, and the pheasants, and the blackcock, and about the big trout that lay nosing up into the swift places, in the cool clear water. And suddenly the lad turned to him, with his handsome face livid with agony and horror, and clutched him convulsively by both arms, and prayed him, for God Almighty's sake——

There that will do. We need not go on. The poor lad was dead in four hours. The cholera was very prevalent at Varna that month, and those who dawdled about in the hot sun, at the mouth of the filthy drains of that accursed hole, found it unto their cost. We were fighting, you see, to preserve the town to those worthless dirty Turks, against the valiant, noble, but, I fear, equally dirty Russians. The provoking part of the Russian war was, that all through we respected and liked our gallant enemies far more than we did the useless rogues for whom we were fighting. Moreover, our good friends the French seem to have been more struck by this absurdity than ourselves.

I only mentioned this sad little incident to show that this Devna life among the pleasant woodlands was not all sunshine ; that now and then Charles was reminded, by some tragedy like this, that vast masses of men were being removed from ordinary occupations and duties into an unusual and abnormal mode of life ; and that nature was revenging herself for the violation of her laws.

You see that we have got through this three weeks more pleasantly than they did at Varna. Charles was sorry when the time came for breaking up the camp among the mountain wood-lands. The more so, as it had got about among the men that they were only to take Sebastopol by a sudden attack in the rear, and spend the winter there. There would be no work for the cavalry, every one said.

It is just worthy of notice how, when one once begins a vagabond life, one gets attached to a place where one may chance to rest even for a week. When one gets accustomed to a change of locality every day for a long while, a week's pause gives one more familiarity with a place than a month's residence in a strange house would give if one were habitually stationary. This remark is almost a platitude, but just worth writing down. Charles liked Devna, and had got used to it, and parted from it as he would from a home.

This brings us up to the point where, after his death and burial, I have described him as riding along the shore of the Bay of Eupatoria, watching the fleet. The 140th had very little to do. They were on the extreme left ; on the seventeenth they thought they were going to have some work, for they saw 150 of the lancers coming in, driving a lot of cattle before them, and about 1,000 Cossacks hanging on their rear. But, when some light dragoons rode leisurely out to support them, the Cossacks rode off, and the 140th were still condemned to inactivity.

Hornby had recovered, and was with the regiment. He had not recognised Charles, of course. Even if he had come face to face with him, it was almost unlikely that he would have recognised him in his moustache. They were not to meet as yet.

In the evening of the nineteenth there was a rumble of artillery over the hill in front of them, which died away in half an hour. Most of the rest of the cavalry were farther to the front of the extreme left, and were "at it," so it was understood, with the Cossacks. But the 140th were still idle.

On the morning of the twentieth, Charles and the rest of them, sitting in their saddles, heard the guns booming in front and on the right. It became understood among the men that the fleet was attacking some batteries. Also, it was whispered that the Russians were going to stand and fight. Charles was sixth man from the right of the rear rank of the third troop. He could see the tails of the horses immediately before him, and could remark that his front-rank man had a great patch of oil on the right shoulder of his uniform. He could also see Hornby in the troop before him.

These guns went moaning on in the distance till half-past one; but still they sat there idle. About that time there was a new sound in the air, close on their right, which made them prick up their ears and look at one another. Even the head of the column could have seen nothing, for they were behind the hill. But all could hear, and guess. We all know that sound well enough now. You hear it now, thank God, on every village green in England when the cricket is over. Crack, crack! Crack, crack! The noise of advancing skirmishers.

And so it grew from the right towards the front, towards the left, till the air was filled with the shrill treble of musketry. Then, as the French skirmished within reach of the artillery, the deep bass roared up, and the men, who dared not whisper before, could shout at one another without rebuke.

Louder again, as our artillery came into range. All the air was tortured with concussion. Charles would have given ten years of his life to know what was going on on the other side of the hill. But no. There they sat, and he had to look at the back of the man before him; and at this time he came to the conclusion that the patch of grease on his right shoulder was of the same shape as the map of Sweden.

A long two weary hours or more was spent like this. Charles, by looking forward and to the right, between the two right-hand men of the troop before him, could see the ridge of the hill, and see the smoke rising from beyond it, and drifting away to the left before the sea-breeze. He saw an aide-de-camp come over that ridge and dismount beside the captain of Hornby's troop, loosening his girths. They laughed together; then the captain shouted to Hornby, and he laughed and waved his sword over his head. After this, he was reduced to watching the back of the man before him, and studying the map of Sweden. It was becoming evident that the map of North America, if it existed, must be on his left shoulder, under his hussar jacket, and that the Pacific Islands must be round in front, about his left breast, when the word was given to go forward.

They advanced to the top of the hill, and wheeled. Charles, for one instant, had a glimpse of the valley below, seething and roaring like a volcano. Everywhere bright flashes of flame, single, or running along in lines, or blazing out in volleys. The smoke, driven to the left by the wind, hung across the valley like a curtain. On the opposite hill a ring of smoke and fire, and in front of it a thin scarlet line disappearing. That was all. The next moment they wheeled to the right, and Charles saw only the back of the man before him, and the patch of grease on his shoulder.

But that night was a night of spurs for them. Hard riding for them far into the night. The field of the Alma had been won, and they were ordered forward to harass the Cossacks, who were covering the rear of the Russian Army. They never got near them. But ever after, when the battle of the Alma was mentioned before him, Charles at once used to begin thinking of the map of Sweden.

CHAPTER LII

WHAT LORD SALTIRE AND FATHER MACKWORTH SAID WHEN THEY LOOKED OUT OF THE WINDOW

" AND how do you do, my dear sir ? " said Lord Saltire.

" I enjoy the same perfect health as ever, I thank you, my lord," said Father Mackworth. " And allow me to say that I am glad to see your lordship looking just the same as ever. You may have forgotten that you were the greatest benefactor that I ever had. I have not."

" Nay, nay," said Lord Saltire. " Let bygones be bygones, my dear sir. By-the-by, Mr. Mackworth—Lord Hainault."

" I am delighted to see you at Casterton, Mr. Mackworth," said Lord Hainault. " We are such rabid Protestants here, that the mere presence of a Catholic ecclesiastic of any kind is a source of pleasurable excitement to us. When, however, we get among us a man like you—a man of whose talents we have heard so much, and a man personally endeared to us, through the love he bore to one of us who is dead, we give him a threefold welcome."

Lord Saltire used, in his *tête-à-têtes* with Lady Ascot, to wish to Gad that Hainault would cure himself of making speeches. He was one of the best fellows in the world, but he would always talk as if he was in the House of Lords. This was very true about Lord Hainault ; but, although he might be a little stilted in his speech, he meant every word he said, and was an affectionate, good-hearted man, and withal a clever one.

Father Mackworth bowed, and was pleased with the compliment. His nerve was in perfect order, and he was glad to find that Lord Hainault was well inclined towards him, though just at this time the Most Noble the Marquis of Hainault was of less importance to him than one of the grooms in the stable. What he required of himself just now was to act and look in a particular way, and to do it naturally and without effort. His genius rose to the situation. He puzzled Lord Saltire.

"This is a sad business," said Lord Saltire.

"A bitter business," said Mackworth. "I loved that man, my lord."

He looked suddenly up as he said it, and Lord Saltire saw that he was in earnest. He waited for him to go on, watching him intently with his eyelids half dropped over his grey eagle eyes.

"That is not of much consequence, though," said Father Mackworth. "Speaking to a man of the world, what is more to the purpose is, to hear what is the reason of your lordship's having sought this interview. I am very anxious to know that, and so, if I appear rude, I must crave forgiveness."

Lord Saltire looked at him minutely and steadily. How Mackworth looked was of more importance to Lord Saltire than what he said. On the other hand, Mackworth every now and then calmly and steadily raised his eyes to Lord Saltire's, and kept them fixed there while he spoke to him.

"Not at all, my dear sir," said Lord Saltire. "If you will have business first, however, which is possibly the best plan, we will have it, and improve our acquaintance afterwards. I asked you to come to me to speak of family matters. You have seen our advertisement?"

"I have, indeed," said Mackworth, looking up with a smile. "I was utterly taken by surprise. Do you think that you can be right about this marriage?"

"Oh! I am sure of it," said Lord Saltire.

"I cannot believe it," said Mackworth. "And I'll tell you why. If it ever took place I *must* have heard of it. Father Clifford, my predecessor, was Petre Ravenshoe's confessor. I need not tell you that he must have been in possession of the fact. Your knowledge of the world will tell you how impossible it is that, in a house so utterly priest-ridden as the House of Ravenshoe, an affair of such moment could be kept from the knowledge of the father-confessor. Especially when the delinquent, if I may so express myself, was the most foolishly bigoted, and cowardly representative of that house which had appeared for many generations. I assure you, upon my honour, that Clifford *must* have known it. And, if he had known of it, he must have communicated it to me. No priest could possibly have died without leaving such a secret to his successor ; a secret which would make the owner of it—that is, the priest —so completely the master of Ravenshoe and all in it. I confessed that man on his deathbed, my lord," said Mackworth, looking quietly at Lord Saltire, with a smile, " and I can only tell you, if you can bring yourself to believe a priest, that there was not one word said about his marriage."

" No ? " said Lord Saltire, pensively looking out of the window. " And yet Lady Ascot seems so positive."

" I sincerely hope," said Mackworth, " that she may be wrong. It would be a sad thing for me. I am comfortable and happy at Ravenshoe. Poor dear Cuthbert has secured my position there during my lifetime. The present Mr. Ravenshoe it not so tractable as his brother, but I can get on well enough with him. But, in case of this story being true, and Mr. Charles Horton coming back, my position would be untenable, and Ravenshoe would be in Protestant hands for the first time in history. I should lose my home, and the Church would lose one of its best houses in the west. The best, in fact. I had sooner be at Ravenshoe than at Segur. I am very much pleased at your lordship's having sought this conference. It shows you have some trust in me, to consult me upon a matter in which my own interests are all on one side."

Lord Saltire bowed. " There is another way to look at the matter, too, my dear sir. If we prove our case, which is possible, and in case of our poor dear Charles dying or getting killed, which is probable, why then William comes in for the estate again. Suppose, now, such a possibility as his dying without heirs ; why, then, Miss Ravenshoe is the greatest heiress in the West of England. Have you any idea where Miss Ravenshoe is ? "

Both Lord Saltire and Lord Hainault turned on him as the former said this. For an instant Mackworth looked inquiringly from one to the other, with his lips slightly parted, and said, " Miss Ravenshoe ? " Then he gave a half-smile of intelligence, and said, " Ah ! yes ; I was puzzled for a moment. Yes, in that case poor Ellen would be Miss Ravenshoe. Yes, and the estate would remain in Catholic hands. What a prospect for the Church ! A penitent heiress ! The management of £12,000 a year ! Forgive my being carried away for a moment. You know I am an enthusiastic Churchman. I have been bound, body and soul, to the Church from a child, and such a propect, even in such remote perspective, has dazzled me. But I am afraid I shall see rather a large family of Ravenshoes between me and such a consummation. William is going to marry."

"Then you do not know where poor Ellen is?" said Lord Saltire.

"I do not," said Mackworth; "but I shall certainly try to discover, and most certainly I shall succeed. William might die on this very expedition. You might prove your case. If anything were to happen to William, I most certainly hope you may, and will give you every assistance. For half a loaf is better than no bread. And besides, Charles also might be killed, or die of cholera. As it is, I shall not move in the matter. I shall not help you to bring a Protestant to Ravenshoe. Now don't think me a heartless man for talking like this; I am nothing of the kind. But I am talking to two very shrewd men of the world, and I talk as a man of the world; that is all."

At this point, Lord Hainault said, "What is that?" and left the room. Lord Saltire and Mackworth were alone together.

"Now, my dear sir," said Lord Saltire, "I am glad you have spoken merely as a man of the world. It makes matters so much easier. You could help us if you would."

Mackworth laughed. "Of course I could, my lord. I could bring the whole force of the Catholic Church, at my back to give assistance. With our powers of organization, we could discover all about the marriage in no time (if it ever took place, which I don't choose to believe just now). Why, it would pay us to search minutely every register in England, if it were to keep such a house in the hands of the Church. But the Catholic Church, in my poor person, politely declines to move all its vast machinery, to give away one of its best houses to a Protestant."

"I never supposed that the dear old lady would do anything of the kind. But, as for Mr. Mackworth, will nothing induce *him* to move *his* vast machinery in our cause?"

"I am all attention, my lord!"

"In case of our finding Charles, then?"

"Yes," said Mackworth, calmly.

"Twenty thousand?"

"No," said Mackworth. "It wouldn't do. Twenty million wouldn't do. You see there is a difference between a soldier disguising himself, and going into the enemy's camp to lie, and it may be, murder, to gain information for his own side, and the same soldier deserting to the enemy, and giving information. The one is a hero, and the other a rogue. I am a hero. You must forgive me for putting matters so coarsely, but you distrust me so entirely that I am forced to do so."

"I do not think you have put it so coarsely," said Lord Saltire. "I have to ask your forgiveness for this offer of money, which you have so nobly refused. They say, every man has his price. If this is the case, yours is a very high one, and you should be valued accordingly."

"Now, my lord, before we conclude this interview, let me tell you two things, which may be of advantage to you. The first is, that you cannot buy a Jesuit."

"A Jesuit!"

"Ay. And the next thing is this. This marriage of Petre Ravenshoe is all a fiction of Lady Ascot's brain. I wish you good morning, my lord."

There are two sides to every door. You grant that. A man cannot be in two places at once. You grant that, without the exception made by the Irish member. Very well then. I am going to describe what took place on both sides of the library door at the conclusion of this interview. Which side shall I describe first?

That is entirely as I choose, and I choose to describe the outside first. The side where Father Mackworth was. This paragraph and the last are written in imitation of the Shandean-Southey-Doctorian style. The imitation is a bad one, I find, and approaches nearer to the lower style known among critics as Swivellerism ; which consists in saying the first thing that comes into your head. Any style would be quite allowable, merely as a rest to one's aching brain, after the dreadfully keen encounter between Lord Saltire and Father Mackworth, recorded above.

When Mackworth had closed the library door behind him, he looked at it for a moment, as if to see it was safe, and then his whole face underwent a change. It grew haggard and anxious, and, as he parted his lips to moisten them, the lower one trembled. His eyes seemed to grow more prominent, and a leaden ring began to settle round them ; he paused in a window, and raised his hand towards his head. When he had raised it half way he looked at it ; it was shaking violently.

"I am not the man I was," he said. "These great field-days upset me. My nerve is going, God help me. It is lucky that I was really puzzled by his calling her Miss Ravenshoe. If I had not been all abroad, I could never have done so well.

I must be very careful. My nerve ought not to go like this. I have lived a temperate life in every way. Possibly a little too temperate. I won't go through another interview of this kind without wine. It is not safe.

" The chances are ten to one in favour of one never hearing of Charles again. Shot and steel and cholera. Then William only to think of. In that case I am afraid I should like to bring in the elder branch of the family, to that young gentleman's detriment. I wish my nerve was better ; this irritability increases on me in spite of all my care. I wish I could stand wine.

" Ravenshoe, with Ellen for its mistress, and Mackworth living there as her master ! A penitential devotee, and a clever man for confessor ! And twelve thousand a year ! If we Jesuits were such villains as the Protestants try to make us out, Master William would be unwise to live in the house with me.

" I wonder if Lord Saltire guesses that I hold the clue in my hand. I can't remember the interview, or what I said. My memory begins to go. They should put a younger man in such a place. But I would not yield to another man. No. The stakes are too high. I wish I could remember what I said.

" Does William dream that, in case of Charles's death, he is standing between me and the light? At all events, Lord Saltire sees it. I wonder if I committed myself? I remember I was very honest and straightforward. What was it I said at last ? I have an uneasy feeling about that, but I can't remember.

" I hope that Butler will keep the girl well in hand. If I was to get ill, it would all rest with him. God ! I hope I shall not get ill."

Now we will go to the other side of the door. Lord Saltire sat quietly upright in his chair until the door was safely closed. Then he took a pinch of snuff. He did not speak aloud, but he looked cunningly at the door, and said to himself—

" Odd !"

Another pinch of snuff. Then he said aloud, " Uncommon curious, by Ged."

" What is curious ? " said Lord Hainault, who had come into the room.

" Why, that fellow. He took me in to the last moment. I thought he was going to be simply honest ; but he betrayed himself by over-eagerness at the end. His look of frank honesty was assumed; the real man came out in the last sentence. You should have seen how his face changed, when he turned sharply on me, after fancying he had lulled suspicion to sleep, and told me that the marriage was a fiction. He forgot his manners for the first time, and laid his hand upon my knee."

Lord Hainault said, "Do you think that he knows about the marriage?"

"I am sure he does. And he knows where Ellen is."

"Why?"

"Because I am sure of it."

"That is hardly a reason, my dear Lord Saltire. Don't you think, eh?"

"Think what?"

"Think that you are—well," said Lord Hainault, in a sort of desperation, "are not you, my dear lord, to put it very mildly, generalizing from an insufficient number of facts? I speak with all humility before one of the shrewdest men in Europe; but don't you think so?"

"No, I don't," said Lord Saltire.

"I bow," said Lord Hainault. "The chances are ten to one that you are right, and I am wrong. Did you make the offer?"

"Yes."

"And did he accept it?"

"Of course he didn't. I told you he wouldn't."

"That is strange, is it not?"

"No," said Lord Saltire.

Lord Hainault laughed, and then Lord Saltire looked up and laughed too. "I like being rude to you, Hainault. You are so solemn."

"Well," said Lord Hainault with another hearty laugh. "And what are we to do now?"

"Why, wait till William comes back," said Lord Saltire. "We can do nothing till then, my dear boy. God bless you, Hainault. You are a good fellow."

When the old man was left alone he rose and looked out of the window. The bucks were feeding together close under the windows; and, farther off, under the shadow of the mighty cedars, the does and fawns were standing and lying about lazily, shaking their broad ears and stamping their feet. Out from the great rhododendron thickets, right and left of the house, the pheasants were coming to spend the pleasant evening-tide in running to and fro, and scratching at the ant-hills.

The rabbits too were showing out among the grass, scuttling about busily. The peacock had lit down from the stable roof, and was elegantly picking his way and dragging his sweeping train among the pheasants and the rabbits ; and on the topmost, copper-red, cedar-boughs, some guinea fowl were noisily preparing for roost. One hundred yards from the window the park seemed to end, for it dipped suddenly down in a precipitous, almost perpendicular slope of turf, three hundred and fifty feet high, towards the river, which you could see winding on for miles through the richly wooded valley ; a broad riband of silver, far below. Beyond, wooded hills : on the left, endless folds of pearl-coloured downs ; to the right, the town, a fantastic grey and red heap of buildings, lying along from the river, which brimmed full up to its wharves and lane ends ; and, over it, a lazy cloud of smoke, from which came the gentle booming of golden-toned bells.

Casterton is not a show place. Hainault has a whim about it. But you may see just such a scene, with variations, of course, from Park-place, or Hedsor, or Chiefden, or fifty other houses on the king of rivers. I wonder when the tour of the Thames will become fashionable. I have never seen anything like it, in its way. And I have seen a great many things.

Lord Saltire looked out on all this which I have roughly described (for a reason). And, as he looked, he spoke to himself, thus, or nearly so—

"And so I am the last of them all ; and alone. Hardly one of them left. Hardly one. And their sons are feeding their pheasants, and planting their shrubberies still, as we did. And the things that were terrible realities for us, are only printed words for them, which they try to realize, but cannot. The thirty mad long years, through which we stood with our backs to the wall, and ticketed as " the revolutionary wars," and put in a pigeon-hole. I wish they would do us justice. We *were* right. Hainault's pheasants prove it. They must pay their twenty million a year, and thank us that they have got off so easy.

"I wonder what *they* would do, in such a pinch as we had. They seem to be as brave as ever ; but I am afraid of their getting too much unbrutalized for another struggle like ours. I suppose I am wrong, for I am getting too old to appreciate new ideas, but I am afraid of our getting too soft. It is a by-gone prejudice, I am afraid. One comfort is, that such a struggle can never come again. If it did, they might have the will to do all that we did, and more.

but have they the power? This extension of the suffrage has played the devil, and now they want to extend it farther, the madmen! They'll end by having a House full of Whigs. And then—why, then, I suppose, there'll be nothing but Whigs in the House. That seems to me near about what will happen. Well! well! I was a Whig myself once on a time.

"All gone. Every one of them. And I left on here, in perfect health and preservation, as much an object of wonder to the young ones as a dodo would be to a poultry-fancier. Before the effect of our deeds has been fully felt, our persons have become strange, and out of date. But yet I, strange to say, don't want to go yet. I want to see that Ravenshoe boy again. Gad! how I love that boy. He has just Barkham's sweet, gentle, foolish way with him. I determined to make him my heir from the first time I saw him at Ranford, if he turned out well. If I had announced it, everything would have gone right. What an endless series of unlucky accidents that poor boy has had.

"Just like Barkham. The same idle, foolish, lovable creature, with anger for nothing; only furious, blind indignation for injustice and wrong. I wish he would come back. I am getting weary of waiting.

"I wonder if I shall see Barkham again, just to sit with my arm on his shoulder, as I used to on the terrace in old times. Only for one short half-hour——"

I shall leave off here. I don't want to follow the kind old heathen through his vague speculations about a future state. You see how he had loved his son. You see why he loved Charles. That is all I wished to show you.

"And if Charles don't come back? By Gad! I am very much afraid the chances are against it. Well, I suppose if the poor lad dies, I must leave the money to Welter and his wife, if it is only for the sake of poor Ascot, who was a good fellow. I wonder if we shall ever get at the bottom of this matter about the marriage. I fancy not, unless Charles dies, in which case Ellen will be reinstated by the priest.

"I hope William will make haste back with him. Old fellows like me are apt to go off in a minute. And if he dies and I have not time to make a will, the whole goes to the Crown, which will be a bore. I would sooner Welter had it than that."

Lord Saltire stood looking out of the library window, until the river looked like a chain of crimson pools, stretching westward towards the sinking sun. The room behind him grew dark, and the marble pillars, which divided it in unequal portions, stood like ghosts in the gloom.   He was hidden by the curtain, and presently he heard the door open, and a light footstep stealthily approaching over the Turkey carpet.   There was a rustle of a woman's dress, and a moving of books on the centre table, by some hand which evidently feared detection. Lord Saltire stepped from behind his curtain, and confronted Mary Corby.

CHAPTER LIII

CAPTAIN ARCHER TURNS UP

" Do not betray me, my lord," said Mary from out of the gloom.

" I will declare your malpractices to the four winds of heaven, Miss Corby, as soon as I know what they are.   Why, why do you come rustling into the room, like a mouse in the dark ? Tell me at once what this hole-and-corner work means."

" I will not, unless you promise not to betray me, Lord Saltire."

" Now just think how foolish you are.   How can I possibly make myself particeps of what is evidently a most dark and nefarious business, without knowing beforehand what benefit I am to receive ?   You offer me no share of booty ; you offer me no advantage, direct or indirect, in exchange for my silence, except that of being put into possession of facts which it is probably dangerous to know anything about.   How can you expect to buy me on such terms as these ? "

" Well, then, I will throw myself on your generosity. I want *Blackwood*. If I can find *Blackwood* now, I shall get a full hour at it to myself while you are all at dinner. Do you know where it is ? "

" Yes," said Lord Saltire.

" Do tell me, please.   I do so want to finish a story in it. Please to tell me where it is."

" I won't."

" Why not ?   How very unkind. We have been friends eight months now, and you are just beginning to be cross to me.

You see how familiarity breeds contempt; you used to be so polite."

"I shan't tell you where *Blackwood* is," said Lord Saltire, "because I don't choose. I don't want you to have it. I want you to sit here in the dark and talk to me, instead of reading it."

"I will sit and talk to you in the dark; only you must not tell ghost stories."

"I want you to sit in the dark," said Lord Saltire, "because I want to be '*vox et præterea nihil*.' You will see why, directly. My dear Mary Corby, I want to have some very serious talk with you. Let us joke no more."

Mary settled herself at once into the arm-chair opposite Lord Saltire, and, resting her cheek on her hand, turned her face towards the empty fire-place. "Now, my dear Lord Saltire," she said, "go on. I think I can anticipate what you are going to say."

"You mean about Charles?"

"Yes."

"Ah, that is only a part of what I have to say. I want to consult you there, certainly; but that is but a small part of the business."

"Then I am curious."

"Do you know, then, I am between eighty and ninety years old?"

"I have heard so, my lord."

"Well then, I think that the voice to which you are now listening will soon be silent for ever; and do not take offence; consider it as a dead man's voice, if you will."

"I will listen to it as the voice of a kind living friend," said Mary. "A friend who has always treated me as a reasonable being and an equal."

"That is true, Mary; you are so gentle and so clever, that is no wonder. See here; you have no private fortune."

"I have my profession," said Mary, laughing.

"Yes, but your profession is one in which it is difficult to rise," said Lord Saltire, "and so I have thought it necessary to provide for you in my will. For I must make a new one."

Poor Mary gave a start. The announcement was so utterly unexpected. She did not know what to say, or what to think. She had had long night thoughts about poverty, old age, a life in a garret as a needlewoman, and so on; and had many a good cry over them, and had never found any remedy for them except saying her prayers, which she always found a perfect specific. And here, all of a sudden, was the question solved! She would have liked to thank Lord Saltire. She would have liked to kiss his hand; but words were rather deficient. She tried to keep her tears back, and she in a way succeeded; then in the honesty of her soul she spoke.

" I will thank you more heartily, my lord, than if I went down on my knees and kissed your feet. All my present has been darkened by a great cloud of old age and poverty in the distance. You have swept that cloud away. Can I say more ?"

" On your life, not another word. I could have over-burdened you with wealth, but I have chosen not to do so. Twenty thousand pounds will enable you to live as you have been brought up. Believe an old man when he says that more would be a plague to you."

" Twenty thousand pounds ! "

" Yes. That will bring you in, you will find, about six hundred a year. Take my word for it, it is quite enough. You will be able to keep your brougham, and all that sort of thing. Believe me, you would not be happy with more."

" More ! " said Mary quietly. " My lord, look here, and see what you have done. When the children are going to sleep, I sit, and sew, and sing, and, when they are gone to sleep, I still sit, and sew, and think. Then I build my Spanish castles ; but the highest tower of my castle has risen to this—that in my old age I should have ten shillings a week left me by some one, and be able to keep a canary bird, and have some old woman as pensioner. And now—now—now. Oh ! I'll be quiet in a moment. Don't speak to me for a moment. God is very good."

I hope Lord Saltire enjoyed his snuff. I think that, if he did not, he deserved to. After a pause Mary began again.

" Have I left on you the impression that I am selfish ? I am almost afraid I have. Is it not so ? I have one favour to ask of you. Will you grant it ? "

" Certainly I will."

" On your honour, my lord ? "

" On my honour."

" Reduce the sum you have mentioned to one-fourth. I have bound you by your honour. Oh, don't make me a great heiress ; I am not fit for it."

Lord Saltire said, " Pish ! If you say another word I will leave you ten thousand more. To the deuce with my honour ; don't talk nonsense."

"You said you were going to be quiet in a moment," he resumed presently. "Are you quiet now?"

"Yes, my lord; quiet and happy."

"Are you glad I spoke to you in the dark?"

"Yes."

"You will be more glad that it was in the dark directly. Is Charles Ravenshoe quite the same to you as other men?"

"No," said Mary; "that he most certainly is not. I could have answered that question *to you* in the brightest daylight."

"Humph!" said Lord Saltire. "I wish I could see him and you comfortably married, do you know? I hope I speak plain enough. If I don't, perhaps you will be so good as to mention it, and I'll try to speak a little plainer."

"Nay; I quite understand you. I wonder if you will understand me when I say that such a thing is utterly and totally out of the question."

"I was afraid so. You are a pair of simpletons. My dear daughter (you must let me call you so), you must contemplate the contingency I have hinted at in the dark. I know that the best way to get a man rejected is to recommend him; I, therefore, only say, that John Marston loves you with his whole heart and soul, and that he is a protégé of mine."

"I am speaking to you as I would to my own father. John Marston asked me to be his wife last Christmas, and I refused him."

"Oh, yes. I knew all about that the same evening. It was the evening after they were nearly drowned out fishing. Then there is no hope of a reconsideration there?"

"Not the least," said Mary. "My lord, I will never marry."

"I have not distressed you?"

"Certainly not. You have a right to speak as you have. I am not a silly hysterical girl either, that I cannot talk on such subjects without affectation. But I will never marry; I will be an old maid. I will write novels, or something of that sort. I will not even marry Captain Archer, charm he never so wisely."

"Captain Archer! Who on earth is Captain Archer?"

"Don't you know Captain Archer, my lord?" replied Mary, laughing heartily, but ending her laugh with a short sob. "Avast heaving! Bear a hand, my hearties, and let us light this taper. I think you ought to read his letter. He is the man who swam with me out of the cruel sea, when the *Warren Hastings* went down. That is who he is, Lord Saltire." And at this point, little Mary, thoroughly unhinged by this strange conversation, broke down, and began crying her eyes out, and, putting a letter into his hand, rose to leave the room.

He held the door open for her. " My dear Mary," he said, " if I have been coarse or rude, you must try to forgive me."

" Your straightforward kindness," she said, " is less confusing than the most delicate finesse." And so she went.

Captain Archer is one of the very best men I know. If you and I, reader, continue our acquaintance, you will soon know more of him than you have been able to gather from the pages of Ravenshoe. He was in person perhaps the grandest and handsomest fellow you ever saw. He was gentle, brave and courteous. In short, the best example I have ever seen of the best class of sailor. By birth he was a gentleman, and he had carefully made himself a gentleman in manners. Neither from his dress, which was always scrupulously neat and in good taste, nor from his conversation, would you guess that he was a sailor, unless in a very select circle, where he would, if he thought it pleased or amused, talk salt water by the yard. The reason why he had written to Mary in the following style was, that he knew she loved it, and he wished to make her laugh. Lord Saltire set him down for a mad seaman, and nothing more. You will see that he had so thoroughly obscured what he meant to say, that he left Mary with the very natural impression that he was going to propose to her.

He had done it, he said, from Port Philip Heads, in sixty-four days, at last, in consequence of one of his young gentlemen (merchant midshipmen) having stole a black cat in Flinder's-lane, and brought her aboard. He had caught the westerly wind off the Leuwin and carried it down to 62°, through the ice, and round the Horn, where he had met a cyclone, by special appointment, and carried the outside edge of it past the Auroras. That during this time it had blown so hard that it was necessary for three midshipmen to be on deck with him night and day, to hold his hair on. That, getting too near the centre, he had found it necessary to lay her to, which he had successfully done, by tying one of his false collars in the fore weather-rigging. And so on. Giving an absurd account of his whole voyage, evidently with the intention of making her laugh.

He concludes thus : " And now, my dear Mary, I am going to surprise you. I am getting rich, and I am thinking of getting married. Have you ever thought of such a thing ? Your present dependence must be irksome. Begin to contemplate a change to a happier and freer mode of life.

I will explain more fully when I come to you. I shall have much to tell you which will surprise you; but you know I love you, and only study your happiness. When the first pang of breaking off old associations is over, the new life, to such a quiet spirit as yours, becomes at first bearable, then happy. A past is soon created. Think of what I have said, before I come to you. Your future, my dear, is not a very bright one. It is a source of great anxiety to me, who love you so dearly —you little know how dearly."

I appeal to any young lady to say whether or no dear Mary was to blame if she thought good, blundering Archer was going to propose to her. If they give it against her, and declare that there is nothing in the above letter leading to such a conclusion, I can only say that Lord Saltire went with her and with me, and regarded the letter as written preparatory to a proposal. Archer's dismay, when we afterwards let him know this, was delightful to behold. His wife was put in possession of the fact, by some one who shall be nameless, and I have heard that jolly soul use her information against him in the most telling manner on critical occasions.

But, before Captain Archer came, there came a letter from William, from Varna, announcing Charles's death of cholera. There are melancholy scenes, more than enough, in this book, and alas! one more to come; so I may spare you the description of their woe at the intelligence, which we know to be false. The letter was closely followed by William himself, who showed them the grass from his grave. This helped to confirm their impression of its truth, however unreasonable. Lord Saltire had a correspondence with the Horse Guards, long and windy, which resulted, after months, in discovering that no man had enlisted in the 140th under the name of Horton. This proved nothing, for Charles might have enlisted under a false name, and yet might have been known by his real name to an intimate comrade.

Lord Saltire wrote to General Mainwaring. But, by the time his letter reached him, that had happened which made it easy for a fool to count on his fingers the number of men left in the 140th. Among the dead or among the living, no signs of Charles Ravenshoe.

General Mainwaring was, as we all know, wounded on Cathcart's Hill, and came home. The news which he brought about the doings of the 140th we shall have from first hand. But he gave them no hope about Charles.

Lord Saltire and General Mainwaring had a long interview,

and a long consultation. Lord Hainault and the General witnessed his will. There were some legacies to servants; twenty thousand pounds to Miss Corby; ten thousand to John Marston; fifty thousand pounds to Lady Ascot; and the rest, amounting in one way or another, to nearly five hundred thousand pounds, was left to Lord Ascot (our old acquaintance, Lord Welter) and his heirs for ever.

There was another clause in the will, carefully worded—carefully guarded about by every legal fence which could be erected by law, and by money to buy that law—to the effect that, if Charles should reappear, he was to come into a fortune of eighty thousand pounds, funded property.

Now please to mark this. Lord Ascot was informed by General Mainwaring that the death of Charles Ravenshoe being determined on as being a fact, Lord Saltire had made his will in his (Lord Ascot's) favour. I pray you remember this. Lord Ascot knew no particulars, only that the will was in his favour. If you do not keep this in mind, it would be just as well if there had been no Lord Welter at all in the story.

Ravenshoe and its poor twelve thousand a year begin to sink into insignificance, you see. But still we must attend to it. How did Charles's death affect Mackworth? Rather favourably. The property could not come into the hands of a Protestant now. William was a staunch Catholic, though rebellious and disagreeable. If anything happened to him, why, then there was Ellen to be produced. Things might have been better, certainly, but they were certainly improved by that young cub's death, and by the cessation of all search for the marriage register. And so on. If you care to waste time on it, you may think it all through for yourselves, as did not Father Mackworth.

And I'll tell you why. Father Mackworth had had a stroke of paralysis, as men will have, who lead, as he did, a life of worry and excitement, without taking proper nourishment; and he was lying, half idiotic, in the priest's tower at Ravenshoe.

CHAPTER LIV

CHARLES MEETS HORNBY AT LAST

OH for the whispering woodlands of Devna! Oh for the quiet summer evenings above the lakes, looking far away at the white-walled town on the distant shore! No more hare-shooting, no more turtle-catching, for you, my dear Charles. The allies had determined to take Sebastopol, and winter in the town. It was a very dull place, every one said ; but there was a race-course, and there would be splendid boat-racing in the harbour. The country about the town was reported to be romantic, and there would be pleasant excursions in the winter to Simpheropol, a gayer town than Sebastopol, and where there was more society. They were not going to move till the spring, when they were to advance up the valley of the Dnieper to Moscow, while a flying column was to be sent to follow the course of the Don, cross to the Volga at Suratow, and so penetrate into the Ural Mountains and seize the gold mines, or do something of this sort ; it was all laid out quite plain.

Now, don't call this *ex post facto* wisdom, but just try to remember what extravagant ideas every non-military man had that autumn about what our army would do. The ministers of the King of Lernè never laid down a more glorious campaign than we did. " I will," says poor Picrochole, " give him fair quarter, and spare his life—I will rebuild Solomon's Temple—I will give you Caramania, Syria, and all Palestine." " Ha ! sire," said they, "it is out of your goodness. Grammercy, we thank you." We have had our little lesson about that kind of amusement. There has been none of it in this American business ; but our good friends the other side of the Atlantic are worse than they were in the time of the Pogram defiance. Either they don't file their newspapers, or else they console themselves by saying that they could have done it all if they had liked.

It now becomes my duty to use all the resources of my art to describe Charles's emotions at the first sight of Sebastopol. Such an opportunity for the display of beautiful language should not be let slip. I could do it capitally by buying a

copy of Mr. Russell's "War," or even by using the correspondence I have on the table before me. But I think you will
agree with me that is better left alone. One hardly likes to
come into the field in that line after Russell.

Balaclava was not such a pleasant place as Devna. It was
bare and rocky, and everything was in confusion, and the men
were dying in heaps of cholera. The nights were beginning
to grow chill, too, and Charles began to dream regularly, that
he was sleeping on the bare hill-side, in a sharp frost, and that
he was agonisingly cold about the small of his back. And
the most singular thing was, that he always woke and found
his dream come true. At first he only used to dream this
dream towards morning; but, as October began to creep on,
he used to wake with it several times in the night, and at last
hardly used to go to sleep at all for fear of dreaming it.

Were there no other dreams? No. No dreams, but one
ever-present reality. A dull aching regret for a past for ever
gone. A heavy deadly grief, lost for a time among the woods
of Devna, but come back to him now amidst the cold, and the
squalor, and the sickness of Balaclava. A brooding over
missed opportunities, and the things that might have been.
Sometimes a tangled puzzled train of thought, as to how
much of this ghastly misery was his own fault, and how much
accident. And above all, a growing desire for death, unknown
before.

And all this time, behind the hill, the great guns, which had
begun a fitful muttering when they first came there, often
dying off into silence ; now day by day, as trench after trench
was opened, grew louder and more continuous, till hearing and
thought were deadened, and the soul was sick of their never-
ceasing melancholy thunder.

And at six o'clock on the morning of the seventeenth, such
an infernal din began as no man there had ever heard before,
which grew louder and louder till nine, when it seemed
impossible that the ear could bear the accumulation of sound ;
and then suddenly doubled, as the *Agamemnon* and the
Montebello, followed by the fleets, steamed in, and laid broad-
side-to under the forts. Four thousand pieces of the heaviest
ordnance in the world were doing their work over that hill,
and the 140th stood dismounted and listened.

At ten o'clock the earth shook, and a column of smoke
towered up in the air above the hill, and as it began to hang
motionless, the sound of it reached them. It was different
from the noise of guns. It was something new and terrible.

An angry hissing roar. An hour after they heard that twenty tons of powder were blown up in the French lines.

Soon after this, though, there was work to be done, and plenty of it. The wounded were being carried to the rear. Some cavalry were dismounted, and told off for the work. Charles was one of them.

The wind had not yet sprung up, and all that Charles saw for the moment was a valley full of smoke, and fire, and sound. He caught the glimpse of the spars and funnel of a great liner above the smoke to the left; but directly after they were under fire, and the sickening day's work began.

Death and horror in every form, of course. The wounded lying about in heaps. Officers trying to compose their faces, and die like gentlemen. Old Indian soldiers dying grimly as they had lived; and lads, fresh from the plough last year, listed at the market-cross some unlucky Saturday, sitting up staring before them with a look of terror and wonder; sadder sight than either. But everywhere all the day, where the shot screamed loudest, where the shell fell thickest, with his shako gone, with his ambrosial curls tangled with blood, with his splendid gaudy fripperies soiled with dust and sweat, was Hornby, the dandy, the fop, the dicer; doing the work of ten, carrying out the wounded in his arms, encouraging the dying, cheering on the living.

"I knew there was some stuff in him," said Charles, as he followed him into the Crown battery; just at that time the worst place of all, for *The Twelve Apostles* had begun dropping red-hot shot into it, and exploded some ammunition, and killed some men. And they had met a naval officer, known to Hornby, wounded, staggering to the rear, who said, "that his brother was knocked over, and that they wanted to make out he was dead, but he had only fainted." So they went back with him. The officer's brother was dead enough, poor fellow; but as Charles and Hornby bent suddenly over to look at him, their faces actually touched.

Hornby did not recognise him. He was in a state of excitement, and was thinking of no one less than Charles, and Charles's moustaches had altered him, as I said before. If their eyes had met, I believe Hornby would have known him; but it was not to be till the 25th, and this was only the 17th. If Hornby could only have known him, if they could only have had ten minutes' talk together, Charles would have known all that we know about the previous marriage of his grandfather; and if that conversation had taken place, he would have known more than any of them, for Hornby knew something which he thought of no importance, which was very important indeed. He knew where Ellen was.

But Charles turned his face away, and the recognition did not take place. Poor Charles said afterwards that it was all a piece of luck—that "the stars in their courses fought against Sisera." It is not the case. He turned away his eyes, and avoided the recognition. What he meant is this :—

As Hornby's face was touching his, and they were both bending over the dead man, whom they could hardly believe to be dead, the men behind them fired off the great Lancaster in the next one-gun battery. "Crack!" and they heard the shell go piff, piff, piff, piff, and strike something. And then one man close to them cried, "God Almighty!" and another cried, "Christ!" as sailors will at such awful times ; and they both leapt to their feet. Above the smoke there hung, a hundred feet in the air, a something like a vast black pine-tree ; and, before they had time to realize what had happened, there was a horrible roar and a concussion which made them stagger on their legs. A shell from the Lancaster had blown up the great redoubt in front of the Redan wall, and every Russian gun ceased firing. And above the sound of the Allied guns rose the cheering of our own men, sounding, amidst the awful bass, like the shrill treble of school-children at play.

Charles said afterwards that this glorious accident prevented their recognition. It is not true. He prevented it himself, and took the consequences. But Hornby recognized him on the 25th in this wise :—

The first thing in the morning, they saw, on the hills to the right, Russian skirmishers creeping about towards them, apparently without an object. They had breakfast, and took no notice of them till about eight o'clock, when a great body of cavalry came slowly, regiment by regiment, from behind a hill near the Turks. Then gleaming batteries of artillery ; and, lastly, an endless column of grey infantry, which began to wheel into line. And when Charles had seen some five or six grey battalions come swinging out, the word was given to mount, and he saw no more, but contemplated the tails of horses. And at the same moment the guns began an irregular fire on their right.

Almost immediately the word was given to advance, which they did slowly. Charles could see Hornby just before him, in his old place, for they were in column. They crossed the plain, and went up the crest of the hill, halting on the high road. Here they sat for some time, and the more fortunate could see the battle raging below to the right. The English seemed getting rather the worst of it.

They sat there about an hour and a half; and all in a moment, before any one seemed to expect it, some guns opened on them from the right; so close that it made their right ears tingle. A horse from the squadron in front of Charles bolted from the ranks, and nearly knocked down Hornby. The horse had need to bolt, for he carried a dead man, who in the last spasm had pulled him on his haunches, and struck his spurs deep into his sides.

Charles began to guess that they were "in for it" at last. He had no idea, of course, whether it was a great battle or a little one; but he saw that the 140th had work before them. I, of course, have only to speak of what Charles saw with his own eyes, and what therefore bears upon the story I am telling you. That was the only man he saw killed at that time, though the whole brigade suffered rather heavily by the Russian cannonade at that spot.

Very shortly after this they were told to form line. Of course, when this manœuvre was accomplished, Charles had lost sight of Hornby. He was sorry for this. He would have liked to know where he was; to help him if possible, should anything happen to him; but there was not much time to think of it, for directly after they moved forward at a canter. In the front line were the 11th Hussars and the 13th Light Dragoons, and in the second were the 140th Hussars,[1] the 8th Hussars, and the 4th Dragoons. Charles could see thus much, now they were in line.

They went down hill, straight towards the guns, and almost at once the shot from them began to tell. The men of the 11th and 13th began to fall terribly fast. The men in the second line, in which Charles was, were falling nearly as fast, but this he could not remark. He missed the man next him on the right, one of his favourite comrades, but it did not strike him that the poor fellow was cut in two by a shot. He kept on wishing that he could see Hornby. He judged that the affair was getting serious. He little knew what was to come.

He had his wish of seeing Hornby, for they were riding up hill into a narrowing valley, and it was impossible to keep

---

[1] If one has to raise an imaginary regiment, one must put it in an imaginary place. The 17th Dragoons must try to forgive me.

line. They formed into column again, though men and horses were rolling over and over at every stride, and there was Hornby before him, sailing along as gallant and gay as ever. A fine beacon to lead a man to a glorious death.

And, almost the next moment, the batteries right and left opened on them. Those who were there engaged can give us very little idea of what followed in the next quarter of an hour. They were soon among guns—the very guns that had annoyed them from the first; and infantry beyond opened fire on them. There seems to have been a degree of confusion at this point. Charles, and two or three others known to him, were hunting some Russian Artillerymen round their guns for a minute or so. Hornby was among them. He saw also at this time his little friend the cornet, on foot, and rode to his assistance. He caught a riderless horse, and the cornet mounted. Then the word was given to get back again; I know not how; I have nothing to do with it. But, as they turned their faces to get out of this horrible hell, poor Charles gave a short, sharp scream, and bent down in his saddle over his horse's neck.

It was nothing. It was only as if one were to have twenty teeth pulled out at once. The pain was over in an instant. What a fool he was to cry out. The pain was gone again, and they were still under fire, and Hornby was before him.

How long? How many minutes, how many hours? His left arm was nearly dead, but he could hold his reins in a way, and rode hard after Hornby, from some wild instinct. The pain had stopped, but was coming on again as if ten thousand red-hot devils were pulling at his flesh, and twenty thousand were arriving each moment to help them.

His own friends were beside him again, and there was a rally and a charge. At what? he thought for an instant. At guns? No. At men this time, Russian hussars—right valiant fellows, too. He saw Hornby in the thick of the mêlée, with his sword flickering about his head like lightning. He could do but little himself; he rode at a Russian and un-horsed him; he remembers seeing the man go down, though whether he struck at him, or whether he went down by the mere superior weight of his horse, he cannot say. This I can say, though, that, whatever he did, he did his duty as a valiant gentleman; I will go bail for that much.

They beat them back, and then turned. Then they turned again and beat them back once more. And then they turned and rode. For it was time. Charles lost sight of Hornby till the last, when some one caught his rein and turned his horse, and then he saw that they were getting into order again, and that Hornby was before him, reeling in his saddle.

As the noise of the battle grew fainter behind them, he looked round to see who was riding beside him and holding him by the right arm. It was the little cornet. Charles wondered why he did so. "You're hard hit, Simpson," said the cornet. "Never mind. Keep your saddle a little longer. We shall be all right directly."

His faculties were perfectly acute, and, having thanked the cornet, he looked down and noticed that he was riding between him and a trooper, that his left arm was hanging numbed by his side, and that the trooper was guiding his horse. He saw that they had saved him, and even in his deadly agony he was so far his own old courteous self that he turned right and left to them and thanked them for what they had done for him.

But he had kept his eyes fixed on Hornby, for he saw that he was desperately hit, and he wanted to say one or two words to him before either of them died. Soon they were among English faces, and English cheers rang out in welcome to their return, but it was nothing to him; he kept his eye, which was growing dim, on Hornby, and, when he saw him fall off his saddle into the arms of a trooper, he dismounted too and staggered towards him.

The world seemed to go round and round, and he felt about him like a blind man. But he found Hornby somehow. A doctor, all scarlet and gold, was bending over him, and Charles knelt down on the other side, and looked into the dying man's face.

"Do you know me, lieutenant?" he said, speaking thick like a drunken man, but determined to hold out. "You know your old servant, don't you?"

Hornby smiled as he recognised him, and said, "Ravenshoe." But then his face grew anxious, and he said, "Why did you hide yourself from me? You have ruined everything."

He could get no further for a minute, and then he said—

"Take this from round my neck and carry it to her. Tell her that you saw me die, and that I was true to our compact. Tell her that my share of our purification was complete, for I followed duty to death, as I promised her. She has a long life of weary penance before her to fulfil our bargain. Say I should wish her to be happy, only that I know she cannot be. And also say that I see now that there is something better and more desirable than what we call happiness. I don't know what it is, but I suspect it is what we call duty."

Here the doctor said, " They are at it again, and I must go with them. I can do no good here for the poor dear fellow. Take what he tells you off his neck, in my presence, and let me go."

The doctor did it himself. When the great heavy gold stock was unbuttoned, Hornby seemed to breathe more freely. The doctor found round his neck a gold chain, from which hung a photograph of Ellen, and a black cross. He gave them to Charles, and departed.

Once more Charles spoke to Hornby. He said, "Where shall I find her?"

Hornby said, " Why, at Hackney, to be sure; did you not know she was there?" And afterwards, at the very last, " Ravenshoe, I should have loved you; you are like her, my boy. Don't forget."

But Charles never heard that. They found Hornby dead and cold, with his head on Charles's lap, and Charles looked so like him that they said, " This man is dead too; let us bury him." But a skilful doctor there present said, " This man is not dead, and will not die"; and he was right.

Oh, but the sabres bit deep that autumn afternoon! There were women in Minsk, in Moglef, in Tchernigof, in Jitemir, in Polimva, whose husbands were hussars—and women in Taganrog, in Tcherkask, in Sanepta, which lies under the pleasant slate mountains, whose husbands and sons were Cossacks—who were made widows that day. For that day's work there was weeping in reed-thatched hovels of the Don, and in the mud-built shanties of the Dnieper. For the 17th Lancers, the Scots Greys, the 1st Royals, and the 6th Enniskillens—" these terrible beef-fed islanders " (to use the words of the *Northern Bee*)—were upon them; and Volhynia and Hampshire, Renfrewshire and Grodno, Podolia and Fermanagh, were mixed together in one common ruin.

Still, they say, the Princess Petrovitch, on certain days, leaves her carriage and walks a mile through the snow barefoot into Alexandroski, in memory of her light-haired handsome young son, whom Hornby slew at Balaclava. And I myself know the place where Lady Allerton makes her pilgrimage for those two merry boys of hers who lie out on the Crimean hill. Alas! not side by side. Up and down in all weathers, along a certain gravel walk, where the chalk brook having flooded the

park with its dammed-up waters, comes foaming and spouting
over a cascade, and hurries past between the smooth mown
lawns of the pleasance. In the very place where she stood
when the second letter came. And there, they say, she will
walk at times, until her beauty and her strength are gone, and
her limbs refuse to carry her.

Karlin Karlinoff was herding strange-looking goats on the
Suratow hill-side, which looks towards the melancholy Volga on
one side, and the reedy Ural on the other, when the Pulk came
back, and her son was not with them. Eliza Jones had got
on her husband's smock-frock, and was a-setting of beans, when
the rector's wife came struggling over the heavy lands and
water-furrows, and broke the news gently and with many tears.
Karlin Karlinoff drove her goats into the mud-walled yard that
night, though the bittern in the melancholy fen may have
been startled from his reeds by a cry more wild and doleful
than his own; and Eliza Jones went on setting her beans,
though they were watered with her tears.

What a strange wild business it was! The extreme east of
Europe against the extreme west. Men without a word, an
idea, a habit or a hope in common, thrown suddenly together,
to fight and slay; and then to part, having learned to respect
one another better, in one year of war, than ever they had in a
hundred years of peace. Since that year we have understood
Eylau and Borodino, which battles were a puzzle to some of us
before that time. The French did better than we, which was
provoking, because the curs began to bark—Spanish curs, for
instance; American curs; the lower sort of French cur; and
the Irish curs, who have the strange habit of barking the louder
the more they are laughed at, and who, now, being represented
by about two hundred men among six million, have rather a
hard time of it. They barked louder, of course, at the Indian
mutiny. But they have all got their tails between their legs
now, and are likely to keep them there. We have had our
lesson. We have learnt that what our fathers told us was true
—that we are the most powerful nation on the face of the earth.

This, you will see, bears all upon the story I am telling you.
Well, in a sort of way. Though I do not exactly see how. I
could find a reason, if you gave me time. If you gave me time,
I could find a reason for anything. However, the result is this,
that our poor Charles had been struck by a ball in the bone of
his arm, and that the splinters were driven into the flesh, though
the arm was not broken. It was a nasty business, said the
doctors. All sorts of things might happen to him. Only one

thing was certain, and that was that Charles Ravenshoe's career in the army was over for ever.

CHAPTER LV

ARCHER'S PROPOSAL

SIX weeks had passed since the date of Captain Archer's letter before he presented himself in person at Casterton. They were weary weeks enough to Mary, Lord Saltire, and Lady Ascot. Lady Ascot was staying on at Casterton, as if permanently, at the earnest request of Lord and Lady Hainault; and she stayed on the more willingly that she and Mary might mingle their tears about Charles Ravenshoe, whom they were never to see again. The "previous marriage affair" had apparently fallen through utterly. All the advertisements, were they worded never so frantically, failed to raise to the surface the particular parish-clerk required; and Lady Ascot, after having propounded a grand scheme for personally inspecting every register in the United Kingdom, which was pooh-poohed by Lord Saltire, now gave up the matter as a bad job; and Lord Saltire himself began to be puzzled and uneasy, and once more to wonder whether or no Maria was not mistaken after all. Mackworth was still very ill, though slowly recovering. The younger Tiernay, who was nursing him, reported that his head seemed entirely gone, although he began to eat voraciously, and, if encouraged, would take exercise. He would now walk far and fast, in silence, with the kind priest toiling after him. But his wilful feet always led him to the same spot. Whether they rambled in the park, whether they climbed the granite tors of the moor, or whether they followed the stream up through the woods, they always ended their walk at the same place—at the pool among the tumbled boulders, under the dark western headland, where Cuthbert's body had been found. And here the priest would sit looking seaward, as if his life and his intellect had come to a full stop here, and he was waiting patiently till a gleam of light should come from beyond.

William was at Ravenshoe, in full possession of the property. He had been born a gamekeeper's son, and brought up as a groom. He had now 10,000*l.* a year; and was going to marry the fisherman's daughter, his own true love; as beautiful, as sweet-tempered a girl as any in the three kingdoms. It was one of the most extraordinary rises in life that had ever taken place. Youth, health and wealth—they must produce happiness. Why no, not exactly in this case. He believed Charles was dead, and he knew, if that was the case, that the property was his; but he was not happy. He could not help thinking about Charles. He knew he was dead and buried, of course; but still he could not help wishing that he would come back, and that things might be again as they had been before. It is not very easy to analyse the processes of the mind of a man brought up as William was. Let us suppose that, having been taught to love and admire Charles above all earthly persons, his mind was not strong enough to disabuse himself of the illusion. I suppose that your African gets fond of his fetish. I take it that, if you stole his miserable old wooden idol in the night, though it might be badly carved, and split all up the back by the sun, and put in its place an Old Chelsea shepherdess, he would lament his graven image, and probably break the fifty guineas' worth of china with his club. I know this, however, that William would have given up his ten thousand a year, and have trusted to his brother's generosity, if he could have seen him back again. In barbarous, out-of-the-way places, like the west of Devonshire, the feudal feeling between foster-brothers is still absurdly strong. It is very ridiculous, of course. Nothing can be more ridiculous or unnecessary than the lightning coming down the dining-room chimney and sending the fire-irons flying about the cat's ears. But there it is, and you must make the best of it.

We are now posted up well enough in the six weeks which preceded the arrival of the mysterious Archer. He deferred his arrival till his honeymoon was completed. His mysterious letter to Mary partly alluded to his approaching marriage with Jane Blockstrop—daughter of Lieutenant Blockstrop of the coast guard, and niece of Rear-Admiral Blockstrop, who, as Captain Blockstrop, had the *Tartar* on the Australian station —and partly to something else. We shall see what directly. For, when Mary came down to see him in the drawing-room there was with him, besides his wife, whom he introduced at once, a very tall and handsome young man, whom he presented to her as her cousin, George Corby.

Did Charles turn in his pallet at Scutari? Did he turn over and stare at the man in the next bed, who lay so deadly still, and who was gone when he woke on the weary morrow?

There was no mystery about George Corby's appearance. When Mary's father, Captain Corby, had gone to India, his younger brother, George's father, had gone to Australia. This younger brother was a somewhat peevish, selfish man, and was not on the best of terms with Captain Corby. He heard, of course, of the wreck of the *Warren Hastings*, and the loss of his brother. He also informed himself that his niece was saved, and was the protected favourite of the Ravenshoes. He had then said to himself, "I am needy. I have a rising family. She is better off than I can make her. Let her stay there." And so he let her stay there, keeping himself, however, to do him justice, pretty well informed of her position. He had made the acquaintance of Captain Archer, at Melbourne, on his first voyage to that port, in the end of 1852; laid the whole matter before him, and begged him not to break it to her at present. Captain Archer had readily promised to say nothing, for he saw Mary the lady of a great house, with every prospect, as he thought, of marrying the heir. But when he saw Mary, after the break-up, in Grosvenor Square, a nursery governess, he felt that he ought to speak, and set sail from the port of London with a full determination of giving a piece of his mind to her uncle, should he hesitate to acknowledge her. He had no need to say much. Mr. Corby, though a selfish, was not an unkind man, by any means. And, besides, he was now very wealthy, and perfectly able to provide for his niece. So, when Archer had finished his story, he merely said, "I suppose I had better send over George to see if he will fall in love with her. That will be the best thing, I take it. She must not be a governess to those swells. They might slight or insult her. Take George over for me, will you, my dear soul, and see how it is likely to go. At all events, bring her back to me. Possibly I may not have done my duty by her."

George was called in from the rocking-chair in the verandah to receive instructions. He was, so his father told him, to go to Europe with Captain Archer, and, as Captain Archer was going to get married and miss a voyage, he might stay till he came back. First and foremost, he was to avail himself of his letters of introduction, and get into the good society that his father was able to command for him. Under this head of instruction he was to dance as much as possible, and to ride to the fox-hounds, taking care not to get too near to the hounds, or to rush at his fences like a madman, as all Australians did. Secondly, he was, if possible, to fall in love with his cousin, Mary Corby, marry her, bring her back, and reside *pro tem.* at Tooralooralyballycoomefoozleah, which station should be swept and garnished for his reception, until the new house at the Jugger-ugahugjug crossing-place was finished. Thirdly, he might run across to the Saxony ram sales, and, if he saw anything reasonable, buy, but be careful of pink ears, for they wouldn't stand the Grampian frosts. Fourthly, he was not to smoke without changing his coat, or to eat the sugar when any one was looking. Fifthly, he was to look out for a stud horse, and might go as far as five hundred. Such a horse as Allow Me, Ask Mamma, or Pam's Mixture would do.[1] And so on, like the directions of the Aulic Council to the Archduke. He was not to go expressly to Durham; but, if he found himself in that part of the world, he might get a short-horned bull. He need not go to Scotland unless he liked; but if he did, he might buy a couple of collies, &c. &c.

George attended the ram sales in Saxony, and just ran on to Vienna, thinking, with the philosophy of an Australian, that, if he *did* fall in love with his cousin, he might not care to travel far from her, and that therefore she might "keep." However, he came at last, when Archer had finished his honeymoon; and there he was in the drawing-room at Casterton.

Mary was not very much surprised when it was all put before her. She had said to Charles in old times, "I know I have relations somewhere; when I am rich they will acknowledge me"; and, just for one instant, the suspicion crossed her mind that her relations might have heard of the fortune Lord Saltire had left her. It was unjust and impossible, and in an instant she felt it to be so. Possibly the consciousness of her injustice made her reception of her cousin somewhat warmer.

He was certainly very handsome and very charming. He had been brought up by his father the most punctilious dandy in the southern hemisphere, and thrown from a boy among the best society in the colony; so he was quite able to make himself at home everywhere. If there was a fault in his manner, it was that there was just a shade too much lazy ease in the presence of ladies. One has seen that lately, however, in other young gentlemen, not educated in the bush, to a greater extent; so we must not be hard upon him. When Lady Hainault and

---

[1] These names actually occur, side by side, in my newspaper (*The Field*), to which I referred for three names. They are in training by Henry Hall, at Hambleton, in Yorkshire. Surely men could find better names for their horses than such senseless ones as these. I would that was all one had to complain of. I hope the noble old sport is not on its last legs. But one trembles to think what will become of it, when the comparatively few high-minded men who are keeping things straight are gone.

Lady Ascot heard that a cousin of Mary's had just turned up from the wilds of Australia, they looked at one another in astonishment, and agreed that he must be a wild man. But when they had gone down and sat on him, as a committee of two, for an hour, they both pronounced him charming. And so he was.

Lord Hainault, on receiving this report, could do no less than ask him to stay a day or two. And so his luggage was sent for to Twyford, and the good Archer left, leaving him in possession.

Lord Saltire had been travelling round to all his estates. He had taken it into his head, about a month before this, that it was time that he should get into one of his great houses, and die there. He told Lady Ascot so, and advised her to come with him; but she still held on by Lord Charles Herries' children and Mary, and said she would wait. So he had gone away, with no one but his confidential servant. He had gone to Cottingdean first, which stands on the banks of the Wannet, at the foot of the North Hampshire mountains.

Well, Cottingdean did seem at first sight a noble lair for an old lion to crawl away to, and die in. There was a great mile-long elm avenue, carried, utterly regardless of economy, over the flat valley, across the innumerable branches of the river; and at the last the trees ran up over the first great heave of the chalk hill : and above the topmost boughs of those which stood in the valley, above the highest spire of the tallest poplar in the water-meadow, the old grey house hung aloft, a long irregular façade of stone. Behind were dark woods, and above all a pearl-green line of down.

But Cottingdean wouldn't do. His Lordship's man Simpson knew it wouldn't do from the first. There were draughts in Cottingdean, and doors that slammed in the night, and the armour in the great gallery used suddenly to go " clank " at all hours, in a terrible way. And the lady ancestress of the seventeenth century, who carried her head in a plate before her, used to stump upstairs and downstairs, from twelve o'clock to one, when she was punctually relieved from duty by the wicked old ancestor of the sixteenth century, who opened the cellar door and came rattling his sword against the banisters up all the stair-case till he got to the north-east tower, into which he went and slammed the door ; and, when he had transacted his business, came clanking down again : when he in turn was relieved by an οἱ πολλοὶ of ghosts, who walked till cockcrow. Simpson couldn't stand it. No more could

Lord Saltire, though possibly for different reasons than Simpson's.

The first night at Cottingdean Lord Saltire had his writing-desk unpacked, and took therefrom a rusty key. He said to Simpson, "You know where I am going. If I am not back in half an hour, come after me." Simpson knew where he was going. Lord Barkham had been staying here at Cottingdean just before he went up to town, and was killed in that unhappy duel. The old servants remembered that, when Lord Barkham went away that morning he had taken the key of his room with him, and had said, in his merry way, that no one was going in there till he came back the next week, for he had left all his love-letters about. Lord Saltire had got the key, and was going to open the room the first time for forty years.

What did the poor old man find there? Probably nothing more than poor Barkham had said—some love-letters lying about. When the room was opened afterwards, by the new master of Cottingdean we found only a boy's room, with fishing-rods and guns lying about. In one corner were a pair of muddy top-boots kicked off in a hurry, and an old groom remembered that Lord Barkham had been riding out the very morning he started for London. But, amidst the dust of forty years, we could plainly trace that some one had, comparatively recently, moved a chair up to the fire-place; and on the cold hearth there was a heap of the ashes of burnt paper.

Lord Saltire came back to Simpson just as his half-hour was over, and told him in confidence that the room he had been in was devilish draughty, and that he had caught cold in his ear. Cottingdean would not do after this. They departed next morning. They must try Marksworth.

Marksworth, Lord Saltire's north country place, is in Cumberland. If you are on top of the coach, going northward, between Hiltonsbridge and Copley Beck, you can see it all the way for three miles or more, over the stone walls. The mountains are on your left; to the right are endless unbroken level woodlands; and rising out of them, two miles off, is a great mass of grey building, from the centre of which rises a square Norman keep, ninety feet high, a beacon for miles even in that mountainous country. The Hilton and Copley Beck join in the park, which is twelve miles in circumference, and nearly all thick woodland. Beyond the great tower, between it and the further mountains, you catch a gleam of water. This is Marksmere, in which there are charr.

The draughts at Marksworth were colder and keener than

the draughts at Cottingdean. Lord Saltire always hated the place : for the truth is this, that although Marksworth looked as if it had stood for eight hundred years, every stone in it had been set up by his father, when he, Lord Saltire, was quite a big boy. It was beautifully done ; it was splendidly and solidly built—probably the best executed humbug in England ; but it was not comfortable to live in. A nobleman of the nineteenth century, stricken in years, finds it difficult to accommodate himself in a house the windows of which are calculated to resist arrows. At the time of the Eglinton tournament, Lord Saltire challenged the whole Tory world in arms, to attack Marksworth in the ante-gunpowder style of warfare; his Lordship to provide eatables and liquor to besiegers and besieged ; probably hoping that he might get it burnt down over his head, and have a decent excuse for rebuilding it in a more sensible style. The challenge was not accepted. " The trouble," said certain Tory noblemen, " of getting up the old tactics correctly would be very great; and the expense of having the old engines of war constructed would be enormous. Besides, it might come on to rain again, and spoil the whole affair."

Marksworth wouldn't do. And then Simpson suggested his lordship's town house in Curzon Street, and Lord Saltire said " Hey?" and Simpson repeated his suggestion, and Lord Saltire said " Hah !" As Charles's luck would have it, he liked the suggestion, and turned south, coming to Casterton on his way to London. He arrived at Casterton a few days after George Corby. When he alighted at the door, Lord Hainault ran down the steps to greet him, for this pair were very fond of one another. Lord Hainault, who was accused by some people of " priggishness," was certainly not priggish before Lord Saltire. He was genial and hearty. There was a slight crust on Lord Hainault. Because he had held his own among the clever commoners at the university, he fancied himself a little cleverer than he was. He in his heart thought more of his second, than Marston did of his double first, and possibly showed it among his equals. But before an acknowledged superior, like Lord Saltire, this never showed. When Lord Saltire talked wisely and shrewdly (and who could do so better than he?), he listened; when Lord Saltire was cross, he laughed. On this occasion Lord Saltire was cross. He never was cross to any one but Lady Ascot, Lord Hainault, and Marston. He knew they liked it.

" Good Ged, Hainault," he began, " don't stand grinning there, and looking so abominably healthy and happy, or I will drive away again and go on to London. Nothing can be in worse taste than to look like that at a man whom you see is tired, and cold, and peevish. You have been out shooting, too. Don't deny it; you smell of gunpowder."

"Did you *never* shoot?" said Lord Hainault, laughing.

"I shot as long as I could walk, and therefore I have a right to nourish envy and all uncharitableness against those who can still do so. I wish you would be cross, Hainault. It is wretched manners not to be cross when you see a man is trying to put you out of temper."

"And how *are* you, my dear lad?" continued Lord Saltire when he had got hold of his arm. "How is Lady Ascot? and whom have you got here?"

"We are all very well," said Lord Hainault; "and we have got nobody."

"Well done," said Lord Saltire. "I thought I should have found the house smelling like a poulterer's shop on Guy Fawkes' day, in consequence of your having got together all the hawbucks in the country for pheasant-shooting. I'll go upstairs, my dear boy, and change, and then come down to the library fire."

And so he did. There was no one there, and he sank into a comfortable chair, with a contented "humph!" in front of the fire, beside a big round table. He had read the paper in the train; so he looked for a book. There was a book on the table beside him—Ruskin's "Modern Painters," which had pictures in it; so he took out his great gold glasses, and began turning it over.

A man's card fell from it. He picked it up and read it. "Mr. Charles Ravenshoe." Poor Charles! That spring, you remember, he had come over to see Adelaide, and, while waiting to see old Lady Hainault, had held his card in his hand. It had got into the book. Lord Saltire put the book away, put up his glasses, and walked to the window.

And Charles lay in his bed at Scutari and watched the flies upon the wall.

"I'll send up for little Mary," said Lord Saltire. "I want to see the little bird. Poor Charles!"

He looked out over the landscape. It was dull and foggy. He wandered into the conservatory, and idly looked out of the glass door at the end. Then, as he looked, he said suddenly, "Gadzooks!" and then, still more briskly, "The deuce!"

There was a splendid show of chrysanthemums in the flower-garden, but they were not what his lordship exclaimed at. In the middle of the walk was Mary Corby, leaning on the arm of a very handsome young man. He was telling some very animated story, and she was looking up into his face with sparkling eyes.

"Othello and Desdemona! Death and confusion!" said Lord Saltire. "Here's a pretty kettle of fish! Maria must be mad!"

He went back into the library. Lord Hainault was there. "Hainault," said he quietly, "who is that young gentleman walking with Mary Corby in the garden?"

"Oh! her cousin. I have not had time to tell you about it." Which he did.

"And what sort of a fellow is he?" said Lord Saltire. "A Yahoo, I suppose?"

"Not at all. He is a capital fellow—a perfect gentleman. There will be a match, I believe, unless you put a stop to it. You know best. We will talk it over. It seems to me to offer a good many advantages. I think it will come off in time. It is best for the poor little thing to forget poor Ravenshoe, if she can."

"Yes, it will be best for her to forget poor Ravenshoe, if she can," repeated Lord Saltire. "I wish her to do so. I must make the young fellow's acquaintance. By-the-by, what time does your post go out?"

"At five."

"Have you no morning post?"

"Yes. We can send to Henley before nine."

"Then I shall not plague myself with writing my letter now. I should like to see this young fellow, Hainault."

George Corby was introduced. Lord Saltire seemed to take a great fancy to him. He kept near him all the evening, and listened with great pleasure to his Australian stories. George Corby was, of course, very much flattered by such attention from such a famous man. Possibly he might have preferred to be near Mary; but old men, he thought, are exacting, and it is the duty of gentlemen to bear with them. So he stayed by him with good grace. After a time, Lord Saltire seemed to see that he had an intelligent listener. And then the others were astonished to hear Lord Saltire do what he but seldom did for them—use his utmost powers of conversation; use an art almost forgotten, that of *talking*. To this young man, who was clever and well educated, and, like most "squatters," perhaps a *trifle* fond of hearing of great people, Lord Saltire opened the storehouse of his memory, of a memory extending over seventy years; and in a clear, well modulated voice gave him his recollections of his interviews with great people—conversations with Sièyes, Talleyrand, with Madame de Staël, with Robespierre, with Egalité, with Alexander, and a dozen others. George was intensely eager to hear about Marat. Lord Saltire and his snuff-box had not penetrated into the lair of that filthy wolf, but he had heard much of him from many friends, and told it well. When the ladies rose to go to bed, George Corby was astonished ; he had forgotten Mary, had never been near her the whole evening, and he had made an engagement to drive Lord Saltire the next morning up to Wargrave in a pony-chaise to look at Barrymore House, and the place where the theatre stood, and where the game of high jinks had been played so bravely fifty years before. And, moreover, he and Lord Saltire were, the day after, to make an excursion down the river and see Medmenham, where once Jack Wilkes and the devil had held court. Mary would not see much of him at this rate for a day or two.

It was a great shame of this veteran to make such a fool of the innocent young bushman. There ought to be fair play in love or war. His acquaintance Talleyrand, could not have been more crafty. I am so angry with him that I will give the letter he wrote that night *in extenso*, and show the world what a wicked old man he was. When he went to his room, he said to Simpson, "I have got to write a letter before I go to bed. I want it to go to the post at Henley before nine. I don't want it to lie in the letter-box in the hall. I don't want them to see the direction. What an appetite you would have for your breakfast, Simpson, if you were to walk to Henley." And Simpson said, "Very good, my Lord." And Lord Saltire wrote as follows—

"MY DEAR LAD,—I have been travelling to my places, looking for a place to die in. They are all cold and draughty, and won't do. I have come back to Casterton. I must stay here at present on your account, and I am in mortal fear of dying here. Nothing, remember, can be more unmannerly or rude than falling ill, and dying, in another man's house. I know that I should resent such a proceeding myself as a deliberate affront, and I therefore would not do it for the world.

"You must come here to me *instantly ;* do you hear? I am keeping the breach for you at all sacrifices. Until you come, I am to be trundled about this foggy valley in pony carriages through the day, and talk myself hoarse all the evening, all for your sake. A cousin of Mary Corby's has come from

Australia. He is very handsome, clever, and gentlemanly, and I am afraid she is getting very fond of him.

"This must not be, my dear boy. Now our dear Charles is gone, you must, if possible, marry her. It is insufferable that we should have another disappointment from an interloper. I don't blame you for not having come before. You were quite right, but don't lose a moment now. Leave those boys of yours. The dirty little rogues must get on for a time without you. Don't think that I sneer at the noble work that you and your uncle are doing: God Almighty forbid; but you must leave it for a time, and come here.

"Don't argue or procrastinate, but come. I cannot go on being driven all over the country in November to keep him out of the way. Besides, if you don't come soon, I shall have finished all my true stories, and have to do what I have never done yet—to lie. So make haste, my dear boy.

"Yours affectionately,
"SALTIRE."

On the second day from this Lord Saltire was driven to Medmenham by George Corby, and prophesied to him about it. When they neared home, Lord Saltire grew distraught for the first time and looked eagerly towards the terrace. As they drove up, John Marston ran down the steps to meet them. Lord Saltire said, "Thank God!" and walked up to the hall-door between the two young men.

"Are you staying in London?" said George Corby.

"Yes. I am living in London," said John Marston. "An uncle of mine, a Moravian missionary from Australia, is working at a large ragged school in the Borough, and I am helping him."

"You don't surely mean James Smith?" said Corby.

"Indeed I do."

"Your uncle? Well, that is very strange. I know him very well. My father fought his battle for him when he was at variance with the squatters about. . . . He is one of the best fellows in the world. I am delighted to make your acquaintance."

Lord Saltire said to Lord Hainault, when they were alone together—"You see what a liberty I have taken, having my private secretary down in this unceremonious way. Do ask him to stay."

"You know how welcome he is for his own sake. Do you think you are right?"

"I think so."

"I am afraid you are a little too late," said Lord Hainault. Alas! poor Charles.

CHAPTER LVI

SCUTARI

ALAS! poor Charles. While they were all dividing the spoil at home, thinking him dead, where was he?

At Scutari. What happened to him before he got there, no one knows or ever will know. He does not remember and there is no one else to tell. He was passed from hand to hand and put on board ship. Here fever set in, and he passed from a state of stupid agony into a state of delirium. He may have lain on the pier in the pouring rain, moistening his parched lips in the chilling shower; he may have been jolted from hospital to hospital, and laid in draughty passages till a bed was found for him; as others were. But he happily knew nothing of it. Things were so bad with him now that it did not much matter how he was treated. Read Lord Sidney Osborne's "Scutari and its Hospitals," and see how he *might* have been, and probably was. It is no part of our duty to dig up and exhibit all that miserable mismanagement. I think we have learnt our lesson. I think I will go bail it don't happen again. Before Charles knew where he was, there was a great change for the better. The hospital nurses arrived early in November.

He thinks that there were faint gleams of consciousness in his delirium. In the first, he says he was lying on his back, and above him were the mast and spars of a ship, and a sailor-boy was sitting out on a yard in the clear blue, mending a rope or doing something. It may have been a dream or not. Afterwards there were periods, distinctly remembered, when he seemed conscious—conscious of pain and space and time —to a certain extent. At these times he began to understand, in a way, that he was dead, and in hell. The delirium was better than this at ordinary times, in spite of its headlong incongruities. It was not so unbearable, save at times, when there came the feeling, too horrible for human brain to bear, of being millions and millions of miles, or of centuries, away, with no road back; at such times there was nothing to be done but to leap out of bed, and cry aloud for help in God's name.

Then there came a time when he began, at intervals, to see a great vaulted arch overhead, and to wonder whether or no it was the roof of the pit. He began, after studying the matter many times, to find that pain had ceased, and that the great vaulted arch was real. And he heard low voices once at this time—blessed voices of his fellow-men. He was content to wait.

At last, his soul and consciousness seemed to return to him in a strange way. He seemed to pass out of some abnormal state into a natural one. For he became aware that he was alive; nay, more, that he was asleep and dreaming a silly, pleasant dream, and that he could wake himself at any time. He awoke, expecting to awake in his old room at Ravenshoe. But he was not there, and looked round him in wonder.

The arch he remembered was overhead. That was real enough. Three people were round his bed—a doctor in undress, a grey-haired gentleman who peered into his face, and a lady.

"God bless me!" said the doctor. "We have fetched him through. Look at his eyes, just look at his eyes. As sane an eye as yours or mine, and the pulse as round as a button."

"Do you know us, my man?" said the gentleman.

It was possible enough that he did not, for he had never set eyes on him before. The gentleman meant only, "Are you sane enough to know your fellow-creatures when you see one?" Charles thought he must be some one he had met in society in old times and ought to recognise. He framed a polite reply, to the effect that he hoped he had been well since he met him last, and that, if he found himself in the west, he would not pass Ravenshoe without coming to see him.

The doctor laughed. "A little abroad still, I daresay; I have pulled you through. You have had a narrow escape."

Charles was recovered enough to take his hand and thank him fervently, and whispered, "Would you tell me one thing, sir? How did Lady Hainault come here?"

"Lady Hainault, my man?"

"Yes; she was standing at the foot of the bed."

"That is no Lady Hainault, my man; that is Miss Night-ingale. Do you ever say your prayers?"

"No."

"Say them to-night before you go to sleep, and remember her name in them. Possibly they may get to heaven the quicker for it. Good-night."

Prayers forgotten, eh! How much of all this misery lay in that, I wonder? How much of this dull, stupid, careless despair—earth a hopeless, sunless wilderness, and heaven not thought of? Read on.

But, while you read, remember that poor Charles had had no domestic religious education whatever. The vicar had taught him his catechism and "his prayers." After that, Shrewsbury and Oxford. Read on, but don't condemn; at least not yet.

That he thanked God with all the earnestness of his warm heart that night, and remembered that name the doctor told him, you may be sure. But, when the prayer was finished, he began to think whether or no it was sincere, whether it would not be better that he should die, and that it should be all over and done. His creed was, that, if he died in the faith of Christ, bearing no ill will to anyone, having repented of his sins, it would not go ill with him. Would it not be better to die now that he could fulfil those conditions, and not tempt the horrible black future? Certainly.

In time he left watching the great arch overhead, and the creeping shadows, and the patch of light on the wall, which shaped itself into a faint rhomboid at noon, and crept on till it defined itself into a perfect square at sundown, and then grew golden and died out. He began to notice other things. But till the last there was one effect of light and shadow which he always lay awake to see—a faint flickering on the walls and roof, which came slowly nearer till a light was in his eyes. We all know what that was. It has been described twenty times. I can believe that story of the dying man kissing the shadow on the wall. When Miss Nightingale and her lamp are forgotten, it will be time to consider whether one would prefer to turn Turk or Mormon.

He began to take notice that there were men in the beds beside him. One, as we know, had been carried out dead; but there was another in his place now. And one day there was a great event; when Charles woke, both of them were up, sitting at the side of their beds, ghastly shadows, and talking across him.

The maddest musician never listened to the "vox humana" stop at Haarlem, with such delight as Charles did to these two voices. He lay for a time hearing them make acquaintance, and then he tried to sit up and join. He was on his left side, and tried to rise. His left arm would not support him, and he fell back, but they crept to him and set him up, and sat on his bed.

"Right again, eh, comrade?" said one. "I thought you was gone, my lad. But I heard the doctor say you'd get through. You look bravely. Time was when you used to jump out of bed and cry on God A'mighty. Many a time I've strove to help ye. The man in *his* bed died while you was like that: a Fusilier Guards man. What regiment?"

"I am of the 140th," said Charles. "We had a bit of a brush with the enemy on the twenty-fifth. I was wounded there. It was a pretty little rattle, I think, for a time, but not of very much importance, I fancy."

The man who had first spoken laughed; the other man, a lad who had a round face once, perhaps, but which now was a pale death's head, with two great staring eyes, speaking with a voice which Charles knew at once to be a gentleman's, said, "Don't you know then that that charge of yours is the talk of Europe? That charge will never be forgotten while the world is round. Six hundred men against ten battalions. Good God! And you might have died there, and not known it."

"Ah, is it so?" said Charles. "If some could only know it!"

"That is the worst of it," said the young man. "I have enlisted under a false name, and will never go home any more. Never more. And she will never know that I did my duty."

And after a time he got strong again in a way. A bullet, it appears, had struck the bone in his arm and driven the splinters into the flesh. Fever had come on, and his splendid constitution, as yet untried, save by severe training, had pulled him through. But his left arm was useless. The doctor looked at it again and again, and shook his head.

The two men who were in the beds on each side of him were moved before him. They were only there a fortnight after his coming to himself. The oldest of the two went first, and two or three days after the younger.

The three made all sorts of plans for meeting in England. Alas! what chance is there for three soldiers to meet again, unless by accident? At home it would have taken three years to have made these three men such hearty friends as they had become in a fortnight. Friendships are made in the camp, in the bush, or on board ship, at a wonderful rate. And, moreover, they last for an indefinite time. For ever, I fancy ; for these reasons. Time does not destroy friendship. Time has nothing whatever to do with it. I have heard an old man of seventy-eight talking of a man he had not seen for twelve years, and before that for twenty-five, as if they were young men together. Craving for his company, as if once more they were together on the deck of the white-sailed yacht, flying before the easterly wind between Hurstcastle and Sconce Point. Mere continual familiarity, again, does not hurt friendship, unless interests clash. Diversity of interests is the death-blow of friendship. One great sacrifice may be made—two, or even three ; but after the first two men are not to one another as they were before. Where men are thrown intimately together for a short time, and part, having only seen the best side of one another, or where men see one another frequently and have not very many causes of difference, friendship will flourish for ever. In the case of love it is very different, and for this obvious reason, which I will explain in a few pages if——

I entered into my own recognisances, in an early chapter of this story, not to preach. I fear they are escheated after this short essay on friendship, coming, as it does, exactly in the wrong place. I must only throw myself on the court, and purge myself of my contempt by promising amendment.

Poor Charles after a time was sent home to Fort Pitt. But that mighty left arm, which had done such noble work when it belonged to No. 3, in the Oxford University eight, was useless, and Charles Simpson, trooper in the 140th, was discharged from the army, and found himself on Christmas Eve in the street in front of the Waterloo Station, with eighteen shillings and ninepence in his pocket, wondering blindly what the end of it all would be, but no more dreaming of begging from those who had known him formerly than of leaping off Waterloo Bridge. Perhaps not half so much.

CHAPTER LVII

WHAT CHARLES DID WITH HIS LAST EIGHTEEN SHILLINGS

CHARLES's luck seemed certainly to have deserted him at last. And that is rather a serious matter, you see ; for, as he had never trusted to anything but luck, it now follows that he had nothing left to trust to, except eighteen shillings and ninepence, and his little friend the cornet, who had come home invalided and was living with his mother in Hyde Park Gardens. Let us hope, reader, that you and I may never be reduced to the patronage of a cornet of Hussars, and eighteen shillings in cash.

It was a fine frosty night, and the streets were gay and merry. It was a sad Christmas for many thousands ; but the general crowd seemed determined not to think too deeply of these sad accounts which were coming from the Crimea just now. They seemed inclined to make Christmas Christmas, in spite of everything ; and perhaps they were right. It is good for a busy nation like the English to have two great festivals, and two only, the object of which every man who is a Christian can understand, and on these occasions to put in practice, to the best of one's power, the lesson of goodwill towards men which our Lord taught us. We English cannot stand too many saints' days. We decline to stop business for St. Blaise or St. Swithin ; but we can understand Christmas and Easter. The foreign Catholics fiddle away so much time on saints' days that they are obliged to work like the Israelites in bondage on Sunday to get on at all. I have as good a right to prophesy as any other freeborn Englishman who pays rates and taxes ; and I prophesy that, in this wonderful resurrection of Ireland, the attendance of the male population at church on week-days will get small by degrees and beautifully less.

One man, Charles Ravenshoe, has got to spend his Christmas with eighteen shillings and a crippled left arm. There is half a million of money or so, and a sweet little wife, waiting for him if he would only behave like a rational being ; but he will not, and must take the consequences.

He went westward, through a kind of instinct, and he came to Belgrave Square, where a certain duke lived. There were lights in the windows. The duke was in office, and had been called up to town. Charles was glad of this; not that he had any business to transact with the duke, but a letter to deliver to the duke's coachman.

This simple circumstance saved him from being much nearer actual destitution than I should have liked to see him. The coachman's son had been wounded at Balaclava, and was still at Scutari, and Charles brought a letter from him. He got an English welcome, I promise you. And, next morning, going to Hyde Park Gardens, he found that his friend the cornet was out of town and would not be back for a week. At this time the coachman became very useful. He offered him money, house-room, employment, everything he could possibly get for him; and Charles heartily and thankfully accepted house-room and board for a week.

At the end of a week he went back to Hyde Park Gardens. The cornet was come back. He had to sit in the kitchen while his message was taken upstairs. He merely sent up his name, said he was discharged, and asked for an interview.

The servants found out that he had been at the war with their young master's regiment, and they crowded round him, full of sympathy and kindness. He was telling them how he had last seen the cornet in the thick of it on the terrible 25th, when they parted right and left, and in dashed the cornet himself, who caught him by both hands.

"By gad, I'm so glad to see you. How you are altered without your moustache! Look you here, you fellows and girls, this is the man that charged up to my assistance when I was dismounted among the guns, and kept by me while I caught another horse. What a cropper I went down, didn't I? What a terrible brush it was, eh? And poor Hornby, too! It is the talk of Europe, you know. You remember old Devna, and the galloping lizard, eh?"

And so on, till they got upstairs; and then he turned on him, and said, "Now, what are you going to do?"

"I have got eighteen shillings."

"Will your family do nothing for you?"

"Did Hornby tell you anything about me, my dear sir?" said Charles eagerly.

"Not a word. I never knew that Hornby and you were acquainted till I saw you together when he was dying."

"Did you hear what we said to one another?"

"Not a word. The reason I spoke about your family is, that no one, who had seen so much of you as I, could doubt that you were a gentleman. That is all. I am very much afraid I shall offend you——"

"That would not be easy, sir."

"Well, then, here goes. If you are utterly hard up, take service with me. There."

"I will do so with the deepest gratitude," said Charles. "But I cannot ride, I fear. My left arm is gone."

"Pish! ride with your right. It's a bargain. Come up and see my mother. I must show you to her, you know, because you will have to live here. She is deaf. Now you know the reason why the major used to talk so loud."

Charles smiled for an instant; he did remember that circumstance about the cornet's respected and gallant father. He followed the cornet upstairs, and was shown into the drawing-room, where sat a very handsome lady, about fifty years of age, knitting.

She was not only stone deaf, but had a trick of talking aloud, like the old lady in "Pickwick," under the impression that she was only thinking, which was a very disconcerting habit indeed. When Charles and the cornet entered the room, she said aloud, with amazing distinctness, looking hard at Charles, "God bless me! Who has he got now? What a fine gentlemanly-looking fellow. I wonder why he is dressed so shabbily." After which she arranged her trumpet, and prepared to go into action.

"This, mother," bawled the cornet, "is the man who saved me in the charge of Balaclava."

"Do you mean that that is trooper Simpson?" said she.

"Yes, mother."

"Then may the blessing of God Almighty rest upon your head!" she said to Charles. "The time will come, trooper Simpson, when you will know the value of a mother's gratitude. And when that time comes think of me. But for you, trooper Simpson, I might have been tearing my grey hair this day. What are we to do for him, James? He looks ill and worn. Words are not worth much. What shall we do?"

The cornet put his mouth to his mother's trumpet, and in an apologetic bellow, such as one gets from the skipper of a fruit brig, in the Bay of Biscay, O! when he bears up to know if you will be so kind as to oblige him with the longitude; roared out:

"He wants to take service with me. Have you any objection?"

"Of course not, you foolish boy," said she. "I wish we could do more for him than that." And then she continued, in a tone slightly lowered, but perfectly audible, evidently under the impression that she was thinking to herself: "He is ugly, but he has a sweet face. I feel certain he is a gentleman who has had a difference with his family. I wish I could hear his voice. God bless him! he looks like a valiant soldier. I hope he won't get drunk, or make love to the maids."

Charles had heard every word of this before he had time to bow himself out.

And so he accepted his new position with dull carelessness. Life was getting very worthless.

He walked across the park to see his friend the coachman. The frost had given, and there was a dull dripping thaw. He leant against the railings at the end of the Serpentine. There was still a great crowd all round the water; but up the whole expanse there were only four skaters, for the ice was very dangerous and rotten, and the people had been warned off. One of the skaters came sweeping down to within a hundred yards of where he was—a reckless, headlong skater, one who would chance drowning to have his will. The ice cracked every moment and warned him, but he would not heed, till it broke, and down he went; clutching wildly at the pitiless, uptilted slabs which clanked about his head to save himself; and then with a wild cry disappeared. The icemen were on the spot in a minute; and, when five were passed, they had him out, and bore him off to the receiving-house. A gentleman, a doctor apparently, who stood by Charles, said to him, "Well, there is a reckless fool gone to his account, God forgive him!"

"They will bring him round, won't they?" said Charles.

"Ten to one against it," said the doctor. "What right has he to calculate on such a thing, either? Why, most likely there will be half a dozen houses in mourning for that man to-morrow. He is evidently a man of some mark. I can pity his relations in their bereavement, sir, but I have precious little pity for a reckless fool."

And so Charles began to serve his friend, the cornet, in a way —a very poor way, I fear, for he was very weak and ill, and could do but little. The deaf lady treated him like a son, God bless her; but Charles could not recover the shock of his fever and delirium in the Crimea. He grew very low-spirited and despondent by day, and, worst of all, he began to have sleepless nights—terrible nights. In the rough calculation he had made of being able to live through his degradation, and get used to it, he had calculated, unwittingly, on perfect health. He had thought that in a few years he should forget the old life, and become just like one of the grooms he had made his companions. This had now become impossible, for his health and his nerve were gone.

He began to get afraid of his horses; that was the first symptom. He tried to fight against the conviction, but it forced itself upon him. When he was on horseback, he found that he was frightened when anything went wrong; his knees gave way on emergency, and his hand was irresolute. And, what is more, be sure of this, that, before he confessed the fact to himself, the horses had found it out, and "taken action on it," or else, may I ride a donkey, with my face towards the tail, for the rest of my life.

And he began to see another thing. Now, when he was nervous, in ill health, and whimsical, the company of men among whom he was thrown as fellow-servants became nearly unbearable. Little trifling acts of coarseness, unnoticed when he was in good health and strong, at the time he was with poor Hornby, now disgusted him. Most kind-hearted young fellows, brought up as he had been, are apt to be familiar with, and probably pet and spoil, the man whose duty it is to minister to their favourite pleasures, be he gamekeeper or groom, or cricketer, or waterman. Nothing can be more natural, or, in proper bounds, harmless. Charles had thought that, being used to these men, he could live with them and do as they did. For a month or two, while in rude coarse health, he found it was possible; for had not Lord Welter and he done the same thing for amusement? But now, with shattered nerves, he found it intolerable. I have had great opportunities of seeing gentlemen trying to do this sort of thing—I mean in Australia—and, as far as my experience goes, it ends in one of two ways. Either they give it up as a bad job and assume the position that superior education gives them, or else they take to drink, and go, not to mince matters, to the devil.

What Charles did, we shall see. Nobody could be more kind and affectionate than the cornet and his deaf mother. They guessed that he was "somebody," and that things were wrong with him; though, if he had been a chimney-sweep's son, it would have made no difference to them, for they were "good people." The cornet once or twice invited his confidence; but he was too young, and Charles had not the energy to tell him anything. His mother, too, asked him to tell her if anything was wrong with his affairs, and whether she could help him; and possibly he might have been more inclined to confide in her, than in her son. But who could bellow such a sad tale of misery through an ear-trumpet? He held his peace.

He kept Ellen's picture, which he had taken from Hornby. He determined he would not go and seek her. She was safe somewhere, in some Catholic asylum. Why should he re-open her grief?

But life was getting very, very weary business. By day, his old favourite pleasure of riding had become a terror, and at night he got no rest. Death forty good years away, by all calculation. A weary time.

He thought himself humbled, but he was not. He said to himself that he was prevented from going back, because he had found out that Mary was in love with him, and also because he was disgraced through his sister; and both of these reasons were, truly, most powerful with him. But, in addition to this, I fear there was a great deal of obstinate pride, which thing is harder to beat out of a man than most things.

And now, after all this half-moralizing narrative, an important fact or two. The duke was very busy, and stayed in town, and, as a consequence, the duke's coachman. Moreover, the duke's coachman's son came home invalided and stayed with his father; and Charles, with the hearty approval of the cornet, used to walk across the park every night to see him, and talk over the campaign, and then look in at the Servants' Club, of which he was still a member. And the door of the Servants' Club room had glass windows to it. And I have noticed that anybody who looks through a glass window (under favourable circumstances) can see who is on the other side. I have done it myself more than once.

CHAPTER LVIII

THE NORTH SIDE OF GROSVENOR SQUARE

JOHN Marston's first disappointment in life had been his refusal by Mary. He was one of those men, brought up in a hard school, who get, somehow, the opinion that everything which happens to a man is his own fault. He used to say that every man who could play whist could get a second if he chose.

I have an idea that he is in some sort right. But he used to carry this sort of thing to a rather absurd extent. He was apt to be hard on men who failed, and to be always the first to say, "If he had done this, or left that alone, it would not have been so," and he himself, with a calm clear brain and perfect health, had succeeded in everything he had ever tried at, even up to a double first. At one point he was stopped. He had always given himself airs of superiority over Charles, and had given him advice, good as it was, in a way which would have ruined his influence with nine men out of ten; and suddenly he was brought up. At the most important point in his life, he found Charles his superior. Charles had won a woman's love without knowing it, or caring for it; and he had tried for it, and failed.

John Marston was an eminently noble and high-minded man. His faults were only those of education, and his faults were very few. When he found himself rejected, and found out why it was so—when he found that he was no rival of Charles, and that Charles cared naught for poor Mary—he humbly set his quick brain to work to find out in what way Charles, so greatly his inferior in intellect, was superior to him in the most important of all things. For he saw that Charles had not only won Mary's love, but the love of every one who knew him; whereas he, John Marston, had but very few friends.

And, when he once set to work at this task, he seemed to come rapidly to the conclusion that Charles was superior to him in everything except application. "And how much application should I have had," he concluded, "if I had not been a needy man?"

So you see that his disappointment cured him of what was almost his only vice—conceit. Everything works together for good, for those who are really good.

Hitherto, John Marston has led only the life that so many young Englishmen lead—a life of study, combined with violent, objectless, physical exertion, as a counterpoise. He had never known what enthusiasm was as yet. There was a vast deal of it somewhere about him; in his elbows, or his toes, or the calves of his legs, or somewhere, as events prove. If I might hazard an opinion, I should say that it was stowed away somewhere in that immensely high, but somewhat narrow forehead of his. Before he tried love-making, he might have written the calmest and most exasperating article in the *Saturday Review*. But, shortly after that, the tinder got a-fire; and the man who set it on fire was his uncle Smith, the Moravian missionary.

For this fellow, Smith, had, as we know, come home from Australia with the dying words of his beautiful wife ringing in his ears: "Go home from here, my love, into the great towns, and see what is to be done there." And he found his nephew, John Marston. And, while Marston listened to his strange, wild conversation, a light broke in upon him. And what had been to him merely words before this, now became glorious, tremendous realities.

And so those who had gone hand in hand down into the dirt and profligacy of Southwark, to do together a work the reward of which comes after death. There are thousands of men at such work now. We have no more to do with it than to record the fact, that these two were at it heart and hand.

John Marston's love for Mary had never waned for one instant. When he had found that, or thought he had found that, she loved Charles, he had in a quiet, dignified way, retired from the contest. He had determined that he would go away and work at ragged schools, and so on, and try to forget all about her. He had begun to fancy that his love was growing cool, when Lord Saltire's letter reached him, and set it all a-blaze again.

This was unendurable—that a savage, from the southern wilds, should step in like this, without notice. He posted off to Casterton.

Mary was very glad to see him; but he had proposed to her once, and, therefore, how could she be so familiar with him as of yore? Notwithstanding this, John was not so very much disappointed at his reception; he had thought that matters were even worse than they were.

After dinner, in the drawing-room, he watched them together. George Corby was evidently in love. He went to Mary, who was sitting alone, the moment they came from the dining-room. Mary looked up, and caught his eyes as he approached; but her eyes wandered from him to the door, until they settled on John himself. She seemed to wish that he would come and talk to her. He had a special reason for not doing so; he wanted to watch her and George together. So he stayed behind, and talked to Lord Hainault.

Lord Saltire moved up beside Lady Ascot. Lady Hainault had the three children—Archy in her lap, and Gus and Flora beside her. In her high and mighty way, she was amusing them, or rather trying to do so. Lady Hainault was one of the best and noblest women in the world, as you have seen already; but she was not an amusing person. And no one knew it better than herself. Her intentions were excellent: she wanted to leave Mary free from the children until their bed-time, so that she might talk to her old acquaintance, John Marston; for, at the children's bed-time, Mary would have to go with them. Even Lady Hainault, determined as she was, never dared to contemplate putting those children to bed without Mary's assistance. She was trying to tell them a story out of her own head, but was making a dreadful mess of it; and she was quite conscious that Gus and Flora were listening to her with contemptuous pity.

So they were disposed. Lord Saltire and Lady Ascot were comfortably out of hearing. We had better attend to them first, and come round to the others afterwards.

Lady Ascot began. "James," she said, "it is perfectly evident to me that you sent for John Marston."

"Well, and suppose I did?" said Lord Saltire.

"Well, then, why did you do so?"

"Maria," said Lord Saltire, "do you know that sometimes you are intolerably foolish? Cannot you answer that question for yourself?"

"Of course I can," said Lady Ascot.

"Then why the deuce did you ask me?"

That was a hard question to answer, but Lady Ascot said:

"I doubt if you are wise, James. I believe it would be better that she should go to Australia. It is a very good match for her."

"It is not a good match for her," said Lord Saltire testily. "To begin with, first-cousin marriages are an invention of the devil. Third and lastly, she shan't go to that infernal hole. Sixthly, I want her, now our Charles is dead, to marry John Marston; and, in conclusion, I mean to have my own way."

"Do you know," said Lady Ascot, "that he proposed to her before, and was rejected?"

"He told me of it the same night," said Lord Saltire. "Now, don't talk any more nonsense, but tell me this, is she bitten with that young fellow?"

"Not deeply, as yet, I think," said Lady Ascot.

"Which of them has the best chance?" said Lord Saltire.

"James," said Lady Ascot, repeating his own words, "do you know that sometimes you are intolerably foolish? How can I tell?"

"Which would you bet on, Miss Headstall?" asked Lord Saltire.

"Well, well!" said Lady Ascot, "I suppose I should bet on John Marston."

"And how long are you going to give Sebastopol, Lord Hainault?" said John Marston.

"What do you think about the Greek Kalends, my dear Marston?" said Lord Hainault.

"Why, no. I suppose we shall get it at last. It won't do to have it said that England and France——"

"Say France and England just now," said Lord Hainault.

"No, I will not. It must not be said that England and France could not take a Black Sea fortress."

"We shall have to say it, I fear," said Lord Hainault. "I am not quite sure that we English don't want a thrashing."

"I am sure we do," said Marston. "But we shall never get one. That is the worst of it."

"My dear Marston," said Lord Hainault, "you have a clear head. Will you tell me this: Do you believe that Charles Ravenshoe is dead?"

"God bless me, Lord Hainault, have you any doubts?"

"Yes."

"So have I," said Marston, turning eagerly towards him. "I thought you had all made up your minds. If there is any doubt, ought we not to mention it to Lord Saltire?"

"I think that he has doubts himself. I may tell you that he has secured to him, in case of his return, eighty thousand pounds."

"He would have made him his heir, I suppose," said John Marston; "would he not?"

"Yes; I think I am justified in saying yes."

"And so all the estates go to Lord Ascot in any case?"

"Unless in case of Charles's reappearance before his death; in which case, I believe he will alter his will."

"Then if Charles be alive, he had better keep out of Lord Ascot's way on dark nights, in narrow lanes," said John Marston.

"You are mistaken there," said Lord Hainault, thoughtfully. "Ascot is a bad fellow. I told him so once in public at the risk of getting an awful thrashing. If it had not been for Mainwaring, I should have had sore bones for a twelvemonth. But—but—well, I was at Eton with Ascot, and Ascot was and is a great blackguard. But, do you know, he is to some a very affectionate fellow. You know he was adored at Eton."

"He was not liked at Oxford," said Marston. "I never knew any good of him. He is a great rascal."

"Yes," said Lord Hainault, "I suppose he is what you would call a great rascal. Yes; I told him so, you know. And I am not a fighting man, and that proves that I was strongly convinced of the fact, or I should have shirked my duty. A man in my position don't like to go down to the House of Lords with a black eye. But I doubt if he is capable of any deep villany yet. If you were to say to me that Charles would be unwise to allow Ascot's wife to make his gruel for him, I should say that I agreed with you."

"There you are certainly right, my lord," said John Marston, smiling. "But I never knew Lord Ascot spare either man or woman."

"That is very true," said Lord Hainault. "Do you notice that we have been speaking as if Charles Ravenshoe were not dead?"

"I don't believe he is," said John Marston.

"Nor I, do you know," said Lord Hainault; "at least only half. What a pair of ninnies we are. Only ninety men of the 140th came out of that Balaclava charge. If he escaped the cholera, the chances are in favour of his having been killed there."

"What evidence have we that he enlisted in that regiment at all?"

"Lady Hainault's and Mary's description of his uniform, which they never distinctly saw for one moment," said Hainault. "*Violà tout.*"

"And you would not speak to Lord Saltire?"

"Why, no. He sees all that we see. If he comes back, he gets eighty thousand pounds. It would not do either for you or me to press him to alter his will. Do you see?"

"I suppose you are right, Lord Hainault. Things cannot go very wrong either way. I hope Mary will not fall in love with that cousin of hers," he added, with a laugh.

"Are you wise in persevering, do you think?" said Lord Hainault kindly.

"I will tell you in a couple of days," said John Marston. "Is there any chance of seeing that best of fellows, William Ravenshoe, here?"

"He may come tumbling up. He has put off his wedding in consequence of the death of his half-brother. I wonder if he was humbugged at Varna?"

"Nothing more likely," said Marston. "Where is Lord Welter?"

" In Paris—plucking geese."

Just about this time all the various groups in the drawing-room seemed to come to the conclusion that the time had arrived for new combinations, to avoid remarks. So there was a regular puss-in-the-corner business. John Marston went over to Mary; George Corby came to Lord Hainault; Lord Saltire went to Lady Hainault, who had Archy asleep in her lap; and Gus and Flora went to Lady Ascot.

" At last, old friend," said Mary to John Marston. " And I have been watching for you so long. I was afraid that the time would come for the children to go to bed, and that you would never come and speak to me."

" Lord Hainault and I were talking politics," said Marston. " That is why I did not come."

" Men must talk politics, I suppose," said Mary. " But I wish you had come while my cousin was here. He is so charming. You will like him."

" He seems to be a capital fellow," said Marston.

" Indeed he is," said Mary. " He is really the most lovable creature I have met for a long time. If you would take him up, and be kind to him, and show him life, from the side from which *you* see it, you would be doing a good work. And you would be obliging *me*. And I know, my dear friend, that you like to oblige me."

" Miss Corby, you know that I would die for you."

" I know it. Who better? It puzzles me to know what I have done to earn such kindness from you. But there it is. You will be kind to him."

Marston was partly pleased, and partly disappointed by this conversation. Would you like to guess why? Yes. Then I will leave you to do so, and save myself half a page of writing.

Only saying this, for the benefit of inexperienced novel-readers, that he was glad to hear her talk in that free and easy manner about her cousin; but would have been glad if she had not talked in that free and easy manner to himself. Nevertheless, there was evidently no harm done as yet. That was a great cause of congratulation; there was time yet.

Gus and Flora went over to Lady Ascot. Lady Ascot said, " My dears, is it not near bed-time ? " just by way of opening the conversation—nothing more.

" Lawks a mercy on me, no," said Flora. " Go along with you, do, you foolish thing."

" My dear ! my dear ! " said Lady Ascot.

"She is imitating old Alwright," explained Gus. "She told me she was going to. Lord Saltire says, 'Maria! Maria! Maria!—you are intolerably foolish, Maria!'"

"Don't be naughty, Gus," said Lady Ascot.

"Well, so he did, for I heard him. Don't mind us; we don't mean any harm. I say, Lady Ascot, has she any right to bite and scratch?"

"Who?" said Lady Ascot.

"Why, that Flora. She bit Alwright because she wouldn't lend her Mrs. Moko."

"Oh, you dreadful fib!" said Flora. "Oh, you wicked boy, you know where you'll go to if you tell such stories. Lady Ascot, I didn't bite her; I only said she ought to be bit. She told me that she couldn't let me have Mrs. Moko, because she was trying caps on her. And then she told nurse that I should never have her again, because I squeezed her flat. And so she told a story. And it was not I who squeezed her flat, but that boy, who is worse than Ananias and Sapphira. And I made a bogey of her in the nursery door, with a broom and a counterpane, just as he was coming in. And he shut the door on her head and squeezed a piece of paint off her nose as big as half a crown."

Lady Ascot was relieved by being informed that the Mrs. Moko, aforesaid, was only a pasteboard image, the size of life, used by the lady's maid for fitting caps.

There were many evenings like this; a week or so passed without any change. At last, there was a move towards London.

The first who took flight was George Corby. He was getting dissatisfied, in his sleepy semi-tropical way, with the state of affairs. It was evident that, since John Marston's arrival, he had been playing, with regard to Mary, second fiddle (if you can possibly be induced to pardon the extreme coarseness of the expression). One day, Lord Saltire asked him to take him for a drive. They went over to dismantled Ranford, and Lord Saltire was more amusing than ever. As they drove up through the dense larch plantation, on the outskirt of the park, they saw Marston and Mary side by side. George Corby bit his lip.

"I suppose there is something there, my lord?" said he.

"Oh dear, yes; I hope so," said Lord Saltire. "Oh, yes, that is a very old affair."

So George Corby went first. He did not give up all hopes of being successful, but he did not like the way things were going. His English expedition was not quite so pleasant as he intended it to be. He, poor fellow, was desperately in love, and his suit did not seem likely to prosper. He was inclined to be angry with Lord Saltire. He should not have let things go so far, thought George, without letting him know; quite forgetting that the mischief was done before Lord Saltire's arrival.

Lord Saltire and John Marston moved next. Lord Saltire had thought it best to take his man Simpson's advice and move into his house in Curzon Street. He had asked John to come with him.

"It is a very nice little house," he said; "deuced well aired, and that sort of thing; but I know I shall have a creeping in my back when I go back for the first week, and fancy there is a draught. This will make me peevish. I don't like to be peevish to my servants, because it is unfair; they can't answer one. I wish you would come and let me be peevish to you. You may just as well. It will do you good. You have got a fancy for disciplining yourself, and all that sort of thing; and you will find me capital practice for a week or so, in a fresh house. After that I shall get amiable, and then you may go. You may have the use of my carriage, to go and attend to your poor man's plaster business in Southwark, if you like. I am not nervous about fever or vermin. Besides, it may amuse me to hear all about it. And you can bring that cracked uncle of yours to see me sometimes; his Scriptural talk is very piquant."

Lord and Lady Hainault moved up into Grosvenor Square, too, for Parliament was going to meet rather early. They persuaded Lady Ascot to come and stay with them.

After a few days, William made his appearance. "Well, my dear Ravenshoe," said Lord Hainault, "and what brings you to town?"

"I don't know," said William. "I cannot stay down there. Lord Hainault, do you know I think I am going cracked?"

"Why, my dear fellow, what do you mean?"

"I have got such a strange fancy in my head, I cannot rest."

"What is your fancy?" said Lord Hainault. "Stay; may I make a guess at it?"

"You would never dream what it is. It is too mad."

"I will guess," said Lord Hainault. "Your fancy is this:— You believe that Charles Ravenshoe is alive, and you have come up to London to take your chance of finding him in the streets."

"But, good God!" said William, "how have you found this out? I have never told it even to my own sweetheart."

"Because," said Lord Hainault, laying his hand on his shoulder, "I and John Marston have exactly the same fancy. That is why."

And Charles so close to them all the time. Creeping every day across the park to see the coachman and his son. Every day getting more hopeless. All energy gone. Wit enough left to see that he was living on the charity of the cornet. There were some splinters in his arm which would not come away, and kept him restless. He never slept now. He hesitated when he was spoken to. Any sudden noise made him start and look wild. I will not go on with the symptoms. Things were much worse with him than we have ever seen them before. He, poor lad, began to wonder whether it would come to him to die in a hospital, or——

Those cursed bridges! Why did they build such things? Who built them? The devil. To tempt ruined desperate men, with ten thousand fiends gnawing and sawing in their deltoid muscles, night and day. Suppose he had to cross one of these by night, would he ever get to the other side? Or would angels from heaven come down and hold him back?

The cornet and his mother had a conversation about him. Bawled the cornet into the ear-trumpet:

"My fellow Simpson is very bad, mother. He is getting low and nervous, and I don't like the looks of him."

"I remarked it myself," said the lady. "We had better have Bright. It would be cheaper to pay five guineas and get a good opinion at once."

"I expect he wants a surgeon more than a doctor," said the cornet.

"Well, that is the doctor's business," said the old lady. "Drop a line to Bright and see what he says. It would be a burning shame, my dear—enough to bring down the wrath of God upon us—if we were to let him want for anything so long as we have money. And we have plenty of money. More than we want. And if it annoys him to go near the horses, we must pension him. But I would rather let him believe that he was earning his wages, because it might be a weight on his mind if he did not. See to it the first thing in the morning. Remember Balaclava, John! Remember Balaclava! If you forget Balaclava, and what trooper Simpson did for you there, you are tempting God to forget you."

"I hope He may when I do, mother," shouted the cornet. "I remember Balaclava—ay, and Devna before."

There are such people as these in the world, reader. I know some of them. I know a great many of them. So many of them, in fact, that this conclusion has been forced upon me—that the world is *not* entirely peopled by rogues and fools ; nay, more, that the rogues and fools form a contemptible minority. I may become unpopular, I may be sneered at by men who think themselves wiser, for coming to such a conclusion ; but I will not retract what I have said. The good people in the world outnumber the bad, ten to one, and the ticket for this sort of belief is "Optimist."

This conversation between the cornet and his mother took place at half-past two. At that time Charles had crept across the park to the mews, near Belgrave Square, to see his friend the duke's coachman and his son. May I be allowed, without being accused of writing a novel in the "confidential style," to tell you, that this is the most important day in the whole story.

At half-past two, William Ravenshoe called at Lord Hainault's house in Grosvenor Square. He saw Lady Ascot. Lady Ascot asked him what sort of weather it was out of doors.

William said that there was a thick fog near the river, but that on the north side of the square it was pleasant. So Lady Ascot said she would like a walk, if it were only for ten minutes, if he would give her his arm ; and out they went.

Mary and the children came out too, but they went into the square. Lady Ascot and William walked slowly up and down the pavement alone, for Lady Ascot liked to see the people.

Up and down the north side, in front of the house. At the second turn, when they were within twenty yards of the west end of the square, a tall man with an umbrella over his shoulder came round the corner, and leant against the lamp-post. They both knew him in an instant. It was Lord Ascot. He had not seen them. He had turned to look at a great long-legged chesnut that was coming down the street, from the right, with a human being on his back. The horse was desperately vicious, but very beautiful and valuable. The groom on his back was neither beautiful nor valuable, and was losing his temper with the horse. The horse was one of those horses vicious by nature—such a horse as Rarey (all honour to him) can terrify into submission for a short time ; and the groom was a groom, not one of our country lads, every one of whose virtues and vices have been discussed over and over again at the squire's dinner-table, or about whom the rector had scratched his head, and had into his study for private exhortation or encouragement. Not one of the minority. One of the majority, I fear very much. Reared, like a dog, among the straw, without education, without religion, without self-respect—worse broke than the horse he rode. When I think of all that was said against grooms and stable-helpers during the Rarey fever, I get very angry, I confess it. One man said to me, "When we have had a groom or two killed, we shall have our horses treated properly." Look to your grooms, gentlemen, and don't allow such a blot on the fair fame of England as some racing stables much longer, or there will be a heavy reckoning against you when the books are balanced.

But the poor groom lost his temper with the horse, and beat it over the head. And Lord Ascot stayed to say, "D—— it all, man, you will never do any good like that," though a greater fiend on horseback than Lord Ascot I never saw.

This gave time for Lady Ascot to say, "Come on, my dear Ravenshoe, and let us speak to him." So on they went. Lord Ascot was so busy looking at the horse and groom, that they got close behind him before he saw them. Nobody being near, Lady Ascot, with a sparkle of her old fun, poked him in the back with her walking-stick. Lord Ascot turned sharply and angrily round, with his umbrella raised for a blow.

When he saw who it was he burst out into a pleasant laugh, "Now, you grandma," he said, "you keep that old stick of yours quiet, or you'll get into trouble. What do you mean by assaulting the head of the house in the public streets ? I am ashamed of you. You, Ravenshoe, you egged her on to do it. I shall have to punch your head before I have done. How are you both ? "

"And where have you been, you naughty boy ? " said Lady Ascot.

"At Paris," said that ingenuous nobleman, "dicing and brawling as usual. Nobody can accuse me of hiding *my* talents in a napkin, grandma. Those two things are all I am fit for, and I certainly do them with a will. I have fought a duel, too. A Yankee Doodle got it into his head that he might be impertinent to Adelaide ; so I took him out and shot him. Don't cry, now. He is not dead. He'll walk lame though, I fancy, for a time. How jolly it is to catch you out here ! I dread meeting that insufferable prig, Hainault, for fear I should kick him. Give me her arm, my dear Ravenshoe."

"And where is Adelaide ? " said Lady Ascot.

"Up at St. John's Wood," said he. "Do steal away, and

come and see her. Grandma, I was very sorry to hear of poor Charles's death—I was indeed. You know what it has done for me; but, by Gad, I was very sorry."

"Dear Welter—dear Ascot," said Lady Ascot, "I am sure you were sorry. Oh! if you would repent, my own dear. If you would think of the love that Christ bore you when He died for you. Oh, Ascot, Ascot! will nothing save you from the terrible hereafter?"

"I am afraid not, grandma," said Lord Ascot. "It is getting too cold for you to stay out. Ravenshoe, my dear fellow, take her in."

And so, after a kind good-bye, Lord Ascot walked away towards the south-west.

I am afraid that John Marston was right. I am afraid he spoke the truth when he said that Lord Ascot was a savage, untameable blackguard.

CHAPTER LIX

LORD ASCOT'S CROWNING ACT OF FOLLY

LORD ASCOT, with his umbrella over his shoulder, swung on down the street, south-westward. The town was pleasant in the higher parts, and so he felt inclined to prolong his walk. He turned to the right into Park Lane.

He was a remarkable-looking man. So tall, so broad, with such a mighty chest, and such a great, red, hairless, cruel face above it, that people, when he paused to look about him, as he did at each street corner, turned to look at him. He did not notice it; he was used to it. And, besides, as he walked there were two or three words ringing yet in his ears which made him look less keenly than usual after the handsome horses and pretty faces which he met in his walk.

"Oh, Ascot, Ascot! will nothing save you from the terrible hereafter?"

"Confound those old women, more particularly when they take to religion. Always croaking. And grandma Ascot, too, as plucky and good an old soul as any in England—as good a judge of a horse as William Day—taking to that sort of thing. Hang it! it was unendurable. It was bad taste, you know, putting such ideas into a fellow's head. London was dull enough after Paris, without that."

So thought Lord Ascot, as he stood in front of Dudley House, and looked southward. The winter sun was feebly shining where he was, but to the south there was a sea of fog, out of which rose the Wellington statue, looking more exasperating than ever, and the two great houses at the Albert Gate.

"This London is a beastly hole," said he. "I have got to go down into that cursed fog. I wish Tattersall's was anywhere else." But he shouldered his umbrella again, and on he went.

Opposite St. George's Hospital there were a number of medical students. Two of them, regardless of the order which should always be kept on Her Majesty's highway, were wrestling. Lord Ascot paused for a moment to look at them. He heard one of the students who were looking on say to another, evidently about himself—

"By Gad! what preparations that fellow would cut up into."

"Ah!" said another, "and wouldn't he cuss and d—— under the operation neither."

"I know who that is," said a third. "That's Lord Ascot; the most infernal, headlong, gambling savage in the three kingdoms."

So Lord Ascot, in the odour of sanctity, passed down into Tattersall's yard. There was no one in the rooms. He went out into the yard again.

"Hullo, you sir! Have you seen Mr. Sloane?"

"Mr. Sloane was here not ten minutes ago, my lord. He thought your lordship was not coming. He is gone down to the Groom's Arms."

"Where the deuce is that?"

"In Chapel Street, at the corner of the mews, my lord. Fust turning on the right, my lord."

Lord Ascot had business with our old acquaintance, Mr. Sloane, and went on. When he came to the public-house mentioned (the very same one in which the Servants' Club was held, to which Charles belonged), he went into the bar, and asked of a feeble-minded girl, left accidentally in charge of the bar—"Where was Mr. Sloane?" And she said, "Upstairs, in the club-room."

Lord Ascot walked up to the club-room, and looked in at the glass door. And there he saw Sloane. He was standing up, with his hand on a man's shoulder, who had a map before him. Right and left of these two men were two other men, an old one and a young one, and the four faces were close together; and while he watched them the man with the map before him looked up, and Lord Ascot saw Charles Ravenshoe, pale and wan, looking like death itself, but still Charles Ravenshoe in the body.

He did not open the door. He turned away, went down into the street, and set his face northward.

So he was alive, and—— There were more things to follow that "and" than he had time to think of at first. He had a cunning brain, Lord Ascot, but he could not get at his position at first. The whole business was too unexpected—he had not time to realize it.

The afternoon was darkening as he turned his steps north-wards, and began to walk rapidly, with scowling face and compressed lips. One or two of the students still lingered on the steps of the hospital. The one who had mentioned him by name before said to his fellows, "Look at that Lord Ascot. What a devil he looks. He has lost some money. Gad! there'll be murder done to-night. They oughtn't to let such fellows go loose!"

Charles Ravenshoe alive. And Lord Saltire's will. Half a million of money. And Charley Ravenshoe, the best old cock in the three kingdoms. Of all his villanies—and, God forgive him, they were many—the one that weighed heaviest on his heart was his treatment of Charles. And now——

The people turned and looked after him as he hurried along. Why did his wayward feet carry him to the corner of Curzon Street? That was not his route to St. John's Wood. The people stared at the great red-faced giant, who paused against the lamp-post irresolute, biting his upper lip till the blood came.

How would they have stared if they had seen what I see.[1]

There were two angels in the street that wretched winter afternoon, who had followed Lord Ascot in his headlong course, and paused here. He could see them but dimly, or only guess at their existence, but I can see them plainly enough.

One was a white angel, beautiful to look at, who stood a little way off, beckoning to him, and pointing towards Lord Saltire's house; and the other was black, with its face hid in a hood, who was close beside him, and kept saying in his ear, "Half a million! half a million!"

[1] Perhaps a reference to "The Wild Huntsman" will stop all criticism at this point. A further reference to "Faust" will also show that I am in good company.

A strange apparition in Curzon Street, at four o'clock on a January afternoon! Gibbon lays great stress on no contemporary historian having noticed the darkness at the Crucifixion. If you search the files of the papers at this period, you will find no notice of any remarkable atmospheric phenomena in Curzon Street that afternoon. But two angels were there nevertheless, and Lord Ascot had a dim suspicion of it.

A dim suspicion of it! How could it be otherwise, when he heard a voice in one ear repeating Lady Ascot's last words, "What can save you from the terrible hereafter?" and in the other the stealthy whisper of the fiend, "Half a million! half a million!"

He paused only for a moment, and then headed northward again. The black angel was at his ear, but the white one was close to him—so close, that when his own door opened, the three passed in together. Adelaide, standing under the chandelier in the hall, saw nothing of the two spirits; only her husband, scowling fiercely.

She was going upstairs to dress, but she paused. As soon as Lord Ascot's "confidential scoundrel," before mentioned, had left the hall, she came up to him, and in a whisper, for she knew the man was listening, said—

"What is the matter, Welter?"

He looked as if he would have pushed her out of the way. But he did not. He said—

"I have seen Charles Ravenshoe."

"When?"

"To-night."

"Good God! Then it is almost a matter of time with us," said Adelaide. "I had a dim suspicion of this, Ascot. It is horrible. We are ruined."

"Not yet," said Lord Ascot.

"There is time—time. He is obstinate and mad. Lord Saltire might die——"

"Well?"

"Either of them," she hissed out. "Is there no——"

"No what?"

"There is half a million of money," said Adelaide.

"Well?"

"All sorts of things happen to people."

Lord Ascot looked at her for an instant, and snarled out a curse at her.

John Marston was perfectly right. He was a savage, untameable blackguard. He went upstairs into his bed-room.

The two angels were with him. They are with all of us at
such times as these. There is no plagiarism here. The
fact is too old for that.

Up and down, up and down. The bed-room was not long
enough; so he opened the door of the dressing-room; and
that was not long enough; and so he opened the door of what
had been the nursery in a happier household than his; and
walked up and down through them all. And Adelaide sat
below, before a single candle, with pale face and clenched lips,
listening to his footfall on the floor above.

She knew as well as if an angel had told her what was
passing in his mind as he walked up and down. She had
foreseen this crisis plainly—you may laugh at me, but she had.
She had seen that if, by any wild conjunction of circumstances,
Charles Ravenshoe were alive, and if he were to come across
him before Lord Saltire's death, events would arrange themselves exactly as they were doing on this terrible evening.
There was something awfully strange in the realization of her
morbid suspicions.

Yes, she had seen thus far, and had laughed at herself for
entertaining such mad fancies. But she had seen no further.
What the upshot would be was hidden from her like a dark
veil. Black and impenetrable as the fog which was hanging
over Waterloo Bridge at that moment, which made the squalid
figure of a young, desperate girl show like a pale, fluttering
ghost, leading a man whom we know well, a man who followed
her, on the road to—what?

The rest, though, seemed to be, in some sort, in her own
hands. Wealth, position in the world, the power of driving
her chariot over the necks of those who had scorned her—the
only things for which her worthless heart cared—were all at
stake. "He will murder me," she said, "*but he shall hear me.*"

Still, up and down, over head, his heavy footfall went to and fro.

Seldom, in any man's life, comes such a trial as his this
night. A good man might have been hard tried in such
circumstances. What hope can we have of a desperate
blackguard like Lord Ascot? He knew Lord Saltire hated
him; he knew that Lord Saltire had only left his property
to him because he thought Charles Ravenshoe was dead; and
yet he hesitated whether or no he should tell Lord Saltire that
he had seen Charles and ruin himself utterly.

Was he such an utter rascal as John Marston made him
out? Would such a rascal have hesitated long? What could
make a man without a character, without principle, without a

care about the world's opinion, hesitate at such a time as
this? I cannot tell you.

He was not used to think about things logically or calmly;
and so, as he paced up and down, it was some time before he
actually arranged his thoughts. Then he came to this conclusion, and put it fairly before him—that, if he let Lord
Saltire know that Charles Ravenshoe was alive, he was
ruined ; and that, if he did not, he was a villain.

Let us give the poor profligate wretch credit for getting
even so far as this. There was no attempt to gloss over the
facts and deceive himself. He put the whole matter honestly
before him.

He would be a fool if he told Lord Saltire. He would
be worse than a fool, a madman—there was no doubt about
that. It was not to be thought about.

But Charles Ravenshoe !

How pale the dear old lad looked. What a kind, gentle
old face it was. How well he could remember the first time
he ever saw him. At Twyford, yes; and, that very same
visit, how he ran across the billiard-room, and asked him who
Lord Saltire was. Yes. What jolly times there were down in
Devonshire, too. Those Claycomb hounds wanted pace, but
they were full fast enough for the country. And what a
pottering old rascal Charley was among the stone walls.
Rode through. Yes. And how he'd mow over a woodcock.
Fire slap through a holly bush. Ha !

And suppose they proved this previous marriage. Why,
then he would be back at Ravenshoe, and all things would be
as they were. But suppose they couldn't——

Lord Ascot did not know that eighty thousand pounds were
secured to Charles.

By Gad ! it was horrible to think of. That it should be
thrown on him, of all men, to stand between old Charley
and his due. If it were any other man but him——

Reader, if you do not know that a man will act from
"sentiment " long, long years after he has thrown "principle "
to the winds, you had better pack up your portmanteau, and go
and live five years or more among Australian convicts and
American rowdies, as a friend of mine did. The one long out-
lives the other. The incarnate devils who beat out poor Price's
brains with their shovels, when they had the gallows before
them, consistently perjured themselves in favour of the
youngest of the seven, the young fiend who had hounded
them on.

Why there never was such a good fellow as that Charley.
That Easter vacation—hey! Among the bargees, hang it,
what a game it was—— I won't follow out his recollections
here any further. Skittle-playing and fighting are all very
well; but one may have too much of them.

"I might still do this," thought Lord Ascot: "I might——"

At this moment he was opposite the dressing-room door.
It was opened, and Adelaide stood before him.

Beautiful and terrible, with a look which her husband had,
as yet, only seen shadowed dimly—a look which he felt might
come there some day, but which he had never seen yet. The
light of her solitary candle shone upon her pale face, her
gleaming eyes and her clenched lip; and he saw what was
written there, and for one moment quailed.

("If you were to say to me," said Lord Hainault once,
"that Charles would be unwise to let Ascot's wife make his
gruel for him, I should agree with you.")

Only for one moment! Then he turned on her and cursed
her.

"What, in the name of Hell, do you want here at *this*
moment?"

"You may murder me if you like, Ascot; but, before you
have time to do that, you shall hear what I have got to say.
I have been listening to your footsteps for a weary hour, and
I heard irresolution in every one of them. Ascot, don't be a
madman!"

"I shall be soon, if you come at such a time as this,
and look like that. If my face were to take the same
expression as yours has now, Lady Ascot, these would be
dangerous quarters for you."

"I know that," said she. "I knew all that before I came
up here to-night, Ascot. Ascot, half a million of money——"

"Why, all the devils in the pit have been singing that tune
for an hour past. Have you only endangered your life to add
your little pipe to theirs?"

"I have. Won't you hear me?"

"No. Go away."

"Are you going to do it."

"Most likely not. You had better go away."

"You might give him a hundred thousand pounds, you
know, Ascot. Four thousand a year. The poor dear fellow
would worship you for your generosity. He is a very good
fellow, Ascot."

"You had better go away," said he quietly.

"Not without a promise, Ascot. Think——"

"Now go away. This is the last warning I give you. Madwoman!"

"But, Ascot——"

"Take care; it will be too late for both of us in another moment."

She caught his eye for the first time, and fled for her life. She ran down into the drawing-room, and threw herself into a chair. "God preserve me!" she said; "I have gone too far with him. Oh, this lonely house!"

Every drop of blood in her body seemed to fly to her heart. There were footsteps outside the door. Oh, God! have mercy on her; he was following her.

Where are the two angels now, I wonder?

He opened the door, and came towards her slowly. If mortal agony can atone for sin, she atoned for all her sins in that terrible half-minute. She did not cry out; she dared not; she writhed down among the gaudy cushions, with her face buried in her hands, and waited—for what?

She heard a voice speaking to her. It was not his voice, but the kind voice of old Lord Ascot, his dead father. It said—

"Adelaide, my poor girl, you must not get frightened when I get in a passion. My poor child, you have borne enough for me; I would not hurt a hair of your head."

He kissed her cheek, and Adelaide burst into a passion of sobs. After a few moments those sobs had ceased, and Lord Ascot left her. He did not know that she had fainted away. She never told him that.

Where were the angels now? Angels?—there was but one of them left. Which one was that, think you?

Hurrah! the good angel. The black fiend with the hood had sneaked away to his torment. And, as Lord Ascot closed the door behind him, and sped away down the foggy street the good one vanished too; for the work was done. Ten thousand fiends would not turn him from his purpose now. Hurrah!

*　　　*　　　*　　　*　　　*　　　*

"Simpson," said Lord Saltire, as he got into bed that evening, "it won't last much longer."

"What will not last, my lord?" said Simpson.

"Why, me," said Lord Saltire, disregarding grammar. "Don't set up a greengrocer's shop, Simpson, nor a butter and egg shop, in Berkeley Street, if you can help it, Simpson. If you must keep a lodging-house, I should say Jermyn Street;

but don't let me influence you. I am not sure that I wouldn't sooner see you in Brook Street, or Conduit Street. But don't try Pall Mall, that's a good fellow; or you'll be getting fast men, who will demoralize your establishment. A steady connexion among government clerks and that sort of person will pay best in the long run."

"My dear lord—my good old friend, why should you talk like this to-night?"

"Because I am very ill, Simpson, and it will all come at once; and it may come any time. When they open Lord Barkham's room, at Cottingdean, I should like you and Mr. Marston to go in first, for I may have left something or another about."

An hour or two after, his bell rang, and Simpson, who was in the dressing-room, came hurriedly in. He was sitting up in bed, looking just the same as usual.

"My dear fellow," he said, "go down and find out who rung and knocked at the door like that. Did you hear it?"

"I did not notice it, my lord."

"Butchers, and bakers, and that sort of people, don't knock and ring like that. The man at the door now brings news, Simpson. There is no mistake about the ring of a man who comes with important intelligence. Go down and see."

He was not long gone. When he came back again, he said:

"It is Lord Ascot, my lord. He insists on seeing you immediately."

"Up with him, Simpson—up with him, my good fellow. I told you so. This gets interesting."

Lord Ascot was already in the doorway. Lord Saltire's brain was as acute as ever; and, as Lord Ascot approached him, he peered eagerly and curiously at him, in the same way as one scrutinizes the seal of an unopened letter, and wonders what its contents may be. Lord Ascot sat down by the bed, and whispered to the old man; and, when Simpson saw his great coarse, red, hairless, ruffianly face actually touching that of Lord Saltire, so delicate, so refined, so keen, Simpson began to have a dim suspicion that he was looking on rather a remarkable sight. And so he was.

"Lord Saltire," said Lord Ascot, "I have seen Charles Ravenshoe to-night."

"You are quite sure?"

"I am quite sure."

"Ha! Ring the bell, Simpson." Before any one had

spoken again, a footman was in the room. "Bring the major-domo here instantly," said Lord Saltire.

"You know what you have done, Ascot," said Lord Saltire. "You see what you have done. I am going to send for my solicitor, and alter my will."

"Of course you are," said Lord Ascot. "Do you dream I did not know that before I came here?"

"And yet you came?"

"Yes; with all the devils out of hell dragging me back."

"As a matter of curiosity, why?" said Lord Saltire.

"Oh, I couldn't do it, you know. I've done a good many dirty things; but I couldn't do that, particularly to that man. There are some things a fellow can't do, you know."

"Where did you see him?"

"At the Groom's Arms, Belgrave Mews; he was there not three hours ago. Find a man called Sloane, a horsedealer; he will tell you all about him; for he was sitting with his hand on his shoulder. His address is twenty-seven, New Road."

At this time the major-domo appeared. "Take a cab at once and *fetch* me—you understand when I say *fetch*—Mr. Brogden, my solicitor. Mr. Compton lives out of town, but he lives over the office in Lincoln's Inn. If you can get hold of the senior partner, he will do as well. Put either of them in a cab and pack them off here. Then go to Scotland Yard; give my compliments to Inspector Field; tell him a horrible murder has been committed, accompanied by arson, forgery, and regrating, with a strong suspicion of sorning, and that he must come at once."

The venerable gentleman disappeared, and then Lord Saltire said,

"Do you repent, Ascot?"

"No," said he. "D—— it all, you know, I could not do it when I came to think of it. The money would never have stayed with me, I take it. Good-night."

"Good-night," said Lord Saltire; "come the first thing in the morning."

And so they parted. Simpson said, "Are you going to alter your will to-night, my lord? Won't it be a little too much for you?"

"It would be if I was going to do so, Simpson; but I am not going to touch a line of it. I am not sure that half a million of money was ever, in the history of the world, given up with better grace or with less reason. He is a noble fellow;

I never guessed it; he shall have it—by Jove, he shall have it !
I am going to sleep. Apologise to Brogden, and give the
information to Field; tell him I expect Charles Ravenshoe
here to-morrow morning. Good-night."

Simpson came in to open the shutters next morning; but
those shutters were not opened for ten days, for Lord Saltire
was dead.

Dead. The delicate waxen right hand, covered with rings,
was lying outside on the snow-white sheet, which was
unwrinkled by any death agony; and on the pillow was a
face, beautiful always, but now more beautiful, more calm,
more majestic than ever. If his first love, dead so many
years, had met him in the streets but yesterday, she would
not have known him; but if she could have looked one
moment on the face which lay on that pillow, she would
have seen once more the gallant young nobleman who came
a-wooing under the lime-trees sixty years agone.

The inspector was rapid and dexterous in his work. He
was on Charles Ravenshoe's trail like a bloodhound, eager
to redeem the credit which his coadjutor, Yard, had lost
over the same case. But his instructions came to him three
hours too late.

CHAPTER LX

THE BRIDGE AT LAST

THE group which Lord Ascot had seen through the glass doors
consisted of Charles, the coachman's son, the coachman, and
Mr. Sloane. Charles and the coachman's son had got hold
of a plan of the battle of Balaclava, from the *Illustrated
London News*, and were explaining the whole thing to the
two older men, to their great delight. The four got enthusiastic and prolonged the talk for some time; and, when it
began to flag, Sloane said he must go home, and so they
came down into the bar.

Here a discussion arose about the feeding of cavalry horses,
in which all four were perfectly competent to take part. The
two young men were opposed in argument to the two elder ones,
and they were having a right pleasant chatter about the corn or
hay question in the bar, when the swing doors were pushed open,

and a girl entered and looked round with that bold, insolent expression one only sees among a certain class.

A tawdry, draggled-looking girl, finely enough dressed, but with everything awry and dirty. Her face was still almost beautiful; but the cheekbones were terribly prominent, and the hectic patch of red on her cheeks, and the parched, cracked lips, told of pneumonia developing into consumption.

Such a figure had probably never appeared in that decent, aristocratic public-house, called the Groom's Arms, since it had got its licence. The four men ceased their argument and turned to look at her; and the coachman, a family man with daughters, said "Poor thing!"

With a brazen, defiant look she advanced to the bar. The barmaid, a very beautiful, quiet-looking, London-bred girl, advanced towards her, frightened at such a wild tawdry apparition, and asked her mechanically what she would please to take.

"I don't want nothing to drink, miss," said the girl; "least ways, I've got no money; but I want to ask a question. I say, miss, you couldn't give a poor girl one of them sandwiches, could you? You would never miss it, you know."

The barmaid's father, the jolly landlord, eighteen stone of good humour, was behind his daughter now. "Give her a porkpie, Jane, and a glass of ale, my girl."

"God Almighty bless you, sir, and keep her from the dark places where the devil lies a-waiting. I didn't come here to beg—it was only when I see them sandwiches that it came over me—I come here to ask a question. I know it ain't no use. But you can't see him—can't see him—can't see him," she continued, sobbing wildly, "rattling his poor soul away, and not do as he asked you. I didn't come to get out for a walk. I sat there patient three days, and would have sat there till the end, but he would have me come. And so I came; and I must get back—get back."

The landlord's daughter brought her some food, and as her eyes gleamed with wolfish hunger, she stopped speaking. It was a strange group. She in the centre, tearing at her food in a way terrible to see. Behind, the calm face of the landlord, looking on her with pity and wonder; and his pretty daughter, with her arm round his waist, and her head on his bosom, with tears in her eyes. Our four friends stood to the right, silent and curious—a remarkable group enough; for neither the duke's coachman, nor Mr. Sloane, who formed the background, were exactly ordinary-looking men; and in front of them were

Charles and the coachman's son, who had put his hand on Charles's right shoulder, and was peering over his left at the poor girl, so that the two faces were close together—the one handsome and pale, with the mouth hidden by a moustache ; the other, Charles, wan and wild, with the lips parted in eager curiosity, and the chin thrust slightly forward.

In a few minutes the girl looked round on them. "I said I'd come here to ask a question ; and I must ask it and get back. There was a gentleman's groom used to use this house, and I want him. His name was Charles Horton. If you, sir, or if any of these gentlemen, know where I can find him, in God Almighty's name tell me this miserable night."

Charles was pale before, but he grew more deadly pale now ; his heart told him something was coming. His comrade, the coachman's son, held his hand tighter still on his shoulder and looked in his face. Sloane and the coachman made an exclamation.

Charles said quietly, "My poor girl, I am the man you are looking for. What, in God's name, do you want with me ?" and, while he waited for her to answer, he felt all the blood in his body going towards his heart.

"Little enough," she said. "Do you mind a little shoe-black boy as used to stand by St. Peter's Church ?"

"Do I ?" said Charles, coming towards her. "Yes, I do. My poor little lad. You don't mean to say that you know anything about him ?"

"I am his sister, sir ; and he is dying ; and he says he won't die not till you come. And I come off to see if I could find you. Will you come with me and see him ?"

"Will I come ?" said Charles. "Let us go at once. My little monkey. Dying, too !"

"Poor little man," said the coachman. "A many times I've heard you speak of him. Let's all go."

Mr. Sloane and his son seconded this motion.

"You mustn't come," said the girl. "There's a awful row in the court to-night ; that's the truth. He's safe enough with me ; but if you come, they'll think a mob's being raised. Now, don't talk of coming."

"You had better let me go alone," said Charles. "I feel sure that it would not be right for more of us to follow this poor girl than she chooses. I am ready."

And so he followed the girl out into the darkness ; and, as soon as they were outside, she turned and said to him,

"You'd best follow me from a distance. I'll tell you why :

I expect the police wants me, and you might get into trouble from being with me.   Remember, if I am took, it's Marquis Court, Little Marjoram Street, and it's the end house, exactly opposite you as you go in.   If you stands at the archway, and sings out for Miss Ophelia Flanigan, she'll come to you.   But if the row ain't over, you wait till they're quiet.   Whatever you do, don't venture in by yourself, however quiet it may look : sing out for her."

And so she fluttered away through the fog, and he followed, walking fast to keep her in sight.

It was a dreadful night.   The fog had lifted, and a moaning wind had arisen, with rain from the south-west.   A wild, dripping, melancholy night, without rain enough to make one think of physical discomfort, and without wind enough to excite one.

The shoeblacks and the crossing-sweepers were shouldering their brooms and their boxes, and were plodding homewards. The costermongers were letting their barrows stand in front of the public-houses, while they went in to get something to drink, and were discussing the price of vegetables there, and being fetched out by dripping policemen for obstructing Her Majesty's highway.   The beggars were gathering their rags together, and posting homewards ; let us charitably suppose, to their bit of fish, with guinea-fowl and sea-kale afterwards, or possibly, for it was not late in February, to their boiled pheasant and celery sauce. Every one was bound for shelter but the policemen.   And Charles—poor, silly, obstinate Charles, with an earl's fortune waiting for him, dressed as a groom, pale, wan, and desperate— was following a ruined girl, more desperate even than he, towards the bridge.

Yes ; this is the darkest part of my whole story.   Since his misfortunes he had let his mind dwell a little too much on these bridges.   There are very few men without a cobweb of some sort in their heads, more or less innocent.   Charles had a cobweb in his head now.   The best of men might have a cobweb in his head after such a terrible breakdown in his affairs as he had suffered ; more especially if he had three or four splinters of bone in his deltoid muscle, which had prevented his sleeping for three nights.   But I would sooner that any friend of mine should at such times take to any form of folly (such even as having fifty French clocks in the room, and discharging the butler if they did not all strike at once, as one good officer and brave fellow did) rather than get to thinking about bridges after dark, with the foul water lapping and swirling about the piers. I have hinted to you about this crochet of poor Charles for a long time; I was forced to do so. I think the less we say about it the better. I call you to witness that I have not said more about it than was necessary.

At the end of Arabella Row, the girl stopped, and looked back for him. The mews' clock was overhead, a broad orb of light in the dark sky. Ten minutes past ten. Lord Ascot was sitting beside Lord Saltire's bed, and Lord Saltire had rung the bell to send for Inspector Field.

She went on, and he followed her along the Mall. She walked fast, and he had hard work to keep her in sight. He saw her plainly enough whenever she passed a lamp. Her shadow was suddenly thrown at his feet, and then swept in a circle to the right, till it overtook her, and then passed her, and grew dim till she came to another lamp, and then came back to his feet, and passed on to her again, beckoning him on to follow her, and leading her—whither?

How many lamps were there? One, two, three, four; and then a man lying asleep on a bench in the rain, who said, with a wild, wan face, when the policeman roused him and told him to go home, "My home is in the Thames, friend; but I shall not go there to-night, or perhaps to-morrow."

"His home was in the Thames." The Thames, the dear old happy river. The wonder and delight of his boyhood. That was the river that slept in crystal green depths, under the tumbled boulders fallen from the chalk cliff, where the ivy, the oak, and the holly grew; and then went spouting, and raging, and roaring through the weirs at Casterton, where he and Welter used to bathe, and where he lay and watched kind Lord Ascot spinning patiently through one summer afternoon, till he killed the eight-pound trout at sun-down.

That was the dear old Thames. But that was fifty miles up the river, and ages ago. Now, and here, the river had got foul, and lapped about hungrily among piles, and barges, and the buttresses of bridges. And lower down it ran among mud banks. And there was a picture of one of them by dear old H. K. Browne, and you didn't see at first what it was that lay among the sedges, because the face was reversed, and the limbs were——

They passed in the same order through Spring Gardens into the Strand. And then Charles found it more troublesome than ever to follow the poor girl in her rapid walk. There were so many like her there: but she walked faster than any of them. Before he came to the street which leads to Waterloo Bridge, he thought he had lost her; but when he turned the corner, and as the dank wind smote upon his face, he came upon her, waiting for him.

And so they went on across the bridge. They walked together now. Was she frightened, too?

When they reached the other end of the bridge, she went on again to show the way. A long way on past the Waterloo Station, she turned to the left. They passed out of a broad, low, noisy street, into other streets, some quiet, some turbulent, some blazing with the gas of miserable shops, some dark and stealthy, with only one or two figures in them, which disappeared round corners, or got into dark archways as they passed. Charles saw that they were getting into " Queer Street."

How that poor gaudy figure fluttered on! How it paused at each turning to look back for him, and then fluttered on once more! What innumerable turnings there were! How should he ever find his way back—back to the bridge?

At last she turned into a street of greengrocers and marine store-keepers, in which the people were all at their house doors looking out: all looking in one direction, and talking so earnestly to one another, that even his top-boots escaped notice: which struck him as being remarkable, as nearly all the way from Waterloo Bridge a majority of the populace had criticised them, either ironically or openly, in an unfavourable manner. He thought they were looking at a fire, and turned his head in the same direction; he only saw the poor girl, standing at the mouth of a narrow entry, watching for him.

He came up to her. A little way down a dark alley was an archway, and beyond there were lights and a noise of a great many people shouting, and talking, and screaming. The girl stole on, followed by Charles a few steps, and then drew suddenly back. The whole of the alley and the dark archway beyond was lined with policemen. A brisk-looking, middle-sized man, with intensely black scanty whiskers, stepped out and stood before them. Charles saw at once that it was the inspector of police.

" Now then, young woman," he said sharply, " what are you bringing that young man here for, eh?"

She was obliged to come forward. She began wringing her hands.

" Mr. Inspector," she said, " sir, I wish I may be struck dead, sir, if I don't tell the truth. It's my poor little brother, sir. He's a dying in number eight, sir, and he sent for this young man for to see him, sir. Oh! don't stop us, sir. S'elp me——".

"Pish!" said the inspector; "what the devil is the use of talking this nonsense to me? As for you, young man, you march back home double quick. You've no business here. It's seldom we see a gentleman's servant in such company in this part of the town."

"Pooh! pooh! my good sir," said Charles: "stuff and non-sense. Don't assume that tone with me, if you will have the goodness. What the young woman says is perfectly correct. If you can assist me to get to that house at the farther end of the court, where the poor boy lies dying, I shall be obliged to you. If you can't, don't express an opinion without being in possession of circumstances. You may detain the girl, but I am going on. You don't know who you are talking to."

How the old Oxford insolence flashed out even at the last.

The inspector drew back and bowed. "I must do my duty, sir. Dickson!"

Dickson, in whose beat the court was, as he knew by many a sore bone in his body, came forward. He said, "Well, sir, I won't deny that the young woman is Bess, and perhaps she may be on the cross, and I don't go to say that what with flimping, and with cly-faking, and such like, she mayn't be wanted some day like her brother the Nipper was; but she is a good young woman, and a honest young woman in her way, and what she says this night about her brother is gospel truth."

"Flimping" is a style of theft which I have never practised, and, consequently, of which I know nothing. "Cly-faking" is stealing pocket-handkerchiefs. I never practised this either, never having had sufficient courage or dexterity. But, at all events, Police-constable Dickson's notion of "an honest young woman in her way" seems to me to be confused and unsatis-factory in the last degree.

The inspector said to Charles, "Sir, if gentlemen disguise themselves they must expect the police to be somewhat at fault till they open their mouths. Allow me to say, sir, that in putting on your servant's clothes you have done the most foolish thing you possibly could. You are on an errand of mercy, it appears, and I will do what I can for you. There's a doctor and a Scripture reader somewhere in the court now, so our people say. *They* can't get out. I don't think you have much chance of getting in."

"By Jove!" said Charles, "do you know that you are a deuced good fellow? I am sorry that I was rude to you, but I am in trouble and irritated. I hope you'll forgive me."

"Not another word, sir," said the inspector. "Come and

look here, sir. You may never see such a sight again. *Our* people daren't go in. This, sir, is, I believe, about the worst court in London."

"I thought," said Charles, quite forgetting his top-boots, and speaking, "*de haut en bas*," as in old times—"I thought that your Rosemary Lane carried off the palm as being a lively neighbourhood."

"Lord bless you," said the inspector, "nothing to this—look here."

They advanced to the end of the arch, and looked in. It was as still as death, but it was as light as day, for there were candles burning in every window.

"Why," said Charles, "the court is empty. I can run across. Let me go; I am certain I can get across."

"Don't be a lunatic, sir," said the inspector, holding him tight; "wait till I give you word, unless you want six months in Guy's Hospital."

Charles soon saw the inspector was right. There were three houses on each side of the court. The centre one on the right was a very large one, which was approached on each side by a flight of three steps, guarded by iron railings, which, in meeting, formed a kind of platform or rostrum. This was Mr. Malone's house, whose wife chose, for family reasons, to call herself Miss Ophelia Flanigan.

The court was silent and hushed, when, from the door exactly opposite to this one, there appeared a tall and rather handsome young man, with a great frieze coat under one arm, and a fire-shovel over his shoulder.

This was Mr. Dennis Moriarty, junior. He advanced to the arch so close to Charles and the inspector that they could have touched him, and then walked down the centre of the court, dragging the coat behind him, lifting his heels defiantly high at every step, and dexterously beating a "chune on the bare head of um wid the fire-shovel. Hurroo!"

He had advanced half-way down the court without a soul appearing, when suddenly the enemy poured out on him in two columns from behind two doorways, and he was borne back, fighting like a hero with his fire-shovel, into one of the doors on his own side of the court.

The two columns of the enemy, headed by Mr. Phelim O'Neill, uniting, poured into the doorway after him, and from the interior of the house arose a hubbub, exactly as though people were fighting on the stairs.

At this point there happened one of those mistakes which so

often occur in warfare, which are disastrous at the time and inexplicable afterwards. Can any one explain why Lord Lucan gave that order at Balaclava? No. Can any one explain to me why, on this occasion, Mr. Phelim O'Neill headed the attack on the staircase in person, leaving his rear struggling in confusion in the court, by reason of their hearing the fun going on inside, and not being able to get at it? I think not. Such was the case, however, and, in the midst of it, Mr. Malone, howling like a demon, and horribly drunk, followed by thirty or forty worse than himself, dashed out of a doorway close by, and before they had time to form line of battle, fell upon them hammer and tongs.

I need not say that after this surprise in the rear, Mr. Phelim O'Neill's party had very much the worst of it. In about ten minutes, however, the two parties were standing opposite one another once more, inactive from sheer fatigue.

At this moment Miss Ophelia Flanigan appeared from the door of No. 8—the very house that poor Charles was so anxious to get to—and slowly and majestically advanced towards the rostrum in front of her own door, and ascending the steps, folded her arms and looked about her.

She was an uncommonly powerful, red-faced Irishwoman; her arms were bare, and she had them akimbo, and was scratching her elbows.

Every school boy knows that the lion has a claw at the end of his tail with which he lashes himself into fury. When the experienced hunter sees him doing that, he, so to speak, "hooks it." When Miss Flanigan's enemies saw her scratching her elbows, they generally did the same. She was scratching her elbows now. There was a dead silence.

One woman in that court, and one only, ever offered battle to the terrible Miss Ophelia: that was young Mrs. Phaylim O'Nale. On the present occasion she began slowly walking up and down in front of the expectant hosts. While Miss Flanigan looked on in contemptuous pity, scratching her elbows, Mrs. O'Neill opened her fire.

"Pussey, pussey!" she began, "kitty, kitty, kitty! Miaow, miaow!" (Mr. Malone had accumulated property in the cat's meat business.) "Morraow, ye little tabby divvle, don't come anighst her, my Kitleen Avourneen, or yill be convarted into sassidge mate, and sowld to keep a drunken one-eyed old rapparee, from the county Cark, as had two months for bowling his barrer sharp round the corner of Park Lane over a ould gineral officer, in a white hat and a green silk umbereller; and

as married a red-haired woman from the county Waterford, as
calls herself by her maiden name, and never feels up to fighting
but when the licker's in her, which it most in general is, pussey;
and let me see the one of Malone's lot or Moriarty's lot ather,
for that matter, as will deny it. Miaow!"

Miss Ophelia Flanigan blew her nose contemptuously. Some
of the low characters in the court had picked her pocket.

Mrs. O'Neill quickened her pace and raised her voice. She
was beginning again, when the poor girl who was with Charles
ran into the court and cried out, "Miss Flanigan! I have
brought him; Miss Flanigan!"

In a moment the contemptuous expression faded from Miss
Flanigan's face. She came down off the steps and advanced
rapidly towards where Charles stood. As she passed Mrs.
O'Neill she said, "Whist now, Biddy O'Nale, me darlin'. I
ain't up to a shindy to-night. Ye know the rayson."

And Mrs. O'Neill said, "Ye're a good woman, Ophelia.
Sorra a one of me would have loosed tongue on ye this night,
only I thought it might cheer ye up a bit after yer watching.
Don't take notice of me, that's a dear."

Miss Flanigan went up to Charles, and, taking him by the
arm, walked with him across the court. It was whispered
rapidly that this was the young man who had been sent for to
see little Billy Wilkins, who was dying in No. 8. Charles was
as safe as if he had been in the centre of a square of the
Guards. As he went into the door they gave him a cheer;
and, when the door closed behind him, they went on with their
fighting again.

Charles found himself in a squalid room, about which there
was nothing remarkable but its meanness and dirt. There were
four people there when he came in—a woman asleep by the
bed, two gentlemen who stood aloof in the shadow, and the
poor little wan and wasted boy in the bed.

Charles went up and sat by the bed; when the boy saw him
he made an effort, rose half up, and threw his arms round his
neck. Charles put his arm round him and supported him—as
strange a pair, I fancy, as you will meet in many long days'
marches.

"If you would not mind, Miss Flanigan," said the doctor,
"stepping across the court with me, I shall be deeply obliged
to you. You, sir, are going to stay a little longer."

"Yes, sir," said the other gentleman in a harsh, unpleasant
voice; "I shall stay till the end."

"You won't have to stay very long, my dear sir," said the

doctor. "Now, Miss Flanigan, I am ready. Please to call out that the doctor is coming through the court, and that if any man lays a finger on him, he will exhibit Croton and other drastics to him till he wishes he was dead, and after that, throw in quinine till the top of his head comes off. *Allons*, my dear madam."

With this dreadful threat the doctor departed. The other gentleman, the Scripture reader, stayed behind, and sat in a chair in the further corner. The poor mother was sleeping heavily. The poor girl who had brought Charles sat down in a chair and fell asleep with her head on a table.

The dying child was gone too far for speech. He tried two or three times, but he only made a rattle in his throat. After a few minutes he took his arms from round Charles's neck, and, with a look of anxiety, felt for something by his side. When he found it he smiled, and held it towards Charles. Well, well; it was only the ball that Charles had given him——

Charles sat on the bed, and put his left arm round the child, so that the little death's head might lie upon his breast. He took the little hand in his. So they remained. How long?

I know not. He only sat there with the hot head against his heart, and thought that a little life, so strangely dear to him, now that all friends were gone, was fast ebbing away, and that he must get home again that night across the bridge.

The little hand that he held in his relaxed its grasp, and the boy was dead. He knew it, but he did not move. He sat there still with the dead child in his arms, with a dull terror on him, when he thought of his homeward journey across the bridge.

Some one moved and came towards him. The mother and the girl were still asleep—it was the Scripture reader. He came towards Charles and laid his hand upon his shoulder. And Charles turned from the dead child, and looked up into his face—into the face of John Marston.

CHAPTER LXI

SAVED

WITH the wailing mother's voice in their ears, those two left the house. The court was quiet enough now. The poor

savages who would not stop their riot lest they should disturb
the dying, now talked in whispers lest they should awaken the
dead.

They passed on quickly together. Not one word had been
uttered between them—not one—but they pushed rapidly
through the worst streets to a better part of the town. Charles
clinging tight to John Marston's arm, but silent. When they
got to Marston's lodgings, Charles sat down by the fire, and
spoke for the first time. He did not burst out crying, or anything of that sort. He only said quietly—

"John, you have saved me. I should never have got home
this night."

But John Marston, who, by finding Charles, had dashed his
dearest hopes to the ground, did not take things quite so
quietly. Did he think of Mary now? Did he see in a moment
that his chance of her was gone? And did he not see that he
loved her more deeply than ever?

"Yes," I answer to all these three questions. How did
he behave now?

Why, he put his hand on Charles's shoulder, and he said,
"Charles, Charles, my dear old boy, look up and speak to me
in your dear old voice. Don't look wild like that. Think of
Mary, my boy. She has been wooed by more than one,
Charles; but I think that her heart is yours yet."

"John," said Charles, "that is what has made me hide from
you all like this. I know that she loves me above all men. I
dreamt of it the night I left Ravenshoe. I knew it the night
I saw her at Lord Hainault's. And partly that she should
forget a penniless and disgraced man like myself, and partly
(for I have been near the gates of hell to-night, John, and can
see many things) from a silly pride, I have spent all my cunning
on losing myself—hoping that you would believe me dead,
thinking that you would love my memory, and dreading lest
you should cease to love Me."

"We loved your memory well enough, Charles. You will
never know how well, till you see how well we love yourself.
We have hunted you hard, Charles. How you have contrived
to avoid us, I cannot guess. You do not know, I suppose,
that you are a rich man?"

"A rich man?"

"Yes. Even if Lord Saltire does not alter his will, you
come into three thousand a year. And, besides, you are undoubtedly heir to Ravenshoe, though one link is still wanting
to prove that."

" What do you mean ? "

" There is no reasonable doubt, although we cannot prove it, that your grandfather Petre was married previously to his marriage with Lady Alicia Staunton, that your father James was the real Ravenshoe, and that Ellen and yourself are the elder children, while poor Cuthbert and William——"

" Cuthbert ! Does he know of this ? I will hide again ; I will never displace Cuthbert, mind you."

" Charles, Cuthbert will never know anything about it. Cuthbert is dead. He was drowned bathing last August."

Hush ! There is something, to me, dreadful in a man's tears. I dare say that it was as well, that night, that the news of Cuthbert's death should have made him break down and weep himself into quietness again like a child. I am sure it was for the best. But it is the sort of thing that good taste forbids one to dwell upon or handle too closely.

When he was quiet again John went on :

" It seems incredible that you should have been able to elude us so long. The first intelligence we had of you was from Lady Ascot, who saw you in the Park."

" Lady Ascot ? I never saw my aunt in the Park."

" I mean Adelaide. She is Lady Ascot now. Lord Ascot is dead."

" Another of them ! " said Charles. " John, before you go on, tell me how many more are gone."

" No more. Lady Ascot and Lord Saltire are alive and well. I was with Lord Saltire to-day, and he was talking of you. He has left the principal part of his property to Ascot. But, because none of us would believe you dead, he has made a reservation in your favour of eighty thousand pounds."

" I am all abroad," said Charles. " How is William ? "

" He is very well, as he deserves to be. Noble fellow ! He gave up everything to hunt you through the world like a blood-hound and bring you back. He never ceased his quest till he saw your grave at Varna."

" At Varna ! " said Charles ; " why we were quartered at Devna."

" At Devna ! Now, my dear old boy, I am but mortal ; do satisfy my curiosity. What regiment did you enlist in ? "

" In the 140th."

" Then how, in the name of all confusion," cried John Marston, " did you miss poor Hornby ? "

" I did not miss Hornby," said Charles quietly. " I had his

head in my lap when he died.   But now tell me, how on earth
did you come to know anything about him ? "

"Why, Ascot told us that you had been his servant.   And
he came to see us, and joined in the chase with the best of us.
How is it that he never sent us any intelligence of you ? "

" Because I never went near him till the film of death was
on his eyes.   Then he knew me again, and said a few words
which I can understand now.   Did he say anything to any
of you about Ellen ? "

"About Ellen ? "

"Yes.   Did Ascot ever say anything either ? "

" He told Lord Saltire, what I suppose you know——"

" About what ? "

" About Ellen."

"Yes, I know it all."

"And that he had met you.   Now tell me what you have
been doing."

" When I found that there was no chance of my remaining
perdu any longer, and when I found that Ellen was gone, why,
then I enlisted in the 140th. . . ."

He paused here, and hid his face in his hands for some
time.   When he raised it again his eyes were wilder, and his
speech more rapid.

" I went out with Tom Sparks and the Roman-nosed bay
horse ; and we ran a thousand miles in sixty-three hours.   And
at Devna we got wood-pigeons ; and the cornet went down and
dined with the 42nd at Varna ; and I rode the Roman-nosed
bay, and he carried me through it capitally ; I ask your pardon,
sir, but I am only a poor discharged trooper.   I would not beg,
sir, if I could help it ; but pain and hunger are hard things to
bear, sir."

" Charles, Charles, don't you know me ? "

" That is my name, sir.   That is what they used to call me.
I am no common beggar, sir.   I was a gentleman once, sir,
and rode a-horseback after a blue greyhound, and we went near
to kill a black hare.   I have a character from Lord Ascot, sir.
I was in the light cavalry charge at Balaclava.   An angry
business.   They shouldn't get good fellows to fight together
like that.   I killed one of them, sir.   Hornby killed many,
and he is a man who wouldn't hurt a fly.   A sad business ! "

" Charles, old boy, be quiet."

" When you speak to me, sir, of the distinction between the
upper and lower classes, I answer you, that I have had some
experience in that way of late, and have come to the conclusion

that, after all, the gentleman and the cad are one and the same
animal. Now that I am a ruined man, begging my bread
about the streets, I make bold to say to you, sir, hoping that
your alms may be none the less for it, that I am not sure that
I do not like your cad as well as your gentleman, in his way.
If I play on the one side such cards as my foster-brother
William and Tom Sparks, you, of course, trump me with John
Marston and the cornet. You are right; but they are all four
good fellows. I have been to death's gate to learn it. I will
resume my narrative. At Devna the cornet, besides wood-
pigeons, shot a francolin——"

It is just as well that this sort of thing did not come on
when Charles was going home alone across the bridge;
that is all I wished to call your attention to. The next
morning, Lord and Lady Hainault, old Lady Ascot, William,
Mary and Father Tiernay were round his bed, watching the
hot head rolling from side to side upon the pillow, and listening to his half-uttered delirious babble, gazing with a feeling
almost of curiosity at the well-loved face which had eluded
them so long.

"Oh, Hainault! Hainault!" said Lady Ascot, "to find him
like this after all! And Saltire dead without seeing him! and
all my fault, my fault. I am a wicked old woman; God
forgive me!"

Lord Hainault got the greatest of the doctors into a corner,
and said—

"My dear Dr. B——, will he die?"

"Well, yes," said the doctor; "to you I would sooner say
yes than no, the chances are so heavy against him. The
surgeons like the look of things still less than the physicians.
You must really prepare for the worst."

CHAPTER LXII

MR. JACKSON'S BIG TROUT

Of course, he did not die; I need not tell you that. B——
and P. H.—— pulled him through, and shook their honest
hands over his bed. Poor B—— is reported to have winked on
this occasion; but such a proceeding was so unlike him, that I
believe the report must have come round to us through one of

the American papers—probably the same one which represented the Prince of Wales hitting the Duke of Newcastle in the eye with a champagne cork.

However, they pulled him through; and, in the pleasant spring-time he was carried down to Casterton. Things had gone so hard with him, that the primroses were in blossom on the southern banks before he knew that Lord Saltire was dead, and before he could be made to understand that he was a rich man.

From this much of the story we may safely deduce this moral, " That, if a young gentleman gets into difficulties, it is always as well for him to leave his address with his friends." But, as young gentlemen in difficulties generally take particularly good care to remind their friends of their whereabouts, it follows that this story has been written to little or no purpose. Unless, indeed, the reader can find for himself another moral or two ; and I am fool enough to fancy that he may do that, if he cares to take the trouble.

Casterton is built on arches, with all sorts of offices and kitchens under what would naturally be the ground floor. The reason why Casterton was built on arches (that is to say, as far as you and I are concerned) is this : that Charles, lying on the sofa in Lord Hainault's study, could look over the valley and see the river ; which, if it had been built on the ground, he could not have done. From this window he could see the great weirs spouting and foaming all day ; and, when he was carried up to bed by William and Lord Hainault, he could hear the roaring of them rising and sinking, as the night-wind came and went, until they lulled him to sleep.

He lay here one day, when the doctors came down from London. And one of them put a handkerchief over his face, which smelt like chemical experiments, and somehow reminded him of Dr. Daubeny. And, he fell asleep ; and when he awoke, he was suffering pain in his left arm—not the old dull grinding pain, but sharper—which gradually grew less as he lay and watched the weirs at Casterton. They had removed the splinters of bone from his arm.

He did not talk much in this happy quiet time. William and Lady Ascot were with him all day. William, dear fellow, used to sit on a footstool, between his sofa and the window, and read the *Times* to him. William's education was imperfect, and he read very badly. He would read Mr. Russell's correspondence till he saw Charles's eye grow bright, and hear his breath quicken, and then he would turn to the list of bankrupts. If this was too sad, he would go on to the share list, and pound away at that, till Charles went to sleep, which he generally did pretty quickly.

About this time—that is to say, well in the spring—Charles asked two questions :—The first was, whether or no he might have the window open ; the next, whether Lord Hainault would lend him an opera-glass?

Both were answered in the affirmative. The window was opened, and Lord Hainault and William came in, bearing, not an opera-glass, but a great brass telescope, on a stand—a thing with an eight-inch object-glass, which had belonged to old Lord Hainault, who was a Cambridge man, and given to such vanities.

This was very delightful. He could turn it with a move of his hand on to any part of the weirs, and see almost every snail which crawled on the burdocks. The very first day he saw one of the men from the paper-mill come to the fourth weir, and pull up the paddles to ease the water. The man looked stealthily around, and then raised a wheel from below the apron, full of spawning perch. And this was the close time. Oho !

Then, a few days after, came a tall, grey-headed gentleman, spinning a bleak for trout, who had with him a lad in top-boots, with a landing-net. And this gentleman sent his bait flying out here and there across the water, and rattled his line rapidly into the palm of his hand in a ball, like a consummate master, as he was. (King among fishermen, prince among gentlemen, you will read these lines, and you will be so good as to understand that I am talking of you.) And this gentleman spun all day and caught nothing.

But he came the next day to the same place, and spun again. The great full south-westerly wind was roaring up the valley, singing among the budding trees, and carrying the dark, low, rainless clouds swiftly before it. At two, just as Lady Ascot and William had gone to lunch, and after Charles had taken his soup and a glass of wine, he, lying there and watching this gentleman diligently, saw his rod bend and his line tighten. The lad in the top-boots and the landing-net leaped up from where he lay ; there was no doubt about it now. The old gentleman had got hold of a fish, and a big one.

The next twenty minutes were terrible. The old gentleman gave him the but, and moved slowly down along the camp-shuting, and Charles followed him with the telescope, although his hand was shaking with excitement. After a time the old gentleman began to wind up his reel, and then the lad, top-boots, and landing-net, and all, slipped over the camp-shooting (will anybody tell me how to spell that word? *Camps-heading* won't do, my dear sir, all things considered) and lifted the fish (he was nine pound), up among the burdocks at the old gentleman's feet.

Charles had the whole group in the telescope—the old gentleman, the great trout, and the dripping lad, taking off his boots and emptying the water out of them. But the old gentleman was looking to his right at somebody who was coming, and immediately there came into the field of the telescope a tall man in a velvet coat, with knee breeches and gaiters, and directly afterwards, from the other side, three children and a young lady. The gentleman in the knee-breeches bowed to the young lady, and then they all stood looking at the trout.

Charles could see them quite plainly. The gentleman in velveteen and small clothes was Lord Ascot, and the young lady was Mary.

He did not look through the telescope any more; he lay back and tried to think. Presently, afterwards, old Lady Ascot came in, and settled herself in the window with her knitting.

"My dear," she said, "I wonder if I fidget you with my knitting-needles? Tell me if I do, for I have plenty of other work."

"Not at all, dear aunt; I like it. You did nineteen rows this morning, and you would have done twenty-two if you had not dropped a stitch. When I get stronger I shall take to it myself. There would be too much excitement and over-exertion in it for me to begin just now."

Lady Ascot laughed; she was glad to see him trying even such a feeble joke. She said—

"My dear, Mr. Jackson has killed a trout in the weirs just now, nine pounds."

"I know," said Charles; "I did not know the weight, but I saw the fish. Aunt, where is Welter—I mean Ascot?"

"Well, he is at Ranford. I suppose you know, my dear boy, that poor James left him nearly all his fortune. Nearly five hundred thousand pounds' worth, with Cottingdean and Marksworth together. All the Ranford mortgages are paid off, and he is going on very well, my dear. I think they ought to give him his marquisate. James might have had it ten times over of course, but he used to say that he had made himself the most notorious viscount in England, and that if he took an earldom, people would forget who he was."

"I wish he would come to see me, aunt. I am very fond of Welter."

I can't help it; he said so. Remember how near death's door he had been. Think what he had been through. How he had been degraded, and kicked about from pillar to post, like an old shoe; and also remember the state he was in when he said it. I firmly believe that he had at this time forgotten everything, and that he only remembered Lord Ascot as his old boy love, and his jolly college companion. You must make the best of it, or the worst of it for him, as you are inclined. He said so. And in a very short time Lady Ascot found that she wanted some more wool, and hobbled away to get it.

After a time, Charles heard a man come into the room. He thought it was William; but it was not. This man came round the end of the sofa, and stood in the window before him. Lord Ascot.

He was dressed as we know, having looked through Charles's telescope, in a velveteen coat, with knee-breeches and leathern gaiters. There was not much change in him since the old times, only his broad, hairless face seemed redder, his lower jaw seemed coarser and more prominent, his great eyebrows seemed more lowering, his vast chest seemed broader and deeper, and altogether he looked rather more like a mighty, coarse, turbulent blackguard than ever.

"Well, old cock," he said, "so you are on your back, hey?"

"Welter," said Charles, "I am so glad to see you again. If you would help me up, I should like to look at you."

"Poor old boy," said Lord Ascot, putting his great arm round him and raising him. "So! there you are, my pippin. What a good old fellow you are, by Gad! So you were one of the immortal six hundred, hey? I thought you would turn up somewhere in Queer Street, with that infernal old hook nose of yours. I wish I had taken to that sort of thing, for I am fond of fighting. I think, now I am rich and respectable, I shall subsidize a prize-fighter to pitch into me once a fortnight. I wish I had been respectable enough for the army; but I should always have been in trouble with the commander-in-chief for dicing and brawling, I suppose. Well, old man, I am devilish glad to see you again. I am in possession of money which should have been yours. I did all I could for you, Charles; you will never know how much. I tried to repair the awful wrong I did you unconsciously. I did a thing in your favour I tremble to think of now, but which, God help me, I would do again. You don't know what I mean. If old Saltire had not died so quick, you would have known."

He was referring to his having told Lord Saltire that he had seen Charles. In doing that, remember, he had thought that he was throwing half a million to the winds. I only tell you that he was referring to this, for fear you should not gather it from his own brutal way of speaking.

I wonder how the balance will stand against Lord Ascot at last? Who ever could have dreamt that his strong animal affection for his old friend could have led him to make a sacrifice which many a more highly organized man would have evaded, glossing over his conscience by fifty mental subterfuges.

"However, my dear fellow," he continued, "it comes to this: I have got the money; I shall have no children; and I shall make no will; therefore it all comes to you, if you outlive me. About the title I can't say. The lawyers must decide about that. No one seems to know whether or not it descends through the female branch. By-the-by, you are not master of Ravenshoe yet, though there seems no doubt that grandma is right, and that the marriage took place. However, whether the estate goes to you, or to William, I offer the same advice to both of you: if you get my money, don't spend it in getting the title. You can get into the House of Commons easy enough, if you seem to care about that sort of fun; and fellows I know tell me that you get much better amusement there for your money than in the other place. I have never been to the House of Lords since the night I took my seat. It struck me as being slow. The fellows say that there is never any chaff, or personalities or calling to order, or that sort of thing there, which seem to me to be half the fun of the fair. But, of course, you know more about this than I."

Charles, in a minute, when he had ineffectually tried to understand what Lord Ascot had been saying, collected his senses sufficiently to say:

"Welter, old boy, look here, for I am very stupid. Why did you say that you should have no children?"

"Of course I can't; have they told you nothing?"

"Is Adelaide dead, Welter?" asked Charles, plucking at the buttons of his coat nervously.

"They ought to have told you, Charles," said Lord Ascot, turning to the window. "Now tell me something. Have you any love left for her yet?"

" Not one spark," said Charles, still buttoning and unbuttoning his coat. " If I ever am a man again, I shall ask Mary Corby to marry me. I ought to have done so sooner, perhaps. But I love your wife, Welter, in a way; and I should grieve at her death, for I loved her once. By Gad! yes; you know it. When did she die?"

"She is not dead, Charles."

"Now, don't keep me like this, old man; I can't stand it. She is no more to me than my sister—not so much. Tell me what is the matter at once; it can't be worse than what I think."

"The truth is very horrible, Charles," said Lord Ascot, speaking slowly. "She took a fancy that I should buy back her favourite old Irish mare, 'Molly Asthore,' and I bought it for her; and we went out hunting together, and we were making a nick, and I was getting the gate open for her, when the devil rushed it; and down they came on it, together. And she broke her back—Oh, God! oh, God!—and the doctor says she may live till seventy, but that she will never move from where she lies—and just as I was getting to love her so dearly——"

Charles said nothing; for with such a great brutal blackguard as Lord Ascot sobbing passionately at the window, it was as well to say nothing; but he thought, " Here's work to the fore, I fancy, after a life of laziness. I have been the object of all these dear soul's anxiety for a long time. She must take my place now."

CHAPTER LXIII

IN WHICH GUS CUTS FLORA'S DOLL'S CORNS

THAT afternoon Charles said nothing more, but lay and looked out of the window at the rhododendrons just bursting into bloom, at the deer, at the rabbits, at the pheasants; and beyond, where the park dipped down so suddenly, at the river which spouted and foamed away as of old; and to the right, at the good old town of Casterton, and at the blue smoke from its chimneys, drifting rapidly away before the soft south-westerly wind; and he lay and looked at these and thought. And before sundown an arch arose in the west which grew and spread; an arch of pale green sky, which grew till it met the sun, and then the wet grass in the park shone out all golden, and the topmost cedar boughs began to blaze like burnished copper.

And then he spoke. He said, " William, my dear old friend—loved more deeply than any words can tell—come here, for I have something to say to you."

And good William came and stood beside him. And William looked at him and saw that his face was animated, and that his eyes were sparkling. And he stood and said not a word, but smiled and waited for him to go on.

And Charles said, " Old boy, I have been looking through that glass to-day, and I saw Mr. Jackson catch the trout, and I saw Welter, and I saw Mary ; and I want you to go and fetch Mary here."

And William straightway departed ; and as he went up the staircase he met the butler, and he looked so happy, so radiant, and so thoroughly kind-hearted and merry, that the butler, a solemn man, found himself smiling as he drew politely aside to let him pass.

I hope you like this fellow, William. He was, in reality, only a groom, say you. Well, that is true enough. A fellow without education or breeding, though highly born. But still, I hope you like him. I was forgetting myself a little, though. At this time he is master of Ravenshoe, with certainly nine, and probably twelve thousand a year—a most eminently respectable person. One year's income of his would satisfy a man I know, very well, and yet I am talking of him apologetic- ally. But then we novel writers have an unlimited command of money, if we could only realize it.

However, this great capitalist went upstairs towards the nursery ; and here I must break off, if you please, and take up the thread of my narrative in another place (I don't mean the House of Lords).

In point of fact there had been a shindy (I use the word advisedly, and will repeat it)—a shindy, in the nursery that evening. The duty of a story-teller is to stick in a moral reflection wherever he can, and so at this place I pitchfork in this caution to young governesses, that nothing can be more incautious or reprehensible, than to give children books to keep them quiet, without first seeing what these books are about.

Mary was very much to blame in this case (you see I tell the truth, and spare nobody). Gus, Flora, and Archy had been out to walk with her, as we know, and had come home in a very turbulent state of mind. They had demanded books as the sole condition on which they would be good; and Mary being in a fidget about her meeting with Lord Ascot, over the trout, and being not quite herself, had promptly supplied Gus with a number of *Blackwood's Magazine*, and Flora with a "Shakespeare."

This happened early in the afternoon. Remember this; for if we are not particular in our chronology, we are naught.

Gus turned to the advertisements. He read, among other things, a testimonial to a great corn-cutter, from a potentate who keeps a very small army, and don't mean any harm :—

" (TRANSLATION.)

" Professor Homberg has cut my corns with a dexterity truly marvellous.

(Signed) " NAPOLEON."

From a country baronet :—

"I am satisfied with Professor Homberg.

(Signed) " PITCHCROFT COCKPOLE,
"Bart."

From a Bishop in the South Sea Islands :—

" Professor Homberg has cut my corns in a manner which does equal honour to his head and his heart.

(Signed) " RANGEHAIETA."

(His real name is Jones, but that is neither here nor there); and in the meantime Flora had been studying a certain part of " King Lear."

Later in the afternoon it occurred to Gus, that he would like to be a corn-cutter and have testimonials. He proposed to cut nurse's corns, but she declined, assigning reasons. Failing here, he determined to cut Flora's doll's corns, and, with this view, possessed himself of her person during Flora's temporary absence.

He began by snicking the corner of her foot off with nurse's scissors. Then he found that the sawdust dribbled out at the orifice. This was very delightful. He shook her and it dribbled faster. Then he cut the other foot off and shook her again. And she, not having any stitches put in about the knee (as all dolls should), lost, not only the sawdust from her legs, but also from her stomach and body, leaving nothing but collapsed calico and a bust, with an undisturbed countenance of wax above all.

At this time Flora had rushed in to the rescue; she felt the doll's body and she saw the heap of sawdust; whereupon she, remembering her "King Lear," turned on him and said scornfully,

"Nero is an angler in the lake of darkness." At this awful taunt, Gus butted her in the stomach, and she got hold of him by the hair. Archy, excited for the first time in his life, threw a box of ninepins at them, which exploded. Mary rushed in to separate them, and at the same moment in came William with a radiant face, and he quietly took Mary round the waist (like his impudence), and he said, "My dear creature, go down to Charles, and leave these Turks to me."

And she left these Turks to him. And he sat on a chair and administered justice; and in a very few minutes, under the influence of that kind, happy, sunny face of his, Flora had kissed Gus, and Archy had cuddled up on his knee, and was sucking his thumb in peace.

And going down to the hall, he found Lady Ascot hobbling up and down, taking her afternoon's exercise, and she said to him, "Ravenshoe, you best and kindest of souls, she is there with him now. My dear, we had better not move in this matter any more. I tried to dispossess you before I knew your worth and goodness, but I will do nothing now. He is rich, and perhaps it is better, my dear, that Ravenshoe should be in Papist hands—at least, in such hands as yours."

He said, "My dear madam, I am not Ravenshoe. I feel sure that you are right. We must find Ellen."

And Mary came out and came toward them; and she said, "Lady Ascot and Mr. Ravenshoe, Charles and I are engaged to be married."

CHAPTER LXIV

THE ALLIED ARMIES ADVANCE ON RAVENSHOE

How near the end we are getting, and yet so much to come. Never mind. We will tell it all naturally and straightforwardly, and then there will be nothing to offend you.

By-and-by it became necessary that Charles should have air and exercise. His arm was well. Every splinter had been taken out of it, and he must lie on the sofa no longer.

So he was driven out through pleasant places, through the budding spring, in one of Lord Hainault's carriages. All the meadows had been bush-harrowed and rolled long ago, and now the orchisis and fritillaries were beginning to make the grass look purple. Lady Hainault had a low carriage, and a pair of small cobs, and this was given up to Charles; Lady Hainault's first coachman declined to drive her ladyship out in the day-time, for fear that the second coachman (a meritorious young man of forty) should frighten Charles by a reckless and inexperienced way of driving.

Consequently Lady Hainault went a-buying flannel petticoats and that sort of thing, for the poor people in Casterton and Henley, driven by her second coachman; and Charles was trundled all over the country by the first coachman, in a low carriage with a pair of cobs. But Lady Hainault was as well pleased with the arrangement as the old coachman himself, and so it is no business of ours. For the curious thing was, that no one who ever knew Charles would have hesitated for an instant in giving up to him, his or her, bed, or dinner, or carriage, or any other thing in this world. For people are great fools, you know.

Perhaps the reason of it was that every one who made Charles's acquaintance, knew by instinct that he would have cut off his right hand to serve them. I don't know why it was. But there is the fact.

Sometimes Lady Ascot would go with him, and sometimes William. And one day, when William was with him, they were bowling quietly along a by-road on the opposite side of the water from Henley. And in a secret place, they came on a wicked old gentleman, breaking the laws of his country, and catching perch in close time, out of a punt, with a chair, and a stone bottle, and a fisherman from Maidenhead, who shall be nameless, but who must consider himself cautioned.

The Rajah of Ahmednuggur lives close by there; and he was reading the *Times*, when Charles asked the coachman to pull up, that he might see the sport. The Rajah's attention was caught by seeing the carriage stop; and he looked through a double-barrelled opera-glass, and not only saw Charles and William in the carriage, but saw, through the osiers, the hoary old profligate with his paternoster pulling the perch out as fast as he could put his line in. Fired by a virtuous indignation (I wish every gentleman on the Thames would do likewise), he ran in his breeches and slippers down the lawn, and began blowing up like Old Gooseberry.

The old gentleman who was fishing looked at the Rajah's red-brick house, and said, "If my face was as ugly as that house, I would wear a green veil;" but he ordered the fisherman to take up the rypecks, and he floated away down stream.

And as Charles and William drove along, Charles said, "My dear boy, there could not be any harm in catching a few roach. I should so like to go about among pleasant places in a punt once more."

When they got home the head keeper was sent for. Charles told him that he would so much like to go fishing, and that a few roach would not make much difference. The keeper scornfully declined arguing about the matter, but only wanted to know what time Mr. Ravenshoe would like to go, adding, that any one who made objections would be brought up uncommon short.

So William and he went fishing in a punt, and one day Charles said, "I don't care about this punt-fishing much. I wish—I wish I could get back to the trout at Ravenshoe."

"Do you really mean that?" said William.

"Ah, Willy!" said Charles. "If I could only see it again!"

"How I have been waiting to hear you say that!" said William. "Come to your home with me; why, the people are wondering where we are. My darling bird will be jealous, if I stay here much longer. Come down to my wedding."

"When are you to be married, William?"

"On the same day as yourself," said William sturdily.

Said Charles, "Put the punt ashore, will you?" And they did. And Charles, with his nose in the air, and his chest out, walked beside William across the spring meadows, through the lengthening grass, through the calthas, and the orchisis, and the ladies' slippers, and the cowslips, and the fritillaries, through the budding flower garden which one finds in spring among the English meadows, a hale strong man. And when they had clomb the precipitous slope of the deer-park, Charles picked a rhododendron flower, and put it in his button-hole, and turned round to William, with the flush of health on his face, and said—

"Brother, we will go to Ravenshoe, and you will be with your love. Shall we be married in London?"

"In St. Petersburgh, if you like, now I see you looking your old self again. But why?"

"A fancy of mine. When I remember what I went through in London through my own obstinacy, I should like to take my revenge on the place, by spending the happiest day of my life there. Do you agree?"

"Of course."

"Ask Lady Ascot and Mary and the children down to Ravenshoe. Lady Hainault will come too, but he can't. And have General Mainwaring and the Tiernays. Have as many of the old circle as we can get."

"This is something like life again," said William. "Remember, Charles, I am not spending the revenues of Ravenshoe. They are yours. I know it. I am spending about £400 a year. When our grandfather's marriage is proved, you will provide for me and my wife, I know that. Be quiet. But we shall never prove that till we find Ellen."

"Find Ellen!" exclaimed Charles, turning round. "I will not go near Ellen yet."

"Do you know where she is?" asked William eagerly.

"Of course I do," said Charles. "She is at Hackney. Hornby told me so when he was dying. But let her be for a time."

"I tell you," said William, "that I am sure that she knows everything. At Hackney!"

The allied powers, General Mainwaring, Lady Ascot, Lord Hainault, and William, were not long before they searched every hole and corner of Hackney, in and out. There was only one nunnery there, but, in that nunnery, there was no young lady at all resembling Ellen. The priests, particularly Father Mackworth's friend Butler, gave them every assistance in their power. But it was no good.

As Charles and William were in the railway carriage going westward, Charles said,

"Well, we have failed to find Ellen. Mackworth, poor fellow, is still at Ravenshoe."

"Yes," said William, "and nearly idiotic. All his fine-spun cobwebs cast to the winds. But he holds the clue to this mystery, or I am mistaken. The younger Tiernay takes care of him. He probably won't know you. But Charles, when you come into Ravenshoe, keep a corner for Mackworth."

"He ought to be an honoured guest of the house as long as he lives," said Charles. "You still persist in saying that Ravenshoe is mine."

"I am sure it is," said William.

And, at the same time, William wrote to two other people telling all about the state of affairs, and asking them to come and join the circle. And John Marston came across into my room, and said, "Let us go." And I said, "My dear John, we ought to go. It is not every day that we see a man, and such a man, risen from the dead, as Charles Ravenshoe."

And so we went.

CHAPTER LXV

FATHER MACKWORTH PUTS THE FINISHING TOUCH ON HIS GREAT PIECE OF EMBROIDERY

AND so we went. At Ravenshoe were assembled General Mainwaring, Lady Ascot, Mary, Gus, Flora, Archy, and nurse, William, Charles, Father Tiernay and Father Murtagh Tiernay, John Marston, and Tommy Cruse from Clovelly, a little fisherboy, cousin of Jane Evans'—Jane Evans, who was to be Mrs. Ravenshoe.

It became necessary that Jane Evans should be presented to Lady Ascot. She was only a fisherman's daughter, but she was wonderfully beautiful, and gentle, and good. William brought her into the hall one evening, when every one was sitting round the fire; and he said, "My dear madam, this is my wife that is to be." Nothing more.

And the dear old woman rose and kissed her, and said, "My love, how wonderfully pretty you are. You must learn to love me, you know, and you must make haste about it, because I am a very old woman, and I sha'n't live very long."

So Jane sat down by Mary, and was at home, though a little nervous. And General Mainwaring came and sat beside her, and made himself as agreeable as very few men beside him know how to. And the fisherboy got next to William, and stared about with his great black eyes, like a deer in a flower-garden. (You caught that face capitally, Mr. Hook, if you will allow me to say so—best painter of the day !)

Jane Evans was an immense success. She had been to school six months at Exeter, and had possibly been drilled in a few little matters ; such as how to ask a gentleman to hold her fan ; how to sit down to the piano when asked to sing (which she couldn't do) ; how to marshal her company to dinner ; how to step into the car of a balloon ; and so on. Things absolutely necessary to know, of course, but which had nothing to do with her success in this case; for she was so beautiful, gentle, and winning, that she might have done anything short of eating with her knife, and would have been considered nice.

Had she a slight Devonshire accent? Well, well! Do you know, I rather like it. I consider it equally so good with the Scotch, my dear.

I could linger and linger on about this pleasant spring at old Ravenshoe, but I must not. You have been my companion so long that I am right loth to part with you. But the end is very near.

Charles had his revenge upon the trout. The first day after he had recovered from his journey, he and William went out and did most terrible things. William would not carry a rod, but gave his to the servant, and took the landing-net. That Ravenshoe stream carries the heaviest fish in Devonshire. Charles worked up to the waterfall, and got nineteen, weighing fourteen pounds. Then they walked down to the weir above the bridge, and then Charles's evil genius prompted him to say, "William, have you got a salmon fly in your book?" And William told him that he had, but solemnly warned him of what would happen.

Charles was reckless and foolish. He, with a twelve-foot trout rod, and thirty yards of line, threw a small salmon fly under the weir above the bridge. There was a flash on the water. Charles's poor little reel began screaming, and the next moment the line came " flick " home across his face, and he said, " By gosh, what a fool I was," and then he looked up to the bridge, and there was Father Mackworth looking at him.

"How d'ye do, my dear sir," said Charles. "Glad to see you out. I have been trying to kill a salmon with trout tackle, and have done quite the other thing."

Father Mackworth looked at him, but did not speak a word. Then he looked round, and young Murtagh Tiernay came up and led him away; and Charles got up on the road and watched the pair going home. And as he saw the tall narrow figure of Father Mackworth creeping slowly along, dragging his heels as he went, he said, "Poor old fellow, I hope he will live to forgive me."

Father Mackworth, poor fellow, dragged his heels homeward; and when he got into his room in the priest's tower, Murtagh Tiernay said to him, "My dear friend, you are not angry with me? I did not tell you that he was come back. I thought it would agitate you."

And Father Mackworth said slowly, for all his old decisive

utterance was gone, "The Virgin bless you, you are a good man."

And Father Mackworth spoke truth. Both the Tiernays were good fellows, though papists.

"Let me help you off with your coat," said Murtagh, for Mackworth was standing in deep thought.

"Thank you," said Mackworth. "Now, while I sit here, go and fetch your brother."

Murtagh Tiernay did as he was told. In a few minutes our good jolly old Irish friend was leaning over Mackworth's chair.

"Ye're not angry that we didn't tell ye there was company?" he said.

"No, no," said Mackworth. "Don't speak to me, that's a good man. Don't confuse me. I am going. You had better send Murtagh out of the room."

Father Murtagh disappeared.

"I am going," said Mackworth. "Tiernay, we were not always good friends, were we?"

"We are good friends, any way, now, brother," said Tiernay.

"Ay, ay, you are a good man. I have done a wrong. I did it for the sake of the Church partly, and partly——well, I was very fond of Cuthbert. I loved that boy, Tiernay. And I spun a web. But it has all got confused. It is on this left side, which feels so heavy. They shouldn't make one's brains in two halves, should they?"

"Begorra no. It's a burning shame," said Father Tiernay, determining, like a true Irishman, to agree with every word said, and find out what was coming.

"That being the case, my dear friend," said poor Mackworth, "give me the portfolio and ink, and we will let our dear brother Butler know, *de profundis clamavi*, that the time is come."

Father Tiernay said, "That will be the proper course," and got him pen and ink, fully assured that another fit was coming on, and that he was wandering in his mind; but still watching to see whether he would let out anything. A true Irishman.

Mackworth let out nothing. He wrote as steadily as he could, a letter of two lines, and put it in an envelope. Then he wrote another letter of about three lines, and enclosed the whole in a larger envelope, and closed it. Then he said to Father Tiernay, "Direct it to Butler, will you, my dear friend; you quite agree that I have done right?"

Father Tiernay said that he had done quite right; but

wondered what the dickens it was all about. We soon found out. But we walked, and rode, and fished, and chatted, and played billiards, and got up charades with Lady Ascot for an audience; not often thinking of the poor paralytic priest in the lonely tower, and little dreaming of the mine which he was going to spring under our feet.

The rows (there is no other expression) that used to go on between Father Tiernay and Lady Ascot were as amusing as anything I ever heard. I must do Tiernay the justice to say that he was always perfectly well bred, and also, that Lady Ascot began it. Her good temper, her humour, and her shrewdness were like herself; I can say no more. Tiernay dodged, and shuffled, and went from pillar to post, and was as witty and good-humoured as an Irishman can be; but I, as a staunch Protestant, am of opinion that Lady Ascot, though nearly ninety, had the best of it. I dare say good Father Tiernay don't agree with me.

The younger Tiernay was always in close attendance on Mackworth. Every one got very fond of this young priest. We used to wait until Father Mackworth was reported to be in bed, and then he was sent for. And generally we used to make an excuse to go into the chapel, and Lady Ascot would come, defiant of rheumatism, and we would get him to the organ.

And then—Oh, Lord! how he would make that organ speak, and plead, and pray, till the prayer was won. And then, how he would send aggregated armies of notes, marching in vast battalions one after another, out into space, to die in confused melody; and then, how he would sound the trumpet to recal them, and get no answer but the echo of the roof. Ah! well, I hope you are fond of music, reader.

But one night we sent for him, and he could not come. And later we sent again, but he did not come; and the man we had sent, being asked, looked uneasy, and said he did not know why. By this time the ladies had gone to bed. General Mainwaring, Charles, William, John Marston and myself, were sitting over the fire in the hall, smoking, and little Tommy Cruse was standing between William's knees.

The candles and the fire were low. There was light outside from a clouded moon, so that one could see the gleam of the sea out of the mullioned windows. Charles was stooping down, describing the battle of the Alma on the hearthrug, and William was bending over, watching him, holding the boy between his knees, as I said. General Mainwaring was puffing his cigar, and saying, "Yes, yes; that's right enough;" and Marston and I were, like William, looking at Charles.

Suddenly the boy gave a loud cry, and hid his face in William's bosom. I thought he had been taken with a fit. I looked up over General Mainwaring's head, and I cried out, "My God! what is this?"

We were all on our legs in a moment, looking the same way. At the long low mullioned window which had been behind General Mainwaring. The clouded moonlight outside showed us the shape of it. But between us and it there stood three black figures, and as we looked at them, we drew one towards the other, for we were frightened. The general took two steps forward.

One of the figures advanced noiselessly. It was dressed in black, and its face was shrouded in a black hood. In that light, with that silent even way of approaching, it was the most awful figure I ever saw. And from under its hood came a woman's voice, the sound of which made the blood of more than one to stand still, and then go madly on again. It said:—

"I am Ellen Ravenshoe. My sins and my repentance are known to some here. I have been to the war, in the hospitals, till my health gave way, and I came home but yesterday, as it were, and I have been summoned here. Charles, I was beautiful once. Look at this."

And she threw her hood back, and we looked at her in the dim light. Beautiful once! Ay, but never so beautiful as now. The complexion was deadly pale, and the features were pinched, but she was more beautiful than ever. I declare I believe that if we had seen a ring of glory round her head at that moment none of us would have been surprised. Just then, her beauty, her nun's dress, and the darkness of the hall, assisted the illusion, probably; but there was really something saintlike and romantic about her, for an instant or so, which made us all stand silent. Alas! there was no ring of glory round her head. Poor Ellen was only bearing the cross, she had not won the crown.

Charles was the first who spoke or moved; he went up to her, and kissed her, and said, "My sweet sister, I knew that if I ever saw you again I should see you in these weeds. My dear love, I am so glad to see you. And oh, my sister, how much more happy to see you dressed like that——"

(Of course he did not use exactly those words, but words to that effect, only more passionate and even less grammatical.

P

I am not a short-hand writer. I only give you the substance of conversations in the best prose I can command.)

"Charles," said she, "I do right to wear weeds, for I am the widow of—(Never mind what she said ; that sort of thing very properly jars on Protestant ears.) I am a sister of the Society of Mercy of St. Bridget, and I have been to the East, as I told you : and more than once I must have been into the room where you lay, to borrow things, or talk with English Catholic ladies, and never guessed you were there. After Hornby had found me at Hackney, I got leave from Father Butler to join an Irish sisterhood ; for our mother was Irish in speech and in heart, you remember, though not by birth. I have something to say—something very important. Father Mackworth, will you come here ? Are all here intimate friends of the family ? Will you ask any of them to leave the hall, Charles ? "

"Not one," said Charles. "Is one of those dark figures which have frightened us so much, Father Mackworth ? My dear sir, I am so sorry. Come to the fire ; and who is the other ? "

"Only Murtagh Tiernay," said a soft voice.

"Why did you stand out there these few minutes ? Father Mackworth, your arm."

William and Charles helped him in towards the fire. He looked terribly ill and ghastly. The dear old general took him from them, and sat him down in his own chair by the fire ; while Ellen stood behind him, with her hood thrown back, and her white hands folded on her bosom. If you have ever seen a stranger group than we were, I should be glad to hear of it.

Poor Mackworth seemed to think that it was expected of him to speak. He looked up to General Mainwaring, and he said—

"I hope you are better of your wound, sir. I have had a sharp stroke of paralysis, and I have another coming on, sir, and my memory is going. When you meet my Lord Saltire, whom I am surprised to find absent to-night, you will tell him that I presented my compliments, and thought that he had used me very well on the whole. Had she not better begin, sir ? or it may be too late ; unless you would like to wait for Lord Saltire."

Father Murtagh Tiernay knelt down and whispered to him.

"Ay ! ay !" he said. "Dead—ay ! so he is, I had forgotten. We shall all be dead soon. Some of us will to hell, General, and some to heaven, and all to purgatory. I am a priest, sir. I have been bound body and soul to the Church from a child, and I have done things which the Church will disapprove of when they are told, though not while they are kept secret; and I tell them because the eyes of a dead man, of a man who was drowned bathing in the bay, haunt me day and night, and say, Speak out!—Murtagh!"

Little Tiernay was kneeling beside him, and called his attention to him.

"You had better give me the wine; for the end is getting very near. Tell her to begin."

And while poor Mackworth was taking some wine (poor fellow, it was little enough he had taken in his life-time), Ellen began to speak. I had some notion that we should know everything now. We had guessed the truth for a long while. We had guessed everything about Petre Ravenshoe's marriage. We believed in it. We seemed to know all about it, from Lady Ascot. No link was wanting in the chain of proof, save one, the name of the place in which that marriage took place. That had puzzled every one. Lady Ascot declared it was a place in the north of Hampshire, as you will remember, but every register had been searched there, without result. So conceive how we all stared at poor Ellen, when she began to speak, wondering whether she knew as much as ourselves, or even more.

"I am Miss Ravenshoe," she said quietly. "My brother Charles there is heir to this estate; and I have come here to-night to tell you so."

There was nothing new here. We knew all about that. I stood up and put my arm through Charles Ravenshoe's, and William came and laid his hand upon my shoulder. The general stood before the fire, and Ellen went on.

"Petre Ravenshoe was married in 1778 to Maria Dawson, and his son was James Ravenshoe, my father, who was called Horton, and was Densil Ravenshoe's gamekeeper. I have proof of this."

So had we. We knew all this. What did she know more? It was intolerable that she was to stop just here, and leave the one awful point unanswered. I forgot my good manners utterly; I clutched Charles's arm tighter and cried out—

"We know about the marriage, Miss Ravenshoe; we have known of it a long while. But where did it take place, my dear young lady? Where?"

She turned on me and answered, wondering at my eagerness. *I* had brought out the decisive words at last, the words we had been dying to hear for six months; she said—

"At Finchampstead, in Berkshire; I have a copy of the certificate with me."

I let go of Charles's arm, and fell back in my chair. My connexion with this story is over (except the trouble of telling it, which I beg you won't mention, for it has given me as much pleasure as it has you; and that, if you look at it in a proper point of view, it is quite just, for very few men have a friend who has met with such adventures as Charles Ravenshoe, who will tell them all about it afterwards). I fell back in my chair, and stared at poor Father Mackworth as if he were a copper disk, and I was trying to get into a sufficiently idiotic state to be electrobiologized.

"I have very little more to tell," said Ellen. "I was not aware that you knew so much. From Mr. William Marston's agitation, I conclude that I have supplied the only link which was missing. I think that Father Mackworth wishes to explain to you why he sent for me to come here to-night. If he feels himself able to do so now, I shall be glad to be dismissed."

Father Mackworth sat up in his chair, and spoke at once. He had gathered himself up for the effort, and went through it well, though with halting and difficult speech.

"I knew of Petre Ravenshoe's marriage from Father Clifford, with all the particulars. It had been confessed to him. He told it to me the day Mrs. Ravenshoe died, after Densil Ravenshoe had told me that his second son was to be brought up to the Protestant faith. I went to him in a furious passion, and he told me about this previous marriage which had been confessed to him, to quiet me. It showed me, that if the worst were to happen, and Cuthbert were to die, and Ravenshoe go to a Protestant, I could still bring in a Catholic as a last resource. For if Cuthbert had died, and Norah had not confessed about the changing of the children, I should have brought in James, and after him William, both Catholics, believing him to be the son of James and Norah. Do you understand?

"Why did I not? I loved that boy Cuthbert. And it was told under seal of confession, and must not be used save in deadly extremity, and William was a turbulent boy. Which would have been the greater crime at that time? It was only a choice of evils, for the Church is very dear to me.

"Then Norah confessed to me about the change of children, and then I saw, that by speaking of Petre Ravenshoe's marriage, I should only bring in a Protestant heir. But I saw, also, that, by using her confession only, I could prove Charles Ravenshoe to be merely a gamekeeper's son, and turn him out into the world, and so I used it, sir. You used to irritate and insult me, sir," he said, turning to Charles, "and I was not so near death then as now. If you can forgive me, in God's name say so."

Charles went over to him, and put his arm round him. "Forgive you?" he said; "dear Mackworth, can you forgive me?"

"Well, well!" he continued, "what have I to forgive, Charles? At one time, I thought if I spoke that it would be better, because Ellen, the only daughter of the house, would have had a great dower, as Ravenshoe girls have. But I loved Cuthbert too well. And Lord Welter stopped my even thinking of doing so, by coming to Ravenshoe. And—and—we are all gentlemen here. The day that you hunted the black hare, I had been scolding her for writing to him. And William and I made her mad between us, and she ran away to him. And she is with the army now, Charles. I should not fetch her back, Charles. She is doing very good work there."

By this time she had drawn the black hood over her face, and was standing behind him, motionless.

"I will answer any more questions you like to-morrow. Petre Ravenshoe's marriage took place at Finchampstead, remember. Charles, my dear boy, would you mind kissing me? I think I always loved you, Charles. Murtagh Tiernay, take me to my room."

And so he went tottering away through the darkness. Charles opened the door for him. Ellen stood with her hood over her face, motionless.

"I can speak like this with my face hidden," she said. "It is easy for one who has been through what I have, to speak. What I have been you know, what I am now is—(she used one of those Roman Catholic forms of expression, which are best not repeated too often.) I have a little to add to this statement. William was cruel to me. You know you were. You were wrong. I will not go on. You were awfully unjust—you were horribly unjust. The man who has just left the room had some slight right to upbraid me. You had none. You were utterly wrong. Mackworth, in one way, is a very high-minded honourable man. You made me hate you, William. God forgive me. I have forgiven you now."

"Yes; I was wrong," said William, "I was wrong. But, Ellen, Ellen! before old friends, only with regard to the person."

"When you treated me so ill, I was as innocent as your

mother, sir. Let us go on. This man Mackworth knew more than you. We had some terrible scenes together about Lord Welter. One day he lost his temper, and became theatrical. He opened his desk and showed me a bundle of papers, which he waved in the air, and said contained my future destiny. The next day I went to the carpenter's shop and took a chisel. I broke open his desk, and possessed myself of them. I found the certificate of Petre Ravenshoe's marriage. I knew that you, William, as I thought, and I were the elder children. But I loved Cuthbert and Charles better than you or myself, and I would not speak. When, afterwards, Father Butler told me, while I was with Lord Welter, before I joined the sisters, or the astounding fact of the change of children, I still held my peace, because I thought Charles would be the better of penance for a year or so, and because I hesitated to throw the power or a house like this into heretic hands, though it were into the hands of my own brother. Mackworth and Butler were to some extent enemies, I think: for Butler seems not to have told Mackworth that I was with him for some time, and I hardly know how he found it out at last. Three days ago I received this letter from Mackworth, and after some hesitation I came. For I thought that the Church could not be helped by wrong, and I wanted to see that he concealed nothing. Here it is. I shall say no more."

And she departed, and I have not seen her since. Perhaps she is best where she is. I got a sight of the letter from Father Mackworth. It ran thus—

"Come here at once, I order you. I am going to tell the truth. Charles has come back. I will not bear the responsibility any longer."

Poor Mackworth! He went back to his room, attended by the kind-hearted young priest, who had left his beloved organ at Segur, to come and attend to him. Lord Segur pished and pshawed, and did something more, which we won't talk about, for which he had to get absolution. But Murtagh Tiernay stayed at Ravenshoe, defying his lordship, and his lordship's profane oaths, and making the Ravenshoe organ talk to Father Mackworth about quiet churchyards and silent cloisters; and sometimes raging on until the poor paralytic priest began to see the great gates rolled back, and the street of the everlasting city beyond, crowded with glorious angels. Let us leave these two to their music. Before we went to town for the wedding, we were sitting one night, and playing at loo, in the hall. (Not guinea unlimited loo, as they used to play at Lord Welter's, but penny loo, limited to eighteen pence.) General Mainwaring had been looed in miss four times running, making six shillings (an almost impossible circumstance, but true), and Lady Ascot had been laughing at him so, that she had to take off her spectacles and wipe them, when Murtagh Tiernay came into the hall, and took away Charles, and his brother Father Tiernay.

The game was dropped soon after this. At Ravenshoe there was an old-fashioned custom of having a great supper brought into the hall at ten. A silly old custom, seeing that every one had dined at seven. Supper was brought in, and every one sat down to table. All sorts of things were handed to one by the servants, but no one ate anything. No one ever did. But the head of the table was empty, Charles was absent.

After supper was cleared away, every one drew in a great circle round the fire, in the charming old-fashioned way one sees very seldom now, for a talk before we went to bed. But nobody talked much. Only Lady Ascot said, " I shall not go upstairs till he comes back. General, you may smoke your cigar, but here I sit."

General Mainwaring would not smoke his cigar, even up the chimney. Almost before he had time to say so, Charles and Father Tiernay came into the room, without saying a word, and Charles, passing through the circle, pushed the logs on the hearth together with his foot.

" Charles," said Lady Ascot, " has anything happened ? "

" Yes, aunt."

" Is he dead ? "

" Yes, aunt."

" I thought so," said Lady Ascot, " I hope he has forgiven me any hard thoughts I had of him. I could have been brought to love that man in time. There were a great many worse men than he, sir," she added, in her old clear ringing tones, turning to Father Tiernay. " There were a great many worse men than he."

" There were a great many worse men, Lady Ascot," said Father Tiernay. " There have been many worse men with better opportunities. He was a good man brought up in a bad school. A good man spoilt. General Mainwaring, you who are probably more honoured than any man in England just now, and are worthy of it ; you who can't stop at a street corner without a crowd getting together to hurrah to you ; you, the very darling of the nation, are going to Oxford to be made an honorary Doctor of Laws.   And when you go into that theatre, and hear the maddening music of those boys' voices cheering you : then, general, don't get insane with pride like Herod, but think what you might have been with Mackworth's opportunities."

I think we all respected the Irishman for speaking up for his friend, although his speech might be extravagant.   But I am sure that no one respected him more sincerely than our valiant, humble, old friend, General Mainwaring.

CHAPTER LXVI

GUS AND FLORA ARE NAUGHTY IN CHURCH, AND THE WHOLE BUSINESS COMES TO AN END

CHARLES's purpose of being married in London held good. And I need not say that William's held good too.

Shall I insult your judgment by telling you that the whole story of Petre Ravenshoe's marriage at Finchampstead was true ? I think not.   The register was found, the lawyers were busy down at Ravenshoe, for every one was anxious to get up to London, and have the two marriages over before the season was too far advanced.

The memorabilia about this time at Ravenshoe, were—The weather was glorious.   (I am not going to give you any more about the two capes, and that sort of thing. You have had those two capes often enough.   And I am reserving my twenty-ninth description of the Ravenshoe scenery for the concluding chapter.) The weather, I say, was glorious.   And I was always being fetched in from the river, smelling fishy, and being made to witness deeds.   I got tired of writing my name.   I may have signed away the amount of the national debt in triplicate, for anything I know (or care. For you can't get blood out of a stone).   I signed some fifty of them I think.   But I signed two, which gave me great pleasure.

The first was a rent-charge on Ravenshoe of two thousand a year, in favour of William Ravenshoe.   The second was a similar deed of five hundred a year in favour of Miss Ravenshoe.

We will now have done with all this sordid business, and go on.

The ladies all had left for town, to prepare for the ceremony.

There was a bachelors' house at Ravenshoe for the last time. The weather was hot. Charles Ravenshoe, General Mainwaring, and the rest, were all looking out of the dining-room windows towards the sea, when we were astonished by seeing two people ride up on to the terrace, and stop before the porch.

A noble-looking old gentleman, in a blue coat and brass buttons, knee-breeches and gaiters, on a cob, and a beautiful boy of sixteen on a horse. *I* knew well enough who it was, and I said, Ho! But the others wondered. William would have known, had he been looking out of the window just then, but by the time he got there, the old gentleman and the boy were in the porch, and two of Charles's men were walking the horses up and down.

"Now, who the deuce is this?" said Charles. "They haven't come far; but I don't know them. I seem to know the old man, somehow; but I can't remember."

We heard the old gentleman's heavy step along the hall, and then the door was thrown open, and the butler announced, like a true Devonshire man—

"Mr. Humby to Hele!"

The old gentleman advanced with a frank smile and took Charles's hand, and said, "Welcome home, sir; welcome to your own; welcome to Ravenshoe. A Protestant at Ravenshoe at last. After so many centuries."

Everybody had grown limp and faint when they heard the awful name of Humby, that is to say, every one but me. Of course I had nothing to do with fetching him over. Not at all. This was the first time that a Humby had had friendly communication with a Ravenshoe for seven hundred and eighty-nine years. The two families had quarrelled in 1066, in consequence of John Humby having pushed against Kempion Ravenshoe, in the grand rush across the Senlac, at the battle of Hastings. Kempion Ravenshoe had asked John Humby where he was shoving to, and John Humby had expressed a wish to punch Kempion Ravenshoe's head (or do what went for the same thing in those times. I am no antiquarian). The wound was never healed. The two families located themselves on adjoining estates in Devonshire immediately after the conquest, but never spoke till 1529, when Lionel Humby bit his thumb at our old friend, Alured Ravenshoe, in Cardinal Wolsey's antechamber, at Hampton, and Alured Ravenshoe asked him, what the devil he meant by that. They fought in Twickenham meadow, but held no relations for two hundred and fourteen years, that is to say, till 1745, when Ambrose Ravenshoe squeezed an orange at

Chichester Humby at an election dinner in Stonnington, and Boddy Fortescue went out as second to Chichester Humby, and Lord Segur to Ambrose Ravenshoe. After this the families did not speak again for one hundred and ten years, that is to say, till the time we are speaking of, the end of April, 1855, when James Humby to Hele frightened us all out of our wits, by coming into the dining-room at Ravenshoe in a blue coat and brass buttons, and shaking hands with Charles, and saying, beside what I have written above—

"Mrs. Humby and my daughters are in London for the season, and I go to join them the day after to-morrow. There has been a slight cloud between the two houses lately" (that is to say, as we know it, for seven hundred and eighty-nine years. But what is time?) "and I wish to remove it. I am not a very old man, but I have my whimsies, my dear sir. I wish my daughters to appear among Miss Corby's bridesmaids, and do you know, I fancy when you get to London that you will find the whole matter arranged."

Who was to resist this? Old Humby went up in the train with all of us the next day but one. And if I were asked to pick out the most roystering, boisterous, jolly old county member in England, Scotland, or Ireland, I should pick out old Humby of Hele. What fun he made at the stations where the express stopped! The way he allowed himself to be fetched out of the refreshment-room by the guard, and then, at the last moment, engaged him in a general conversation about the administration of the line, until the station-master was mad, and an accident imminent, was worthy of a much younger man, to say the least. But then, in a blue coat and brass buttons, with drab small clothes, you may do anything. They are sure to take you for a swell. If I, William Marston, am ever old enough, and fat enough, and rich enough, I shall dress like that myself, for reasons. If my figure does not develop, I shall try black br—ch—s and gaiters, with a shovel hat, and a black silk waistcoat buttoned up under my throat. That very often succeeds. Either are better than pegtops and a black bowler hat, which strike no awe into the beholders.

When we all got to town, we were, of course, very busy. There was a great deal of millinery business. Old Humby insisted on helping at it. One day he went to Madame Tulle's, in Conduit Street, with his wife and two daughters, and asked me to come too, for which I was sorry at first, for he behaved very badly, and made a great noise. We were in a great suite of rooms on the first floor, full of crinolines and that sort of thing, and there were a great many people present. I was trying to keep him quiet, for he was cutting a good many clumsy jokes, as an old-fashioned country squire will. Everybody was amused with him, and thoroughly appreciated his fun, save his own wife and daughters, who were annoyed ; so I was trying to keep him quiet, when a tall brown-faced, handsome young man came up to me and said—

"I beg a thousand pardons; but is not your name Marston ? "

I said, " Yes."

"You are a first cousin of John Marston, are you not ?—of John Marston, whom I used to meet at Casterton ? "

I said, " Yes ; that John Marston was my cousin." But I couldn't remember my man, for all that.

"You don't remember me ! I met you once at old Captain Archer's, at Lashbrook, for ten minutes. My wife has come here to buy fal-lals for Charles Ravenshoe's wedding. He is going to marry my cousin. My name is George Corby. I have married Miss Ellen Blockstrop, daughter of Admiral Blockstrop. Her eldest sister married young Captain Archer of the merchant service."

I felt very faint, but I congratulated him. The way those Australians do business shames us old-country folk. To get a heavy disappointment and be married in two months week is very creditable.

bushmen are rough fellows," he said. (His manners really charming. I never saw them beaten.) "But you country fellows must excuse us. Will you give me the re of your acquaintance? I am sure you must be a good for your cousin is one of the best fellows I ever knew."

would be delighted." And I spoke the truth.

ll introduce you to my wife directly," he said ; "but the fact she is just now having a row with Madame Tulle, the milli here. My wife is a deuced economical woman, and she nts to show at the Ravenshoe wedding in a white moiré-antique, which will only cost fifty guineas, and which she says will do for an evening dress in Australia afterwards. And the Frenchwoman won't let her have it for the purpose, because she says it is incorrect. And I hope to Gad the Frenchwoman will win, because my wife will get quite as good a gown to look at for twenty guineas or so."

Squire Humby begged to be introduced. Which I did.

"I am glad, sir," he said, "that my daughters have not heard your conversation. It would have demoralised them,

sir, for the rest of their lives. I hope they have not heard the
argument about the fifty-guinea gown. If they have, I am a
ruined man. It was one of your Australians who gave twelve
hundred guineas for the bull, 'Master Butterfly,' the day
before yesterday ? "

"Well, yes," said George Corby, "I bought the bull. He'll
pay, sir, handsomely, in our part of the world."

"The devil he will," said Squire Humby. "You don't
know an opening for a young man of sixty-five, with a blue
coat and brass buttons, who understands his business, in your
part of the country, do you ? "

And so on. The weddings took place at St. Peter's, Eaton
Square. If the ghost of the little shoeblack had been hovering
round the wall where he had played fives with the brass
button, he might have almost heard the ceremony performed.
Mary and Charles were not a handsome couple. The enthusiasm of the population was reserved for William and Jane
Evans, who certainly were. It is my nature to be a
Jack-of-all-trades, and so I was entrusted with old Master
Evans, Jane's father, a magnificent old sea-king, whom we
have met before. We two preferred to go to church quie
before the others, and he, refusing to go into a pew, fo
himself a place in the free seats, and made himself comf
So I went out into the porch, and waited till they cam

I waited till the procession had gone in, and ther
that the tail of it was composed of poor Lord Charles
children, Gus, Flora, and Archy, with their nurse.

If a bachelor is worth his salt, he will make himself
I saw that nurse was in distress and anxious, so I
with her.

Archy was really as good as gold till he met
accident. He walked up the steps with nurse
possible. But even at first I began to get anxiou   Gus
and Flora. They were excited. Gus wouldn't   the
steps ; but he put his two heels together, and jump   them
one at a time, and Flora walked backwards, looking at him
sarcastically. At the top step but one Gus stumbled ;
whereupon Flora said, "Goozlemy, goozlemy, goozlemy."

And Gus said, "You wait a minute, my lady, till we get into
church," after which awful speech I felt as if I was smoking in
a powder magazine.

I was put into a pew with Gus, and Flora, and Archy. Nurse,
in her modesty, went into the pew behind us.

I am sorry to say that these dear children, with whom I

had had no previous acquaintance, were very naughty. The ceremony began by Archy getting too near the edge of his hassock, falling off, pitching against the pew door, bursting it open, and flying out among the free seats, head foremost. Nurse, a nimble and dexterous woman, dashed out, and caught him up, and actually got him out of the church door before he had time to fetch his breath for a scream. Gus and Flora were left alone with me.

Flora had a great scarlet and gold church service. As soon as she opened it, she disconcerted me by saying aloud, to an imaginary female friend, " My dear, there is going to be a collection ; and I have left my purse on the piano."

At this time also, Gus, seeing that the business was well begun, removed to the further end of the pew, sat down on the hassock, and took from his trousers' pocket a large tin trumpet.

I broke out all over in a cold perspiration as I looked at him. He saw my distress, and putting it to his lips, puffed out his cheeks. Flora administered comfort to me. She said, " You are looking at that foolish boy. Perhaps he won't blow it, after all. He mayn't if you don't look at him. At all events, he probably won't blow it till the organ begins ; and then it won't matter so much."

Matters were so hopeless with me that I looked at old Master Evans. He had bent down his head on to the rail of the bench before him. His beautiful daughter had been his only companion at home for many years, for his wife had died when Jane was a little bare-legged thing, who paddled in the surf. It had been a rise in life for her to marry Mr. Charles Ravenshoe's favourite pad-groom. And just now she had walked calmly and quietly up the aisle, and had stopped when she came to where he sat, and had pushed the Honiton-lace veil from her forehead, and kissed his dear old cheek : and she would walk back, directly as Mrs. William Ravenshoe. And so the noble old privateer skipper had bent down, and there was nothing to be seen there, but a grey head and broad shoulders, which seemed to shake.

And so I looked up to the east end. And I saw the two couples kneeling before the clergyman. And when I, knowing everything as I did, saw Charles kneeling beside Mary Corby, with Lord Ascot, great burly, brutal giant, standing behind him, I said something which is not in the marriage service of the Church of England. After it all, to see him and her kneeling so quietly there together ! We were all happy enough that day. But I don't think that any one was much happier than I. For I knew more than any one. And also, three months from that time, I married my present wife, Eliza Humby. And the affair had only been arranged two days. So I was in good spirits.

At least I should have been, if it had not been for Lord Charles Herries' children. I wish those dear children (not meaning them any harm) had been, to put it mildly, at play on the village green, that blessed day.

When I looked at Gus again, he was still on the hassock, threatening propriety with his trumpet. I hoped for the best. Flora had her prayer-book open, and was playing the piano on each side of it, with her fingers. After a time she looked up at me, and said out loud—

"I suppose you have heard that Archy's cat has kittened?" I said, "No."

"Oh, yes, it has," she said. "Archy harnessed it to his meal cart, which turns a mill, and plays music when the wheels go round; and it ran downstairs with the cart; and we heard the music playing as it went; and it kittened in the wood-basket immediately afterwards; and Alwright says she don't wonder at it; and no more do I; and the steward's-room boy is going to drown some. But you mustn't tell Archy, because, if you do, he won't say his prayers; and if he don't say his prayers, he will," &c., &c. Very emphatically and in a loud tone of voice.

This was very charming. If I could only answer for Gus, and keep Flora busy, it was wildly possible that we might pull through. If I had not been a madman I should have noticed that Gus had disappeared.

He had. And the pew door had never opened, and I was utterly unconscious. Gus had crawled up, on all fours, under the seat of the pew, until he was opposite the calves of his sister's legs, against which calves, *horresco referens*, he put his trumpet and blew a long shrill blast. Flora behaved very well and courageously. She only gave one long, wild shriek, as from a lunatic in a padded cell at Bedlam, and then, hurling her prayer-book at him, she turned round and tried to kick him in the face.

This was the culminating point of my misfortunes. After this, they behaved better. I represented to them that every one was just coming out of the vestry, and that they had better fight it out in the carriage, going home. Gus only made an impertinent remark about Flora's garters, and Flora only drew a short, but trenchant, historical parallel between Gus and Judas Iscariot; when the brides and bridegrooms came down the aisle, and we all drove off to Charles's house in Eaton Square.

And so, for the first time, I saw all together, with my own eyes, the principal characters in this story. Only one was absent. Lord Saltire. I had seen him twice in my life, and once had the honour of a conversation with him. He was a man about five feet eleven, very broad shouldered, and with a very deep chest. As far as the animal part of him went, I came to the conclusion, from close and interested examination for twenty minutes, that he had, fifty or sixty years before, been a man with whom it would have been pleasanter to argue than to box. His make was magnificent. Phrenologically speaking, he had a very high square head, very flat at the sides : and, when I saw him, when he was nearly eighty, he was the handsomest old man I had ever seen. He had a florid, pure complexion. His face was without a wrinkle. His eyebrows were black, and his hair seemed to refuse to be grey. There was as much black as grey in it to the last. His eye was most extraordinary—a deep blue-grey. I can look a man as straight in the face as any one ; but when Lord Saltire turned those eyes on me three or four times in the course of our interview, I felt that it was an effort to meet them. I felt that I was in the presence of a man of superior vitality to my own. We were having a talk about matters connected with Charles Ravenshoe, which I have not mentioned, because I want to keep myself, William Marston, as much out of this story as possible. And whenever this terrible old man looked at me, asking a question, I felt my eyebrows drawing together, and knew that I was looking *defiantly* at him. He was the most extraordinary man I ever met. He never took office after he was forty. He played with politics. He was in heart, I believe (no one knows), an advanced Whig. He chose to call himself Tory. He played the Radical game very deep, early in life, and, I think, he got disgusted with party politics. The last thing the old Radical atheist did in public life was to rally up to the side of the Duke in opposition to the Reform Bill. And another fact about him is, that he had always a strong personal affection for Sir Francis.

He was a man of contradictions, if one judges a man by Whig and Tory rules ; but he was a great loss to the public business of the country. He might have done almost anything in public life with his calm clear brain. My cousin John thinks that Lord Barkham's death was the cause of his retirement.

So much about Lord Saltire. Of the other characters mentioned in this story, I will speak at once, just as I saw them sitting round the table at Charles and William Ravenshoe's wedding.

I sat beside Eliza Humby. She was infinitely the most beautiful, clever, and amiable being that the world ever produced. (But that is my business, not yours.) Charles Ravenshoe sat at the head of the table, and I will leave him alone for a minute. I will give you my impressions of the other characters in this story, as they appeared to me.

Mary was a very charming-looking little person indeed, very short, and with small features. I had never seen her before, and had never heard any one say that she was pretty. I thought her very pretty indeed.

Jane Evans was an exceedingly beautiful Devonshire girl. My eye did not rest very long on her. It came down the table to William, and there it stopped.

I got Eliza Humby to speak to him, and engage him in conversation while I looked at him. I wanted to see whether there was anything remarkable in his face, for a more remarkable instance of disinterested goodwill than his determining to find Charles and ruin himself, I never happened to have heard of.

Well, he was very handsome and pleasing, with a square determined look about the mouth, such as men brought up among horses generally have. But I couldn't understand it, and so I spoke to him across Lizzie, and I said, casting good manners to the winds, " I should think that the only thing you regretted to-day was, that you had not been alongside of Charles at Balaclava ; " and then I understood it, for when I mentioned Charles and Balaclava, I saw for one instant not a groom but a poet. Although, being a respectable and well-conducted man, he has never written any poetry, and probably never will.

Then I looked across the table at Lady Ascot. They say that she was never handsome. I can quite believe that. She was a beautiful old woman certainly, but then all old women are beautiful. Her face was very square, and one could see that it was capable of very violent passion ; or could, knowing what one did, guess so. Otherwise there was nothing very remarkable about her, except that she was a remarkably charming old lady.

Nothing more. In fact, the whole group were less remarkable and tragical-looking than I thought they would have been. I was disappointed until I came to Lord Ascot, and then I could not take my eyes off him.

There was tragedy enough there. There was coarse brutality and passion enough, in all conscience. And yet that man had done what he had done. Here was a puzzle with a vengeance.

Lord Ascot, as I saw him now, for the first time, was simply a low-bred and repulsive-looking man. In stature he was gigantic, in every respect save height. He was about five feet nine, very deep about the chest. His hair was rather dark, cut close. His face was very florid, and perfectly hairless. His forehead was low. His eyes were small, and close together. His eyebrows were heavy, and met over his nose, which was short and square. His mouth was large ; and when you came to his mouth, you came to the first tolerable feature in his face. When he was speaking to no one in particular, the under lip was set, and the whole face, I am sorry to say, was the sort of face which is quite as often seen in the dock, as in the witness-box (unless some gentleman has turned Queen's evidence). And this was the man who had risked a duke's fortune, because " There was some things a fellow couldn't do, you know."

It was very puzzling till he began to speak about his grandmother, and then his lower lip pouted out, his eyebrows raised, his eyes were apart, and he looked a different man. Is it possible that if he had not been brought up to cock-fighting and horse-racing, among prize-fighters and jockeys, that he might have been a different man ? I can't say, I am sure.

Lord and Lady Hainault were simply a very high-bred, very handsome, and very charming pair of people. My cousin knows them both very intimately, and he says there are not two better people in the world.

Charles Ravenshoe rose to reply to General Mainwaring's speech, proposing the brides and bridegrooms, and I looked at him very curiously. He was pale, from his recent illness, and he never was handsome. But his face was the face of a man, whom I should fancy most people would get very fond of. When we were schoolfellows at Shrewsbury, he was a tall dark-haired boy, who was always laughing, and kicking up a row, and giving his things away to other fellows. Now he was a tall, dark, melancholy-looking man, with great eyes, and lofty eyebrows. His vivacity, and that carriage which comes

from the possession of great physical strength, were gone ; and
while I looked at him, I felt ten years older. Why should
I try to describe him further? He is not so remarkable a man
as either Lord Ascot or William. But he was the best man I
ever knew.

He said a few kind hearty words, and sat down, and then
Lord Ascot got up. And I took hold of Lizzie's hand with
my left ; and I put my right elbow on the table and watched
him intensely, with my hand shading my face. He had a coat
buttoned over his great chest, and as he spoke he kept on
buttoning and unbuttoning it with his great coarse hand. He
said—

" I ain't much hand at this sort of thing. I suppose those
two Marstons, confound them, are saying to themselves that I
ought to be, because I am in the House of Lords. That John
Marston is a most impudent beggar, and I shall expect to see
his friend to-morrow morning. He always was, you know. He
has thwarted me all through my life. I wanted Charles
Ravenshoe to go to the deuce, and I'll be hanged if he'd let
him. And it is not to be borne."

There was a general laugh at this, and Lord Ascot stretched
his hand across General Mainwaring, and shook hands with my
cousin.

" You men just go out of the room, will you ? " (the servants
departed, and Lord Ascot went to the door to see they were
not listening. I thought some revelation was coming, but I
was mistaken.) " You see I am obliged to notice strangers,
because a fellow may say things among old friends which he
don't exactly care to before servants.

" It is all very well to say I'm a fool. That is very likely, and
may be taken for granted. But I am not such a fool as not
to know that a very strong prejudice exists against me in the
present society."

Every one cried out, " No, no ! " Of all the great wedding
breakfasts that season, this was certainly the most remarkable.
Lord Ascot went on. He was getting the savage look on his
face now.

" Well, well ! let that pass. Look at that man at the head
of the table—the bridegroom. Look at him. You wonder
that I did what I did. I'll tell you why. I love that fellow.
He is what I call a man, General Mainwaring. I met that
fellow at Twyford years ago, and he has always been the same
to me since. You say I served him badly once. That is true
enough. You insulted me once in public about it, Hainault.

You were quite right. Say you, I should not talk about it to-day. But when we come to think how near death's gates some of us have been since then, you will allow that this wedding day has something very solemn about it.

"My poor wife has broken her back across that infernal gate, and so she could not come. I must ask you all to think kindly of that wife of mine. You have all been very kind to her since her awful accident. She has asked me to thank you.

"I rose to propose a toast, and I have been carried away by a personal statement, which, at every other wedding breakfast I ever heard of, it would be a breach of good manners to make. It is not so on this occasion. Terrible things have befallen every one of us here present. And I suppose we must try all of us to—hey !—to—hah !—well, to do better in future.

"I rose, I said, to propose a toast. I rose to propose the most blameless and excellent woman I ever knew. I propose that we drink the health of my grandmother, Lady Ascot."

And oh ! but we leapt to our feet and drank it. Manners to the winds, after what we had gone through. There was that solemn creature, Lord Hainault, with his champagne glass in his hand, behaving like a schoolboy, and giving us the time. And then, when her dear grey head was bent down over the table, buried in her hands, my present father-in-law, Squire Humby, leapt to his feet like a young giant, and called out for three times three for Lord Ascot. And we had breath enough left to do that handsomely, I warrant you. The whole thing was incorrect in the highest degree, but we did it. And I don't know that any of us were ashamed of it afterwards.

And while the carriages were getting ready, Charles said, would we walk across the square. And we all came with him. And he took us to a piece of dead white wall, at the east end of St. Peter's Church, opposite the cabstand. And then he told us the story of the little shoeblack, and how his comical friendship for that boy had saved him from what it would not do to talk about.

* * * * * *

But there is a cloud on Charles Ravenshoe's face, even now. I saw him last summer lying on the sand, and playing with his eldest boy. And the cloud was on him then. There was no moroseness, no hardness in the expression ; but the face was not the merry old face I knew so well at Shrewsbury and Oxford. There is a dull, settled, dreaming melancholy there still. The memory of those few terrible months has cast its shadow upon him. And the shadow will lie, I fancy, upon that forehead, and will dim those eyes, until the forehead is smoothed in the sleep of death, and the eyes have opened to look upon eternity.

Good-bye.

THE END

Richard Clay & Sons, Limited, London and Bungay.